W9-CRO-769

The Great Ordeal

Also by R. Scott Bakker

THE PRINCE OF NOTHING SERIES

The Darkness That Comes Before, *Book One*

The Warrior-Prophet, *Book Two*

The Thousandfold Thought, *Book Three*

THE ASPECT-EMPEROR SERIES

The Judging Eye, *Book One*

The White-Luck Warrior, *Book Two*

WRITING AS SCOTT BAKKER

Neuropath

Disciple of the Dog

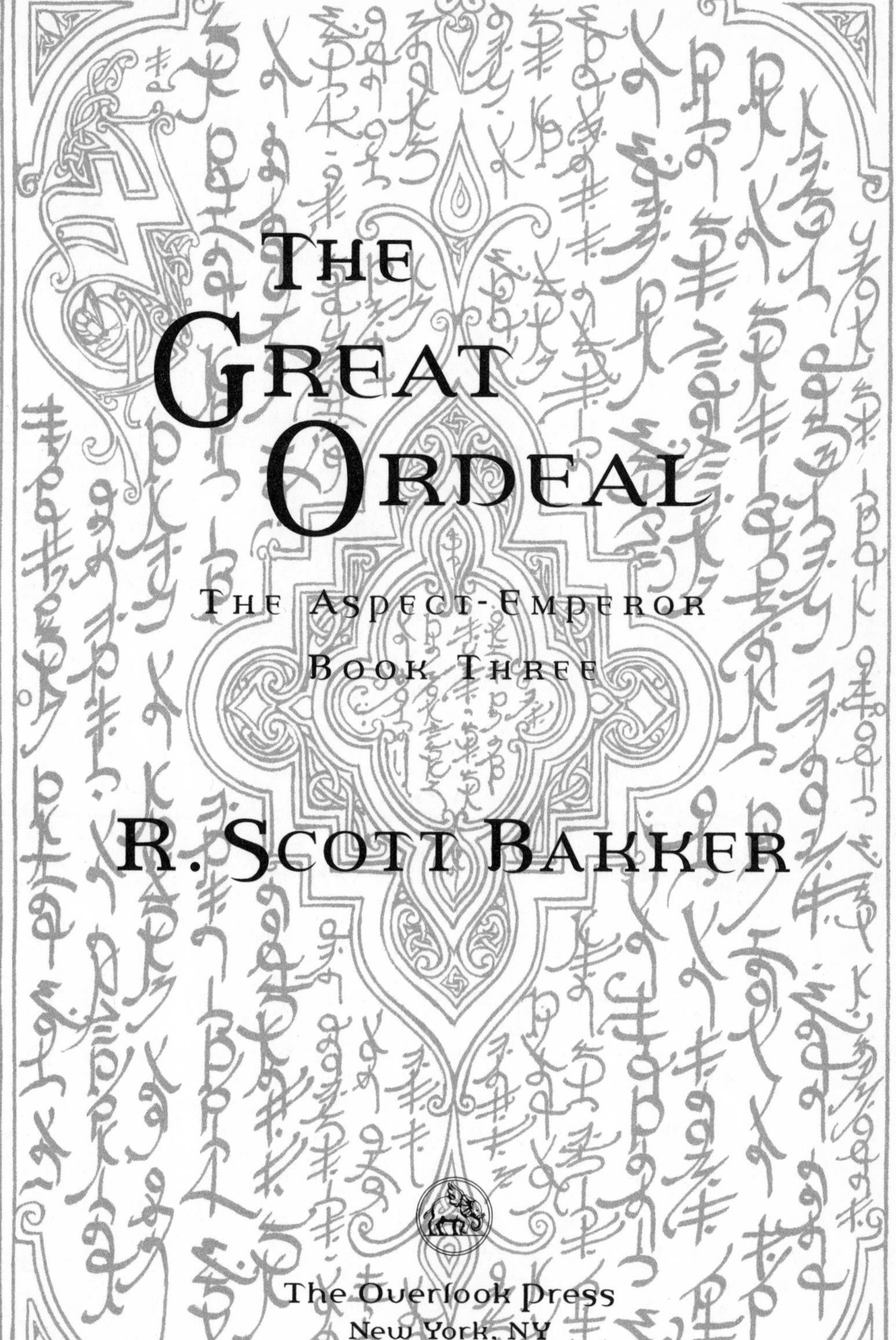

The Great Ordeal

The Aspect-Emperor

Book Three

R. Scott Bakker

The Overlook Press
New York, NY

This edition first published in hardcover in the United States in 2016 by
The Overlook Press, Peter Mayer Publishers, Inc.
141 Wooster Street
New York, NY 10012
www.overlookpress.com
For bulk and special sales, please contact sales@overlookny.com
or write to us at the above address.

Cataloging-in-Publication Data is available from the Library of Congress

Type formatting by Bernard Schleifer
Manufactured in the United States of America
First Edition
1 3 5 7 9 8 6 4 2
ISBN 978-1-4683-0169-4

To Frank and Ken

Contents

Appendices

What Has Come Before . . .

THE PRINCE OF NOTHING

Wars, as a rule, fall within the compass of history. They mark the pitch of competing powers, the end of some and the ascendancy of others, the ebb and flow of dominance across the ages. But there is a war that Men have waged for so long they have forgotten the languages they first used to describe it. A war that makes mere skirmishes out of the destruction of tribes and nations.

There is no name for this war; Men cannot reference what transcends the short interval of their comprehension. It began when they were little more than savages roaming the wilds, in an age before script or bronze. An Ark, vast and golden, toppled from the void, scorching the horizon, throwing up a ring of mountains with the violence of its descent. And from it crawled the dread and monstrous Inchoroi, a race who had come to seal the world against the Heavens, and so save the obscenities they called their souls.

The Nonmen held sway in those ancient days, a long-lived people that surpassed Men not only in beauty and intellect, but in wrath and jealousy as well. With their Ishroi heroes and Quya mages, they fought titanic battles and stood vigilant during epochal truces. They endured the Inchoroi weapons of light. They survived the treachery of the Aporetics, who provided the Inchoroi with thousands of sorcery-killing Chorae. They overcame the horrors their enemy crafted: the Sranc, the Bashrag, and most fearsome of all, the Wracu. But their avarice at last betrayed them. After centuries of intermittent war, they made peace with the invaders in return for the gift of ageless immortality—a gift that was in fact a fell weapon, the Plague of Wombs.

In the end, the Nonmen hunted the Inchoroi to the brink of annihilation. Exhausted, culled of their strength, they retired to their underworld mansions to mourn the loss of their wives and daughters, and the inevitable extinction of their glorious race. Their surviving mages sealed the Ark, which they had come to call Min-Uroikas, and hid it from the world with devious glamours. And from the eastern mountains, the first tribes of Men began claiming the lands they had abandoned—Men who had never known the yoke of slavery. Of the surviving Ishroi Kings, some fought, only to be dragged under by the tide of numbers, while others simply left their great gates unguarded, bared their necks to the licentious fury of a lesser race.

And so human history was born, and perhaps the Nameless War would have ended with the fading of its principals. But the golden Ark still existed, and the lust for knowledge has ever been a cancer in the hearts of Men.

Centuries passed, and the mantle of human civilization crept along the great river basins of Eärwa and outward, bringing bronze where there had been flint, cloth where there had been skins, and writing where there had been recital. Great cities rose to teeming life. The wilds gave way to cultivated horizons.

Nowhere were Men more bold in their works, or more overweening in their pride, than in the North, where commerce with the Nonmen had allowed them to outstrip their more swarthy cousins to the South. In the legendary city of Sauglish, those who could discern the joints of existence founded the first sorcerous Schools. As their learning and power waxed, a reckless few turned to the rumours they had heard whispered by their Nonman teachers—rumours of the great golden Ark. The wise were quick to see the peril, and the Schoolmen of Mangaecca, who coveted secrets above all else, were censured, and finally outlawed.

But it was too late. Min-Uroikas was found—occupied.

The fools discovered and awakened the last two surviving Inchoroi, Aurax and Aurang, who had concealed themselves in the labyrinthine recesses of the Ark. And at their hoary knees the outlaw Schoolmen learned that damnation, the burden that all sorcerers bore, need not be inevitable. They learned that the world could be shut against the judgment of Heaven. So they forged a common purpose with the twin abominations, a *Consult*, and bent their cunning to the aborted designs of the Inchoroi.

The Mangaecca relearned the principles of the material—the Tekne. They mastered the manipulations of the flesh. And after generations of study and searching, after filling the pits of Min-Uroikas with innumerable corpses, they realized the most catastrophic of the Inchoroi's untold depravities: Mog-Pharau, the No-God.

They made themselves slaves to better destroy the world.

And so the Nameless War raged anew. What has come to be called the First Apocalypse destroyed the great Norsirai nations of the North, laying ruin to the greatest glories of Men. But for Seswatha, the Grandmaster of the Gnostic School of Sohonc, the entire world would have been lost. At his urging, Anasûrimbor Celmomas, the High King of the North's mightiest nation, Kûniüri, called on his tributaries and allies to join him in a holy war against Min-Uroikas, which Men now called Golgotterath. But his Ordeal foundered, and the might of the Norsirai perished. Seswatha fled south to the Ketyai nations of the Three Seas, bearing the greatest of the legendary Inchoroi weapons, the Heron Spear. With Anaxophus, the High King of Kyraneas, he met the No-God on the Plains of Mengedda, and by dint of valor and providence, overcame the dread Whirlwind.

The No-God was dead, but his slaves and his stronghold remained. Golgotterath had not fallen, and the Consult, blasted by ages of unnatural life, continued to plot their salvation.

The years passed, and the Men of the Three Seas forgot, as Men inevitably do, the horrors endured by their fathers. Empires rose and empires fell. The Latter Prophet, Inri Sejenus, reinterpreted the Tusk, the First Scripture, and within a few centuries, the faith of Inrithism, organized and administered by the Thousand Temples and its spiritual leader, the Shriah, came to dominate the entire Three Seas. The great Anagogic Schools arose in response to the Inrithi persecution of sorcery. Using Chorae, the Inrithi warred against them, attempting to purify the Three Seas.

Then Fane, the self-proclaimed Prophet of the so-called Solitary God, united the Kianene, the desert peoples of the Great Carathay, and declared war against the Tusk and the Thousand Temples. After centuries of jihad, the Fanim and their eyeless sorcerer-priests, the Cishaurim, conquered nearly all the western Three Seas, including the holy city of Shimeh, the birthplace of Inri Sejenus. Only the moribund remnants of the Nansur Empire continued to resist them.

War and strife ruled the South. The two great faiths of Inrithism and Fanimry skirmished, though trade and pilgrimage were tolerated when commercially convenient. The great families and nations vied for military and mercantile dominance. The minor and major Schools squabbled and plotted. And the Thousand Temples pursued earthly ambitions under the leadership of corrupt and ineffectual Shriahs.

The First Apocalypse had become little more than legend. The Consult and the No-God had dwindled into myth, something old wives tell small children. After two thousand years, only the Schoolmen of the Mandate, who relived the Apocalypse each night through the eyes of Seswatha, could recall the horror of Mog-Pharau. Though the mighty and the learned considered them fools, the Mandate's possession of the sorcery of the Ancient North, the Gnosis, commanded respect and mortal envy. Driven by nightmares, they wandered the labyrinths of power, scouring the Three Seas for signs of their ancient and implacable foe: the Consult.

And as always, they found nothing.

Some argued that the Consult had finally succumbed to the toll of ages. Others that they had turned inward, seeking less arduous means to forestall their damnation. But since the Sranc had multiplied across the northern wilds, no expedition could be sent to Golgotterath to settle the matter. The Mandate alone knew of the Nameless War. They alone stood guard, but they suffocated in a pall of ignorance.

The Thousand Temples elected a new, enigmatic Shriah, a man called Maithanet, who demanded the Inrithi recapture Shimeh, the holy city of the Latter Prophet, from the Fanim. Word of his call spread across the Three Seas and beyond. Faithful from all the great Inrithi nations—Galeoth, Thunyerus, Ce Tydonn, Conriya, High Ainon and their tributaries—travelled to the city of Momemn, the capital of the Nansurium, to swear their swords and their lives to Inri Sejenus. To become Men of the Tusk.

And so the First Holy War was born. Internal feuds plagued the campaign from the outset, for there was no shortage of those who would bend the holy war to their selfish ends. The Inrithi host marched victorious nonetheless, winning two great victories over the heretic Fanim at Mengedda and Anwurat. Only with the Second Siege of Caraskand and the Circumfixion of one of their own would the Men of the Tusk find common purpose. Only when the Men of the Tusk discovered in their midst a *living* prophet—a man who could see into the hearts of Men. A man like a god.

Anasûrimbor Kellhus.

Far to the north, in the very shadow of Golgotterath, a group of ascetics called the Dûnyain had concealed themselves in Ishuäl, the secret redoubt of the Kûniüric High Kings ere their destruction in the First Apocalypse. For two thousand years the Dûnyain had pursued their sacred study, breeding for reflex and intellect, training in the ways of limb, thought, and face—all for the sake of reason, the Logos. They had dedicated their entire existence to mastering the irrationalities of history, custom, and passion—all those things that determine human thought. In this way, they believed, they would eventually grasp what they called the Absolute, and so become true self-moving souls.

But their millennial isolation was at an end. After thirty years of exile, one of their number, Anasûrimbor Moënghus, reappeared in their dreams, demanding they send to him his son Kellhus. Knowing only that Moënghus dwelt in a distant city called Shimeh, the Dûnyain dispatched Kellhus on an arduous journey through lands long abandoned by Men—to kill his apostate father.

But Moënghus knew the world in ways his cloistered brethren could not. He knew well the revelations that awaited his son, for they had been his revelations thirty years previous. He knew that Kellhus would discover sorcery, whose existence the forefathers of the Dûnyain had suppressed. He knew that given his abilities, Men would be little more than children to him, that Kellhus would see their thoughts in the nuances of their expression, and that with mere words he would be able to exact any devotion, any sacrifice. He knew, moreover, that eventually Kellhus would encounter the Consult, who hid behind faces that only Dûnyain eyes could see—that he would come to see what Men with their blinkered souls could not: the Nameless War.

The Consult had not been idle. For centuries they had eluded their old foe, the School of Mandate, using doppelgängers—spies who could take on any face, any voice, without resorting to sorcery and its telltale Mark. By capturing and torturing these abominations, Moënghus learned that the Consult had not abandoned their ancient plot to shut the world against Heaven, that within a score of years they would be able to resurrect the No-God and bring about a *new* war against Men, a Second Apocalypse. For years Moënghus walked the innumerable paths of the Probability Trance, plotting future after future, searching for the thread of act and consequence that would save the world. For years he crafted his Thousandfold Thought.

Moënghus knew, and so prepared the way for his Dûnyain-born son, Kellhus. He sent out his world-born son, Maithanet, to seize the Thousand Temples from within, so that he might craft the First Holy War, the weapon Kellhus would need to seize absolute power, and so unite the Three Seas against the doom that was their future. What he did not know, could not know, was that Kellhus would see *further* than him, think beyond his Thousandfold Thought ...

That he would go mad.

Little more than an impoverished wayfarer when he first joined the Holy War, Kellhus used his bearing, intellect, and insight to convince ever more Men of the Tusk that he was the Warrior-Prophet, come to save mankind from the Second Apocalypse. He understood that Men would render anything to him, so long as they believed he could save their souls. He also befriended the Schoolman the Mandate had dispatched to observe the Holy War, Drusas Achamian, knowing that the Gnosis, the sorcery of the Ancient North, would provide him with inestimable power. And he seduced Achamian's lover, Esmenet, knowing that her intellect made her the ideal vessel for his seed—for sons strong enough to bear the onerous burden of Dûnyain blood.

By the time the battle-hardened remnants of the First Holy War laid siege to Shimeh, Kellhus had achieved absolute authority. The Men of the Tusk had become his Zaudunyani, his Tribe of Truth. While the Holy War assailed the city's walls, he confronted his father, Moënghus, mortally wounding him, explaining that only his death could realize the Thousandfold Thought. Days later Anasûrimbor Kellhus was proclaimed Holy Aspect-Emperor, the first in a millennium, by none other than the Shriah of the Thousand Temples, his half-brother, Maithanet. Even the School of Mandate, who saw his coming as the fulfillment of their most hallowed prophecies, knelt and kissed his knee.

But he had made a mistake. Before reaching the Three Seas and the Holy War, his passage across Eärwa had delivered him to the lands of the Utemot, a Scylvendi tribe renowned for warlike cruelty. Here he had struck a murderous compact with the tribe's chieftain, Cnaiür urs Skiötha. Moënghus had also fallen into the hands of the Utemot some thirty years prior, and had used the then adolescent Cnaiür to murder his chieftain father and effect his escape. The youth had spent tormented decades pondering what had happened and had come to guess the inhuman truth of the Dûnyain. So it was that Cnaiür and Cnaiür alone knew the dark secret of Anasûrimbor Kellhus. Before his death, the barbarian revealed these truths to none other than Drusas Achamian, who had long harboured heartbreaking suspicions of his own. At the coronation, before the eyes of the entire Holy War, Achamian repudiated Kellhus, whom he had worshiped; Esmenet, whom he had loved; and the Mandate masters he had served. Then he fled into the wilderness, becoming the world's only sorcerer without a school. A Wizard.

Now, after twenty years of war, conversion, and butchery, Anasûrimbor Kellhus prepares to realize the penultimate stage of his father's Thousandfold Thought. His New Empire spans the entirety of the Three Seas, from the legendary fortress of Auvangshei on the frontiers of Zeum to the shrouded headwaters of the River Sayut, from the sweltering coasts of Kutnarmu to the wild rim of the Osthwai Mountains—all the lands that had once been Fanim or Inrithi. It was easily the equal of the old Ceneian Empire in terms of geographical extent, and far more populous. A hundred great cities, and almost as many languages. A dozen proud nations. Thousands of years of mangled history.

And the Nameless War is nameless no longer. Men call it the *Great Ordeal.*

THE JUDGING EYE

Achamian

For twenty years Drusas Achamian has kept a painstaking record of his Dreams of the First Apocalypse.

He lives as an exile, the world's only Wizard, on the savage northeastern frontier of the empire Anasûrimbor Kellhus has raised about his supposed divinity. The Sranc once besieged his half-ruined tower with regularity, but the scalpers have driven the inhuman creatures over the mountains, chasing the Holy Bounty. For years now Achamian has lived in peace, hunting his sleep for hints and rumours of Ishuäl, the hidden fastness of the Dûnyain. If he can find Ishuäl, he believes, he can answer the question that burns so bright in so many learned souls ...

Who is the Aspect-Emperor?

This peace is shattered when Anasûrimbor Mimara, the daughter of his former wife, arrives demanding he teach her sorcery. Her resemblance to her mother, Esmenet—the harlot who has become Empress of the Three Seas—returns the old Wizard to all the pains he sought to escape. He refuses her demand, bids her to leave time and again, but she defies him and takes up a vigil outside his tower.

Mimara, who has never forgiven her mother for selling her into slavery as a child, has fled the Imperial Court with no intention of returning. She possesses the ability to see the fabric of existence and so the power to learn sorcery—and this, she has decided, is the one thing that will lift her from the mire of shame and recrimination that is her life. She tells herself she has nothing else ...

But she also possesses a different kind of sight, one both more precious and more significant: on rare occasions, she can see the *morality* of things, the goodness and the evil inherent to them. She has what the ancients called the Judging Eye.

Day and night she howls at his tower, demanding that he teach her. The first time he comes down, he strikes her. The second time he tries to reason with her. He explains his lifelong quest to discover the truth of her stepfather Anasûrimbor Kellhus, how he seeks the location of Ishuäl because it is the Aspect-Emperor's birthplace, and the truth of a man, Achamian insists, always lies in his origins. He tells her how his Dreams have slowly transformed, abandoning the epic atrocities of the First Apocalypse, and focusing more and more upon the mundane details of Seswatha's ancient life. Because of this, Achamian now knows *how* to find Ishuäl: he **must** recover a map that lies hidden in the ruins of ancient Sauglish, far to the north.

"You have become a prophet," Mimara tells him. "A prophet of the past."

And then, desperate to win his tutelage, she seduces him.

Only in the shameful aftermath does she tell the old Wizard that he has dwelt upon his suspicions for too long. The Aspect-Emperor has already embarked on his quest to destroy the Consult and so save the world from a Second Apocalypse. The Great Ordeal marches.

Achamian abandons Mimara at his tower and strikes out for Marrow, the nearest scalper outpost. Here he contracts a company called the Skin Eaters to join his quest, deceiving them with promises of the Coffers, the ancient Library's famed treasury. The Captain of the company, a veteran of the First Holy War named Lord Kosoter, troubles him, as does Cleric, his mysterious Nonman companion. But time is short, and he can think of no one else who would accompany him on such a mad trek. He must somehow reach the Library of Sauglish, and thence Ishuäl, before the Great Ordeal reaches the gates of Golgotterath. The scalper company departs shortly thereafter, planning to cross the Osthwai Mountains into the Sranc-infested North.

Mimara, however, is not so easily dissuaded. She shadows the scalpers without appreciating the cunning of their forest craft. She is discovered, and Achamian is forced to save her, saying that she is his wilful daughter. Fearing she will reveal his true purposes, the old Wizard at last relents. He allows her to accompany him on his quest and agrees to teach her sorcery.

Shortly afterward they learn that a spring blizzard has closed the passes through the Osthwai Mountains, perhaps delaying them for weeks—for too long. Only one path remains open to them: the accursed halls of Cil-Aujas.

The company camps before the entrance to the derelict Nonman Mansion, plagued with apprehensions. Then, with the coming of dawn, they descend into the heart of the mountain. For days they wander the wrecked halls, led by Cleric and his ancient memories. Deep in the Mansion, Mimara finally confesses her sporadic ability to see the morality of things, and Achamian, obviously troubled, tells her that she possesses the *Judging Eye*. She presses him to tell her more, but the old Wizard refuses. Before she can berate him properly, the company discovers that the Mansion is far from abandoned.

Sranc assail them with fury and countless numbers. Despite the sorcerous toll exacted by Cleric and Achamian, the company is overcome, and the survivors are forced to flee down into the bowels of Cil-Aujas. Achamian is knocked unconscious by a Chorae-bearing Sranc. Mimara kills the creature and pockets the sorcery-killing artifact. They flee through the mines that riddle the foundations of the mountain, and find themselves on the scorched rim of a burning lake. The Sranc pour after them, a howling tide. They flee along a stair, and would certainly perish, were it not for Cleric and his sorcerous might. Their route sealed behind them, they find themselves in an ancient slave pit, huddling among the bones of a dead dragon. Only a handful survive.

While they recover themselves, Cleric dispenses *Qirri*, an ancient Nonman remedy. Mimara finds herself staring at her Chorae. It is void and terror to her sorcerous eyes, yet she persists gazing. The Judging Eye opens, and the thing is miraculously transformed. Suddenly she *sees* the Chorae for a true, white-burning *Tear of God.* She turns to Somandutta, the scalper who has become her protector with the Wizard incapacitated. But he sees nothing ...

Then she notices the stranger sitting in their midst.

Cleric recognizes the figure as the shade of Gin'yursis, the ancient Nonman King of Cil-Aujas. The wraith dons the Nonman as if he were clothing, possesses him. While the company stands watching in dread, the Qirri finally revives the old Wizard. Recognizing their peril, he begins screaming at them to flee.

Again they race into the black, while something dark and nebulous and godlike pursues them. In desperation, Achamian brings the ceiling crashing down, sealing the company even deeper within the dread Mansion.

They find themselves at the bottom of a vast well, what Achamian remembers as the Great Medial Screw from his ancient Dreams, a stair that plumbs the whole mountain. The sky is little more than a prick of light above them. The battered Skin Eaters rejoice. All they need do is climb ...

But Gin'yursis rises from the deeps to claim them, dragging hell itself as his mantle.

Mimara's Judging Eye opens, and she raises high her Tear of God, somehow knowing ...

The Great Ordeal

Far to the north, young Varalt Sorweel finds himself staring down upon the boggling might of the Southron Believer-Kings. He is the only son of Varalt Harweel, the King of Sakarpus, who has resisted the Aspect-Emperor's demand to yield his ancient city and its famed Chorae Hoard. Standing with his father on the high curtain walls, the adolescent realizes that he and his people are doomed. Then, miraculously, a stork—a bird that is holy to the Sakarpi—appears on the battlements above his father. After a moment of uncanny communion, King Harweel turns and commands that Sorweel be taken to safety. "See that no harm comes to him!" he cries. "He will be our final swordstroke! Our vengeance!" Dragged away screaming, the young prince watches sorcerous flames engulf the parapets and his father upon them. A desperate flight ensues, and it seems that the *Aspect-Emperor himself* pursues them through the chaotic streets.

The pursuit ends in the apparent safety of the citadel. Blasting through walls, Anasûrimbor Kellhus effortlessly kills Sorweel's protectors. He approaches the adolescent Prince, but rather than seizing or striking him, he *embraces* him. Tells him that he is forgiven.

The city secure, the Great Ordeal prepares for the long march across the trackless wilds. Sorweel finds himself desolate for the loss of his father and the shame of his new circumstances. As the new King of Sakarpus, he is naught but a tool of the New Empire, a way for the Aspect-Emperor to legitimize his tyranny. Before the host departs, none other than Moënghus and his eldest son Kayûtas visit him in his palace. They tell him he is to join the Ordeal as the symbol of his nation's commitment to their holy cause. The following day Sorweel finds himself part of the Scions, a horse company composed of princely hostages from across the rim of the New Empire. This is how he meets and befriends Zsoronga ut Nganka'kull, the Successor Prince of Zeum.

A Mandate sorcerer named Eskeles is assigned to tutor Sorweel in Sheyic, the common tongue of the Three Seas, and through him the young King learns the reasons why so many worship the Aspect-Emperor so fervently. For the first time he begins to doubt his father ... What if the Aspect-Emperor spoke true? What if the world was about to end?

Why else would someone so cunning march so many Men to their doom?

Sorweel is also provided a slave named Porsparian to attend to his needs, a wizened old man who is anything but the submissive thrall he pretends to be. One night Sorweel watches him tear away the turf and mold the face of the Goddess Yatwer from the dirt. Before his eyes, mud bubbles up as spit from her earthen lips. The slave palms this mud and smears it across the incredulous King's cheeks.

The following morning Sorweel attends a Council of Potentates with Zsoronga and Eskeles. His dread waxes as he watches the Holy Aspect-Emperor move from lord to lord, declaring the truths they think hidden in their souls. He fears what will happen when the man sees the hatred and treachery smoldering in his own. But when Anasûrimbor Kellhus comes to him, he *congratulates* Sorweel for grasping the truth, and before all those assembled declares him one of the Believer-Kings.

The all-seeing Aspect-Emperor, Sorweel realizes, is blind to the truth of his soul.

Esmenet

Far to the south in Momemn, the capital of the New Empire, Esmenet struggles to rule in her husband's absence. With Kellhus and the bulk of his armed might faraway, the embers of insurrection have begun to ignite across the Three Seas. The Imperial Court regards her with condescension. Fanayal ab Kascamandri, the Padirajah of what had been the heathen Kianene Empire before the First Holy War, grows ever more bold on the fringes of the Great Carathay Desert. Psatma Nannaferi, the outlawed Mother-Supreme of the Cult of Yatwer, prophecies the coming of the White-Luck Warrior, the godsent assassin who will murder the Aspect-Emperor and his progeny. Even the *Gods*, it seems, plot against the Anasûrimbor Dynasty. Esmenet turns to her brother-in-law, Maithanet, the Shriah of the Thousand Temples, for his strength and clarity of vision, yet she wonders why her husband would leave the Mantle in *her* incapable hands, when his brother is Dûnyain like himself.

She also has the travails of her own family to contend with. All her eldest children have gone. Mimara has fled—to Achamian, she hopes and prays. Kayûtas, Serwa, and her stepson, Moënghus, ride with their father in the Great Ordeal. Theliopa remains with her as an advisor, but the girl is scarcely human, she is so narrow and analytical. The next youngest, the mad and murderous Inrilatas, Esmenet keeps imprisoned atop the Andiamine Heights. Only her very youngest, the twins Samarmas and Kelmomas, provide her with any comfort. She clings to them as if they were flotsam in a shipwreck, not realizing that Kelmomas, like his brother Inrilatas, has inherited too many of his father's gifts. The boy has already driven away Mimara with the cunning of his insinuations. Now he plots deeper ways to secure sole possession of his mother's heart.

He will tolerate no rivals.

In the city of Iothiah, meanwhile, the White-Luck Warrior reveals himself to Psatma Nannaferi, who summons all her High Priestesses to plot the destruction of the Anasûrimbor. None other than Yatwer, the monstrous Mother of Birth, moves against the Aspect-Emperor. As the Goddess most favoured by slaves and caste-menials, she commands tremendous temporal power. Unrest spreads among the servile poor throughout the Empire.

Even as the first rumours of this sedition reach his mother in Momemn, young Kelmomas continues his own devious insurrection. Where before he had driven Mimara away, now he engineers the death of his idiot twin, Samarmas, knowing that grief for his loss will make his mother even more desperate for his love.

Agonized by the death of Samarmas, Esmenet turns to her brother-in-law, Maithanet, frantic for the thought of a *God* hunting her family. He reminds her that the Gods can see neither the No-God nor the coming Apocalypse, and so perceive her husband as a threat instead of the Saviour.

At his bidding, Esmenet summons Sharacinth, the officially sanctioned Matriarch of the Yatwerians, to the Andiamine Heights with the intention of setting the Cult against itself. When they fail to cow the woman, Kellhus himself arrives, and breaks her will to resist with the sheer force of his presence. The blubbering Matriarch yields, promising to wrest her Cult from Psatma Nannaferi. The Aspect-Emperor returns to the Great Ordeal, dismaying his Empress with his lack of grief for the death of Samarmas, his son.

Kelmomas sets out that very night and, using his Dûnyain gifts, murders Sharacinth and her retinue. Rumours of her assassination travel quickly, igniting the embers of sedition among the slaves and caste-menials. Riots erupt across the Three Seas.

Esmenet does turn to Kelmomas for comfort. At night, she takes to embracing him in her bed while the smell of smoke and the sound of screaming waft through windows. Intoxicated with success, the young Prince-Imperial begins plotting against his uncle, Maithanet, who alone possesses the ability to see through his deception.

THE WHITE-LUCK WARRIOR

Achamian

The horror of Cil-Aujas lies as much within them as behind. Achamian, Mimara, and the Skin Eaters descend the heights into the vast forests the scalpers call the Mop. The old Wizard presses Mimara, desperate to discover how she had overcome the evil shade of the Nonman King, but she demurs, resenting him for his refusal to explain the Judging Eye. Achamian attempts to make amends a short time after, but a second scalper company, the Stone Hags, ambushes them, and the matter is forgotten. The Skin Eaters have scarce travelled a fraction of the way to the Coffers, and they are decimated. The men take to mutinous muttering, and Achamian finds himself advocating *for* their Captain, as much as he despises the man's homicidal understanding of "discipline."

Days later, they hear cries filtering through the forest gloom, and Achamian spies the Stone Hags caught upon a distant ridge battling more Sranc than they can hope to overcome. Later that night, the survivors come upon the Skin Eaters. Chaos and conflict rule, then the skinnies come shrieking out of the forest blackness. Mimara finds herself apart from the others, almost certainly doomed, but Somandutta appears before her, and in an inhuman display of skill, handily slays the Sranc assailing her. Soma is a *skin-spy*, she realizes, but their straits are such that she waits until they reach the relative safety of Fatwall, an Imperial outpost they find abandoned and burning, before telling Achamian. The old Wizard confronts the Nilnameshi caste-noble, who flees the ruined fortress rather than parlay. Vast numbers of Sranc descend upon the ruined tower they take as their citadel, and the Skin Eaters endure a night of gibbering slaughter.

The subsequent days see them travel fast through the foliated underworld of the Mop, thanks to the way the Qirri quickens their limbs—fast enough to break the body and spirit of those surviving Stone Hags who have joined them. Mimara shares stories of her life upon the Andiamine Heights with Achamian, and the two outcasts come to an unspoken accord, an affection borne of trial and shared affliction. But Mimara is not long in violating this trust. The thing called Soma has been tracking them all along. It surprises her alone in the gloom, tells her she must murder the Captain to prevent Cleric from killing them. It also tells her that she is pregnant. Overlooking the ruins of ancient Kelmeol, the thing encounters its Consult master, who bids it to continue tracking the scalper company, and to continue *protecting Mimara*—all the way to Golgotterath if need be. "*All* the prophecies must be respected," the Synthese says, "the false as much as the true."

The Mop behind them, the scalpers begin the long, arid trek across the Istyuli Plains. The days become more feverish, the nights more crazed, and it seems to Mimara that she alone is aware of the madness slowly consuming them. Cleric's ritual dispensation of the Qirri has become a raucous, even rapturous affair, far more religious than medicinal. The Nonman's sermons have become both more ominous and profound. Despite her reluctance, Mimara presses Achamian on the issue, begs him to abandon the Skin

Eaters, to flee as far from Cleric and his Qirri as they can, only to sob with relief when he argues why they must stay. They march into the very wake of the Great Ordeal, encounter a supply company—Men they murder to pass undetected.

Not long afterward, Mimara meets with the thing called Soma once again, though now it has taken *her own form*. She demands that it tell her what is happening; it presses her to ask Cleric about the *Qirri*, to discover what it is. Before she can ask the thing why, Achamian appears, and the skin-spy flees leaping into the night, pursued by the Wizard and his sorcerous might. Achamian is furious, convinced the creature meant to replace her. She lies to him, tells him nothing about her previous encounters with the thing.

More and more she can feel the unborn child within her, and its presence seems to fortify her against whatever consumes the others. She dares question the company's Sergeant, Sarl, whose sanity was snapped in twain in the depths of Cil-Aujas. He tells her nothing of Cleric, but he does reveal that the Captain somehow *knows* her true identity. There can no longer be any doubt: the Skin Eaters are an instrument of the Holy Aspect-Emperor.

When the scalpers congregate to receive their Qirri the following night, she astounds them all by *refusing* her portion. Nothing is made of it, but in the pitch of night she awakens to find Cleric gazing down at her. She asks what the Qirri is, and he tells her that it's the ashes of some long-dead Nonman hero. When she asks *who*, he bids her *taste* to see. And so she succumbs to the drug once again—and in doing so discovers what they have been consuming for the length of their mad and onerous quest ...

The ashes of Cu'jara Cinmoi.

As the Captain leads them ever deeper into the dead North, they finally come upon the trail of the Great Ordeal: field upon field of burnt and hewn Sranc. Mimara asks Achamian how he could still doubt Kellhus. Was this not proof that he waged war against Golgotterath? This, combined with the truth of the Qirri, proves too much for the old Wizard, and that evening *he* denies Cleric's dispensation of the cannibal ash. Mimara awakens to cries in the night, finds the Captain and the Nonman binding and gagging the Wizard. She throws herself at them, only to be seized by Galian and the others, who immediately set about stripping her clothes. The Captain falls upon them in a fury, killing one, raging at the others, telling them that *damnation* awaits any who harm her. The Judging Eye opens, and she sees what sin has made of Lord Kosoter, something infernal for the numberless atrocities he has committed. So it seems that a wheezing demon falls to its knees at her feet, calling her Princess-Imperial, and imploring that she save them from damnation.

The Captain is not simply a Zaudunyani fanatic, he is an agent of the Aspect-Emperor, one of her stepfather's countless slaves. But as inclined as he is to worship her, he possesses no inclination to *heed* her. He refuses to release Achamian—or to reveal the nature of his mission. All she knows is that it involves following through on *Achamian's quest*. Even with the old Wizard bound and gagged, they continue the trek to the Library of Sauglish and the legendary Coffers.

The surviving Skin Eaters find themselves divided along the line of this revelation. Galian and his cohorts—those who care nothing for matters of faith—become more and more mutinous. Only their awe of Cleric—and craving for Qirri—seem to constrain them. They make no secret of their carnal designs. With Achamian incapacitated, the crazed Captain has become her sole refuge. So she plies the man as they march ever nearer the ancient Library, searching for some weakness, something she can use to win Achamian's freedom. When the man proves immovable, she turns to Cleric, going so far as to shave her hair in an attempt to seduce him—anything that might change their dismal fortunes.

This is how she learns the astonishing truth of his identity. Cleric is none other than *Nil'giccas*, the last of the Nonman Kings.

She dares tell Achamian as much. Taking advantage of darkness and preoccupation, she crawls to a point behind where the old Wizard lays trussed and gagged. She tells him of the child—his child—in her womb. She tells him of her love ... her hope.

The Captain discovers her, whips her with his belt before the leering others. But in doing so, he simply reminds her *who she has always been*: someone who cannot be broken for violence alone, someone who always has "one sip remaining." The following morning, the Judging Eye opens, reveals the degrees of damnation awaiting each of her captors—none more than the Captain. And she understands that the tragedy of *their* circumstance dwarfs her own.

Though her silence gulls the scalpers into thinking her broken, their eventual arrival at the Library of Sauglish finds her strong, resolved in a manner she had never known.

Fearing treachery, the Captain bids Cleric accompany Achamian to the Library alone while he and the others hang back, holding Mimara as surety. As much as the prospect of leaving Mimara behind terrifies the old Wizard, he cannot but see the arrangement as a profound opportunity, given what Mimara has told him of Cleric. Seswatha was an ancient friend of Nil'giccas, the King of Ishterebinth: perhaps he can use his knowledge of the ancient Sohonc Grandmaster to prise the Erratic from the Captain's homicidal influence. So they depart, and Mimara finds herself stranded with the last four surviving Skin Eaters aside from Lord Kosoter—Sarl, Pokwas, Xonghis, and Galian—as well as the sole surviving member of the Stone Hags, Koll.

Achamian plies the Nonman as they pick their way through the wooded ruins of Sauglish, bidding him time and again to recall *who he really is*: Nil'giccas, the Last Nonman King, anything but Cleric, the slave he has become. Too late does he realize his mistake: tragedy and farce, atrocity and slaughter: only these can make an Erratic remember. By declaring Seswatha's ancient love in Seswatha's own voice, Achamian has simply whetted the ageless Nonman's appetite for loss. When they at last reach the ruined Library, they find the entrance to the legendary treasury of the Sohonc destroyed. If the surrounding blight were not sign enough, the smell and the spoor are unmistakable: Wracu ...

A Dragon has made a den of the Coffers.

Mimara remains with the Captain in the camp, watching apprehensively as Galian, emboldened by Cleric's absence, begins *baiting* his legendary leader. The surviving scalpers, it seems, have been plotting mutiny for some time, biding their time, waiting for this very opportunity. Horrified, she watches them cut down Lord Kosoter, a man she had thought immortal for sheer ferocity. The last of the Skin Eaters turn to her ...

Cleric and the old Wizard, meanwhile, dare enter the ruined maw of the Coffers, where they find Wutteät, the famed Father of Dragons, coiled about a great heap of Far Antique treasure. Achamian attempts to bargain with the Wracu, offering to exchange Truth for the map to Ishuäl.

"TURN FROM THIS PLACE," the beast croaks. "TURN! COME TO ME WHEN THE WORLD HAS TRULY ENDED."

As the leader of the mutiny, Galian is the first to assault Mimara. He tears her clothing away, promises to kill the unborn infant in her womb ...

Achamian and Cleric assail the undead Dragon in tandem—Man and Nonman, as in days of ancient old. The Coffers become a furnace of killing light.

No more than a league distant, the Judging Eye opens, and Mimara apprehends the extent of Galian's damnation, the eternity of torment that awaits his final heartbeat. She tells him what she sees, and he hesitates for the certainty of her warning, the pity in her gaze. Then he is flopping across the humus, writhing about the knife in his back. Mimara looks up and sees that Koll, the sole, travel-wasted survivor of the Stone Hags, has saved her.

Together, Achamian and Cleric drive Wutteät roaring from the Coffers, fleeing like a moth afire into the skies. Thinking their triumph might seal some compact between them, Achamian once again appeals to the Nonman Erratic, to *Nil'giccas*, but the Last Nonman King has already forgotten. Cleric turns his fearsome sorceries upon the old Wizard.

Stunned, Mimara watches Koll battle Galian's confederates, Xonghis and Pokwas. Sarl retreats, hugging his beloved Captain's severed head, cackling and crooning nonsense. Koll, she realizes, *is not Koll at all*, but *Soma*—or, rather, the skin-spy that had replaced him so very long ago.

An agent of the Unholy Consult has saved her ... Why?

Cleric hammers Achamian with ancient and inhuman sorceries, howling out his final, cryptic sermon as he does so. The Last Nonman King wants only to die, the old Wizard realizes, for he attacks only, and raises no sorcerous defenses. The antique Hero has given Achamian a choice: kill him, or be killed.

Between Xonghis and Pokwas, the thing called Koll is overmatched, but the two scalpers have overlooked Mimara, who is nowhere near as helpless as she appears. Using their distraction, she kills the two scalpers with Galian's sword. One cannot raise walls against what has been forgotten.

Heartbroken, Achamian strikes Nil'giccas from the sky above him.

Mimara runs to where the thing called Koll lies, demanding to know why it has saved her. But Sarl falls upon the thing with his knife, cackling about the bounty for "spiderfaces". The forest burns about the sordid scene.

The old Wizard returns to the scalper camp in horror and dismay, only to be overjoyed to find Mimara alive. Together they flee to the Library of Sauglish. They raise a bier to provide Nil'giccas a proper funeral. As the

Last Nonman King's body burns, they ransack the Coffers, find the ancient map described in Achamian's dreams, the map to Ishuäl—the hidden stronghold of the Dûnyain, the birthplace of the Holy Aspect-Emperor.

They gather the ashes of Nil'giccas to replenish their supply of Qirri, then set out on the final leg of their journey. Now far from the lodestone of the Great Ordeal, they are once again beset by Sranc. They persevere, gain the Demua Mountains, and at last surmount the glacier overlooking the vale of the Dûnyain. At long last, they see it, *Ishuäl* ...

Itself a gutted ruin.

The Great Ordeal

Once the victim of forces beyond his comprehension, Sorweel now finds himself the *agent* of such forces as well. He remains a victim so far as he remains the "guest" of the Aspect-Emperor, the demon who murdered his father, conquered his city, and plundered the famed Chorae Hoard. But he has become an agent through the occult ministrations of his slave, Porsparian, who had rubbed the spit of Yatwer, the Dread Mother of Birth, across his cheeks and so rendered his sedition invisible to the Anasûrimbor. But now that Sorweel can hide his heart, what should he do?

Leaving the Pale of Sakarpus behind, the Great Ordeal marches into the arid emptiness of the Istyuli Plains. Not a single Sranc opposes them.

Aimless, Sorweel gives himself over to the camaraderie of the Scions. Though Sheyic, the common tongue of the host, defeats him, he is a young warrior among young warriors—even more, a young hostage among young hostages—and the language of boyish, martial yearning transcends all tongues. If he cannot avenge his father or fathom the Dread Mother's design, then he will ride out and test himself with his new comrades.

He will ride in his enemy's war.

Exalt-General Proyas, meanwhile, confers with Kellhus, who informs him the time has come for the Great Ordeal to break up to facilitate foraging. Even more alarmingly, he reveals that the New Empire crumbles in their absence. With all his power concentrated in the Great Ordeal, his old enemies grow ever more bold. To assure the Ordealmen suffer no distractions, no fear for the loved ones they have left behind, he declares an embargo on all sorcerous communications with the Three Seas.

Henceforth, the Great Ordeal marches both divided and alone.

The Scions ride out to the southwest of the Army of the Middle North, tasked with securing game—a mission the young hostages bemoan for its safety. Nevertheless, Sorweel's knowledge of the Istyuli allows them to track and destroy a wandering Sranc clan. They discover and begin following a great elk trail shortly thereafter, only to find the herd that authored it butchered across the plain. Eskeles, who continues to teach Sorweel the rudiments of Sheyic on the trail, recognizes the carnage as the consequence of a Hording, a massing of Sranc. But only Sorweel, relying once again on his knowledge as a native of the plains—and impossible communications with the Dread Mother—can see the true significance of the slaughter. The Consult, he tells the wondering Mandate Schoolman, prepares an ambush. Days later, they find an entire legion of Sranc hidden to the south of the Great Ordeal.

Now divided into four armies, the host plumbs the great, vacant heart of the Istyuli. The outriders begin returning with tales of Sranc congregating just over the northern horizon, a vast and raucous Horde strewn across the path of all four armies, growing ever more numerous as clan after clan joins its inchoate retreat. Soon all the Ordealmen can see the great, bilious clouds of dust the creatures have kicked across the horizon: the Shroud. Soon all can hear the shrieking cacophony from afar.

Kellhus, meanwhile, begins meeting with Proyas in his private chambers, where he confesses to things that have long troubled the Exalt-General's heart. Achamian, he tells the Believer-King, was right about him all along.

As the Scions race back to warn the Great Ordeal, Sorweel at last confides in Zsoronga, who has been wary of him ever since the Aspect-Emperor declared him one of the Believer-Kings. Sorweel tells his friend about Porsparian—and more importantly, about Yatwer, the Mother of Birth—begging for whatever insight he has to offer. Zsoronga tells him he is *Narindari*, a divine assassin sent to murder Anasûrimbor Kellhus.

Sorweel is denied the luxury of ruminating on his friend's mad assertion. The Scions push their ponies to the limits of endurance in an attempt to reach the Great Ordeal ahead of the Consult Legion. The Scions find themselves fleeing across treacherous ground through the darkness, their numbers dwindling as more and more of their exhausted mounts fail. When Eskeles is thrown, Sorweel leaps from his pony to assist the portly Mandate Schoolman. Sranc overrun them, cluster about the sorcerer's

Wards. Eskeles panics, but Sorweel remains calm, instructs the man to find some means of warning Anasûrimbor Kayûtas and the Army of the Middle-North. The sorcerer casts a Bar of Heaven, revealing the Legion to the embattled Norsirai, and so saving a mighty fraction of the Great Ordeal.

The following morning Sorweel and Zsoronga swear an oath to be as brothers, boonsmen until death. Kayûtas declares him a hero, saying that his actions had saved the Army of the Middle-North from almost certain destruction. What Zsoronga said earlier was true, the young Believer-King realizes: the Dread Mother of Birth *positioned* him within the Great Ordeal. In typical Anasûrimbor fashion, Kayûtas follows his praise with the demand that he kill his slave, Porsparian. The Great Ordeal is running out of food, the man explains, and the Aspect-Emperor has commanded that his Believer-Kings put down all their noncombatant servants and slaves.

Sorweel bids Porsparian to follow him into the grisly tracts of dead Sranc, planning to release rather than murder him. But it is the old Shigeki who leads *him* into the bloody wrack. The slave clears a pocket of turf, then begins unearthing bones from the soaked muck: a skeleton that takes on the ghostly image of the *Mother* herself. Skeletal hands reach into a vacant womb and draw out a strange pouch, which Sorweel takes in trembling hands. Porsparian throws himself upon a spear before the youth can question him.

Sorweel investigates the leather pouch in his tent later that evening, knowing what it contains even before he draws it open: a Chorae. Zsoronga had called him *Narindari*, an assassin of the Gods.

Every assassin needs a weapon.

Later that night he seeks out Anasûrimbor Serwa, the Grandmistress of the Swayali, on the pretext of thanking her for saving him. She cannot see that he lies, nor can she sense the Chorae within the pouch the Mother of Birth has given him. He departs knowing that in the entire World, he alone possesses the means both to deceive—and to kill—the Aspect-Emperor.

The Great Ordeal continues crawling north toward the ever-withdrawing Horde. The desolation of the Istyuli gradually gives way to the knuckled landscape of ancient Sheneor, a High Norsirai nation prominent in the Holy Sagas, and the Ordealmen rejoice for finally reaching the outskirts of scripture. At the behest of their Aspect-Emperor, the Schools begin what comes to be called the Culling, drawing up in long lines and floating out over the masses of the Horde, killing and burning as many of the obscene creatures as they possibly can. The slaughter is great, but as the Horde withdraws, it scoops up ever more clans: the Culling can do little more than slow the foul mustering of their foe.

Summoned to the Umbilicus, Proyas finds Kellhus preparing to receive an embassy of Nonmen from Ishterebinth. Claiming to speak for Nil'giccas, King of Ishterebinth, the emissary declares that his people will add their voice and shield to the Great Ordeal, but only if Kellhus manages to retake the ancient fortress of Dagliash, and sends them three hostages according to the ancient Law of Niom: a son, a daughter, and an *enemy*, one who can gainsay any deception.

Sorweel learns that he is to be that third hostage the following morning, a "false enemy," Serwa assures him. The news so dismays Zsoronga that he refuses to believe it at first, arguing that the Dread Mother will find some way to keep Sorweel near the Aspect-Emperor. But the Goddess fails to intercede. Swearing to return, Sorweel charges his friend with keeping Her gift, the Chorae-concealing pouch, safe while he is gone.

Serwa must rely on Metagnostic Cants of Translocation to convey herself, Sorweel, and her eldest brother to Ishterebinth in a swift and safe manner. Her diluted blood, however, means that she, unlike her father, must sleep several watches between each casting. And so they cross the ruined breadth of ancient Kûniüri, stepping from horizon to horizon in blinding flashes of sorcerous light, but only twice daily. Sorweel comes to know both brother and sister in the intervals between, waiting for Serwa to muster her strength for their next leap across horizons. He is unnerved by the sheer number of facts arguing the righteousness of Anasûrimbor Kellhus and his cause. Even more, he begins to fear his burgeoning passion for the man's extraordinary daughter.

The Great Ordeal, meanwhile, continues its northward march. As it climbs toward the flank of the Neleöst, the preponderance of Sranc in the retreating Horde shifts from the east, the flank occupied by the Army of the Middle-North, to the west, the flank occupied by the Army of the South under King Sasal Umrapathur of Nilnamesh. Such are the numbers of Sranc drawn from the northeastern plains of the High Istyuli that the Aspect-Emperor deploys Saccarees and the Mandate to reinforce Umrapathur, thus stoking the jealousy of Carindûsû, Grandmaster of the Vokalati. When the retreating Horde is backed against the quick waters of the River Irshi, King Umrapathur occupies the ruined stronghold of Irsûlor, trusting to its heights to hold back the masses that now fairly encircled the Army of the South. Carindûsû leads his School north, thinking that together the Vokalati and the Mandati could drive the trapped Sranc multitudes to their death in the River Irshi. But rather than implode before the line of sorcerous destruction, the Sranc surge *toward it*, race through and around it. The whole horizon seems to fall screaming upon Irsûlor. The sorcerers cease their fruitless advance, begin racing back to defend King Umrapathur and the imperilled Army of the South. But they are too late: knowing the Irshi would force the Horde to strike, the Consult unleash a Bashrag legion they had concealed. Irsûlor is already an island of armoured humanity in a Sranc ocean when the Bashrag shatter the line. Sranc leap screaming in their wake. The Men of the Ordeal are broken into battling pockets that are utterly consumed one by one.

By the time the first Mandati and Vokalati return, only Umrapathur and his household survive upon Irsûlor's summit. Saccarees joins with Carindûsû in burning the endless Sranc surging from all points upon Umrapathur's shorn stronghold. But Carindûsû goes mad for shame and grief, and sorcerous *battle* breaks out between the Vokalati and the Mandate. The summit is overrun, and King Umrapathur dies defiled. Saccarees slays Carindûsû, and the surviving sorcerers of the Vokalati and the Mandate flee Irsûlor.

Even as this catastrophe unfolds in Sheneor, Sorweel awakens in Kûniüri. Unable to find either Serwa or Moënghus, he follows what are at first faint cries on the wind. He finds them, brother and sister, naked and prone upon the forest floor, locked in carnal embrace. He abuses himself for the sight. Even as his seed drops hot across his fist, the Imperial siblings *spy him*, and Sorweel is caught in the commission of a shame unlike any he has suffered. He flees their derision, rages for hatred and humiliation.

Following the disaster at Irsûlor, the Holy Aspect-Emperor reunites the Great Ordeal, and marches to the holy heights of Swaranûl. Upon its summit, he tells the mourning Believer-Kings their supplies have been exhausted, and that, henceforth, they have no choice but to begin eating Sranc.

Esmenet

Second Negotiant Malowebi, a Mbimayu Schoolman become diplomat, has been sent by the Great Satakhan of High Holy Zeum to assess Fanayal and his Fanim army—all that remains of the once mighty Kianene Empire—as potential allies in the struggle against Anasûrimbor Kellhus. Despite all the Bandit Padirajah's boasts, the only thing about Fanayal that manages to impress Malowebi is the existence of Meppa, the Last Cishaurim.

Young Kelmomas, meanwhile, observes his mother's struggles in the Imperial Synod. A messenger arrives bearing dire tidings from Shigek: news that Fanayal has invaded the Sempis River valley, and has already overthrown the walls of Iothiah. Shaken, Esmenet dissolves the Synod and takes Kelmomas to her apartments, where she reveals the entrance to the network of secret passages that riddle the whole of the Andiamine Heights. Their palace has hollow bones. In the event of any crisis, she tells him, he is to await her in these tunnels.

The following day Kelmomas overhears his mother asking Theliopa about Maithanet. Esmenet has come to distrust her brother-in-law, and wants to know how she could possibly sound his true intentions. Theliopa is unsure, but she knows that aside from their father the only soul who could do such a thing is *Inrilatas*, Kelmomas's mad brother. Of all the Imperial siblings, none possesses more of Father's strength than Inrilatas, or less ability to manage it. For years now he has been imprisoned in his room at the summit of the Andiamine Heights.

Esmenet decides to use him to test the loyalty of her husband's brother, the Holy Shriah of the Thousand Temples. Kelmomas decides to talk to Inrilatas first. At first he tries to convince the chained adolescent that he must *kill* their Uncle, but Inrilatas can see through him. He can even see the soul of Samarmas within him, whispering warnings! Kelmomas retreats in dismay, but not without leaving a small file behind him ...

Malowebi, meanwhile, tours the savaged streets of Iothiah with Fanayal, as repulsed by the brutality of the Fanim as he is amazed the great and ancient city was taken at all. He is impressed: by Fanayal's martial instincts and acumen, by the ferocity of his warriors, and by the awesome power of Meppa, the Last Cishaurim. But it is the *weakness* of the New Empire that impresses him most of all. The Aspect-Emperor, he realizes, has left it all but defenceless.

Esmenet visits Inrilatas, asks him if he would sound the truth of his uncle's heart. Though she is usually immune to his wiles, he manages to slip past her defences, speak truths that make her heart roil. But he agrees to do what she wishes, to question Maithanet, but only so long as Kelmomas *alone* is in attendance.

In Iothiah, Malowebi watches as Fanayal reviews the captives and apportions them among his Grandees. Psatma Nannaferi, the Mother-Supreme of the Yatwerian Cult, is dragged before the Bandit Padirajah. Her youthful beauty transfixes all present, yet she speaks and carries herself as an old crone. Where other captives had wept and begged, she stands tall and laughs, declaring that all of Fanayal's accomplishments are due to the Dread Mother of Birth. Meppa intercedes, and in the course of their exchange Malowebi realizes that *Yatwer indeed inhabits her*, that the Hundred Gods truly ruled these events. The Fanim are no more than puppets, Nannaferi declares, props to prepare the way for the White-Luck Warrior.

Witless to the peril, beguiled by her beauty, Fanayal takes her as his own portion.

Kelmomas begins exploring the shadow palace that lies in the bones of the Andiamine Heights. Esmenet, meanwhile, enters into negotiations with Maithanet possessing a greater confidence in her own abilities. She insists that he submit to Inrilatas's questioning as a condition of their future cooperation. When Maithanet asks her how she came by her suspicions, she merely replies, "Because you are Dûnyain." Maithanet agrees to the interrogation, but reminds her, as Theliopa already has, that the boy's madness renders any determination he might make moot.

As per Inrilatas's instructions, Maithanet and Kelmomas alone enter his chamber. Maithanet surprises the two brothers by jamming the door behind them, locking all three of them together. The mad adolescent immediately begins by asking the Holy Shriah whether he intends to murder their mother. Maithanet denies this, repeatedly, but Inrilatas's questions morph, begin turning on ever more subtle observations. "Uncle Holy", as the Imperial siblings refer to him, admits that he has always been concerned by the way their father has, over the years, allowed his concern for Esmenet to compromise the Shortest Path ...

The way Kellhus has allowed *love* to cloud the Thousandfold Thought.

Maithanet is unimpressed, pointing out that whatever Inrilatas can see, his father has already seen. He declares the interrogation yet another example of Esmenet's failing reason. "Mother?" Inrilatas asks, surprising both his brother and uncle. "You think Mother arranged this?"

Kelmomas stands horrified as Inrilatas reveals his crimes to their uncle, how he first murdered Samarmas and then Sharacinth. Why would his brother betray him this way? Maithanet, genuinely surprised, turns to the eight-year-old, demanding to know what he has done. This is when Inrilatas strikes, whipping his chains about his uncle's throat, strangling him. But Maithanet employs a blade concealed upon his elbow to stab the adolescent, killing him.

The door is battered down, and Esmenet enters to find her son dead. Kelmomas accuses Maithanet of murdering Inrilatas after he revealed his intent to usurp her. Uncle Holy storms from the palace, which has been thrown into uproar.

Later that night, Esmenet calls Lord Sankas to her chambers, asks him to contract an assassin.

So she finds herself stealing through the streets of Momemn in disguise several days following. Imhailas, Exalt-Captain of the Eothic Guard, leads her to a derelict tenement in a district not unlike the one she had lived in during her days as a prostitute. She meets with the Narindar alone in his room to spare any of her servants the threat of damnation, not knowing that the assassin Sankas had contracted in truth lies murdered underneath the bed—not knowing that she parlays with the *White-Luck Warrior*.

Even as the man agrees to murder Maithanet, horns ring out over the city ... battlehorns. She races back to the palace in terror, only to discover that her home has been *taken* by the Shrial Knights. Maithanet has finally struck. Imhailas has to drag her away, such is her terror for Kelmomas and Theliopa. The Exalt-Captain takes her to Naree, a Nilnameshi prostitute who has become his lover, and demands that she shelter the Empress.

And so Esmenet finds herself a fugitive in the very Empire she ruled, reliving her own past. Naree wants no part in the affair, but harbours the Empress for the love she bears Imhailas. For weeks Esmenet hides thus, fretting for her surviving children, raging for impotence, and bearing sundry indignities at the hands of her reluctant host. Imhailas is her sole source of information regarding the outside world, and his tidings never fail to dismay her. No matter how hard he pressures her, she refuses to flee her city.

Kelmomas witnesses the violent fall of the Andiamine Heights to the Shrial Knights through the innumerable spy-holes his father has installed throughout the palace. He takes the hidden network of passages as his new home, mourns the loss of his mother almost as much as the loss of his secret. As his hunger gets the better of him, he begins to ambush solitary Knights, dragging them into his hidden lair, devouring them until they spoil.

Malowebi, meanwhile, confers via sorcerous dreams with the Satakhan of High Holy Zeum on the matter of Fanayal, Meppa, and the manifest weakness of the New Empire. The Mbimayu emissary counsels caution: the fact that Kellhus has emptied the Imperial larder in his mad quest to destroy Golgotterath suggests that he *genuinely believes* the Second Apocalypse is upon them. Nganka'kull, however, sees opportunity, commands Malowebi to promise the support of Zeum should Fanayal succeed in his daring plan.

Imhailas returns to Naree's room after a long sojourn bearing news that no one knows what has come of Kelmomas. Esmenet fairly swoons, but her Exalt-Captain catches her, once again begs her to flee the city and raise an army from elsewhere across the Three Seas. But Esmenet suddenly recalls the secrets of her palace home. So long as Kelmomas remains hiding in the Andiamine Heights, there is no way she can leave Momemn. Imhailas relents, obviously exasperated.

Naree makes love to Imhailas that night—to spite *her*, Esmenet realizes. The indignity of listening combined with her terror for her son is too much, and she begins weeping. The Gods do war against her! At that moment the door is kicked open and Shrial Knights surge into the room. Esmenet is thrust to her knees, watches horrified as Imhailas is beaten to death before her. A Collegian throws five gold kellics at the shrieking Naree, then leaves one silver kellic as well, as a memento, he says, of the Empress she betrayed.

Maithanet's own bodyguard, the Inchausti, march Esmenet through the early morning streets to the Temple of Xothei. The frightful passage quickly transforms into a humiliating parade as more and more of Momemn awakens to word of the Empress's capture. Riot breaks out by the time they finally gain the great three-domed Temple's gate.

In chains, she is led into the gloom of the interior, to the central dais with its golden idols of the Ten, where she finds Maithanet awaiting her. He demands to know why she had Inrilatas try to assassinate him, and when she replies that she had nothing to do with it, *he realizes that she speaks true*. To Esmenet's astonishment, he falls to his knees and begs her *forgiveness*. Maithanet confesses that Kellhus's design defeats him as much as her, and that he now thinks that Kellhus had known all along that his Empire would collapse in his absence, and so had abandoned them to their own fates. He calls out to the surrounding lords and ministers, announcing the reconciliation of the Tusk and the Mantle. With wonder Esmenet watches dozens of Shrial and Imperial Apparati stride from the gloom toward her. The Shriah hears a noise, turns toward the idols. Standing in the one place overlooked, the *White-Luck Warrior* plunges a knife into his breast.

Uproar seizes the assembly, but Esmenet seizes *them*, decrying Maithanet as a traitor and a heretic—the murderer of the Aspect-Emperor's son. She speaks *oil* as Kellhus had taught her, saying not what was true, but what most needed to be believed. She is the only remaining link to their holy Warrior-Prophet, so when she screams at them to kneel, those assembled comply.

They all hear it in the ensuing silence, the throb of Fanim war-drums, and Esmenet realizes …

Fanayal attacks Momemn.

Prologue: Momemn

And naught was known or unknown, and there was no hunger.
All was One in silence, and it was as Death.
Then the Word was spoken, and One became Many.
Doing was struck from the hip of Being.
And the Solitary God said, "Let there be Deceit.
Let there be Desire."

—*The Book of Fane*

Late Summer, 20 New Imperial Year (4132, Year-of-the-Tusk), Momemn

For all the tumult of the Unification Wars, for all the rigours of motherhood and imperial station, Anasûrimbor Esmenet had never ceased to read. Of all the palaces her divine husband had seized for her comfort, not one had wanted for material. She had marvelled at the bleak beauty of Sirro in the arid shade of Nenciphon, dozed with the labourious precision of Casidas in the swelter of Invishi, scowled at the profundities of Memgowa in the chill of Oswenta. Smoke often plumed the horizon. Her husband's Holy Circumfix obscured walls, festooned shields, pinched naked throats. His children would watch her with His omnivorous eyes. The slaves would wash and scrub away the blood, paint, and plaster over the soot. And whenever opportunity afforded, she devoured what she could, the great classics of Early Cenei, the polyglot masterpieces of the Late Ceneian Empire. She smiled at the rollicking lays of Galeoth, sighed for the love poetry of Kian, bristled at the race chants of Ce Tydonn.

But for all the wisdom and diversion these forms possessed, they hung in the aether of fancy. Only *history*, she discovered, possessed a nature that answered her own. To read history was to read about *herself* in ways both concrete—Near Antique accounts of the Imperial Ceneian Court often pimpled her skin, so uncanny were the resemblances—and abstract. Every history and chronicle she consumed answered to the same compulsions, the same crimes, same hurts, same jealousies and disasters. The names were different, as were the nations, languages, and ages, and yet the same lessons remained, perpetually unlearned. It was almost *musical* in a sense, variations playing against ruinous refrains, souls and empires plucked like the strings of a lute. The peril of pride. The contradiction of trust. The necessity of cruelty.

And over time, one lesson in particular came to haunt her, a moral that—for her, at least—could only appal and dismay ...

Power does not make safe.

History murders the children of weak rulers.

The crow of battlehorns, so different from the long-drawn yaw of prayer-horns across the city.

Momemn was in uproar. Like a bowl of water set upon the floor of a racing chariot, it quivered and spit and swamped its rim. Anasûrimbor Maithanet, the Holy Shriah of the Thousand Temples, was dead. Fanim drums throbbed against gaseous hearts, made menace of the west. The Imperial Apparati and Shrial Knights ran to secure the Imperial Capital—to open the armouries, to rally the bewildered, to man the great curtain walls. The Blessed Empress of the Three Seas, however, ran to secure her heart ...

Her son.

"*Kelmomas hides yet in the palace* ..." Maithanet had said ere her assassin had struck.

"*What? Alone?*"

The gold-armoured Inchausti—who had paraded her mere watches before as their carnival captive—now escorted her as their imperial sovereign. Given the mobs besieging Xothei, they had elected to leave the temple through a series of mouldering, secret tunnels, what had been sewers during another age. Their Captain, a tall Massentian named Clia Saxillas, led them to an exit somewhere north of the Kamposea Agora, where they discovered the streets overrun with the very masses they had sought to avoid—souls as bent on finding loved ones as she.

For the better part of a watch, her world was confined to roiling gutters of humanity, troughs teeming with frantic thousands. Tenements towered dark and indifferent above the chaos. Her dead brother's elite guardsmen battled to maintain a square about her, jogging where the streets afforded, otherwise cursing and clubbing their way through the surge and trickle of untold thousands. At every turn, it seemed, she found herself stepping over the fallen, those unfortunates unable or unwilling to make way for their Blessed Empress. Captain Saxillas thought her mad, she knew, running to the Andiamine Heights at such a time. But to serve the Anasûrimbor was to execute madness in the name of miraculous success. If anything, her demands cemented his loyalty, confirmed the divinity he thought he had glimpsed in Xothei's great gloomy hollows. To serve divinity was to dwell among fractions of what was whole. Only the consistency of creed distinguished the believer from the mad.

Either way, his Shriah was dead and his Aspect-Emperor was away at war: *she* alone possessed his loyalty. She was the vessel of her husband's holy seed—the Blessed Empress of the Three Seas! And she would save her son, even if it meant that Momemn burned for want of leadership.

"*He isn't what you think he is, Esmi.*"

So it was with a mother's terror that she rushed down the baffled streets, cursed and cajoled the Inchausti whenever the press slowed their advance. Of all the afflictions she had endured while in hiding, none had gouged so deep as the loss of Kelmomas. How many watches had she spent, her throat cramping, her eyes fluttering, her whole being hung about the fact of his absence? How many prayers had she offered to the inscrutable black? How many promises of whatever? And how many horrific scenarios had come floating back in return? Idles drawn from the murderous histories she had read. Little princes smothered or strangled. Little princes starved, blinded, sold as novelties to catamite slavers ...

"Beat them!" she howled at the Shrial Guardsmen. "Bludgeon your way through!"

Our knowledge commands us, though our conceit claims otherwise. It drives our decisions and so harnesses our deeds—as surely as any cane or lash. She knew well the grievous fate of princes in times of revolt and overthrow. The fact that her husband's Empire crashed down about her was but one more goad to find her son.

The Fanim would have to wait. It mattered not at all that Maithanet had remained true to her husband, had genuinely thought *hers* the more treacherous soul. What mattered was that his servants had thought the same, that they still ran amok, and that one of them might find her son! She had seen their cruelty firsthand—watched them murder her beloved Imhailas! She knew as well as any woman could the way Men were prone to scapegoat others for their humiliation. And now that Maithanet *was dead*, who could say how his followers might avenge him, which innocents they might seize to token their grief and fury?

Now that Maithanet was dead.

She faltered at the thought, raised her hands against the turmoil, saw the grape stain of Shrial blood etching the whorl of her left palm. She closed her eyes against the surrounding commotion, willing the image of her little boy. Instead she saw the Narindar assassin standing almost naked between the golden idols, the Holy Shriah of the Thousand Temples supine at his feet, his blood black as pitch about points of reflected white.

Her husband's brother. Maithanet.

Dead. Murdered.

And now Fanim drums tripped racing hearts ...

Momemn was in uproar.

At long last they emerged from the canyon streets onto the relative openness of the Processional, and the Inchausti instinctively began trotting. Not even the mass panic could dilute the Rat Canal's famous reek. She saw the Andiamine Heights climbing soundless above the Imperial Precincts, her hated home, marmoreal walls clean in the sunlight, copper rooves gleaming ...

She looked wildly about, saw no signs of smoke, no mark of invasion. She glimpsed a small girl wailing over a woman prostrate on the hard cobble. Someone had painted Yatwer's Sickle upon the child's swollen cheek.

"*Mumma! Mumma-mumma-mumma!*"

She turned away, forbade herself any pang of compassion.

The Holy Shriah of the Thousand Temples was dead.

She could not think of what she had done. She could not regret.

Forward, to her hated home. That was the direction of her war.

The hush of the Imperial Precincts never failed to amaze her. The Scuäri Campus radiating outward, heating the air. Monuments, mottled black and green. Lintels hanging intricate against the sky. Columns soaring, jailing interiors that promised cool shadow and obscurity.

It made her screams all the more stark, shocking.

Kel!

Please!

Kel! It's sa-safe, my love! Your mother has returned!

She has prevailed!

Your Uncle is dead ...

Your brother is avenged!

She had no idea when she began crying.

The Andiamine Heights climbed before her, a palatial heap of rooves and columns and terraces, the marble bright in the high morning sun, the copper and gold shining.

It seemed haunted for quiet.

Kel! Kelmomas!

She forbade the Inchausti from following her. Any protest they might have nursed went unspoken. She wandered with a kind of stunned, disbelieving gait into the gloomy halls of the Apparatory. She seemed to float more than walk, such was her horror ... Hope is ever the greatest luxury of the helpless, the capacity to suppose knowledge that circumstances denied. So long as she remained a captive in Naree's apartment, Esmenet could always suppose that her little boy had found some way. Like a slave, she could grow fat on faith.

Now only truth lay before her. Truth and desolation.

Kelmommaaaaas!

Silence ... the visceral sense of void that attends any once-vibrant place emptied of motion and life. The apartments had been looted. The gilded panels were dull in the shuttered gloom, the censors cold, filled with fragrant ash—even the scenes stitched across the tapestries hung chill and fallow. Dried blood smeared and skinned the polished floors. Boot prints. Hand prints. Even the profile of a face, immortalized in chapped brown. Down every hallway, it seemed, she chased pale gleams that vanished as she drew near.

It was but a shell, she realized—a many-chambered skull. Her home.

Kel!

Her voice scratched at the vacant depths, too hoarse to echo.

It's m-m-meeee!

She had started her search in the Apparatory because of the way the palace's network of secret passages tracked its every room and niche. If there was one place, she had reasoned ... One place!

Mommy!

For all his blessed humanity she did not doubt the resourcefulness of her little boy. Out of all of them, he was the most hers—the *least* Dûnyain. But he possessed some modicum of his father's blood still. *Divine* blood.

Accursed.

Kelmomas!

Nothing could be so absent—so *missing*—as a lost child. They dwell so close, more *here* than here, ducking fingers that would tickle, convulsing with laughter, gazing with thoughtless adoration, lazing on your knees, on your hip, or in the crook of your arm, their body always *there*, always waiting to be clasped and hoisted, pressed against the bosom they took as their throne. Let the Inchausti scowl! Let men disapprove! What did they know of *motherhood*, the mad miracle of finding your interior drawn from you, clinging and bawling and giggling and learning everything there was to learn anew?

Damn you!

She stood motionless in the ransacked gloom, her ears pricked in the wake of her abraded voice. The Fanim drums pulsed on the edge of hearing. Her breath rasped.

Where are you?

She began sprinting down the marmoreal corridors, a hope where *he* should be, a horror where *he* should be, a missing breath, an unbalanced step, a look that could only roll, never focus, for the simple want of *him* ...

Kel! Kel!

She flew through the palace proper, the gilded labyrinth that was her home, more an assemblage than a coherent soul, wracked by sobs, laughing, crying out in the lilting voice of play. This was how the uncouth invaders would find her, a remote fraction of her soul realized. This was how the Fanim would find the Blessed Empress of the Three Seas, alone in her palace, cooing, shrieking, cackling, at last pried apart by a barking world.

She ran until a knife sliced the back of her throat, until spears gored her flanks. She ran until her feet became panicked refugees, each fleeing the other—until her wind seemed a beast that loped beside her, tongue lolling.

Kel!

She fell hard, not so much tripping as collapsing. The floor swatted her face, skinned her knees—then soothed these hurts with a bottomless cool.

She lay gasping in a slow-spinning heap.

She could hear it all, the mutter of the courtiers and the ministers, the laughter of caste-noble dandies, the swoosh of preposterous gowns, the barefooted patter of slaves. She could see *him* strolling toward her, though she knew his appearance only from the profile stamped on his coins: *Ikurei Xerius*, striding oblivious, ludicrous in his gold-silk slippers, gloating more than smiling ...

She bolted upright on a sharp intake of breath.

Masculine voices filtered up through the barren halls.

Your Glory! Glory!

The Inchausti?

She cast her eyes about the gloom, realized she lay in the vestibule of the Upper Palace.

She stood, exhaustion hard in her limbs. She walked to the battery of oaken shutters that fenced the opposing colonnade, unlatched and drew a section of them aside, squinted at the broad balcony beyond. Sparrows chirped and squabbled about a marble amenity basin. The pastel sky throbbed with the promise of retribution and war. Beneath its perpetual haze, Momemn riddled the distance with street and structure.

Plumes of smoke ribbed the horizon.

Dark clots of horsemen scoured the surrounding fields and orchards.

Refugees mobbed the gates.

Horns peeled, but whether they summoned or warned or rallied, she did not know ... or care.

No ... a fraction whispered.

Something ruthless dwells within every mother, a capacity borne of plague and tribulation and children buried. She was impervious; the hard realities of the World merely broke their nails for clawing. She turned away, strode back into the shadowy palace with a kind of weary resignation—as though she played at something that had cracked her patience long before. She had not so much abandoned hope as shouldered it aside.

She found the towering doors to the Imperial Audience Hall ajar. She wandered in, walked small beneath the soaring stonework. She pondered all the loads teetering, and the Sumni harlot within her wondered that such a place *could be her house*, that she lived beneath ceilings impregnated with Chorae, gilded in silver and gold. The sky framed the monumental dais with stages of pale brilliance. Dead birds bellied the netting that had been strung across the opening, as dry as flies. The upper gallery lay in graven shadow, while the polished expanses gleamed below. The tapestries strung between the columns seemed to sway, one for each of her dread husband's conquests. The scene tapered into gold instead of black in the corners of her eyes.

She considered duty, the way she would have the Shrial Knights who had murdered Imhailas executed. She thought of Naree and the savagery that awaited her. She smirked—a heartless smile—at the timid cruelties that had once hedged her own submissive nature.

No more.

She would speak oil and demand blood. Just like her divine husband.

Glory! Glory!

She walked soundless across the great floor, approached the dais, her eyes fending the brilliance of the sky beyond. The Circumfix Throne was little more than a silhouette ...

She did not see him until she was almost upon him.

Her son. Her mighty Prince-Imperial.

Anasûrimbor Kelmomas ...

Curled within the arms of her humble, secondary throne. Asleep.

Bestial with filth. Demonic with blood.

Her desperation flung her past her revulsion. She seized him, embraced him, shushed him as he keened and wailed.

Mummeee ...

Mum-mummeee ...

She drew her cheek across the cold tangle of grease and hair. "Shush ..." she gasped, as much for her sake as for his. "I am the only power remaining."

The sky beyond the Mantle caught her eye, and with it, a consciousness of her city, great Momemn, capital of the New Empire. Faraway drums counted the tandem racing of their hearts, mother and son.

Let it burn.

For this one moment at least.

The Blessed Empress of the Three Seas heaved at the glorious little shoulders and arms, pulled her weeping boy into her very being.

Where he belonged.

CHAPTER ONE

Aörsi

IV. The Game is the part of the whole that reenacts the whole as the whole. It therefore recognizes nothing outside itself, as we recognize nothing outside what we recognize.

—The Fourth Canto of the *Abenjukala*

We are born of tangled lovers, reared in the snarl of kin. We are ravelled to our desires, roped to our frailties and our sins. We are caught upon the hooks of others as upon the thistle of ourselves, looped and twisted, here brushed into lucent fibres, there bound in woolen obscurities.

And they come to us as combs and scissors.

—*Contemplations*, SIRRO

Late Summer, 20 New Imperial Year (4132, Year-of-the-Tusk), the northeast shore of the Neleöst

The living should not haunt the dead.

"The *meat* ..." Mirshoa said to his cousin, Hatturidas. They trudged side-by-side through the sun-spoked dust, Kishyati, vassals of Nurbanu Soter by virtue of their uncle, the ailing Baron of Nemuk, borne here for reasons far more complicated than piety or fervour. Men marched *together*, as aggregate souls, sons among the sons, fathers among the fathers. They never knew what compelled them, so they fastened on the occasioning words, and so transformed their bondage into artifice, a thing freely chosen.

"What of it?" Hatturidas replied after the jnanic interval indicating disapproval.

He had no desire to *think* of the meat, let alone discourse upon it.

"My ... my *soul* ... It grows more disordered because of it."

"That, at least, is in order."

Mirshoa glared at his cousin. "Tell me you don't feel it!"

Hatturidas continued tramping. Beyond him, thousands of his brother Jaguars toiled, and innumerable others beyond them as well, bent beneath packs and arms and armour. The World seemed to roll as a ball beneath them, so vast was the Great Ordeal.

Mirshoa lapsed back into rumination, which was unfortunate, because the man could not reflect without speaking.

"It's like my soul is naught but ... but smoked glass ..."

Wherever words should *not* go, that was where Mirshoa was sure to follow them. Be it the carnal nature of Inri Sejenus or the most effective purificatory rite for menses, his voice would barge and blunder, his eyes animate, growing wider even as those listening narrowed. Mirshoa was a hapless soul, a man numb to too many edges to avoid being cut. Ever since their childhood, Hatturidas had been his shepherd and his shield, "Taller by a thumb," his mother would always say, "wiser by a century ..."

"It's like something ... simmers, Hatti ... Like I'm a pot on coals ..."

"Skew the lid, then. Cease this bubbling!"

"Enough with your sarcasms! Tell me you *feel* it!"

The Shroud always hung on the horizon now, mountainous veils piling to where they became powder, obscuring every distance save the Sea.

"Feel what?"

"The *meat* ... The meat making you ... *shrink* in proportion to who you were the day before ..."

"No ..." Hatturidas said, wagging his bearded jaw. He hoisted his testicles in the exaggerated barracks way. "I grow *larger*, if anything."

"You're a fool!" Mirshoa cried. "I've marched across Eärwa with a mad wretch!"

Hatturidas could even hear *them* sometimes, a noxious croon rolling on the wind ...

The countless mouths of the Horde, screaming.

He spared his cousin an indulgent glance, the look of one who has always been stronger.

"And so you will march *back*."

The Men of the Three Seas did not so much eat as *feast* on the flesh of their vile and wicked enemy.

Following the reunification of the host at Swaranûl, the Great Ordeal followed the arthritic coastline of the Neleöst, the Misty Sea, advancing on a ponderous, northwestern arc. The Horde withdrew before the Shining Men as always, amorphous miles of howling Sranc, starving for the exhaustion of the earth beneath, keening for the promise of Mannish congress on the wind. But where the outriders had once chased, running down or driving away the more famished clans, and where the Schoolmen had simply massacred, hanging low above fields of screaming turmoil, they now *hunted* the beasts—worked a grisly harvest.

Cadres of sorcerers strode deep into the billowing clouds, intent not so much on destroying as *herding*, striking wedges, then driving what numbers they could toward the echelons of horsemen who followed. Some Sranc invariably fled south and east, only to find themselves dashing headlong into waves of galloping lancers. The skirmishes were as brief as they were brutal. Screeching creatures hacked and skewered in a shadowy world of violence and dust. Afterward, the horsemen—be they Imperial Kidruhil, caste-noble knights, or tribal plainsmen—would pile the dead into conical heaps, hundreds of them, until they dotted the blasted hillocks and pastures of the coast. There they would stand, cairns of fish-white carcasses, gathering flies and carrion birds, awaiting the shining tide that approached from the southwestern horizon. The clash of cymbals. The screech and bellow of signalling horns. The rumble of marching thousands.

The Host of the Believer-Kings.

According to scripture and tradition, no flesh was more polluted than that of the Sranc. Not pig. Not even dog or monkey. *The Holy Sagas* related the tale of Engûs, an ancient Meörnish Prince who saved his tribal household by fleeing into the high Osthwai and bidding them to consume their monstrous foe. The Sranc-Eaters, they were called, and they were damned as no soul could be short of sorcerers, witches, and whores. According to

Sakarpi legend, the vale where they took refuge was mortally cursed. Those who sought it thinking they would find gold (for the wont of rumour is to attribute riches to the damned) were never seen again.

Despite this, despite the native revulsion and disgust, nary a word of protest was raised among the Ordealmen. Perhaps it was the measure of their faith. Perhaps it was simply the nature of Men to celebrate one day what they had abominated the day before, so long as their hungers were sated.

Perhaps meat was simply meat. Sustenance. Who questioned the air they breathed?

The flesh was dense, pungent to smell, in some ways sour and in others sweet. The sinews in particular were difficult to gnaw through. Some among the Inrithi took to chewing the gristle throughout the day. The entrails were heaped in odious piles, along with those pieces—feet, viscera, and genitalia, mostly—too difficult or unsavoury to eat. If fuel was plentiful enough, the heads would be burned in oblation.

The rank and file simply portioned the beasts and cooked them over open fires. With the carcasses so divided, it became impossible to distinguish the limbs from those of Men. Everywhere one travelled, whether through the timbered tents of the Galeoth, or the garish parasol cities of the Conriyans and Ainoni, one saw arms and legs sweating over grease-fuelled fires, blackened fingers hanging slack over light. But if the resemblance troubled any, they dared not speak it.

The caste-nobility, as a rule, demanded more in the way of preparation and variety. The carcasses were beheaded and hung from their heels on timber scaffolds to properly drain. These racks could be seen throughout the encamped Ordeal, rows of white and violet bodies hanging from their heels, graphic for their nakedness. Once drained, the beasts were butchered in the manner of cattle and sheep, then served in ways that disguised the troubling humanity of their forms.

Within days, it seemed, the entire host had set aside its scruples and fell to their grisly fare with relish, even celebratory enthusiasm. Tongues and hearts became the preferred delicacies among the Nansur kjineta. The Ainoni prized the cheeks. The Tydonni took to boiling the creatures before searing them over flame. To a man they discovered the peculiar mingling of triumph and transgression that comes upon those who battle against *what they would eat.* For they could not bite without suffering some glimmer of the affinity between Sranc and Men—the sordid spectre of cannibalism—and they could not chew and swallow without some sense of predatory *domination.* The immeasurable Horde, which had been the object of so much foreboding and terror, became small with hilarity and devious wit. At the latrines they traded jokes about justice and Fate.

The Men of the Ordeal feasted. They slept with sated bellies, with the assurance that their most primitive needs had been secured. They awoke drowsy, without the dull and alarming hollow of starvation.

And a wild vitality crept through their veins.

There was a grove of oaks that became sacred with the passage of summer in Ishuäl. As green sickened into orange and dun, the Dûnyain made ready, not as yeoman preparing for winter, but as old priests welcoming even older Gods. They sat among the trees according to their station, knees out, their feet pressed sole to sole, the skin of their shaved skulls alive to the merest air, and they gazed into the boughs with a fixity that was not human. They cleared all thought from their soul, laid awareness bare to its myriad engines, and they watched the oak leaves fall ...

Each of them possessed gold coins—remnants of a long-forgotten hoard—very nearly worn smooth of image and insignia, but yet possessing the ghosts of long-dead Kings. Sometimes the leaves dropped of their own volition, rocked like paper cradles across motionless air. But usually high-mountain gusts unmoored them, and they battled like bats, danced like flies, as they rode the turbulence to the ground. The Dûnyain, their eyes dead with the absence of focus, let their coins fly—a flurry of sparks traced the raw sun. Without fail, some fraction of the leaves would be caught and pinned to the flagstones, lobed edges curled like fingers about the gold.

They called it the Tracery, the rite that determined who among them would sire children and so sculpt the future of their terrible race.

Anasûrimbor Kellhus breathed as Proyas breathed, tossing coinage of a different sort.

The Exalt-General sat before him, legs crossed, hands clutching knees through the pleats of his war-skirt. He looked at once alert and serene, the General of a host that had yet to be truly tested, but beyond this appearance, gusts raked him as surely as they had raked the Tracery Grove. Blood flushed heat through the man's veins, steeped his extremities with alarmed life. His lungs drew shallow air.

Horror wafted from his skin.

Kellhus watched, cold and impervious behind indulgent, smiling eyes. He sat cross-legged also, his arms hanging loose from his shoulders, his hands open across his thighs. The Seeing Hearth lay between them, flames rushing into a luminous braid. Despite his manifest repose, he leaned forward imperceptibly, held his chin at the angle appropriate to expectation, as if awaiting some pleasant diversion ...

Nersei Proyas was but a rind in his eyes, a depth as thin as a heartbeat was long. Kellhus could have reached out and *behind* him, manipulated the dark places of his soul. He could have summoned any sentiment, any sacrifice ...

But he hung motionless instead, a spider with its legs pinched close. Few things were so mercurial, so erratic, as Thought filtering through a human soul. The twist and skitter, the tug and chatter, sketching forms across inner oblivion. Too many variables remained unexamined.

He began as he always began, with a shocking question.

"Why do you think the God comes to Men?"

Proyas swallowed. Panic momentarily frosted his eyes, his manner. The bandages on his right arm betrayed archipelagos of crimson.

"I-I don't understand."

The anticipated response. Questions that begged explanation opened the soul.

The Exalt-General had changed in the weeks following his first visit to Anasûrimbor Kellhus' spare quarters. His gaze had become equine with uncertainty. Fear now twitched through his every gesture. The tribulation of these sessions, Kellhus knew, had eclipsed any trial the Great Ordeal could offer. Gone was the pious resolve, the air of overtaxed compassion. Gone was the weary stalwart, the truest of all his Believer-Kings.

All Men possess their share of suffering, and those bearing the most are bent as with any great load. But it had been *words*, not wounds, that had robbed the Exalt-General of his old, upright demeanour, possibilities, as opposed to any atrocity of the real.

"The God is Infinite," Kellhus said, pausing before the crucial substitution. "Is It not?"

Apprehension crimped the clarity of Proyas's gaze.

"Of-of course ..."

He is beginning to dread his own affirmations.

The Greater Proyas, at least, understood where they must lead.

"Then how could you hope to conceive Him?"

Instruction could be a joint undertaking, a pursuit, not just of thoughts and claims, but of the *insights* that motivated them; or it could be a forced concession, like those cruel tutors exacted beneath raised canes. Kellhus had been forced to rely on the latter more and more as the years had passed, for the accumulation of power was at once the accumulation of complexity. Only now, relieved of the burdens of his Empire, could he resume the former.

Only now could he witness a faithful soul, an *adoring* soul, thrash in mortal crisis.

"I-I suppose I cannot ... But ..."

Soon, he would lift his coin from Proyas ... Very soon, only the wind could take him where he needed to go.

"But what?"

"I can conceive *you*!"

Kellhus reached into his beard to scratch a false itch, reclined so that he sat propped on his elbow. These simple gestures of discomfort, openly displayed, immediately summoned a corresponding ease in the Exalt-General, one that utterly eluded the man's awareness. Bodies spoke to bodies, and short of flinching from raised fists, the worldborn were utterly deaf to what was said.

"And *I*, the Most Holy Aspect-Emperor, can conceive God. Is that it?"

The man leaned according to the angle of his desperation. "How else could it be? This is why Men lavish such attention on idols, is it not? Why they pray to their ancestors! They make ... make *tokens* of what lies near ... Use what they know to grasp what they cannot."

Kellhus sipped his bowl of anpoi, watching the man.

"So this is how you conceive me?"

"This is how *all* Zaudunyani conceive you! You are our *Prophet*!"

Behave like one.

"So you think that I conceive what you cannot."

"Not think, *know*. We're but squabbling children absent you and your word. I was *there*! I *partook* in the conceit that ruled the Holy War before your revelation! The ruinous folly!"

"And what was my revelation?"

"That the God of Gods *spoke to you*!"

Eyes losing focus. Imagery boiling up out of oblivion. Probabilities like crabs scuttling on the shores of what was unknown.

"And what did It tell me?"

And again it dimpled his depths the way a chill stone might the surface of a warm pool, saying *It* rather than *He*.

"The God of Gods?"

Such preposterous *care* was required. Action and belief turned each upon the other in ways so intimate as to be inextricable. Proyas did not simply believe, he had *killed thousands* for his Faith. To concede, to recant, was to transform all those executions into *murders*—to become not simply a fool, but a *monster*. To believe fiercely is to do fierce things, and nothing fierce happens without suffering. Nersei Proyas, for all his regal demeanour, was the most ferocious of his countless believers.

No one had so much to lose as him.

"Yes. What did It tell me?"

Thrumming heart. Wide, bewildered eyes. And the Aspect-Emperor could see comprehension brimming in the darkness that came before the man. Soon, the dread realization would come, and the coin would be lifted ...

New children would be sired.

"I-I ... I don't understand ..."

"What was my revelation? What secret could It whisper into an ear so small as mine?"

There is a head on a pole behind you.

Brutalities spin and scrape, like leaves blasted in the wind.

He is here ... with you ... not so much inside me as speaking with your voice.

There is a head on a pole behind you.

And he walks, though there is no ground. And he sees, though his eyes have rolled into his brow. Through and over, around and within, he flees and he assails ... For he is here.

Here.

They seize him from time to time, the Sons of this place, and he feels the seams tear, hears his scream. But he cannot come apart—for unlike the Countless Dead his heart beats still.

His heart beats still.

There is a head on a pole behind you.

He comes to the shore that is here, always here, gazes without sight across waters that are fire, and sees the Sons swimming, lolling and bloated and bestial, raising babes as wineskins, and drinking deep their shrieks.

There is a head on a pole behind you.

And he sees that these things are *meat*, here. Love is meat. Hope is meat. Courage. Outrage. Anguish. All these things are meat—seared over fire, sucked clean of grease.

There is a head on a pole.

Taste, one of the Sons says to him. *Drink.*

It draws down its bladed fingers, and combs the babe apart, plucking him into his infinite strings, laying bare his every inside, so that it might lick his wrack and wretchedness like honey from hair. *Consume* ... And he sees them descending as locusts, the Sons, drawn by the lure of his meat.

There is a head ... and it cannot be moved.

So he seizes the lake and the thousand babes and the void and the massing-descending Sons and the lamentations-that-are-honey, and he rips them about the pole, transforms here into *here*, *this-place-inside-where-you-sit-now*, where he has always hidden, always watched, where Other Sons, recline, drinking from bowls that are skies, savouring the moaning broth of the Countless, bloating for the sake of bloat, slaking hungers like chasms, pits that eternity had rendered Holy ...

We pondered you, says the most crocodilian of the Sons.

"But I have never been here."

You said this very thing, it grates, seizing the line of the horizon, wrapping him like a fly. Legs click like machines of war. *Yesss* ...

And you refuse to succumb to their sucking mouths, ringed with one million pins of silver. You refuse to drip fear like honey—because you have no fear.

Because you fear *not* damnation.

Because there is a head on a pole behind you.

"And what was your reply?"

The living shall not haunt the dead.

"What was your revelation?" Proyas cried, anger twisted into incredulity. "That the No-God would return! That the end of all things was nigh!"

He was *immovable* in the eyes of his Exalt-General, Kellhus knew, the stake from which all strings were bound and all things were measured. Nothing could be so gratifying as his approval. Nothing could be so profound as his discourse. Nothing could be so dense, so *real*, as his image. Ever since Caraskand and the Circumfixion, Kellhus had ruled Proyas's heart, become the author of his every belief, the count of his every kindness, his every cruelty. There was no judgment, no decision the Believer-King of Conriya could make without somehow consulting the impression Kellhus had left in his soul.

In so many ways, Proyas was the most reliable of all those he had yoked to his will—the perfect instrument. And he was a cripple for it.

"And you are certain of this?"

To make him believe the first time had been labour enough. Now he must make him believe *anew*, cast him into a different shape, one that served a far different—and far more troubling—purpose.

Revelation was never a simple matter of authority because Men were never so simple as sodden clay—something that could be rolled blank and imprinted anew. There was fire in deeds, and the world was nothing if not a kiln. To act upon a belief was to cook its contours into the very matter of the soul. The more extreme the act, the hotter the fire, the harder the brick of belief. How many thousands had Proyas condemned to die in his name?

How many massacres had fired the beliefs Kellhus had pressed into his soul?

"I'm certain of what you've told me!"

It did not matter, so long as those tablets were smashed ... irretrievably broken.

Kellhus gazed not at a man so much as a heap of warring signals: distress and conviction; accusation and self-loathing. He smiled the smile that Proyas unwittingly begged him not to smile, shrugged as if they discussed nothing more than mildew and beans. The spider flicked open its legs.

"Then you are certain of too much."

The very words that had caused the Greater Proyas to barricade the soul of the Lesser.

Tears lacquered the man's gaze. Bewildered incredulity slackened his face.

"I ... I-I ... don't ..." He bit the words against his lower lip.

Kellhus looked down into his bowl, spoke as though rehearsing an old meditation.

"*Think*, Proyas. Men *will* so they can become one with the Future. Men *want* so they can become one with the World. Men *love* so they can become one with the Other ..." A fractional pause. "Men are forever famished, Proyas, famished for *what they are not* ..."

The Holy Aspect-Emperor had leaned back so the fire rising white and scintillant between them would frame his aspect.

"What ..." Proyas asked on emptied lungs, "what are you saying?"

Kellhus grimaced in a rueful, *it-could-not-be-otherwise* manner.

"We are the *antithesis* of the God, not the reflection."

Confusion. Confusion was ever the herald of genuine insight. As the Greater Proyas churned, a chorus of discordant voices, the Lesser Proyas *found himself that song*, a clamour that he could only conceive as one. When those voices at last embraced one another—he would find himself remade.

Rapid breath. Fluttering pulse. Hands clenched, fingernails scoring sweated palms.

So close ...

"And this—" Proyas blurted, only to catch himself, as much for his terror as for the burning hook in his throat.

"*Speak*. Please."

A single, treacherous tear fell into the folds of the Believer King's luxurious beard.

At last.

"This is why you c-call the God-of-Gods ..."

He sees ...

"Call Him ... '*It*'?"

He understands.

Admission was all that remained.

It.

The name of all things inhuman.

When applied to the inanimate world, it meant nothing. No whinge of significance accompanied its utterance. But when applied to *animate* things, it became ever more peculiar, ever more fraught with moral intimation. And when used to single out apparently human things, it roared with a life all its own.

It festered.

Call a man "it" and you were saying that *crime* can no more be committed against him as against a stone. Ajencis had called Man "*onraxia*", the being that judged beings. The Law, the Great Kyranean claimed, belonged to his very essence. To call a man "it" was to kill him with words, and so to oil the actions that would murder him in fact.

And the God? What did it mean for the *God of Gods* to be called an "it"?

The Holy Aspect-Emperor watched his most trusted disciple flounder in the wrack of these considerations. Few tasks were so onerous as to make a man believe the new, to think thoughts without precedent. It was an irony so mad as to be an absurdity, that so many would forfeit their *lives* sooner than their beliefs. It was ardour, of course. It was loyalty and the simple hunger for the security of the Same. But more than anything, it was *ignorance* that delivered conviction beyond the pale of disputation. Ignorance of questions. Ignorance of alternatives.

No tyranny was so complete as blindness. So with each of these sessions Kellhus merely raised more questions and posed more contradictory answers, and watched the once solitary track he had cut into Proyas vanish into the trampled earth of possibility ...

He raised a hand into the dim air, gazed upon the nimbus of gold shining about them.

Such a remarkable thing.

So hard to explain.

"It comes to me, Proyas. In my sleep ... *It* comes ...."

A statement pregnant with both meaning and horror. Kellhus often did this, answered his disciples' questions with observations that seemed relevant only because of their ornamental import and the odour of profundity. Most failed to even notice his evasion, and those few who glimpsed it assumed they were being misdirected for some divine reason, in accordance with some greater design.

Nersei Proyas simply forgot how to breathe.

A glance toward his trembling fingertips.

Two more balled fists.

"The God ..." was the most the Exalt-General could say.

The Holy Aspect-Emperor smiled in the manner of those more bereaved than undone by tragic ironies.

"Is nothing human."

An empire of his soul ...

This was what his father's Thousandfold Thought had made.

"So the God–?"

"Wants nothing ... *Loves* nothing."

A pattern conquering patterns, reproducing on the scales of both insects and heavens; heartbeats and ages. All bound upon him, Anasûrimbor Kellhus.

"The God doesn't care!"

"The God is beyond care."

He was as much a creature of the Thought as it was a creature of him. For it whispered as it danced, threading the stacked labyrinths of contingency, filing through the gates of his daylight apprehension, *becoming him*. He *declared*, and the patterns went forth, making wombs of souls, reproducing, taking on the cumbersome complexities of *living life*, transforming the dancing of the dance, begetting heresies and fanaticisms and mad delusions ...

Forcing more declarations.

"So then why does He demand so much of us?" Proyas blurted. "Why entangle us with judgments? Why *damn* us!"

Kellhus drew up his manner and expression to answer the bodily cacophony of his warlike disciple, becoming the perfect counterpoint: ease to rebuke his disorder, repose to shame his agitation, all the while *reading*, counting the cubits of his disciple's pain.

"Why is wheat sewn and harvested?"

Proyas blinked.

"Wheat?" He squinted as though ancient. "Wha-what are you saying?"

"That our damnation is the Gods' harvest."

For twenty years now, he had dwelt in the circuit of his father's Thought, scrutinizing, refining, enacting and being enacted. He had known it would crash into ruin after his departure ...

Known that his wife and children would die.

"What? What?"

"Men and all their generations–"

"No!"

"–all their aspirations–"

The Exalt-General bolted to his feet, flung his bowl across the chamber. "*Enough!*"

No flesh could be sundered from its heart and survive. All of his empire was doomed–was *disposable*. Kellhus had known this and he had prepared. No ...

It was the hazard of the converse that had eluded him ...

"The World is a *granary*, Proyas ...

The fact that his heart would also crash into ruin.

"And we are the bread."

Proyas fled his beloved Prophet, flew from the mad, glaring presence. The Umbilicus had become a labyrinth, turns and leather portals, each more disorienting than the last. Out–he needed *out*! But like a beetle in the husk of a beehive, he could only throw himself this direction and that, chasing forks squeezed into extinction. He reeled like a drunk, dimly aware of the tears stinging his cheeks, the ridiculous need to feel shame. He barged between startled servants and functionaries, bowled over a slave. If he had paused to think, he could have found his way with ease. But the desperation *to move* ruled all because it blotted all.

Proyas fairly toppled clear the entrance. He shrugged away the hands of the Pillarian who rushed to assist him, fled into the greater labyrinth that was the Ordeal.

We are the bread ...

He needed time. Away from the tasks of his station, all the insufferable details of command and administration. Away from the stacked carcasses of Sranc. Away from the hymns, the embroidered walls, the faces, the shield-pounding ranks ...

He needed to ride out alone, to find some *lifeless* place where he could ponder without interruption ...

Think.

He needed to–

Hands seized his shoulders. He found himself standing face-to-face with *Coithus Saubon* ... The "Desert Lion" in the flesh, blinking at him as he had when they stood in the glare of the Carathay so very long ago.

His counterpart ...

"Proyas ..."

Even his *nemesis* in certain respects.

The man regarded him–and his state–with the amused incredulity of someone finding evidence that confirmed low opinions. He still possessed the broad-shouldered vigour of his youth, still cropped his hair short, though it was now white and silver. He still wore the Red Lion of his father's House on his surcoat, though a Circumfix now framed its fiery contours. He still lived in his hauberk, though the chain was now fashioned of nimil.

For a moment, Proyas could almost believe that nothing of the past twenty years had actually happened, that the First Holy War still besieged Caraskand on the Carathay's cruel limit. Or perhaps that was what he wanted to believe–a kinder, more naive reality.

Proyas drew a hand across his face, winced for the wet of his tears. "What ... what are you doing here?"

A narrow look. "The same as you, I suspect."

The Believer-King of Conriya nodded, found no words to speak.

Saubon frowned in an affable, grinning way. "The same as you ... Yes."

A chill air swept across them, and Proyas's nostrils flared for the taint of meat, both cooking and rotting.

Sranc meat.

"He summons me for private counsel as well ..." Saubon explained. "He has for months now."

Proyas swallowed, understanding full well, but not comprehending at all.

"Months now?"

The World is a granary ...

"More rarely when the Ordeal was still broken, of course."

Proyas stood blinking. Astonishment had furrowed his brow and forehead as a gardener's claw.

"You have been speaking with-with ... *Him?*"

The Norsirai King stiffened in obvious affront. "I am Exalt-General, same as you. I raise my voice in relentless honesty, as do you. I have sacrificed as much of my life! More! Why should he set *you* apart?"

Proyas stared like an idiot. He shook his head with more violence than he intended, the way a madman might, or a sane man plagued by hornets or bees. "No ... *No* ... You are right, Saubon ..."

The Believer-King of Caraskand laughed, though a bitterness sharpened his humour into a scowl.

"I apologize," Proyas said inclining his chin. Their animosity had always imposed a formality between them.

"And yet it dismays you to see *me* here."

"No ... I–"

"Would you declare as much to our Lord-and-Prophet? Pfah! You have always been too quick to flatter yourself with the fact of his attention."

Proyas felt like a child for the red-rimmed sting of his glare.

"I ... I don't understand."

How does one sum their impression of complicated others? Proyas had always thought Saubon headstrong, mercurial, even curiously fragile, given to bouts of near-criminal recklessness. Saubon was a man who could never quite outrun his need to *prove*, even in the all-seeing gaze of Anasûrimbor Kellhus ...

And yet here the man stood, so *obviously* the stronger of the two.

The tall Norsirai raised his chin in the boasting, Galeoth way. "You have always been *weak*. Why else would he draw you under his wing?"

"Weak? *Me?*"

A faint smile. "You were tutored by a sorcerer, were you not?"

"What are you saying?"

Saubon began backing toward the mountainous silhouette of the Umbilicus. "Perhaps he doesn't instruct you ..." he called before turning to stride away.

"Perhaps he draws the poison from your soul."

He and Saubon had clashed innumerable times over the years, disputed points both inane and catastrophically consequential. The breaches in jnan were beyond counting: the bellicose Galeoth had even called him *coward* in the Imperial Synod once, shamed him in the eyes of all those assembled. And the same could be said of the field, where his counterpart seemed to make sport of violating the terms he negotiated in their Lord-and-Prophet's name. In a pique of rage, Proyas had gone so far as to *draw* on the fool after he seized Aparvishi in Nilnamesh. There had been a similar incident in Ainon after Saubon sacked the estates of dozens of caste-nobles Proyas had already sworn to the Zaudunyani! He had gone to Kellhus after this last, thinking that surely the "Mad Galeoth" had gone too far. But he found only rebuke.

"You think I overlook your frustration?" Kellhus had said. "That I *fail to see*? If I do not speak of it, Proyas, it is because *I have no need*. All the ways Saubon falls short on your string are the ways he mobilizes those he leads. What most irks you most, *best serves me*."

Proyas had trembled for hearing this, physically shook! "But my Lor–!"

"I'm not shaping warlords to *rule* my Holy Empire," Kellhus had snapped. "I'm fashioning generals *to conquer Golgotterath* ... to overthrow wicked heights, not treat honourably with heretics."

Proyas had laboured to foster a greater spirit of generosity between Saubon and himself after this incident. They had even become comrades in some respects. But if the weeds of grievance had been torn up, the roots still remained. A wariness. A skepticism. An inclination to begin shaking his head in negation.

Saubon, after all, remained Saubon.

Now Proyas watched the man recede and vanish into the blackness of the Imperial Pavilion and found that he could not move. So he stood in the mazed ways just beyond the precincts of the Umbilicus, at first staring, then at last *hiding*, sitting crouched between stained canvas panels, sitting *anchored*. Reflecting upon it afterward, Proyas would realize the *purity* of his vigil, one that belied the carnival of thoughts and apprehensions that tormented his soul. Afterward, he would realize the man called Proyas had not waited at all ...

The Greater Proyas had.

For the space of two watches he sat in the dust, gazing, his every blink pricking his eyes.

The Umbilicus formed the radial hub of the Great Ordeal, the point of intersection for all the avenues that twined and forked like arteries across the desolate plains. He watched the files of Men dwindle into broken threads, then ambling particles, warriors who seemed to have no errand, only a vagabond restlessness. Very many glimpsed him in the shadows, and no matter what their reaction, be it a glance or a leering grin, a curious viciousness seemed to haunt their manner. So Proyas watched the light shed by the Nail of Heaven glow across the worn and weathered tent-tops instead, averting his gaze so that the passersby seemed little more than shades—rumours of Men.

He recognized Saubon before properly seeing him, so distinct was his leaning, broad-shouldered gait. Starlight dusted the summits of his hair and beard, moonlight complicated the chain-mail draped about his far shoulder. Torchlight painted the substance of him orange and brown.

Proyas made as though to call out, but his breath became as a stone, something too heavy to move. All he could do was watch, sitting like a child or dog in the dust.

The Believer-King of Caraskand walked with blank purpose, like a man reviewing some bland yet loathsome chore standing between him and his slumber. Proyas could feel himself shrink with the man's every step—what kind of shameful madness was this? Cringing like a beggar, fearful of a thrashing when starvation threatened him more. What had delivered him to such a low place?

Who?

Saubon walked obliviously until the obtuse angle between them became square. Then, as though his senses were canine, he turned to Proyas.

"You waited all this time ... here ... for me?"

Proyas peered into his face, searching for some sign of his own wax-kneed uncertainty. He saw none.

"There's discord between us," Proyas called out, dismayed by the weakness of his voice. "We must speak."

The Norsirai studied him. "There's discord, yes ... but not between you and I." He took two steps and crouched before him, close enough to touch with outstretched fingers.

"What ails you, Brother?"

Proyas fought the anguish scaling his face. He ran a hand across his cheek and jaw, as if to catch any treacherous ticks. "Ails me?" He had the impression of profound misunderstanding, of running afoul assumptions so mistaken as to be comic.

Saubon regarded him with a kind of gloating pity.

"The *things* he tells you," Proyas finally said, his voice conspiratorial. "Does it not ... *trouble* ... what you once believed?"

Saubon pursed his lower lip, nodded. A torch staked nearby flared in a spasm of wind. Curlicues of gold swam and flickered across the Believer-King of Caraskand.

"I am troubled, aye. But not so much as you."

"So he has told you!" Proyas hissed, finally grasping the reason behind his mad vigil.

A grave nod. "Yes."

"He told you about the God of Gods!"

King Coithus Saubon scowled; bird-footed shadows rutted his temples. "He told me you would be waiting here ... for me."

Proyas blinked. "What? You mean he ... he ..."

The Norsirai Exalt-General reached out a bare hand, clenched him firmly on the shoulder.

"He told me to be kind."

Chapter Two

Injor-Niyas

One cannot console those who pretend to weep.

—Conriyan Proverb

Late Summer, 20 New Imperial Year (4123, Year-of-the-Tusk), the northern Demua Mountains

"Come ..." Serwa said, her brother already wind-whipped and towering at her side.

Sorweel hesitated as always. It seemed an insult clutching her, feeling the slim body that his heart had never ceased to ponder, even when fury made his jaw ache and his ears roar. For no matter how *hard* he hated, his lust refused to leave him.

It was always the same. No sooner would a realization come to him than the warring dogs of his soul would tear it into something bewildering. He had thought his path clear. He was *Narindar*, as Zsoronga had said, an assassin of the Hundred. The Mother of Birth herself had anointed him, hiding him from the unnatural scrutiny of the Anasûrimbor, provisioning him with the weapons he needed, even raising him to the exalted station he required. Accursed or no, his Fate had drawn relentlessly *nearer*. Then the Nonmen embassy had arrived bearing the terms of their alliance with the Great Ordeal, and the dogs set their grinning teeth to his heart once again. She had told him herself: he was to be a Hostage of Ishterebinth, held captive with Serwa and her eldest brother, Moënghus.

Sorweel found himself thrown—sorcerous leap after sorcerous leap—across the ruins of ancient Kûniüri with the daughter of his father's murderer, somehow more infatuated after every stone cast. And he had thought *that he might love her*, dared imagine a different future, one that assassinated him instead of her father …

Only to discover her shuddering in the arms of her brooding, warrior brother.

"Horse-King … It is time to go."

Sorweel hesitated for his hatred, but he yielded for want of recourse as much as for want of *her*. So he slung his right-arm about her waist, felt the heat of her body as an iron drawn from the fire. Thoughts chattering, he listened as her voice made a pipe of the World. Lights spun as they always spun, glittered like glass wrack tossed into the white heights of the sun, and he unravelled as he always unravelled, from the pith outward, his very existence flashing like the light of a mirror between horizons.

They had crossed the Demua Mountains this way. Sorweel, the false Believer-King, and the insane children of the Holy Aspect-Emperor, leaping from slope to precipice, skin and nerves alive to the cold, lungs burning for some unfathomable sharpness in the air—peak to gasping peak, always perched on the edge of the void. The whole world seemed tossed, the ground hooked and hanging, barked of everything save rims and ravines of snow. He huddled with them, his numb fingers latched about his shoulders, hugging what heat his breast and gut could muster, pulling against the shivers that would shake him into more snow. And he found he could not distinguish between his terrors, the vertigo of the scarps soaring about and below them, and the plummet of his heart.

He gazed across the stark, his hatred spinning like a tossed coin, and he watched winds scour the nearby summits, endlessly inhaling snow to the east. He felt their incestuous presences pressed close, Serwa small and Moënghus great, both hot with blood and life, huddling against all the thin and empty edges the same as he … and he wished them dead.

All he need do is *push*, he thought. One push and he could die here at his ease, the heat of him emanating outward, drawn on as a drink by the voids surrounding. A brief clash of panic and limbs. A sharp intake of breath.

And no one ever need *know*.

And then, one sorcerous step and it was gone, this world of stone and ice and gaping plummets. They were back into the forests, the ground steep to be sure, but terraced and overgrown, a place where no one need fear standing.

The trees were cramped for altitude, and the grasses and bracken were thinned for gravel. Streams roped the rutted heights above, shooting with waters cold enough to pinch fingertips and crack teeth. The three of them sat wordless for some time, savouring the warm and easy air. Serwa dozed against the crook of her arm. Moënghus switched his glower between the vista and his thumbs. Sorweel stared out, watching the scrawl of ridges flatten into a less troubled horizon.

"What do your people know of Injor-Niyas?" Serwa eventually asked.

Her voice, he realized, always descended upon him. It never reached out.

He said nothing, turned to the west to spare himself the cruel hilarity of her gaze. He hated her more, he decided, in the sunlight.

"Father," she continued, "says that it is our *lesson*, that the ghouls are a cipher for the extinction of Men."

Staring away was his only reprieve. He could not look at them without cringing for shame, just as he could not sleep without dreaming of their congress. Only by turning his back to them could he think those thoughts that let him breathe. How he was Narindar, an instrument of the dread Mother of Birth. How he was the knife that would kill their demonic father and deliver them to their ruin. The very knife!

He had even begun praying to Her in the knotted watches before sleep.

Deliver them, Mother ...

What he had seen was a crime—of that he had no doubt. Incest was anathema in all nations, all households—even the Anasûrimbor, who more than any other had to appease the mob. They were *afraid*, Sorweel had come to realize. They feared their *father* would see their crime in his face ...

But they also feared, he had decided, what their father might see in *their* faces. This, Sorweel realized, was the only thing keeping him alive. He had no idea how much they could or could not hide, but he knew that *murder* was no small thing, not even for the likes of them. Perhaps they only had so much faith in their ability to deceive their accursed father. To murder a man—such an act left hard tracks in any soul. So they had elected to sin in sand, to drive him away, let the wild accomplish what they dare not, and let their wandering blow the spoor of guilt from their soul.

So they baited him, laughed and tormented. They played games—endless games!—all of them meant to shame, to infuriate! Over the Demua and now upon the bourne of fabled Ishterebinth, last of the great Nonmen Mansions.

They were running out of time.

"This World once belonged to the Nonmen," she was saying, "the way it now belongs to Men—to *you*, Sorweel." He could feel her remorseless gaze upon him. "What Fate will you seize?"

Wind whisked sharp through the grasses.

"That one is easy," Moënghus said, standing on a grunt. He leaned to swat pine needles from his leggings. He clasped Sorweel's shoulders in two embattled hands, shook him with mock camaraderie. "The *purple* one."

Sorweel twisted out of the man's grip, swung at his face—missed. The Prince-Imperial lunged and shoved him—hard enough for his legs to tangle like thrown rope. Sorweel crashed backward across the ground, scuffed an elbow against a stump of granite. Lightning deadened his hand.

"What?" Moënghus bellowed. "Why do you persist? Run, little boy—*Run!*"

"You ca-call *me* cursed!" Sorweel cried. "Me?"

"I ca-call you wretched. *Weak*."

"Tell me, then! Where do *incests* burn? What part of Hell has your *holy* father reserved for you!"

A lupine grin and careless shrug. "The one where your father keens like a pregnant widow ..."

From whence does the power of words come? How can mere breath and sound strike the rhythm from hearts, the stone from bones?

"*Podi!*" Serwa called to her brother. "*Yus'yiril onpara ti ...*"

Even though there was warning in her voice, Moënghus laughed. He glared at Sorweel for a moment, then, spitting, turned to descend the slopes. Sorweel watched the light and shadow break across his receding back, his heart a cracked and cooling cauldron.

He turned to the Swayali witch, who gazed at him with a fixity that should have shamed both of them. Out of spite, he welcomed her peer. Sunlight traced glowing threads through her hair.

"*How?*" she finally asked.

"How what?"

"How could you still ... *love* us?"

Sorweel looked down, thought of Porsparian, his dead slave, rubbing the mud and spit of Yatwer across his face. *This* was what she saw, he realized, the spittle of the Goddess, a magic that was no magic—a *miracle*. They picked and sneered and goaded, and yet saw only what their dread father had seen: the adoration proper to a Zaudunyani Believer-King. Hatred strapped his heart, his being, and yet she saw only desire.

"But I *despise* you," he said, returning her gaze.

She continued peering for several heartbeats.

"No, Sorweel. You do not."

As if hearing the same inaudible thing, they both looked to the clearing, their eyes sorting between the slow drifting points of fluff.

Resolutions, promises, threats. These things whispered make hearts strong.

No one need hear. No one save the Goddess.

Deliver them, Mother. Deliver them to me.

Shame is a great power. Even in the womb, we shrink from the furious glare of the father, the horrified glance of the mother. Before we draw our first wailing breaths, we *know*; the taunts we will flee, the alchemy of more refined derision, and the way it dwells in the meat of us, little pockets of despair, making foam of our heart, of our limbs. One can hold anguish in their teeth, fury in their brow, their eyes, but shame occupies us *whole*, fills our shrinking skin.

Weakening even as it awakens.

Part of Sorweel's dilemma lay in the span between their sorcerous leaps, the way he so often found himself *watching* her while she dozed to recover her strength. She was a different soul when she leapt, one that murmured in fright, grunted for exertion, cried out in murky horror. Eskeles had also borne the curse of the Dreams, had also endlessly suffered as he slept. But then Eskeles had been nowhere near as serene as Serwa when he was awake. His nocturnal travails in no way contradicted his sunlit humanity. Sorweel could not hear Serwa whimper or sob without swallowing some kind of pang in his throat.

When she slept it seemed he could see her as she *could be*, if only he could tear down the conceits of her gifts and station. What she *should* be were he strong and she weak.

After she roused herself, they made one last sorcerous leap from the shoulders of the Demua to a hill that was more a monstrous stump of elevated stone, a pillar hewn at the base. Ivies thatched the clearings. Great oaks and elms raftered the gloom, their roots parsed about immense blocks of stone. Mossy ground wheezed beneath their feet. Elephantine roots spanned the cavities that inexplicably pocked the terrain, trailing ringlets of dulcet moss. The air was hard with the smell of things rotted soft. The light was diffuse and marbled with shadow, as if refracted through uneasy waters.

"I have no recollection of this place," Serwa said, wandering ahead.

"At last," Moënghus chided, "we can enjoy some death and ruin without being lectured."

Birdsong whistled through the greening heights. Sorweel found himself squinting at the glare of the sun through the canopy.

"The ghouls are older than old ..." she called into the dank hollows. "I wager even they've forgotten ..."

"But are they *happy* for it?" her brother answered. "Or merely perplexed?"

The branching shadows climbed from his breast to his face, like some great black vein. Sunlight painted a thousand white circles about the rim of his nimil corselet. He was often like this, Sorweel had learned, before the melancholy that made him so mercurial struck. Glib. Sarcastic in the manner of those returning to some despised toil.

Serwa stepped between two massive blocks, drew her hand across scabbed and pitted planes, along fractures worn as smooth as stones thrown up by oceans. She walked the way she was prone, at once waifish and intent, hard in the manner of souls absolutely assured of her power. It made her seem cruel.

"The stone carries an ancient bruise ... a ... *mustiness* ... older and more faint than any I have ever seen."

But then everything she did made her seem cruel.

"Let the dead be dead," her brother muttered.

Her reply was muted for the intervening greenery, but no less musical. "*One cannot raise walls against what has been forgotten ...*"

The white-eyed warrior looked directly at him, smirking. "She was always Father's favourite."

Sorweel stared down at scabbed and stained knuckles.

"Who was Harweel's favourite?" the Prince-Imperial pressed, mocking.

Serwa's voice climbed from the mossy, arboreal gloom. "*This place was abandoned before Arkfall ...*"

"I was his only son," Sorweel replied, at last looking to the black-haired Anasûrimbor.

There is a darker understanding between Men, shapes that can only be discerned in the absence of women–in the absence of light. There is a manner and a look and a tone that Men alone can see, and it exists as much between brothers as it does enemies from across seas. It needs no voice to be bellowed, no colour to be unfurled, only momentary solitude between masculine souls, a cinching of the air between them, a mutual glimpse of all the murders that had made each possible.

"Yes," Moënghus said, his tone ferrous. "I heard them speak of it in Sakarpus."

Sorweel licked his lips rather than breathe. "Speak of what?"

"How good Harweel squandered his seed on your mother."

They shared a single hard breath between them, the one drawing in what the other expelled.

"They said her womb ..." the Prince-Imperial continued, "died before she did ..."

A fog rose up within the youth, one that chilled his skin for interior heat.

"What happens here?" Serwa said, stepping from behind one of the monstrous oaks. Neither man was surprised. Nothing escaped her notice for long.

"*Look* at him, Sister ..." Moënghus said without breaking eye contact. "Tell me you do not see hate ..."

Pause. "I see only what I have alw–"

"He even clenches his pommel! Threatens to draw!"

"Brother ... We have discussed this."

What were they talking about?

"If he were to strike me dead now!" Moënghus cried. "Would you believe it then?"

"All hearts are divided! You know this. And you kno–"

"He! *Hates*! Look at hi–!"

"*You know that I always see deeper*!" the Grandmistress of the Swayali cried.

"Bah!" the towering Prince-Imperial spat, turning on his heel.

Sorweel stood rigid, his fury not so much blunted as cracked into gravel for confusion. He watched Moënghus's broad back dip and dwindle across the sun-striped floor.

"Madness!" the youth spat to the girl. "Both of you are mad!"

"Or *maddened*," Serwa said.

He turned to her, saw the same imperturbable expression he always saw.

"Am I such a riddle?" he asked on a snarl.

She stood upon a canted slab, its back carpeted in black-green moss, its edges caked in white lichen. She seemed taller than him because of it … mightier. A lone lance of sunlight bathed her face, made her glow like her accursed father.

"You love me …" she said, her voice flat as her gaze.

Rage, as if he were a catapult and her voice the release.

"I think you are an incestuous whore!"

She flinched, and some vicious fraction of him exulted.

But her retort fell as liquid brilliance from her mouth, rose as steam from the surrounding gloom.

"***Kaur'silayir muhiril*** …"

Sorweel stumbled back, first for astonishment, then for articulations of seizing light. His feet pedalled air. He was thrown back, pinned against a great rutted oak. Her voice crashed upon him from all angles, as if he were a leaf tossed in the tempest of her will. Rancourous light flashed from her gaze, bright as the obscured sun. An obsidian nacre framed her, a black that twigged and branched as if chasing cracks into the very cut of existence. Falcons of gold battled her whipping hair.

And she was upon him, not so much traversing as cutting down the interval between them, seizing his shoulders, setting his skin afire with her light, sucking all air from his breast with her emptiness, looming with the compressed weight of mountains, compelling, *demanding* …

"***What are you hiding***?"

Her lips opened about the surface of the sun.

His words rose on the back of blackness to meet her demand.

"*Nothing* …"

Not as toil, as freedom.

"***Why do you love us***?"

"*Because I hate what you hate ...*" Like words spoken on pipe-smoke. "*Because I believe ...*"

On the breath following a kiss.

Ink had clotted and conquered his periphery, folding the vein-spangled wood and the airy spheres beyond into oblivion. She alone remained, a titanic presence, her eyes flaring like Nails of Heaven.

"***Can you not see our contempt?***"

A word like a wave to a friend.

"*Yes.*"

She leaned forward, wrath incarnate, terror incarnate, and he was blown as paint across the bark.

"***I think not.***"

His head arched back in abject terror, he could only stare down his cheeks at her catastrophic aspect, only moan his lament, his blubbering shame. His water spilled as hot as blood. His bowel.

And in a span of a heartbeat it was all gone.

Her sorcery. His honour.

"Why?" she was crying. "Why would you love *us*? *Why*?"

Shivers blew through him, twirled like a breeze. He had soiled ...

"Can't you see we're *monsters*!"

Soiled himself. He glimpsed something uncertain, even vulnerable in her gaze ... Fear?

Trembling for ... for ...

The reek of his own unmanliness rose about him ...

The proof.

The first sob, wrenched from his breast by an ethereal fist. "*Wh-who?*" he coughed, his face grinning for madness. Degradation, crashing through, crushing against. Then, all of it.

Everything.

Losing Harweel. His little brother hot in his callused palm. Losing his inheritance, his people. The image of them—sinuous and obscene. Sitting with Zsoronga in the fading light, listening to Obotegwa forgetting to breath. The glistening cleft. Watching the Sranc-faced Goddess claw muck from her own womb. The brandishing—the bestial heat! The growl that climbed to the tip. Crying out as Porsparian threw his throat upon a spear. The lunging bliss! Fierce with ... Taut with ... Riven. Cringing in a cavern of inhuman faces, clutching Eskeles, the whole world roaring, raving, gibbering ...

Threads of seed branching hot across knuckled shame. His father flapping as a vexed goose—afire.

His mother grey as stone.

His seed! His nation! The smell of shit and shit and shit—

Let-me-kill-let-me-kill—

He was on his knees, bent forward, bobbing as if priming his gut to vomit. But he understood little or nothing of this—or anything. The keening noises that cracked from his chest were not his own. Not more ...

Proof.

She stood gazing down upon him, cold and indistinct.

"*Who?*" his throat scratched, his voice wheezed. A sound like cattle lowing.

"Love us ..." she said, turning aloof from his spectacle. "If you must."

He had shrunk beneath the mighty oak, curled against its cruelty, folding more and more of himself into the indistinct roar. And still her voice plucked him with ... with ...

I have Compelled him!

Confusion.

What more would you have me do? What I have Compelled the ghouls will Compel also. He loves us.

Her brother's voice was indistinct, too much of the roar to rise above it.

Father misjudged the depth of his wound.

But it mattered not at all, the clarity of her accursed voice.

Our Father is wrong about more than you know ... The World overmatches him as it does us or anyone ...

He understood none of it ...

He simply carries the battle deeper.

And the world swayed in spirals, slow and warm.

My face dwells beneath your face ... Shush and you will see ...

And the Mother hummed and stroked. With his own hands she bathed him.

Hush ...

Hush, my sweet.

"Momma?"

Eternity dwells within you. A power indistinguishable from what happens ...

"Am I mad?" he asks.

Mad ...

And ever so holy.

"The Quya," Serwa was saying, "are not to be trifled with."

Sorweel sat heedless of the plummet before him, gazing westward with swollen eyes. He had crept to a crater pooled with water following his humiliation, bathed as she had slept and Moënghus had skulked across their inland island. For what seemed a watch he had lain floating upon ancient black, numbed to the cold, listening to the slurp of his own motions, the sound of his own breathing. Not a thought had passed through him. Now, his hair damp, his breeches still sopping, he stared dumbfounded at their destination in the distance. It erupted from the table's edge of the horizon, a silhouette only slightly darker than the sky gaping violet about it: a mountain stranded on a carven plain.

Ishterebinth. The final refuge of the ghouls.

He had dreamed of the Nonmen in his youth, as had every Son of Sakarpus. The Priests called them inhuman, the False Men, who had offended the Gods by usurping the divine perfection of their form, for making like women with men, and—most heinous of all—for stealing the secret of immortality. One Girgallic Priest in particular, Skûtsa the Elder, used to delight in regaling the children with descriptions of their wickedness during After-Temple. He would draw out the ancient scrolls, reading first in the ancient dialects, then providing lurid translations. And they would seem scriptural, the Nonmen, obscene for all the ways they surpassed Men, and yet somehow belonging to the wild and dark world in a way that Men could not, a race born of the blackest, most primeval recesses, harbouring a malice that would see them burn for all eternity.

"Sranc with souls," Skûtsa once declared in fit of palsied disgust. "Only the *patience* of their lies distinguish them!"

And the horror that cracked in his voice had become tinder for dreams more fiery still.

Now he sat dull and chill, staring at the apparition of the Last Mansion as Serwa explained why they would have to travel the remaining distance on foot.

"You forget the toll. I would be too weak to protect you after we arrive."

"Then take us to that wooded hillock," Moënghus said. "We can stay hidden until you recover. I wager it's two watches to the Mountain from there."

"And if the Cant is seen? You would gamble everything to spare your feet?"

"The Shortest Path, Sister."

They climbed down the encircling cliffs, and struck north and east across forest floors even more pillared, pitted, and rotted than those upon Nameless. Every so often they encountered the hulks of immense elms, dead and decrepit, climbing knuckled to neck-cramping heights, bark hanging like sack-cloth from sweeps of bone. Neither Serwa nor her brother made any comment, even passing beneath rafters of shorn branches.

Heroes had been his fare, growing up—the recounting of triumphs, not humiliations. Sorweel was surprised, the way all degraded Men are surprised, to find that a *station* awaited him, that the degraded had a place reserved. He was the one who trailed, the one who was avoided. He was the one not spoken to, and only regarded to scold or to settle some point of comedy or ridicule. The remarkable thing was that he need not even contemplate these facts to grasp them, that this knowledge had always dwelled within him. The world never wants for abused souls.

Moënghus slackened his pace to draw beside him, but acknowledged him in no way beyond his forbidding proximity. In all such exchanges, it was the place of the degraded soul to first implore.

"What did she do to me?" Sorweel finally asked, watching the shadows dapple across Serwa's pack and shoulders some twenty paces before them.

"A Cant of Compulsion," the man replied after consideration.

Ghosts of what had happened plagued his innards.

"But ... how cou—"

"Could she make you shit your breeches?" The hewn face turned to look down upon him, but with curiosity, not derision. There was something otherworldly about his white-blue eyes ...

Scylvendi eyes, Zsoronga had told him.

"Yes."

The Prince-Imperial puckered his lips in thought, glanced ahead. Sorweel followed his gaze, glimpsed *her* face turning like a shell in a wave. She had heard them, despite the filtering birdsong, the twig-combing breeze. This he knew.

"How does hunger make you eat?" Moënghus asked, still peering after her.

They slept beneath dead elms that night with only the distance of the mountain wolves and their nocturnal wail to mark the leagues they had travelled. The following morning they threaded forest galleries so deep as to seem tunnels; they could scarcely see the sky, let alone gauge their progress. Giolal, the land was called, the famed hunting preserves of the Injori Ishroi. They trekked in silence for the most part. Sorweel walked without thought, at first, as though he were a being of glass, paralytic for fear of breaking. When he finally dared ruminate, images of the previous day came to him as cramps of shame and humiliation, and he could do little more than dwell on preposterous and petty schemes to secure revenge. But even then, the inkling had germinated within him ... the knowledge that something more than their incestuous love affair moved the Imperial siblings.

It even occurred to him that he was *meant* to catch them making love ...

The day was all but exhausted when they finally crested a ridge that afforded a view. Sorweel had climbed a clutch of gargantuan boulders, their northern shelves chapped with lichens. It almost seemed another arcane leap, so sudden was the view.

Ishterebinth ... at last. *Ishterebinth* ... mountainous upon the ramping of lesser hills, its bulk obscuring the sky before them. The sun hung low on the horizon to the south, a blooded orb. The Mansion reared into its waning brilliance, so that its ascending scarps and slopes were stamped with the contrast of ink on cream vellum. The scale was such that his heart refused to credit it at first.

A *mountain* ... skinned and hewn, its every surface shorn into planes and pitted ... with apertures, terraces, and graven images—graven images most of all. Such detail that it pained the eye to probe it.

Sorweel crawled forward on all fours.

"How could such a thing be?" he asked, his voice glutinous for disuse.

"Endless life," Serwa said, "is endless ambition."

The forest knotted the terrain immediately below them, climbed several of the mountain's foundational phalanges before ending in what appeared to be whole tracts of dead trees. The posture of the mountain was that of a penitent, a kneeler whose thighs were outstretched. A road parsed the centre, paved with white stone and curiously ribbed with columns and roofless vaults, though most of the latter (and even some of the former) had collapsed at some point. Even from this distance, Sorweel could see figures labouring up its length, a file of mites that reached all the way to the Mansion's shadowed groin, where masses seemed to congregate beneath cliffs of stacked imagery. Two massive figures flanked the maw of the entrance, the face of the latter rising above the line of shadow, staring out to the southern horizon, orange and crimson and impassive.

"Sorcery ..." Serwa remarked to her brother. "The whole is sopped in the Mark."

"What do we do?" Moënghus asked, his gaze rapt upon the Mansion.

The Swayali witch spared the man a grim look, said nothing. She sat upon the lip of the ridge-line, swung her feet over the edge.

And then Sorweel *heard* it blooming like a sheet hung in the wind, low and fluting, yet bearing the gravel of misery nonetheless.

"What's that?" he called. "That sound ..."

Now that his soul had fastened upon it, it gripped the throat of all sound, a profound *wrongness* on fine summer air.

"The Mountain weeps," Serwa replied, already upon the ground. "It's the Weeping Mountain."

They spent watches labouring through the dwindling light, ascending wooded slopes and gravelled spines. There was no talk of stopping. The forest did not so much end as *die*, the trees stripped of greenery, the ground pestled barren. Only the Nail of Heaven illuminated their way across the ruin. They teetered across dead-falls, stumbled over mats of unearthed roots. Branches ragged the starry arches of the night.

Despite the diurnal heat, the quiet of winter stole over the world.

Ishterebinth loomed to their right, slowly drawing to their fore as Serwa led them over the back of its eastern thigh. Sorweel's mother had shown him an ancient heirloom once, a seal carved out of ivory, a relic of some Southron potentate, she had said. She had pulled him into the bowl of her crossed legs, laughing as she explained its peculiarities with her chin on his shoulder. She called it a "ziggurat", a miniature of the false mountains that certain pickish Kings, loathe to surrender their bodies to the pyre, constructed for their tombs. What had fascinated him were the hundreds of miniature figures that had been etched into its terraced sides: it scarcely seemed possible that any artisan could render images so small. For some reason, the detail hooked his soul like a burr, and he was sure he had tested his mother's patience, considering each of the figures—some no larger than a babe's nail clippings—and speculating, "Look-look! *Another* warrior, Mama! This one with spear *and* shield!"

Ishterebinth was no false mountain, and aside from its flat summit, it possessed none of the ziggurat's geometric simplicity. There was a lurid wildness to the size and arrangement of its imagery, an unkempt intensity to its detail, that utterly contradicted the tidy and sane parade of figures about the ivory terraces, the slaves toiling about the base, the kingly court promenading about the pinnacle. Even still, he felt a mote, crawling toward something too *immense* to be wrought. Each time he scaled Ishterebinth with his gaze, some past premonition of that boy—still drowsy with the certainty that his mother and father would live forever—sparked within him. He would even smell the attar-of-spruce wafting from the censor, hear the evening orisons ...

And he would wonder whether it were simply some mad nightmare ...

Wake up ... Sorwa, my sweet ...

Life.

His eyes burned and his blinks had become wilful by the time they gained the great road they had spied from afar—the Halarinis, the Grandmistress called it, the Summer Stair. Sorweel and Moënghus both shrank to a crouch, glimpsing a torchless procession of figures along its length. Serwa, however, continued trudging forward the same as before.

"They're Emwama," she said turning in a pirouette that added no interval to her pace. With that she resumed her forward stride, utterly feckless. Moënghus followed, a heavy hand now upon the pommel of his broadsword. Sorweel lingered for a moment, glancing up at the granitic immensity of their destination, then resumed the place the Anasûrimbor had reserved him, the station of shame and hate.

Serwa called out a brief string of arcane syllables, and an eye of piercing brilliance opened a mere span above her, chasing shadows from the objects of its glare.

The Emwama sickened him.

Sorweel knew what they were, or at least what they were *supposed* to be: the Mannish servitors of the Nonmen—slaves. But whatever they were, they had long since ceased being Men. Deer-eyed and round-faced. Stunted both in form—the tallest scarcely reached his elbows—and intellect. They were clad as rustics for the most part, though a few wore gowns that bespoke some kind of rank or function. Those travelling up the mountain bore astonishing loads, everything from wood to game to stacked rounds of unleavened bread. Short of breasts there was scarcely any way to distinguish the males from the females, save that a number of the latter carried sleeping infants in slings braided out of their remarkably voluminous hair.

From the outset, they crowded about the three travellers, great eyes wide and glistening, gaping like astounded children, and chattering in an insensible tongue, their lilting voices as deformed as their stature. Despite the uproar, they managed to keep their distance—at least at first. Their native shyness quickly waned, and the boldest jostled closer and closer. Eventually several dared to reach out wondering fingers, as if intent on touching what they could not quite believe. Serwa, especially, seemed to be the object of their adoring curiosity. Finally she barked at them in a tongue reminiscent of the one she used canting, but utterly unlike that of the Emwama.

They understood nonetheless. Several moments of screeching turmoil ensued as the misbegotten creatures fought to grant them what seemed some ritually prescribed space. Afterward, it almost seemed a miracle, the way the mob accumulated more and more misshapen souls and yet somehow managed to respect the invisible perimeter Serwa had imposed about them. Within a watch the mob they had gathered extended far beyond the outermost ring of Serwa's sorcerous light. For those confined to the dark, there was no way they could be anything more than illuminated glimpses of sharper, more sacred archetypes, and yet somehow they managed not to crowd their stunted brethren.

But it was the stink, more than anything, that fondled Sorweel's gut, for it was *human* through and through, no different than the stink of Men of the Ordeal gathering for march: at times earthen and almost benign, with various corners acrid and sweet, at times tar-like with the musk of unwashed armpits, thick enough to taste. Had they smelled any other way, be it forest moss or moulting snakes or unmucked stalls, he could have looked upon all their myriad differences as features proper to their form, things belonging to an essence distinct from his own. But their smell, like a carpenter's plumb, revealed them for what they were: inbred grotesqueries. Their eyes were bulbous, their spines crooked, their skulls simian. His horror, in some small measure, was the horror of the husband who is presented a deformed son.

There was no concealing such disgust. "Think of the difference between your cattle," Serwa called to him at one point, "and the elk who rule the plain." He understood instantly what she meant, for there was something at once bovine and doughty about the Emwama, the incurious hardiness of those bred to serve ruthless masters.

"More like dogs to wolves," Moënghus shouted in reply. He brandished a fist in mock fury, laughed at the scrambling panic its shadow caused among the halflings.

Sorweel glanced to the breathless spectacle of Ishterebinth above and before and was shocked by his ire. The old Girgallic Priests were always railing about the wickedness of the World in Temple, not as something to lament, but as something to celebrate. "Clean hands cannot be cleansed!" they would cry, reading from the *Sacred Higarata*. An unpolluted world was a world without martial honour, a world without sacrifice or compensation. The glory lay in the adulteration of the waters.

But this ... this was a pollution that begged no glory, an evil that could beget only tragedy—travesty. The evils of the World, he was beginning to realize, were more complicated than the goods by far. To the debauchery of the Anasûrimbor, he could now add the deformity of the Emwama. Perhaps pious fools confused simplicity for pious truth for good reason.

The World was not so elementary as Sakarpus, where there were Sranc and there were Men and nothing but dumb beasts in between.

Are you such a fool, Sorwa?

No.

No, Father.

Sorweel did his best to ignore the diminutive throngs. The three travellers climbed, leaning into the incline, though it seemed they were borne as flotsam on the stream of heads and shoulders and packs that Serwa's light carved from the mobbed darkness. They laboured past the pillars that flanked the road. It was as if they had been carved of soap, so indistinct were the figures engraved upon them. The only feature they shared, aside from dimension, was a visage beneath the capitals, each one of them worn fish-like by the ages, and facing what Sorweel assumed was south, regardless of the turns in the road's direction.

"Where Men hold places holy, the Nonmen extol *passages* ..." Serwa explained, spying his wondering gaze. "The Summer Stair was a *temple* to them once ..."

The Believer-King glanced at her, only to have his eyes yanked to the peak of the column rising behind her as she paced him in the crush—to the *stork* standing pale and gracile against the infinite vacancy of the night. Fear did not suffer his gaze to linger.

"To walk this road was to be purified," she continued, her own eyes probing the mountainous heights before them, "cleansed of anything that might pollute the Deep."

He shuddered for the meaty deformity of the Emwama.

So they gained the Cirrû-nol, the legendary High Floor of Ishterebinth, accompanied by the children of a degenerate race. The mountain had swallowed the Nail of Heaven as they approached. Even raising a hand to block the glare of Serwa's light, Sorweel could discern little more than the bruising black. He could make out monstrous faces, each hanging high enough to cramp his neck and staring out at a diagonal to the south, the same as those gracing the processional pillars. He did not so much see as assume the cyclopean bodies beneath. A hush, at once anxious and reverent, fell across the Emwama. They began looking about the gloomy expanse, casting hectic glances into what he guessed was the maw of the gate. The disrepair of the Summer Stair had prepared him for the wreckage they found. But not even the plodding, drawn-out nature of their approach, nor the obscuring darkness, could deaden him to the scale, the lunatic enormity ...

Such a place.

The shiver began as a tickle, more in his breath than his body, but within heartbeats, it owned him to his bones. He clutched his shoulders, clamped his teeth against any chatter.

"Imagine our ancient forefathers," Serwa said to him, her face strange with sharp lines of light and shadow. "Imagine them storming such a place with shields of leather and swords of brittle bronze."

He looked to her uncomprehending.

"Many think the ghouls did not so much fall to the Tribes of Men," she explained, gazing across the surrounding heights, raising her face to the clarity of her arcane light, "as bare their throats to them."

He felt all the more at sea learning facts such as these. His ignorance was smaller without them.

"May our tribe be so lucky," Moënghus muttered. Towering over the Emwama, he resembled some wild-maned warrior of yore, one of the "restive multitudes" so often referenced in the Holy Tusk.

A silence seized the ensuing moments, remarkable for the hundreds of Emwama crowded about them. There was noise, of course, the shrill of nocturnal insects, the dull of coughs and sniffs, but the soul has a way of hearing *past* these mundane things, of listening for what *should* be heard. Sorweel even looked up, convinced the Surillic Point hissed. He glimpse white wings kiting across the light's upper limit, vanishing ... A shiver fell through him.

He glanced to the siblings, as if fearful of discovery.

The Prince-Imperial stared at his sister, who had advanced several paces ahead, scanning the black. Though Sorweel had never thought otherwise, the Swayali Grandmistress's command now seemed absolute.

"What are you thinking?" Moënghus asked.

"These Emwama are a good sign ..." she replied without returning his look. "But the ruin is worrisome ... Much has changed since Seswatha stood in this place."

"Ruin?"

She turned to him, her face as inscrutable as ever. Her mouth opened. Her eyes sparked like twin Nails with the first impossible syllable. "***Teirol—***"

She snapped her head back to face the Mansion, extending her arms as if to seize its immensity in proxy. The Emwama before her wailed and scattered ...

The Surillic Point winked out.

A *line* took its place, brilliant enough to parse the violet blackness, an incision of light, appearing instantly at all stages, from the floor below her arms to the very summit of the void, and *broadening*, as if a door as tall as creation slipped open ...

A Bar of Heaven. Like that raised by Eskeles on the desolate tracts of the Istyuli; only, where his had illuminated leagues of bestial Sranc, hers revealed a far different host, one hung as if from hooks of stone.

Moënghus cursed, barked at his sister in the same unknown tongue.

"We are the children of the Aspect-Emperor ..." she said tonelessly. "Light is our birthright."

Strange hoots broke out among the Emwama, and a chest-thumping not unlike applause.

Sorweel simply blinked and gaped.

"Once it was called Ishoriöl, the Exalted Hall," Serwa was saying, her voice pitched above the babbling murmur of the Emwama. "Of all the Great Mansions, only Siöl could claim more glory ..."

So near to the Weeping Mountain it seemed the light had inked a cavern across the sky. Only the great faces were as he imagined. The warlike bodies he had imagined beneath were in fact priestly, limbs like cliffs clothed in monkish robes, hands clasped low as if to assist someone climbing, outermost knees jutting as opposing turrets. Trees mobbed the crooks of their arms, some bent into claws, others upright. Scrub and grasses thronged anywhere the graven cloth was hooked into gullies, so that the twin immensities seemed draped in gardens. The faces themselves were plainly Nonmen, though they seemed uncanny for staring to the south rather than out and over the processional. Growth clotted eyes like skiffs.

"For an Age it bequeathed its wisdom to our race, dispatching its immortal sons, the Siqu, to advise our kings, train our artisans, teach our scholars ... Nil'giccas foresaw the doom of his race, and knew that we would outlive them ..."

The main entrance lay between the titanic figures, famed Minror the Unholy—the Soggomantic Gate. But two other portals flanked it, each half the size, each set beneath scarps of engraved riot. Their nimil doors lay askew, dazzling the dingy stone and wrack about them, but their mouths remained black for shadow. Wicked Minror also lay askew, a wall as savage as broken glass stacked and fused, only consisting of plates of soggomant—thousands of golden fragments looted from the Ark. But where the Bar of Heaven could scarcely plumb the depths of the lesser gates, here it beamed like a candle held to the socket of an eyeless man, revealing a monumental hall gagged with ruin. The legendary gate that had sealed the Mountain against the Great Ruiner had been destroyed from within ...

"Then Mog-Pharau came," she continued, "and all the nations of the North were swept away. Nil'giccas withdrew, and these very gates were sealed shut. Ishoriöl became Ishterebinth, the Exalted Stronghold. All surviving knowledge of the Tutelage passed to the South with Seswatha."

Ishterebinth, he realized, had not so much been stripped of its natural skin as clothed in the mad intricacies of its soul. History. Icon and Image. Faith. All the things the Anasûrimbor bandied about with a philosopher's contempt for belief had been writ into living rock, panel after panel, line after line. The only difference was that it was not script, though his eye everywhere insisted on seeing it as such. Nor was it engraving ...

It was *statuary*, countless images, endless pageants, somehow prised out of the mountain's hide. Sorweel knew this because of the very ruin that so concerned Serwa. Some sections had sloughed away like decrepit plaster, whereas others had been pocked by titanic impacts, revealing graven recesses deep enough for a man to hide. And he realized: for all its mad, bloated artifice, Ishterebinth was a place of senescence and death. Slowly, inexorably, weather and weight and assault were stripping it—*denuding* it. Channels scored the mountainous facades, tributaries where plummeting stonework had collected into rivers of artifice and gouged ravines through the granite embroidery. Debris lay heaped about the foot of every scarp, in some places as high or higher than Sakarpus's walls. Broken meaning.

"The Stronghold is Exalted no longer," Moënghus called out in wry warning.

Sorweel shared his misapprehension. An ally who could not keep his own walls was no ally.

"The ghouls are many things, Brother. Some less than Men, some more, and some incomprehensible."

The Prince-Imperial grinned. "What are you saying?"

Sorweel could tell that for all the deference Moënghus showed his sister, he still saw her as the pestering child she had once pretended to be.

A dark look from his sister. "Only that *humility* would better serve our father."

Moënghus cast a contemptuous glance at Sorweel.

"And if they decide that Father has violated the Niom?"

"Nil'giccas was Seswatha's *friend*."

Her tone remained poised, as always, at the pitch of indifference, but Sorweel somehow knew she was less than convinced.

"Bah! *Look* at this place, Serri! Look! Is this the House of a *sane* king?"

"No," she admitted.

The Emwama milled about them, watching with a wonder marred for the perverse size of their eyes.

"You remember what Father told us," Moënghus pressed. "The confused always seek the security of *rules*. That was why the Niom was so important, why this"—a thumb thrown in Sorweel's direction—"kag's *hatred* was so important!"

The Grandmistress scowled. "What do you want me to do?"

"What I wanted from the beginning!"

"No, Podi."

A moment of fierce appraisal passed between the siblings, and somehow Sorweel knew that Moënghus *meant to kill him*—here and now if he could.

"Is that the Dûnyain in you, Serri? Or is it *Mother*?"

"I said, *no*."

Moënghus glared at Sorweel with barely constrained fury.

"*Yul'irisa kak-kak meritru* ..." he grated to his sister.

And though Sorweel understood none of it, in his soul's ear he heard, *If I snap his neck anyway?*

"It would make no difference."

Something in her tone hooked the gazes of both men.

The ghouls. They were coming.

So they stood breathless on the High Floor beneath the Soggomantic Gate, the Believer-King and the children of the Aspect-Emperor. A murmur passed through the throngs, even though only those Emwama near the fore could have possibly seen the approach of their ageless masters. Terror has its own vision. A kind of cringing eagerness overcame the creatures, one that reminded Sorweel of beaten dogs. They did not so much crowd the three travellers as shrink against them, their smiles garish and false beneath looks of shy dread. One even clutched his hand—child fingers, only horned and callused like a man's.

Sorweel found himself returning the insistent squeeze. And in a moment of madness he understood that the siblings hadn't tormented him because he had witnessed their incest—the incest had been the torment! They had afflicted him because the terms of the Niom demanded that he *hate the Anasûrimbor* ...

Because they needed evidence of what the Goddess would never let them see.

And now they thought themselves doomed.

What had he done? The youth stood riven. The Nonmen of Ishterebinth issued from the lesser gate to the right, an otherworldly file. Where the stone and lichens sopped the light, they reflected it, flashing small and iridescent beneath the vast, graven heights. Their gait betrayed neither urgency nor alarm.

Moënghus cursed, his great frame taut.

"Say nothing," Serwa admonished the two men. "Do as I do."

The False Men gathered more radiance as they approached, such was the burnish of their gown-length hauberks. Hairless as porcelain. Eyes like obsidian. Pale as melting snow. The mere image of them constricted Sorweel's breast. Fair of face. Narrow of hip and broad of shoulder. Imperious without the least pretension—the assurance of an indisputable ascendancy in grace and glory as much as form. With their every step, something clawed Sorweel from the inside, a panic as old as his Race—a *recognition*, not of something other, but of something *stolen*. Where the Emwama disgusted for being less, the Nonmen repelled for being *more*, for achieving what were *human* sums, a measure writ into every Mannish soul. *This* was what made them False, inhuman ...

The way they made *beasts* of Men.

Small wonder the Gods demanded their extermination.

The ghouls began fanning across the mall behind the foremost of their number, the one with small pelts of fur hanging against his chest. The Bar of Heaven glared above everything, a column hewn from the sun, so tall as to chase shadows into puddles about booted feet. The Nonmen hauberks, which had seemed chitinous mirrors, now made powder of the light, which coursed serpentine and scintillating up and down their forms. Black pommels jutted above their shoulders. Small moans and curious, keening whispers broke out among the Emwama. The little fingers in his hand curled into claws.

Sorweel's heart began hammering.

"Say *nothing*," the Swayali witch murmured.

The Nonman with the necklace of pelts—*human scalps*, Sorweel numbly realized—began barking incomprehensible words, his voice deep and ariose. The great mob of Emwama fell to their faces in almost perfect unison, so much so it seemed the ground itself had dropped. Sorweel lurched for vertigo, clenched his now empty hand. Both he and Moënghus looked to Serwa, but she seemed every bit as perplexed as they.

"*Anasûrimbor Serwa mil'ir*," she called out. "*Anasûrimbor Kellhus ish'alurij pil—*"

The Nonman barked out another command—in the Emwama tongue, Sorweel realized—but there was no response from the prostrate masses. The otherworldly figure paused some ten paces before Serwa, his nimil skirts shimmering where they swayed, his marmoreal face devoid of passion. His companions formed a loose and cadaverous assembly behind him.

"*Niomi mi'sisra*," Serwa ventured once again, her tone searching and conciliatory. "*Nil'gisha soimi—*"

"*Hu'jajil!*" the Nonman cried.

Serwa and Moënghus fell almost immediately to their knees, dropped their faces to the cracked ground. Witless, Sorweel was late in following, which was why he saw the Emwama behind Moënghus rise and, as quick as a dog slaps its tail, club the base of his skull. He cried out, tried to leap clear of the pungent little beasts, but the small callused hand had seized him once more—as did innumerable others, wrenching, twisting, pinching, striking. He heard Serwa frantically shouting in Ihrimsû. He glimpsed Moënghus somehow roaring back to his feet, shrugging the wretches from his great shoulders, swinging one from a strapped arm—

But an impact knocked all vision from him, snatched away his legs.

Clawing. Screeching. Stink and blackness.

CHAPTER THREE

Momemn

Men, who belong to nature, apprehend their nature as Law when it seems to them to be restrained, and as nature when it seems to them to be unruly. Thus do some Sages say that a lie, merely, divides Men from Beasts.

—MEMGOWA, *The Book of Divine Acts*

Early Autumn, 20 New Imperial Year (4132, Year-of-the-Tusk), Momemn

"Catch," the Whore of Momemn calls across sunlight …

But the peach is already in his hand.

In the vast and vacant gloom of Xothei, the Gift-of-Yatwer stands motionless beside the idol of his Mother, watching several doddering priests raise and bear the carcass of their Shriah away. Three of them spit upon the floor at his feet. He looks back as the Inchausti lead him away, sees himself standing in the shadow of his gilded Mother.

Horns rifle the sky. Hoe and Earth! Hoe and Earth! Wicked Momemn lays blotted, struck from the Book for its iniquities. The Empress calls across the remains of the sun. "Catch …"

He does not so much wash as rinse the blood from his hands.

A thin and oddly-apparelled girl joins their company, Theliopa, whose subtlety has been honed into simplicity. "Someone who was there when it happens," he explains to her, even as he watches her vanish beneath crashing black.

The Empress tosses a peach … "Catch."

The fingers he submerges are brown, and yet crimson blooms through the water.

The Empress peers into his mien. "What you did … How could it be possible?"

Ruby-red beads hang quivering from the pads of his fingers. He cranes his ear down to listen: the water chirps ever so faintly. The ripples bloat out across all creation.

All Creation.

Blaring horns. A black city roiling, bracing.

"Catch."

The rooves slump, first to one knee, then another. The Mother sheds her tear, gives what has been given. He watches himself cast what is broken, sees the Aspect-Emperor stumble, then vanish beneath the Mother's heel.

He turns from the Sea, where the sun splints the back of dark waters, and he gazes out to the summer-weary fields of the south; he sees himself standing upon a greener hill, gazing at where he now stands at the Empress's side.

His Mother gathers him in clacking arms of ruin.

Kellhus would often chide Esmenet for her perpetual misgivings. He would remind her that Men, despite any chest-thumping declaration to the contrary, sought servitude to the simple degree they hungered for power. "*If you cannot trust in your station,*" he would say, "*at least take heart in their greed, Esmi. Dispense your authority as milk, and they will come racing as kittens … Nothing makes Men so meek as* ambition."

And race after her they did.

She had assumed it had been the Inchausti calling after her as she had searched the Andiamine Heights. But as she wandered back down the darkened halls with Kelmomas, she encountered Amarsla, one of her body-slaves, who collapsed wailing at her feet. "I found her!" the old matron began crying to the frescoed ceilings. "Praise Seju, *I found her*!" And *others* began to emerge from the gilded maze, first an Eothic Officer whose name she could not recall, then lumbering Keopsis, the Exalt-Counter …

Despite the general panic, word of Maithanet's death and her de facto restoration had swept through the streets of Momemn, and those souls dispossessed by her brother-in-law's coup began flocking back to the Imperial

Precincts, their erstwhile home. Fairly a dozen trailed her and Kelmomas by the time they reached the Scuari Campus, where dozens *more* awaited, a motley that cheered with wild abandon. Clutching Kelmomas to her waist, she stood sobbing with disbelief and gratitude ...

Then set about seizing the collective reins they offered.

She disengaged the bestial apparition that was Kelmomas, commended him, despite his wailing protestations, to the ministrations of Larsippas, one of the palace physician-priests. He needed to be cleansed, dressed, and fed, certainly, as well as examined for illness or infection. His skin was Zeumi dark, stained as if he had hidden in a vat of dye. He wore nothing more than his bed-time smock, the linen transformed into leather for the laminations of filth. His hair, once flaxen and immaculate, was as black as her own, here matted into manure-like clumps, there twined into rat tails. The expressions of those recognizing him for the first time were universally appalled. Some even went so far as to sign finger charms, as though she had plucked him from death and damnation rather than hiding and squalor.

"Mumma, *no*!" he blubbered.

"Do you hear those drums?" she asked, clasping his shoulders and kneeling before him. "Do you understand what they mean?"

The boy's blue eyes seemed even more bright, more canny, shining from blood-swart cheeks.

He isn't what you think he is ...

The small Prince-Imperial nodded reluctantly.

"Finding you safe was simply the beginning, Kel," she said. "Now I must *keep* you safe! Do you understand, Sweetling?"

"Yes, Mumma."

She cupped his cheek and smiled reassurance. Larsippus drew him away, shouting for someone to draw water. She allowed herself three doting heartbeats before setting aside motherhood and taking up the Empire—becoming the very thing that those watching so desperately needed her to be: Anasûrimbor Esmenet, the Blessed Empress of the Three Seas.

The Inchausti comprised the sum of her military. She would later discover that the Pillarians had died to a man defending her home and her children. Apparently some Eothic Guardsmen had surrendered, but shame would delay their appearance. Of the Imperial Apparati she had seen at Xothei, a good number had also followed her to the palace—those who had known her well enough to trust her forgiving nature, she would later realize. The others, those who had fled out of fear of retribution, she would never see again.

She began by embracing Ngarau, the old and indispensable Grand Seneschal she had inherited from the Ikurei Dynasty.

"My House is out of order," she said, gazing into the eunuch's pouched eyes.

"No longer, my Glory."

Dark and lurching, Ngarau began moving among the assembly, bellowing commands. Migrations toward various quarters of the palace and elsewhere immediately began thinning the crowd, leaving only kneeling soldiery and Imperial Apparati behind. Phinersa, her erstwhile Master of Spies, knelt among them, his svelte form clad in the black-silk robes he had made his uniform. When she turned to regard him, the small man proved as nimble at falling to his face as he was at everything else.

"You knew nothing of the coup?" she cried at the maul of black hair.

"I knew nothing," he said into the cobble. "I *failed* you, my Glory."

"Stand up," she exclaimed, her voice cracking for disgust, not so much at Phinersa as at the tragic toll of the insanity that had seized them all. Chaos and revolt across the Three Seas. Innumerable deaths, near as well as far. Sharacinth. Imhailas. Inrilatas ...

Samarmas.

"You heard what Maithanet said at Xothei?"

"Yes," the man replied, his voice muted, his clean-shaven face blank with care. She had expected him to leap into his old, insinuating manner as much as too his feet, but he remained wary. "That you and he were to be reconciled."

Which would make *her* the savage one, the more murderous Anasûrimbor.

"No," she said, staring at him carefully. He had the cheek and jaw of a soft man, she decided. "That the *Empire was never meant to survive ...*"

Because her displeasure was clear, the Master of Spies bowed his head to the degree demanded by jnan—no more. Esmenet looked to the other Apparati kneeling at points about her on the Scuari Campus.

"That was a lie!" she cried in a clear, bold voice. "That was *proof* of the cancer that had poisoned his soul! Would my husband abandon his wife?

Would the Holy Aspect-Emperor leave his *children* to their ruin? If he foresaw the collapse of his Holy Empire, then surely he would have hidden his wife and children away!"

Her voice rang bright across the stone expanse. She saw Vem-Mithriti, her sorcerous Vizier, hobbling to join the motley assembly, his black and gold robes of the Imperial Saik comically distended for the winds off the Meneanor.

"And that means our Lord-and-Prophet foresaw quite the opposite! That he prophecied our *triumph*, that Momemn would break the back of the Fanim Dog—that the mightiest Empire of our age would survive!"

Silence, save for the rhythmic throb of Fanim war-drums ... But there was wonder and worship enough in their look, she supposed.

She looked back to her Master-of-Spies, afforded him a momentary glimpse of her terror.

"Do you know what happens?" she asked on a murmur.

He shook his head, looked out to the line of the walls. "They struck my chains scarce a watch before yours, my Glory."

She clenched his arm in a spontaneous gesture of reassurance.

"All of us must be strong now," she said. "Strong and cunning."

The Inchausti Knights milled in the near distance, watching from the monumental stair of the Allosium Forum. She raised an arm, beckoned their white-bearded commander, Clia Saxillas. The Massentian officer moved with the haste appropriate to his station, and no more. She bid the man rise after he had kissed her knee.

"I assassinated your Shriah," she said.

The caste-noble stared at her sandaled feet. "Aye, my Glory."

"Do you hate me?" she asked.

He dared look into her eyes. "I thought I did."

The pulsing drums as much as exhaustion made her gaze indomitable. The man blinked, looked to the ground with more fear than reverence. And at that moment it seemed she could *feel* it radiating about her, looming above and leaning out ...

The shadow of her accursed husband.

"And now?"

The man licked his lips. "I am not sure."

She nodded.

"The Inchaustic Knights guard me and my children now, Saxillas ... You are my new Exalt-Captain."

The man hesitated for the merest heartbeat, an instant that revealed the profundity of his grief, the fact that he mourned the death of his Shriah the way another might mourn the death of a beloved father.

"Deploy your men," she continued. "See that the Imperial Precincts are secured." She paused a moment, her thoughts fraught with the enormity—perhaps *impossibility*—of the task that lay before her ...

The drums throbbed ... recounted the horrors of Caraskand.

"Then retrieve my assassin from Xothei."

Uncle Holy is dead! Dead-dead-dead, tucked into bed!

On and on his thoughts capered, but the Voice was in no mood. It disapproved of his humour.

I could smell it in her look ... He told her something!

But not enough! the boy chortled within. *Not! Even! Close! Ooh, bad throw, Uncle Holy! Such a pity! Bad, bad throw! Now the number-sticks are mine!*

To all outward appearances, Anasûrimbor Kelmomas was an ailing ten-year-old boy, a divine son of the Holy Aspect-Emperor driven to heartbreaking extremis by the wickedness of his once-beloved uncle. The insipid ingrate, Larsippus, drew him through the corridors to the palace lazaret, alternately snarling instructions to the menials he had commandeered, and murmuring dulcet reassurances to his divine ward.

"And He has soooo very many Hands," the gaunt man was saying. The Prince-Imperial's failure to register anything did not surprise the man. They did not hear all that much, little boys who had survived what this poor child had survived. They spoke even less. "He is as cunning as he is cruel. We just need to cleanse you, search for signs of His touch. But not to fear ..."

Perhaps Disease had fondled the boy's soul as well.

And how was Mother able to kill him? the Voice asked. *She has no Strength!*

What does it matter?

There's more *happening here! More than we know!*

So? You're forgetting they're all dead now, *Sammi! All of those who could* see!

And it seemed miraculous, the prospect of untainted impunity—glorious invisibility! To cuddle snuggle-warm in Mother's arms, to whisper knives hot in her ear, to roam unhindered, unrestrained, through the darkling halls, the blind streets. He could play and play and play—

Father can still see.

Father was forever the pall across his jubilation.

"Shush ..." Larsippus was saying, his braying voice huffing for the effort of sounding gentle. "Nothing to fear at all ..."

So? He's as good as dead.

How so?

Because dead is just someplace else, someplace too far away to ever come back from ...

Golgotterath is not so far. Father will *come back ...*

This lent his false sobs the pang of reality. *And how could* you *know? What makes you so smart?*

Because He came back from Hell.

Stories! Rumours!

Mother believes them.

The wraith floated in from the gloom of the Imperial Audience Hall and stepped into shimmering, sunlit materiality: her daughter, Anasûrimbor Theliopa, garbed in a blue, pearl-spangled gown hooped into the shape of an overturned fuller's basin. Esmenet laughed at the sight of her, not so much for the absurdity of her dress as for the absurdity of finding it so beautiful—so *true*. She hugged the sallow blond girl tight, breathed deep her earthen scent—Thelli had never ceased smelling like a little girl. Esmenet even savoured the way the woman went rigid rather than reciprocate the embrace.

She cupped Theliopa's cheeks, blinked tears hot enough for the two of them. "We have much to speak about," she sighed. "I need you now more than ever."

And even though Esmenet had expected as much, it *stung*, the lack of any answering passion in the girl's angular expression. Theliopa could only miss her the way a geometer would miss his compass, such was the girl's share of her father's spoils.

"Mother ..."

She had no time for this, for *he* had caught her eye. Esmenet pressed her daughter aside to consider the second soul the Inchausti had delivered ...

Her impossible assassin.

What was it he had called himself? *Issiral* ... the Shigeki word for "fate". It was easily the most unlucky name she had ever heard ... and yet *Maithanet* was dead. Her boy was *avenged.*

The Narindar strode into the angular sunlight and halted, stood upon the terrace threshold the way he had stood between the idols of War and Birth in Xothei. He had a strange mauled-beyond-his-years look, perhaps because his trim beard belonged to a younger generation. He was naked save for the grey cloth bound about his loins, and *remote* in the way of violent and imperturbable men. The short hair that had raised her hackles when she had first contracted the man—priests of Ajokli were forbidden to cut their hair—now occasioned relief. She had no wish for the world to know she harboured a devotee of the Four-Horned Brother. In fact, he would have looked a slave were it not for an unnerving air of *relentlessness* about him, the sense that absolutely nothing outside his cryptic ends mattered, be it scruple, let alone comfort or security. She thought of what Lord Sankas had said, the way Narindar saw events as wholes. She wondered whether the Consul had managed to flee to Biaxi lands.

Issiral's right hand was bloodied, a token of the calamity he had wrought mere watches ago.

The calamity she had authored through him.

"You may cleanse your hands in the basin," she said, nodding at the graven pedestal to his left.

The man wordlessly complied.

"Mother ..." Theliopa said from her periphery.

"Join Phinersa and the others," Esmenet directed the girl, watching the Narindar's hands vanish beneath shimmering water. "He will tell you what little we know."

All was bustling activity about the mother and daughter, urgent and yet all the more muted for it. She had chosen the Postern Terrace behind the Imperial Audience Hall to establish her command, not simply for the view it afforded of her besieged city, but because it forced everyone she summoned to contemplate her husband's Holy Chair, the Circumfix Throne, before coming to kneel before her. A small multitude now milled about the balustrade—merchants, officers, spies and advisors—peering out to the surrounding hills, pointing, exchanging questions and observations. A steady stream of messengers passed back and forth from the murk and glister of the Imperial Audience Hall. Harried looks were exchanged with sharp words. Three Kidruhil signallers stood at the ready with their bronze longhorns, one missing his horsehair helm, the other with his arm in a crimson sling. Porters had arrived with the first of the drink and food mere moments before.

The Whore had favoured her—at least so far. They knew very little as of yet, save that Momemn remained inviolate. The streets yet surged, but the campuses of the Cmiral and the Kamposea Agora appeared all but deserted. Smoke rose from the Lesser Ancilline Gate, but she had been told the fire was due to a mishap.

Fanayal, it seemed, had known nothing of the internecine turmoil that engulfed the city. Maithanet had fairly stripped the ramparts to better bully the mob, anticipating that her capture would provoke riots. Had Fanayal stormed Momemn directly, the mat of street and structure below would already be a ruinous battleground. But the Bandit Padirajah had chosen to take Jarûtha as his base and secure the countryside surrounding the Imperial Capital instead—affording her time she desperately needed. As surreal, as *horrific*, as it was watching bands of wild enemy horsemen scour the distance, the sight flushed her with an almost delirious sense of relief. So long as the heathen filth remained out *there*, Thelli and Kelmomas were safe.

She watched the Narindar stare at his cleansed hands, then lower his ear as if listening ... for some further portent? He was every bit as eerie and unsettling as he had been that fateful day she had contracted him ... the day of Maithanet's coup.

The man finally turned to meet her gaze.

"What you did ..." she began, only to trail.

His look was bold in the manner of children.

"What you did," he repeated, but not as if he were confused by her meaning. His voice was as unremarkable as his appearance, and yet ...

"How?" she asked. "How could it be possible?"

How could a mere man murder a *Dûnyain*?

He pursed his lips in lieu of shrugging.

"I am but a vessel."

And it pimpled her skin, this answer. Were she a caste-noble, she would have been oblivious. Only a soul reared in slums and gutters, a caste-menial or a slave, could understand the dread import of what he meant, for only such souls understood the horror of the Four-Horned Brother ... Ajokli.

Only the most desperate turned to the Prince of Hate.

The Blessed Empress of the Three Seas signed a charm that only Sumni harlots would know. By happenstance a slave scurried between them bearing a shallow basket stacked with peaches. She plucked one from the man's passage, whether to allay or to conceal her anxiety she did not know. "Catch," she called, tossing it to the Narindar.

The man picked it from the sky. Then, closing both of his hands about it, he raised it above his open mouth and violently squeezed, so that he might drink its nectar directly, in the uncouth Shigeki manner.

Esmenet watched with a kind of appalled fascination.

"I want you to remain here in the palace," she said as he lowered the pulped fruit. Sunlight limned the runnels of juice across his shaved chin.

At first she thought he looked at her, but then she realized that he looked *beyond*, as if spying something on the distant hills ...

"With me," the Blessed Empress of the Three Seas said, biting a pensive lower lip.

The man continued staring around her edges. Shouting rose up through the Imperial Audience Hall, fractured for the accumulation of echoes. At last they had found him, Caxes Anthirul, her Home Exalt-General, the man who had capitulated to Maithanet—who would have assured her doom, had the Whore been less generous.

The Narindar, Issiral, lowered his head in cryptic obeisance.

"I will consult my God," he said.

Kelmomas breathed like a child asleep, lay motionless like one, his limbs akimbo above tangled sheets, his eyes shut in the slack manner of dreaming souls, but his ears were pricked to the mazed darkness, and his skin tingled, alive to the promise of her touch.

She stalked the apartments beyond, exhausted, he knew, yet restless with the alarums of her day. He heard her clasp the decanter on the Seolian sideboard, the one stamped with the serpentine dragons that so fascinated him from time to time. He heard her sigh in gratitude—gratitude!—that the thing had been filled.

He heard the silken gurgle of a bowl deeply filled. The gasp between compulsive swallows.

He heard her staring out into vertigo, the wine-bowl clink to the floor.

Inwardly, he clucked for glee, imagining her acrid smell and her embrace, at first timid, then growing more fierce with the waxing of her desperation. He was clean, his skin scrubbed pink with cinnamon-scented soaps, then rinsed in dilute tinctures of myrrh and lavender. She would hold him, tighter and tighter, and then she would weep, for fear, for loss, but for gratitude far, far more. She would clutch him and sob, her lips pursed against any audible wail, and she would exult in the beatific glory of her *living* son ... she would tremble and she would gloat and she would think, *So long as I have him ...*

So long as I have *him*.

She would rejoice as she has never rejoiced, marvel at the miraculous deformity of her Fate. And as the excesses of her passion dwindled, she would hang numb and awake, listening to the enemy's drums on the night air. She would comb his hair with absent fingers, assuming the solitary authority of all mothers abandoned by their husbands. She would muster the countless injustices she had suffered and she would lash them into a semblance of order. And she would plot ways to *keep him safe*, never knowing, never dreaming ...

She would think herself *heroic*, not so much to reward efforts made as to goad efforts *required*. She would torture anyone who needed to be tortured. She would kill anyone who needed to be killed. She would be whatever her sweet little boy needed her to be ...

Protector. Provider. Comforter.

Slave.

And he would lay besotted, breathe and breathe and breathe ...

Pretend to sleep.

The Andiamine Heights clattered and hummed with subterranean industry, alive once again—resurrected. The Blessed Empress sauntered to the bedroom, drawing the long pins from her hair.

A fraction of her will be watching, his accursed brother whispered.

Silence!

Uncle Holy told her something.

Five golden kellics flashing in Naree's dark palm.

Imhailas vanishing with the heat of his blood.

The Collegian sneering at the girl, saying, "*And here's a silver to* remember *her by …*"

Esmenet could not blink without seeing these and other desperate things as she made her way up the marble stair. It made her dizzy thinking of the darkness of those days, mourning Inrilatas, fretting for Kelmomas and Thelli, fearing her brother, the Holy Shriah of the Thousand Temples. The soldiers had fled upon her appearance, leaving the wrought-iron camp lanterns they had placed for her benefit swaying like dowser sticks. Her shadows bobbed, angles splitting and combining as she climbed the steps. Hooves rained as hail across the street outside. Officers bawled at their formations. No one expected problems, but with the tumult of the days, she had decided to err on the side of precaution. Almost dying in one riot was enough.

Besides, it was important that she arrive *as she was*, Anasûrimbor Esmenet, the Blessed Empress of the Three Seas. She savoured the joy of the triumphant return, the petty jubilation of returning as master to a place where she had been a slave. The *Empire* climbed these stairs as much as she!

She paused at the top of the stair, amazed that she recognized so little of the place. But then Imhailas had taken her here at night and in a panic, and she had not stepped foot outside Naree's apartment until the Shrial Knights had dragged her out screaming and weeping weeks later. She looked about, realizing that she had never been on this stair, or in this hall, not really. The camp lanterns made a grotesquerie of the uneven plastering. The emerald paint had begun peeling back in a singular direction, so that it resembled something reptilian.

She saw her daughter waiting by the apartment door, her face pale even for this gloom. Theliopa's gown (yet another one of her own manufacture) consisted of black and white lace pleats, packed so dense as to resemble closed codices in places, and everywhere strung with tiny black pearls. Her flaxen hair had been pinned high into a matching headdress. Esmenet smiled for the simple relief of seeing someone she truly trusted. This was the way it was with tyrants, she knew, how their trust was whittled down until only blood remained.

"You've done very well, Thelli. Thank you."

The girl blinked in her odd way.

"Mother. I can see what you-you are about to do."

Esmenet swallowed. She hadn't expected *honesty*. Not here.

"And what of it?"

She wasn't sure she could stomach it.

"I would beg you to reconsider," Theliopa said. "Don't do it, Mother."

Esmenet approached her daughter.

"What do you think your father would say?"

The shadow of a scowl marred the blank fixity of Theliopa's gaze.

"I hesitate to say, Mother."

"Why?"

"Because I know it will harden you-you *against* what must-must be done."

Esmenet laughed in mock wonder.

"Such is the grudge I hold against my husband?"

Theliopa blinked, paused in calculation.

"Yes, Mother. Such is the grudge."

It suddenly seemed that she dangled from a hook.

"Y-you have no inkling of what I suffered here, Thelli."

"I see a great deal in your face, Mother."

"Then what would you have me do? What your *father* would do?"

"Yes!" the girl cried with surprising vehemence. "You must *kill her*, Mother."

Esmenet gazed at her beloved daughter in reproach, if not disbelief. She was past being surprised by her extraordinary children.

"Kill her? And for what? For doing *the very thing I would have done*? You see only the consequence of the life I have lived, daughter. You know nothing of the blood and bitumen that fills a bowl so cracked as your mother! You know nothing of the *terror*! Grasping and grasping for *life*, for bread, for medicine, for the gold needed to secure these things with dignity. Killing her would be killing myself!"

"But why would you-you confuse yourself with this woman? Sharing the same-same weal does nothing to change the fact that *you are the Empress*, and she-she is the whore who betrayed you, that had-had Imhailas murd—"

"Shut up!"

"No, Mother. Momemn *is besieged.* You are *Father's* vessel, the one anointed to rule-rule in his absence. *All eyes are upon-upon you*, Mother. You must-must gratify them, show them the strength they need to see. You must-must be ferocious."

Esmenet gazed at her daughter, stupefied by that word, "ferocious."

"Think of *Kelmomas*, Mother. Imagine if he had died *because of that woman.*"

The fury had always been there, of course, the *will* to make suffer, to gloat and glory in vengeance. Her soul's eye had witnessed Naree die countless ways for what she had done—enough to make a habit of bloody imagery. The girl *had* betrayed her, had *sold* her life and the lives of all those she loved for silver. It all came rushing back, a cringing, noxious tide, the girl's petty cruelties, her peevish need to humiliate a deposed queen, a mourning mother ...

Esmenet looked to her beloved and inhuman daughter, watched the girl read and approve the savage turn in her thought, saw the clenched jaw where slack eyes had been.

"If you wish, I will do it for you, Mother."

Esmenet shook her head, caught each hand in the other to prevent either from floating away. She could taste the words she had spoken months ago, the oath they had contained.

"*It means that your life—your* life, *Naree—belongs to me ...*"

"She's my burden. You said so yourself."

Theliopa raised the pommel of a knife she produced as if by magic from the intricacies of her gown.

Esmenet could *taste* the thing when she inhaled, or at least so it seemed. She clutched the handle, felt a cloud of gas for the heft of it, the lethal solidity. Her husband's eyes watched her from her daughter's angular face. She flinched from them, looked down out of some unnameable instinct. She turned to the door, numb, barged through on a deep breath.

The chipped, yellow-painted walls. The tawdry simulation of opulence. The tincture of too many bodies and too little bedding.

The Inchausti had been no more gentle this visit than the Shrial Knights had been the previous. The girl's shelves had been ransacked, her furnishing smashed and thrown as wrack in the corners.

Esmenet had returned, this time steeped in the very power she had fled from before. It seemed mad that the floorboards did not creak, the walls did not groan, for the presence of one who could burn everything down.

Naree lay crouched in the corner to the right and opposite, naked save for a rag she clutched beneath her chin. The girl immediately began keening in terror, but not for recognizing her Blessed Empress—that would come later—but for understanding that once the rapists left, the executioner always followed.

One of Ngarau's runners found his body at daybreak of the seventh day of the siege, at the bottom of an ancillary stair. The victim had chosen anonymous attire, but he was too well known on the Andiamine Heights not to be immediately recognized: Lord Sankas, Consul of Nansur, Patridomos of House Biaxi, and confidante of the Blessed Empress.

Esmenet had hoped the Patridomos would simply reappear, drawn like the others by word of her restoration. And now *here he was* sprawled across a blackening sheet of blood below the Reverse Gallery of the Apparatory—the path she had directed him to take what seemed a lifetime ago.

"Perhaps-haps he merely tripped," Theliopa offered, wearing nothing but a smock—scandalous attire for any Princess-Imperial other than her. She looked like those mad Cultic ascetics who confused mortification of flesh for cultivation of spirit, angular with bones, strung with veins.

"And what of his broadsword?" Phinersa asked mildly. "Did it simply fly loose its scabbard?"

The Blessed Empress of the Three Seas could only gawk at the inert form.

Sankas ...

He had dressed to travel incognito, bereft of any insignia, wearing a simple white-linen tunic beneath a blue-felt robe that had slipped loose one arm in the fall, and now lay bundled to one side of him. The tunic had wicked the blood, clotting violet and black like bandages about his edges, so that he seemed *inked* in place, as much an artistic conceit as a corpse ...

Sankas was dead!

She had tasked Phinersa with finding him on the day of her restoration. She needed the Patridomos, not simply because of his prestige and prodigious clout within the Congregate, but because he was one of the few independent power brokers she could trust. *Sankas had secured the Narindar for her*, which meant he had wagered his very soul *against* the Holy Shriah of the Thousand Temples—for her!

She would find Phinersa's subsequent report less than satisfactory. Like so many others, Lord Sankas had gone into hiding following the coup. But where most had been forced to shelter within the city, he had escaped the city altogether, commandeering one of his House's many grain ships and sailing no one knew where—anywhere across the Three Seas, given the enormous extent of his holdings (not to mention how well he had married off his seven daughters).

She looked to her Exalt-Captain, Saxillas, who continued wearing his Inchaustic accoutrements despite her explicit request. What was it with these men?

"How could something like this happen?"

The Shrial Knight dared meet her gaze, more dismayed than alarmed, more baffled than furious.

Was he going to be a problem?

"Errors, lapses ..." she said. "These things are *inevitable*, Saxillas. This is why I need men who know *how to fail*, men who know how to cope with mishaps and disasters, and most importantly of all, *how to make them right*."

"Forgiveness, my Glory," he said, falling immediately to his knees.

She rolled furious eyes at Theliopa and Phinersa.

It's beginning all over again, a treacherous fraction of her soul whispered.

"Oh, get up!" she snapped at the man. She gazed to the top of the stair, squinted at the morning glare. For a long moment she could scarcely breathe. She could feel it kindle in her bowel once again, the cloying terror of intrigue and conspiracy. The conviction that Sankas was coming *to see her*, that he bore *mortal tidings*, floated like smoke through a body that seemed nothing but a shell of clothing and skin.

An imperial emptiness.

"Find who did this, Saxillas," she said. "Regain your honour. Redeem your Lord-and-Prophet's *faith*."

The Nansur caste-noble stood dumbfounded, either realizing he had just been threatened with *damnation*, or simply witless as to how he should proceed. He was incompetent, Esmenet realized, as so many honourable men were. She squelched the urge to scratch and scream. Why? Why was *trust* ever the cost of cunning?

"Mother?" Theliopa asked.

As always, the Fanim drums throbbed eternal. Heathens were ever on the horizon, she realized, whetting their knives, plotting her destruction. Heathens were always watching around the corner.

"Dress yourself," she said to her beloved, misbegotten daughter. "You look a common whore."

"Wha–?" Vem-Mithriti, her ancient Grand Vizier, coughed out as he hurried down the hallway toward them. His hobbling gait seemed to strike them dry with pity.

"What's this ..." he gasped, "I hear about ... murder ..."

"Come, old grandfather," Esmenet said, stepping out to usher him back the way he had come. "We're finished here."

Without warning, the sound of distant horns filtered down with the light ... Horns of assembly ...

Horns of war.

Theliopa made toward Kelmomas the instant she set foot in the Sacral Enclosure, striding from brilliance to cool shadow as she passed beneath the various garden bowers. She paused several paces away, as if at an imaginary threshold of an imaginary room he occupied. The young Prince-Imperial turned to her with a questioning smile, regarded the spectacle of her appearance. Fins–lacquered felt, trimmed with virginal pearls, three to a shoulder. Bodice embroidered in cloth of silver, cinched viciously about her waist. Skirt like a yaksh, turquoise silk stretched across hoops and ribs.

An old madwoman, he thought. Theliopa dressed like an old madwoman.

He stood, brushed the dirt from his knees. A gust swished through the hibiscus tree above them. An autumn insect buzzed between.

Something has gone wrong, the Voice whispered.

He nodded to the sky, to the rhythmic, almost sub-audible boom pulsating across the sky. "The Fanim can't *really* get us, can they?"

She strode forward, as if taking this comment as permission to enter his imaginary room. She came to a pause just to the left of where he had buried the third guardsmen he had killed ...

And eaten.

"They-they build siege engines," she said. "When they are done, we shall see."

She was watching him closely—far more intently than he could ever remember, in fact.

Perhaps she can smell them rotting in the dirt ...

She doesn't have that *Strength*!

"Who is that *man*, Thelli, the one dressed in a slave's cloth?"

She all but peered, her suspicion now so obvious as to be comical.

"That is the Narindar Mother contracted to assassinate our uncle."

"I *knew it*!" he cried, surprised at the honesty of his elation. "*Narindar* ... He's the one!

He's the one that saved us!"

Anasûrimbor Theliopa continued to gawk.

"What's wrong, Thelli?" he finally said, throwing up his arms the way Mother often did when confounded by her daughter's strange ways.

She answered in a rush, as if his question had opened the very door she leaned against. "You think-think I can't see, that-that Father's blood runs too-too thin in my veins."

The Prince-Imperial scowled and laughed—the way a daft eight-year-old should. "What are yo—?"

"Uncle Holy *told me*, Kel."

Enemy drums pounded across the skies.

"Told you what?"

She looked like a thing graven, the goddess of some lesser race. "I know what happened with Inrilatas, with Sharacinth and-and—" She halted on a sharp intake of breath, as if a razor tumbled in her wind.

"With Samar-marmas."

Fear. He would have *liked* to have seen *fear* on her face, some inkling of peril, anything that might reflect his *power*, but he saw what he *needed* instead—thoughtless confidence.

Say nothing. Appear weak.

She amazed the boy by managing to kneel stiffly at his feet, despite the apparatus of her skirt. For the first time he realized the cunning she put into their manufacture, the myriad springs and folding armatures. Her manly scent enclosed him.

"Tell me, Kel," she said.

He could stab her now if he wanted.

She looked a pale monstrosity, her eyes slightly bulbous, their lids rimmed pink, her angles slightly cadaverous—everything about her wandered the verge of disgust. And her skin seemed *so thin* for its pallor, a tissue he could rip away with his fingernails ... if he so wished.

"I need-need to know ..."

The bottomless indifference of her gaze was the only thing that terrified.

"Was it *you* who killed Lord Sankas?"

He was genuinely stupefied.

She gazed at him with piscine relentlessness, her pale blue eyes dead, void of passion. And for the first time he *felt* it ... the menace of her inhuman intellect.

Let her watch ... his twin murmured.

"Did you wander last night?" she asked.

"No."

Let her see ...

"You slept?"

"*Yes.*"

"And you had no idea that Lord Sankas was returning?"

"None!"

She maintained her implacable gaze, her manner as stilted and as relentless as an automata, her face as blank as a sunflower opened to receive the sun.

"What?" he cried.

Theliopa popped to her feet without reply, turned away with a swish of her ridiculous gown.

"And if I *had* murdered him?" he called after her.

She paused on the hook of his voice, turned to regard him once more.

"I would have informed Mother," she said plainly.

He was careful to look down to his thumbs. Dirt had inked the whorls across the pads, the ruts about the knuckles. How long would it take, he wondered, to bury her out here? How long would he have?

"Why haven't you told her already?"

He could feel her scrutiny now—and he was amazed to think how he had utterly ignored it all these years. As long as he could remember, she had always been too focussed to *not* be oblivious, and now ...

Now she had become the next eye to pluck.

Pale skin was always more intense, somehow, bleeding ...

"Because the Capital needs its Empress," she said, her voice falling from the shadow of his bangs, "and you, little brother, have made her too *weak* ... too heartbroken to bear knowing your crimes."

For all the anxious contrition he had slathered across his manner and expression, Anasûrimbor Kelmomas cackled within. His twin brother fairly screamed.

Truth.

Always such a burden ...

A small table draped in white silk stood unattended in the centre of the road some thirty paces from where Esmenet stood upon the Maumurine Gate. A swan-necked decanter had been placed upon it, blue glass caught in a cage of wrought gold, set with seventeen sapphires. A golden bowl sat empty beside it.

The Fanim had delivered their demand to parlay shortly after daybreak. The embassy had been led by no less than Surxacer, the youngest son of Pilaskanda, who had ridden fearlessly within bowshot and cast a spear bearing the missive upon the spot where the table now stood. The message had been terse and to-the-point: the fourth watch past the sun's summit, the Padirajah of the Kianene Empire would meet with the Blessed Empress of the Three Seas at the Maumurine Gate to discuss the terms of "mutual peace."

It was a *ruse*, of course—or so everyone on her warcouncil had assumed. They thought her decision to treat the offer as if it were *earnest* mad, she knew, more for the incredulous burr in their voices than any seditious comment. No soul dared test her authority anymore, even when they perhaps should.

So she found herself crowded upon the breastwork above the gate and between Maumurine's towers, dwarfed by sheer faces of stone.

"So what is your stratagem?" her Exalt-General, Caxes Anthirul, murmured at her side.

"Listen to what he has to say ..." she replied, wincing at the loudness of her voice. The war-drums were louder, more raw and less surreal beyond the baffles of the city. "Take his measure."

"And if he's merely trying to draw you out?"

She had hated Caxes Anthirul while a fugitive in hiding, cursed him for casting his sticks with her brother-in-law. At the time, his defection to the Thousand Temples had broken the back of any hope she might have had of overcoming Maithanet and saving her children. She had even rehearsed all the torments she would visit upon him, once her husband returned to set things aright. It spoke to the perversity of circumstance, so maudlin was the comfort she found in his presence, now. Fate was not so much a whore as a whore-maker, snapping the pious like twigs, warming Herself in the fires that had been honour.

Even festooned in regalia, Caxes Anthirul looked nothing like the champion painted by reputation. He was deceptively dull-eyed, one of those men prone to conceal their cunning in a bleary gaze, and the combination of his girth and clean-shaven jowls made him look more palace eunuch than famed hero of the Unification. Nevertheless, he belonged to that reassuring breed of soldiers who wholly understood their role as *instruments* of power. House Caxes was a southern Nansur family, with extensive interests in and around Gielgath. And like many bloodlines lacking any commercial or ancestral stake in the Capital, the Caxes were notoriously loyal—to *whomever* happened to be in power.

"I've been told my Imperial duty is to *run*," Esmenet finally replied.

Perhaps she simply preferred the company of whores. After all, she had married one.

"In war, the only duty is to *prevail*, Blessed Empress ... All else is calculation."

"My husband told you that, didn't he?"

The man shook with silent laughter, shivered with mirrored light.

"Aye," he replied with a sidelong wink. "More than once."

"Lord Anthirul? Are you saying you actually *approve*?"

"It's good to share in the risks of your men," Anthirul said. "Their commitment will only reflect as much of your commitment as they can *see*, Blessed Empress. Your courage is nothing to them barricaded in the palace, but *here* ..." He glanced to the hundreds of Columnaries massed about and above them. "Word will spread."

She frowned up at the man.

"You said as much yourself in Xothei ..." he continued, his tone matched by a peculiar seriousness in his gaze. "*He picked you.*"

It surprised her always, the assumption that Kellhus could not err ...

"The stories of this," he said, casting his bleary gaze back out toward their enemy, "will serve to remind them."

Or deceive.

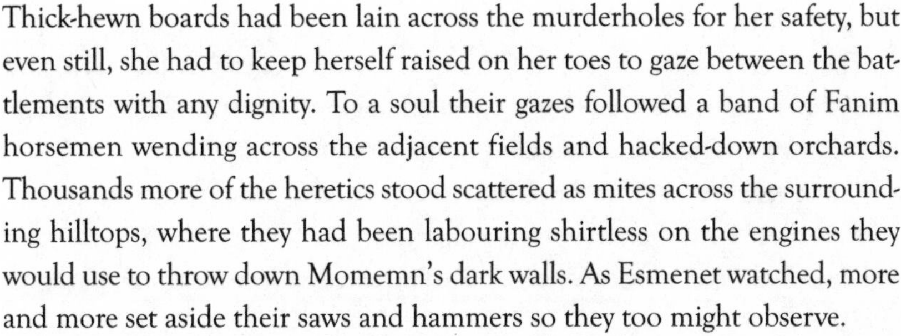

Thick-hewn boards had been lain across the murderholes for her safety, but even still, she had to keep herself raised on her toes to gaze between the battlements with any dignity. To a soul their gazes followed a band of Fanim horsemen wending across the adjacent fields and hacked-down orchards. Thousands more of the heretics stood scattered as mites across the surrounding hilltops, where they had been labouring shirtless on the engines they would use to throw down Momemn's dark walls. As Esmenet watched, more and more set aside their saws and hammers so they too might observe.

The sun burned bright, but the air possessed the hurried chill belonging to a later season. From the Andiamine Heights, she could almost pretend that everything yet shambled along the same ruts as before. Not so here. She had forgotten what it was like to gaze across perilous regions, to stand upon the verge of her power's dissolution. Here, within the walls, one was executed for taking her family's name in vain; and just *there*, one was murdered for speaking her family's name in any other way.

Estimates of the size of Fanayal's host varied. Phinersa insisted that no more than twenty to twenty-five thousand Kianene proper rode with the Bandit Padirajah, as well as a mutinous motley of some fifteen thousand others, ranging from non-Kianene Fanim faithful driven into exile, to bandit desert tribesmen—many of them Khirgwi, bent on little more than plunder. Had Momemn lain on the seaward edge of a plain, their numbers could have been guessed quite handily, but as it stood, the combination of the surrounding hills and their astonishing mobility allowed them to conduct their siege without revealing much about their size or disposition. The Imperial Mathematicians only had rumour and the smoke of obscured fires to go on. Using the ancient method of continually averaging their most recent estimates against the sum of their former counts, they had come to circle a number approaching thirty-thousand ... a good deal less than the forty-five thousand her Master-of-Spies insisted.

Given that she scarcely possessed eight thousand trained souls with which to defend the Home City, she found neither number reassuring—even less so given the rumours of *Cishaurim* pulling down the walls of Iothiah. Her Vizier-in-Proxy, Vem-Mithriti, who stood withered in his voluminous black-silk robes mere paces away, had sputtered for fury claiming she had nothing to fear. The flecks of his spittle, however, had argued otherwise. Excess passion was the perennial vice of gulls, and war, much like gambling, fed upon gulls.

The image of the advancing Fanim war-party hooked her like yarn, and then she saw it, the White Horse on gold hanging below the Twin Scimitars of Faminry ... The fabled standard of the Coyauri.

"Such reckless courage," the Exalt-General said.

And their Lord, Fanayal ab Kascamandri.

"*The Padirajah himself comes!*" a voice cried from the tower parapets above.

This changed everything.

"So he really means to parlay?" Esmenet asked.

Phinersa replied from her left. "The God has granted us a miraculous opportunity either way, my Glory."

She turned to Anthirul, who still stared out, his manner meditative and battle-seasoned, his lips pursed as if he cracked seeds between his front teeth.

"I concur," he finally said, "though my heart repents it."

"You mean *kill him*," she said.

The Home Exalt-General at last looked down, matched her gaze. He approved of her hesitation, she could tell—almost as much as Phinersa disapproved. Was it because she was a woman, a vessel wrought to give what men take?

"Think of how many you might save simply by taking his skin!" Phinersa cried to the back of her neck, speaking, as he often did, like one who takes umbrage for *reason's* sake rather than his own.

Either way, he was becoming too familiar.

She turned to her daughter instead, who stood dutifully—too dutifully, it occurred to Esmenet—a pace behind the men that fairly encircled her mother.

The flaxen-haired girl looked at her blandly. The rumble of hooves climbed from the throbbing drums. "I would do what Father would do."

"Yes!" Phinersa cried, his composure nearly undone.

Her Master-of-Spies was afraid, she realized. Genuinely afraid ...

And Esmenet realized that *she was not.*

This bid to parlay was nothing more than a trap, one that the Fanim themselves expected to fail, or so her timid Imperial stalwarts would have her believe. War had a jnan all its own, an etiquette wherein the failure to afford your enemy the opportunity to be foolish was itself a failure. Fanayal was simply "testing his hook bare," as the saying went, throwing his line on the off chance he might catch *her* ...

She was a *woman* after all.

But now it appeared that Fanayal was offering *her* the opportunity to do the same ...

Which meant that the invitation was *not* simply a ruse to assassinate her.

And since he had most certainly *not* come to be assassinated in turn, it meant that Fanayal ab Kascamandri, the far-famed Bandit Padirajah, genuinely *wanted* to parlay ...

But why?

"Make preparations," she told Anthirul. "We kill him *after* we hear what he has to say ..."

The thought of murder pained her, but only momentarily. Smoke still marred points across the entirety of the landward horizon. As yet, no one knew what kind of destruction they had wrought, only that it was both heinous and extensive. She would kill Fanayal, *here*, then she would hunt his vermin race to the very limit of everywhere. She would clot the Carathay with the blood of their sons, so that her son never need suffer them again ...

She would commit this act. She knew this with ruthless certainty. After so many years soaked in the rumours of her husband's butchery, she was due her own measure.

Her eyes fluttered about the thought of Naree.

"When I say, 'Truth shines,'" she told her shining Home Exalt-General. She glanced to the Fanim as if seeking totemic verification. Her breath, which had been miraculously relaxed all this time, tightened for realizing the desert horsemen had almost completed their journey ... "Kill him then."

Some thirty riders spilled across a final berm, then jerked their trotting mounts down the road. Most sported the long moustaches and conical helms of their people. Otherwise they looked savage—almost Scylvendi—for their eclectic attire, some shining for plundered hauberks, others dull and dark for their arduous journey. Their horses possessed the many-veined, angular look of malnourishment, ribs tiger-striped for shadow. They had ridden as hard as Anthirul had said, which meant they were exhausted as Anthirul supposed. Their failure to storm and take Momemn when they had the chance was written into them.

The Fanim company fanned as wide as the ditches allowed, then broke into a full gallop—a calculated act of bravado, she was certain, but formidable nonetheless.

A memory of Shimeh passed as a shudder through her, a glimpse of Kidruhil cut down in the brilliant calligraphy of Achamian's light.

The criminals thundered toward the small table, racing into their shadows, becoming a dark and elongated mass. Dust roiled about flexing legs and haunches. She was so convinced they would bowl the table over that she began cursing them even as they reined to a chaotic and yet collective stop. A great, transparent wing of dust unfurled before them, threatened to swoop over the very breastwork where she stood, before the eternal winds off the Meneanor shrugged it inland.

Riven, she watched the desert warriors resolve from their lean silhouettes. She had planned to greet them with jnanic decorum, disarm them with feminine solicitation. She found herself peering from man to man instead, searching for *him* ...

He was easy to find, given that he looked so much like his brother, Massar, who had been Whelmed, and even now marched with her husband toward Golgotterath. The elaborate goatee, the narrow, hooked-nose virility, the sharp, deep-set eyes: these immediately marked him as a Son of Kascamandri. Otherwise he alone dressed in a way that recalled his father's glory, wearing a golden helm crowned with five quills, and a corselet of shimmering nimil over a yellow-silk Coyauri tunic.

Her fury overcame her. "*Trespasser*!" she screeched. "Flee to your wasted homes! Or I shall litter the desert with your people's bones!"

A moment of astounded silence.

The Fanim began laughing.

"You must forgive my men," the Padirajah called through the huffing remnants of his own hilarity. "We Fanim let women rule our hearths and"—he wobbled his head in mock indecision—"our beds." More gales of laughter erupted from around and behind him. He looked about with a sly and boyish open-mouthed smile. "You sound ... *ridiculous* to them."

Esmenet could feel her entourage clench in embarrassment and outrage around her, but she was too old a whore to be rattled by *this* kind of contempt or derision. Her shame, after all, was at once *their* shame. Where wives were left guessing, whores *knew*: the harder the laughter, the more pathetic the weeping.

"What is it Fane says?" she called back in mock agreement. "Cursed are those who mock their mothers?"

A single guffaw from some fool high on the eastward tower. Otherwise, the Padirajah's very own war-drums counted out the beats of his speechlessness.

"You are no mother to me," he finally said.

"And yet you *act* my son, nonetheless," she called down in inspiration, "a son bearing grievances."

Fanayal regained a wary version of his previous smile.

"I suspect you are accustomed to such grievances," he replied. "You are a *hard* mother. But not to my people, Empress. Ours is not a house any *idolater* can set back in order."

Where the derision from earlier had simply passed over her, this bruised for some reason.

"Then why bother parlay?"

A pained squint, as if suffering her had already become something inevitable.

"The *Ciphrang*, Empress Mother. Kucifra, the *demon* who lies with you in angelic guise, who begets monsters in your womb—your *husband*! Yes ... He has forced such *cunning* on me as you could not *believe*. I can scarce fathom it myself, forsooth! The indignities I've suffered, the accursed acts I have seen with mine eyes! I fear your husband has been an affliction ..."

He had paced his magnificent white charger westward about the table and its golden burdens as he spoke. Now he wheeled the horse about with a mere flick of the reins.

"Each lesson has cut us, aye! But we have *learned*, Empress, learned to pack ruses inside of ruses, to forever think, '*What will they think?*' before thinking anything at all!"

Esmenet frowned. She glanced at Phinersa, his counsel plain in the urgency of his look.

"You still haven't answered my question," she called out.

Fanayal's smile was as thin as his moustaches.

"But I *have* Empress."

And Anasûrimbor Esmenet found herself staring at a face that was *no longer the Padirajah's* ... but had become, rather, the face of someone altogether *different*, someone whose chin, cheeks, and scalp had been shaven—and who inexplicably wore a band of graven silver over his eyes ...

Skin-spy?

An asp bent into a gleaming black hook. Blue flaring light. She threw hands across her eyes.

"*Water!*" someone was bellowing. "*He bears the Wat—!*"

Bowstrings thrummed in panicked seriatim.

Cishaurim?

Caxes Anthirul scooped her in his great arms, bore her backward and down.

Axes of movement and light, bald sky and black-stone expanses swung on a pendulum, blotted by searing brilliance. Sounds too spastic, too brief to be shrieks, air bursting from flesh.

The shielding bulk of the Exalt-General was wracked as though a bull gored him. Vem-Mithriti was singing, his voice bassooned with age. And Theliopa was dragging her from the rent and ruined bodies, fire swinging like capuchins up across the girl's gown into her hair.

"*Kill him!*" someone was screaming. "*Kill the devil!*"

A Columnary bearing a cloak tackled the burning girl to the floor. Esmenet rolled back into her daughter's sudden absence, cracked her skull. She scrambled to her hands and knees, saw arrows flitting across open space, raking the tracts below.

Vem-Mithriti stepped from the ruined breastwork into open air, phantom bastions hanging before him. He looked as frail as sticks beneath the voluminous lung that was his black-silk gown—frail *and* unconquerable, for as he stepped out he turned, and she saw the lightning kindled in his palms, forehead, and heart. For all the years that winded his voice, his speech hewed true, clipping great and terrible Analogies raw from the aether.

"*Kill the devil!*"

She saw Caxes Anthirul's bulk on the ragged edge.

She saw Phinersa standing dumbstruck, realized he had but one arm.

She saw the nameless Waterbearer—the *Cishaurim*!—rise up to meet the decrepit Grand Vizier. She saw the black asp that was his eye hook from his collar, gleaming like oiled iron.

Her slippers skidded on blood, yet she managed to find her feet.

She felt no fear.

Lightning leapt between Schoolman and Cishaurim, a brilliance that bleached the ramparts white. Hair lifted across her body.

The Indara-Kishauri hung impassive, watching the brilliant onslaught as if through some kind of window ... He leapt skyward as if yanked, swung about ...

He wasn't simply *any* Cishaurim, she realized. He was a Primary ...

Which meant that Vem-Mithriti was dead ...

Her stubbornness had killed them all!

She drew her own ceremonial knife, began hacking at the coats of her bodice. Heartbeats passed before she even realized what she was doing. One of the officers cowering behind her leapt forward to seize her wrist, but she twisted free, brandished her knife, resumed sawing through the accursed fabric, pricking and cutting herself time and again for panicked haste.

Casting a luminous glance back toward her, the old sorcerer stepped about to keep himself between her and the Cishaurim. The old fool! His singing stammered about a wheezing cough ...

A great Dragonshead reared from his outstretched hands, ethereal scales gleaming in the sun ...

Esmenet could scarcely see, but she was sure the Waterbearer advanced on the old man from on high. At last she hooked a crimson finger about the leather cord she wore against her naked waist—she fairly cried out for relief.

She glimpsed their nameless assailant above Vem-Mithriti's shoulder. Sunlight flashed along the silvered curve of his visor. The asp was black as ink, a cursive slip of the quill. A shower of archery deflected about him. He did not so much as flinch as the Dragonshead dipped toward him ...

Cataract, as brilliant as the sun.

She cut the cord, yanked it hard enough to lacerate skin. She felt the heat of it slip from her navel.

It swung as a stone in a sling ... the Chorae.

So very few remained in the Three Seas. She nearly shrieked for realizing she had to cut it free, glanced up ...

The Indara-Kishauri simply *walked through* the old sorcerer's inferno, his visor mirroring crimson and gold ...

Esmenet pricked her finger to the bone. The Chorae slipped to the ground.

The Waterbearer closed on the howling Anagogic sorcerer, threw up his hands as if to *grapple* ...

The Blessed Empress bent at the waist, scooped the thing into her palm ...

Looked up.

Saw her ancient Grand Vizier hanging upon the void immediately before her, his Wards sloughing into oblivion, his howling song cut short, spears of incandescent Water erupting from points across his skull and gown, then slumping like something too rotted to hang, dropping away from the enigmatic *Cishaurim*, who simply stepped *through* everything the old man had been, to set foot on the shattered parapet before her ...

She cast the Chorae.

Glimpsed her reflection in the silver visor, broken across the graven water ...

Saw the iron sphere sail past his cheek, drop into the void beyond his right shoulder.

And she smiled for dying in such a way. Debacle for debacle.

But the Cishaurim jerked—a shaft with Imperial fletching had materialized from his left breast. The asp flailed like a black rope.

Two more arrows chipped across the golden hauberk in rapid succession.

Then another appeared from his right arm.

The force pulled him backward. He tripped over debris, vanished over the edge ...

Only to fall *outward*, away from them, on an arc that bellied low over ground strewn with the Fanim who had failed to beat their horses clear her archers' range.

The Blessed Empress of the Three Seas stood gazing after him, windswept and astounded.

"Our Mother!" Theliopa was crying, her voice piping high and shrill. "Our Mother has *saved us*!"

The table stood untouched some twenty paces below. The wind dandled the embroidered tassels beneath the rim, yanked them inland, toward steppe and desert, away from the eternal sea.

The drums of her enemy beat across the horizon.

Chapter Four

Aörsi

Thieve wearing one mask, murder wearing another; the face beneath will be forgotten.

—Ainoni Proverb

Faith is the name we give to our determination.
A search for things better known whilst weeping,
And understood not at all.

—*The Goat's Heart*, Protathis

Early Autumn, 20 New Imperial Year (4132, Year-of-the-Tusk), the northeast shore of the Neleöst

Dreams came, dark tunnels beneath weary earth ...

A ridge against the night sky, curved like a sleeping woman's hip.

And upon it two silhouettes, black against clouds of stars, impossibly bright.

The figure of a man seated, crouched like an ape, legs crossed like a priest.

And a tree, branches swept up and out, vein-forking across the bowl of the night.

And the stars revolve about the Nail of Heaven like clouds hurried across winter skies.

And the Holy Aspect-Emperor of the Three Seas stares at the figure, stares at the tree, but cannot move. The firmament cycles like the wheel of an upturned cart.

The figure seems to perpetually sink for the constellations rising about him. He speaks, but his face cannot be seen.

I war not with Men, it says, *but with the God.*

"Yet no one but Men die," the Aspect-Emperor replies.

The fields must burn to drive Him forth from the Ground.

"But I tend the fields."

The dark figure stands beneath the tree, begins walking toward him. It seems the climbing stars should hook and carry him in the void, but he is like the truth of iron—impervious and immovable.

It stands before him, regards him—as it has so many times—with *his* face and *his* eyes. No halo gilds his leonine mane.

Then who better to burn them?

For Sranc, the ground was meat, and so the desolation of the land was complete. The Neleöst had fallen unnaturally calm, lapping the grey beaches with swampish lassitude. It climbed into a distance bleak for want of feature, the line of the horizon smeared from existence, so that Creation coiled without demarcation into the greater scroll of the sky. Their left flank secure, the Men of the Circumfix crossed the southern marches of what had once been Aörsi, the most warlike of the great High Norsirai nations. Illawor, the province had been called, and in ancient times, it had been quilted with fields of sorghum and other hardy cereals. The Ordealmen spied the ruins of what they thought were small forts peppered across the despoiled landscape, but were in fact ancient byres. Every homestead had been a bastion in ancient Aörsi ere the First Apocalypse. Men slept with their swords, wives with their bows. Children were taught how to commit suicide. *Skûlsirai*, they called themselves, the "Shield-People".

Now the Great Ordeal chased the Horde across the waste that remained of their land, consuming those Sranc they butchered as they marched. New names were needed, given the revulsion and disgust milled into their existing epithets. To eat Sranc or skinnies or muckers was to eat excrement or vomit or even worse. The Ainoni began calling them "Catfish", for the slicked skin, the pallor, and because they swore the beasts tasted like the black rivers roping the Secharib Plains. But the name soon fell into disfavour. Despite the advantage of euphemism, it seemed too flaccid a term to capture the madness of eating the creatures.

"Meat" soon became the term of choice, at once generic and visceral, a symbolic condensation of both the *fact* of their obscenity and the *point*. To eat was to dominate, to conquer as they needed to conquer. But it was *horror* as well, for their nightly feast could be nothing other than horror, the encampment dazzled with bonfires, greasy for shadow, adorned with innumerable dismemberments, butchered Sranc swinging on ropes, heaped into seeping piles, their innards coiled in oily puddles of violet and black.

None could say precisely when it happened, when feast had become bacchanal, when dining had become something more than chewing and swallowing—something darker. At first, only the most sensitive souls among them could discern the difference, how a growl seemed to perpetually hang from the back of their throat, and a savagery from the back of their soul—a furious inkling that others seemed more and more prone to act out. Only they could sense that the Meat was changing them and their brothers—and not for the better. What had been wary became ever more reckless. What was measured became garish by imperceptible degrees.

Perhaps no event demonstrated this creeping transformation more dramatically than the matter of Sibawûl te Nurwul. With the reunification of the Great Ordeal, the Cepaloran Chieftain-Prince found himself ever more irked by the bombast of his rival, Halas Siroyon, General of the Famiri auxiliaries. The Famiri had accumulated a fearsome reputation over the previous weeks. Their disdain for armour easily rendered them the swiftest of the Ordeal's horsemen, and with Siroyon riding the legendary Phiolos at their fore, they had proven themselves peerless suppliers of Meat. Lord Sibawûl begrudged even this modest glory. On occasion he could be heard complaining that the very thing that made them such effective "cattlemen"—their lack of armour—was also what made them useless in actual battle.

Hearing word of these complaints, Siroyon confronted his Norsirai counterpart, wagered that he could lead his Famiri deeper into the shadow of the Horde than the blond Cepaloran would ever dare. Sibawûl agreed to the wager, even though it was not his nature to hazard the lives of his men over such obvious points of honour. He accepted because he and his cousins had spied the beginning of an *interval* opening in the circuit of the Horde the day previous, and he saw a means of redeeming himself in Siroyon's petulance. His back had since healed, but his flogging several weeks previous had all but crippled his pride.

And indeed, the Whore smiled on him. The following dawn revealed a great cleft in the Horde's horizon-engulfing line, a point where the gaseous ochre-and-black had been smeared into vacancy. For those who daily ranged the raucous margins of the Horde, the break was as plain as the morning sun, but Sibawûl and his Cepalorae had set out *before sunrise*. By the time Siroyon grasped what his rival was doing, Sibawûl was already flying into the bower of the Shroud, a distant point leading a distant rake of thousands. Bellowing, the General led his Famiri in pursuit, riding so hard that dozens were killed for being thrown. The land was dishevelled, scalloped by streams and humped with knolls of bared stone, some with the remains of ancient cairns teetering on their summits. The Horde had stamped the scrub into never-ending carpets of dust and twigs. Siroyon only managed to spy Sibawûl and his Cepalorae from a few rare heights—enough to know he had lost his rash wager. He should have relented, but pride drove him forth, the kind indistinguishable from terror of shame. Even if he conceded the glory to Sibawûl, he could at least outshine the man with descriptions of what *they* had seen. Sibawûl had never been one to expound on his glories. As a student of jnan, Siroyon suffered no such scruple.

Lord Sibawûl led his whooping Cepalorae into the very maw of the Horde, and it seemed a thing of madness to venture where hitherto only Schoolmen had dared tread. The howl deafened. The billowing heights of the Shroud *encompassed* them. The stampeded earth yielded to more and more desiccate grasses and scrub. Dead Sranc peppered the less-battered ground, limbs jutting about gaping mouths. This in itself was a shock, given that the creatures generally devoured their fallen. The horsemen almost instantly spied ruins draped ahead of them in the ochre gloom, structures like jaws snapped open across the earth, one inside another. They passed over the remnants of ancient walls, and a new dread claimed their hearts. The thanes rose their voices in futile query, even protest, understanding that the Horde had parted about a place that Sranc would sooner die than tread, a place famed in the *Holy Sagas* ...

Wreoleth ... the fabled Larder-of-Men.

But Lord Sibawûl could not hear his champions, and rode ahead with the bearing of one who presumes the absolute loyalty of his beloved. So the horse-thanes of Cepalor followed their Lord-Chieftain into the accursed city, between the rotted black teeth of her walls, beneath the gutted skulls of her towers. Scrub webbed the ground, forcing their ponies to barge through bird-bone lattices. A kind black moss encrusted what stone and structure that survived, transforming the ruins into a sinister procession. The city seemed a pillaged necropolis, the many-chambered monument of a people who had not so much lived as dwelt.

The blond-braided horsemen filed through the ruin in columns, glancing about in numb incredulity. The Shroud climbed the neck-straining heights about them, plumes through mists, spilling like ink in water across the vault of heaven. Their lips tingled for the Horde's yammering roar. Many held their cheeks to their horse's neck, spitting or vomiting, so vile was the stench on the wind. A few hid their faces for weeping.

Without explanation, Sibawûl veered southward and led his Cepalorans back to the molar line of the city's southern fortifications. He led them to a section that had been swamped by some millennial tide of earth, and the horsemen formed a long line across the summit, the way they would mustering for a charge ...

The riders gazed out over thronging, twisted miles, countless figures packed in orgiastic proximity, worm-pale and screeching. To the sweeping eye it shivered for lunatic motion and detail, a world of depraved maggots, at once larval and frantic, trowelled across the contours of a dead and blasted plain. To the eye that darted, it horrified for images of licentious fury, Sranc like hairless cats spitting and wailing, nude figures kicking across the ground, rutting, scratching and scratching at earth plowed into fecal desolation.

They felt iron-girt children, the hard Sons of Cepalor. They had all witnessed the onslaught of the Horde—witnessed and survived. They had all gazed across nightmare miles, screaming regions illumined in the glare of sorcerous lights. But never had they seen the Horde *as it was*. For months they had ridden like mites into the shadow of an unseen beast, thinking first they *pursued*, then *hunted*, what lay concealed behind the pluming cliffs. Now they fathomed the deranged vanity of their Lord, and the doom he had delivered them. This was why Sibawûl te Nurwul, for all his celebrated restraint and cunning, had ridden to Wreoleth's southern bourne. This was what he had wanted to brandish to his peers, to the Holy Aspect-Emperor ...

Testimony of the Beast.

To a man they understood. They pursued no more than they hunted. They simply followed the way starving children follow perilously loaded wains, waiting for fortune to feed them. And even as they watched the Sranc *spied them*. They could see it, passing like a gust across distant fields of wheat, the awareness of Men, the temptation. The thunderous caterwaul, the screeching fore of it at least, waned and warbled, and was then redoubled as the innumerable creatures lunged toward the Cepalorae.

The horsemen battled with panicking mounts. Their mouths opened in cries that could not be heard. Alarums. Pleas. Some even cursed the callow arrogance of their illustrious Lord. But Sibawûl, who could see if not hear their consternation, ignored them. He stared at the surging Horde, his face blank—the look of one testing the validity of dreams.

The Sranc seemed a singular thing, a millipede skin, celled with howling mouths, haired with crude arms, chapped and scaled with black armour. As one they charged, their numbers so vast as to make the twenty-three hundred Cepalorae seem a twig before the flood. They unmoored the very ground beneath the Ordealmen, so that Wreoleth, far from a rock awaiting the tide, seemed a raft floating toward doom. Sibawûl watched without word or expression. Several horse-thanes screamed at him. Dozens of Vindaugamen—a shameful handful—fled. Others wheeled their balking ponies in preparation. The Nymbricani braced themselves against their cantles, lowered their lances. Even as they watched, the Sranc flying at the fore of the rush faltered, drawn up by some inexplicable terror. Many of the Cepalorae even glanced at the sky behind them, thinking that perhaps the Holy Aspect-Emperor had come. More and more of the creatures began screaming, scrambling backward, as if an invisible line had been scrawled about the circuit of the dead city. But all the world behind them was *hunger* in near infinite repetition, the obscene desire to savage and couple with their ancient foe. The horrified ones were shoved and trampled—some were even cut down, such was the frenzy. Sranc climbed their brothers, some to rush the horsemen on the mound, others to escape them, and countless abominations died in the crush. Abject madness consumed the frontal masses, forming a rind of cannibalistic fury. Only when it reached the very foot of the ancient fortifications did the surge stall ...

The *Holy Sagas* had spoken true. Wreoleth had been carved into the very *being* of the Sranc, a terror mightier than any of their prodigious lusts. They would sooner die, sooner fall upon their crazed kin, than set foot upon its ground. Here the last of the High Norsirai had huddled safe and yet not safe, their numbers dwindling as the Consult raided them for fresh captives time and again. Here they had eked out a wretched, waiting existence, livestock for the wicked hungers and whims of the Unholy Consult.

The horrified Cepalorae gazed across the thrashing spectacle, the countless white faces, inhuman beauty clenching into puckered outrage, packed and receding, on and on, becoming watercolour impressions for the fog of fecal dust. Full-grown men wept, wondered that Fate would dangle them so near the end of all things. Others laughed, emboldened, despite their dread, to stand with such impunity before the geologic extent of their foe.

Those on the eastern flank cried out soundlessly, pointed to the glower of lights through the ochre sheers. The Culling, they realized—the Schoolmen had come! And they realized they looked upon what their sorcerous brother-in-arms always saw with the grinding of the days. The keen-sighted glimpsed a triune of dark-skinned sorcerers robed in billows striding the low skies in echelon, each wielding a phantom dragon. They were white and violet garbed Vokalati, those Sun-wailers, as they were called, who had survived Irsûlor and the madness of their Grandmaster, Carindûsû.

According to legend, this was when the Chieftain-Prince first glimpsed the Sranc masses surging to their *southeast* and grasped the shape of their new peril.

The arcane mutter of sorcery wormed through the gut of the Horde's thunder. Even as the Cepalorae cheered, the Horde roiled, and dust erupted from the rabid tracts. The horsemen could even see the Sranc scooping dirt and gravel into the sky, creating a fog that obscured all but the brilliance of jetting and blooming fire. Silhouettes burned and flailed. Many among the horsemen raised a ragged cheer thinking the Vokalati had come to save them.

But Sibawûl knew better, knew the Schoolmen had possibly sealed their doom. The Sranc instinctively spread out when afflicted from above, the way skirmishers might beneath a hail of archery. But where human formations counted the extra area taken in yards, the Horde encompassed *miles*. It ballooned and billowed across the desolate dimensions whenever the Schoolmen rained ruin down upon them. Many were the times he and his riders had retreated watching the Culling vanish into the Shroud.

The Horde was about to reclaim Wreoleth.

Sibawûl galloped behind his warriors, slapping the rumps of their ponies with the flat of his blade, crying out words that could not be heard with an urgency that was easily seen. And so the Cepalorae fled, each man crouched low on his saddle, flaxen war-braids lashing his back and shoulder. They galloped down slots of ruin, blundered through copses of thistle, chalk juniper, and plains bracken. With horror, they watched the vast palms of dust close in prayer across the sky before them, the sun fade into a pale disc. Caterwauling thousands flooded into the passage the Men had followed not more than a watch before. Gloom fell across Wreoleth, at once septic and chill, and the proud horsemen of Cepalor called out for terror and despair.

Halas Siroyon, who had gained the interval's mouth only to see its throat close, would glimpse Sibawûl and his Cepalorae from afar, and it would seem that he gazed across *worlds*, from a terrain crabbed for density to one blurred for gaseous obscurity—a glimpse from a dream. He was driven back, and his bare-chested riders suffered grievously for the javelins and arrows of the loping Sranc. The chroniclers would write that Phiolos, the greatest of all horses, caught one shaft in the shoulder and another in the rump, while his less-renowned master flaunted one in his left thigh.

The Shroud closed about all knowledge of Lord Sibawûl and his kinsmen. Wreoleth lay as an abscess in the viscera of the Horde.

A day and night passed before the Horde relinquished the accursed Larder. Accusations were traded in the Eleven Pole Chamber. The Believer-Kings petitioned their Holy Aspect-Emperor, who admonished them, saying, "Sibawûl may be the fiercest among you, but the temper of the soul matters little when the peril is unnatural. The weak are spared, while the bravest are unmanned. Pray to the God of Gods, my brothers. Only fell Wreoleth can show what it has wrought."

Grief-stricken, Siroyon would be the first to dare the second opening of the interval the following morning. He would find his rival—and the nine-hundred and twenty-three Cepalorae who survived with him—bereft of wit or calculation. Of the missing, nothing was ever learned, for the survivors refused to speak on *any* matter, let alone what they had endured. If they responded to hails at all, it would be to look *through* their interrogator, into whatever deeps and distances that had made slack rope of their souls.

The Ordeal had drawn near to legendary ruins by this time, so that word of Sibawûl's survival passed as lightning through the Holy Host of Hosts. A booming cheer seized the masses, one that pained the throats of those who caught any glimpse of the harrowed Cepalorae. Expressions are ever the measure of weal and woe. A simple look is often enough to fathom the scale, if not the specifics, of what some other soul has suffered, to know whether they have triumphed or merely persevered, wavered or capitulated outright. The look of the Cepalorae communicated something more horrible than suffering, something incommunicable.

That night, when Sibawûl answered the summons of his Holy Aspect-Emperor in Council, the gathered Believer-Kings found themselves appalled by the man's transformation. Proyas embraced him, only to recoil as if at some whispered rebuke. At the behest of Anasûrimbor Kellhus, Saccarees related the legend of Wreoleth according to Mandate lore. The Grandmaster spoke of how Mog-Pharau had stamped his chattel with a terror of the place so that its inhabitants might be spared, "as grain is spared the millstone." Wreoleth, he explained to the anxious assembly, had been the *granary* of the Consult, and its Sons suffered as no other Son of Men had suffered.

"What say you?" Siroyon finally cried to his rival.

Sibawûl levelled a gaze that could only be called dead.

"Hell ..." he replied, his voice dropping from his mouth like sodden gravel from a spade. "Hell kept us safe."

Silence fell across the Umbilicus. Framed by the sorcerous twining of the Ekkinû, the Holy Aspect-Emperor peered at Sibawûl for five long heartbeats. He alone seemed untroubled by the vacancy that now dominated his manner.

Anasûrimbor Kellhus nodded in cryptic affirmation, as if understanding rather than affirming what he had glimpsed. "Henceforth," he said, "you shall do as you will in matters of war, Lord Sibawûl."

And so the Chieftain-Prince of Cepalor did, leading his tribal cohorts out before the tolling of the Interval every day, returning with sacks of white skin, which he and his kinsmen consumed raw in the dark. They stoked no fire, and seemed to avoid those fires belonging to their neighbours. They no longer slept, or so the rumours charged. Word of their unnatural ferocity on the fields spread, how the Sranc fled from them no matter what their numbers. Wherever Sibawûl and his pallid horsemen congregated, the Ordealmen shunned them. The more superstitious fingered charms upon spying them—some even threw arms over their own faces, convinced that dead eyes saw only dead men.

All came to fear the Sons of Cepalor.

There was a head upon the pole behind him.

To remake Men, Kellhus had come understand, one had to recover what was most simple in them—what was basic. The greatest poets eulogized childhood, extolled those who found innocence untrammelled within. But without exception they seized only on the simplicities that flattered and consoled, ignoring all the ways children resemble beasts. Animals were by far the better metaphor. Men did not so much remain children *at heart*, as they remained *brutes*, a collection of reflexes, violent, direct, blind to all the nuances that made men Men.

To remake Men, one had to tear down their trust in complication, force them to shelter in instinct and reflex, reduce them to what was animal.

Proyas had good reason to look hunted.

"You're saying that ... that ..."

Kellhus exhaled, and so reminded his Exalt-General to do the same. This time, he had bid Proyas to sit at his side rather than opposite the hearth: to better exploit bodily proximity. "Damnation has claimed Sibawûl and his countrymen."

"But they *live*!"

"Do they? Or do they dwell somewhere between?"

Proyas gazed appalled. "But h-how ... how could such a thing *happen*?"

"Because fear pries open the heart. They suffered too much terror upon ground too steeped in suffering. Hell forever gropes, forever pokes at the limits of the living. In Wreoleth, it found and seized them."

There was a head upon the pole behind him. If he could not turn to see it, it was because it lay behind his *seeing* ... Behind all seeing.

"But-but ... surely *you* ..."

He held his disciple in the palm of his intellect.

"Surely I could *save* them?" A pause to let the import roil. "The way I saved Serwë?"

Something between anguish and exasperation cramped his Exalt-General's face. To strip a soul to its essentials, one had to show the complication of the complicated—this was the great irony of such studies. Nothing is more simple than complication become habit. What was effortless, thoughtless, had to become fraught with doubt and toil.

As it should.

"I ... I don't understand."

He could sense it even now, the head on the pole behind him.

"There are many I have failed to save."

There was no denying the indulgence of the exercise. Once Kellhus had mastered the multitudes, once the polity derived its might from him, he had no longer required manipulations so fine as this. Years had passed since he had undertaken a Study so immediate as the soul of a single man.

And for all the implacable serenity of his Dûnyain soul, it stirred memories of the First Holy War, the turbulent span when such scrutiny had comprised the *sum* of his Mission. Since the Fall of Shimeh, no soul (not even Esmenet) had warranted such attention.

The instinct to bigotry that had nearly killed him in Caraskand had quickly come to heel, to serve, compelling acquiescence, silencing critics, even murdering enemies. For years, he had grappled the great beast that was the Three Seas, pinned it to earth, and with gifts and brutalities he had *trained* it, until his name only need be uttered—until his tyranny had become indistinguishable from his *being*. This allowed him to move from nations to truths, to turn his intellect full upon the maddening abstracta of the Daimos, the Metagnosis, and the Thousandfold Thought.

He had pierced the obscurantist veils, grasped the *metaphysics* of Creation, transformed meaning into *miracles*. He had walked the ways of Hell, returned bedecked in trophies. No one, not even the legendary Hero-Mage of ancient Ûmerau, Titirga, could rival his arcane might.

He had learned of the head on the pole.

Domination. Over lives and nations. Over history and ignorance. Over *existence itself*, down through the leaves of reality's countless skins. No mortal had possessed such might. His was a power and potency that not even the Gods, who must ration themselves across all times, could hope to counter, short of scooping themselves hollow and forever dwelling as phantoms ...

No soul had so owned Circumstance. He, and he alone, was *the Place*, the point of maximal convergence. Nations hung from his whim. Reality grovelled before his song. The *Outside itself* railed against him.

And yet for all of it *darkness still encircled him*, the obscurity of before, the blackness of after.

For those who worshipped him as a god, he remained a mortal man, possessing but one intellect and two hands—great, perhaps, in proportion to his innumerable slaves, but scarcely a mote on the surface of something inconceivable. He was no more a prophet than an architect or any other who wrenches his conception into labourious reality. All the futures he had raised had been the issue of his toil ...

He suffered visions, certainly, but he had long ceased to trust them.

"I was *there*, Master ..." Proyas said. "I saw. No one could have saved Serwë!"

Kellhus held him in the clasp of endless engines.

"Do you mean her life, or her *soul*?"

The nets of muscle sheathing him flexed into the sigil of horror.

"Does it trouble you, Proyas?"

And he was shadow-play, his disciple, the light of cosmic enormities bent small across the surface of a tear. He was an oak leaf, riding the yaw and twizzle of drafts, hanging above the rumour of whirlwinds ...

A glimpse through the aperture we confuse for life ...

"D-does what ... what trouble me?"

He was anything but a Man.

"To know that Serwë burns in Hell."

Slaves brought them their repast: small medallions of sizzling Sranc meat, seasoned with blueberries and wild scallions rooted from the seashore. The meat was improbably tender and sweet. The Place called Anasûrimbor Kellhus told his heartbroken disciple a tale of prophets as they ate, the way the bottleneck of their mortality invariably distorted visions they thought took the compass of the Heavens. The infinite could only be experienced in butchered approximation, he said, and communicated with rank fraudulence. "Men are bent on clarity and proportion, even when there is none to be found," he explained. "They offer up *broken* visions, Proyas, and call them perfect and whole." A grandfather's rueful smile, canny and adoring. "What else *can* Men see, when their eyes are so small?"

The challenges come as squalls of bewildered anger. "But then-then how is the God to tell us ... tell us *anything*?"

A forgiving frown on a long-drawn sigh, the kind that speaks of wars not quite survived.

"That is *the* conceit, is it not? The assumption that prophets deliver word of the God *to Men*."

Proyas sat motionless for three heartbeats.

"Then what is their purpose?"

"Is it not plain? To deliver word of Men *to the God*."

Men are made, and Men are born, and ever do the proportions escape them. They can only guess at themselves, never see, only infer the lines they inhabit from the crooks they glimpse in others. Proyas had been cursed by the fact of his birth, then doomed all the more by what life would make of him. His was a *wondering* soul, philosophical in the Near Antique sense. But it was also an exacting one, a soul that demanded clarity and resolution. As a babe he had slept in his mother's arms no matter what the court or domestic furor. The clamour meant nothing to him, so long as beloved arms held him tight, so long as the beloved face smiled down.

The living shall not haunt the dead ...

For twenty years this had been what Kellhus had given him: the drowsy slumber of certainty.

"*But why*?" Proyas cried.

The time had come to rouse him, deliver him to the horror of the Real.

"Your question is your answer."

Golgotterath suffered none to slumber.

"No!" the man barked. "No more *riddles*! Please! I beg you!"

Kellhus smiled with wry and mortal reassurance, the way a gentle and fearless father might to fortify his sons against his passing. He turned from the paroxysm of shame that had seized his disciple, grasped the decanter at his side to pour the man anpoi.

"You ask this because you seek reasons," he said, passing the *chanv*-laced drink to the Believer-King. "You seek reasons because you are incomplete ..."

Proyas glared as a wounded child over the edge of the bowl as he drank. Kellhus felt the concoction bloom warm and sweet over his own tongue and throat.

"Reason is naught but the twine of thought," he continued, "the way we bind fragments into larger fragments, moor the inhaling now to what is breathless and eternal. The God has no need of it ..."

Logos.

Proyas still did not understand, but he had been mollified by the tone of consolation, if nothing else. An anger yet animated him, one belonging to boys who are hectored beyond fearing their older brothers. But despite everything, his *hope*—the long-abused ache to know—yet occupied the bricked heights of his soul ...

Waiting to be overthrown.

"To be *all* things, Prosha, the God must be at once greater than itself, *and less*."

"Less? Less?"

"Finite. A *man*. Like Inri Sejenus. Like me ... To be *all things*, It must know ignorance, suffer suffering, fear and confus—"

"And *love*?" the Exalt-General fairly cried. "What of love?"

And for the first time that evening, Anasûrimbor Kellhus was surprised.

Love was the logic that conserved *Life* as opposed to Truth ... the twine that bound hosts and nations from the myriad moments of Men.

"Yes ... Most of all."

Love, far more than reason, was his principle tool.

"Most of all ..." Proyas repeated dully, his voice digging through the sand of torpor, the exhaustion of a clinging intellect, staggered heart. "Why?"

He does not want to know.

The Place called Anasûrimbor Kellhus snuffed all extraneous considerations, aimed its every articulation at the soul drowning in the air before him.

"Because of all the passions, nothing is so alien to the God as love."

There was a head on a pole behind him.

What would Nersei Proyas, first among the Believer-Kings, *make of the Truth*?

This was the object of the Study.

The carpeted earth did not so much reel as *wrench*, Kellhus knew, wringing things too fundamental too bleed. Confusions. Questions eating questions, cannibalizing the very possibility of asking. And *inversions*, blasphemous in and of themselves, but utterly ruinous in their implication.

Upside-down prophets who deliver word of Men to the Heavens?

An *inside-out* God?

Calamitous insights never arrive whole. They are like the wires that the Ainoni forced into the gullets of captured runaway slaves, things that twist and pierce, that become ever more entangled with the motions of normal digestion—things that *strangle from the inside*, and so kill, organ by anguished organ.

Twenty years of abject devotion overturned, spilled. Twenty years of certitude, so deep, so profound, as to *make murder holy*.

How? How would the Zaudunyani respond to the overthrow of their most cherished beliefs?

The man's eyes fluttered about welling heat. "B-but ... but *what you say* ... H-how is a man to worship?"

Kellhus said nothing at first, awaited the inevitable questioning look.

"Doubt," he said, seizing his disciple's gaze within the iron fist of his own. "Query, not as Collegians or Advocates query, but as the *bewildered* query, as those who genuinely seek the limits of what they know. To ask *is to kneel*, to say, 'I end *here* ...' And how could it be otherwise? The *infinite is impossible*, Proyas, which is why Men are so prone to hide it behind reflections of themselves—to give the God beards and desires! To call It 'Him'!"

He raised a gold-haloed hand to his brow, feigning weariness. "No. Terror. Hatred of self. Suffering, ignorance, and confusion. *These are the only honest ways to approach the God*."

The Believer-King dropped his face, hitched about a low sob.

"*This* place ... where you are now, Prosha. ***This is the revelation***. The God is not comfort. The God is not law or love or reason, nor any other instrument of our crippled finitude. The God has no voice, no design, no heart or intellect ..."

The man wept as if coughing.

"It is *it* ... Unconditioned and absolute."

A soft keening, a sound that was both question and accusation.

How?

The Place called Kellhus watched the Believer-King vanish into what he was, observed the very order of the man dissolve as a clot of sand in quick waters. Deviations were noted. Assumptions were revised. Possibility bloomed across the whole, the branching of branches, new multiplicities for the hard knife of actuality to cull ...

Origins were isolated.

"And the *wages?*" the man barked through lips stringed with snot and spittle.

Yes, my friend. What of salvation?

"There is no recompense," the Place said, "save knowing ..."

"Knowing that we know nothing!"

"Exactly."

"So–?"

Sorrow and scrutiny.

"You see it. After all these years you finally understand."

A moment of stunned gazing, swollen face swaying as though staring from the deck of a foundering vessel. The man did not need to speak for the Place to hear the name.

Achamian.

The Place smiled, as if things catastrophic could be gentle ironies all the same.

"The teacher you renounced ..."

A grimace seized the man's expression of wronged incredulity. Jaw pulled down. Lips cramped about a soundless cry. Spittle strung like spider's silk across the void of his mouth ...

"*He* is the prophet you sought all along."

The Place held its weeping slave, rocked him in its arms. The smell of burnt lamb wicked through the closed confines of the chamber.

"Then what are you."

Spoken with lament, without the intonation of a question. Spoken the way beloved dead are removed from the place of mourning.

"A deceiver," the Place said. "False ..."

"No–"

"I am *Dûnyain*, a Son of Ishuäl. I am the product of a monstrous decision made two thousand years ago, a decision to breed Men as Men breed cattle and dogs, to remake them *in the image of intellect* ..."

He pulled the man to the side, and down, so that his bearded face lay like a plate on his lap.

"I was sent forth to hunt down and kill my father," the Place said, "who had been sent out before me ..." He paused to brush a greying lock from the man's brow. "When I discovered the weakness of Men, I understood that my father would command enormous power ... that I would need the strength of nations to overcome him."

Warring patterns. Everything turned upon the way patterns owned the souls of Men. Truth, as surely as Luck, simply sorted the conquered from the dead.

"So I began *acting* a prophet, even as I denied being one, knowing that my intellect would astound you and your brothers, that eventually you would *make* me your prophet ..."

"No! Tha–"

"Thus I seized my nation, the First Holy War ..."

The Place drew a long-fingered hand across the side of the Believer-King's face, temple to jaw. They seemed unreal to the man, it knew, those fierce and unruly days. The residue dwelt within him, the imprint of bearing witness, sparked to life from time to time in dreams and reveries. Pebbles from an ocean, but nothing else. Like all other survivors, he was perpetually stranded, forever thrown.

"My father had anticipated this, had known that the trial of my journey would transform me, that the assassin who had departed Ishuäl would arrive his *disciple*."

Petulant fury. Toddler defiance. "No! This *canno*—!"

"But there was something he failed to realize ..."

Swollen indecision. Hope reaching out through anguish and asphyxiation, clutching for the reversal that would return everything to what had been. "What? *What?*"

"That my trial would drive me mad."

"*But you are my Lord! M-my salvation!*"

"Caraskand ... The Circumfix ..."

"*No—cease! Stop this! I'm-I'm begging you! Pleas—*"

"I began seeing ... phantasms, hearing voices ... *Something began speaking to me.*"

"*Please … I-I ...*"

"And in my disorder, I *listened* ... I did what it commanded."

Sobs wracked the man, the convulsions of a bereaved child. But these words yanked something through Proyas, as if he had been wound by a windlass and released. The Place relaxed its grip, lowered him back to its lap. The man's bloodshot eyes fixed him heedless of any shame or fury.

"I killed my own father," the Place said.

"The God! *It has to be the* God! The God spe—"

"*No*, Proyas. Gird yourself. Peer into the horror!"

I tend the fields ...

A glutinous breath. The squint of a soul attempting to squint away its own misgivings. "You think th-this voice is ... is *your own*?"

And burn them.

The Place smiled the negligent smile of those who could have no stake in feuds so minor.

"The truth of a thing lies in its origins, Proyas. I know not *from whence this voice comes*."

Hope, beaming with a hand-seizing urgency. "Heaven! *It comes from Heaven!* Can't you see?"

The Place gazed down at its most beautiful slave.

"Then Heaven is not sane."

The Place bid the man strip and he stripped.

Even after so many years of hardship, the man's frame remained upright and unbroken. He was lean, the way all Ordealmen were lean; shadow inked the overlay and anchoring of his every muscle. Black hair matted the olive-pale skin of his chest. It thinned to a line as it descended the hollow of his belly, then bloomed about his groin and thighs. His phallus lay grey and inert.

The disciple hung his head, crushing his beard. His gaze was swollen and uncomprehending.

The Place drew its robe up and aside, welcomed the kiss of unencumbered air. It approached the man from behind, reached out to clutch the pulse racing in his throat.

The truth of a thing ... it whispered.

It drew its member across the man's buttocks ...

Savoured the flutter beneath its fingertips ...

Then the insertion. The stench of feces and sizzling lamb. The cough that was really a sob ...

Deep ... until all that remained was *one* place, the congress of Greater Souls.

It seized the man, lifted him from his feet. It used him as he had never been used before.

There was a head upon a pole behind him.

All souls wander. No matter what track they follow, it is never their own.

Faith is thrust upon us all. Even the suicide, who makes a fetish of refusal and a conceit of lamentations, has faith. Even the ironist, who would mock all creation to better sun his thistles. Even he *believes* ...

Faith is as inescapable as Men are small. They are borne breath by breath, a bubble in oily oblivion. No compass is so puny as the now, and yet it is the estate of man, his ephemeral empire. Faith. Faith alone binds him to what was and what will be—to what *transcends*. Faith alone clasps hands with what is other and *holds firm*. It is as inevitable as suffering, as compulsory as breath.

Only its object varies ...

The *in what*.

Proyas had believed in Anasûrimbor Kellhus, had assumed he dwelt within a World *without horizons*, where all the hidden things had been counted and enslaved. He was here and he was now, as meagre as any Man, but he was everywhere and eternal as well—*so long as he believed*. What horror could the World hold for him, standing at the Holy Aspect-Emperor's right hand? No matter where he travelled, no matter what atrocities he committed, *the God was for him*.

But no longer.

The ground had pitched, and all things now fell to the horizon. Proyas did not so much flee as plummet from the Umbilicus, did not so much walk as drop through the canvas-sheeted ways of the encampment, so steep had his world become ... the scarp it had always been.

The God had never been for him. It was a spider ... Infinite and inhuman.

Kellhus was not His Prophet.

Faith was deception, the mean and the base groping for the epic and the glorious—proof against idiot insignificance, against *truth*.

Ever had he hung upon the beating of a single, witless heart. Ever had he been flotsam in the mad surge of events, another battered now, reaching, clutching for a surety that did not exist.

Ever had he been used, exploited! Ever had he been a fool! A fool!

Ever had he fallen thus ...

He fell to his knees among the shag-hide tents of the Nangaels, raised fists to the catamite images that clogged his eyes. Upon this ledge he huddled, sobbing for loss and degradation ...

Faith was the small aping immensity, the remote painted across the near, the triumph of conceit over terror.

The most blessed ignorance.

And it was no more.

Terror had been a drug when Proyas was young.

Ever had he been a hero as a youth, dazzled by the great souls of legend; ever was he bent on proving his bravery, not to others, but to himself. His mother would sometimes weep for the hazards he dared: scaling the mortices of the Atikkoros, taunting the bulls used by a troupe of Invitic acrobats, and climbing every tree opportunity afforded, not simply into the bower, but to the skinny peak, where the wind would pitch him as an iron ingot upon a stalk of milkweed.

His favourite had been a grandiose oak that everyone called Wheezer for the hoarse noise it made when the wind possessed the proper temper. The tree's original peak had been sheared away, leaving the lesser half of what had been a fork, an upward arching branch that provided the footing he used to surmount Wheezer the way he could no other tree. There he would hang swaying, his heart racing, his hands and head fuzzy for floating exhilaration, Aoknyssus reaching out in grim and intricate stages, and it would all seem to be for him—him! He must have climbed the hoary old beast at least a hundred times without incident. And then, one dour, autumnal day, it simply *cracked*. He still felt the twang of mortal terror recalling it, the clutch of cold sweat across his skin. He still caught his breath ...

Swinging *out* and dropping *down*, doomed until a skein of lower branches miraculously caught the broken bough. He found himself hanging, legs kicking out over void. The entire palace would hear his scream (he would spend some three months hating Tyrûmmas, his older brother, for endlessly mimicking his cry. He could remember pondering, in the first few instants, which was the greater horror, dropping to his death, or hanging exposed as more and more shocked and scowling faces gathered beneath ...

"Are you daft, boy? I said *take* my hand."

And then, from nowhere it seemed, there was *Achamian*, standing as though upon invisible ground, *floating*, reaching out with ink-stained fingers.

"Never!"

"You would rather break your neck?"

"I would rather splint my soul!"

Even in extremis, the portly Schoolman's look betrayed the same exasperated wonder that the boy so often provoked on flat ground.

"I fear you're too young to die for your scruples, Prosha. One must have a wife to widow, children to orphan."

"You're *damned*! All Schoolmen are damned!"

"Which is why your father plunders his treasury to pay us. Now *take* my hand. *Take it*!"

"*No*!"

He was regularly astounded pondering this incident as a grown man. Perhaps others would find cause for pride in bravery, but not Proyas. If terror had been a plaything for him as a boy, a thing to be baited and teased, it was out of ignorance far more than for courage, the preposterous assurance that nothing *truly* untoward could happen to *him*. Tyrûmmas's watery death would ignite the pyre beneath that confidence, teach him the terror *of terror*.

"Well ..." the canny sorcerer had said, "you can wait for the God of Gods to reach down to save you ..."

"What do you mean?" Proyas had cried, too breathless to be clever. Some twenty cubits clacked its jaws beneath him. The bark had already begun to bite.

"Or ..." Akka continued, pausing for effect.

"Or *what?*"

Drusas Achamian splayed his inked fingertips wider still, and Proyas noticed that he chewed rather than pared his nails. "You can take the hand He has put before you."

There had been *love* in the sorcerer's look, a father's bottled fear. He would never admit to the flare of love he had felt in that moment, and he would cringe from its memory the way he cringed from thought of carnal shames.

He dared raise a hand, shifting the entirety of his weight to his other grip, snapping the branch ...

He had no recollection of the ground slapping him unconscious. He would get his splint, but for his left leg, not his soul. Everyone said it was a miracle that he had survived. His mother told him that Achamian had cried out louder than she had as he plummeted. For years following, various caste-nobles would mimic the cry—a kind of effeminate whoop—when the Schoolman barged by ...

Neither he nor Achamian so much as mentioned the episode.

And now he fell once again.

Proyas staggered through the slums of the Shigeki, the parasols of the Antanamerans, the scissoring timbers of the Kurigaldmen. The ways were largely abandoned, so he had little need to conceal his distress. Still, a consciousness of his appearance rose whenever he neared the battered pavilion of some Lord. Shame and ... a gloating. What had happened? What was happening? He began cackling. It seemed his heart would combust, leap into open flame, for the merest remembrance of what had transpired!

The Whore smiled, and no soul hailed him.

Stars dusted the black bowel of the void. The Ordeal matted the visible world beneath, a mosaic broken to the contours of the land, each contingent a tessera set in the mortar of labyrinthine paths. It all seemed mad to him now, the heaps of Sranc parts, particularly crooked hands and horned feet, the countless versions of the Circumfix, gold, crimson, and pitch. It all seemed ... *frail*, fraught with a simmering licentiousness, as if there were a *greater* Ordeal beyond the one he could see. He could feel strewn across nocturnal miles, the wrack of a more profound host, one senseless of pious decrees and righteous declarations, bound by nothing more than the coincidence of low appetites ...

I ...

A bestial impatience.

He crouched in a ravine and wept for a short time, gagged for memory and human offal.

I am forsaken.

That faith belonged to the foundation was a truth that Proyas had lived more than fathomed. It was the *human ground*, a thing too onerous not to be broken and divided between names: "love" in the union of disparate souls, "logic" in the union of disparate claims, "truth" in the union of desire and circumstance ...

"Desire" when it reached out, seeking.

All I have known ...

He huddled against rock and clay, a little place, croaking alone in the dark, wracked with grief, assailed by fear and imagery.

False.

The sun, he thought, would bring flies.

The Enathpanean district of the camp was a crowded helter clustered across the break and heave of the land, notable only for the admixture of Galeoth tents, crude and sturdy, and the rambling Khirgwi marquees of the native Enathpaneans. He found Saubon's pavilion before realizing he'd been searching for it. The Red Lions splayed across its canvas panels glowered black in the Nail of Heaven's soulless light. The glimpse of golden illumination about the entrance flap heartened the Exalt-General, though he had yet to understand what had brought him here.

Given the dearth of fuel, all fires were forbidden after the prandial watch. Nevertheless, three men, Knights of the Desert Lion by their soiled surcoats, leaned about a small fire set several paces before the pavilion, bent like boys dripping wax on ants. Proyas recognized all three as Saubon's captains: his Swordbearer, Thipil Mepiro, a diminutive Amoti famed for his duelling prowess; his towering Shieldbearer, Ûster Scraul, a thin, stammering Kurigalder called "the Bard" for his eloquence in battle; and his famed Spearbearer, Thurhig Bogyar, a red-maned Holca warrior, apparently descended from Eryelk the Ravager no less.

Something about their manner—an inward leering, a hunching against—troubled Proyas.

"What happens here?"

Even their response to his challenge troubled him, the way they shared looks between themselves, as if no authority could matter outside their small circle.

A Sranc head gleamed in the lap of the enormous Holca.

"I said," Proyas repeated in abrupt fury, "*what happens here*?"

All three turned to him as if upon the same slow swivel. The Law demanded they fall to their faces; instead they fixed him with murderous looks. Bogyar drew a cloth across his grisly prize. Knights of the Desert Lion were notoriously ill-mannered: "Saubon's Brigands" some called them. Where almost every Believer-King built their household from caste-noble stone, Saubon, who had never forgiven the Whore for making him the *seventh* son of foul old Eryeat, had made the gutter his quarry.

"The *Law* awaits your ans—"

A powerful and familiar voice called from the pavilion just beyond—the Desert Lion himself.

"Proyas? What are you doing here?"

Saubon stood before the swaying entrance flap, his grey hair still flattened for his helm, but stripped to his leggings otherwise.

"I've come to confer with my brother, Brother," Proyas said, sparing him little more than a glance. "But these dogs ne—"

"Answer to *me*," Saubon snapped. He hooked open the flap of his pavilion on a long arm. "We all make our own way."

"And they have chosen the one with whips," Proyas said evenly. He glared at Saubon in the ruthless, New Imperial manner, the one that brooked no exceptions. The habits of command, at least, had not abandoned him.

The Believer-King of Caraskand muttered some kind of Galeoth curse. Mepiro, Scraul, and Bogyar had watched the exchange like the overweening sons of a doting and unscrupulous father. But their arrogance—or, more likely, their failure to disguise it—was too much. Saubon's scowl faded into something remote. They had over-played their sticks, and Proyas watched the realization knock the presumption from their faces with no little satisfaction.

The covered head forgotten, the three Bearers scrambled to press their foreheads against the packed earth. Their fire dwindled as if for the absence of attention—sputtered ...

First the first time, Proyas wondered that he could see so well in the dark. Whence had such an ability come?

"Come," Saubon called, motioning him to the entrance flap. "They will know the Law on the morrow. You have my assurance, *brother*."

When it came to treating with subordinates, Ketyai caste-nobles were more remote and summary than their Norsirai counterparts. Vassals who made themselves visible with some trespass became invisible the instant their punishment was meted. No pleas were heard, no remonstrations of penitence or innocence. And unless the affair was public or ceremonial, no crowing displays were made, no gloating declarations ...

Nevertheless, Proyas paused above the prostrate knights, at once perplexed and trembling for outrage.

Saubon scowled at the indecisive spectacle, but said nothing.

Winded and dismayed, Proyas barged past his counterpart, found himself standing within the lantern-illumined pavilion, utterly abandoned by the confidence he'd commanded but moments before. Pale light climbed the walls, the canvas so blotted and weather-stained as to resemble maps scraped of names and ink. Something like Zeum loomed over the lantern set beside his simple bed. Nilnamesh hung skewered by the centrepost. The floor was bare, dead and earthen, and only the most rudimentary furnishings populated the golden gloom. The air was close, smelled of sweat, lamb, and hay rotted to dust. A blond youth stood meekly beneath the two hanging lanterns, his cheeks neither nude nor bearded.

Saubon strode past Proyas, barked, "Leave!" at the youth, who promptly fled. With a groan, the Galeoth warrior dropped to his rump on his cot, glanced at Proyas for a heartbeat before lowering his face to a broad bowl between his feet. He scooped water across his brow and cheeks.

"You've been to see *him* again," he said, blinking into the basin. "I can tell."

Proyas stood speechless, not knowing why he had come.

Saubon raised his face in scowling appraisal. He absently clutched the rag at his side, began towelling his beard and chest. He nodded to the platter of greying meat on the camp table to Proyas's right.

"Be-before ..." the Believer-King of Conriya stammered. "Y-you said he told you the truth."

A careful look. "Aye."

"So he told you that he wasn't ... a ..."

Saubon drew the towel down his face. “He told me he was something called ‘Dûnyain.’”

“That all of this was some kind of vast ... *calculation*.”

The bitten eyes gazed forward. “Aye. The Thousandfold Thought.”

It seemed the lanterns should wink out for the absence of air.

“So *you know*!” Proyas cried. “How? How is it you can be ... be ...”

“Untroubled?” Saubon said, tossing the rag to the ground. He studied Proyas, elbows propped on his knees. “I’ve never been a believer like you, Proyas. I have no *need* to know what lays at the bottom of things.”

They breathed.

“Even to save the world?”

A scowl and a grin warred for possession of Saubon’s face. “Is that what we do?”

Proyas choked on the sudden impulse to scream. What was happening? What was happening?

“Wha-what *is he doing*?” he cried, flinching for the unmanly crimp in his tone, and yet finding himself compounding the treachery with a rush of more white-skinned words: “I-I ne-need ... *I need to know* what he’s doing!”

A long, inscrutable look.

“*What is he doing*?” Proyas nearly screeched.

Saubon shrugged his shoulders, leaned back. “I think he tests us ... prepares us for something ...”

“So he *is* a Prophet!”

As intelligent as he was, a kind of barbaric immodesty had always characterized Coithus Saubon, a vulgar need to lord over those who were his equals. Even in the presence of their Holy Aspect-Emperor, his inclination was to smirk. Now the first spark of genuine alarm humbled his gaze.

“You’ve dwelt in his shadow as long as me ...” A bark of laughter that was supposed to sound confident. “What *else* could he be?”

Dûnyain.

“Yes ...” Proyas replied, nausea welling through him. “What else could he be?”

Some Men are like this. They would rather scoff, turn aside the plea they hear in other voices to better disguise the penury of their own. It takes them time to set aside the ephemeral arms and armour of the court. For twenty years he and Saubon had dwelt in the revelatory light of Anasûrimbor Kellhus. For twenty years they had discharged his commands with thoughtless obedience, delivering innumerable Orthodox to the sword, setting the fleshpots of the Three Seas alight. *Together* they had done this, the Right and Left Hands of the Holy Aspect-Emperor. Forsaking wives and children. Breaking all the Laws that had come before. And in all that time they had wondered only at the *tragic folly* of those they had killed. How? How could Men turn aside their eyes, when the God's light was *so plain?*

They were in this *together* as well. Not even the proud and impetuous Coithus Saubon could feign otherwise.

"The way I see it," the Galeoth Exalt-General said slowly, deliberately, "he's preparing us for some kind of *crisis* ... A crisis of faith."

It seemed sacrilegious, even blasphemous, taking a ... *tactical* attitude to their Lord-and-Prophet. But it also seemed far more canny, far more *awake*—certainly more than the caged slurry of his own thoughts.

"Why do you say that?"

Saubon stood, absently raked his fingers across his scalp.

"Because we are living *scripture*, for one ... And scripture, if you haven't noticed, dwells on grievance and disaster ..." Again he expressed the attitude of second-guesses, the one that looks past what words mean to consider what they *accomplish*. "And because he says so *himself*, for another. He scarcely speaks without referencing Celmomas and the doom of the Great Ordeal's ancient namesake ... Yes ... Something is coming ... Something *only he knows about*."

Proyas stared breathless. It seemed he could not move without stirring the memory of his bruises.

"But ..."

"After all this time, you still don't fully understand him, do you?"

"And you do?"

Saubon swatted the air the way Galeoth were prone when irked by questions. "You think me stubborn," he said. "Mercenary. Your *lesser* counterpart. I know this—*he* knows this! I take no offense because I think you stubborn and insufferably pious. And so we counsel one against the other continuously, each heaving upon the rope of disparate reason ..."

"So?"

"This is *theatre*!" Saubon cried, throwing wide his strapped arms. "Can't you see? We are all mummers here! *All* of us! Prophet or not, our Holy Aspect-Emperor must control *what* Men *see* ... All of us have *roles* to play, Proyas, and no one gets to *choose* which."

"What are you saying?"

"That our parts remain to be written. Perhaps you're to be the fool ... or the traitor ... or the long-suffering doubter ..." A bleary gaze, filled with hilarity and rheumy spite. "Only *he* knows!"

Proyas could only stare at the man.

Saubon grinned. "Perhaps you must be *weak* to survive the catastrophe to come."

Proyas shuddered—the substance of him rippled like water in a kicked pan. His exhalation was audible, ragged with turmoil. Lantern-light pricked. Tears spilled hot down his cheeks. He glared angrily at Saubon, knowing the sight would astound him.

"So ..." he began, only to stumble upon a crack in his voice. "So what is *your* role then?"

Saubon watched him carefully. It would be the first and only time Proyas would see pity on his face. The man's blue eyes, which had become all the more fierce for the rutting of his skin and the greying of his brows, clicked to his bare toes, which he flexed as if to better grip the ground. "The same as you, I suspect."

Proyas wondered at the belt cinched about his chest. "How could you know this?"

Saubon shrugged. "Because he tells us the same things."

A stabbing shame accompanied these words. All breath and motion fell from the Believer-King of Conriya.

Some secrets are too vast to be hoisted. A space must be cleared.

"Did he—?"

Madness. This couldn't be happening ...

Saubon scowled. "Did he what?" A barking laugh. "*Bugger* me?"

All the air ... All the air *had been breathed.*

A gaze that had been anxious and incredulous was now simply stupefied. The Galeoth Believer-King exploded in a fit of coughing. Water dribbled from his nose.

"*No* ..." he gasped.

Proyas had thought he had been looking at his counterpart, but when

Saubon moved, paced to the threshold hands to his head, he found his gaze fixed on the vacant space the man had occupied.

"He says he's *mad*, Saubon."

"He-he *told* you this?"

Their rivalry, such as it was, suddenly seemed the most profound of their many bonds. In an inkling, they had become brothers in a perilous land. And it occurred to Proyas that perhaps *this* was what their Lord-and-Prophet desired: that they finally set aside their meagre differences.

"*He buggered you?*" Saubon cried out.

It was a crime among the Galeoth, using a man as a woman. It was a shame like no other. Among all the buzzing terrors, Proyas realized that he would forever bear this taint in Coithus Saubon's eyes. That he would, in some measure, be a woman. Weak. Unreliable in the ways of manhood and war ...

A strangeness had seized Saubon's expression, the bundling of some crazed fury. "*You lie!*" he exploded. "He *told* you to say this!"

Proyas simply matched his gaze, observed more than watched the man's rage crack and crumble against his blank constancy. And he realized that even though he had been the one to suffer their Aspect-Emperor's violent embrace, it was *Saubon* who would be the most grievously tested ...

The one most pitted against the bigotries of his soul.

The statuesque Norsirai paced, his every tendon pulled taut, a thousand strings grooving his pale skin. He glanced about, frowning in the manner of addled drunks or senile old men, as if things obvious had been misplaced. "It's the *Meat*," he muttered on a sob. Without warning he leapt, batted the platter and its morsels across the gloomy interior. "*This accursed Meat!*"

The violence of the act startled both of them.

"The more you consume ..." Saubon said, staring at clawed hands. "The more you ... you *hunger*."

Confession has its own calm, its own strength. Only ignorance is so immovable as resignation. Proyas had thought this strength his, especially given the bewildered frailty that had preceded it. But grief welled through him as he made to speak, and the desperation that cramped his expression seized his voice.

"Saubon ... What's *happening*?"

Speechless horror. One of the lanterns sputtered; light wavered over the ochre continents and archipelagos stained across the canvas walls.

"Tell no one of this," Coithus Saubon commanded.

"You think I don't know as much!" Proyas cried in sudden fury. "I'm asking you *what we're supposed to do*?"

The man nodded, as much wilderness as wisdom flashing in his gaze. It almost seemed they took turns, each tethering the fraught excesses of the other, like two snarled kites trying to find some kind of crippled equipoise.

"What we have always done."

"But he's telling us to ... to ... *not to believe*!"

Out of everything, this was the most unbelievable ... unforgivable.

"*That* is the test," Saubon said. "The trial ... It has to be!"

"Test? Trial?"

A look too beseeching to be convincing.

"To see if we continue to *act* when ..." Saubon said, "when we have *ceased to believe* ..."

They traded exhalations.

"But ..."

They both could feel it, the taint of the meat, a cruel and vicious spring coiled within their every thought and breath. The meat. The Meat.

Yesss.

"Think, Brother ..." Saubon said. "What *else* could it be?"

They had no choice but to believe. Faith is inescapable ... and nowhere more so than in the commission of some mighty *sin*.

"We stand so close ..." Proyas murmured.

Only its object varies ... the *in what*.

"Lean into the oar, Brother," Saubon said, his voice rent between dread and ferocity. "*Golgotterath* will decide."

Be it God ... Man.

"Yes ..." Proyas said on a shudder. "Golgotterath."

Or nothing.

CHAPTER FIVE

Ishuäl

The father who does not lie is no father at all.

—CONRIYAN PROVERB

Between the truth that aims uncertainly, and the deceit that aims true, scholars no less than kings cling to the latter. Only madmen and sorcerers have truck with Truth.

—*The Cirric (or 'Fourth') Economy*, OLEKAROS

Early Autumn, 20 New Imperial Year (4132, Year-of-the-Tusk), the Demua Mountains

"*Nau-Cayûti* ..." one of the wretches croaked.

"*Nau-Cayûti* ..." another rasped, rocking like a worm.

"*Such a prizsse* ..."

Achamian rolled to his knees, coughed. Manacles clamped his neck, wrists, ankles. A circle of figures leaned close about him, black with confusion. Beyond, the world lurched with shadow and gold. A reeking breeze laved his naked back, pinched his gut and pulled vomit to his throat.

He convulsed with a different body, gagged about a string of burning spittle. Memories of a darkling flight crowded his eyes, claws hooked about his limbs, wings shearing hard air, a blasted landscape reeling out to the horizon.

"*Such-such a prizsse ...*"

"*He-he-heeee ...*"

More memories came, like ice packed about his heart and lungs. His wife, Iëva, plundering his loins with wanton abandon. The Inchoroi, Aurang, cracking him from his sarcophagus, hauling him into the heavens. Golden bulkheads rearing from bastions of cruel stone, their surfaces stamped in endless, alien filigree ...

Golgotterath, the Great Prince realized. He was in Min-Uroikas, the dread Ark-of-the-skies ...

Which meant he was worse than dead.

"My father!" he cried, staring about witless. "My father will yield *nothing* for my return!"

"*Return ...*" one of the wretches gasped.

"*There is no return ...*" another added.

"*No escape ...*"

The Wizard gazed wildly about. Ten ancient men encircled him, their skin sucked tight about their ligaments, their eyes bleary with mucous and misery. They wagged their heads—some bald, some wisped with snow-white strands—as if trapped nodding at the surface of a long, nightmarish slumber. One chewed his own bottom lip, so that blood sheeted his chin.

At first he thought they sat huddled—but he quickly realized they possessed *no limbs*, that they had been bound like larva to cradle-like sconces of stone. And he understood that these ten men were Men no longer, but wheels in some kind of *contrivance*, arcane and abominable.

At once, the Great Prince realized *who* it was who truly scrutinized him—as well as who had betrayed him.

"My wife," he groaned, testing the mettle of his chains for the first time. "Iëva!"

"*Has committed ...*" one of the ancient mouths warbled.

"*Such crimes ...*"

"What was her price ..." he coughed. "Tell me!"

"*She sheeks only ...*" the bloody one bubbled.

"*To save her soul ...*"

Laughter, thin and eerie, passed through the wretches, like the lash through the whip, one rising from the trailing of another.

The Great Prince cast his gaze beyond them, toward the gold-girdered walls. He saw hooded light rising across faraway structures, surfaces gleaming through darkness, stamped with infinite detail, packed into inexplicable forms. A sudden awareness of distance and dimension struck him ...

Dizzy, gaping spaces.

He fell to his right elbow, so sudden was the vertigo. They *floated*, he realized. The ancient amputees had been arrayed across a platform of some kind—one rendered of the same unearthly metal as the Ark. Soggomant, foul and impenetrable. He saw golden reliefs through the scuffs in the offal beneath him, warring figures, leering and inhuman. And the form, opposing S's hooked about the arms of a V ...

A shape no Son of the House Anasûrimbor could fail to recognize: the Shield of Sil.

They floated upward through some kind of shaft, one impossibly vast, a gullet broad enough to house the King-Temple whole. The Horns, Nau-Cayûti realized ...

"A *marvel* ..." one of the wretches croaked, a momentary light flaring and fading in his eyes.

"*Is it not?*"

They ascended what Siqu called the *Abskinis*, the Groundless Grave ...

"*The Iyiskû ...*"

"*They made this ...*"

"*To be their ...*"

"*Sssshurrogate world ...*"

The vast well that plumbed Golgotterath's Upright Horn.

"*Now ... now ...*"

"*It belongs to me ...*"

They climbed to the world's most wicked summit, where none but the dead and the damned descended.

"*The very ...*"

"*Stronghold ...*"

"*Of ssssalvation!*"

Rage, delirious and titanic, seized the old Wizard's limbs and voice. He howled. He cast his naked body whole, wrenched and heaved with the strength that had made him unconquerable on so many fields of battle.

But the Wretches only drooled and laughed, one after the other.

"*Nau-Cayûti ...*"

He drew his feet beneath him, squatted, strained roaring, until his limbs flushed and quivered. He hurled all his being ...

"*Thief* ..."

The iron links creaked, but did not yield.

"*You hath returned* ..."

"*To the house* ..."

"*From which you hath stolen* ..."

He slumped in dismay, gazed sneering at the wretches. Different faces worn into the same face by decrepitude. Different voices throttled into the same voice by senescence and age-old hatred. Ten Wretches, *one* ancient and malevolent soul.

"Damnation awaits you!" the Great Prince roared. "Eternal torment!"

"*Your pride* ..."

"*Your strength* ..."

"*Are naught but kindling* ..."

"*For the Lust* ..."

"*Of the Derived* ..."

The Great Prince's thoughts raced through the old Wizard's soul.

"*They shall glory* ..."

"*In your misery* ..."

Rising ... rising through stench and darkness. A vast throat, ribbed in gold, descending. "*Damnation*!" Nau-Cayûti bellowed. "How long can you cling, wicked old fool?"

"*Your eyes* ..."

"*Shall be put out* ..."

"*Your manhood* ..."

"*Shall be cut from you* ..."

"*And I shall give you over* ..."

"*To my children* ..."

"*To their rutting fervour* ..."

And Nau-Cayûti laughed, for fear was all but unknown to him. "How long before Hell has its say?"

"*You will be shattered* ..."

"*Beaten and degraded* ..."

"*Your wounds will bleed* ..."

"*The black of my children's seed* ..."

"Your honour will be cast ..."

"As ash ..."

"To the high winds ..."

"Where the Gods shall gather it!" the Great Prince boomed. "The very Gods *you flee!*"

"And you will weep ..."

"At the last ..."

The Shield of Sil climbed high into the dark, toward a gold-shining aperture. Chained within a mightier frame, the old Wizard screamed with lunatic defiance, roared with a strength not his own.

"And when all is done ..."

"You will tell me ..."

"Where your accursed tutor ..."

"Has concealed ..."

"The Heron Spe—"

Then brightness, blinking and chill.

The cough of too-cold air too sharply drawn.

Night had fallen quickly once they had descended the far side of the glacier, forcing them to camp just below the frosted heights. They had settled upon a ledge that was lifeless save for the tattooing of lichens across the sunward faces. They had fallen asleep clutching each other—for hope as much as for warmth.

Now, rubbing his eyes, the old Wizard saw Mimara hugging her knees on the mounded lip, staring out across the distance, toward the ruined talisman of Ishuäl. She was draped in rotted furs, the same as he, but where he had elected to wear his looted nimil corselet beneath his pelts, she wore the gold-scaled hauberk she had retrieved from the Coffers over hers. She spared him a curious glance, nothing more. She looked boyish for her hair, he thought.

"I dr-dreamed ..." he said, hugging his arms against a shiver. "Dreamed of *him*."

"Him?"

"Shauriatas."

He had no need of explanations. Shauriatas was the curse-name of

Shaeönanra, the cunning Grandmaster of the Mangaecca, the intellect who discovered the last surviving Inchoroi and resurrected their World-breaking design.

Shauriatas. The Lord of the Unholy Consult.

The surprise in her eyes was fleeting. "How's he doing?"

The old Wizard screwed his face into a scowl, then coughed in laughter. "Not quite himself."

The vale plummeted and piled across the morning distance, gullies and ravines pinned one to the other on tumbling angles, ramps matted with conifers, shouldering scarps that climbed to the clouds.

Ishuäl perched over the lowland creases, its towers and walls overthrown, little more than a socket where a jewel was supposed to be.

Ishuäl ... The ancient sanctuary of the Kûniüric High Kings, hidden from the world for an entire age.

He had not known what to expect when he and Mimara had crested the glacier the previous day. He had some understanding of time, of the mad way the past formed an invisible rind about the present. When life was monotonous—*safe*—what happened and what *had* happened formed a kind of slurry, and the paradoxes of time seemed little more than a philosopher's fancy. But when life became *momentous* ... nothing seemed more absurd, more *precarious*, than the now. One ate, as one always ate, one loved and hoped and hated the same as before—and it all seemed impossible.

For twenty years he had cloistered himself with his Dreams, marking progress in the slow accumulation of nocturnal variance and permutation. The growth of his slave's children became his only calendar. His old pains evaporated, to be sure, and yet everyday had seemed to be *that* day, the day he cursed Anasûrimbor Kellhus and began his bloody-footed trek into exile, so little had happened since.

Then Mimara, bearing long-dead torment and news of the Great Ordeal ...

Then the Skin Eaters with their evil and blood-crazed Captain ...

Then Cil-Aujas and the first Sranc, who had driven them into the precincts of Hell ...

Then the madness of the Mop and the long, manic trail across the Istyuli Plains ...

Then the Library of Sauglish and the Father of Dragons ...

Then Nil'giccas, the death of the Last Nonman King ...

So he had wheezed and huffed to the glacier's summit in the calamitous shadow of these things, not knowing what to think, too numb and bewildered to rejoice. For so long the very World had been the mountain between them, and his limbs and heart trembled for climbing ...

Then, there it lay: *Ishuäl*, the sum of labourious years and how many lives; *Ishuäl*, the birthplace of the Holy Aspect-Emperor ...

Blasted to its foundations.

For a time he simply blinked and blinked. The air was too chill, his eyes too old. The sun was too bright, dazzling the icy heights. No matter how hard he squinted, he could not see ...

Then he felt Mimara's smaller, warmer hands enclose his own. She was standing before him, gazing up into his face.

"There's no cause to weep," she had said.

But there was.

More than enough.

His laughter forgotten, he now gazed at the wrecked fortress, his eyes clicking from detail to detail. The great blocks, scorched and fractured, spilling down the encircling slopes. The heaped debris ...

Dawn silence thundered in his ears. He found himself swallowing against a hollow pinned to the back of his throat. *So much* ... was all he could think, but whether he meant toil or suffering or sacrifice, he could not say.

The despair, when it came, crashed through him, bubbled through his bowel. He looked away in an effort to master his eyes. *Fool!* he cursed himself, worried that he had outgrown his old weaknesses only to inherit the frailties of old age. How could he falter at such a time?

"I know," he croaked, hoping to recover himself by speaking of his Dream.

"What do you know?"

"How Shauriatas survived all these years. How he managed to cheat Death ..."

And damnation.

He explained how the Consult sorcerer had been ancient even in Far Antique days, little more than a dread legend to Seswatha and the School of Sohonc. He described a hate-rotted soul, forever falling into hell, forever deflected by ancient and arcane magicks, caught in the sack-cloth of souls too near death to resist his clutching tumble, too devoid of animating passion.

A pit bent into a circle, the most perfect of the Conserving Forms ...

"But isn't trapping souls an ancient art?" she asked.

"It is ..." Achamian replied. He thought of the Wathi doll he once owned—and used to save himself from the Scarlet Spires when everyone, including Esmenet, had thought him dead. He had been reluctant, then, to think of the proxy that had been trapped within it. Had it suffered? Was it yet another of his multitudinous sins?

One more blemish for Mimara to glimpse with her Judging Eye?

"But souls are exceedingly complicated," he continued. "Far more so than the crude sorceries used to trap them. The intricacies of *identity* are always sheared away. Memory. Faculty. Character. These are cast into the pit ... Only the most base urges survive in proxies."

Which was what made them such useful slaves.

"So to have your soul caught ..." She trailed, frowning.

"Is to be twice-damned ..." he said, trailing at the behest of a queer reluctance. Few understood the monstrosity of sorcery better than he. "To have your hungers enslaved in the World, while your thoughts are tormented in the Outside."

This seemed to trouble her. She turned back to the vista, her brow furrowed. He followed her gaze, yet again felt his heart slump at the sight of Ishuäl's cracked foundations rising above the black carpet of pine and spruce.

"What does it mean?" she asked of the wind.

"The Dream?"

"No." She glanced at him over her shoulder. "The *timing*."

Now it was his turn to fall silent.

He thought, as he always did when he became agitated, of the Qirri. A querulous part of him groused, wondering why Mimara should bear the Nonman King's pouch, when *he* was the leader of their piteous company—their Slog of slogs. But like an old dog caught in the rain yet one more time, he shook away these peevish thoughts. He had come to understand the narcotic ash over the months of his addiction, at least enough to distinguish *its* thoughts from his own.

Mimara was right. To dream such a thing *now* ...

What could it mean?

To suffer this Dream the very day he would at last *set foot in Ishuäl*. To not only *see* Shauriatas, but to learn the *true* fate of Nau-Cayûti—or something of it. What could it mean to learn the truth of one great Anasûrimbor's death, just before discovering the truth of another, even greater Anasûrimbor's birth?

What was happening?

He sat rigid, his breath pinched by the sense of things *converging* ...

Origin to ending.

What came after to what came before.

"Come," Mimara called, standing, brushing grit from her ragged trousers. The sickle of her belly caught an errant lance of sunlight ... The old Wizard momentarily forgot how to breathe.

A chevron of geese soared above, barking southward.

"We have bones to inspect," she said with the weariness and resolve of a long-suffering mother.

They pick their way down through the remains of an ancient moraine, climbing between boulders that chance had arrayed in descending barricades. Mimara follows the old Wizard, her eyes keen for any glimpse of the ruined fastness through the raggish trees. Ishuäl had been raised on the low hip of a mountain to the southwest, forcing them to descend into the very basement of the vale, before resuming their climbing approach. Periodically, she sees decapitated towers and sections of truncated wall rising between the dark crowns. The teetering stone looks ancient and wind-blasted, bleached sterile for countless ages of exposure. An eerie silence permeates the surrounding forest.

"What will we do now?" she asks with a vague air of surprise. With the Qirri, it seems only the merest whim separates what is spoken from what is merely thought. More and more she finds herself verbalizing ill-considered things.

"What we *are* doing!" the old Wizard snaps without so much as glancing at her.

It's okay, little one ...

She understands his dismay. For him, finding the map in the ruined Library had been a kind of irrefutable sign, divine indication that *he had not acted in vain.* But when he had finally crested the glacier, when he finally peered across the vale and found the destination he had hunted in his

Dreams for twenty years *ruined*, his newfound conviction had tumbled from him, whipped away on the high mountain wind.

Papa had a scary dream.

Drusas Achamian knew the cruelty of Fate—perhaps more profoundly than she. Perhaps they had been lured here simply to be broken—a punishment for vanity perhaps, or for nothing at all. The Holy Sagas were literally filled with such stories of divine treachery. "The Whore," she once read in Casidas, "will carry you through wars and famine in glory, only to drown you for tripping in a ditch." She remembers smiling at the passage, taking heart in the laying low of the high and mighty, as if the punishment of the exalted was at once the vengeance of the weak.

What if the Dûnyain were extinct? What if they had travelled all this way, ushered all those men—those scalpers—to their deaths *for nothing at all?*

The thought almost makes her laugh, not out of any callousness, but out of *exhaustion*. Toil, harsh and relentless, has a way of twisting hope into self-consuming circles. Battle peril long enough, she has learned, and you will come to see salvation in your doom.

The quiet seems to intensify as they near the broken sanctuary. A ringing seeps into her ears. Out of some reflex, they close the space between them, so that they continually bump and brush each other. They begin measuring their steps, leaning and ducking as much to remain hidden as to avoid dead branches. They begin creeping as though approaching an enemy camp, their footfalls inaudible save for the smothered pop of twigs beneath the matted pine needles. They peer through the branching gloom.

After scaling cliffs, glaciers, and mountains, the slopes and defilades about the fortress should have seemed insignificant. They tower instead, pitched to angles that only their souls can perceive. Squinting up the broken incline, she glimpses dead stone in sunlight, wind she cannot feel combing through thronging weeds and sapling trees. It seems they climb a burial mound.

She thinks of the Qirri, the pinch of bitter bliss, and her mouth begins watering.

They come to the debris robed about the foundations. The trees yield to mountain sunlight ... Dazzling sheets.

And they find themselves in the wind, standing on the ruined perimeter, staring across a sight she can scarce believe.

Ishuäl ... She is breathless for thinking it.

Ishuäl ... An empty name spoken from the far side of the world.

Ishuäl ... Here. Now. About her eyes. Beneath her feet.

The birthplace of the Aspect-Emperor ...

Of the Dûnyain.

She turns to the old Wizard and sees *Drusas Achamian*, the hallowed Tutor, the infamous Exile, clad in rotting pelts, wild with the filth of endless escape. Sunlight flashes for glimpses of Nil'giccas's nimil hauberk. Sunlight flashes from his wetted cheeks.

Fear stabs her breast, he looks so frail and wretched.

He *is* a prophet of the past. Mimara knows this now—and it terrifies her.

When she had made this declaration so many months ago—impossible months—she had spoken with the insincerity of those who speak to appease. She had answered the unaccountable instinct, one that all Men share, to brace wavering souls with vainglorious pictures of what might be. She had spoken out of haste and expedient greed, and yet somehow, she had spoken true. *Dreams* had summoned him to Ishuäl. Dreams had sent him to Sauglish for the means to find it. Dreams *of the past* had driven him, not visions of the future ...

For the old Wizard knew nothing of the future, save that he feared.

When she paused to recollect their long-suffering journey, it seemed she possessed *two* sets of memories: the one embodied, where she had thrown heart and limbs at the world, and the other disembodied, where everything happened, not out of desperation or heroic effort, but *out of necessity*. She wondered that the same thing could possess such contradictory appearances. And with a kind of dismay, she realized that between the two, her experience of striving and overcoming were the more false.

Fate had her—had *them*. Anagkë, the Whore, would midwife her child ...

She fairly weeps for thinking it.

No matter how fierce or cunning or deliberate her struggles, no matter how much it *seems* she cut trails of her own making, she follows tracks laid at the founding of the World ... There can be no denying it.

One can sooner climb free the air than escape Fate.

And with this realization comes a peculiar kind of melancholy, a resignation that was at once a *commission*, a *willingness to be used* that troubled her with memories of the brothel. Everything, the prick at the bottom of her lungs, the mandible of mountains fencing the near distance, even the character of the light, carries the numb pinch of eternity. She would strive. She would spit and strain and fight ... and she would know it was nothing more than a gratifying illusion. She would cast herself into the belly of her own inevitability.

What else is there?

Fight, little one, she whispers to the miracle that is her belly. *Fight for me.*

Breathless, wordless, they pick their way over a destroyed segment of wall. They pause, winded by things more profound than mourning or exhaustion. The old Wizard slumps to his knees.

The sanctuary had been all but razed. Berms of rubble are all that remain of the walls. Masonry ramps and carpets the interior, thrown like wrack by some surging sea. Even still, it seems she can *see* the place: the cyclopean scale in the width of the foundations, the craftsmanship in the polished faces, the design in the lay of the wreckage.

Citadel. Assembly yard. Dormitories. Even a grove of some kind.

The fractured stone is pale, almost white, throwing the black of soot and scorching into sharp relief. Pockets weeping ash. Surfaces scaled in charcoal. The itch of sorcerous residue stains everything in tones that cannot be seen—colours both impossible and foul.

"How?" she finally dares ask. "Do you think—"

She catches herself, suddenly hesitant to voice her wondering. She doesn't so much distrust Achamian himself as his heartbreak.

Your father is reckless ...

The wind whisks across the ruined expanses, pricks cheeks for grit.

The old Wizard hauls himself to his feet, totters for a moment. "I'm a fool ..." he croaks.

He says that too often to mean it. You'll learn.

Achamian curses and wipes at his eyes, tugs on his beard—more in fury than reflection. "He's been one step ahead of me all along!" he cries. "Kellhus!" He claps his head, wags his beard in incredulity. "He wanted me here ... *He wanted me to see this!*"

She scowls.

"*Think*," he grates. "Kosoter. The Skin Eaters. He *had to know*, Mimara! He's been *leading* me all along!"

"Akka, come," she says. "How could such a thing be possible?"

For the first time she hears it in her voice, the tones of a mother—the mother she will soon be.

"My notes!" he cries in dawning horror. "The *tower*! He came to my tower! He *read my notes*, discovered I was hunting Ishuäl in my Dreams!"

She looks away, repelled by the violence of his self-pity, and resumes wandering between the mounds. She ponders the growth thronging from the ruin's every seam: weeds drying with the season, scrub like wicker, even small twisted pines. How many years since ruin had come and gone? she wonders. Three? More?

"Are you saying he came *here*?" she called to the watching Wizard. "Destroyed his birthpla—?"

"Of course he did!" he snaps. "Of-course-of-course-*of-course*! To cover his tracks. To prevent me from discovering his origin—perhaps ... But *think*. How could he rule in utter security so long as the Dûnyain still lived? He *had* to destroy Ishuäl, girl. He had to kick away the ladder that had raised him so high!"

She isn't so sure. But then she never is.

"So *Kellhus* did this?"

The old Wizard spouts curses rather than reply—speaking some language she cannot fathom, and sounding all the more foul-humoured for it. He begins waving his arms and pacing as he shouts.

She spins on her heel to consider the ruined fortress in a single look ...

Everything Achamian said bore the ring of truth, so why does she disagree?

She turns to encircling mountains, imagines what it would look like, seeing her stepfather stride across the bleached heavens, bearing light and fury. She can almost hear his voice crack across the firmament, calling on his Dûnyain brothers ...

She looks back to the razed foundations—to Ishuäl.

Spite, she realizes. Brute hatred destroyed this place.

The old Wizard has fallen silent behind her. She turns, sees him sitting with his back against a great block of stone, staring at nothing, clutching at his forehead, combing his scalp with his fingers. And somehow she knows: Anasûrimbor Kellhus has long ceased being a man for Drusas Achamian—or even a devil for that matter. He has become a *labyrinth*, something that misleads every breath, mazes every direction. Something that can never be escaped.

But there are other powers. Spiteful powers.

She *smells* it first ... the ghost of rot. A waist-high section of wall conceals it, though she realizes she has seen it all along in the wandering arc of ruin heaped about its rim. A strange kind of astonishment trills through her, like finding a horrible scar on a new lover.

"Akka ..." she calls weakly.

The old Wizard glances up in alarm. She expects him to either ignore or rebuke her, but something in her tone, perhaps, hooks his concern.

"What is it?"

"Come ... Look ..."

He is quick in trotting to her side—almost too quick. She has never grown accustomed to the nimble alacrity that the Qirri has lent his old bones. All such reminders trouble her ... in a vague way.

So reckless with his heart, little one.

They stand side-by-side, gazing into the maw of a great pit.

The hole falls at a steep angle rather than straight down, with the ruin piled like a cowl about its ceiling edge, and the floor descending like a tongue opposite. It resembles a gigantic burrow, not unlike the one leading to the Coffers in the Library. Blackness fills its throat, almost tangible for the surrounding brightness, viscous with threat.

Achamian stands stupefied. She is not sure what draws her to climb the far side. Perhaps she has lost her stomach for deep and dark places. Regardless, she picks her way to the crest, which overlooks the far limit of the fortress, and finds herself staring down a vast incline of branches—only they are not branches ...

Bones, she realizes.

Sranc bones.

Innumerable. So many that their sum has eclipsed the scale of manufactured things and become one with the mountain's foundations. An enormous ramp, broad and shallow enough to bear a wain near the peak, dropping scores of feet, flaring out like a skirt, spilling into the forests.

She turns voiceless to the old Wizard, who scrambles to join her on the summit of the pitch.

He stares as she stares, trying to comprehend ...

The mountain wind tousles his beard and hair, twisting and wagging its iron-grey tails.

"The Consult," he murmurs from her side, his voice thin with dread. "The Consult did this."

What was going on?

"This was where they pitched the fallen ..." he continues.

In her soul's eye she sees Ishuäl as it must have been: cold walls climbing from vast heaps of dead. But even as the image rises, she dismisses it as impossible. They found no bones among the ruined fortifications, which suggests the walls were destroyed *before* any mass assault.

She looks at him sharply. "And the battle?" Even as she speaks, her fingers are working to release the pouch from her belt ...

Qirri ... Yes-yes.

The Wizard glances toward the great pit, shrugs without sincerity.

"Beneath our feet."

She has the premonition of rotted ground, and a dread fills her. The ruined fortress merely barks the surface, she realizes. The tracts buried beneath are riddled with far-flung veins and hollows, like termite-infested wood.

The hole runs deep, she realizes. Cil-Aujas deep.

A shudder rocks her balance from her. She stumbles, catches herself.

"Ishuäl ..." she begins, only to trail in indecision.

"Is but the *gate*," the old Wizard says, his eagerness outrunning his apprehension.

She turns to him with a beseeching look, but he is already clambering back the way he came, his eyes bright with rekindled hope.

"Of course ..." he mutters. "Of course! This is a *Dûnyain* stronghold!"

"So?" she calls down, standing welded upon the heaped rubble.

"So nothing is what it appears to be! *Nothing*!"

Of course.

Within heartbeats he has rounded the wreckage and found his way back to the pit's black maw. He pauses, looks up to her both frowning and squinting. The ruins radiate out about them, buzzing in the sunlight. They gaze at each other across the interval, exchanging unasked questions.

At last his eyes click to her waist, where her right hand pensively fingers the pouch.

"Yes-yes," he says roughly. "Of course."

⸻

Renewed, they creep into the darkness together.

She can still feel the panic, cold enough to prick, but her thoughts have become woolen with relief, as if she has found leisure at the end of some arduous task. The Qirri is forever dredging up inappropriate passions, it seems, moving her soul at angles to her circumstances. The tunnels they plumb are entirely unlike the ancient obsidian marvels they explored in Cil-Aujas, but they are the same nonetheless. Halls that flee the sun. Chutes into blackness. Graves.

And despite her terror, she finds that she does not care.

Blessed be the Nonman King ... his residue ...

They descend at a shallow angle. The old Wizard's Surillic Point bleaches their surroundings with white detail. Detritus and scabbed ruin clot the floor. The walls are so scored she cannot but glimpse the shrieking legions of Sranc that had once trod them. Otherwise, the stonework is both meticulous and devoid of ornamentation.

They slip deeper into the earth, a bead of white in dungeon blackness. The air remains rank, the odour of dead things mouldering, rot drained to the dregs. Neither of them speak. The same questions move their souls, ones that only the black depths can answer. To speculate aloud, it seems, would be to waste precious wind. Who knew what air dwelt below? What foulness?

The light soundlessly shoulders away the dark, revealing a pocked and blasted region a cavity where everything tingles with sorcerous residue. Some kind of gate, she realizes, glimpsing the mangle that had once been an iron portal. They had happened upon an underworld bastion of some kind.

"They brought the ceilings down ..." the old Wizard says, his eyes probing the cragged hollows above them. "All this has been excavated."

"What do you think happened?"

"The Dûnyain," he says, speaking in the airy way of someone describing images drawn from the Soul's eye. "They fled the walls above when they realized they were overmatched. They sealed themselves in the tunnels below. I'm guessing they brought the ceilings down when the Consult assaulted this gate."

Her eyes roam the pitted surfaces, confirming.

"To no avail," she says.

A grim, beard-crushing nod. "To no avail."

The tunnels complicate beyond the destroyed gate, chambers like nodes, opening onto further corridors. Mimara finds her earlier presentiment of immensity confirmed. Somehow she just knows that the tunnels go on and on, forking and twining, veining the mountain foundations with complexity and confusion. Somehow she knows they have been designed to defeat comprehension as much as courage ...

That they stand at the threshold of a labyrinth.

"We must mark our way," she tells the old Wizard.

He glances at her, frowning.

"This place is Dûnyain," she explains.

They wander across littered floors, a bead of illumination bumping and shuffling through the black. An aging Wizard and a pregnant woman.

Cil-Aujas howls from some deep pit in her memory, rendering the silence that much more palpable, enough to squeeze her chest, freight her limbs. And it strikes her that she never truly surfaced, that the long mad flight through the Mop and across the Istyuli were but a different underworld, the endless skies a different ground, as crushing as any mountain. She tries guessing at the function of the chambers they pass through, recess after recess, walls scorched, floors chapped with desiccated gore. The spaces yield to the relentless light, lines firm and straight, reaching out with geometric perfection. Most are blasted, their contents stamped to ruin, kicked into corners. But one possesses iron racks, some kind of restraints for human forms, arranged in a radial arc. Another appears to be some kind of kitchen.

The Wizard marks every room with the charcoal nub of an abandoned torch. Crude chevrons tipped on their side, always pointing to the obscurity before them.

They pass through several more chambers, breathing cobweb-air. They clamber down a half-ruined stairwell, enter the throat of what seems a long corridor. Fragments of bone and debris gravel the floors.

She tries to imagine the Dûnyain. She has heard tales of her stepfather's martial skill, how it dwarfed even that of the skin-spies, so she sees *Soma* in her soul's eye, only in Dûnyain guise, battling through Sranc and blackness, his sword sketching impossible figures in the screeching dark. When the images fade she falls to pondering Koll, the final face worn by the thing called Soma, and the madness of Sauglish.

She wonders that a Consult abomination would save her.

"Nothing ..." the old Wizard murmurs beside her.

She turns to him with a curiosity she feels only with her face.

"No ornament," he explains, running a knobbed hand across the wall nearest to him. "No symbol. Nothing ..."

She looks to the walls and ceiling, feels the surprise of considering things noticed but not pondered. The sorcerous light is crowded and bright about them, darkening in stages as her eyes stray into the near distance. Everything is bare and ... perfect. Only the random marks of conflict score them—the mad quill of discord.

The contrast unnerves her. The descent into Cil-Aujas had been a descent into chaotic meaning, as if strife and loss and *story* had composed the heart of the mountain.

There is no story here. No reminders. No hopes or regrets or vain declarations.

Only blank assertion. The penetration of density by mazed space.

And she realizes ...

They explore the bowel of a far different mansion. One less human.

Ishuäl.

Even before they enter, it seems that she *knows* this room. She—a child of the brothel.

It lies waiting, a square of pure black at the end of the corridor. The absence of resistance surprises her as she steps across the threshold, as if the hairs on her arms and cheeks had warned her of some invisible membrane.

The point of light slides effortlessly before them, gouging deep hollows from the blackness. They both stand breathing and staring. The ceiling is so low and broad as to seem a different floor. What seem to be lidless sarcophagi line the arc of the walls, dozens of large pedestals hewn from living rock, receding into the deeper gloom. But where the buried dead are typically lain with ankles bound, foot-to-foot, these sarcophagi flare outward: pinning their occupants spread-eagled, providing a space between ...

A place.

She swallows against a nail in the back of her throat. Stepping across a shattered sword, she approaches the nearest pedestal to her right. Bones and dust, dimpled and ragged like sheets of rotted skin, crowd the interior. Jawless skulls tipped on their sides. Ribs like halved hoops, implying torsos far broader than her embrace. Femurs like clubs, still threading the iron straps that had once restrained them. Pelvises, rising like antlers from the detritus ...

Whale bones she finds herself thinking ...

Once, during her second year in the brothel, an Ainoni caste-noble named Mipharses had fallen in love with her—at least as much as any man could fall in love with a child-whore. He would lease her for days at a time, long enough for her to dare dream—despite the suffocating misery of his bed—of escaping the brothel and becoming a wife. Once he took her down the River Sayut on his pleasure barge, through the idyllic channels of the delta, to a cove filled with what he called Narwhales, fish that were not fish, white and ghostly beneath the lucid distortions of the surface. She had been frightened and enthralled in equal measure: the beasts periodically blasted from the surface, where they would seem to hang in an armless twist before crashing back into the window blue.

"This is where they come to mate," Mipharses said, pressing as much as holding her to his lap. "And die ..." he added, pointing to a swale of beach beneath the overgrown shore.

And there she saw the carcasses, some bloated and blackened like sausages, others little more than bones cast up like flotsam in a storm.

Bones like these bones.

"Does the Sea pitch them up after?" she had asked. She never fails to cringe when she recalls the tenderness of her look and manner during these years. She never fails to curse her mother.

"The Sea?" Mipharses had replied, smiling the way some men are prone when sharing vicious truths with coddled women. She would never forget the way his yellow teeth contradicted the ludicrous perfection of his oiled and pleated beard. "No. They swim here to die ... Beasts can sense their ending, little dear. That is what makes them nobler than Men."

And looking at him she had agreed. Far nobler.

She hears the Wizard's boots scuff the floor behind her.

"What is this place?" he calls with a kind of querulous wonder.

A tingling horror stops her reply.

"These bones ..." he continues. "Other than the skulls, they aren't ... *human*."

The very air sparks. It seems that she sways, even though she stands as rigid as a shriving pole.

"Yes," she hears herself say. "They *are* ..."

As human as the Dûnyain could be.

In the war of light and shadow that is her periphery, she glimpses the old Wizard gazing at her in numb alarm.

She turns her back to him, cradles her abdomen in her hands.

The Eye opens ...

A dizzying moment. Vision wars against vision, one world crisp with edge and grit, the other milky with warring angles, the budding of things long hidden ...

And she sees it, *Judgment*, implacable and absolute, bleeding like dye through the sack-cloth of the mundane. She sees it, the world become a jurist's scroll, and she cannot but read ...

Damnation.

The shattered sword near the entrance: she sees the progression of hands that once clasped the pommel, the parting flesh, the plunging point, the mewling screams of its soulless victims, the glittering perfection of the lines it once sketched through pockets of subterranean gloom.

An invisible palm presses her cheek, forces her gaze across what she does not want to see ...

The torment of the Whale-mothers.

Between women and men, women possess the lesser soul. Whenever the Eye opens, she glimpses the *fact* of this, the demand that women yield to the requirements of men, so long as those demands be righteous. To bear sons. To lower her gaze. To provide succor. The place of the woman *is to give*. So it has always been, since Omrain first climbed nude from the dust and bathed in the wind. Since Esmenet made herself a crutch for stern Angeshraël.

But the horror the Eye reveals before her ...

The insect obscenity of their innocent forms. Bulbous, their flesh little more than quivering cages. Women bred into monstrous instruments of procreation, until they had become little more than pouches slung about their wombs.

The misery. The huffing and moaning. The mewling screams. The inhuman men filing to their assignations, utterly heartless and insensate. The slapping of hip and genitalia. The animality of coupling stripped to its essential germ, to the milking pitch of insemination ...

Sadism without desire. Cruelty—unimaginable cruelty—absent the least will to inflict suffering.

An evil that only the Inchoroi could surpass.

And when her gaze flinches, she sees that this crime is no aberration, but rather an inevitable and extreme implication of what rules the whole. Everywhere she looks she sees it with heart-scratching clarity, rising like bruises beneath the world's tender skin. Craft. Cunning. The devious pitch of intellect, domineering, devoid of compassion or humility ...

And the *will*—the blasphemous will most of all. The deranged hunger *to become God.*

She begins trembling. "Akka ..." she hears herself gasp. "You-y-you ..." She trails to recover her voice and her spit. Tears flood her cheeks.

"*You were right.*"

Even as she says this a part of her balks—the part that knows how desperately he has yearned to hear these words ...

The Holy cares nothing for the designs of Men. And their appetites, it denies outright. The Holy, at all turns, demand the *sacrifice of mortal projects*, the carrying of burdens that slow, even kill. The Holy was the path of detours, even dead ends. The road that punished for following.

"What are you saying?" the old Wizard croaks.

She blinks, then blinks again, but the Eye refuses to close. She sees rolling heads, masticating mouths. The Whale-mothers, tongueless and screaming ... The lean men arched like shitting dogs.

She sees the unspeakable evil that is the Shortest Path.

"This place ... The Dûnyain ... Th-they ... *They are evil* ..."

She turns to him, glimpses the horror rising behind his charred face.

"You-you ..." he begins in a thin voice. "You *see* this wi—?"

A roaring crashes through her, a thunder beyond the reach of her ears. Her edges blacken, pursue her inward. Sensation shrinks ... then blooms in proportions titanic and absurd. Suddenly *she sees Him*, her stepfather,

Anasûrimbor Kellhus I, the Holy Aspect-Emperor, high on his throne, wreathed in darkness and fury, a malignant cancer cast across the far corners of the world ...

Doom incarnate.

Suddenly she sees the *Truth* of the old Wizard's terror. A Dûnyain ruled the World—a *Dûnyain!*

She reels as if struck, so sudden, so absolute is the inversion of her understanding. Her Sheära corselet, which has always amazed her for its arcane weightlessness, suddenly drags as iron upon her shoulders.

For so long Momemn has been the luminous summit, the hub that ferried light to the more shadowy extremities of the Empire. Despite her hatred, it has always seemed both the source and the rule—for it is ever the want of the heart to make *home* its measure of measures. But now it *pulsed* with dread implication, glutinous with foul blackness, a leprous counterpoint to Golgotterath, another stain blotting the world's mapped places.

"My mother!" she cries, seeing her flicker like a candle flame beneath the rising night. "Akka! We have to find her! *Warn her!*"

The old Wizard stands gaping, astounded—as well as blasted with the wages of his damnation in the Eye. Everywhere, all around them, torment and perdition, radiating like stones kicked from the Fire. Has the entire world been consigned to Hell?

She tries to blink away the Eye—to no avail. She finds herself fumbling with her own urgency, so long has it been since anything abstract has pierced the Qirri's numbing swaddle.

The Wizard was right. The *very World* ... The World already hangs from the gibbet ...

One final swing and its neck is broken.

"Wha-what?" the damned soul before her stammers. "What are you *saying?*"

Then the Eye closes, and the judgment of things is rinsed into the outlines of vision, into nonexistence. The facts of Drusas Achamian blot the value, and she sees him bewildered, bent with age, cracked by a life of sorcerous insurrection. He holds her by the shoulders, close despite the proximity of her Chorae to his breast. Tears glaze his rutted cheeks.

"The Eye ..." she gasps.

"Yes? *Yes?*"

Then she glimpses it over his frayed shoulder.

A shadow flitting between stacked debris. Pale. Small.

A Sranc?

She hisses in alarm. The old Wizard looks about frowning, his eyebrows pulled into a shaggy stoop above his gaze.

"There ..." she whispers, pointing toward a slot between the bone-laden sarcophagi.

The old Wizard peers into the anxious gloom. With a flourish of his fingers he throws his Surillic Point into the chamber's deeper regions. She leans against the vertigo of sweeping shadows.

They both glimpse the figure, their hearts pounding to the same terror. They see the eyes glitter, the face squint with blank wonder.

Not a Sranc.

A boy ... A boy with his head shaved in mockery of Nil'giccas.

"*Hiera?*" he calls, as if utterly unperturbed by his discovery. "*Slaus ta heira'as?*"

It torqued the old Wizard's ears, so long had it been since he last heard the tongue outside his Dreams.

"Where?" the boy had asked. "Where is your lantern?"

Achamian even recognized the peculiar intonation—though from twenty, as opposed to two thousand, years past. The child spoke *Kûniüric* ... but not in the ancient way, the way Anasûrimbor Kellhus had spoken it so long ago.

The child was Dûnyain.

Achamian swallowed. "C-come out," he called, straining to speak about the bolt of horror and confusion in his throat. "You have nothing to fear from us."

The child stood from his feckless crouch, stepped from behind the sarcophagus that obscured him. He wore a man's woolen tunic, the grey fabric belted and cinched to fit. He was slender, and from the look of him, tall beyond his years. He gazed avidly at the Surillic Point above, held out his hands as though testing the light for raindrops. Three fingers had been lopped from his right hand, making a crab's claw of his thumb and forefinger.

He turned to appraise the two interlopers.

"You speak our tongue," he said mildly.

Achamian stood rigid, unblinking.

"No, child. You speak *my* tongue."

Sit. This is the imperative of old men when the World besieges them. Retire from the confusion, consider it in dribs and drabs rather than grapple with it whole. Sit. Recover your wind while pondering.

Mimara had found his dread answer. In the space of heartbeats she had confirmed a *lifetime* of fears. But witless incomprehension seemed the most he could summon by way of reply. Stammering indecision where horror and dismay should have ruled.

This boy represented a different kind of confirmation—and conundrum.

So while Mimara remained rooted to where she stood, Achamian took a seat on a block of ruin, a perch that set his face a hand's span below that of the standing child.

"You are Dûnyain?"

The boy seemed to search his gaze. "Yes."

"How many of you remain?"

"Just me and one other. The Survivor."

"And where is he?"

"Somewhere in the Halls beneath us."

The floor now tingled beneath the old Wizard's boots.

"Tell me ... What happened here?"

Achamian asked this even though he *knew* what had happened here, even though he could reconstruct its stages in his soul's eye. But for the nonce he was old and he was terrified, and there was courage in the asking of questions—or at least the semblance of it.

"The Shriekers came," the boy replied, his manner mild unto blank. "I was too young to remember ... much ..."

"So how do you know?"

"The Survivor told me."

The old Wizard pursed his lips. "Tell us what he told you."

There is always a dare in the eye of bold children, an arrogance that comes with lacking the weakness of more worried elders. The crab-handed boy's fearlessness, however, was devoid of demonstration.

"They came and they came, until the whole valley seethed. The Shriekers threw themselves at our walls, and the slaughter was great. We heaped their corpses to the battlements. We threw them back!"

Mimara watched from his periphery, not comprehending, but from the keen cast of her gaze, understanding all the same. So little separates tales of woe.

"Then the *Singers* came," the boy continued, "walking across empty air, shouting in voices that made lanterns of their mouths. They pulled down the walls and the bastions, and the surviving brethren withdrew into the Thousand Thousand Halls ... They could not contend with the Singers."

The "Shriekers"were obviously Sranc. The "Singers," Achamian realized, had to be Nonmen Quya, Erratics who had turned to the Consult in the pursuit of murder and memory. He could see the battle unfold as the boy spoke: mad Quya, screaming light and fury as they walked over the high pines, endless mobs of Sranc surging below. It seemed mad and strange and tragic, that such a war could be waged so far from the knowledge of Men. It did not seem possible that so many unknown souls could die unknown deaths.

Without sorcery or Chorae, the Dûnyain, for all their preternatural ability, were helpless before the Erratics. So they fled into the labyrinth they had spent one hundred generations preparing, made a citadel of what the boy called the "Thousand Thousand Halls." The Quya pursued them, he said, crashing through barricades, flooding the corridors with killing lights. But the brethren simply fell back and back, retreating ever deeper into the complexities of the maze.

"For all their might," the boy continued in his monotone drawl, "the Singers were easily confused. They lost their way, wandered howling. Some perished for thirst. Others went mad, and brought the ceilings down upon themselves in their desperation to escape ..."

It seemed Achamian could feel them, ancient lives ending in blindness and suffocation ...

Explosions in the deep.

His diction flawless, the boy explained how the invaders mustered legion after legion of Sranc, poured them into the labyrinth, crazed and screaming, the way yeomen might try to drown rodents in their burrows.

"We lured them deep," he said, his voice utterly devoid of the passions and hesitations that belong to childhood. "Left them to starve and thirst.

We killed and we killed, but it was never enough. There was always more of them. Shrieking. Snarling ..."

"We fought them for years."

The Consult had made a screaming cistern of the Thousand Thousand Halls, filled the labyrinth until it could hold no more, and death spilled over. The boy could actually remember the latter stages of the underworld siege; corridors packed with listless and dying Sranc, where the brethren need only step and spear to move on; chutes and stairwells choked with carcasses; the flights and the assaults, wave after endless wave, ferocious and unrelenting, so much so that brother after brother would finally falter and succumb.

"And so we perished one by one."

The old Wizard nodded in sympathy he knew the boy did not need.

"Everyone except you and the Survivor ..."

The boy nodded.

"The Survivor carried me in," he said. "The Survivor walked me out. The Logos has always burned brightest within him. None among the brethren stood so close to the Absolute as he."

Mimara had stood rooted this whole time, her face blank, alternately studying the boy and peering out into the surrounding gloom.

"Akka ..." she finally murmured, staring into the dark.

"And what is his name?" Achamian asked, ignoring her. The boy's description of the Survivor troubled him for some reason.

"Anasûrimbor," the boy replied. "Anasûrimbor Koringhus."

This name seized Mimara's attention as violently as it seized the old Wizard's heart.

"Akka!" she fairly shouted.

"What is it?" he asked dully, his wits addled by stacking implications. Ishuäl destroyed. The Dûnyain evil. And now ... *another* Anasûrimbor?

"He *distracts* you!" she cried in a strangely hooded voice.

"What?" he asked, leaping to his feet. "What are you saying?"

Her eyes pinned wide with fear, she pointed into the blackness draping the depths of the chamber before them. "Someone watches us!"

The old Wizard squinted, but could see nothing.

"Yes," the boy said at his elbow, though there was no way he could have understood Mimara's Sheyic. How had he let the child come so close?

Close enough to strike ...

"The Survivor has come."

Hope dwindles.

Yesterday, Achamian had been but a son cringing beneath his father's angry shadow. Yesterday, he had been a child sobbing in a mother's anxious arms, looking into her eyes and seeing love—and helplessness. To be a weak child—cursed with an eye for the impractical, for the profound and the beautiful. To continually remind your father of what he despised in himself. To be a surrogate for paternal self-loathing.

Yesterday, he had been a Schoolman, begging and conniving, awakening to find himself strangled, his eyes clotted with two thousand years of grief. Yesterday, he had been the husband of a whore, loving against the pitch of circumstance and fanatical horror. To be a weak man, cursed with convictions that others could scarcely conceive, let alone consider. To be a laughingstock, a cuckold, counted treacherous among your brothers.

Yesterday, he had been a Wizard, measuring days with his resentments and ruminations, scrawling errant messages that not even fools would read. Yesterday, he had been a mad hermit, a prophet in the wilderness, lacking the heart to act on his own mad declarations. To have a question that was at once a hatred... To have a love that was at once a loss ... and a cry for vengeance.

Yesterday, he had beheld Ishuäl.

The intruder's shadow strode toward them, gathering substance and detail with every step.

Never had he felt so defeated ... so old.

Too much ...

The crab-handed boy lingered close enough to murder.

Too much ...

His own wind rattled the cage of his lungs, bolted for escape.

The light seemed to seize the figure, hoist his terrifying visage from the gloom of the Thousand Thousand Halls. But he did not surface *as he should* according to swales of smooth skin and muscle. Illumination tripped across ridges of braided tissue, edged the crater of a missing cheek, gleamed across exposed gums and the remnants of teeth. Shadow inked innumerable hooks and gouges, the knotted scribble of children who had more time than papyrus.

The spoor of a thousand mortal battles, of a Dûnyain in extremis, pursuing the intangible lines of survival and triumph through countless threshing swords, playing the margins of his own flesh, ignoring all but the most lethal incisions, so that he might kill and kill and *overcome* ... Endure.

They are evil ... So said the Eye.

The Survivor was a grotesquery. Even still Achamian could *see* through the skein of hideous scarring: the lineage, the bones and *blood* of antique Kings.

"You know my father," the Dûnyain said, his voice as deep and melodious as Truth. "Anasûrimbor Kellhus ..."

Drusas Achamian retreated, his limbs moving without his volition. He stumbled, literally crashed onto his rump.

"Tell me ..." the grotesquerie said.

Yesterday, the old Wizard had sought to deliver the World from destruction.

"Has he grasped the Absolute?"

CHAPTER SIX

Momemn

And there did a Narindar find him and kill him, pricking him with a poison needle behind the ear. Word passed throughout the Empire, and the multitudes were filled with wonder that an Aspect-Emperor could be sorted in his own garden. Within a fortnight, foul assassination had become manifest prophecy, and no action was taken against the Cult of the Four-Horned Brother. All the World wished the matter forgotten.

—*The Annals of Cenei*, CASIDAS

It is said of the Nansur that they fear their fathers, love their mothers, and trust their siblings, but only so far as they fear their fathers.

The Ten Thousand Day Dynasty, HOMIRRAS

Early Autumn, 20 New Imperial Year (4132, Year-of-the-Tusk), Momemn

"*Noooo* ..." the Padirajah howled.

Malowebi stood staring across the cluttered gloom of the grand pavilion, stranded three steps inside its threshold by protocol. Fanayal stood at his own bedside, staring down at the death throes of his Cishaurim, Meppa—or as his people knew him, Stonebreaker. The Padirajah, who had always seemed lean and youthful, now seemed fatted with his fifty-plus years. Psatma Nannaferi lounged upon a brocaded settee nearby, her dark eyes glittering like quicksilver on the gloom's phantom verge. Her gaze never left the ailing Padirajah, who held his face turned from her—deliberately it seemed. She watched and watched, her expression one of genuine expectancy and sly contempt, as though she awaited an adored part of a well-rehearsed tale, one featuring the villain she most despised. It almost made her seem as youthful as she should seem.

Gleaming edges and surfaces cluttered the encircling shadows, glimpses of plunder, the Padirajah's share of Iothiah. Fired pottery. Heaps of clothing. Brocaded furnishings. From where the Mbimayu Schoolman stood, the scene almost seemed cobbled from these fragments, debris bricked into Creation ...

The stage where the fabled Fanayal ab Kascamandri reckoned his doom.

"Nooo!" he cried to the prostrate form. The Twin Scimitars of Fanimry, the gold-on-black banner of his nation and faith, had been kicked across the floor, and now lay neglected beneath his feet, one more looted carpet. The White Horse on Gold, the famed Coyauri flag that Fanayal used as his personal standard yet hung, but scorched and tattered for the very battle that had laid Meppa low ...

Malowebi had already overheard Fanayal's wild desert warriors murmuring and arguing amongst themselves. The Whore Empress had done this, they said. Kucifra's *woman* had struck the Last Cishaurim down ...

"What will they say?" the Yatwerian witch cooed, still watching him from her settee. "How far can you trust them?"

"Bridle your tongue," Fanayal murmured. He leaned as if hung from hooks, peering at his fallen Cishaurim. The Padirajah had wagered *everything* on the man that lay dying on his silk sheets below—every favour his God had afforded him.

The only real question now was what happened next.

Malowebi had known men like Fanayal in Zeum, souls that leaned more on things *unseen* than seen, that made idols of their ignorance so they might better strut and proclaim whatever court trifle they happened to covet unto obsession. From the very beginning of the man's insurrection—for more than twenty years!—Fanayal ab Kascamandri had cast himself opposite Anasûrimbor Kellhus. Men cannot but measure themselves against their enemies, and the Aspect-Emperor was nothing if not ... formidable. So Fanayal had styled himself the *holy antagonist*, the Chosen Hero, fated to slay dread Kucifra, the-Light-that-Blinds, the Demon who had broken the back of his faith and his race. He had set himself a task that only the alarming power of his Waterbearer could complete.

Despite his vanity, the eldest son of Kascamandri truly was an inspired leader—of that Malowebi had no doubt. But it was Meppa who had been the *miracle*, the Second Negotiant realized. The Last Cishaurim. Short of him, Fanayal and his desert horsemen could scarcely do more than hurl insults at the cyclopean walls of their Imperial Zaudunyani foes. *Meppa* had been the one to conquer Iothiah, not Fanayal. The bellicose son of Kascamandri had sacked a defenceless city, no more.

Without Meppa, Fanayal had no hope of overcoming the Imperial Capital. And so he found himself trapped in a contradiction of fact and ambition. Momemn's monstrous black walls were all but impregnable. He could tarry, but there was no way to starve a coastal city into submission. Meanwhile, the countryside became ever more resolved against him. For all their grievances, the Nansur had not forgotten their generational hatred of the Kianene. Simply feeding his motley army was becoming ever more difficult, ever more bloody. Desertions, especially among the Khirgwi, were all but inevitable. Even as the Empress mustered and redeployed Columns, the Fanim army was sure to dwindle. Perhaps Fanayal could prevail in an open contest with an Imperial Zaudunyani army. Meppa's sacrifice had killed the formidable Caxes Anthirul, at least; perhaps some fool would lead the Imperials in the Home Exalt-General's stead. Perhaps the Bandit Padirajah could, with the dregs of his long-hunted desert people, conjure one of those miraculous victories that had been the glory of his ancestors ...

But to what end, if the great cities of the Nansurium remained closed to him?

The circumstances could not be more dire, and yet Malowebi fairly cackled for pondering them. The usefulness of the Fanim only extended as far as their ability to challenge the Empire. Short of Meppa, then, High Holy Zeum *had no use for Fanayal ab Kascamandri.*

Short of Meppa, Malowebi could go *home.*

He was free. He had waited upon this growing cancer long enough. Time to forget these pompous and pathetic sausages—to begin plotting his revenge on Likaro!

"Your Grandees think you *daring* ..." Psatma Nannaferi crooned. She reclined with opiate indifference across the settee, wearing a silk shift that clothed her alluring nethers in shadow, nothing more. "But *now* they see."

Fanayal wiped a callused hand across the mud of his expression.

"*Shut up*!"

A screech that blooded throats, pimpled skin ... and promised mayhem.

The Yatwerian witch growled in laughter.

Yes ... Malowebi silently resolved. *Time to leave*.

The Dread Mother was here!

But he stood transfixed. The pavilion threshold lay no more than three paces behind him—he was fairly certain he could slip out without notice. Men like Fanayal rarely forgave those insolent enough to witness their weakness and hypocrisy. But they were also prone to punish the merest slights as mortal transgressions. As the son of a cruel father, Malowebi knew well how to be at once present and invisible.

"*Yesss* ..." the Yatwerian witch cooed with lolling contempt. "The White-Luck conceals so very many things ... so many *frailties* ..."

She was right. Now that the number-sticks had finally betrayed him, what had seemed inspired audacity, even providence, stood revealed as recklessness. But why would she say such a thing? Why speak any truth at all, when it could only be provocation?

But this was the problem with all matters entangled in the machinations of the Hundred: the *advantage* was never to be seen.

Only madness.

Yes! Time to leave.

He could use his Cants to fold himself into the night, begin the long trek ho—

"*Idolatrous whore*!" Fanayal screamed, showering Meppa's inert form with spittle. It betrayed the profundity of his horror, Malowebi realized, the way he chose to rage at the empty space before him rather than face the malevolent temptress. "This is *your* doing! Witch! The Solitary God rebukes me! Punishes me for taking you into my bed!"

Malowebi started for the contradiction of seething fertility and stringy, old crone laughter. Even in the shadowy confines of Fanayal's pavilion, she seemed *illuminated*, a thing drawn out of chill waters, raw, tasteless for being ... so *clean*.

"Then *burn* me!" she cried. "The Fanim share that custom with the Inrithi at least! Forever burning *those who Give*!"

Padirajah finally whirled, his face twisted. "Fire is merely how it *ends*, witch! First I cast you as a rag to my warriors, let them rut and stamp your sex into mud! *Then* I hoist you high above the bramble flame, watch you writhe and shriek! burst into a beacon warning of all that is foul and wicked!"

The old woman's laugh became silent.

"Yes!" she croaked. "Give ... me ... all ... their ... seed! All their *fury* bound to the Mother's pitiless womb! Let your *entire nation* lean hard upon me! Groan as grinning dogs! Let them know me as *you* have known me!"

The Padirajah lunged toward her, only to be hung from his wrists, held as if leashed to opposite corners of the pavilion. He craned his head about, crying out, groaning. At long last his wide, palpating eyes found Malowebi where he stood riven between shadows. For a moment, the Padirajah seemed to *implore* him—but for things too great for any man to bodily yield.

The look slipped into oblivion. Fanayal collapsed to his knees before the vile seductress.

Psatma Nannaferi wailed her amusement. The nails of her darkling look scratched the Mbimayu Schoolman's image—for the merest instant only, but it was enough, enough for him to glimpse the crimson filigree of *veins*, the uterine webs she had sunk as roots into the Reality surrounding.

Flee! Run you old idiot!

But he already understood that it was too late.

"*Share* me!" she shrieked. "Burn meeee! Do it!" A sound like a dog's growl, close enough to send the Zeumi's skin crawling against his foul robes. "*Do it!* And watch your precious Snakehead *die*!"

Ice ached in the craw of his bones. Malowebi understood the truth of her infernal hilarity—and the truth of everything that had transpired with it. The Dread Mother *had been among them all along*. That fateful day in Iothiah, *they* had been delivered to Psatma Nannaferi, not vice versa.

The time to flee had itself fled long ago.

"What are you saying?" Fanayal asked, his face bereft of dignity, his knees wide across the carpets.

"The black blasphemer knows!" she chortled, throwing her chin in Malowebi's direction.

Curse Likaro!

"Tell *me*!" the Padirajah cried, all the more pathetic for attempting to sound imperious.

A black-hearted smirk.

"*Yeeeessss*. Your every ambition, the whole pathetic empire of your conceit, is bound to me, Son of Kascamandri. What you take from me, you cut from yourself. What you gift to me, you gift to yourself ..." Her eyes roamed the shadowy spaces about them. "And," she said, her voice dropping to a croak, "to your *Mother* ..."

"But can you save him?" Fanayal cried.

A teasing laugh, as though from a girl smitten by a lover's foibles.

"Of course," she said, leaning forward to caress his swollen cheek. "My God *exists* ..."

Malowebi *had* fled that night—eventually.

He watched her bid Fanayal reach two fingers between her thighs. His breath abandoned him. His very heartbeat became entangled on the rapturous violence of her reaction ...

He watched the Padirajah withdraw his fingers, stare in abject horror at the blood clotted upon them. Psatma Nannaferi curled as a pampered cat upon the settee, her eyes drowsy.

"*Press it into his wound* ..." she said on a languorous breath. Her eyes were already closed.

Give.

Fanayal stood as a man precarious upon a mountain's summit, unsteady, astounded, then he turned to the Last Cishaurim.

And Malowebi fled, his gown stained about the thighs. He fairly flew across the encampment, slinking through shadows, cringing from all for shame. In the safety of his tent he tore off all his elaborate accoutrements, stood shivering and naked in his own stink. He would not remember falling asleep.

When he awoke, he found his index and forefinger stained cherry red.

He was no fool. As little as he knew about the Dread Mother of Birth, he knew well enough what perils lay ahead. He was what his people called "wairo", snared by the Gods. According to the Kûburû, the most ancient lore of his people, the calamity of wairo lay in the caprice of the Hundred. But the Mbimayu had a more nuanced and therefore more frightening explanation. Where Men had to forever toil, forever accumulate the wages of their labour to hope for their descendant's prayers, the Gods stood outside the very possibility of *individual acts*. The substance of their limbs was nothing other than the *passage of events themselves*. They gripped and steered the World through bounty, yes, but through *catastrophe* far more. Wars. Famines. Earthquakes. Floods.

These were their Hands, both holy and terrible.

Which was why those judged wairo were often driven into the wild. When he was but nine, Malowebi had found a dead woman curled about the base of a great cypress on his grandfather's estate. Her rot had dried—the Parch had been hard that year—but her ligaments yet held and this, with her clothing, lent her a horrific substance. Weeds surged about her edges, as well as places in-between. His grandfather refused to have her moved when he showed him. "*No animal has touched her*," he had said, his eyes wide with urgent wisdom. "*She is wairo*."

And now he himself was wairo ... accursed.

So if he returned uninvited to the Padirajah's grand pavilion, it was because he had never left ...

Days had passed. Meppa was on the mend. Fanayal had emerged unscathed from that monstrous night—at least as much as he. Malowebi had all but hidden in his tent, wracking his soul for some kind of solution, cursing both the Whore of Fate and Likaro—the latter far, far more than the former. Likaro's posturing, Likaro's fawning, and most of all Likaro's *deceit*—these had brought this calamity down upon him!

But such wounds could be picked for only so long before bandages had to be sought. He was a Disciple of Memgowa; he knew any hope of remedy required the very thing he was missing: *knowledge*. And as the Whore would have it, the only source of that knowledge was the very source of his peril: Psatma Nannaferi. Only *she* could tell him what happened. Only she could tell him what he needed to *give* ...

Gaining access to Fanayal's pavilion was easy enough: no one guarded it anymore.

And *she* lay within it always, like some kind of holy spider.

Malowebi had always been of the boldest of his brothers, the first to leap into cold or uncertain waters. The way he reckoned, he could die witless like that wairo he found as a boy, or he could die knowing what ensnared him, and most importantly, whether there were any terms of escape. And so on a diver's breath he struck from his tent and made toward the Padirajic standard, the Twin Scimitars on Black, hanging motionless above the intervening pavilions. "Die knowing," he muttered to himself, as if still not entirely convinced. He paused on a start, waited out a flurry of some fifty dusty riders. The hillside obscured Momemn, though the toil and incomplete siege towers strung along the heights made the Imperial Capital's oppressive presence plain. A part of him could scarce believe his embassy had taken him this far—within sight of the Andiamine Heights! It seemed mad to think that the Harlot Empress slumbered mere leagues away.

He imagined delivering Anasûrimbor Esmenet to Nganka'kull in chains, not because he believed it could happen, but because he would much rather imagine Likaro gnashing his teeth than what presently awaited him in the gloom of Fanayal's pavilion. It almost seemed miraculous, the brevity of his trek. Flapping his arms against the dust in the wake of the riders, marching resolutely through the immobility his sudden appearance occasioned in the dozens who glimpsed him, bearing toward the scrolled awning and gold-embroidered flaps ... and then, impossibly, *there he was*, standing precisely where he had stood that night the accursed Waterbearer *should* have died.

The air was stuffy, ripe for the smell of a chamber pot. Sunlight gilded the network of bellied seams above, shedding grey light across the thickets of furniture and baggage. Malowebi spent several heart-pounding moments searching the confusion. Where the great oak bed had commanded the interior that night, it was simply more clutter now. Save for misplaced pillows and twisted sheets, the mattress was empty ... as was the settee next to it ...

Malowebi cursed himself for a fool. Why did Men assume things froze in place when they denied them the grace of their observation?

Then he saw her.

So close that he gasped audibly.

"What do you want, blasphemer?"

She sat no more than four paces to his left, staring into the mirror of a cosmetics table, her back turned against him. He had no clue why he stepped toward her. She could hear him just as well from where he stood.

"How *old* are you?" he blurted.

A smile creased the delicate brown face in the mirror.

"Men do not sow seed in autumn," she said.

Her black hair toppled sumptuous about her shoulders. As always, she dressed to whet rather than blunt desire, naked save gauze wrapped about her hips and a hookless turquoise jacket. To simply lay eyes upon her was to be fondled.

"But ..."

"I loathed the covetous eyes of Men as a child," she said, perhaps watching him through the mirror, perhaps not. "I had *learned*, you see, learned what it was they would take. I would see girls like the one staring at me now, and I would think them nothing more than whipped dogs, creatures beaten until they *craved* the rod ..." She raised a cheek to a waiting pinky, smeared what looked like gold-dust across the outskirts of her plump gaze. "But there's knowing, and there's *knowing*, like all things living. Now I understand how the earth *rises* to the seed. Now I fathom *what is given* when Men take ..."

Her smoky image puckered purple-stained lips.

"And I am *grateful*."

"B-but ..." Malowebi fairly sputtered. "She ... I mean, *She* ..." He paused upon a bolt of terror, recalling his glimpse of *veins* flung sodden across all the visible spaces the night the Last Cishaurim should have died. "The Dread Mother ... *Yatwer* has wrought all this!"

Psatma Nannaferi ceased her ministrations, watched him carefully through the reflection.

"And yet none of you fall to your knees," she said on a coquettish shrug.

She played him the way a dancing girl might, but one who cared nothing for the heft of purses. A bead of sweat slipped from his kinked hair down his temple.

"She has given you the Sight," the Mbimayu sorcerer pressed. "You *know* what will happen ..." He licked his lips, trying hard not to look as terrified as he was. "*Before* it happens."

The Mother-Supreme continued daubing lamp-black across her lids.

"So you *believe*."

Malowebi nodded warily. "Zeum respects the ancient ways. We alone worship the Gods *as they are*."

A grin that could only belong to an old and wicked heart.

"And now you wish to know *your* part in this?"

His heart rapped his breastbone for racing.

"Yes!"

The lamp-black, combined with the ancient age of the mirror, made empty sockets of her eyes. A brown skull watched him now, one graced with a maiden's lips.

"Your doom," the hollow said, "is to *bear witness*."

"B-bear? Witness? You mean *this*? What happens?"

A girlish shrug. "Everything."

"Everything?"

She swivelled about on one buttock to face him, and despite the pace between them, her near nudity pressed sweaty and flat against his yearning, her sable lines became cliffs for the extent of his desire. Never had he so yearned to fall!

The Yatwerian Priestess smiled coyly.

"He will *kill* you, you know."

Horror and compulsion. She emanated the heat of plowed earth in hot sun.

Malowebi fairly sputtered. "Kill-kill *me*? Why?"

"For taking," she said as if cradling candy on her tongue, "what was given."

He stumbled backward, fought her allure as though caught in laundered veils ...

The Emissary of High Holy Zeum fled.

Laughter, like sand scoured against sunburned skin. It nipped all his edges as he bounced hip and shin against the intervening clutter.

"*Witness*!" an old crone shrieked. "*Witnessss*!"

His pulse slowed until beaten by a different heart. His breath deepened until drawn by different lungs. Watching with the constancy of the dead, Anasûrimbor Kelmomas settled into the grooves of another soul ...

If it could be called such.

The man his mother called Issiral stood in the heart of his unlit chamber, watch upon watch, motionless, dark eyes lost in some bleak nowhere. The Prince-Imperial, meanwhile, kept secret vigil above, staring down through the louvres. He lowered his avian vitality to the same deep rung, made his every twitch a noon shadow.

And he waited.

Kelmomas had watched many people through the spyholes of the Apparatory, and their comic diversity had never ceased to surprise him. The lovers, the tedious loners, the weepers, the insufferable grinners: it seemed an endless parade of newfound deformities. Watching them step from their doors to consort with the Imperial Court had been like watching slaves bind brambles into sheaves. Only now could he see how wrong he had been—that this diversity had been apparent only, an illusion of his ignorance. How could he not think Men various and strange when Men were his only measure?

Now the boy knew *better*. Now he knew that every human excess, every bloom of manner or passion, radiated from a single, blind stem. For this man—the assassin that had somehow *surprised* Uncle Holy—had paced out the *true beam* of possible and impossible acts.

And it was not human ...

Not at all.

The spying had started as a game—a mischievous trifle. Mother's guilt and preoccupation assured that Kelmomas had his run of the palace. The vagrant suspicions that darkened her look from time to time meant he could no longer risk tormenting any of the slaves or menials. So what *else* was he supposed to do? Play with dirt and dolls in the Sacral Enclosure? Spying on the Narindar would be his hobby, the boy had decided, a diverting way to squander watches while plotting the murder of his older sister.

The first afternoon had alone convinced him *something* was amiss with the man—something more than the fact of his red-stained earlobes, trim beard, or short-cropped hair. By the second day it had become a game within a game, proving he could match the man's preternatural feats of immobility.

After the third day there was no question of *not spying*.

The matter of his sister had become an open sore by this time. If Theliopa told Mother then ...

Neither of them could bear think what might happen!

Anasûrimbor Theliopa was the threat he simply could not ignore. The Narindar, on the other hand, was nothing less than *his saviour*, the man who had rescued him from his uncle. And yet, day after day, every time opportunity afforded, he found himself prowling the hollow bones of the Andiamine Heights searching for the man, spinning rationale after rationale.

She had not fully fathomed the extent of his intellect, Thelli. She had been witless of her peril, yes. And so long as that remained the case, she had no cause to carry through on her evil threat. Like all idiots, she preferred her cobble deeply grooved. Momemn needed a *strong* Empress, especially now that the Exalt-Cow, Anthirul, was dead. So long as the siege continued, he and his brother should be secure enough ...

Besides, saviour or not, *something was wrong about this man.*

His reasons marshalled, bright before his soul's eye, his hackles would settle, and he would hang as a hidden moon about the planet of this impossible man.

Time would pass, perhaps a watch or so, then some itinerant terror would shout, *Thelli knows*!

He would blink away images of those he had eaten.

Crazed cunt!

He had initially approached the challenge she represented with calm, even *elation*, like a boy set to climb a dangerous yet well-known and beloved tree. He certainly knew the bough and branch of Imperial intrigue well enough. Two of his brothers and his uncle lay dead by his hand—two Princes-Imperial and the Holy Shriah of the Thousand Temples! How much difficulty could a stuttering *skinny* like Anasûrimbor Theliopa pose?

Sranky, Inrilatas used to call her. Inri was the only one who had ever made her cry.

But that elation soon faded into frustration, for Thelli proved no normal tree. She never left Mother's side during daylight—never!—which meant the Inchaustic cloud protecting the Empress protected her as well. And she spent every night without exception barricaded in her apartment ... *Awake* as far he could tell.

But before anything, he had begun to worry about his Strength. The more Kelmomas mulled the events of the previous months, the less he seemed to own them, the more glaring his impotence became. He cringed at the lazy way Inrilatas had toyed with him, humoured him for boredom's sake, or how Uncle Holy had plumbed him to the pith once alerted. The fact was it had been his *uncle* who had killed Inrilatas, not Kelmomas. And how could he claim credit for his uncle's assassination when the actual assassin hung stationary upon the shadows just below?

For all his gifts, the young Prince-Imperial had yet to learn the *disease* that was contemplation, how more often than not it was *ignorance of alternatives* that made bold action bold. He spied upon the Narindar, matching him immobility for immobility, pulling every corner of his being into the straight line that was the assassin's soul—every corner, that is, save his intellect, which asked again and again, *How can I end her?* with the relentlessness of an insect. He lay unblinking, the taste of dust upon his tongue, scarcely breathing, peering between interleaved fronds of iron, raging at his twin, ranting, and even, on occasion, weeping for the unbearable injustice. And so he *spun* within a motionless frame, pondering, until pondering so polluted his pondering he could bear ponder no more!

He would marvel at it afterward, how the mere act of plotting Thelli's murder had all but assured her survival. How all the scenarios, all the spitting disputes and aggrandizing declamations, had been a mere pretext for this eerie war of immobility he had undertaken against the Narindar ... Issiral.

He was all that mattered here, Fanim siege or no Fanim siege. The boy just *knew* this somehow.

After endless watches of blank reverie, utter inactivity, the man would simply ... do something. Piss. Eat. Take ablution, or on occasion, his leave. Kelmomas would lay watching, his body senseless for being so long inert, suddenly the man would ... *move*. It was as shocking as stone leaping to life, for nothing betrayed any prior will or resolution to move, no restlessness, no impatience borne of anticipation ... *nothing*. The Narindar would just be *moving*, exiting the door, stalking the frescoed corridors, and Kelmomas would scramble, cursing his prickling limbs. He would fly after him *through* the very walls ...

And then, for no apparent reason, the assassin would simply ... stop.

It was narcotic for simply being *so strange*. Several days passed before Kelmomas realized that no one ... *no one* ... ever witnessed the man acting this way. In the presence of others he would be remote, taciturn, act the way a terrifying assassin should, always careful to assure the others of his humanity, if nothing more. Several times *it was Mother* who encountered him, coming about a corner, through a door. And no matter what she said, if she said anything at all (for in certain company she would rather not encounter the man at all), he would simply nod wordlessly, then return to his room, and stand ...

Motionless.

Issiral ate. He slept. He shat. His shit stank. The general terror of the slaves was to be expected, as was the hatred of Uncle Holy's many intimates at the Imperial Court. But what was more remarkable still was the degree to which the man went *unnoticed*, how he would sometimes tarry in one spot, unseen, only to inexplicably pace five steps to his left, or his right, where he would stand unseen as a gaggle of scullery slaves passed teasing and whispering.

The enigma soon began to tyrannize the Prince-Imperial's thoughts. He started dreaming of his vigils, reliving the stark discipline that occupied his days, except that when his *body* turned about to slip back in the labyrinthine tunnels, *his soul would somehow remain fixed by the louvres*, and he would simultaneously watch and crawl away, riven by a horror that plucked him to his very vein, the World shrieking as the face in the flint turned and ever so slowly swivelled up to match his incorporeal look—

As the game continued, this became one more thing to fret and dispute in the academy of his skull. Were his dreams warning him of something? Did the Narindar somehow *know* of his observation? If he did, he betrayed absolutely no discernible sign. But then the man betrayed no sign of *anything*.

Watching the man simply whetted the edge of this concern, especially as Kelmomas came to fathom just *how much the assassin knew*. How? How was the man able to so unerringly intercept his mother, to know, not simply where she was going without any communication whatsoever, but the *precise path* she would take?

How could such a thing be possible?

He was *Narindar*, the boy reasoned. A famed Missionary of the evil Four-Horned Brother. Perhaps his knowledge was *divine*. Perhaps that was how he had managed to overcome Uncle Holy!

This sent him to his mother's Librarian, an eccentric Ainoni slave named Nikussis.

Nikussis was a slight, dark-skinned man—every bit as skinny as Theliopa, in fact. Possessed of some murky ability to spy insincerity, he was one of very few worldborn souls who could somehow see past the boy's capering glamour. The man had always treated him with an air of reserved suspicion. During one fit of despair, Kelmomas had actually considered murdering the man for this very reason, and he had never quite relinquished the idea of using him to test various poisons.

"They say one stalks these very halls, my Prince. Why not ask *him*?"

"He refused to tell me," the boy lied glumly.

A squint of approval.

"Yes, that doesn't surprise me."

"He told me the ways of Gods do not answer the ways of Men ..."

Lips like oiled mahogany, pursing into a smile pained for inversion. Disgust never looked so happy.

"Yes-yes ..." Nikussis said with the sonorousness of wisdom correcting youth. "He spoke true."

"And I said the ways of my Father *are* the ways of *the* God."

Fright never looked so delicious.

"And ... ah ..." A half-concealed swallow. "What did he say?"

Terror, the boy had long since realized. Fear was his father's *true* estate, not adoration or abjection or exaltation. Men did what he, little Anasûrimbor Kelmomas, bid them to do out of terror of his father. All the yammer about love and devotion was simply cotton to conceal the razor.

The Librarian hung pale on his response.

"The assassin said, Let your Father ask then."

The eyes of skinny people bulged when they were frightened, he realized watching Nikussis. Would Thelli's eyes bulge? Was she even *capable* of fear?

"So I cried out, '*Sedition*!'"

He screeched this last word, and was gratified by how the old Librarian started—the fool almost kicked the sandals from his feet!

"Wha-wha-what did he say then?" Nikussis stammered.

The young Prince-Imperial shook his head in false incredulity.

"He shrugged."

"Shrugged?"

"Shrugged."

"Well-well it is good then that you came to see me, young Prince."

The famished idiot fairly babbled everything he knew of the Narindar after that. He spoke of great slums of envy and avarice, hatred and malice, how thieves and murderers marred every congregation of Men, souls as wicked as the soul of Anasûrimbor Kelmomas was noble, as polluted as his was pure. "The Tusk says the Gods answer to our every nature, manly or not. There is no Man saved for virtue, no Man damned for sin, save what dwelleth in the Eye of their God. And just as there are wicked healers, so too are there holy murderers ..." He tittered in admiration of his eloquence—and Kelmomas understood instantly why Mother adored him.

"And none are so wicked or so holy as the Narindar."

"And?" the Prince-Imperial asked.

"And?"

"I *already know* all this tripe!" the boy cried, openly wroth. What was wrong with the fool?

"Wha-wha-what would you hav—?"

"Their *power*, you fool! Their *strength*! How is it they can kill the way they kill?"

Every man was a coward—this had been his great lesson hiding in the bones of the Andiamine Heights. Just as every man was a hero. Every sane man conceded something to fear—the only question was one of how much. Some Men begrudged crumbs, rampaged as lions over the merest trifle. But most—souls like Nikussis—one had to *cut* to draw out the thrashing hero. Most came by their courage far too late, when only shrieking and raving remained.

"The-they say the Fo-Four-Horned Brother *Himself* picks them ... orphans ... alley urchins, younger than even you! They spend their lives traini—"

"*Every* boy trains! All kjineta are born to war! What makes these boys *special*?"

Men like Nikussis, bookish souls, had at best a shell of obstinate arrogance. All was pulp beneath. He could be bullied with impunity—so long as his skin remained intact.

"I-I fear I-I don't und—"

"What *lets a mere mortal ...*" He paused to swallow away the murderous quaver in his voice. "What lets a mere mortal walk into Xothei and stab Anasûrimbor Maithanet, the Holy Shriah of the Thousand Temples, in the breast? How could such ... a thing ... be ... *possible?*"

The overstuffed scroll-racks blunted his voice, rendered it deeper and softer than it was. The Librarian gazed at him in false appreciation, nodding as if he at last understood ... The Prince-Imperial was *bereaved*. The boy had *loved* his uncle—of course!

Nikussis did not *truly* believe this of course, but the man needed some tale to balm the fact of his capitulation to such a child. Kelmomas chortled, realizing that henceforth the Librarian *would like him*—or at least tell himself as much—simply to save his dignity from himself.

"You me-mean the Unerring Grace."

"The *what?*"

The brown face blinked. "Th-the ... uh ... *luck* ..."

A measure of fury darkened the Prince-Imperial's scowl.

"You know the rumours ..." Nikussis began, hesitating. "Fr-from before ..." he nearly blurted. "The tales of the ... of the-the ... White-Luck Warrior hunting your father?"

"What of it?"

The Librarian's eyelids bounced with his chin. "The greatest of the Narindar, those possessing the blackest hearts ... those they say *become* their mission, indistinguishable from Death. They act not of will, but of necessity, never knowing, always doing that which must be done ..."

At last! At last the buffoon spoke of something *interesting*.

"So you're saying their luck is ... is *perfect?*"

"Yes. Yes."

"Every throw of the sticks?"

"Yes."

"So the man who murdered my uncle ... he's ..."

The Librarian's eyes narrowed into their old selves. It was his turn to shrug.

"A Vessel of Ajokli."

The Librarian need tell him nothing of Ajokli. The Thief. The Murderer.

The Grinning God.

Anasûrimbor Kelmomas slipped back into his murky interval, walked unseen, less than a shadow at the limit of all the golden spaces between, back to his Empress mother's apartment. Breathing came easy.

You remember.

He shimmed and he crept, dashed down the hidden halls, and climbed and climbed. Never, it seemed, had he belonged more to this planar void between vital and stupid things. Never had he been more make-believe.

Why do you refuse to remember?

The boy paused in the black. *Remember what?*

Your Whelming.

He continued his ascent through the cracks of his hallow house.

I remember.

Then you remember that beetle ...

He had wandered from Mother, followed a beetle he had found clicking across the floor into the shadowy reaches of the Allosium forum. He could still see the dwindling gleam of the candlewheel tracking the creature's carapace as it tipped across the tiles ... leading him deeper.

To the Four-Horned Brother rendered in polished diorite.

What about it?

He could see Him in his dark climb heavenward, squatting fat and evil in his socket Godhouse—and watching the beetle the same as he. *Both* of them had been grinning!

That was an offering, the accursed voice said.

He had spoken to the bulbous figure, then, crouching beneath it, he had used his fingernails to clip off two of the beetle's legs. Together they had watched it chip round and round.

That was a joke!

His father was a vessel of the God of Gods! He could share *jokes* with the Grinning God if he pleased! He would pinch Yatwer's teat if he pleased!

And how He laughed.

The boy froze in the dark—this time absolute—once again ....

Evil Ajokli *had* laughed.

They had laughed together, he and the Grinning God. He smiled at the recollection.

So? The Gods court us ...

He had the Strength! He was every bit as divine!

The Prince-Imperial resumed climbing, his smile a fading bruise upon his face. His twin had fallen silent, perhaps immersed in the self-same hum that made empty bladders of his limbs. Only when he slipped out of the maze and into his mother's bedchamber did he recognize the extent of his horror.

The stories they told about Ajokli in Temple were always the same. He was the Trickster, the one who, unlike Gilgaöl, *took without contest or honour*. His escapades would enthrall the young, who loved nothing more than to dupe and prowl about the judgment of their fathers. Each exploit would always *seem* harmless, always *seem* comical, and so he and the other children would chortle, sometimes even *cheer* for the Grinning God.

But this was the trap, the lesson, the moment when the horrific *truth* of the Four-Horned Brother would yaw bottomless, the moment when the death and damnation of beloved innocents would begin—and when the children realized *they too* had been seduced, tricked into *celebrating* the vile and the wicked. What was sleek, what was supple, what was so roguishly *human* would slip as garments to the floor, revealing a primordial and poisonous God, one grown mountainous for consuming endless ages of grief and hatred.

And they would laugh, the boy and his bodiless twin, laugh at the terrified looks, the tearful remonstrations, the frantic prayers. They would laugh that it was always the same, that the halfwits *would always be tricked* by the exact same story, let alone similar ones. They would puzzle at the absurdity of cheering a thing one heartbeat and lamenting it the next—at the fact that souls could *yearn for contrition*, for the judgment of more elder fools. Who cared whether people died? If the stories were ancient, then everyone was dead in them anyway. Why wait huddled on your knees, when you could have fun?

Ajokli, the boy had decided, was by far the most sensible of the Hundred. Perhaps He wasn't so much *evil* as ... misunderstood.

Only now did the Prince-Imperial understand. Only now could he fathom their terror, the knifing breath of sudden, catastrophic realization. To be gulled in stories is to be armed in life.

Kelmomas often thought of himself as a hero, as the one soul doomed to prevail. The death of his brothers and his uncle had simply confirmed the assumption. Everything spoke to his ascendancy! But stories, he knew, were as treacherous as sisters, luring thought into labyrinths of smoke, coercing it down this perfumed corridor and that, all the while sealing the unseen portals shut. For the sake of simple ignorance, every victim assumed themselves the hero, and without exception, death was their enlightenment, damnation their prize.

The Gods always ate those who failed to feed.

A different boy stood pining for his mother in the Empress's sumptuous bedchamber, one whose ears had finally been pricked to the faraway rumble of more dreadful things, gale storms hanging upon horizons that parsed him to the yolk.

A guttering lantern cast light as shredded gauze, shining across a bed that was empty save the shadows of snakes tangled through the sheets. Golden illumination filtered from the antechamber and sitting room beyond. Kelmomas found himself walking thoughtlessly toward the sound of his mother's voice.

"*Any price* ..." she murmured to some unidentified soul. But whom? She only resorted to meetings in her chambers when she required utter secrecy ...

"So ..." she continued, her voice urgent, bound as tight as a sacrificial goat, "what does the Four-Horned Brother say?"

Kelmomas stopped.

He had drawn past the marble post set into the scalloped corner. He could see her, dressed in her evening habitual, reclined backward on her gold-stitched, Invitic divan, bathed in the white of whale-oil, staring at a point toward the middle of the room. Her beauty fairly struck him breathless, the twinkle of Kutnarmi diamonds across her headdress, the brushed gleam etching her curls, the flawless caramel of her skin, the rose-silk folds of her gown, the dimpled gleam chasing the seams ...

So perfect.

He stood as a wraith in the shadowy margin, his pallor more that of desolation than the blood of ancient northern kings. He had wandered into the house of Hate; he had maimed a beetle presuming to teach a lesson. And now Hate had wandered into his house presuming to teach in turn.

He's here ... the voice murmured. *We delivered Him to Mother.*

Issiral. The Four-Horned Brother stalked the halls of the Andiamine Heights.

And in his soul's eye he could see Him standing opposite, Immortal Malice, smoking with the density of Creation ...

Her face snapped toward him—the shock fairly knocked him from his skin. But she looked through him—for an instant it seemed the horror of his dream had been made real, that he hung as vision only, something incorporeal ... Insubstantial. But she squinted, her eyes baffled by the lantern glare, and he realized that she saw nothing for limits that were all her own.

Kelmomas shrank into the blackness, slipped about the corner.

"Drafts," Mother explained absently.

The boy fled back into the frame of the palace. He hid in the deepest marrow, where he wept and wailed for the imagery that shrieked beneath his soul's eye, the torrid glimpses of Mother penetrated, violated time and again, her beauty battered from her face, her skin perforated, bleeding like gills, maps of blood cast across her precious urban frescoes ...

What was he to do? He was just a little boy!

But she's the only one!

Shut-up-shut-up-shut-up!

Rocking in his own arms. Wheezing and snuffling.

Only her! No one else!

Nooooo!

Clutching and clutching, grasping void ...

Who will love us now?

But Mother lay on the bed slumbering as she always did when he finally returned, curled on her side, the knuckle of her index finger drawn to her lips. He stared at her for the better part of a watch, an eight-year-old wisp rendered smoke from murk, his gaze more fixed than was human.

Then at last he rooted into the circuit of her embrace. She was so much more than warm.

She exhaled and she smiled. "*This isn't right ...*" she murmured on the thick edge of slumber. "*Letting you ... run wild as a beast ...*"

He clutched her left hand in both of his own, squeezed with the desperation of the real. He lay larval in her embrace. With every breath he hewed nearer oblivion, face numb, head thick with recent sobs, his eyes two scratches soothed. Gratitude held him ...

His own Unerring Grace.

That night he dreamed the same dream of the Narindar. This time the man took two instant strides to stand immediately below the grill, leapt, and skewered his eye.

CHAPTER SEVEN

Ishterebinth

Lies are but clouds, giants that blow and rage only to pass, always to pass. But the Truth is the sky, everlasting and elusive, a shelter in the day, an abyss in the night.

—*The Limping Pilgrim*, ASANSIUS

Late Summer, 20 New Imperial Year (4132, Year-of-the-Tusk), Ishterebinth

Anasûrimbor Serwa was no more than three when she realized that it all *gave way*, the World. She would find her eye drawn to the threads of white knotted across all things illuminated, and she would know, *This is not real*. And since her memories began at three, it had always been thus. The Unreality, as she called it, had forever sapped her surroundings. "See, Mama?" she would cry, "Look-look! None of it is *real*!" Sometimes she would even dance and traipse, singing, "Everything is False! Everything! Only! Seems!"

Such displays had terrified her mother, who begrudged her children her husband's rapacious gifts. The fact that her daughter could care so little for her fear meant that she possessed her husband's heart as well.

It had been unfathomable then, The Unreality, more an ethereal assemblage of inkling and intuition than anything explicable. A certainty of breakneck plummets across flat ground. An intimation of perspectives hidden in the creases of what could be perceived. A profound incompleteness in the warp and weft of *whatness*, making smoke of the ground, paper of the sky, lazy scarves of whole horizons. It would strike her in the *gleam* of things in particular, the wires of white that looped about everything illuminated: the pools of shining marble beneath the sun wells, the afternoon radiance that dazzled their dinners on the Postern Terrace throughout the summer. The glint of reflections while bathing.

She was six when it began infecting *people* as well. Her mother had been the first to succumb, but only because she was the nearest, the most damaged. The Empress's periodic furies were famous among the siblings. Father terrified them, but like a God, his perpetual absence made that terror easy to ignore. Mother, on the other hand, had *afflicted* them. She would tolerate no "little Ikureis", she continually said, her term for children spoiled for luxury and the fawning of others. And so she harried them for minutiae, small failures in expression or demeanour that she alone could perceive. "What child speaks thus?" became her refrain.

And so they learned from a very young age to be the sons and daughters their mother perpetually demanded they be ... to no avail, of course. It was enduring yet another one of these maternal sermons that Serwa suddenly found she *understood*. The giddy clarity of the insight made her laugh aloud–which in turn had earned her a horrified slap, one which would have sent her bawling before, but merely served as evidence on this occasion. The endless defects Mother enumerated were nothing but *pretexts*, the little girl realized, excuses to provoke and to punish. The Blessed Empress wanted them to feel as she felt–she needed them to be helpless because she needed them to *need her*. The weeping child clings with the most desperation, loves with immolating fierceness ...

Mother punished not to educate or to redress any of the innumerable wrongs alleged, but to uncover *evidence of herself in her children*, some portion that did not belong to her hated husband.

Her mother, young Serwa had realized, *was not real*. She acted for reasons she knew not, spoke words she did not understand, pursuing ends that she could neither fathom nor bear. The mother she had loved (as far as she could love) quite simply *did not exist*. That mother, Serwa realized, was a puppet of something larger, darker, something that merely manufactured scruple to prosecute its base demands.

The Empress did not change because she could not change: she had borne too many injuries to learn from any one of them. She chided and struck her children the way she always had. But never again would Serwa—or her siblings (for they shared everything)—*suffer* her affliction. They knew her the way an old miller might know an even older mill: as a mechanism grinding the same grains in the same ways. Understanding her particular Unreality had allowed them to rule her as profoundly as Father had ruled her—even more!

After apprehending the Unreality in her mother, Serwa began glimpsing it in other souls as well—*all* souls, in fact. Slaves or potentates, it did not matter. Soon everyone had become a motley of loose things, scraps bound in uncertainties, like the rag bundles that beggars scrounged and bartered for drink. Mimara most of all. Moënghus certainly. Thelli. Even Kayûtas when he was taxed. Their words, their resolutions, their hatreds and their loyalties, were all things she could draw out as she pleased, scrutinize, knot to some other scrap or throw away.

Soon the Unreality had come to possess everything and everyone ... except, of course, Inrilatas (who had never been real in the first place). And Father.

In all the World only *Father* was real.

The episode with Mother had occurred while he was away campaigning in Ce Tydonn, but he would see it instantly upon his return two months later. "Ho, now, little Witch," he had said, bidding her to leap into his arms. "How is it you've grown so much taller than your brothers?"

"But I have Mother's bones!" she had protested.

"No, Serwa. You do not."

And so she learned that hers was a greater eye watching from a mightier angle. She could see *around* the things that outran the limits of lesser souls. And to see a thing was to possess power over it—this was the truth behind the Unreality. The World was Real only to the degree it resisted Desire, and she, like her Dûnyain father, could crush the resistance of the Real. More importantly, she *desired what she willed*—and nothing more.

"You have outgrown the Andiamine Heights, little Witch."

"But where can I go?"

"To Orovelai, so that you might outgrow the Swayali as well."

"And then, Papa?"

"Then you will find your own place, dwell where none can touch you."

"Where?"

"Why, *here*," Father said, grinning—for her benefit she now knew. He had placed the pad of his index finger between her brows—to this very day she could feel the boring pressure of that touch. "Only for Real."

So it was the ghouls looked and looked and could not find her.

So it was that she *sang* to them in the murk—mundane songs, for the Agonic clasped about her throat, but no less sorcerous in effect. Songs conceived in Nonman souls, spoken in Nonman tongues, recalling Nonman sins, Nonman losses. The more monstrous the indignity, the more frantic, the more gentle, the more loving her song.

And it appalled as much as terrified her tormentors, the fact that a mere mortal, a frail daughter of Man, could so transcend their age-old cunning and art.

That she could forgive them their crimes, let alone their ancient hatred of Men.

Sorweel had lost the numbers of the days.

There had been much screaming and animal terror at first, passages through tunnels, tunnels upon tunnels, some slung through ruin, some utterly black, and leering, ghoulish faces, a carnival of anguished passion. He remembered dreaming of suffocation.

How long had it been? Watches? Months?

Then, abruptly, something like wakefulness came to him—something almost conscious.

Eerie, singsong incantations mobbed the air, palpable for their chill. Murk blotted the indeterminate spaces, hollows fatted only by the echo of shouts and anguish. Breathing was difficult. Something ... iron, had been strapped about his cheeks. His arms had been bound behind his back, each wrist to each elbow, tight enough for his shoulders to ache. He could hear Serwa *singing* ... Somewhere. Posts perhaps a span taller than a man populated the dark, each black with the gloss of obsidian. Lintels joined them, forming a grid of empty squares across the void above, and making thresholds of every other step taken across the cracked floors. All the space he could see had been carved into ritual *crossings*, creating a chamber that was always entered, always exited ... and as he would find out afterward, never truly occupied.

"The Niom has been betrayed," a voice accused from nowhere.

The Thresholds, the ghouls called it, a place *that was no place*, where the Nonmen of Ishterebinth sought to conceal their most appalling crimes from the Hundred ...

The youth had not the least inkling how he knew this.

"You are no enemy of the Aspect-Emperor."

A Sranc face hung against the blackness immediately before him, watching with glistening intensity. The white lips opened, and he glimpsed the merest gleam of fused Sranc teeth before light dazzled him. The watching eyes became incisions upon the sun. A third strand of sorcerous singing seized Sorweel's ears from the inside.

"You love his Issue," his accuser continued. The Asker, as he would come to call him. "You yearn for the Witch, Anasûrimbor Serwa."

He was taller than the rest, gracile as a woman, save that his hips were narrow and his shoulders were broad. He alone stood as was proper (though why Sorweel should know as much escaped him), hands clasped in the small of his back. He alone was Ishroi.

I hate them, the youth replied, somehow, for he had no awareness of breath or lips.

He could hear Moënghus weeping ... Somewhere near. He heard only what he was meant to hear, he realized.

"And yet you fear for them."

Yes ...

And there was bliss, answering as he did. For the first time he could remember, he felt unfettered—free! The Sranc regarded him, and for all the wonder of its light, Sorweel had never known anything so *reasonable*. What it wanted to take was simply identical to what he needed to give—what could be more reasonable?

"Because you love them?"

No.

"Then why?"

Because the Dread Mother has cursed them.

There were pauses like this, when the Asker fell silent, and the Sranc-faced Singer simply watched, its eyes shining like sunlight.

"The one Men call Yatwer?"

Take care, he chastised the ghoul, puzzled that he could speak something so dire whilst so profoundly at ease. *She does not count you among Her children.*

The Sranc Singer turned momentarily to the Asker, then swivelled back to him. Its neck was human, and obscene for it.

"The Dread Mother speaks to you?"

As I speak to myself.

The Asker's face appeared above the Singer's shoulder. What looked like *tears* brimmed from its black eyes, spilled upon a single blink, and it seemed more wickedness, that such beasts should weep.

"And what does She say?"

The sorcerous voice swelled upon a wailing phrase; Sorweel suffered a torsion of the eyes, as if a second, peering soul saw what he saw falling. The voice that answered had the sound of bare feet scuffing, old women wheezing ...

That you are False.

The two white faces leaned closer.

"And the Aspect-Emperor ... What does she say of him?"

That She hath poured for him two *portions—a soul filled, and a soul anointed.*

There was as much curiosity as horror in the Asker's aquiline face.

Oinaral ... the youth somehow remembered or realized or ... he was not quite sure. He knew only that his interrogator was named Oinaral ...

That he *recognized* him.

"And you ... Are you Filled or Annointed?"

I am the one Anointed.

"Anointed to kill the Aspect-Emperor?"

And something rebelled within him. A sudden reluctance cramped his shining will.

The Sranc face wailed about a bolus of light, as if labouring to pry away the obstruction, but it was immovable, immune.

An *opening* leaned before him, obscured all that was dark and dying. And he saw *her*, his beloved *mother* sitting at the westward window of the Lookery, lost in some faraway thought. The dusk made a scarlet plate of the Plain beyond her, burnishing the very earth the Great Ordeal would pock with latrines years later.

Sorweel stood arrested on the threshold. Her distance belonged to one of those adult reveries that children are apt to ignore, but her kerchief lay slack in her hand across her skirted lap, the one she used to catch her coughing, the one she always kept bundled in an angular fist. It almost seemed sinful, seeing the linen of its pinched knees pried apart. He glimpsed what he thought were rose petals.

She started at the sight of him. The kerchief vanished beneath clenched hands. He met the terror in her gaze, matched it, understanding at that instant the truth of the rose petals.

Her horror melted into concern, then beamed into adoring reassurance—mothers sacrifice nothing so much as their sorrow and fear. Her hands wrung the kerchief into a horseshoe.

"**Tell the abomination** ..." she croaked through bulbous earth. "**To give what has been given.**"

Words he did not remember.

He blinked between worlds. The Sranc face toiled now, twisted about unheard exhortations, brilliant exhalations.

"Tell us!" the Asker bawled.

For the first time Sorweel saw the inconsistency between what it mouthed and what he heard.

Serwa was singing something soft, reassuring ... Somewhere.

"You need not Compel me," the young King of Sakarpus gasped. "The Niom has been observed."

"I am Harapior," the Nonman had said.

Serwa knew him, both from the High Floor beneath the Soggomantic Gate and from her Dreams. All had heard of the Lord Torturer in Seswatha's day.

"They said I would be among the first to Succumb ..." he continued, "back when this Age was young. They thought what was horror for them was horror for all. They could not see how *honour*, the pride that throws souls upon the anvil, was what fed the Dolour." The shadow had laughed in whispers. "Their honour had blinded them."

He had dragged her face up by the maul of her hair.

"So they dwindle, mortal whore, and ... I ... *remain* ..."

He grasped her jaw in a hot hand. He did not think she could see him, such was the gloom. He thought he terrorized her, an entity in the black … a malice in the deep.

He did not understand her Father.

He crouched, brought his lips to hers, close enough that she could feel their inhuman heat. He cooed into her mouth as if it were an ear—or the entrance to the place where she lay hidden.

"I *remain*, child … Now we shall see what song you sing for me."

Cries filtered through the honeycombed dark, myriad and deep, choruses cracked into countless strands of lament, rising raw with outrage and incredulity, fading hoarse into misery and exhaustion. Souls most ancient … reliving … and reliving … forever caught upon the shoals that had wrecked them.

Ishterebinth, Sorweel realized in dim, rolling horror. Ishterebinth had them.

They were lost among the Lost.

Four ghouls bore him through the riddled deep, two holding the pole to which his arms were bound, and two walking before. They loomed as cruel and evasive shadows for the most part, smoke to the glimpse, stone to the touch. Their pace remained constant whether he lurched with them or hung limp, his booted toes scrawling across the floors. Lights rose like beads on a string from the linear gloom—*peerings*, he realized, the sorcerous lanterns of the Nonmen. Halls and galleries, all squeezing his breast for the inkling of monstrous depth. Graven images rebuked his every bobbing glance, pageant upon dead pageant, figures stiff with ancient manner, faces leering and passionless.

Something was amiss. His legs seemed incidental, things too slick to be held fast. His eyes *no longer blinked*. He spent what seemed the better part of a watch trying to determine if he even breathed.

Did he breathe?

There was much that he seemed to know, even though he could not reason without spinning into confusion. He knew the sun had finally set upon the Nonmen as Serwa had feared, that they had outlived their allotment of sanity. He knew they had cast their lots *against* the House of Anasûrimbor …

That they tortured Serwa and Moënghus in the deep.

A great and broken voice welled from the blackness of a portal passing to his right.

"W-wake ... Please wake up!"

They turned down an enormous processional, a pillared gallery that was an underworld road. For the first time he realized the utter absence of scent. A portal loomed before them, a monumental gate framed by a graven bestiary. A guard stood at the foot of the nearest column. He was draped in an elaborate gown of nimil chain like all the others, motionless save for his head, which he rolled with his chin against his breast, muttering. The ensconced lights bobbed across his scalp.

"How, my love ... How could you think that a flower could ...could ..."

They passed through the murk of a narrow, defensive passageway. The shadow of the mountain fell away, and they found themselves on a balcony wrought from black iron, set on the waist of an enormous, globular hollow, a chamber great enough to house the Blackwall Citadel entire.

He stood upon the Oratorium, he realized, in the legendary audience chamber called the Concavity, the bastion that Nil'giccas had raised against madness and forgetting. A dozen peerings flared from points about the interior equator, anchoring ethereal and overlapping spheres of illumination. The iron platform hung over the curved plummet, as long and broad as a warship's deck. Dozens of Ishroi watched his entrance from points across its grilled expanse, pale and hairless as marble, nude beneath gowns of resplendent nimil chain. But the approach of the Exalted Bark, the famed floating dais of the Nonman King, had seized the youth's dazzled attention. As he watched, it levitated across the vacant heart of the Concavity, rotating as though on a gentle breeze. It was about the size of a river scow, a gilded counterpart to the Oratorium platform. The sacred Aeviternal Seal, the Shield-of-the-Mountain, bisected it, a great coin fraught with icon and imagery rising about the Black Iron Seat, the legendary throne of Ishterebinth.

The Exalted Bark descended as if turning upon an ethereal screw, revealing the figure ensconced within the eruption of horns and quills comprising the Black Iron Seat. The young king of the Lonely City set eyes upon *Nil'giccas*, the Great King-upon-the-Summit, gowned in scales of gold, dripping as if pulled from some pool, and regarding *him* with marmoreal inscrutability.

The youth returned his scrutiny, numbed by a dawning realization ...

The Bark slowed as it closed the interval between it and the Oratorium. The sound of hidden linkages scraped the air. The grilled floor shuddered beneath his feet.

The ghoul upon the Black Seat ... Somehow he *knew* it was *not* Nil'giccas.

But how could that be when they were entirely indistinguishable from one another—or Sranc for that matter?

The Ishroi surrounding him and his keepers crouched in unison, pressed their faces against their knees. Left to stand on his own, Sorweel wobbled, found that he also recognized many of the illustrious court about him. The radiant Cilcûliccas, named the Lord of Swans for his preposterous luck. The crimson armoured Sûjara-nin, the Farthrown, a Dispossessed Son of Siöl. Cu'mimiral Dragon-gored, who was called Lord Limper ...

How? How could he know souls—*inhuman* souls—he had never seen before?

He turned to peer at the Nonman King, who now stood before the Seal-and-Seat, doused and gold-gleaming before all ... and found that he knew him as well.

Nin'ciljiras, Son of Ninar, Son of Nin'janjin.

How could he know this Nonman at all?

Let alone *hate* him.

"We are the dwindling light ..." the Nonman King called in ritual invocation. "The darkling soul ..."

Unnerved by the passions Nin'ciljiras provoked, Sorweel cast his look to the text and imagery hewn from the Concavity's walls ... and was stunned. He could *read* the text ... *recognize* the images ...

"Walkers of the Ways Beneath."

Nin'ciljiras turned to a black basin set upon a pedestal just to the right of the Black Iron Seat. He raised a bowl that trailed threads too viscous to be water. Facing the crouched assembly, he doused himself in shining oil. The liquid pulsed in a sheet across his face, cracking into rivulets about the seams of his golden hauberk.

"Beseechers of Wisdom."

For the first time Sorweel noticed the naked little Emwama child at the foot of the lunatic throne, gazing out with the same too-wide eyes that had repulsed the youth at the Gates of Ishterebinth, cringing beneath the wicked profusion of iron spines.

"Haters of Heaven ..."

His voice hung but for a heartbeat, then the congregated Ishroi spake,

"SONS OF FIRST MORNING ..."

in reverberating unison.

"ORPHANS OF LAST LIGHT."

The Nonman King made an absent gesture, then, trailing a skirt of droplets, returned to the Black Iron Seat, where he became surreal for the contrast. The ghouls who had born Sorweel through the Mountain now hoisted him upright, dragged him beneath the gold-glistening aspect. The Emwama child retreated like an oft-struck cat, crouched shivering no more than a length away.

The Nonman King gazed upon him with what seemed bewildered contempt. A ghoul dressed in a welter of black silks knelt to the right of the Seat, began whispering into his ear. It was *Harapior*, the youth realized in dismay, his necklace of human scalps bunched as feathers about his cheeks. Listening to him, Nin'ciljiras raised his gaze to the similarly dressed ghoul standing on Sorweel's immediate right: the Asker, his interrogator from the Thresholds ...

Oinaral Lastborn.

"The Assay has been completed?" Nin'ciljiras asked Oinaral in a brass voice.

The Nonman lowered his face. "The Niom has been honoured, Tsonos. The manling has sworn to murder the Aspect-Emperor."

The King's gleaming brow furrowed.

"Harapior says he is *more*. More than an Enemy."

A pause that seemed to lean against all hearts.

"Yes ... One of the Hundred acts through him."

This loosed a susurrus of exclamation among the gathered Ishroi.

The Nonman King affected indifference, turned to ladle more oil upon his scalp. "The Fertility Principle," he said tilting his profile to strings of pulsing translucence.

"Yes," Oinaral replied. "The one the Tusk names Yatwer."

The shining face turned.

"Do you know what this means, Oinaral Oirûnarig?"

A pause.

"Yes."

The Nonman King now stared at Sorweel frankly, though without directly meeting his return gaze. "Do you think this is why the Anasûrimbor sent him to us? He knows that Fertility moves against him, does he not? Perhaps he suspects Her interest in this one."

An apprehension struck the Horse King, one both spear-sharp and inchoate. Was that what he was? Something *wielded* like axe or hoe? A dumb instrument?

Narindar, Zsoronga had called him. Holy assassin.

"The youth has been under the Aspect-Emperor's thrall for months," Oinaral explained, his tone rigid in a way that revealed the extent of his animosity for not mellowing. "Why exile a threat that is more easily killed?"

The Nonman King gazed upon the Lastborn with alarm and scowling indecision. How strange it was to witness human passion on the face of a Sranc. How natural and obscene.

"So Her track runs through *us* ..." Nin'ciljiras said.

Sorweel heard the legendary assembly stir behind him, the murmuring clamour of souls too ancient to be astonished, yet astonished all the same.

"We are now bound to this one," Oinaral called through the clamour. "Irrevocably."

The Nonman King turned to the basin once again, doused himself while the uproar of the Ishroi waxed and faded across the Iron Oratorium. "Lord Cilcûliccas!" he finally called over Sorweel's head. "What say the Quya?"

The Lord of Swans stepped from his fellows. The bolt of Injori silk he wore affixed to his shoulder and wrapped crosswise about his torso was so fine as to become crimson paint where it flattened against his nimil gown.

"Oinaral Oirûnarig speaks true, Tsonos," he said.

The Nonman King pondered the legendary Quya with open distaste, then returned his gaze to Sorweel's keeper. "And what of the brother and sister?"

Sorweel suffered another swell of apprehension, like pins pricking just deeper than ice-numbed skin.

"The son knows nothing," Oinaral said. "Tsonos."

"And the daughter?"

The son of famed Oirûnas paused. "Surely Harapior has told you ..."

An oily smile.

"I would hear *your* thoughts, Lastborn."

Oinaral shrugged. "What your allies told yo—"

"You mean *our* allies!" Nin'ciljiras snapped.

The Nonman tested his sovereign with three heartbeats of silence. "Nothing sorcerous can compel her," he finally replied. "Nothing. Even more, she has proven entirely indifferent to Harapior's ... other inducements. Indeed, if anything, *she torments him.*"

"That is a lie!" Harapior cried from his station beside the Black Iron Seat.

"It must trouble you," Oinaral said, "the way the Goddess so effortlessly followed this boy into the Thresholds, into the place where your tresspasses cannot be seen. Do you tremble, Lord Torturer, knowing your infernal room has hidden nothing from their eyes—*that all your crimes have been counted?*"

Harapior stood sputtering—and obviously terrified.

Oinaral turned from him in disgust, shouting, "She is *proof!*" to the assembled Lords of Ishterebinth. "Proof of her father's blood! Proof tha—!"

"*Enough!*" Nin'ciljiras screeched.

Murmuring alarm hung as a cloud about the platform. Sorweel could do naught but roil in animal terror ... Other inducements? *Weeks?* What was happening here?

How could he *know* all these ghouls?

"*We are one Mansion!*" Nin'ciljiras keened, glaring wildly, then turning to his oil for respite once again. "*One!*" He raised his face to better savour the looping chill, then paused to regard the brown-eyed Emwama child, who promptly tried to huddle into invisibility.

"What do you advise?" Lord Cilcûliccas called from the assembly.

"That we *honour* the Niom," Oinaral began, "as we have across each and every Age befo—"

"And *what?*" the Nonman King grated. "*Ally ourselves with* Men! The beasts that burned Holy Siöl, scattered her Sons! That cut Gin'yursis' throat! What? You would have us cling to mere words, when all of us, Erratic and

Intact"—he looked about in triumph—"*can be saved from Hell?*"

Oinaral Lastborn said nothing.

The Son of Ninar grimaced as if at some discomfort of the bowel. "I tire of this, Oinaral Oirûnarig. I tire of perpetually treating for your soul, always sparing you horror ... as you care to define it ..."

He had raised his gaze to the assembled Ishroi as he spoke—his true audience, Sorweel realized. A bead of oil hung from either hairless brow, each gleaming with a miniature replica of the assembly.

"I weary of pandering to your delicacies while we—*we*!—dwell in such fear of Hell as to become Hell unto ourselves, husks—*husks*!—about a roaming madness. We! We are the bulwark! That is why we crumble! While you are cosseted? Relieved of the martial obligations of your Kinning? Your *Race*? *Spared* so you might be spared our curse?"

A heartbeat of silence, fraught with inhuman intimations.

"I am spared your glory and your respect," Oinaral Lastborn replied, his manner mild. "That much is true. But no one is spared the treachery of *your* blood, *Son of Viri*."

Something *sharp* crept into the gaze of Nin'ciljiras then, and Sorweel understood, not simply the brute meaning of the words, but the circumstantial intricacies as well. The ghoul who was King was the grandson of *Nin'janjin* ...

Nil'giccas was no more. What remained of Ishterebinth had been cloven in two.

"Such words meant death not so long ago," Nin'ciljiras said in a voice like a wire.

Oinaral snorted in amusement.

"We age better than our meanings, it se—"

"*You shall accord me as you accorded my cousin*!" Nin'ciljiras screamed wroth. "You! Shall! *Accord*! You shall reckon my holy station, for it flows from the blood of the Kinning Most High-and-Deep, the Kinning of Kings! *I*! I am the last Son of Tsonos in this House, and *only Tsonoi may rule*!" He threw down his arm in a gesture that was both alien and familiar, sending a spatter of oil across the black grillwork. "I alone can claim the blood of Imimorûl!"

"Then perhaps," Oinaral said mildly, "the Canons of the Dead serve only the dead."

"*Sacrilege!*" the Nonman King raved. "*Sacrilege!*" His voice scraped across the near curves of the Concavity, hung as reeds upon the high air. At first Sorweel assumed the outburst meant doom for the ghoul called Oinaral Lastborn, but the bewildered, hunted expression of the Nonman King assured him otherwise. His overseer did not so much risk as *provoke*, Sorweel realized. He did not so much dare as *demonstrate* ...

The fact that Nin'ciljiras was being eaten by the Dolour before their very eyes.

"None here contest your right, Tsonos," Lord Cilcûliccas declared, stepping forward to intervene, scowling at Oinaral as he did so—but not in fury. He towered over Sorweel to stand before the Lastborn, his nimil hauberk a lucid contrast to the sordid gold worn by Nin'ciljiras—a *soggomant* hauberk, the youth dimly realized. A great deal was shared in their momentary, mutual look. The Quya clapped a white hand upon Oinaral's shoulder, fairly wrenched the Nonman to his knees before turning to join him.

All those across the Iron Oratorium joined in their obeisance, knelt with their fingers clasped across the small of their backs.

"Y-yes," Nin'ciljiras said, scowling for confusion. "We are one Mansion! What better sentiment with which to conclude?"

"But the matter of this mortal and Fertility remains unresolved," Cilcûliccas said to the Nonman King.

Nin'ciljiras squinted at the Lord of Swans, scowled as if the matter were inconsequential. He angrily waved away Harapior's attempt to intervene.

"Yes-yes-yes ..." he said with an air of phony impatience.

And Sorweel realized that the Nonman King *could not remember* ... that he attempted to disguise this fact in a more general contempt for details.

"So we are *agreed* then?" Cilcûliccas said.

"Yes ... Of course."

The resplendent Quya stood, nodding as if in acquiescence as he did so. "O' Tsonos, your wisdom is ever our beacon. If war has overthrown the Niom, how are we to treat this Son of Men? How should we protect our Mountain from the wrath of the Hundred?"

Oinaral kept his eyes fixed upon the floor throughout this exchange. Sorweel could not help but notice the way Cilcûliccas continued squeezing his shoulder in reassurance with his large, pale hand.

"Yes! Yes! He is a Blessed Ward of Ishterebinth," Nin'ciljiras declared.

"A King of Men, and a God-entangled enemy of our enemy ... He is not to be obstructed."

Sorweel fairly snorted aloud, given that his arms remained bound about a pole wedged behind his back.

The Lord of Swans stood, his silk bolt wrapped as blood around him, beaming with insincere admiration. The peerings glinted across his nimil gown, shattered by thousands of miniature swans.

"You are most wise, Tsonos. He will, of course, require a Siqu ..."

Why did he feel that somewhere unseen and unknown, he *burned*?

What had these creatures done to him?

Sorweel watched the alabaster lips of Harapior hanging at Nin'ciljiras' ear, snipping off one inaudible—and sinister, he could not but think—fact after another. The Concavity, he realized, was not so different from any Mannish court, riven with subterranean conflict and intrigue, games of influence and power. Oinaral had played not so much to preserve an overwrought dignity as to lay his King's incompetence bare—and for stakes greater than the single coin that was his life. The confederacy of Lord Cilcûliccas proved that some kind of conspiracy was afoot.

Any hope of saving Serwa, the youth realized, lay with these two ghouls.

They cut his bounds while the Nonman King sat fungal upon the Black Iron Seat, watching bloodless. Sorweel stood plagued with the same disorientation as earlier, testing his joints, swinging sensation back into his hands. The congregated Ishroi and Quya stared without the least scruple, their black eyes glittering, their obscene gowns scintillant in the sorcerous light. The sameness of their faces lent insanity to the spectacle. And yet Sorweel found he could recognize others: Vippol the Elder, another Siölan refugee and most gifted of the surviving Quya. Moimoriccas, long-called Earth-Eater for his ensorcelled cudgel, Gimimra, the famed "Graver", which struck the very ground from beneath his foe's feet. He recognized others as well, somehow distinct even though their pallor and beauty rendered them identical—and to more than just one another. Even as a fraction of his soul recognized individuals, another fraction insisted they were *just another breed of Sranc*—one framed, not as apes or dogs, but as strapping, catamite Men.

For a Son of Sakarpus—a true child of the Pale no less—they could be nothing else.

Without warning, the shining assembly fell as one to one knee ...

"Our House embraces thee, Sorweel, Son of Harweel," the chorus intoned.

The youth found he simply *knew* the ritual reply ... somehow.

"Let all ... grace ..."

He fairly coughed for the alien workings of his mouth and throat—for abusing the apparatus of speech, he numbly realized, speaking *their blasphemous tongue* ... Horror clenched the moment in a suffocating fist.

"Find all ... all honour ..."

What was happening here?

He turned to Oinaral, his Siqu, frantically seeking guidance now that bondage and coercion had retired from the mad field. But the Lord of Swans had already secured the man's attention, holding hands to his womanish cheeks, as a man might a beloved child. Even as the condescension repelled the youth, a deeper inkling *approved*, knowing how such intimacies of rank conserved the sacred hierarchies.

"Recall what happened ..." Cilcûliccas murmured to his ward.

Oinaral acknowledged the High Quya with a lingering look, then, clasping Sorweel's arm, he quickly drew the youth from the ghoulish regard of the Nonman King and his underworld court. A thin barrage of entreaties followed in their wake, some strident, others pathetic for being so tremulous.

"*Cu'cirrurn*!"

"*Gangini*—!"

"*Aurili*—!"

Names, he realized. They called out names as invitations.

"Say nothing ..." Oinaral muttered as he hustled him into the murk of the exit. "It will only inflame them." What had been a cavernous immensity was suddenly low and looming, ceilings pitted with images of love and outrage.

"Inflame?" the youth managed.

"Aye," Oinaral said, his eyes fixed forward, his stride brisk, yet unalarmed. "Those who teeter upon the Dolour, especially. You must avoid speaking to my brothers."

"Why?"

"Because they would love you, if they could."

Sorweel thought of the pathetic Emwama child cringing at the foot of the Black Iron Seat.

"Love me?"

Oinaral Lastborn walked three paces before turning to him, looking down without quite matching his gaze—much as the Nonman King had. "You are not safe here, Son of Harweel. You will find only madness in the embrace of Ishterebinth."

A numbness confounded his frown.

"So the oath of Ishterebinth means nothing?" he asked.

Oinaral Lastborn did not answer. They passed beneath the mirror sheen of the Concavity Gate, and Sorweel hunched for the intimation of hanging stone immensities. The peerings etched no more than pockets of graven image in either direction, transforming the underworld road into a necklace beaded by twilight worlds and primordial times. The Inner Luminal, it was called, the Hall that would become a euphemism for their King, Nil'giccas, after the construction of the Concavity.

"I know things ..." Sorweel said, only to be perplexed by the sound of his own voice.

Oinaral led him opposite the way they had originally came, deeper, he somehow knew, into the Weeping Mountain.

"How do I know these things?"

Oinaral strode at a brisk pace, said nothing.

Sorweel hastened after him, marvelling at the panels passing overhead, triumphs and tragedies, stacked one upon the other to the ceiling vaults above, the rising layers of a doomed race. Before, the scenes had been intelligible insofar as they offended, wholly debauched. Now they all but exploded for *recognition*, each glimpse a peering into times and worlds. Lovers reclined in forbidden liaison (for her breasts were bared) at a banquet for the Feast of the Mere. The annual Embassy between Nil'giccas and Gin'yursis, the great assembly of Injori Ishroi in the High Halls of Mûrminil ...

How he had hated the sullen, ashen halls of Cil-Aujas!

For the first time, Sorweel understood the sage-stumping miracle that was knowledge, the condensed *opacity* that was its substance. He *knew* these things, and aside from its rank impossibility, this knowing was indistinguishable from any other, so obscure were the machinations of the soul. These memories were *his*, rising from the very point of him, even though they could belong only to this underworld.

What was happening?

These walls were interwoven with minutiae, roped with power, glory blotting glory, and lust and tenderness and contemplation populating all. He could read them as surely as he could read the murals of his ancestral home.

"You did this by hand ..." he blurted to Oinaral—his Siqu—who had drawn paces ahead.

He received scant regard from the Nonman, less than a glance. "I fail to understand."

"You spent *thousands of years* doing this! These engravings ..."

The wonder of such a task. It seemed he could even *see* it in his soul's eye, something both more and less than images, the chisel, the mallet, and the toiling thousands, the compulsion leaping as contagion through the surviving Mansions, the demand to unearth some fragment of themselves from dead stone.

"Aye," Oinaral admitted. "An entire Age. We are not so fractious as Men. We live our lives as tribute ... not prizes."

"Such a toil," Sorweel said, boggled by the enormity of such a task.

"To secure such life we had left," Oinaral replied. "If a fortress be raised of stone, then we would make a *fortress* of our Memory, of all that we had lost. We succumbed to the imperial urge, the brute certainty that what is large is unassailable."

"Madness!" Sorweel cried—once again with a passion he could not recognize.

Oinaral had stopped, and now loomed before him, his breastbone even with Sorweel's forehead, his black-silk gown open to reveal the nimil mail he wore beneath.

"All mighty endeavours beg contradiction," he said, frowning. He turned to the very line of panels Sorweel had made the object of his gesture. "Look ... Look between the moments of glory, and you find moments of a far different sort ... *Look*, husbands dandling children ... wooing lovers ... appeasing wives ..."

He spoke true. Scenes of the small had been hewn into the sublime procession, but it seemed the eye had to *look* to find them, not for lack of prominence, but because they were *not* historical, things recognizable in *form* merely. Tokens of what was ineluctable.

"We were *losing it all*," the Nonman continued. "All the delights that grace hard life, be they carnal or paternal or anything that cobbles life with joy *were drifting into oblivion*. Do not be so quick judge, Son of Harweel. Madness is often the only sanity left, when hope alone serves the living."

Sorweel's hands no longer tingled, though they shook for rage and incredulity ...

"You *squandered* it!" he barked stamping. "Squandered the last age remaining!"

Oinaral appraised him without expression, a Sranc with a wise man's soul. The light of the nearest peering daubed his eyes with points of white.

"This is not you speaking."

"You *fools*! You set aside sword and scroll for this? How could you do such a thing?"

The Siqu flinched for the violence of his expostulation, resumed his haunting regard.

"Raise your hands, Son of Harweel ... Touch your face."

A tickle, like that of a feather, caught the youth's throat. He coughed, once again without the least sense of face and mouth.

"I ..." he said helplessly. His face?

Oinaral either nodded or simply lowered the white oval of his chin. "Touching your face has not occurred to you because It *does not want you to*. The Union happens faster when the Donning Soul remains ignora—"

"It?" Sorweel interrupted on welling panic. "*It* ... doesn't want me to?"

"Touch your face, Son of Harweel."

Had they all gone mad in his absence?

"What has happened here, Cousin?" he cried. "What has become of the Holy Kinnings? How can you speak of these things without *shame*?"

"I will explain everything ..." Oinaral said, smiling reassurance. "You need only touch your face."

Sorweel at last raised his hands, frowning, perplexed ...

And found his face missing.

Not missing ... *replaced*.

A stunned heartbeat. His fingertips recognized the silken polish of nimil, which always seemed warmer than the air. He swept frantic hands across curves and swales of metal, all of it stamped in intricate symbols …

A faceless helm of some kind?

Mammalian panic. Suffocation. He seized the thing, wrenched at it in futility. It seemed continuous with his skull!

"Get it off!" Sorweel cried to the watching ghoul. "*Get it! Off!*"

"Calm," Oinaral said with what seemed the supreme assurance. The graven walls bobbed about him.

"*Get it off!*"

With one hand, he wrenched a fistful of nimil-mail from Oinaral's breast, while the panicked other skittered across the helm, thumbing every crease, every crevice, searching for some kind of seam or latch or strap—something!

"Take it off now!" he cried. "Honour your Embrace!"

Oinaral clasped his wrist, held his hand fixed between them.

"*Calm*," he repeated. "*Recall yourself*, Sorweel, Son of Harweel."

"I can't breathe!"

He began thrashing as one drowning. The Nonman grinned for effort, revealed a wetted expanse of fused teeth. Glare and grip—something irresistible lay in the combination, an inhuman resolve.

"I will honour my Mountain's Embrace," he said through a grill of exertion. "None are more true than the False Men, so long as they are Intact. But if I do take the helm from you …"

Even in his panic, the youth saw a shadow float through the ghoul's gaze.

"What? What?"

"Anasûrimbor Serwa is dead."

Words that slapped, that cracked his knees as twigs.

He slumped kneeling.

And it gave way. What was real began turning about the peerings, the vignettes on the walls, and the *engravings within*, the childish antics, the mortal sorrows, all pulled apart, strewn as wreckage amid a life far more terrible, images of degenerate glory, epic savagery, golden horns goring the sky, all spinning into a great gyre …

But the black-gowned Nonman had hauled him back to his feet, crying, "Walk! Walk, Son of Harweel!"

And he was reeling down the pillared processional, glimpsing swatches of floor passing between his battered boots.

"Jealousy and vigilance ..." Oinaral said, pacing him in the gloom between great lanterns. "*These* will save you. Jealousy of the life that is yours, vigilance for the life that is not."

Sorweel pawed the ensorcelled helm once again, drawing his fingers across the intricate filigree stamped into the metal ... His head was *entombed*, and yet he could see! It was as if he traced the surface of perfectly transparent glass, but distorted somehow, like his soul simply could not admit to *seeing through*, so that it seemed he reached out *behind* what existed, grasped what was near from about the back of distance.

"The Sons of Trysë called it the Cauldron," the Siqu explained. "The Sons of Ûmerau, the Embalming-Skull ..."

Sorweel lowered his hands and saw what appeared to be the terminus of the Inner Luminal ahead, some three lanterns ahead.

"We have always called it the Amiolas," the gaunt Nonman continued. "Many have worn it, but I fear too many years have passed since last it suckled life ..."

"It contains a soul!" the youth gasped in renewed panic.

"A shade, a soul shriven of depth, one that slumbers until it dreams."

"You mean-mean ... planted within someone living!"

"Yes."

"So I'm possessed? My soul isn't my own?"

Oinaral walked three, meditative paces before replying.

"Possession is an imprecise metaphor. One and one make one, with the Amiolas. You are no longer the soul you once were. You are something new."

The Horse-King staggered alongside his Siqu, groping, fending. He *had* to be who he was. Was he not *dead* otherwise? *He had to be who he was*! But how? How could a soul sit in judgment of itself and say, I am this, and not that? Where lay the vantage? The point prior to all pointing? How did one catch the catching hand?

"To parlay one must understand," the Nonman was explaining. "To understand *one must be*. So the Amiolas weds the soul of its wearer to the ancient shade of the Ishroi trapped within it ..."

He was not who he was!

"This is how you speak my tongue, know my Mansion and my Race ..."

Perhaps it was the exhaustion. Perhaps it was the simple sum of his loss. Regardless, a child within kicked at his lungs, his heart. A sob welled up, a battering grief ... and caught somewhere short of expression—somewhere short of the lips he could not feel. He convulsed about the absence of air.

Suffocation. The story-braided walls curled into blackness. He was dimly aware of falling to his knees once again ...

Oinaral Lastborn was kneeling before him, darkling eyes bright with concern.

"You must *never weep*, Son of Harweel. The Amiolas would sooner die than weep."

But ... but ...

"You wear a *prisonhouse* upon your head, Manling, an arcane dungeon for one of the proudest, most reckless souls in the history of my Race. Immiriccas Cinialrig, the Goad, the Malcontent, great among the Injori Ishroi. He was sentenced to death by Cu'jara Cinmoi during our feud with the Vile—a sentence commuted by Nil'giccas. His was our most ruthless soul, Son of Harweel. And aside from the Inchoroi, he punished none with such cruelty as himself."

But the vertiginous gyre had returned, engulfing him in its dread turn. The youth looked up from the dragging blackness, saw Oinaral Lastborn drain as milk into spinning clamour.

"I—!" Sorweel cried.

I must—

Harapior could not bear to gag her. She sang as his wife once sang from dishevelled pillows, contemplating love and sorrow, a voice like a breath clad in light, near enough to tickle, far enough to pretend to sleep.

She sang to what was naked and weak.

Anasûrimbor Serwa was too real to suffer such as him. His shadow laboured on the horizon of what she willed, toiled astounded, for he had thought her body his implement, the lever he would use to overturn her soul. But he could find no skin to break, no need to starve, no gaze to dim. He could find *no strings*! She was chained abject before him, yet she was nowhere to be found.

Her words fell as a patter of acid upon his heart.

Lilting was her heart,
turbulent was her soul,
moon upon silk upon waters

She sang not to him but to what made him. She sang to the darting eye, the trembling hand, the taut lip. She beckoned to them, and they heeded her song, twisted and yawned like lazy weeds.

Bloomed.

he raised her as fire,
lowered her as snow,
lay cheek against her cheek,
lips not quite
touching,

For even the stoniest of Nonman had long been broken into sand and loam.

drawing two breaths,

She poured her voice in pitchers, sang to what was sodden.

exhaling one.

She laid her hoe to his ground, and set her seed deep.

CHAPTER EIGHT

Ishuäl

No matter the insanity, tomorrow always has a hand.

—NILNAMESHI SAYING

Better blind in Hell than speechless in Heaven.

—ZARATHINIUS, *A Defence of the Arcane Arts*

Early Autumn, 20 New Imperial Year (4132, Year-of-the-Tusk), the ruins of Ishuäl

Another dream drawn from the sheath.

The sea rises up, chokes us into oblivion. The earth cracks, crushes our bones. The forests burn, suck the screams from our throats. Men are bred for the small, so when great things happen, transcendent things, they have naught but stupor and awe to keep them—which is to say, nothing at all. Even the will to pray fails them, and they can only gawk at the murderous immensity—gape.

No-no-no-no-no ...

Drusus Achamian stood rapt, staring with eyes that burned for the lack of blinking. Shame had rooted him, horror without compare. He stood pinned to what he was, to treacheries committed and obligations failed.

The Fields of Eleneöt reached out beneath black skies, churning with threshing limbs, the flash of bronze arms and armour. The Sohonc, who were to be their grace, their salvation, fended the hooking flight of dragons. Gnostic lights limned and parsed the heights below the pall of clouds. Wracu fell screaming from the black, disgorging geysers of shining fire. Sranc teemed and thronged, assailed the Kûniüri shield-walls, not according to their former nature, but with a new and devious cunning, sacrificing themselves with insect incomprehension, building ramps and promontories with the piling of their own carcasses, and racing over these to spear deep into the fracturing ranks of Men. Bashrag tossed bodies like so many rags.

Everywhere he looked, disaster stung the old Wizard's eyes. Men falling, curling about entrails. Men shrinking into howling, battling clots. Men running in panicked waves, knocked face-first to the turf, hacked and speared by the white-skinned rush behind them. Standards dragged down, gonfanons that mapped clans within tribes, tribes within nations. The Knights-Chieftain overrun. Proud Lord Amakûnir. Clever Prince Weodwa. The might and glory of the High Norsirai, the arrogant panoply, everywhere broken, everywhere collapsing, fleeing.

And roping fat and black across the horizon, roaring, the *Whirlwind* ...

Mog-Pharau. Tsuramah.

Speaking, roaring through a thousand thousand throats, innumerable screams bound to a singular will, a chorus all the more obscene for its inexplicability.

TELL ME ...

A sob kicked its way between the High-King's teeth. It was happening ...

WHAT DO YOU SEE?

Exactly as Seswatha had said.

Anasûrimbor Celmomas II, the White-Lord of Trysë, the Last High-King of Kûniüri, staggered as though struck by some great blow.

Achamian fell to his knees ...

WHAT AM I?

Through the din, he could hear the consternation behind him, the cries of incredulity, the calls to withdraw, abscond with their High-King. "The fields are lost!" a voice bellowed from behind him. "Lost! All is lost!" Someone seized his shoulder, tried to haul him back, away from his dread wages. He threw off the hand, ran *toward* the massacre instead ...

There was nothing to do but die.

His had always been a heroic soul. Many times had he rushed ahead of his royal household, to buttress some failing point in the lines, to shatter a wavering foe.

But this was no act of heroism.

The flurries of Men running toward him could not be rallied, so profound was their panic. They were but the human crest of an inhuman wave, an onrush of innumerable, fish-skinned beasts, their faces crushed into expressions of exaltation and fury. The first of his kinsmen flew past the High-King bereft of shield or weapons, tearing at the harnesses of their scale hauberks. The runners behind them vanished beneath the hacking onslaught.

Still sprinting, Anasûrimbor Celmomas cast his first javelin into the vicious flood, loosed his great, ensorcelled blade, Glimir, and leapt into the slavering rush alone ...

Where he delivered scything death, his famed blade's edge not so much hewing as *passing through*, parting flesh and lacquered hides as if they were smoke. Again and again he shouted his beloved son's name. Again and again he threw his heartbreak into Glimir's great swing. The Sranc fell as his harvest, collapsed into slop and twitching portions. The ground wheezed and twitched about him. And for a moment, it seemed he had stemmed the inhuman rush, that he had rallied *Fate*, if not his men. Sranc skidding, falling, flying apart like rotted fruit. The Last High-King grinned for the simplicity, for the purity and the futility.

This was how he died. This! This! A pious Son of Gilgaöl to the last ...

It happened, as it always happened, too fast to be truly perceived. The glimpse of the Sranc chieftain vaulting from the backs of the fallen, over Glimir's fatal arc, knees rising as its hammer descended ...

The helm was struck from his head. Anasûrimbor Celmomas dropped back into harems of dead, not so much senseless as heartbeats behind his awareness. He watched, with eyes hooked to the edge of oblivion, as lines of burning lights caught the Sranc chieftain's second blow, transformed the beast into a wagging, squealing shadow. The High-King heard the mutter of Gnostic sorceries, and the resounding "Life and light!" war-cry of the Knights of Trysë ...

And the Whirlwind.

WHAT ...

The play of line and blur, the shadows of Men, incandescences blooming out of the deep ...

AM ...

Hands hooking his armpits, and the sense of rising buoyant above the grit and intricacy.

I ...

The taste of blood and char on his own lips.

Seswatha's face bounced across the sky's corners, grave with horror, drawn with exertion.

He was being drawn to safety—he knew as much, and he mourned.

"Leave me," Achamian gasped, and though his eyes peered up at his old friend, they somehow saw around and *behind* him.

"No," Seswatha replied. "If you die, Celmomas, everything is lost."

How strange it all looked, the last moments of the World. So trivial—so *small* ... Even his friend, the famed Grandmaster of the Sohonc, his snub nose at odds with his long jaw, his beard adolescent-thin, hermit-white. He seemed an imposter, a Bardic fool, dressed to mock the might and gravity of his patrons ...

TELL ME.

The peal of faraway horns scored the thunder of the Whirlwind.

Celmomas smiled blood. "Do you see the sun? Do you see it flare, Seswatha?"

"The sun sets," the Grandmaster replied.

"Yes! Yes. The darkness of the No-God is not all-encompassing. The Gods see us yet, dear friend. They are distant, but I can hear them galloping across the skies. I can hear them cry out to me. You cannot die, Celmomas! You must not die!"

And Achamian heard the words without hearing, the breath-warble of unvoiced words.

Brave King ...

"They call to me. They say that my end is not the world's end. That burden, they say, is *yours*. Yours, Seswatha."

"No," the Grandmaster whispered.

And the crack in the heavens opened, the clouds blown down and away like smoke from an incense-bowl. Light showered the ground, whitening, gleaming, rimming the edges of the surrounding tumult.

Light showered *through* ...

"The sun! Can you see the sun? Feel it upon your cheek? Such revelations are hidden in such simple things. I see! I see so clearly what a bitter, stubborn fool I have been ..."

For there it was, as obvious as vision, the catalogue of his folly, the thousand scorned insights, the revelations condemned as delusion. Celmomas reached through it, clutched the shadow of the Grandmaster's hand.

"And to you, you most of all, have I been unjust. Can you forgive an old man? Can you forgive a foolish old man?"

Seswatha lowered his forehead to his royal rings, kissed his numb fingertips.

"There's nothing to forgive, Celmomas. You've lost much, suffered much."

Tears spliced an illuminated world.

"My son ... Do you think he'll be there, Seswatha? Do you think he'll greet me as his father?"

"Yes ..." Seswatha replied roughly. "As his father, and as his king."

And there was such comfort in this lie, a swooning relief, a swell of ferocious, paternal pride. "Did I ever tell you," Achamian said, "that my son once stole into the deepest pits of Golgotterath?"

"Yes," the Sohonc Grandmaster replied blinking. "Many times, old friend."

"How I miss him, Seswatha!" Achamian cried, his eyes hooking back, rolling. "How I yearn to stand at his side once again."

A silhouette resolved from the high-hanging brilliance ... a figure, riding in majesty and divine glory.

"I see him so clearly," the High-King gasped. "He's taken the sun as his charger, and he rides among us. I see him! Galloping through the hearts of my people, stirring them to wonder and fury!"

Gilgaöl, War, come to claim him ... Come to *save*, despite everything.

"Shush ... Conserve your strength, my King. The surgeons are coming."

The vision's eyes were fury, his hair the tangle of warring nations, and his teeth were as whetted blades. A crown gleamed above his brow, four golden horns, clutched in the arms of four nubile virgins—the Spoils. Bones and bodies clotted the ravines of his grim expression. And his cloak smoked with the burning of fields.

Gilgaöl, the Dread Father of Death, the All-Taker.

Brave, broken King ...

He did not so much fly toward the High King as *grow*, bigger and bigger, bloating until he blotted the Whirlwind, crowded the very sky. Fire sheathed and pulsed across his four horns, streams that plummeted in skyward oblivion. He opened his hands, and lo! Another stood within the curved palms, another man, bright as a ceremonial knife. A Norsirai, though his beard was squared and plaited in the fashion of Shir and Kyraneas. His dress was strange, and his arms and armour bore the glint of Nonmen metals. Two decapitated heads swung from his girdle ...

Behold the son of a hundred fathers ...

Behold the end of the World ...

"He says ... says such sweet things to give me comfort. He says that one of my seed will return, Seswatha—an Anasûrimbor *will return* ..."

A cough that was a convulsion wracked the High-King and the old Wizard could feel clotted things float loose within. Blood foamed against the back of his throat. He pulled his next breath as through a burning reed. Then the darkness at last came out of hiding, spilled from all quarters into his life and vision.

"At the end of th—"

Drusas Achamian awoke screaming.

Drusas Achamian is tender. As much as Mimara loves him for this, she recoils whenever he awakes crying out. Where hard life makes some maudlin to the point of weeping at mere memory, it grants others a curious immunity to suffering. Like the slaves who work the charcoal pits, their skin grows hardened to the pinch of fire and coals, insensible to burning things.

"I saw so—" he begins, only to be throttled by waking phlegm. He gazes at her with idiot need.

She looks away, expressionless. She knows the cruelty of his Dreams—as well as anyone who's not a Mandate Schoolman, she knows. Even still she cannot bring herself to ask after the matter, let alone comfort him.

A part of her has forgotten how. The judging portion.

So she gazes across the mountain slopes as he collects himself, staring with sham curiosity at the high-climbing flanges of stone. The Dûnyain watch from perches in the nearby ruin, two faces in her periphery, unnerving for their blank vigilance.

She finally believes what Achamian has always insisted. She knows they see the souls behind human expression the way architects see behind the facades of great buildings. She knows that they see her hatred, her murderous intent—she knows that every word she speaks brings them infinitesimally closer to mastering her ...

She does not care, let alone worry. What was cunning was wicked also: they could do naught but bare their souls to the Judging Eye. And even if the Eye failed, she had swooned for the evil visited upon the Whale Mothers. There could be no undoing the foul umbrage stamped into her heart. If she could not see, she would hate.

The question was Achamian. What would that blank vigilance make of him? Had his heart been likewise hardened?

Or had the long toll finally emptied his purses?

Am I too harsh with him, little one?

The eastern sky is a luminous silver plate behind the mountains, but the world in the interval remains gloomy and cool. The old Wizard sits for a time, his head slung from his shoulders, his hair a ragged curtain about his lap. He snuffles from time to time—evidence of weeping. As much as it shames her, some inner miscreant scoffs. Never has it taken so long for him to recover.

She waits, trying to smooth the irritation and impatience from her expression. Unknowingly, her hands clutch the globe of her lower belly—rest where they belong.

How, she wonders. How can she compel him to be as hard as he has to be? As strong as she *needs* him to be.

"I-I dreamed ..." he finally offers in a voice strung with phlegm. He flinches as if she has thrown something sharp with her gaze, falls silent. He does not so much as glance at the Dûnyain. "I dreamed in-in the ... *old way*," he continues with greater resolution ..." His look turns inward, becomes even more haggard, more put upon. "I had almost forgotten. The visions, the smell and sound ... Everything vanishes upon awakening ..." He licked his lips, gazed at the gnarled back of his left hand. This is another of his weaknesses: his need to explain his weakness. "Everything save the passions ..."

At last she replies. "You mean you dreamed of the First Apocalypse?"

"Aye," he said, his voice fading to a murmur.

"You were Seswatha once again?"

This yanked his chin upward. "No ... *No* ... I was Celmomas! I dreamed his ... his Prophecy."

She stares at him with flat, expectant eyes.

No. Your father isn't mad. He just sounds that way—even to himself!

"I know ..." he begins, pausing to rub his eyes despite the filth of his fingers. "I *know*. I know what it is we must do ..."

"And what is that?"

He purses his lips. "The Eye ..."

For some reason this fails to alarm her. "What about it?"

He studies her for a careful moment, far more himself, now.

"We must continue north, intercept the Great Ordeal ..." He pauses to gather wind. "You must ... You must gaze upon Kellhus with the Eye."

He speaks with the air of entreaty, as if convincing her to undertake yet another mad gambit. But there is finality in his voice also, a weary sense of coming, despite stubbornness and stupidity, to an obvious conclusion.

"And for what?" she asks, her tone more clipped than she wishes. "To see what I already know?"

He frowns about popping eyes. "Know?"

The perversity is not lost on her. To doubt his words, his mission, for so long, then to suddenly see it with a clarity that he could never hope to attain—only to discover that she does not believe in *him*.

She sighs. "That the Aspect-Emperor *is evil*."

The words hang on idylls of mountain breeze. The old Wizard fairly gapes.

"But how could you ... how could you *know* such a thing?"

She turns to the Dûnyain where they sit above them, gazes in a bold manner. The two merely return her regard with a kind of absolute immobility.

"Because he is Dûnyain."

She can see the old Wizard glaring in her margins, baffled and alarmed.

"No, Mimara," he says after what seems a long moment. "*No*. He *was* Dûnyain."

This sparks a surprising fury in her. Why? Why must he always—*always*!—give away the coin of his doubt? He would make the world rich and himself a pauper, if he could.

She turns back to him with a kind of sly anger.

"There's no outrunning what they are, Akka."

"Mimara ..." he says, as if she were her tutor. "You're confusing acts for essences."

"It's a sin to *use!*"

They are truly arguing now. He parses his words with careful condescension.

"Remember Ajencis. 'Use' is simply a way to *read* ... Everybody 'uses' everybody, Mimara—always. You need only look with certain eyes."

Certain eyes.

"You cite Ajencis?" she scoffs. "You make *arguments*? Old fool! *You* dragged us all the way out here. You! The truth of man lies in his origins, you said. And now, when I have gazed upon those origins—with the *very Eye of God*, no less!—you argue that they *mean nothing*?"

Silence.

"You were right about him all along!" she presses, at once upbraiding and beseeching. "*You*, Akka! You turned to your heart in your pain, in your outrage, *and your heart spoke true*!"

The Aspect-Emperor is evil.

"But—?"

"Can't you see? That room—the bones of the Whale Mothers!—that is the *truth* of what Kellhus has done to my mother—*to your wife*! He has made a tool of her womb, a bauble of her heart! What greater crime, greater *monstrosity*, could there be?"

And for the first time she glimpses the deeper tracts of her own outrage, the stab and twinge of her own sins against her mother. Esmenet, undone by her own astrologer mother, ruined by the famine that forced her to sell her daughter, undone by the masculine cruelty of the Imperial Court, and ruined by her false husband most of all ...

Her *false* God.

And Mimara had sought only to *punish* her—her only blood!

Something—a horror—seized her breath at that moment, a sudden, cavernous accounting of all the harms she had authored. The time her mother had tried to teach her the rudiments of sowing, and Mimara had intentionally pricked her finger. How she used stories of her molestation to batter her mother with heartbreak and shame. The way she called out her mother's fears and misapprehensions, accused her of being too weak, too polluted, to aspire to the glory of her Imperial station. "*Empress? Empress? You can scarce rule your face, let alone an empire!*"

The way she had laughed as her mother fled sobbing ...

You can scarce rule your face ...

She can see her mother weeping in her soul's eye, curling about silk pillows in lieu of trust and love. Rebuffed, rebuked, shamed time and again. And alone, always alone, no matter whom she clung to ...

Only *this man*, Drusas Achamian, had truly loved her, truly sacrificed for her. Only he had extended the *dignity* that was her due, and she had been tricked into betraying him ...

Turned into another Whale Mother.

Mimara cannot swallow, cannot breathe, so overwhelming is the sense of *commission*, the weight of things tragic and irrevocable. She has seen it herself with the Eye, the inexplicable vision in the Mop, so she knows that *she is saved*. But that knowledge has become indistinguishable from skin-scratching, hair-rending shame. She *should* be damned, cast into everlasting fire ...

A ship creaks on the wine-dark sea, a slaver ship ...

Mummy ... the little girl sobs, listening to the shuffle of boots across the timber floors.

"Anasûrimbor Kellhus is Dûnyain," the woman says to the old Wizard, speaking to silence the riot that is her heart.

Mummeeee please!

"As much as these two."

Please make them stop.

The old Wizard has seen through her anger, glimpsed the hope-cracking turmoil beneath. She can tell by his hesitation.

"What are you saying?" he finally asks.

Her voice shocks her, it sounds so measured and cool. "That you must kill them."

He knew. He knew all along that this was what she demanded. She could tell—like a Dûnyain.

"Murder."

She turns to the two onlookers, knowing they could see her dark intent, and not caring in the least. She barks with laughter, a sound that earns a look of scowling alarm from the old Wizard.

She smiles at the man, husband and father, and feels at once vicious and victorious.

"There's no murdering a Dûnyain."

They sat side-by-side on the rump of what had been the northwest tower, observing the old man and his pregnant woman arguing below. The sun glared from between eastern peaks, cool for the emptiness and the wind, climbing inexorably from the pockets of night. The spruce breathed. Rising light etched the ridge-lines and branching ravines, drawing angles steep with the contrast of encroaching shadow.

"What do they say?" the boy asked.

The Survivor replied without interrupting his study. Their language defeated him, yet the other, nonverbal tongues of their souls spoke with an almost painful clarity—like the Shriekers, only more complicated. The pounding hearts and wringing hands. The rictus of muscle about their eyes their lips. The frequency of blinks ...

"The woman argues our destruction."

The boy was unsurprised. "Because she fears us."

"They both fear us—the man more than the woman. But she hates us in a way the old man is not capable."

"She is stronger?"

The Survivor need only look to nod. "She is stronger."

The implication was plain. If she were stronger, then she would carry the dispute.

"Should we flee?" the boy asked.

The Survivor closed his eyes, glimpsed bodies convulsing in holes—memories, not possibilities.

"No."

"Should we kill them?"

For all the complexities of this extraordinary turn, the Survivor had no need of the Probability Trance to dismiss this course of action.

"The old man is a Singer. We are overmatched."

He had been among those on the battlements when the invaders had floated from the forest galleries, advanced across empty space, their mouths and eyes afire. He need not blink to see his brethren tossed from the walls, pinioned by lines of scorching white.

"Then we should flee," the boy concluded.

"No."

Ignorance. This had been the cornerstone of the Brethren, the great rampart they had raised against what comes before. They had raised darkness against darkness, and it had proven a catastrophic miscalculation. Only so long as the World *remained ignorant of them*, could they remain secure against it, let alone isolate and pure.

History. History had come in the form of inhuman legions, creatures as bound to their crazed passions as the Brethren were free. History had come as death and destruction.

Ishuäl had fallen long before her walls had been pulled down, the Survivor knew. The Dûnyain had been destroyed long before they had sheltered in the deepest deeps of the Thousand Thousand Halls. The World had learned of them, somehow, and had counted them a mortal threat.

The time had come to discover why.

"Then what?"

"We must accompany them. We must leave Ishuäl."

The boy lacked all but the most rudimentary instruction, such had been their straits over the years. He could track the *passions* of the woman and the old man easily enough, but the thoughts and significances utterly eluded him. He could scarcely attain the Divestiture, the first stage of the Probability Trance. He was Dûnyain by virtue of his blood, not his training.

It would have to be enough.

"Why?" the child asked.

"We must seek my Father."

"But why?"

The Survivor resumed his implacable scrutiny of the old man and his pregnant woman.

"The Absolute has fled this place."

The Thousand Thousand Halls plumbed the earth to the bowel, rising high into the encircling mountains, innumerable miles of passage hewn from the living rock. For two thousand years the Dûnyain had toiled, reaching forever deeper, etching mathematical conundrums into the earth's very fundament. They used the labour to condition the body, to teach the soul how to ponder independent of menial tasks. They used the labyrinth to sort those who would live from those who would die, and those who would work from those who would train and father. It refashioned the strong, and it buried the weak. The Thousand Thousand Halls had been their first and most cruel judge, the great sieve through which the generations spilled, collected and discarded.

How could they know it would be their salvation?

The Shriekers had come without the least warning. There had been anomalies the previous years, members of the Brethren sent out never to be seen, others found dead in their cells—suicides. An absence had moved among them, the shadow of contaminants not quite disposed. Their isolation had been compromised—they knew this much and nothing more. They did not trouble themselves with the implications, understanding the dead had taken their lives for *purity's* sake. To interrogate the circumstances of their deaths would simply undo their sacrifice—and perhaps necessitate another. To embrace ignorance, even one so hallow as their own, was to embrace *risk*. A garden was not a garden absent the possibility of things going to seed.

The Shriekers descended upon Ishuäl in violence and fury. The valley was evacuated, the gates barred, and for the first time confusion and discord ruled the Dûnyain. To dwell as they dwelt in a world groomed to its barest essentials, where the course of leaves could provoke scandal, had weakened them in ways they could never imagine. They could feel it, watching the savage cohorts stream down the mountains, their vulnerability to things wild and disordered. To live *lives* within the circuit of expectation, without any real comprehension of surprise, the way it breaches, throws the soul back in wincing disarray. They realized they had become something *delicate* in their millennial pursuit of the Unconditioned.

Some, a few, simply walked into the swords of their enemy, such was their soul's disorder. But the others rallied—discovered that the assaulting world was, in its way, more delicate still.

The sun bright. The air gusting between the gaping heights. The battlements choked with motion and fury. The catwalks slicked in blood. The slopes matted with the miscreant fallen ...

The Survivor had stepped between arrows and javelins, running down the miraculous course between flying points and edges, and he had struck the life out of *hundreds*. Tendons severed. Throats cut. Limbs lopped. Horns cawed low and sonorous over the screaming yammer, while he and his brothers battled in exquisite silence, striking and leaping and dipping across the heights, almost tireless, almost invulnerable, almost ...

Almost.

The World was wild with Cause, true, *but it could be overcome*. How could so few exact such a toll otherwise? The ferocity of the inexplicable attack waned, then faded. The Shriekers relented, slunk howling back into the forests. And despite everything, the Survivor had thought the Dûnyain *confirmed*: in their discipline, in their training and their doctrine—even in their fanatical solitude ...

Then the Singers had come, shouting in voices of *light and fire*, and the extent of their delusion had been made clear.

That which comes before determines that which comes after ... This had been the sacred rule of rules, the all-embracing dictum, the foundation upon which the whole of their society—their *flesh* as much as their doctrine—had been raised.

Demolished in the space of a heartbeat.

The Survivor had watched, not so much stupefied as numbed. Unlike the Shriekers, who had descended the eastern glacier, the Singers had appeared out of the west, mail-armoured figures filing across *empty air*. Each bore a lozenge of light within their mouths—one so bright it seemed they chewed miniature suns. They sang, their voices like a waterfall boom, hanging indecipherable, the sound falling inward from all directions, as if they called from beyond the very frame of the World.

No miracle could be more violent. Words—*words* had called forth death and energy from *emptiness*. He had watched that which comes *after* determine what comes *before*. He had witnessed the rank impossibility that the Manuscripts called *sorcery*, the overthrow of his every assumption. And what was more, it seemed that he could *see* its residue, as if its exercise stained somehow, cast shadows across the light of the mundane world.

The Singers approached their hallowed bastions, their voices thundering in white unison, rising with impossible resonances, echoing across spaces and surfaces that simply did not exist. And the Brethren had stared without breath or comprehension.

This, the Survivor would later realize. This was the moment of their destruction. The instant *before* the looms of glittering light had crowned Ishuäl's heights with fire and destruction. The lull preceding ... when each of the Brethren realized *they had been deceived*, that the compass of their *lives* let alone their assumption had been little more than errant fancy ...

The towers of Ishuäl burned. And they fled through the groves and gardens, withdrew into the bosom of the Thousand Thousand Halls.

Took shelter in the very judge that had so utterly failed them.

The Siege and Fall of Ishuäl ...

The loss: a mere place. What was this compared to the revelation that accompanied it?

That which comes after *could determine* that which comes before ... The *impossible* made *manifest*. The world was an arrow with one and only one direction, or so they had believed. Only the Logos, only reason and reflection could bend the world's inexorable course. Thus the Dûnyain and their hallowed mission: to perfect the Logos, to grasp the origins of thought, bend the arrow into a perfect circle, and so attain the Absolute ...

Become a self-moving soul.

Free.

But the Shriekers and their Singers cared nothing for their doctrine—only for their extinction.

"Why do they hate us?" the boy asked, not for the first time. "Why do so many wish to destroy us?"

"Because in our deception," the Survivor replied, "we *became a truth*, one too terrifying for the World to countenance ..."

For years the Brethren had battled through the Thousand Thousand Halls, entombed in blackness and butchery, living by touch and sound, disguising their scent by wearing the skins of their enemy. Killing. Slaughtering ...

"What truth?" the boy pressed.

"That freedom is the measure of the darkness that comes before."

He had fallen like fangs upon them, sent them gushing to the dust. Limbs like chains tearing the seams of his unseen enemy. Hands like vindictive teeth. He stepped between their frenzied exertions, cut and cutting. Their blood was thinner than that of the Brethren, but it clotted faster. It tasted more of tin than copper.

"They think themselves free?"

The reek. The mewling screams. The thrashing. For years, he had battled through the bowels of the earth. The innumerable cuts as the lines he pursued had become wanton with desperation.

"Only so long as we are dead."

He had been *broken*—the Survivor understood this.

He had gone mad for enduring.

The Thousand Thousand Halls had swallowed the Brethren whole, delivering them one by one to the homicidal ardour of their enemy. Every one of them had fought, using all the skill and cunning two thousand years could muster. But not one of them doubted the conclusion of their fell battle.

The Dûnyain were doomed.

The old and the young fell first—one miscalculation was all it took, so capricious were the margins. Some were killed outright, vanishing into rutting heaps. More died of sepsis from their wounds. A few even became lost, despite having survived the labyrinth in their youth. The cataclysmic sorceries of the Singers, in particular, threw whole galleries from their mathematical hinges. These wandered out of light and life.

Sealed in.

And so the Dûnyain dwindled.

But somehow the Survivor had persevered. No matter how sopped with blood, his strength had never failed him. No matter how ruinous the destruction, he never lost his way—and more importantly, never found himself shut in. He always prevailed, always emerged, and always tended to the babe he had stolen into the depths with him.

Feeding him. Teaching him. Hiding him. Snuffing thousands to keep him safe. He had risked speaking, lest the boy's ears forget how to listen and comprehend. He had even dared lantern light, lest the boy's eyes forget how to see.

He, the *one most burdened*, would be the only one to survive.

For a time the Shriekers had seemed inexhaustible, a never-ending infusion of lives both crazed and disposable. More, always more, released in numbers so tidal they became incalculable, overwhelming even the most elegant of traps: concealed pits, rigged ceilings, abyssal chasms.

But then, as inexplicably as every other turn in the war, their numbers abated. The final dregs were abandoned altogether, left to wander howling until thirst and hunger claimed them. Fewer and fewer, until those he found simply gasped across the floors.

The last cry had been piteous, a screech so wretched as to sound human.

Then the Thousand Thousand Halls fell silent.

Perfectly silent.

The Survivor and the boy wandered the black with impunity after that. But they never dared the surface, even via those chutes they thought undiscovered. Too many had died that way. They wandered and the boy grew, hale despite his underworld pallor.

Only when the last of their stores failed them did they dare the long climb to the surface. They abandoned their underworld temple, their hallowed prison.

The Survivor had emerged in the obliteration of everything he had known, Ishuäl, his brow furrowed against an alien sun. For the first time in his life, he stood *naked*, utterly exposed to the indeterminacy of the future. He scarcely knew *who he was*, let alone what he should do.

The boy had gawked at a world he could not remember, stumbled and swayed for vertigo, such was the pull of empty space. "Is that the ceiling?" he had cried, squinting up at the sky.

"No," the Survivor replied, beginning to realize that the *obvious* was the greatest enemy of the Dûnyain. "The World has no ceiling ..."

And he looked to his sandalled feet, stooped to pick a seed from a crotch in the debris. The nut of some tree he did not recognize.

"Only floors ... more and more ground."

Earth for roots. Skies for endless branching, reaching ...

Grasping.

Using a black iron cleaver, he felled a tree that had been a sapling ere the Shriekers had come, so he might count the years of their entombment ...

And so know the age of his son.

He was not who he was, the Survivor. Too much had been taken.

"What do we do now?" the boy had asked that first day in the sun.

"Tarry ..." he said.

That which comes *after*, he now knew, determined that which comes before. Purpose was no illusion. *Meaning was real.*

"Tarry?"

"The World has not finished with Ishuäl ..."

And the boy nodded in belief and understanding. He never doubted the Survivor, though he remained wary of the madness within him. He could not do otherwise, such was the screaming, the indiscriminate slaughter.

There was the day he told the boy to stop breathing, lest the clouds alert their enemy. There was the day he gathered a hundred stones, then wandered through the forest, killing ninety-nine birds.

There were many such days—for he could not stop saving ... killing ...

He was not who he was.

He was a seed.

And now *these people* ...

They looked like Dûnyain, but they were not.

The boy had fled to him immediately after spying the old man and the pregnant woman descend into the valley. Together they had followed the couple's progress toward Ishuäl, tracking the bubble of silence their presence opened in the forest. They watched them wander forlorn through the ruins. When the two descended into the Upper Galleries, they closed the distance, hanging at the very limit of their inexplicable light. Soundless, they shadowed them, stealing what glimpses coincidence afforded.

"Who are they?" the boy had whispered.

"Us ..." the Survivor had replied. "As we once were."

Though he understood nothing of what the strangers said, the Survivor easily discerned the outlines of their mission. Ishuäl had been their destination. They had come *seeking* the Dûnyain, and had found only desolation.

The old man had been stunned and heartbroken, but not the pregnant woman. She had come, the Survivor decided, for reasons she did not understand. And she fretted not for the destruction of Ishuäl, but for the ruin of the old man.

The father of the child within her.

These insights had anchored the scenarios that flashed beneath his soul's eye, the possibilities. When he and the boy revealed themselves, *she* would be the one to intercede, to domesticate the old man's fear and suspicion.

For the Survivor had glimpsed *relief* in the old man, as well. The loitering blinks, the slacking gaze, the slowing heart of a terror averted ...

Terror of the Dûnyain.

She would be the one to throw open the gates of their trust—that much, at least, had been obvious.

Then they entered the Fathering.

The Survivor had watched her from the blackness, too distant to absorb more than the shape of her demeanour. He saw her stumble as though suddenly struck blind, then gaze witless across the stone beds, the bones of the Dûnyain women. Incomprehension ... Horror ...

Hatred.

A passion as profound as any he had witnessed, seizing her from ... nowhere.

She too was mad.

But the old man did not know this. The old man had come to *believe* in her madness, to take her assessment as his own. Even as she spoke, the Survivor realized that the time for observation had come to an end. They had no choice but to intervene if they were to master this extraordinary turn of circumstance.

She was passing a judgment that the old man did not share—yet.

So he sent the boy out to them.

It belonged to his madness to second-guess decisions regarding the boy. A kind of clamour had swelled within the Survivor, watching him approach the two strangers. The child seemed more frail than he was, more desolate. And out of some darkness came a cold assurance of murder, the wayward conviction that he had sent the boy to his doom ...

But these were not Shriekers. They were *humans*, the clotted canvas the Dûnyain had scraped clean. They hungered for understanding, not blood and anguish. They sought knowledge of what had happened to this place ... to Ishuäl.

When the boy called out, they listened, stood pricked with hooded apprehension.

And when the old man *responded in their tongue*, the Survivor realized that something *deep* connected these travellers to the Dûnyain. Something ancient. Something that came before.

When the boy had told the old man his name, Anasûrimbor, he realized that something *living* connected them as well. Something that inspired endless terror.

It could only be his father.

"Mimara ..." the old Wizard croaks. "What ... What you *ask* ..."

She understands the threshold she has crossed. She feels the irony. For so many years she mocked the Zaudunyani, for their interminable bowing and scraping, for their adulation, and for their round-eyed *sincerity* above all. Only now does she understand the *truth* that their delusions aspire to.

She has pondered the Judging Eye obsessively over the months, probed it like a tongue counting missing teeth. Was it a curse? A gift? Would it break her? Would it exalt? For so long she has sought to understand it, not realizing that it was *itself* understanding. She had lost herself in the labyrinth of hints and implications, asking things that no soul so slight, so mortal, could every hope to comprehend.

These questions, she now knew, were simply that, questions, words thrown across the face of human ignorance. The mere appearance of honesty ...

But *now*—now she understands: Fanaticism is indistinguishable from knowledge of good and evil.

To possess the Eye is to *know* who should live and who should die—as certainly as a man knows his own hand! And to know is to stand without worry or constraint, to *be* in the obstinate, inexhaustible way of inanimate things. To be immovable, unconquerable ... even in death.

"You have no choice, Akka," she says, her voice steeped in murk and compassion. "They are *Dûnyain* ..."

She grips his paralytic hand, and it seems necessary and inevitable, the horror and indecision that numbs his expression, slackens his gaze.

"You *know* the peril they represent. Better than any man living."

The Survivor watched, impassive and immobile upon the warming slope of masonry. He spoke only to respond to the inquiries of the boy, who continued to struggle with the thoughts beneath the cacophonous flare of human passion.

"His suspicion of us is old ..." the boy noted.

"Yes. Decades old."

"Because of your father."

"Yes, because of my father."

"But her suspicion is new."

"Yes. But it is more than suspicion."

"She despises us ... Because of something she witnessed?"

"Yes. In the Upper Galleries."

"In the Fathering?"

An image of her standing limned in marine light, dishevelled and forlorn, fury and condemnation boiling over the pots of her eyes.

"She thinks us obscene."

"But why?"

"Because the Brethren make tools of all things, even wombs."

The boy turned to him. Sunlight picked random filaments from the stubble dusting his scalp. "You have never spoken of this before."

"Because our women are dead."

The Survivor explained how, in the First Great Analysis, the ancient Dûnyain had jettisoned all the customs that bound them so they might contemplate the Shortest Path without prejudice or constraint. Because of the differences in intellect between them, they recognized the onerous obstacle posed by paternity and physiognomy. Training was not enough. The assumption that the Absolute could be grasped through mere *thinking*, that Men were born with the native ability to grasp the Infinite, was little more than vain conceit. The flesh, they realized. Their souls turned on their flesh, and their flesh *was not capable* of bearing the Absolute. They had realized that *breeding* was the only sure route, so it was decided that men and women would be bred according to the fitness of their progeny.

"Over the centuries, the sexes were transformed," he said, "each according to their share of our burden."

The boy gazed at him, so open, so weak compared to what he should have been, and yet as impenetrable as a stone compared to the worldborn couple.

"So she resembles the First Mothers?"

A single, slow blink. An image of branches. The sound of the dying masticating in the dark.

"Yes."

The Shriekers had chewed their own limbs in the end, suckled on the teat of their own leaking life, dying as they did in the blind deeps of the Thousand Thousand Halls.

Mimara fumes. From whence does the will to argue—to *contradict*—arise?

Over the years she had argued not so much with her fists as *from* them. No matter how slight the confrontation, she always held them balled so tight as to score her palms with indentations of her fingernails. She had scoffed from her neck and upper chest, the one stiff with indignation and the other tight with anxiousness. She had sneered from her jaw, her eyes slack with the threat of tears.

Never had she contended, as she did now, from her *belly* ...

From the very root of all that mattered.

"The *Scylvendi* ..." the old Wizard says with an air of seizing upon some jewel in his thought. "Cnaiür urs Skiötha ... Moënghus's *true* father. He travelled half Eärwa without succumbing to Kellhus. We don't need to do this! We don't need to do this precisely *because we know* that they are Dûnyain!"

"The Scylvendi," she snorts. Pity jostles to the fore of her battling passions. "And where is he now, Cnaiür urs Skiötha?"

A look of shock. Achamian has grown accustomed to her alacrity, the swiftness of her tongue and intellect. How could he not, fending her barbs as he has across the very breadth of Eärwa? But for all her cleverness, she has never possessed genuine strength, let alone the potency of conviction—only anger.

"Dead," the former Schoolman admits.

"So knowing is no surety against them?"

She is using his own arguments now—from their first meeting in Hûnoreal, when he tried to convince her that she was an agent of her stepfather, whether witting or not.

"No," the old man concedes.

"Then we have no choice!"

Damnable woman!

"No, Mimara ... *No!*"

She finds herself squeezing her abdomen, such is her fury.

"But I *have seen them*! With *the Eye*, Akka!" The contempt, the outrage and righteous indignation—none of these are here own. Truth owns everything now.

Her belly.

"I have seen them with the Eye!"

Such a carp! Relentless. As clever as she was cruel. And now, *bloodthirsty*. She even seemed a remorseless warrior-maiden, her hair cropped, the scales of her Sheära corselet glinting in the sun.

A part of him scoffed and marvelled, asked what had so bent her sense of right and wrong. But these thoughts were less than sincere, ways to shroud the *understanding* that hulked beneath ...

The fact that she was right.

They *were* Dûnyain. If they left them behind, what religion would they manufacture? What nation would they seize? If they took them along—as prisoners or companions—how could he and Mimara *not* be enslaved?

Only now, it seemed, could he appreciate the peril of dwelling within the circuit of such a dwarfing intellect. How could one be free in the presence of such beings? How could one be anything other than a child, manipulated at every turn?

These were questions he had pondered long watches over the years. Even in abstraction and retrospect, they had seemed onerous. And how could they not? when they always watered at the well of Esmenet ...

He was a man who had *surrendered his wife*!

But to ask such questions now in the *living presence* of the Dûnyain made them seem more than mortal.

Because they *were*, he realized. More than lives depended on how he answered ...

He forced himself to regard the two, boy and man, against the grain of the sudden aversion that welled within him. It was always better, a fraction of him had decided, to look *around* those you might kill.

The shadows were retreating, shrinking toward the very sun that routed them. Given the higher perch of the Dûnyain, the old Wizard could see the line of bright and gloom draw down across the two. Where they once seemed a piece with the ruined tower's foundations, now they seemed quite apart. The boy sat hugging his knees, a posture too careless to be anything other than premeditated. The Survivor sat in the manner of teamsters long on the wagon, leaning forward, elbows on knees. His woolen smock seemed to absorb the sunlight without remainder. His skin was striped and hooked for the random play of scars, the result of some artist's disordered folly.

Both matched his gaze with the selflessness of dogs pricked to the possibility of scraps. They seemed forlorn, pathetic, a scarred monstrosity and a crippled boy stranded on the wilder limits of the World ... Enough to stir a sense of shuffling compassion.

He says ... says such sweet things to give me comfort ...

This was deliberate, the old Wizard knew. Their posture and demeanour could be *nothing other* than deliberate ploys, chosen to maximize their chances for survival–and domination.

He says that one of my seed will return, Seswatha—an Anasûrimbor will return ...

Could it be mere coincidence? To dream of the Prophecy on the eve of coming to Ishuäl would have been significant enough, but to do so *from the High-King's eyes*? And on the morn where he must decide the fate of an *Anasûrimbor*–the full-blooded Dûnyain son of Kellhus no less!

"What does it matter?" Mimara cried in impatience. "When the very World is at stake, what does it matter, two–two!–meagre heartbeats? What does it matter if *you* send them to their damnation?"

The old Wizard snapped his attention back, glared at her ...

He had heard these words before. He lowered his gaze, pinched the bridge of his nose with thumb and forefinger. It seemed he could see Nautzera, stern and frail and scathing in the gloom of Atyersus, saying, "*I guess, then, you would say that a* possibility, *that we're witnessing the first signs of the No-God's return, is outweighed by an* actuality, *the life of a defector—that rolling the dice of apocalypse is worth the pulse of a fool!*"

That was how it all began, it now seemed. All those years ago, with the Mandate's mission to spy on Maithanet–another Anasûrimbor. Ever since, he had lived in a world of ciphers, as cryptic as they were fatal, charting the doom of civilizations with rank guesses ...

Small wonder so many augurs went mad!

"Mimara—relent ... Please, I beg you! I-I cannot ... just ... murder ..."

"Murder?" she cried with mock hilarity. Everything about her radiated disapproval. There had been something about her ever since he had awoken, something as grim as it was relentless and remote.

Something very nearly *Dûnyain*.

Despite the harshness of her humours, he had never thought of her as *cruel*—until now. Was it the Eye, as she said? Was it the safety of the World, or the child she bore in her womb?

"*All* are murdered in the end!" she said. "How many have *you* killed to come this far, hmm, Wizard? Dozens? *Hundreds*? Where was your compunction then? The Nangaels who found us on the plain, the ones you pursued, why did you murder them?"

A glimpse of panicked horsemen, whipping their mounts across shelves of dust.

"To ..." he began, only to falter.

"To safeguard our mission?"

"Yes," he admitted, glaring into his palms, thinking of all the lives ...

"And did you hesitate?"

"No."

He had never tallied them, he realized. He had never bothered estimating, let alone counting all those he had killed. Could the World be so violent? Could he?

"Akka ..." she said, calling more to his gaze than to him. "*Akka* ..."

He looked into her face, shuddered for a sudden premonition of Esmenet. And in the mad way of so many small revelations he understood that *she* was the reason he had accepted Nautzera's mission all those years ago. Esmenet. She was the reason he had gambled Inrau's life and soul—and lost.

"This ..." Mimara was saying, "this *life* ... is naught but a detour. Deliver them to their destination!"

Those lips. He could never have imagined that those lips could argue murder.

Qirri. He needed his Qirri.

He wiped his face and beard with an unsteady palm. "It is not-not my ... my place."

"They are *already* damned!" she cried. "Irrevocably!"

His temper cracked—finally. He found himself on his feet, roaring down at her.

"*As! Am! I!*"

For an instant, he thought this would catch her short, thrust her cheek to jowl with the consequences of what she was asking. But if she hesitated, her reasons were her own.

"So then," she said on a ruthless shrug, "you have nothing to lose."

And only a world to save.

A child.

"*Empitiri asca!*" the pregnant woman began crying, glancing at the Survivor and boy with varying measures of horror and fury. "*Empitiru pallos asca!*"

The argument, which had been animated since the beginning, became increasingly shrill. The gulf of tongues defeated the Survivor, but the sentiment did not. She was bidding the old man to *recall his mission*. They had suffered much, these two travellers, both in the sum and fraction of their lives. Enough to demand some kind of accounting—or, at the very least, fidelity to the motives that had driven them to such extremes.

Murdering them, she was saying, was the only way to keep faith with what they had sacrificed ...

With those they had killed on the way.

The old man began cursing and stomping. Accelerated heart rate. Tears clotting eyes. At last he turned to where the Survivor and the boy sat on the humped debris, mustering the will to murder ...

"Should you not intervene?" the boy asked.

"No."

"But you said yourself: She is stronger."

"Yes. But for all she has suffered, mercy remains her primary instinct."

The old sorcerer, his skin blackened for filth, his beard wire-white, stood braced beneath his cloak of ragged pelts, gazing at them in turbulent indecision.

"So she is weak after all."

"She is worldborn."

Something swelled within the old man, a crippled ferocity ...

After the Brethren had thrown back the Shriekers' first assault, they had pried opened the creature's skulls. They had been careful to take captives, both for the purposes of interrogation and study. The Neuropuncturists quickly realized the Shriekers weren't natural. Like the Dûnyain, their neuroanatomy bore all the hallmarks of *artifice*, with various lobes swollen at the expense of others, the myriad articulations of Cause branching into configurations alien to all other earthly beasts. Structures that triggered anguish in everything from lizards to wolves elicited *lust* in the Shriekers. They possessed no compassion, no remorse or shame or communal ambition ...

Again, like the Dûnyain.

But there were differences as well, every bit as dramatic as the similarities, only more difficult to detect for their structural subtleties. Of all the regions known to Neuropuncture, none was so difficult to chart or probe as the Outer Sheath, especially those portions crowded behind the forehead. After centuries spent mapping Defectives, the Brethren had discovered that this structure was naught but the outer expression of a far larger mechanism, a great net cast across deeper, more primitive tracts. Cause. Cause soaked the skull through the senses, ran in cataracts that were unwound into tributaries, only to be knotted and unravelled again. At turns superficial and profound, it was siphoned and tapped into a tangle that could only be likened to a marsh, Cause splintered into imperceptible eddies and swirls, currents wrapped across the inner circumference of the skull, before draining back into the cataracts once again.

The first Neuropuncturists called it the Confluence. It was—for them—their primary resource and their greatest challenge, for it was nothing other than the *soul*, the light they coaxed into ever more brilliance with each passing generation. The Confluence was the structure that distinguished even the most malformed of the Defectives from beasts. And the Shriekers possessed none. Cause coursed through them in rills and tributaries and rivers without so much as touching the light of the soul.

They were creatures of darkness, the Brethren realized. Utter darkness. Not one sky dwelt within their skulls. Not one thought.

As much as they resembled the Dûnyain, the Shriekers were actually their antithesis, a race honed to give perfect expression to the darkness that comes before. Where the Dûnyain reached for infinity, the Shriekers embodied zero.

This old man who would kill them, the Survivor knew, dwelt somewhere in the shadowy in-between. The woman had poured her Cause into the cup of his skull, where it had rushed and swirled, before soaking into the dim swamp of his soul. And now it was about to drain into action.

The old man dropped his chin to his breast, crushing his wild, white beard. He began speaking the way the Singers had spoken, words that sparked light, a voice that rose not from the mouth, but from the limit of everything surrounding. He had pinched shut his eyes against tears. Now open, they flashed like twin Nails of Heaven.

" ... ***irsuirrima tasi cilliju phir*** ..."

"Cling to me," the Survivor commanded the child. "Simulate love and terror."

The boy did as he was told.

Thus they stood, a scarred monstrosity and a crab-handed child, stranded and helpless. The old man hesitated, anarchic and unkempt, little more than a rind wrapped about shining power.

The Survivor wondered that light could throw shadows in full sun. The boy feigned an involuntary cry.

The pregnant woman watched, her right hand clutched about her belly. The Survivor need only glance at her to hear the thrumming heartbeats, born and unborn ...

Finally, she called out.

CHAPTER NINE

Ishterebinth

But what could be more essential than the belly and the whip? Where I dwell, these are the blatant movers of our souls; words are little more than garlands. So I say Men must suffer in ways that words can retrieve lest they die. That is the simpler truth.

—AJENCIS, Letter to Nikkyûmenes

Late Summer, 20 New Imperial Year (4123, Year-of-the-Tusk), Ishterebinth

He could not feel the pillow.

Sorweel lay in bed—a grand one, hewn from image-pitted stone—and yet he could not feel the pillow.

But there was *sunlight*, pale for being filtered so deep … and the inconstant flux of chill and astringent air.

They were in the Apiary, he realized, the highest halls of Ishterebinth. He threw aside sheets thin as web, hoisted himself to the bed's edge. He raised his hands to the faceless helm he already knew was there—the body entertains hopes all its own. The Amiolas held him as absolutely as before.

Eyes imprisoned, he nevertheless peered into the chamber's dimmer recesses, blinded by the brightness of the shaft above him. The bed sat upon a raised corner, some three steps above what appeared a cramped library otherwise, teetering shelves of codices, and iron scroll-racks crude enough to speak of human manufacture, heaped with scrolls of endless variety, some no more than rolled rags, others winking with the glister of nimil, silver, or gold.

He discerned the Nonman last, and fairly leapt in his skin when he did so, for Oinaral had been nearest all along, obscured by the bed's draperies. He stood as motionless as the marble that he so resembled in hue and density, holding a long nimil blade to the light, turning it as though to follow the luminous bead pulsing along its edge.

Holol, Sorweel realized. The sword was named Holol—"Breathtaker".

"What do you do?"

"Gird for war," the Nonman replied without so much as a glance.

And Sorweel saw that he wore a second, heavier hauberk over the gown of nimil chain he had worn before. He noted the oval shield leaning against what appeared a workbench just beyond the Ghoul, almost absurd for the density of signification stamped into it.

"War?"

With a quickness that was nothing short of surreal, the Nonman leapt to stand before him, his blade extended, pressing the Amiolas at a point that would have blinded him, had his face been uncovered. And yet, Sorweel sat absolutely still, curiously unalarmed—possessed of a bravery, he realized, that was not his own.

"I fear you have come to us at an inopportune time, Son of Harweel," Oinaral Lastborn said, his voice deadly and even.

"And why is that?"

"Our time is over. Even I, the Lastborn ... even I can feel it begin ..."

The dark gaze dulled for turning inward.

"You mean the Dolour."

Oinaral scowled; the faintest of tremors passed through his arm. Light decanted the length of the arcane Cûnuroi blade.

"The Intact huddle," he said in a voice more wrung of passion than calm, "drip with the years into the very confusion they so fear. But the Wayward ... *they set out*, paddle until they lose sight of all compassionate shores ... seeking to recover themselves in shame and horror."

Oinaral did not so much as move, and yet his manner sagged somehow. "Many ..." he said on a breath nearly human. "Many find their way to *Min-Uroikas* ..."

Incredulity stomped the breath from the youth, an outrage not his own.

"What are you saying?"

Oinaral lowered his gaze. The wicked white length of Holol dipped not at all.

"Cousin!" Sorweel cried, his voice not his own. "Tell me you jest!"

Dismay. Outrage. And shame—*shame* before all.

Flee to Min-Uroikas?

Then fury. He had assumed his own hatred peerless: a father dead, an honour and a nation trammelled. But what he felt now crackled as a live bonfire within him, a fury that could pop bones and crack teeth, pulp fists for punishing insensate stone!

Flee to *Min-Uroikas*? For what? To treat with the Hated? The *Vile*? How could such a thing be possible?

"You *lie*! Such a thing cou—!"

"Listen to me!" Oinaral shouted down the length of the sword. "*Thousands* have found their way to Min-Uroikas! Thousands!" He grimaced for something approximating wrath and became, for a fleet instant, truly Sranc-faced. "And *one* of them has found his way back!"

Nin'ciljiras ... Sorweel realized. And upon this ringing fact, the fury was sucked away.

Ishterebinth has fallen to Golgotterath!

He had known this, but ...

A sudden cold washed through him then, a resolve both fathomless and grim. Rather than grope in the vain hope of throwing off the yoke of another, more vital soul, rather than sort himself from himself, he had to find someway to master the *new* soul he had become. Serwa and Moënghus were doomed, otherwise.

"Then why raise Holol against me?"

Oinaral glared. "Cilcûliccas demands that I slay you."

"The Lord of Swans? Why?"

"Because you are for Min-Uroikas, Son of Harweel, though you know it not."

Sorweel leaned forward, pressed the Amiolas hard against the point of Holol.

"Then why *hesitate*?"

Oinaral gazed down upon him in drawn horror. It both unnerved and *thrilled* the youth, the sword's gleaming taper, the luminous tip grinding, nimil-scored and nimil-blunted, a mere thumb's breadth from his brow.

The arid slap of wings. They both started. The Holol chipped across the wrought face as Sorweel yanked his head to squint into the shaft above them. The white was so bright as to be liquid, but Sorweel saw the terrifying silhouette nonetheless, unmistakable for the knifing beak and swan-long neck.

A stork battled in the chute's throat, then was gone.

"Because only Fate," Oinaral Lastborn said, "can redeem the piteous soul of my Race."

"But Father ... Sorweel is one of your Believer-Kings. Will they not interrogate him?"

"Yes," the Holy Aspect-Emperor had conceded.

"So they will discover the Niom has been betrayed, and all our lives will be forfeit."

"That is why you must teach him to hate the Anasûrimbor."

"How?"

"I murdered his father. And you, little Witch, have conquered his heart."

"I have conquered nothing."

Scrutiny, so piercing as to make the night moan.

"And yet, hate will come easy to him."

"I am *not* for Golgotterath!"

Sorweel raced after Oinaral into the baroque chill of the Apiary. He as yet had no idea what the Nonman intended—the ghoul had hustled him out of his chambers without explanation.

"Then who *are* you for?" the Nonman asked.

"My line ... My nation!"

Oinaral cut an imposing figure: his shield slung across his back, a hauberk over his chain gown, and a padded harness—fur pounded into felt—about his shoulders and chest. Holol hung in its scabbard from his hip, its haft propping the palm of his right hand. He appeared both fearsome for his resemblance to Sranc, and *proper*—for reasons Sorweel could only attribute to the Amiolas. An Injori Ishroi of yore.

"Then you are for the Anasûrimbor," he declared.

"No! I am destined to be his assassin!"

"Then you would doom your line, your nation."

"How? How could you know this?"

This earned a scowling glance. "How could I *not* know this, Manling? I was *there*. I was Siqu ere the heartbreak of Eleneöt. *I saw the Whirlwind walk* with mine own eyes—the Sranc move of *one dread will*! I saw the smoke of Sauglish on the horizon, watched the fires of mighty Trysë reflected in the waters of Aumris. I saw it all ... the thousands shrieking upon the piers, the raving onslaught, the mothers casting their babes against stone ..."

His voice had grown wan as he spoke; *how* paling before the ferocity of *what*.

"Everyone knows of the Great Ruiner," Sorweel retorted. "The question is how could you know he *returns*? Or that the Anasûrimbor alone can forestall him?"

"It has been prophe—"

"*I* have been prophecied!"

A vague apprehension slackened the inhuman gaze.

"These are difficult matters for any Man ... let alone one so young as you."

"You forget. My soul is neither young nor human so long I wear this accursed thing on my head."

Oinaral strolled in silent meditation, looking, for all his warlike accoutrements, the meticulous sage his brothers had condemned him to be. Sorweel understood then how much he could *trust* the Son of Oirûnas. Ever is manner the oracle of the man. Ever does our carriage betray our souls. The Lastborn did not steer or cozen, he assayed tragic alternatives, grappled with uncertainties entirely his own. *Different* ignorances.

What Sorweel felt was too numb to count as hope. Oinaral was not steeped in the ancients—*he was one*. His questions stood upon floors planked in countless answers.

This, the youth realized, was what the Nonmen had always been to Men ... Guides ...

Fathers.

"Emilidis abhorred all his miraculous works," the Nonman finally said, "but none so much as the Amiolas. He made certain that no one could forget its nature."

"But *why*?" Sorweel cried. "Why should I believe your myth over the living decree of Yatwer? Why should I doubt the Almighty Goddess that stalks me daily, raises me up, shelters me from evil? You heard my confession: her spit has baffled his eye, allowed me to sow lies where all other men stand exposed! And yet you claim that *he*, my father's *murderer* has the truer vision?"

Oinaral held him in his sour regard. "If I were tell you," he began, "that your mother had taken a lover before your birth, and that this lover was your *true* father, what would you te–?"

"Impossible!" Sorweel coughed in disbelief. "Outrageous!"

"*Exactly*," Oinaral said, speaking with the intensity of insight. "The possibility is *unthinkable*."

"I ask for explanations, and you besmirch my paternity?"

"I say this because the No-God *is just such a possibility* for your Goddess, your Mother of Birth. The No-God is a prospect She cannot think, cannot know, cannot discern, no matter how violently it remakes the World. To exist across all times is to be oblivious to the Eschaton, the *limit* of those times, and Mog-Pharau *is that limit*. The Eschaton."

He glanced at the frowning youth, then gestured to one panel among the many that fretted the walls, to a scene where Ishroi threw down Bashrag and Sranc before the Horns of Golgotterath–but was it Pir Pahal or Pir Minginnial?

"The No-God stands *outside* inside and outside," Oinaral continued. "The Gods of your idols could not foresee its coming two thousand years ago. When It walked the World in actuality they saw only the ruin that was its shadow–*ruin they blamed on other things*! The priests of Men cried out and out and out, for naught. The masses huddled in the Temples wailing, and their Gods–your Gods!–heard only madness or mockery ..."

Sorweel gaped faceless. The Amiolas, which had been an insufferable burden, seemed the only thing holding him upright.

"What are you saying? That *Yatwer* is deceived?"

"More. I'm saying that given Her nature, She *cannot but* be deceived."

"Impossible!"

Oinaral merely shrugged. "Necessity always seems such to the ignorant."

Sorweel reeled, suppressed an urge to bellow his exasperation. How? How could a boy simply awaken one morning and find himself beset by such perversities? Prophets who were not prophets, but were saviours all the same? Gods who ruled as blindly as Kings?

At every turn! Whenever he found some kernel of resolve, whenever he thought he had glimpsed the *truth* of his straits, the *World said otherwise* ... How? How had he become such a lodestone for madness and contradiction?

"You wear the Amiolas, Son of Harweel. The knowledge dwells within you, as certain as suffering itself. The Unholy Consult seeks the destruction of the World ..."

He need not reflect to know the canny Nonman had spoken true. The memories were *there*, mountainous with portent and implication, heartbreak and hatred, but like gears belonging to a different mill they remained inert, immovable, like something that could only be scratched, never seized.

"You bear the Weal, the same as us ..."

And he simply knew ... knew that Oinaral Lastborn spoke true ... The Incû-Holionas had come to exterminate all souls ... and the Gods could not see it at all ...

The Dread Mother was blind.

They descended to the Fourth Observance, one of the more ancient halls of Ishterebinth. Sorweel glimpsed yet another panel depicting Min-Uroikas—Golgotterath—this one hewn from stone grained like violent waters. The Mountain loomed obdurate about them, a crushing forever caught in suspension. His thoughts bobbed and twitched like butterflies, absurd for being so insubstantial in a crypt so massive.

Ishterebinth.

"They plot our extinction ..." the youth said.

"Yes," Oinaral Lastborn replied, his voice timbered in too many passions.

"But why? Why would anyone war for such an insane outcome?"

They crossed another baroque junction. The sound of nearby weeping momentarily scraped the walls.

"Salvation," the Nonman said. "There is no reprieve from such sins as they have committed."

An implacable fury swelled through Sorweel's limbs, an urge to throttle —to strike! But it was cracked for the absence of foes, broken into aimless urgency.

"They seek ..." he said, using calm words to force calm into his demeanour. "They seek to save themselves from ... from damnation?"

"You know this as well," Oinaral said. "You only balk because of its *implication* ..."

"Implication? What implication?"

He could scream, such was the absurdity of it all.

"Because it means the Anasûrimbor is almost certainly your Saviour."

And there it was. The Amiolas need not blot his sense of breathing.

The Mother-of-Birth had doomed him to assassinate a Living Prophet, the *true Saviour*.

Effigies of her father often came to her in the blind watches, glimpses, episodes. She would dwell upon them so as to stop her ears against her brother's odd shrieks, reliving her own past as she relived Seswatha's in her sleep. And sometimes, when the rigours of her captivity waxed ascendant, she found herself rehearsing conversations that did not exist. Her father would come to her bearing bread, water. He would rinse skin she could not feel, ask her how she was now captive in a place so pitiless, so dark.

"Hate had not come easy," she would tell him. "His love for me was ... was ..."

"So is this the end, little Witch? Are you so ready to forget?"

"Forget ... What do you mean?"

"That you are my daughter."

A Nonman huddled naked on the corner of the next intersecting hall, his face buried in tangled arms and knees. The nearest peering illuminated the bulb of the wretch's head, rendered him a thing of white wax and motionless shadow. He seemed a part of the Mountain. Were it not for the pulse of a lone vein, Sorweel would have sworn the ghoul dead.

Oinaral took no notice.

"A Man once told me that hope dwindles with age," the Siqu said after a handful of paces. "That was why, he said, the ancients were happy."

Sorweel could only reply out of numb habit. "And what did you say?"

"That there was hope, and there was *hope for*, and that this was what made the ancients happy ... hoping for."

Deafening silence.

Sorweel simply continued walking, blank for being overmatched by this latest revelation.

"You do understand, do you not, Son of Harweel?"

"I can scarce understand *my* burden. What am I supposed to make of yours?"

Oinaral nodded.

"Those of us who became Siqu so long ago did so because *we knew this day would come* ... this, the day of our Dissolution. We did what we did so that we might finally relieve ourselves of hope's burden, and let it pass *into our children* ..."

A wonder had accompanied these words, one demanding scrutiny as much as reverence. Such a world Sorweel had stumbled into, filled with so much darkness and sorrow and truth.

"Children ...You mean Men."

Halls branched through the blackness, untrod, Sorweel somehow knew, for thousands of years.

"I will tell you what Immiriccas could not know," the ancient Siqu said, staring into the depths of the Observance. "There comes a point where all the old ways of making sense just slough away. You persist in your daily ablutions, your ritual discourse and habitual labour, but an irritation claims you, the suspicion that others conspire to mock and confuse. This is all that you feel ..."

Massacres lined their passage, the toil of making dead.

"The Dolour itself is invisible ... all you ever see are cracks of fear and incomprehension where before all was seamless ... thoughtless ... certain. Soon you dwell in perpetual outrage, but are too fearful to voice it, because even though you know everything is the same, you no longer trust those you have loved to agree, so spiteful they have become! Their concern becomes condescension. Their wariness becomes conspiracy.

"And so the Weal becomes the Dolour, so the Intact become the Erratic. Think on it, mortal King, the way melancholy is prone to make you cruel, impatient of weaknesses. Your soul slowly disassembles, fragments into disconnected traumas, losses, pains. A cowardly word. A lover's betrayal. An infant's last, laboured breath. And for the heroes among us, the heartbreak commensurate with their breathtaking glory ..."

Oinaral lowered his head as if at last conceding to some relentless weight. "This is how you know that you stand before the *least* of my Race," he voice raw. "The fact that I stand lucid and Intact before you."

Their boots sent echoes muttering into the excavations buried about them.

"And that is why Nil'giccas is dead and gone ..." Oinaral said on cracking passion. "He warred valiantly—I know this because for long centuries I was his Book. It was he who contrived the Bark and the Concavity, who made the Seal-of-the-Mountain a floating jewel. None toiled against the Dolour so mightily—or piteously—as he. The more he came apart, the more he demanded that his surroundings bind him together. But nothing could remedy his dissolution ...

"*Depravity*, Son of Harweel. Only depravity retrieves the Wayward soul. No one knows why, but only horrors can render it whole, the commission of atrocities. You recover yourself for a slender interval, and you despair, crack for shame at the dishevelled beast you have become, *and you rejoice*. You *live!* The hunger for life burns far stronger in us than in Men, Son of Harweel. The suicides among us are miraculous, rare names in the Great Pit of Years ...

"And so Nil'giccas—the most Illumined of our ancient Heros—took to *depravity* ..."

Oinaral fell silent. His gait even slowed, as if he dragged his ruminations across the floors behind him.

"What did he do?" Sorweel asked.

A momentary glance to the littered floors—detritus leached from the porous walls.

"He took to the Emwama—a practice that Nin'ciljiras continues. That oil he pours upon his face and head is distilled from the fat of his victims. Atrocity! Simply to warrant his claim to be Intact!"

The Siqu cast his right arm down in the Injori gesture of disgust and symbolic ablution. "But this is to be expected from a Son of Viri, the line of Nin'janjin. But from Nil'giccas? The Blessed Man-Tutor?"

"So what did you do?" the youth asked, understanding that Oinaral gave him a confession in lieu of explanation.

"I feared. I mourned. I cautioned. Finally I *threatened*. When he persisted, I abandoned him."

The Siqu walked riven now, his fists clenched, his neck finned above the folds of his nimil coif.

"And this would be *all that he would remember* ... My betrayal ..."

The youth could feel his own heart swell.

"*Second Father*!" Oinaral boomed, his voice crashing through the black tunnels, ripping through the film of shadows. "Lover! Sharer of Secrets! I abandoned thee!"

The Nonman collapsed to his knees, and Sorweel glimpsed his own image slip across Oinaral's nimil shield as he pitched forward in kneeling anguish—

The reflection seized him about the throat.

Head sealed within the eldritch helm, a cauldron pitted with inscription ...

And a face where there should be no face, as if shining *across* the skein of nimil sigils ...

A Nonman face.

"He would have died a thousand deaths for me!" the Siqu cried. "And in his darkest watch, *I abandoned him*!"

Sorweel gazed hapless. "But he had succumbed to depravity ... What else was there to be done?"

"*The ancient learn no lessons*!" Oinaral roared. In a blink he was back upon his feet, looming martial over the stunned youth. "A *mortal* should know as much! You do not punish the aged as you would children! Doing such simply salves your own conceit! Indulges your own malice!"

His eyes rolled ceiling-ward. His face clenched into something indistinguishable from a Sranc, and in a heartbeat Sorweel understood that the skinnies had been cut *directly* from them, that they were but the most horrific fragment of the ancient being before him—a demented mockery!

Such a blight the Inchoroi had been.

"I was *weak*!" Oinaral cried. "I punished him for failing to be what he had always been! I punished him for wronging *me*!" He seized Sorweel by his stained tunic, wrenched him into his spittle. "Don't you see, Manling? All of this *is my fault*! I was the last rope remaining, his only tether!"

Confusion clouded the Siqu's fury. He let slip Sorweel's tunic, looked to the ground, blinking, shaking.

"What happened to him?" the youth asked. "What did he do?"

Oinaral whirled away in what resembled—to human eyes—childish shame. Sorweel turned away, but more to avoid his own reflection across Oinaral's shield than out of respect.

"He fled ..." the Nonman moaned into the graven walls, hunched as though paring his fingernails. "Vanished the fortnight following. I abandoned our beloved King, and he abandoned his sacred Mansion, the last surviving Son of Tsonos ... until Nin'ciljiras returned."

"But he would have fled regardless ..."

"Only a fraction flee the Mountain ... Some retreat into the Holy Deep, where they dwell in the blankness of the black, with no meaning to pain them. And others, the thousands of wretches below us, simply dwell, wander the compass of their most primitive habits, circling hearths they cannot remember, endlessly crying out, endlessly gathering and dropping the smashed pottery of their souls ..."

The youth could not but wonder whether this would be all that remained of him ... or Serwa ... ere this latest nightmare were through.

"I alone am to blame," the ancient Siqu declared to the miniature glories.

"But you said as much yourself. One need not leave the Mountain to flee. What would it matter if Nil'giccas roamed the mines or the Mere? He had fled already, Cousin. Nin'ciljiras would have been acclaimed regardless."

The Son of Oirûnas finally turned to him. His cheeks gleamed. Pink rimmed his black-glittering eyes. He was a wise soul, the youth knew, but one jealous of its madnesses.

"How many remain Intact?" Sorweel asked.

The Nonman hesitated for an instant, as if loathe to yield the topic of his heartbreak. Renewed resolution deadened his expression.

"Scarcely a dozen. Several hundred others dwell, like Nin'ciljiras, in the twilight between."

"So few."

Oinaral Lastborn nodded. "The wound the Vile struck was mortal, though it would take three Ages for the poison to prevail. Our very immortality was our extinction." Something, the irony perhaps, hooked his lips into a sneer. "We have dwelt with Apocalypse since before Far Antiquity, Son of Harweel. I fear we have at last embraced it."

The glare had been so bright as to make straw of everything that gleamed, and chalk of all that was indistinct. Ordealmen laboured across the plain, each soul bearing his shadow beneath him. Their dust conspired to create a second Shroud, dwarfish and insubstantial.

"And if Ishterebinth *has* fallen to the Consult? What then, Father?"

A grave look.

"You are my daughter, Serwa," Anasûrimbor Kellhus replied. "Show them my portion."

Nin'ciljiras had come without explanation, Oinaral explained, disgorged by the very horizon that had swallowed him an Age previous when he and the other Dispossessed Sons of Viri had fled the Judgment of the Seal. The son of Ninar had come in all due humility, invoking the Canon of Imimorûl, demanding a hearing before the Aged. Some had sought to kill him, to execute the sentence Nil'giccas had passed. But his return so soon after the disappearance of the King was no coincidence. Nin'ciljiras had found Ishterebinth in uproar, for never had a Mansion wanted for a Son of Tsonos! So the Aged, those upon the Dolour's mad bourne, seized upon the cur, immediately declared him, fearing strife and rebellion otherwise—sorrows that would all but toss them to madness. What could any of the Younger do? They had no voice in matters of Canon. They remained Intact entirely because they *had no honour*, for honour was nothing but the summit of life, and they had lived not at all. Aside from sneers, what could they command in the presence of *heroes*?

"I was a child when the Second Watch was disbanded," Oinaral explained. "I remember seeing *him*, Nin'janjin, the Most-Accursed Son, standing as a brother beside Cu'jara Cinmoi in the glory of the Siölan Mall. I alone *recall* the terms of our wicked capitulation!"

So Oinaral could only watch in horror as Nin'ciljiras, Scion of Nin'janjin, was bled as Nil'giccas was once bled upon the Holy Seal of Ishoriöl, and so became the King of the Exalted Stronghold. And he knew with a certainty that was a sickness in his gut what would follow, how Min-Uroikas would figure ever more in the usurper's discourse and declaration, how possibilities mentioned would become, in the fullness of months and years, promises sworn.

How Ishterebinth would one day awaken a fief of Golgotterath ...

Sorweel had fairly swooned for incredulity, listening as he did with a composite soul. What disaster? What catastrophe could warrant degradation so outrageous as this? To beg scraps from the palm of the Vile! Lick the hands that had tortured and murdered their wives! Their daughters! To fall as cannibals upon honour and glory!

"Outrage!" he barked from hunched shoulders. "*They are the Vile!*"

Oinaral seized his shoulder, drew him to a halt. "*Name* yourself, Son of Harweel ... Take possession of what you think."

"*They are the Vile*," the Horse-King cried. "How? How could any forgetting be so profound?"

"All forgetting is so profound," the Siqu replied.

They passed from the Observances into the Pith proper, where the corridors were expansive and the ceilings oppressive. The peerings were few and far between, but for some reason the gloom embalmed more than it exposed. Guttural hymns floated from the galleries about them, a solemn chorus singing from the *Holy Juürl*. The stone seemed dulcet, as bright as teeth for the polish of trailing hands. Bestiaries adorned the walls, ancient totems from days even the Great Pit of Years could not reckon. The engravings were more shallow, the figures rendered as large as the surfaces that bore them—a welcome reprieve from the incessant assault of detail. Sorweel could recognize the creatures easily enough—bear, mastodon, eagle, lion—but each had been rendered as if occupying all positions *at once*—crouching, leaping, running—so that they seemed curious kinds of *suns*, their torsos become discs, their many limbs the emanations of light.

"Serwa ... Moënghus ... What will happen to them?"

It frightened him, the way her name pinched his throat for speaking.

"They will be Apportioned."

Somehow he knew what this meant. "Divided as spoils ..."

"Yes."

"To be loved ..." the youth said, at once horrified and unsurprised. "Then murdered."

"Yes."

"You must do something!"

"The Aged coddle me," Oinaral said, "make grand gesture of all the strife I am spared. At least some ember of them, they proclaim, shall glow long into the black. But for all their fatuous celebration, I am despised just the same. Thus the bitter irony of my curse, Son of Harweel. I am the greatest shame my Kinning has known, a reclusive Scribe among grasping Heroes, and yet only I recall the distinction between honour and corruption ..."

The Injori Ishroi rolled his head about his chin as if facts could seize throats.

"Only I can remember *what shame is*!"

And it amazed Sorweel that this underworld could be so similar to his own. Men forever ornamented their words with more words, claiming to be moved by compassion, eloquence, and reason, when in sooth the station of the speaker was their only care. If anything rendered the Nonmen "false," he decided, it was their nobility, their solidarity, their steadfast refusal to contravene the claims of their fathers ...

Their utter contempt for things *convenient*.

"This is why you need me to overthrow Nin'ciljiras?" the young Believer-King asked. "The bigotry of the Aged?"

Oinaral stared forward, his marmoreal profile expressionless. "Yes."

"But if your word counts for nothing, what could the word of Men do?"

"I do not need you to speak, Son of Harweel."

"Then what *do* you need me for?"

The Siqu refused to meet his gaze, gesturing instead to a great stair that plummeted into blackness and living rock to their right—the Inward Stair, Sorweel realized. Light flared at the terminus below, but nowhere along the passage.

"To survive," Oinaral replied.

"I don't understand," Sorweel said as they descended into the gloom. The wondrous bestiary ornamenting the halls above had yielded to the same crammed welter of history. But where the miniature dioramas stood a fair cubit and were stacked parallel to the floors elsewhere, these issued at an angle upon every step, ribbing the ceiling with epic scenes of strife and glory.

"You are God-entangled."

Sorweel could scarcely feel his own frown. "I fear my doom lies in a different direction, Oinaral."

"Doom has no direction, Son of Harweel. The time and place of your death has been assigned, no matter when or where you find yourself."

The thought unnerved the youth, despite all the months he'd squandered mulling it.

"So?" he asked on a thin voice.

"To be doomed is also to be an *oracle* ..."

"A way to read the future?"

The dark eyes appraised him.

"In a manner, yes ... I know only that you cannot die within the Weeping Mountain."

The youth scowled. Was this what he had meant about Fate before?

"You want to use me as your *charm*!" he cried. "As proof against your own death!"

The tall Siqu descended some ten steps before answering. His elaborate coat and gown shimmered in the nearing light. His shadow climbed the steps behind him.

"Where we go ..." he began, only to pause as if caught upon some obscure scruple.

"I cannot survive where we go," he resumed, "unless I stalk your shadow—your Fate."

"And where do we go?" Sorweel asked, raising a hand against the breaching light, for though the stair continued, its cloistered, subterranean passage had come to an end. The oppressive ceilings fell away ...

If evasion had been his design, then the Siqu had timed his confession perfectly. Even with the knowledge afforded by the Amiolas, the spectacle struck him speechless. Hundreds of peerings burned as a constellation of little suns, so bright as to dazzle the eyes, shedding light across the whole of what was called the Ilculcû Rift, a vast, diagonal wedge of emptiness struck into the Mountain's heart. The Inward Stair flared outward across the lower slope, broadening into something truly monumental, and descending to the lowest trough of the Ilculcû. But the wonder lay above, stamped deep into the opposite face of the Rift: the famed Hanging Citadels of Ishterebinth.

"We dwindle," Oinaral said, "but our works remain ..."

Sorweel found himself gawking for awe, even though Immiriccas had despised the ostentation. The opposite depths of the Mountain, Sorweel knew, were riddled with the palatial complexes of the Injori Ishroi, a maze of underworld manors, all opening onto the hanging face of the Ilculcû, forming a great and eclectic ceiling, one possessing numberless embrasures, dozens of colonnades and terraces—a veritable scarp of gilded and graven structure! A labyrinth of iron platforms subtended it all, hanging like nets pinned to a fisherman's ceiling, descending in stages, conjoining all of the strongholds. Some sported balustrades, but most hung as plates in air, lavishly furnished in places, sparsely in others, all of it bound into a surreal commons. The Believer-King could see dozens of figures through and across the haze of grilled floors, some congregated, some paired as lovers, and a great number solitary.

Discourse hung as a thin mutter upon the air. Periodic shouts of grief pealed across the gulf.

"Behold," Oinaral said, his tone bitter and bent, "Mi'punial's Famed Hidden Heaven ..."

"The Sky-Beneath-the-Mountain," Sorweel replied in awe. "I remember ..."

He looked to his Siqu, not quite credulous of his certainty. "I remember *singing* ..." he said, fumbling between thoughts and images not his own. "I remember the peerings ablaze, the horns pealing morning bright—and the whole Rift booming with sacred song!"

"Aye," Oinaral said, turning his head away.

"The Ishroi and the Indentured would congregate across the Sky-Beneath," Sorweel continued, "and they would sing ... from the *Hipinna*, mostly ... Yes ... for that was the favourite of the wives and the children ..." And it seemed he could hear it, the holy chorus, at once thunderous and sweet, magical for the seamless compounding of hearts and voices, passion struck from the mire of the flesh, raised to the mystic purity of the Ecstasis. He found himself looking from side to side across the expanse of the Inward Stair, noticing for the first time the small mounds of debris scattered across its entirety. "We would vanish into our songs," he said, glimpsing things some other soul had seen, "and the Emwama ... they would assemble on these very steps, and *weep* for the beauty of their masters!"

Sorweel turned to the ancient Siqu. "They worshipped us then ... Adored the hand that whipped them."

"As they do now," Oinaral said darkly. "As they are bred."

"And the singing?" the soul that had once been Sorweel asked. "Has song fled the Mountain, my Brother?"

The Siqu paused upon one of the strange, small piles of debris. He chipped his boot against the fibrous mass, expelling something that clattered down the steps at an angle before and below Sorweel ...

The bowl of a human skull.

"Song has fled the Mountain," the ghoul said.

The gloom was such that only forms could be discerned at any distance. Anasûrimbor Serwa knew him by the wary scruple of his passage, how he never followed quite the same path to where she hung. The Thresholds had been wrought to baffle the Gods, a place where the Nonmen might escape as a thief into a crowd, and Harapior, more than any of the others, lived in terror of what sins might find him. Just as he, more than any other, found terror and torment in her singing.

Glory was a drug to them, her father had said. She never need fear them so long as she remained extraordinary.

She sang as she always sang ... another ancient Cûnuroi hymn.

"My wife, Mirinqû, would sing thus," the Lord Torturer said, "as she prepared my kit before battle." He had paused just outside the penultimate threshold; now he grimaced for crossing, stood riven in her presence. "That very song, that very way ..."

He raised and lowered his left hand, blinked two tears from his eyes.

"In her voice ..."

Wrath clawed his expression.

"But your singing was not so *exact* in the beginning ... No ... Not at all."

He lowered his wax-white face in contemplation.

"I know what you do, Anasûrimbor witch. I know that you sing to torment your tormentors. To heap yet more turmoil upon our blasted hearts."

He stood impassive, absolutely still, and yet wild violence emanated from him.

"But *how* you do it—that is the question that consumes my brothers." He drew his black eyes up. "How does a mortal girl, a captive hidden from sun, sky—even the Gods!—become the terror of the Ishroi, throw all Ishterebinth into uproar?"

He bared fused teeth.

"But I know. I know what you are—the secret of your obscene line."

He knew of the Dûnyain, she realized.

"You sing Mirinqû's songs because of what I have said. You sing with her-her ... her *voice* because of what I remember! You are the captive, yet it is I who confesses—who *betrays*!"

There could be no more doubt as to who ruled in Ishterebinth.

Again he reached out; again his will fell short her skin. He balled the hand into a shaking fist, raised it to her temple. Monstrous passion deformed his face.

"I would draw my blade *now*!" he screeched. "You would sing then, I assure you!"

And he warred with himself, Lord Harapior, swayed and moaned for tides of disordered passion. He lowered his face once again, stood gasping, clenching and unclenching his fists, listening to the dulcet call of long-dead daughters and wives.

"But your rumour has spread too far," he grated in a broken voice. "They speak only of you throughout the Mountain ... the daughter of Men who has tortured the Torturer."

He stood breathing, folded a final tremor into the serenity of immortal hatred.

His manner became that of a thumb testing a vicious edge.

"You will have no voice left, Anasûrimbor, ere you find peace in the Weeping Mountain."

The peerings faltered, then became no more than husks surfacing in the gelid light of Holol, which Oinaral held point-out as they descended into the Chthonic Manse, the riddled heart of the Weeping Mountain. They passed great veins of quartz, and the sword dazzled the shelves of lucent statuary, visions that awed the youth, but left him no less boggled. The empire of the ghouls was nothing if not *time*, the stacking of Ages in the mist. But what could walls sheathed in miraculous simulacra provide eyes that could not see?

The ghouls had chiselled their souls into their walls for naught. They had remade the Mountain in their image for naught. They had presumed they could render the spirit *material*, make of it something hard as stone, all for naught. The deeper Oinaral Lastborn led Sorweel, the more the pageants heaped upon the walls shouted tragic vanity.

If his human portion was baffled, the inhuman portion was *appalled:* the thought of his brothers huddled as aggrieved misers over their dwindling hoard of memories. It was the penance of the besotted, souls bent upon the vindication of suffering, the *proof of persecution* that would seal their claim against Fate. They had been condemned by a folly that was theirs and *theirs alone*, and so they had committed the most human of humanity's numberless sins ...

They had blamed Heaven.

Sorweel need only prick his ear to the black to sound the wages of their folly. For where Nonmen had once toiled singing, they now wailed as bewildered beasts in the dark. Oinaral had spoken true: song had fled these halls long, long ago. Only paeans and dirges graced the Mountain now.

Thousands had once populated these levels, the bulk of the Injori. Below the Hanging Citadels of the Ishroi and far greater in extent, the Chthonic Manse had housed the Indentured, those born into the Sworn Kinnings. This had been the unheralded but no less vital heart of Ishterebinth. Throngs had streamed beneath the peerings, packed the concourses of the Lesser Rifts. Sorweel could remember the perpetual sound of *rain*, not for any actual rainfall, but for the noise of endless industry broken across adorned walls, filtered until nothing but vapour reached the ear.

Now only dark and derelict passages remained, turn after turn, the walls belted with meaningless, miniature parades, the floor strewn with debris—bones among them. Gone was the light—Oinaral actually took care to avoid corridors housing the glow of isolate peerings. Gone was the swarm of regimented activity. And gone was the sound of cleansing rain ...

For it was here that the Weeping Mountain took its name.

Sakarpus had wept the night and day following the triumph of the Aspect-Emperor, and though the chorus had immersed him, Sorweel had heard nothing save his own lamentations writ wide. No matter how distant, the wail on the wind could only be his own because the loss it declared was also his own. The losses of the Nonmen, however, lay far beyond his ken. His skin pimpled for the unnatural tenor. His ear recoiled for the lunacy of the screech. He could hear it in each tormented aria, the punishments of millennia whittled to the point of *now*, vast life concentrated into anguished slurry—horrors reverberating in a drum a thousand years dead. A dead wife. A treacherous lover. A disastrous rout. Sorweel could own none of these losses—and who could, given the mad individuality of each? Time itself had flown apart in the bowel of the Weeping Mountain. And so he heard fragments, a choir of crazed overreactions, torment, heartbreak, floating devoid of sense or origin. "*The left leg is broken*!" one voice bobbed across the turbulence. "*The knee is not the knee*!"

"*Don't look*!" another voice erupted. "*Turn aside thine eyes*!"

The cacophony gathered density the deeper they fathomed, becoming an all-permeating roar, a wash of thousands thrashing as a snake caught upon a pitchfork. Neither Sorweel nor Oinaral ventured to speak. The Siqu led. Sorweel followed rigid with apprehension, starting at each new howl that issued raw from the black beyond Holol's white light. The wailing grew louder, and with it, the madness thickened as cream, until he found himself reeling for a melancholy all his own, as if the multiplication of laments heard from without rendered them indistinguishable from sorrow within.

Sorweel clutched his hands against tremors, clenched his voice into a burning ball.

"An endless funeral ..." he found himself gasping. "A *blasted tomb*! How could anyone dwell in such a place?"

"Gird your loins, Son of Harweel. The tempest is yet to come ..."

Sorweel stopped, watched Oinaral and his point of light draw ahead of him.

"*Enough*!" he cried. "No more games! Tell me! Where are you taking me? *What is your design?*"

The Nonman turned to study him for a long moment—too long.

"I'm not a fool," Sorweel continued. "I've survived months among the Anasûrimbor bearing murder in my heart! You refuse to lie—this is how I know you possess honour ... and because these ... *memories* I have assure as much. I knew you as a boy!" He paused to glare at the Nonman. "You cannot lie, Oinaral Lastborn, so you defer, evade ... Why? If not to lure me *too deep*, past some point of return."

A dark, glittering look. "This is what you think?"

"I think this is *as far as I go*. I think our time of reckoning has come!"

A shy, even anguished, edge crept into the porcelain expression. "Even if it costs the lives of the girl an—?"

"*Enough*!" the Believer-King erupted. "Enough! What is it you so fear to tell me? What *awaits* us in the dark?"

Oinaral cast an apprehensive look about them.

"We search for my father," he said, bereft of expression, hope.

This caught Sorweel by surprise. The inhuman lament reverberated in the interval. The Cauldron lay numb as void, as if the bone of his skull had been knitted into it.

"Oirûnas?" he asked, knowing this name as surely as that of Niehirren Halfhand or Orsuleese the Faster, or any other Heroic Lord of the Plains. Oirûnas Oirasig, Survivor of the First Watch, and Master of the Second. With his twin brother, Oirinas, among the most renowned of the Siölan Ishroi.

"He still lives?"

Solemn hesitation. "Yes."

"But surely he's ..." Sorweel began, only to pause on a sudden scruple.

He knew the pain of lost fathers. The ache.

But the Nonman seemed unmoved. "The Dolour has claimed him entirely," he said. "Yes."

They stared at each other across the desolate hall, Man and Nonman.

"This is why you need me?" Sorweel said. "To survive your ... your *father*?"

"Yes," the ancient Siqu replied, averting his darkling gaze. "To beg of him one last legendary deed."

So they walked, Man and Nonman.

Buried. Wandering the entombed heart of Ishterebinth, the Weeping Mountain. *Encased.* Enveloped by graven lattices of glory and orgiastic excess. Trampled by bootless meaning, otiose hope. The brute reality was dismaying enough, but the *immateriality* of the underworld trek was by far the worse. The losses.

How? How had we been laid so low?

The Nonman Siqu explained everything, how they travelled through the Chthonic to reach the Vast Ingressus, the massive well that sank through the greater part of the Weeping Mountain. Oinaral had not seen his father since the Hero had forsaken the Citadels a millennium previous, but he had heard rumour enough to know that he lived, and to believe that he wandered the Mere—the Holy Deep. For all the disorder of their souls, the Erratics remain shackled to animal necessity. This was why Sorweel and Oinaral had so far only *heard* them, why the lamentations had remained before them. Save for a few, the Wayward congregated about the Ingressus, where they scavenged what food they could.

The caterwaul waxed. Oinaral flinched at first sound of the clacking, stone hammering stone. He paused, stood white and rigid in Holol's light, listening to the noise repeat as relentlessly as a wheel ...

Clack ... Clack ... Clack ...

"Time is short," he finally called. "We must run!" He seized Sorweel by the arm, drew him into the black passage before them—into the immured cacophony.

"What?" the Believer-King cried, stumbling after him. "What is it?"

"The Boatman comes!" Oinaral replied, breaking into a trot while holding the luminous point of Holol out before them.

Clack ... Clack ... Clack ...

Graven surfaces unspooled in the light. They crossed a reception hall of some kind, one reduced to scorched wrack for fire or sorcery. In the sweep of shadows, Sorweel glimpsed a nude figure huddled amid the debris.

"So we take the Haul?" he asked, not quite fathoming.

Another nude figure in the black, this one standing, pounding its face into the doll-sized imagery before him. Sorweel saw a whole panel roll beneath the light, the figures smashed like teeth from jaws, the remaining roots smeared with blood.

"*Run!*" the Nonman cried over his shoulder.

A hair-raising screech. The light struck two filth-smeared figures locked upon the soiled floor, strangling, each striving to rape or murder the other. Sorweel's boot cracked through a rib cage, and he pitched forward to the ground—realized that what he had assumed ash and dust was in fact excrement. He glimpsed movement in the blackness, the shine of Sranc scalps. The gloom howled.

Oinaral stooped to assist him. His light seemed to pick out random images of horror.

"*Cousin!*" Sorweel shouted—a cry punched from him by horror and incredulity. "*This cannot be!*"

But wailing had conquered all heights of sound. They stood in the Wormery, he realized, where the famed silks of Injor-Niyas were manufactured for the Kings of lands as distant as Shir and Kyraneas. The Ingressus was close ... Very close!

A wretch stepped out of the howling blackness and fell upon Oinaral's nimil-armoured knee, his ribs inked in shadow, so famished as to resemble a Sranc in body as well as mien. The Siqu turned in revulsion and horror, struck the piteous soul upon the brow with Holol.

Clack ... Clack ... Clack ...

Figures tossed in the greater gloom about them.

They ran about a great mound of ruin—some bricked structure toppled. A portcullis jutted from the shattered blocks, nine black-iron teeth pointed as pitchfork over a shoulder, each adorned in severed Nonman heads in varying stages of decay.

Oinaral cast his gaze about, then gestured for Sorweel to climb. He followed the Siqu to the ruin's summit, the Horde's screech resonating within the unholy Cauldron. Holol's radiant point shed a chiaroscuro of shadows across the floors beneath them. Pallid figures leapt into existence in the interstices of light, ghouls become larval with grief, wailing, rocking, slapping offal across their cheeks and skulls. Gesticulating hands. Fused teeth about howling maws. Skin blackened for filth and feces. Rictus after anguished rictus, hundreds of them, all hairless and fungal white, bobbing like buoys across the murky expanse. And the spectacle brought the youth to his knees, struck him to the root. Rot had become his marrow, cinders his heart ...

These! These were their wages! The fruit of their mad conceit, their blasphemous folly!

The unthinkable had come to pass. The People of Morning were truly dead.

The Nonman's light flew out across space, revealing the hulks of columns and piers, stations gutted and gigantic, heights of graven glory hanging cadaverous over writhing floors.

Clack ... Clack ... Clack ...

His bearing apparently secured, Oinaral dropped down the mound's side, then led him across ground heaped with centuries of midden and crawling with famished Erratics. Sorweel danced about them as one might lepers, stumbled over a famished ghoul leaning over a violet corpse, tearing at the black nipple with canine abandon. Many were oblivious to their passage, rapt with some long extinct horror. Sorweel saw one cradling void like an infant, another caressing stone like a lover. But many others noticed, some with the dull mien of those peering about immovable grief, others caught upon the Holol's light as fish upon a lure, black eyes glittering ...

Many of these began standing.

Clack ... Clack ... Clack ...

Sorweel gawked about, stumbling after the Siqu, who turned to him while still trotting. His shout need not be inaudible.

Run!

A sorcerous mutter somehow steamed through the mad Lament ...

And Sorweel was running hard upon the heels of the glittering Nonman warrior, pitching over midden slopes. Once again he glimpsed the Amiolas reflected in Oinaral's oval shield. Once again he glimpsed the spectral horror of Immiriccas gazing back upon him. And the Believer-King stopped amid a clutch of grovelling wretches, astonished and appalled.

Was he dead?

What–what? What was happening here?

Oinaral receded into the deeps, his light slouching across the countless aggrieved. A wall of ascending arches reared before Nonman Siqu, curved about void. His mail coats glittered like something out of legend ...

Shadow fell across the young Believer-King.

What happened?

A bloodred light sparked *behind him*–and he whirled about, recalling the sorcerous singing. He saw dozens of Erratics, naked and rag-bound, staggering over and through their brothers while bounding as wild apes toward him. He saw a figure gowned in rags a fair distance behind, his mouth and eyes flaring white, a piercing, crimson bolus scribbling between his upraised hands. There was a crack like thunder. Something happened he could not quite fathom, let alone describe–something like light blowing the blood from all the intervening bodies. A warble passed through the screaming chorus.

Hot fluid slapped across him.

Somehow Oinaral had him in an iron clasp and was drawing him backward.

Clack ... Clack ... Clack ...

"*Hell!*" he screamed at the Siqu. "*I'm in Hell!*"

But the ghoul could not hear him.

Chapter Ten

Dagliash

The song of Truth is the cracking of Desire. Only when Men weep do they know.

—CANTICLES, 6:6, *The Chronicle of the Tusk*

Give them dirt, and they will multiply.

—AÖRSI PROVERB

Late Summer, 20 New Imperial Year (4132, Year-of-the-Tusk), High Illawor

Harsunc. The Fish Knife.

This was what the Aörsic Knights-Chieftain called the River Sursa, for this was what the waterway resembled, especially when glimpsed from the rampart heights of Dagliash in the glare of evening: a long thin blade of silver cutting the lifeless wastes of Agongorea from the spare Erengaw Plains, the eastern bank nearly straight; and the western bank, the one prone to flooding, curved as though from years of whetting.

Fish was also the belittling cognomen the ancient Aörsi had used for the Sranc—their version of *skinnies*. "The Fish," the war-bitten would say, "must first jump the Knife." They spoke the way all warlike Men speak, filled with bluff and hatred, saying only what was injurious to their foe, deriding (as they should) all that was lethal and true. In their simple and dangerous hearts, the River Sursa was always *theirs*, always the instrument of Men.

But in truth the Harsunc possessed *two* deadly edges. Since the days of Nanor-Ukkerja, the blood of innumerable Men had mucked her banks, souls lost in battles whose names were carved on cracked and buried stone. Chronicles told of bloated bodies jamming the river's throat, of great rotting sheets that skinned the waters for days, even weeks, before decay and the relentless current finally delivered them to the gullet of the Misty Sea.

The Harsunc was as apt to be defended as crossed—to run red as purple. "If it is our Knife," Nau-Cayûti asks his cocksure generals in the *Kayûtiad*, "then why have we raised Dagliash to watch over it?"

Indeed, it would be the *wrong edge* that would prove the most keen in the end. The No-God would end the millennial dispute. Dagliash would be wrecked. All the Bardic metaphors, the generational meanings, the midnight tales of dread and glory would burn with the cities of the High Norsirai. The River Sursa, to the extent it was referred to at all, became the "Chogiaz", what the Sranc had named it in their obscene tongue. Two thousand years would pass ere Men breathed meaning into its spare aspect once again. Two thousand years would the Knife wait for the Great Ordeal to dare its ancient and murderous edges.

The Ordealman trudged onward, crossing the vast swamp the Horde had made of the River Migmarsa, so passing from High Illawor into Yinwaul—from a land scarcely mentioned in the *Holy Sagas*, to one mentioned as much as any other. The Horde continued its withdrawal, gathering and retreating before the shining hosts. The great smoke that had concealed it, the dust of a million stamping feet, thinned as the ground became stonier, so that it seemed the horizon steamed more than billowed before the pursuing horsemen. At times they could even glimpse the beasts, pale masses seething, multiplied until they matted the contours of the land. Hillocks and knolls overrun, vales choked, distances plumbed, *encompassed.* Everywhere great masses shifting and sloughing, as if the very world moulted. Men gazed stupefied, neither fearing nor wondering, for most lacked the means to truly comprehend what they witnessed. They knew only that they were *dwarfed*, little more than insignificant specks in the thrall of jealous enormities. Their lives, they understood, mattered only in their *sum*. And since this is the grim truth of all human life, the insight possessed the character of revelation.

And it came to seem holy, eating Sranc. To consume them was to partake of the Horde.

To eat meaning.

And so they rode, day in and day out, crossing the trampled, lifeless miles, pacing and pondering their innumerable foe. They watched the Schoolmen stride the low sky, a necklace of brilliant lights strung across the horizon. Their gazes danced from flash to flicker, point to burning point. Some took to watching the way the lights steeped and burnished the pluming veils above. Some watched the obscene thousands perishing below, mites engulfed in sweeping fire. Periodically, they turned in their saddles to study the columns of the Great Ordeal, the assemblies glittering in the high sunlight. The visions made fanatics of them all.

They *had* come to the ends of the earth. They *did* war to save the very World.

There could be no doubting in the penumbra of such mad spectacle ...

The justness of their cause. The divinity of the Holy Aspect-Emperor.

Only their strength remained in question.

Gradually, so slow as to defeat the discrimination of many, a different pitch had crept into the Horde's thundering howl, a plaintive edge, more panicked than crazed, almost as though the Sranc *knew* they were being eaten. The Schoolmen who strode the low skies in the Culling found they could now *glimpse* the seething fields they scoured, parsed, and blasted. Where for weeks and months the beasts had seemed to elude and frustrate the pursuing horsemen, now they seemed to genuinely flee.

"They *fear* us!" a joyous Siroyon declared in Council.

"No," the Holy Aspect-Emperor said, ever quick to dispatch assumptions that might lead his men to dismiss their foe. "They scream according to their hunger and exertion and nothing more. Now that our bellies are full, our advance has quickened. We have merely twisted the lute-strings tight."

But for many, there could be no denying the growing desperation of their Adversary. Time and again, the Holy Aspect-Emperor cautioned his Believer-Kings, reminding them that Sranc *were not Men*, that straits hardened them, that starvation fuelled their ferocity. Even still, a new daring took root among the more feckless skirmishers. They believed they knew their foe as well as any ancient Knight-Chieftain: his ebb, his flow, his more treacherous vicissitudes. And as always, the assumption of knowledge licensed a growing sense of impunity.

What was more, a dark and destructive will had impregnated their thoughts—*all* their thoughts—a need, a *hunger*, to visit catastrophic destruction upon their foe, to reap him as wheat, to gather him into infinite sheaves, and gorge upon him in ecstasy. "Think!" they would cry to one another in private. "Think of the *feast*!"

Seeing these dark inklings, the Holy Aspect-Emperor harangued them in council, upbraiding them for their recklessness. On several occasions he even went so far as to invoke the Martial Prohibitions, and condemned several caste-nobles to the lash. Time and again he called their attention to *how far they had come*. "Who?" he would cry, his voice booming through the Eleven Pole Chamber. "Who among you will be the first to have come *so far* only to perish in rank folly? Who among you shall earn the honour of *that* song?"

And then, when the Ordeal had reached the eastern frontier of Illawor, he stabbed his finger on the great, illuminated map his Believer-Kings so often bickered over, and drew his haloed finger down the Fish Knife, the fabled Harsunc, inked in bold black. It was too deep to be forded, too broad for Sranc to swim; even those not privy to the reports of the Imperial Trackers knew as much.

Soon, the Horde would be *caught* before them.

It would defend Dagliash no matter what.

"What feast," the Holy Aspect-Emperor asked his Believer-Kings, "will be served up then?"

The timbers pitched. Proyas's stomach climbed his ribs, then dropped.

Two days previous the Ordeal had come upon a forest of poplars—or the remnants of one—in the wake of the Horde. Given the mists enveloping the shoreline, the apparition of savaged trees had seemed more an omen than a boon. But come nightfall the blessing they represented had become plain. The carpenters set to repairing innumerable wains and other accoutrements. Their idle brothers, meanwhile, cavorted about genuine bonfires, whooping into the void. Agmundrmen and others fashioned great spits, which they used to roast Sranc whole. Flames climbed the height of Momemn's walls for the whoosh of grease. The encampment, long condemned to chill and gloom for the lack of fuel, blazed for the light of innumerable fires, and Men ambled as though drunk, their beards shining for gluttony, their gazes bright for something too vicious to be called jubilation.

Only the Schoolmen and the Shrial Knights refrained from partaking in the bacchanal. But while the former remained within their enclaves as always, the latter set about cutting and appropriating the best timber they could find. Under the watchful gaze of Lord Ussiliar, they toiled through the night, dressing and dowelling and binding, fashioning a platform large enough to deck a Cironji war-galley.

The Raft, they called it.

Now Proyas stood upon it with his fellow Believer-Kings, swinging over emptiness on a mummer's stage, gazing stupefied across the teeming leagues, for the day possessed the arid clarity of summer's abdication. For all the miracles he had witnessed over the years, this seemed the most preposterous. Even the Grandmasters among them appeared visibly awestruck. Many present had seen the now legendary Throwing-of-the-Hulls, when Kellhus emptied Invishi's harbour by raising and casting burning ships whole at Prince Akirapita's Chorae-equipped bowmen. Although that episode was the greater spectacle, they had spied it from afar. *This*, however, this had the intimacy of a father's embrace, and the profundity of unhinged *ground*, vaulting not simply as a person, *but as a place*. Proyas watched others exchange small looks of wonder, heard the murmur of astonishment and glee.

Couras Nantilla, who stood next to him, clutched his arm as if to say, *See! See!*

But Nersei Proyas saw only the power and nothing of the *proof*. Small commiserations like Nantilla's grasp simply recalled the consolation lost and the rank turmoil gained: the knowledge that *he was no longer Zaudunyani*, even though he belonged to them all the same. These Men who had been his brothers were now gulls ... fools bent on suffering for their delusions!

And so his heart was broken even as it bounced on a string of giddy drops and steep, aerial turns.

Out of instinct, he aspired to the blank mien and manner that is the refuge of all lost souls in public. But melancholy possesses a spite all its own, and seeks to reveal itself regardless of what the soul wills. Kellhus brought the Raft about, Yinwaul fell away, and the Neleöst bobbed across the whole of the horizon. The angle of the sunlight also changed, and Proyas turned, startled to find himself standing in another's shadow. It was

Saubon. His hand upon the rail, the Galeoth loomed before him, standing so as to shield him from the others.

"Dour befits our terrible station," the man muttered under his breath, "but not *tears* ..."

Proyas averted his face, pawed away the wetness. His eyes had felt muddy, but then they always felt muddy of late. For a heartbeat he stood as one broken, utterly abject in Saubon's alarmed gaze. Then he found it, the old arrogant posture, the mien and stance of a great man possessing warrant both temporal and divine—the most profound assurance known to Men. He communicated his gratitude to Saubon with a lingering look.

What was happening?

The encampment blurred as cobbles underneath a carriage. Thousands clotted the battered land, all of them crying out, creating a roar that was scooped by the velocity of their passage overhead. To a soul they shouted out, bellowed in praise and adulation of their False Prophet. Dark and pale and sunburned faces. Mouths pitting beards. Thickets of axes and spears and swords threshing into oblivion.

And then, in a heartbeat, it was all gone, a commotion fading to vapour behind them. The racing ground snapped asunder, and the Raft hurtled out over the turbulent plate of the Neleöst Sea ...

At the fore of the Raft, Kellhus stood facing backwards, facing *them*, his eyes sparking brilliance even in the direct sun. He held his arms out low to his side, as if balancing upon a beam. He alone neither swayed nor stumbled, but rather leaned and straightened as one with the timber deck. The golden discs about his hands could only be glimpsed intermittently; the halo about his head not at all. The wind whisked his hair into a golden snarl, tugged his silk robes into ancient skin, innumerable creases and lobes fluttering across the white gleam of the sun.

Who? Who was this man who had conquered so wide, so deep?

Timbers groaned as they tilted toward the west. A new distance rose up and around his godlike silhouette: the dishevelled bulk of the Urokkas—or what they could see of the mountains through the tailings of the Shroud. The Raft lurched toward them, toward Dagliash.

Who was Anasûrimbor Kellhus?

Had Achamian been right about him all along?

Hanging no higher than a carrack's mast, they could feel the Neleöst on their skin, taste the ghost of brine and spray. The Sea swept out, and for all its torment below, receded into the featureless perfection of a geometer's rule. The coastline lay on their right ...

As did the Horde.

Dragged south by the prevailing winds, the Shroud extended miles out to Sea. It seemed a thing painted, immense strokes of ochre and dun daubed across the northern horizon. The shores in advance of the Ordeal were barren. They saw nothing save land that had been stamped and rooted and denuded, that is, aside from a lone company of Kidruhil, who cheered in miniature, brandishing lances and shields at their miraculous passage. The Shroud loomed ever higher, stacking hazes and plumes that cricked the neck for gazing. For a time their Holy Aspect-Emperor stood lucid and shining in the rising sun, framed by the gloom of caliginous, sky-spanning veils.

The million-throated howl breached the rush of wind and the boom of surf. Proyas noticed Siroyon pulling a kerchief to his mouth and nose. The Shroud swallowed them. Coughing obscurity. The barks and screams of innumerable throats, braided into a pitch that siphoned burning liquid into ears. The stench was intolerable, base and glutinous with rot, acrid with feces. Despite the foulness, the Lords of the Ordeal peered toward the shoreline to a man. Even Proyas could feel it, the sense of peeking behind curtains both monumental and forbidden, a clamour to glimpse the catastrophic fact of their foe ...

The soul-numbing numbers.

His eyes watering, Proyas glimpsed the crawling tracts, disjointed visions of a thousand thousand caterwauling shadows. The land itself seemed to smoke, though nothing burned beyond the throats and stomachs of the onlookers.

Aside from Kellhus, only Kayûtas and Sibawûl seemed unaffected. The latter actually turned to regard Proyas the instant of his glimpse, and it seemed mad that eyes could be so dead in a fume that pricked everything living. Most all present pawed at the corners of their eyes. Teeth ached for the loudness of the inhuman chorus. Skin tingled. King Hogrim hacked convulsively. Temus Enhorû, Grandmaster of the Saik, fell to his knees retching. Lord Soter did a comic jig to avoid the spatter, cried something in Ainoni about understanding sorcerers with no stomach for the sea.

The Shroud gradually thinned and parted, as did the feverish crescendo of the Horde's roar. Armour that had flashed in the sun was now flat and pale. Grey soiled their plaited beards. Black wedged the corner of their mouths.

Men spat into the rushing Sea. The Urokkas leapt into clarity about their holy steersman, more squat and sullen than majestic.

"Hark!" Kellhus called through glaring light. "Witness the undoing of the Horde!"

His plan was every bit as simple as the cumbersome size of the Ordeal demanded. Inexorably retreating toward the River Sursa, the Horde had withdrawn *about* the Urokkas rather than into them. The idea was for the Schools to strike out across the low peaks, where they would defend the slopes against the bulk of the Horde to the north, drowning the passes and ravines in arcane fire. The Men of the Ordeal, meanwhile, would advance along the broken shores to the south, their flank secure. At some decisive instant, the Holy Aspect-Emperor would use the Raft to deliver a cohort of warriors *into* Dagliash, where, with the Swayali, he would transform the mountain the Nonmen called Iros, and the Norsirai, Antareg, into a beacon of death. "When the Fish collapse upon Dagliash as their final refuge," their Lord-and-Prophet said, "they will find only iron and fire!"

They saw the sedimentary bloom of the Sursa before they saw the river itself, a vast bruise blackening the aquamarine plate of the Sea. The granitic immensity of Antareg reared into their line of sight, cliffs stacked upon cliffs rising from the surf. Dagliash dominated its summit, a fist brandished against the Sea: cyclopean walls devoid of battlements but otherwise intact, their sheer bulk betraying the naivete of their ancient makers; great square hollows that had been towers and bastions. More than any ruin he had seen, it showed how time was itself a caustic solution, something that consumed edges, made sediment of complexity.

It was hard not to be astonished by the elegant genius of the plan: As the Ordealmen cleared the shoreline, the Horde to the north would shovel *itself* into the furnaces stoked by the Schools. The proud horsemen of the Ordeal, so long confined to skirmishing with their foe, would be loosed in pitched battle at long last. Slaughter and terror would herd them toward the drowning waters of the Sursa.

"Our Lord-and-Prophet has become our butcher!" Prince Nurbanu Ze cackled, his humour too familiar, his elation too avid.

The Meat owned some more than others. At some point following their departure, their hunger to close with their foe had become more unseemly than noble. Proyas himself could feel it thickening his voice and stoking his fury: the throb of carnal lust, a coital tremor passing through all things anxious and hateful. No one need speak it to know—not anymore. Coupling and killing had been kicked from the places once allotted in their souls, as if, in eating their foe, *they were becoming him.*

He could see it in their hooded, leaning looks, the shadow of something eager and indecent. Coithus Narnol, Saubon's older brother and King of Galeoth, scanned the heights, his mouth open like a witless dog. The Mysunsai Grandmaster, Obwë Gûswuran, peered out to the Shroud beyond the humped and broken line of the Urokkas, his back not so much turned as canted away from the assembly. Their Holy Aspect-Emperor, Proyas realized, had not so much charged them with an onerous task as laid out a wicked banquet.

Disbursing glory was all that remained.

"Lord-and-Prophet!" Proyas cried, shocked by the near sob that cracked his voice. "I beg of you! Yield the glory of Dagliash *to me!*"

The assembled Lords and Grandmasters made no secret of their surprise. In all their years vying for their Holy Aspect-Emperor's favour, not once had Proyas thrown his lot in with theirs. Saubon scowled openly.

Kellhus, however, continued hurtling backward into the vista without acknowledging him. The Raft slowed as it approached the ancient fortress, climbing in stages to match the height of the cliffs. Surf crashed and hissed below. The scarps framed him, details dropping as the Raft ascended. The halos about his hands were clearly visible against the watercolour darks, like the ghosts of gold-foil.

"Thus far our foe has naught but nettled us," Kellhus declared to his Believer-Kings, his eyes blind for luminous meaning, light gazing into infinity. "Even Irsûlor was but a gambit for them, a trifle wagered with little expectation. Were it not for our arrogance, our dissension, Umrapathur would be here with us now ..."

"Lord-and-Prophet!" Proyas cried. "I *beg you please*!"

This earned him curious looks from Kayûtas and Apperens Saccarees, not to mention an elbow from Saubon. Others, like Nurbanû Soter and Hringa Vûkyelt, merely acknowledged his infraction with frowns.

"Dagliash is *where they will fight,*" Kellhus continued, ignoring his infelicity, "where the Unholy Consult will try to gore rather than bleed our Great Ordeal ..."

It's peculiar, the way the *truancy* of an act can command the soul that wills it, the way Men sometimes throw more effort behind their errors rather than retreat from them. If wrong cannot be made right, at least it can be made *real.*

What did it matter, the honour of Dagliash, if disgrace was the toll of attaining it? And yet, never in his life had Proyas so needed a thing—or so it seemed, hanging above the hulking ruins.

"Here it was," Kellhus said, "the Nonmen first saw the Incu-Holoinas cut open the sky. Here it was the Inchoroi committed the first of their ghastly and numberless crimes ..."

The Raft now circled the fortress, wafting sideways so that the gutted bastions remained square to the Holy Aspect-Emperor's back. Clots of black armoured Sranc streamed from various orifices, mobbing the walls.

"Viri ... Great among the Nonmen Mansions, lies dead beneath the foundations of these walls, the underworld fastness of Nin'janjin. The very ground is chambered, riddled as an infested stump ..."

"*Please*!" the Believer-King of Conriya heard himself cry, hoarse and plaintive. "After all I have given!"

You owe me this!

The Holy Aspect-Emperor of the Three Seas finally turned to regard him, chips of sun glaring from his eyes.

"Hitherto, the Consult could not move in force against us," he said. "They could only wait, use the Horde and their cunning to bleed us. Now the Great Ordeal stands upon their very threshold. *Agongorea* lies yonder, the Field Appalling, and beyond that, G*olgotterath itself* ..."

"Grant *me* the honour!" Saubon cried out after sparing Proyas an outraged look.

"No!" Proyas shouted. "*No!*"

But others had begun calling out as well, a greedy cacophony. What had been pity, distaste, had become umbrage, a determination to *outdo*. Suddenly it seemed he could taste the *grease* of the place, the pumice sear ...

Dagliash was larded with Meat.

"If our Foe hopes to keep us from their foul Gate!" Kellhus boomed over all. "*They will strike here!*"

Now it was the fortress that seemed the one floating.

Proyas threw himself to his knees before Anasûrimbor Kellhus's feet, the first among his surging, shouting peers. It was not devotion that impelled him, nor even the will to prove oneself fanatical, for these things had been stripped from him. Only the hunger ...

The *necessity.*

"Pleeease! I beg you!"

The need for something simple.

Zeal, it was often said, dwelt in the *deeds* and not the words of Men.

But Proyas knew this was not true, knew that one could never sort the words from the deeds, if only because *words were deeds*, acts committed, possessing consequences as mortal as any fist or knife. But knowing a thing and understanding it were never quite the same. To know the power of words was one thing, but to *witness* that power, to first hear the words spoken and to then see the souls dance ... Words land as hammers.

And yet, to observe a thing always is to observe a thing not at all. Proyas had seen Anasûrimbor Kellhus harangue countless souls across the breadth of the Three Seas—thousands of exhortations across dozens of years, battles, and nations—without understanding the least of what happened. And how could he when he stood among those exhorted? When it was his heart caught upon the hook of that beloved voice, carried from glory to hope to outrage? Far from the surest way to fathom their power, *being moved* by words was to lose all awareness of motion, to think oneself *immovable.*

So he witnessed what he had seen countless times for the *first* time: Anasûrimbor Kellhus addressing the Host of Hosts, not as Warrior-Prophet or even Aspect-Emperor, but as *Dûnyain*, the most astonishing fraud the World had ever known, whetting souls already too keen to be called sane ...

For they were in the thrall of the Meat, the Ordealmen. They heaved as mobs, leapt and howled and gesticulated as individuals. Some even had to be restrained by their brothers, such was the intensity of their fury and adulation. To watch was to be at once frightened, heartened—and even aroused.

The Raft had been raised upon posts and fashioned into a podium. The Lords of the Ordeal stood assembled upon it, decked in whatever regalia that remained to them. Their myriad nations swallowed all visible creation about them—heads become beads become grains of sand, all crying out in lust. Closing his eyes, Proyas could scarcely distinguish their howl from that of the Sranc, save that it boomed more than screeched across the Vaults of Heaven.

The Horde of Men, hailing an inhuman beacon ...

A Dûnyain.

Anasûrimbor Kellhus dangled high above the Raft, crisp and brilliant in a play of vague and watery lights. When he spoke, his voice was somehow portioned between all souls, so that each man heard him as a friend making observations over their shoulder.

"When a man is abandoned ..."

Proyas stood at Saubon's side at the Raft's forward edge, gazing out across the mobbed tracts. He had often wondered at the contradiction of these sermons, the way the humility they preached never failed to provoke displays of wild and vicious pride ...

"When he bleeds for cutting, weeps for loss ..."

He had even dared ask Kellhus about it once, in the dark hours following the defeat at Irsûlor. The Holy Aspect-Emperor had explained how suffering pays different wages to different Men: wisdom, for souls such as his own, the resignation belonging to philosophers and lepers; and for souls such as theirs, *righteousness*, the knowledge that they could exact from others what had been taken from them.

But even this, Proyas now knew, had been another flattering lie, another conceit, another provocation to savagery.

"When a man is fearful, witless for confusion ..."

Righteousness had been what he wanted all along. Kellhus had said as much himself. If *wisdom* had truly been what he wanted, he would have never turned out Achamian.

"When he is MOST SMALL ... only THEN can he fathom the proportion of the God!"

Proyas watched the mottled landscape surge, strain, and roar. Nangael thanes, red-faced and screaming. Eumarnans wagging crescent swords across the beam of the morning sun. Agmundrmen clapping their ash bows. He could remember the swelling joy he had once felt witnessing such sights, the besotted gratitude, the bloodthirsty certainty, ferocious and predatory, as if death could be brought about by mere willing ...

Now bile leapt to the back of his throat.

"*Why?*" he spat at Saubon without looking.

The man's face turned in his high periphery.

"Because I am a mighty warrior."

"No! Why you—you!—*over* me?"

Mere weeks ago the possibility of bickering like this would have been unthinkable. But somehow, somewhere, a twist had complicated the line of what had been thoughtless and unquestioned.

The Meat had climbed into all things.

"Because," his fellow Exalt-General grated, "Men are reckless with things they hate."

"And what, pray-tell, is it I hate, brother?"

A grinning sneer.

"Living."

"***Luxury blots it!***" the Holy Aspect-Emperor cried from on high, his voice parsing across the thundering tracts, at once booming and cooing.

"***Comforts conceal!***"

Pinpoint lights shone across whatever polish yet existed in the arms and armour of the Ordealmen. The shouting warbled and faltered, then trailed into miraculous silence. The Southron Men gaped in astonishment, for their Holy Aspect-Emperor both exhorted them from above, *and regarded them from each and every mirrored surface*, as though he in fact stood *everywhere*, hidden at right angles to what could be seen. Be it the dimpled plane of the shield covering the back of the man before them, a helm's mercurial sheen, or a sword's shaking length, there it was, *apprehending each*, their beloved Warrior-Prophet's bearded face, a thousand thousand aspects, exclaiming ...

"***GIFTS ONLY DECEIVE!***"

The Host of Hosts erupted.

"You think I seek death?" Proyas cried to Saubon.

"I think you seek excuses to die."

These words fairly winded the Believer-King of Conriya.

"And why would that be?"

"Because you are *weak*."

"Weak, is it? And you are strong?"

"Stronger. Yes."

They fairly faced each other now, enough to draw the attention of their fellow Believer-Kings. "And why is that?"

"Because I never needed to *believe* in him to serve him ..." A Galeoth snort, the one that so marked him as a barbarian in high company. "Because I've been throwing the number-sticks all along!"

And with that, all fight slipped from Proyas—as did any other species of will. He turned from the tall Norsirai. A numb detachment tugged his gaze from point to point across the mob, face to rapturous face, some vicious, others pained—their teeth bared in the manner of the Saved. The light of their Prophet's face gleamed blue across beards and wet-cheeks. Many wept, while others ranted, bellowed declarations, their brows scored with the common hatred that was the wage of their devotion.

"***You are one with the God only when you suffer!***" the voice from over their shoulders cried.

Proyas glimpsed the numberless chips of luminous blue—the reflection of Anasûrimbor Kellhus in their eyes. Man after man, rank after rank, formation after formation, the same shining blue dots ...

Fading as the false reflections faded before them.

"***WHEN! YOU! SACRIFICE!***"

Booming waves of adulation.

"You could never understand!" Saubon cried in his ear.

"Understand what?"

So much of the issue between Men turns on who is weary and who is in need.

"Why he made me *your* equal!"

There was honesty in this, enough to seize his attention entire.

Saubon wagged his hand in a contemptuous gesture, at once indicating and dismissing the crazed spectacle about them. "All this time you thought he warred to bring about Righteousness! Only now do you see how wrong you were." The Norsirai Exalt-General spat, darkening an archipelago of timber between Proyas's booted feet. "Piety? Zeal? Bah! *These are simply his tools*!"

Incredulity, too raw to be hooded. "Tools for wha ...?"

Proyas trailed, his voice caught out high and angry against a sudden silence. He looked up, his eyes drawn by the peripheral presentiment that all the World did the same. The breath was yanked from his breast ...

"You despair," Saubon grated in his ear, "because like a child you thought that Truth alone could save the World ..."

For in fact, he alone looked up.

"But it is *strength* that saves, Brother, not Truth ..."

He alone could see their Lord-and-Prophet hanging above them.

"And strength burns brightest upon Lies!"

To a man the Ordealmen had been captured by the blue-and-golden images shimmering from all but the most meagre polish, the tackiest gloss about them. Their Holy Aspect-Emperor hung in plain sight and yet *unseen*, head thrown back, the light of meaning pulsing from his mouth, singing words that no soul could comprehend ...

And yet they heard, "***THIS, YOUR SACRIFICE—YOUR ORDEAL!***"

They leapt in rapture, cowered in worship.

Every reflection glimpsed exhorted, boomed, "***THE GOD KNOWS YOUR MEASURE!***"

The Men of the Three Seas screamed, jubilant, deranged.

The Meat ... Proyas thought, too cold to betray his gagging horror.

The Meat had taken Anasûrimbor Kellhus.

They wheezed in the dark, misbegotten lungs drawing foul, misbegotten air. Hulking, lurid thoughts heaved in their hulking, tripartite skulls. Lice teemed. They peered and peered through glutinous eyes, but saw nothing save the dark. They bristled, clacked teeth, barked warnings in their crude tongue. Like old dogs nursing old pains, they periodically snapped and roared, clawed the blackness of innumerable others ...

On and on, forking through the deeps, wheezing in the dark, shaking matted, black-bison manes ...

Waiting.

CHAPTER ELEVEN

Momemn

I. The Game enacts the form of Creation. To be is to be for the Game.

II. The parts of the Game are the whole of the Game, given the rules that compel them. The parts and the rules comprise the Elements of the Game.

III. There are no moves [acts] in the Game, only the changing permutations of Elements.

—Opening Cantos of the *Abenjukala*

Bonfires shed no daylight.

—SCYLVENDI PROVERB

Mid-Autumn, 20 New Imperial Year (4132, Year-of-the-Tusk), Momemn

So long as he *watched*, the little boy reasoned. So long as he continued spying on the Narindar, he would be safe.

Anasûrimbor Kelmomas had become a solitary sentinel, charged with a vigil he dare not explain to anyone, and which only he could keep. What had begun as a mere diversion, a distraction from far more pressing concerns like his sister, had now become a mortal mission. *The Four-Horned Brother* walked the palatial corridors, bent on some dark design the boy could not fathom—save that it somehow involved him.

So he continued, even expanded his campaign of secret observation. Day after day, he lay motionless, peering at the man standing motionless in his dark chamber, or, those rare times the assassin elected to roam the palace, he scurried after him through the mazed bones of the Andiamine Heights. And when exhaustion finally forced him back to his mother's bed, he curled riven with terror, convinced the Narindar somehow *watched him*. Day after day, he did this, matching the man in his every particular, a step to shadow his every step, a breath to shadow his every breath, until they came to seem a *tandem* soul, a singular thing divided between light and shadow, evil and good.

Just *why* watching the assassin should keep him safe, Kelmomas could not say. He had boggled himself innumerable times trying to reckon his circumstances, particularly what it meant to always and only do *what had already been done*—what the Librarian had called the "Unerring Grace." Since he belonged to what happened as much as anything else, what difference did it make whether he watched the man hidden or not? Kelmomas possessed a keen appreciation of the impunity intrinsic to acts committed outside the knowledge of others. To spy as he spied was, in some strange and elusive sense, to *own* the one spied upon. It sometimes seemed they were bugs, the people he watched, clicking through routines so blind they could be mechanical. He had often thought that watching the inhabitants of the palace as he did was like watching the great gears and armatures of the Emaunum Mill, a vast contraption that endlessly groaned and clacked onward, chasing tooth and socket and groove, utterly blind to the mischief dwelling within it. A rock was all that he needed, or perhaps a pocket filled with sand, to bring the entirety to a cracking halt.

This was what it meant to spy, *these were the wages*. The power of life and death and all the plunder that lay between. Were the Narindar a man like any other he would have been hapless, vulnerable to whatever stratagem the Prince-Imperial might concoct. To spy on another was to seize what was blind from the unseen margins, to lure and to dupe, to *rule* ...

The way he ruled Mother.

But the Narindar was not a man like any other. In fact he was scarcely a man at all. The recognition would descend upon the boy from time to time, tease goose-pimples from his skin, bully his breath into a cringe: the

Four-Horned Brother stood in the shadows immediately below him, the wicked Father of Hate.

The puzzles fairly drove him mad: What were the wages of *spying on a God?*

The assassin possessed the Unerring Grace. How else explain the string of impossibilities he had observed? The boy *wanted* to believe he possessed a Grace all his own, but the secret voice was always quick to remind him that he possessed the Strength and that this was a far different thing than Grace. They endlessly bickered points such as these in the carapace of his skull ...

But if there's no hiding from Him, why doesn't He simply kill me?

Because He plays you!

But how could a God *play at anything?*

Because that is what he feeds upon 'ere you die, the grain of your experience.

Fool! I asked how, *not why!*

Who can say how the Gods do what they do?

Maybe because they can't!

And when the ground shakes, when mountains explode, or the seas rise up?

Pfah. The Gods do *these things? Or do they simply know they will happen before they happen?*

Perhaps there's no difference.

And this was the rub, he came to realize. What did it mean to act without willing? What *could* it mean? When Kelmomas reflected on his own actions, he always found himself steered to the incontrovertible fact of his soul. *He* fathered his actions. *He* was the primal source, the indisputable origin ...

The problem was that *everyone* thought as much, to varying degrees. Even slaves ...

Even Mother.

One afternoon the Narindar abruptly turned his head as if to look at someone standing before his chamber door—which he never bolted. Then he was at the door, pausing, looking back to where he had stood moments before. Then he was striding out into the corridor beyond, forcing the young Prince-Imperial to scramble the way he always did, scampering through the black slots, shimming up to the next iron grating to spy his enigmatic quarry. For all his diabolic implication, the assassin was by far the easiest to track of the souls the boy had pursued through the palace. He walked with the measure of a lifelong soldier, his pace welded to some constant and transcendent tempo. No one dared accost him. And he passed through points of congestion with the smoky ease of a phantom.

On this occasion he left the regimented grid of the Apparatory and passed into the chaos of the Lower Palace, into the stores, one of the few places where the network of secret tunnels did not go. The panicked Prince-Imperial found himself stranded at an intersection of hallways, watching the Narindar recede into obscurity, becoming no more than a dimming succession of glimpses in the intermittent lantern-light.

Then, as he strode upon the very limit of visibility, Kelmomas thought he saw him step *sideways*, vanish into an alcove of some kind. The boy lay at the grill for some time, peering to no avail and debating what he should do. After weeks of shadowing the man with no problem, what did it mean to lose him here and now?

Was this how it happened?

He's known all along! Samarmas cried. *I told you*!

Was this how Grinning Ajokli would avenge his sacrilege?

I told you!

Was this how everything had already happened?

He lay shaking in terror, all but immobilized when the great train of bearers—caste-menials by the look of them—began filing immediately below him, talking in hushed murmurs, huffing for the great baskets of apples they bore upon their shoulders. The smell filled the deep halls, crisp and sour. Nothing shouted the impotence of the Fanim and their siege more loudly than the streams of soldiers and provisions arriving by sea. They laboured past, dim, dark Men, bearing apples as swollen as Mother's lips, crimson unto purple and green. The gossamer hairs across the boy's body fixed him as surely as nails. He lay watching the head of the train climb the hallway toward the alcove where the assassin lay hidden. But the flotilla of intervening baskets obscured the lead bearer, leaving only the absence of turmoil to indicate that the Narindar merely observed the same as he. The passage of so many bodies had whipped the lanterns into momentary brilliance, and so Kelmomas clearly saw the last man pass the point where he thought the assassin lay concealed. The bearer toiled on unaware and unmolested, save that he stumbled, and sent an apple from his basket. The fruit hung waxen red and green for a moment, before spinning to the floor and kicking back down the corridor, gleaming as it bounced.

A hand reached out and snatched it.

And the Narindar was striding back the way he came, glowering into emptiness, taking vacant bites of the apple as he approached. The white of the apple's flesh bobbed overbright in the murk. Kelmomas lay as stiff as a dead cat. He did not breathe for the entirety of the assassin's transit.

Only at that moment did he truly understand the dread proportion of his circumstance.

Everything has already happened …

The young Prince-Imperial took to hand-wringing in his mother's chambers that night. Even Mother, for all her preoccupation, glimpsed his agitation through the veneer he typically wore to court her adoration.

"There's no cause to fear," she said, sitting next to him on the bed, cupping his cheek and pulling his head to her bosom. "I *told* you, remember? I *killed* their Waterbearer. Me!"

Hands on either shoulder, she pressed him back to display her marvelling smile.

"Your mother killed the Last Cishaurim!"

She had wanted him to clap his hands and cheer, and perhaps he would have, were it not for the swollen urge to chew out her tongue …

There was so much he had to teach her!

"Now they have no hope of overcoming our walls, Sweetling. We grow fat, fed by the sea, while the whole Empire rallies across the Three Seas! Fanayal. Was. A. Great. Fool. He thought he would reveal our weakness, but in sooth he has only shown the *savages* who would rule in our stead!"

Kelmomas had heard it all before of course, how Father, for all the demands he made of the provinces, "smashed no idols." But the boy had never considered the Fanim an actual threat. If anything he had come to see them as *allies* in his war against his sister—and imbecilic ones at that. The only fear they instilled was the fear they would simply melt away, for the day they decamped was also the day his hag-cunt-sister would betray him—*Thelli*! Even if Mother refused to believe her at first, sooner or later she *would*. Despite her peculiarities, despite her inability to emote, let alone love, Theliopa was the one soul Mother trusted above all others.

Kelmomas could feel his body retreat into a weeping cage for pondering the consequences. It was too much … too much …

Necessity impaled him. Necessity piled upon mad necessity.

Never, it seemed, not even in the darkest of the dark cannibal days following Uncle Holy's coup, had he been so oppressed, so maliciously and monstrously abused. Even Mother had become an affliction! Taking Thelli's word over his! *Over his*!

There was so much Father had failed to teach her. There was so much she had yet to learn.

The Postern Terrace deserted, Esmenet leaned against the balustrade, her eyes closed to the evening glare, her face alive to the mellow heat. The last of her Exalt-Ministers and their Apparati had dissolved into the solution of the city. Ngarau, perhaps sensing her humour, had withdrawn with all the slaves in tow. She had even kicked off her slippers so she might savour the dwindling of day through the soles of her bare feet. Only her Inchausti remained, discrete and motionless sentinels, men who would die, as Caxes Anthirul had died, to keep her safe.

And it seemed *miraculous* what she had accomplished ...

Would that she understood any of it.

Rehearsing events, she had found, simply made them more baffling. But word of these atrocities and miracles—overthrowing Maithanet, killing the Last Cishaurim—had spread, sparking an even more profound wonder. The minstrels *were singing of her*, the caste-menials had shrugged away the Yatwerian foment and were claiming her as their own. Zaudunyani across the Three Seas now made her their example, testimony of the divinity of their cause. Pamphlets were distributed. Numberless bless-tablets were stamped and fired with her name. She became Esmenet'arumot, *Esmenet-unbroken* ... Mother of the Empire.

"'*The dogs besiege our mother*!'" Phinersa had told her the other morning. "This is what they cry in the streets. '*Our mother is in peril*! *Our mother*!' They pull their hair and beat their breasts for you!" The Water, it seemed, had burned away whatever reserve of arrogance Phinersa had possessed with his arm. Her Master-of-Spies, she had come to realize, was the kind of man who gave in proportion to his sacrifice—*this* was likely why Kellhus had chosen him to serve her. The more Phinersa lost in her name, the more he would commit to her next throw. That same night she discovered that he had sent an array of palm-sized tablets—different blessings—to her apartments. Years ago, seeing her face upon what the faithful called "silver empresses" and the apostates "shiny harlots" had left her numb, devoid of shame or pride. But she wept for seeing these crude plates, for seeing her name wedged as something prized, something *holy* ...

Something unconquerable.

And how could she not, when she was a harlot in a land that held them accursed? A *Sumni* whore, no less, a bright beacon of Thousand Temples hypocrisy ...

How could she be anything but broken?

In the histories she had read, the authors always attributed events to *will*, if not that belonging to the principles, then to the Hundred. The stories were stories of *power*: caprice was something she always had to read *into* accounts. The great Casidas, of course, was the sole exception. As a onetime galley slave, he understood *both sides* of power, and so possessed a keen eye for the conceits of the powerful. His *Annals of Cenei* had knotted her innards night after night for this very reason: Casidas understood the truth of power in times of strife, how history was a blind thresher. He himself described it as, "a perpetual battle fought in the pitch of an eternal night, shadowy Men hacking at hints in the gloom and all too often"—she would never forget the phrase—"reaping their beloved."

Esmenet also understood the sordid tangle of immunity and vulnerability that comes with power—well enough to be interminably stranded upon their divide. She was no fool. She had lost too much to trust to any consequence, let alone her ability to command the hearts of Men. The name the mob called may now be hers but the woman they invoked simply did not exist. She *had* made this reversal possible, it was true, but more as a wheel makes a chariot possible, and not as a charioteer. She had provided her Empire with a name to focus their belief, and scarce more.

She hadn't even killed the Last Cishaurim ... not in sooth.

Perhaps this explained her addiction to the verandah behind her husband's throne—to standing, as she stood now, in this very *place*. Lingering here, she could *almost* believe the legend she had become, this mad myth of herself. Looking out over her city, she could indulge the fancy, the grandest of all the grand conceits, the tale of the *hero*, the soul that somehow wricks free the thousand hooks of circumstance, that somehow hangs above the fray, ruling without being ruled ...

She closed her eyes, greeted the mellow warmth of the sun across her face ... the feeling of *orange*.

With every passing day more and more Columnaries disembarked, swelling the garrison. General Powtha Iskaul had already struck sail with the battle-hardened Twenty-ninth. The three Arcong Columns she and Anthirul had sent to retake Shigek had been recalled, and had travelled at least as far as Asgilioch. Without his Waterbearer, Fanayal hesitated, if not wavered outright, even as his men clotted the southern hilltops with ever more siege engines. To simply eke out his existence, he had no choice but to endlessly provoke the surrounding countryside: thousands of retired Zaudunyani warriors were mustering in the neighbouring provinces, and tens of thousands more across the Three Seas ...

It mattered not at all *how* her fortune had come about, only *that* it had come about.

The Blessed Empress of the Three Seas dared gaze against the evening glare, peer from point to point across the intricate urban vista, at Momemn, the famed Child of dark Osbeus, seat of Anasûrimbor Kellhus, the mightiest conqueror since Triamis the Great. The River Phayus parsed the northern limit on her right, a vast brown snake scaled in evening brilliance. The Girgallic Gate marked the western limit in the distance before her, squat towers scorched black for proximity to the sinking sun. The Maumurine Gate towered equally conspicuous on the southern limit, if only for the hood of wooden hoardings that had been raised about it following her encounter with the Cishaurim.

The air already possessed the arid evening absence of haze that seemed to strip the sense of distance from otherwise dim landmarks. But even as the sun blinded her to the western core of the city, it inked the regions surrounding with ever-greater clarity. The shadows of the distant siege towers joined the thatched black marking the spine of the hills. The once-dreaded Tower of Ziek cast the boroughs to the east of its square bulk into premature night. So too did the three gilded domes of mighty Xothei enclose more and more of the Cmiral's campus in shadow.

Leaping from place to place with her look somehow made the dwindling of the light plain. And Esmenet realized that *she could see it happen*, the coming of night. She saw those final squares and lanes of sun-bright ground we all see, only scattered in countless thousands across her city. Looking about, she could see them dwindle according to the flattening sunlight. And as the edges retreated up the walls, the darkness became as *liquid*, a flood welling from all points already in shadow, submerging lesser structures and streets, then greater, climbing in counterpoint to the slow plummet of the sun.

Night was the foundation, she realized, the deathless state. The soul had no more than its tongue pressed against the complexity of Creation. She thought of her assassin, her Narindar, and how he had to dwell in the darkest night of all. This was why killing Maithanet had seemed so miraculous, so easy: because it had been no different than any other assassination—because *being Dûnyain didn't matter*. Being her husband didn't matter.

Breathing becomes bright when we cease thinking.

As often happens, the hot glare of evening winked into the chill glow of dusk in a heartbeat. What was warm pressure fled into the cool vacancy of night. Esmenet shivered for the cold and the horror ... for being a flea upon the back of calamity. She was a reader of Casidas. The ruins of ancient Cenei lay upriver, fields upon fields of fallow stone, the debris of a capital easily as great as her own. The ruins of Mehtsonc lay farther inland still, little more than a network of forested mounds, the legendary glory that was Kyraneas, indistinguishable from the earth ... more gravel in the ground.

Momemn lay at the mouth of the Phayus, against the dark immensity of the Meneanor Sea. The Empires of the West had, the scholars said, run out of river.

Esmenet peered out over Momemn, watched the torches and candles and plates ignite across the indigo leagues, each conjuring a small golden world, most within windows, but some on street-corners and rooftops. Lives scattered as coins, she thought, thousands of jewels. A treasury of souls.

She had no idea who would write the history of her and her family. She prayed that it would not be anyone so clear-eyed as Casidas.

CHAPTER TWELVE

Ishterebinth

To lose is to cease to exist for the Game; to be as dead. Since the Game is always the same Game, rebirth belongs to the survivor. The dead return as strangers.

—Fifth Canto of the *Abenjukala*

Early Autumn, 20 New Imperial Year (4132, Year-of-the-Tusk), Ishterebinth

Ishoriöl. O' Exalted Hall!

How glorious she had been! Famed for her silks, her chain, her song, and for the way her Ishroi rode horses rather than chariots into war. Sons from all the Mansions of Eärwa travelled to its fabled gates to beg knowledge of her craft. Only Cil-Aujas could boast a greater population, and only Siöl, the House Primordial, could boast more sublime learning or warlike glory.

How bright the peerings had blazed! How the concourses had thronged! How the air had rumbled with discourse and play! And *here*, within the Great Entresol, the cavernous chamber where the Ingressus served the great belly of the Chthonic, here more than anywhere. All had been enamelled in white—a gloss that banished all shadows, delivered clarity to every corner. The black painted Hauls hung from their nimil chains, some moored to black-iron gangways, others rising and falling, each the size of a river barge, the sorcerous Heavers muttering their incessant song upon the stern. The sky was nothing but a pinprick at the terminus of the Ingressus so very far above, twinkling like a second Nail of Heaven, a sublime measure of holy *depth*. Activity everywhere. Crowds milling across the Pier Floor. Overseers sipping liqueurs upon their balconies. Trains of Emwama bearers crisscrossing the gang-stages, loading and unloading the holds of the hanging ships. The sound of cracking whips, careless voices laughing. The bumblebee hum of the Injori lutes ...

Women and children ... laughing.

Clack ... *Clack* ... *Clack* ...

Widowed fathers screaming.

How? The Believer-King's eyes rolled up and across the vacancy of the Great Entresol, the walls once smooth and draped with garlands now pitted with insufferable images. This was Ishterebinth! Oinaral held him fast beneath his left arm and chest, dragged him among the threshing of fungal shadows. How could this nightmare be true? He rolled his head about to see masses more stark in Holol's constant light, nested like plucked birds up and down the midden swales that choked the Pier Floor. About them, the Great Entresol somehow bundled the Lament into a vast and horrific resonance, one that probed his ears with hot fingers.

Clack ... *Clack* ... *Clack* ...

What had Nil'giccas done to him?

A pursuing shadow seized his attention. Sorweel turned and saw a lurching figure ... saw *him* ...

Mu'miorn.

Walking naught more than a pace from his dragging heels. Naked. Emaciated. The youth had no clue how these ghouls could tell one from the other, and yet the face hanging above him was more familiar—more *known*—than his own. Tender lips, now savaged with ulcers. Hard brow now scored with filth. But the always-injured eyes were the same, as were the tears silvering his cheeks. Mu'miorn! ruined, wrung to the last embers of his life, scarcely more than an anguished cloud. Mu'miorn, reeling after him, a dark intensity in his eyes ... a recognition.

And horror delivered the Believer-King to what was soundless in the caterwauling air, a place where shriek defeated shriek, and the sepulchral quiet of the *Deep* could be heard. Something cut him from the inside, peeled away some inner rind ...

For he had *loved* this wretched apparition, lain within his hot-skinned embrace night upon night. He had teased. He had played. He had shouted within him, even as his shout looped opalescent across his skin. He had cursed him for jealousy's sake, struck him for his betrayals, and knelt weeping at his knees, begging forgiveness. Though stranded upon the mere threshold of manhood, the long-suffering Son of Harweel knew the love of turbulent *centuries*, the epochal cycles of addiction and exhaustion, outrage and ecstasy ...

"*Mu'miorn*!" he cried out in futility.

Disgust, for making as a woman with a man. Revulsion. And heartbreak. And horror.

Horror and more horror.

Clack ... Clack ... Clack ...

Mu'miorn staggered and wept, spittle hanging from his gagging mouth. He could not *believe*, Sorweel realized. He could not believe!

"*It's me*!" the youth cried, arching against Oinaral's ruthless pull, tugging at the ghoul's mailed arm. But all at once Mu'miorn stumbled, crumpled about the lewd filth of his groin, then folded as a rug beneath the ghoulish figures vying behind him, vanished underfoot ...

Sorweel howled, wrenched himself clear the Lastborn's grasp, found himself scrambling upon his rump, helpless before the woebegone figures lurching toward him. Mouths working. Pallid skin blackened by filth. Eyes seizing upon different memories of degradation and hatred and sorrow—an inhuman will to avenge! Oinaral was not senseless to his plight. Holol appeared above the Believer-King, a wick of silver bearing a point of blazing radiance. And the cadaverous throng recoiled before it, raised arms in warding, blinked against the points of white pricking their eyes. An assembly of shrieking dead.

"*Mu'miorn*!"

Oinaral Lastborn stepped about him, drove the wretches stumbling back with his light. Sorweel crawled back as a crab over the offal, frantically peering between pallid and battered shins for sign of his lover. His left hand dropped into emptiness. He fell back, nearly pitched into the abyss for pursuing his arm. He rolled about instead, ribs bruising upon the drop, found himself gazing into the voided bowel of the Mountain, into the ink obscurity of the Holy Deep.

They had come to the ends of the Pier Floor.

Holol had waxed, becoming bright unto blinding, or so it seemed, for Sorweel could see the pale contours of the Great Entresol, the vast arches leaning out like slabs of sky, the chains hanging dead, the derelict gangways and stages, some twisted like twigs in cobwebs. Skeletal gantries cast shadows across the curve of the image-pitted walls. Innumerable figures huddled keening across the heaped quarters of the Pier Floor, along the raised balconies and colonnades and down the steps of the Helical, wending into abyssal blackness.

Clack ... Clack ... Clack ...

His eye caught upon the Displacement, the fracture that formed a ragged hoop about the entirety of the Entresol, a rupture in the very bone of the World. Where the Ark had all but wrecked Viri, it had struck but a single, gargantuan break through the entirety of Ishoriöl, a disfigurement that was at once a monument forever memorializing the fiends who had wrought such ruin and misery ...

The horrid Gaspers ... The *Inchoroi* ...

Wrath. Ever had *wrath* been his fame and foundation. And ever had it been his weakness and his strength, the goad that rendered him reckless and heroic in equal measure, an imperial hatred, wild and unrestrained, a rapacious will to visit woe and destruction upon his foes. The *Despiser*, his Kinning had named him, Immiriccas the Malcontent, and it spoke to the darkness and violence of the Age that such could be a name of pride and glory.

They were the object of his fury—the Vile! *They* had done this. Everything that had been stolen had been stolen by them!

Fury, wild and blind, the kind that battered bones to gravel, swelled through the Believer-King, crashed molten through his limbs. And it renewed him. It made him *whole*. For hatred, as much as love, blessed souls with meaning, a more terrible grace.

He pressed himself about, saw Oinaral Lastborn standing mere cubits from the edge, sweeping Holol from side to side, his nimil coats shimmering, his porcelain scalp and mien white as snow. His ashen kinsmen lurched and thronged about him, each sullied face reflecting antique horrors. They hemmed the brilliant arc of the sword, at once dazzled and bullied. Several already lay dead or bleeding at their stamping feet.

And dismay stamped the youth's fury to mud, for it seemed perverse that any glory should remain. The mail-draped Siqu seemed a figure out of legend, a glittering remnant of the past fending a bestial and desolate future—proof of doom *fulfilled.*

Clack ... Clack ... Clack ...

The youth glanced up, realizing that the Great Entresol housed a *second light*, one descending from on high, more luminous than that belonging to the arcane sword. Gazing up, he saw a broad-bellied Haul, black-hulled as in days of old, the light of its peering breaching the rim of the Ingressus. He made to alert Oinaral, only to glimpse *Mu'miorn* once again, breaking from the piteous congregation, leaping toward him, only to catch his cheek upon the Siqu's holy sword.

The brilliance dimmed, and in the abrupt gloom Sorweel saw his beloved's head *glowing* as a bulb of violet and crimson. Mu'miorn fell away, relinquished Holol's glaring light, slumped pallid upon the midden ground ...

The Son of Harweel reeled on the edge ...

Embraced the Lament as his own.

O' Ishoriöl, your Sons alone had made a fetish of Summer, loathing the endless Winter that was upon them. They had walked as Angels among the stink and hair of mortal Men. "Turn to the Children of the Day," they had been the first to cry. "Minister to the People of Summer, for the Night is upon us. Imimorûl is dead! The Moon no longer hears our paeans!"

O' Ishterebinth, your Sons alone had *believed in Men*, for Cil-Aujas had thought them beasts of burden, and Siöl, akin to Sranc, degenerate forgeries of themselves, polluted and debased. "Kill them," they had cried, "for their seed is quick, and they teem as vermin across the hide of the World!"

But your Sons had known—your Sons had *seen*. If not Men, what other vessel might bear the nectar of their learning, the Song of their doomed race?

"Teach them," the Blessed Siqu called.

"Or consign our Sum to Oblivion."

"*Mu'miorn!*" the in-between soul that had once been Sorweel cried.

Clack ... Clack ... Clack ...

Gloom hooded the Great Entresol, and Mu'miorn vanished among tangled shadows. Holol had been sheathed. Luminance filtered down from above. Pallid bodies roiled in the black.

Oinaral lunged toward him, resplendent before the horrid surge. He leapt into him, tackled him about the breast ... The youth glimpsed the Haul, bulbous black framed by ceilings stark with illumination. They sailed past the floor, and *emptiness* pulled them down and away.

They plummeted, weightless.

Oinaral's arm yanked him gallows-hard, held him dangling as they somehow swung out over the cavernous void.

The Holy Deep.

He choked for want of wind. He made to cry out, but for which madness he did not know. Oinaral had somehow managed to wrap his free arm about one of the fallow nimil chains. Now they swung on a giddy ellipse.

The lunatic depths of the Great Entresol howled about them.

Clack ... Clack ... Clack ...

Mu'miorn ...

O' Ishoriöl, would a different doom have followed? Would the World have turned otherwise had the Mansions of your kin listened?

For the *Vile* had come unto Men in the wilds of Eänna, delivered the very ministry your Sons had so urgently argued. The *Vile* had sat upon the earth to carve joints with the absurd Prophets of Men, whispered deceit in the guise of secrets, wove the thread of their wicked design into the fabric of their custom and belief. The Vile, *not the Exalted*, had shown them how to make inscription of speech, and so had chiselled alien malice upon the heart of *an entire Race*.

The *Vile* had armed them with the Apories that were so wasted upon Sranc.

What had they thought, the remaining Sons of Siöl, as the Mannish vermin rampaged through the glorious halls of the House Primordial? What had they thought, the remaining Sons of Cil-Aujas, when they retired from the fields of Mir'joril, and barred the Gates of their Mansion?

What had they thought of this last great insult, this final atrocity inflicted by their conquered foe?

Had they seen *error* ... or just more injustice?

And so the Lust to Teach was rekindled among your Sons—O' Ishoriöl, a *second* folly! "A Tutelage of the Bright to undo the Tutelage of the Vile!" the first Siqu declared to your great King. And Cet'ingira Deepseer more than any other made glister of his treachery, saying unto Nil'giccas, "Let me make a ministry of the wisdom we have purchased with our doom. For among them are souls as wise as our own."

Aye. As foolish.

And as terrified of damnation.

Oblivion on a swing.

Clack ... Clack ... Clack ...

Sorweel hung limp, the rim of the Cauldron biting his breastbone, shuddering only to weep for his lover and his Race. All was black below. The Haul lowered in surreal stages above, a shadow that took the illuminated depths of the Great Entresol as its halo. It floated down to the shrieking rim of the Pier Floor then below. Without warning, Oinaral's frame flexed against his own, and they began to sway as a pendulum, Man and Nonman.

Vertigo clawed his gut, scratched a greater awareness from the mud of his grief. The light emerged from obscurity, chased the Haul's shade down their forms, and Sorweel glimpsed his own shadow crisp and confounded across the walls of the Ingressus, swinging coupled across sewage-clotted imagery. The peering affixed above the vessel was an explosion of radiant hair for tears he could not feel. He glimpsed only battered gunwales, soiled decks, the heaped carcasses of pigs ...

And a hooded figure, standing immobile directly beneath the light.

Clack ... Clack ... Clack ...

The Haul sank. Oinaral's exertions became more violent, savage even, and their gyrations pulled them out on a fatter arc. He could feel the Nonman's strength failing; he knew that if all else were silent, he would hear the ghoul heaving and spitting air like a bull. He sagged to Oinaral's abdomen, and he knew that he need only do *nothing*, and the Siqu's arm would yield him to the gaping below, make of him a gift to the Holy Deep ...

And the knowing suffused him with far more hope than horror.

Release me ...

His breast slipped from Oinaral's clasp.

Return me to your bosom, Mother.

But the Siqu managed to catch his left arm. He swung out limp on the chain's arc.

The way is too hard.

He felt, rather than heard the Nonman scream above him.

Your son is too weak.

And he could *feel* what was about to happen, feel himself cartwheeling through blackness, clipping the sides as a doll cast down a well. He could feel the fatal plummet that was *release*–

A *bird* blasted up out of the blackness, its great white wings thrashing, the yellow knife of its beak aimed at heaven. The peering etched it in clean light above, a *stork*, a miraculous vision of *life*–

Sorweel seized Oinaral's wrist–out of brute reflex more than resolution. He swung wide and kicking over the void. The Great Entresol resonated with bottled screams.

The iron band of the Nonman's grip vanished. He toppled, flew *into the peering* as though into the sun, missed it by the breadth of an arm, crashed into the stacked carcasses. He rolled to planks of sodden wood, looked about wildly.

Clack ... Clack ... Clack ...

Every surface seemed aglow for the brilliance of the peering. Oinaral lay riven on his back upon a bed of butchered animals, convulsing arms and legs out, mouth wide and gasping. His nimil coats blazed as water beneath morning sunlight. His eyes fluttered.

Immiriccas pondered killing him for what he had done.

You wear a prisonhouse *upon your head, mortal ...*

But Sorweel found his gaze drawn to the *other*, the night-cloaked figure that stood directly beneath the peering–for the mouth of the hood now regarded them. The Boatman regarded them, his mouth working as though reciting words–to a song.

Clack ... Clack ... Clack ...

An emaciated hand drew back the cowl, and the Son of Harweel was amazed. The peering flashed across bare white scalp, and the eyes watched from the shadow of hairless brows ... The Boatman was a Nonman—the fact of this emanated from him. And yet he was *ancient*, his cheeks creased, his sockets pouched as infirm breasts. Mortality pursed the whole of his hard, cruel mien.

He stared as one who searches for the relatives of those he hates.

Clack ... Clack ... Clack ...

And the Haul went down.

The Boatman, his blasted skin luminous in the light, had not ceased staring at them—singing all the while. The Lament subsided in imperceptible degrees, became less and less distinct from the endless boom of falling waters, more and more haunting, an appalling backdrop for the growl of Boatman's song:

O' Siöl! Dark is the harbour of your womb,
A lion has arisen, and your children hide.
A dragon has descended, and your children flee.
O' Siöl! O' barren House Primordial!

So we squatted upon our haunches,
Bathed our arms in the black water,
We swore oaths of hatred against them.
We spurned our prayers,
And the emptiness that ate them.

It was an ancient song, and obscure. It sawed on the ears, the heart, bearing more the stain of melancholy than the substance, and yet possessed of unnerving passion all the same.

Clack ... Clack ... Clack ...

What was near was all too bright, enough to make a scowl of the merest inward glance. Halos hung about every surface, be it bitten wood, links of iron, or porcine swales. The Boatman seemed even more a horror, given how deeply the light inked his senescence in shadow. So Sorweel and Oinaral found their eyes driven outward, to the walls of the Ingressus, where distance and graven image had declawed the peering light. The walls climbed about them, hoop after hoop of reliefs carved at least a forearm deep, slowly climbing into oblivion above and resolving from oblivion below. They remained silent long after the dwindling of the Lament above had permitted easy speech. Each stared out from their portion of the bark's stern, disbelieving what had just happened. Sorweel leaned blank against the gunwale, listening to the clatter of machinery, the creak of links and joists about the grisly load.

The Haul descended on a great nimil chain. Two great iron wheels revolved at its heart, purchasing length from above by consuming slack from below. Gears locked into the wheels released a mighty hammer against an iron anvil, generating the rhythmic crack that had punctured the Lament above. The noise itself was difficult to describe, save that it was sharp enough to wince ears, and somehow left the taste of metal upon the tongue. Given the dread nature of their descent it seemed alarming and horrifying, a drawing of attention in a place where only those as soundless as shadows could hope to survive.

Clack ... Clack ... Clack ...

Iron bars jutted from points short the prow and stern, converging upon a black-iron collar that pinched the chain between two smaller wheels above—a stabilizing device of some kind. The peering hung from this, a radiance too bright to possess detail.

And directly beneath it, the hale yet withered Nonman stared and sang:

O' Siöl! What love hath thou remaining?
What fury hath thou loosed? What destruction?
We who know the ground, plot in its bones,
Prepare to grapple the endless, Eating Sky!

"The Boatman ..." Sorweel at last ventured to Oinaral. He had no wish to speak of what had happened, but neither did he wish to be alone with thoughts that were not his own. "I don't remember him."

"The Amiolas knows him," the Siqu replied without turning. A violet stain lay upon his cheek, a swatch of dried blood curved like a flower petal. The youth recoiled from thoughts of Mu'miorn, the violence of a grief that was not his own. "We were always a long-lived race," the Siqu continued, "and he was ancient ere Nin'janjin returned, a wonder even, ere Sil first tempted his nephew, the Tyrant of Siöl. The Inoculation did not work for any of the aged save him ..."

"*Morimhira* ..." Sorweel gasped in a realization that confounded him. The legendary Father-of-Orphans—as famed as any among the Exalted. Morimhira, the violent uncle of Cu'jara Cinmoi, who had cut short the Verse of innumerable lives back in the luxurious days before the Ark, when Mansion yet warred against Mansion.

"Yes," Oinaral said. "The Most Ancient Warrior."

So decrepit.

"How has he come to look like this?"

So human.

"The Inoculation worked, but not entirely. Since no disease can claim him, he is deathless ..."

"But not ageless."

The Siqu glanced to the darkness below. "Aye."

"But how could he ..." The youth trailed in confusion. His knowledge seemed a book whose spine had unravelled—or worse, *two* books. All he had were sheaves scattered and heaped, facts and episodes. With his every knowing, it seemed, he became more disordered, not less, as if every page pulled open was another page torn.

"How has he escaped the Dolour?" Oinaral said, guessing his question. He shrugged his great shoulders. "None know. Some think he was the *first* to suffer it, that his acts had been so violent and his life so long that he was *already Erratic* ere the Second Watch was abandoned, and that this ... natural derangement ... has rendered him immune to the violence of what the others suffer. He does not speak, though he understands much of what is said. He does not grieve or weep—at least not outwardly."

"And he cares for them now? The others? Feeds them?"

The bald head shook in negation beneath the motionless white point of the peering gleaming upon it.

"No. The Emwama tend to the Chthonic. The Boatman goes where they cannot. He ministers to those who wander the Holy Deep."

Clack ... Clack ... Clack ...

"Like your father, Oirûnas."

Oinaral was several heartbeats in replying.

"He completes a Fathoming each day, every day ..." he said. "What was once a holy pilgrimage before the Chthonic was abandoned. Some say he does penance for all those he killed before the coming of the Vile."

"What do you say?"

The Siqu turned to him—daring the ethereal visage of Immiriccas, Sorweel now knew.

His visage.

"That a wild labyrinth lays about him," the Lastborn said, glancing as if in gesture to the blackness, but in truth out of aversion to his aspect. "And he cleaves to the only path that recognizes his feet."

The Haul descended to the cracking of hammers and the Boatman's rust-iron voice.

Facing the sun, there Imimorûl dug a great well,
And bid his children enter.
In the bone of the world, there he conjured song and light,
And his children feared no more the starving Sky.

Here! Here Imimorûl drew down the face of the mountain,
Bid us seize the halls of the House Primordial—here!
Here lies a home that cleaves the tempest asunder,
A home that breaks the shining beak of the dawn.

So the Most Ancient Warrior sang. And Sorweel learned that the earth was mazed, the ground riddled with cavernous hollows. It seemed horrific somehow, that intervals should haunt the foundation of foundations. This was the *ground*, he realized in numb disbelief—the *ground*!—and they travelled *through* it, cranked into its black maw. The changes in the engravings seemed instant when he finally noticed them, but he somehow understood they had come about gradually, figure by sculpted figure. At some point in the descent, when the Lament yet resounded perhaps, the stone populace of the walls *had begun to notice them*. One by one the fist-sized faces turned, and the cubit-tall figures began to form ranks against the observing void. By the time Sorweel observed the change, the little sculptures had already barricaded the panels, standing, watching, face after indistinguishable face.

Clack ... Clack ... Clack ...

The soul divided between Sorweel and Immiriccas gaped in horror.

"None know how or why the stone-eaters responsible carved them thus," Oinaral said from his periphery, perhaps sensing his unease, perhaps not. "The stone-eaters themselves said they did it to honour the Fathoming, as a goad to self-examination and an accounting of sins. To apprehend memorials without, they said, was to neglect the testimony of what lies within."

Sorweel shuddered, such was the effect of the thousands of motionless faces.

"And you do not believe them?"

"Their expressions ..." the Siqu said, his voice as searching as his gaze. "There is too much hatred in them."

But the youth could see no expression in any of them at all. They simply watched, great rings of miniature faces, band stacked upon murky band, their eyes so indifferent as to be dead, so numerous as to be one. The Lament yet lay clear upon the air, a morass of shouts and wails, a racket barbed so as to hook as burrs upon more lucid souls. And the contradiction raised his hackles, the sight of judgment *given* and the sound of judgment *received ...*

And he realized the Fathoming had always been a thing of dread for Immiriccas, whose aversion to reflection approached loathing. Action should be enough!

But for him to stand in judgment of Immiriccas was at once for Immiriccas to stand in judgment of him. *Who he had been* the dismal months preceding came in a cringing flood, images churning as foam. Mewling when blood should have been spilled. Bemoaning what should have been avenged. Questions like sparrows battling in his breast, leaving him winded. Sorweel shrank from the ancient and inflamed gaze, the immovable eye of the Ishroi, even as he bowed before the thousands stacked in great rings about the walls of the Ingressus ...

Clack ... Clack ... Clack ...

The Haul descended, and Sorweel fell a second time, into deeps no less irrevocable. *Humanity* had been his ground, his implicit ordering frame, and like so very many things human, it could only command so long as *it remained unseen*. Thus are pride and courage so eager to example witless faith: only *not knowing* allows Men to be what they need to be. So long as Sorweel had remained *ignorant* of his countless mortal frailties, they could secure him thoughtless foundation. But now that he had fathomed himself from a *greater* vantage, a far mightier and more noble frame, he could *only* see himself as anxious and deceitful, craven and imbecilic, crooked and grotesque, an ape that lurched in mockery of the *true rule*.

The Nonmen.

The lions fled, and there they rested content,
And they placed yokes upon the groaning Emwama,
Who placed yokes upon the braying beasts,
And brought forth abundance for the Sons of Siöl

Judgment ever belongs to the greater. He saw himself the way the Injori Ishroi saw Men in days of ancient old, as strutting beasts, by turns devious and absurd, rotting even as they lived, shouting boasts from atop their barrow-graves. Weed or flower, it did not matter, for their time was too short to count anything but the dregs of glory. Henceforth, his would always be a miscreant life.

And so the last of the boy left to the Son of Harweel died in the Weeping Mountain.

The walls of the Umbilicus had been dyed black to make stark the gilded halos about his head and hands. Perhaps no soul in the Empire aside from herself and her elder brothers knew this.

"And if I should fail? What then, Father?"

His presence had dwarfed for intensity more than dimension. His look passed through her the way it always had, twin cables strung taut across the interval that was her soul.

"Spend your final breath on prayer."

She became *real*, kneeling before him like this, just as she had as a little girl. Always.

"For me?"

"For everything."

Clack ... Clack ... Clack ...

The Lament gradually faded into the boom of waters. They continued sinking, a vacant bulb of illumination dropping into viscous black. Sorweel abandoned his position, sat upon the deck opposite the stacked carcasses, his head—or the Cauldron, rather—bent against the glare. If Oinaral wondered at his silence, he made no sign. The Nonman stood leaning from the stern as before, a pale shadow decked in armour lurid with scintillant light. Perhaps he too grappled with misgiving and unwelcome insight. Perhaps he too sounded waters the intellect could only muddy.

The youth lay slack, hung in incredulity. An image of Serwa floated beneath his soul's eye, and his blood ran cold.

The Boatman began a different dirge, another song the Amiolas remembered, an epic lay of love in the shadow of extinction. Sorweel turned to him. He was scarcely more than a silhouette for the radiance above, an apparition of smoke rising into sunlight.

She stripped and she clothed him,
but she fed him not,
and with her brother,
they became runners beneath the Starving,
fleeing into the wilds of Ti,
where the rivers vanish,
in the cruel shadow of the House Primordial.

Sorweel lay drowsing as he listened, his body a thing forgotten, at once bound upon the rack and entombed in clay. Watching the Boatman, he saw a *scuttling of shadows about his feet* ... He thought it a cat, at first, for he had seen innumerable cats upon the river barges of his home. Then the first of the figures strode from the Boatman's shadow and into horrific reality.

Clack ... Clack ... Clack ...

There, less than two lengths from where he lay against the deck, a *living stone statue* stood no more than a cubit in height ...

It was one of the countless Ishroi chiselled from the walls, dressed much as Oinaral, rendered in exquisite detail, save where scabbed by ancient happenstance. The little face held him in its chipped regard.

Sorweel could not call out, could not *move*, whether for the want of limbs or volition he would never know.

A second graven doll joined the first, this one naked and missing the top third of its head.

And then a third joined them. And more, appearing along the summit of the pig carcasses immediately before him, miniature stone ghouls glaring down eyeless. He could hear even more, their march like a thousand little hammers tapping across the deck.

The peering flared soundless and white, cast a garland of crisp little shadows from their stone feet.

Clack ... Clack ... Clack ...

He could not scream out any warning.

But someone had seized his shoulders—someone was shouting his father's name! The Siqu—Oinaral ...

"*Awaken*! On your *feet*, Son of Harweel!"

Sorweel clawed his way up, casting wildly about for any sign of the stone effigies. He looked to the Lastborn in confusion, glimpsed a pale, naked figure drop wheeling and kicking into the abyss a mere toss from the Haul. He turned to the Siqu in astonishment, to confirm that he had seen what he had seen. But Oinaral was already squinting upward, his hand held so as to cast a shadow across his eyes. Sorweel joined him, found himself dazzled by the peering. Another pallid figure materialized, plummeting from visibility into obscurity within a heartbeat—close enough for the youth to start. It seemed he had locked gazes with the hurtling wretch, glimpsed the mien of someone awakening ...

He stood blinking against his own disordered soul.

Clack ... Clack ... Clack ...

"What happens?" he gulped as much as called.

"I do not kno—"

Another flash of battling white. Sorweel glimpsed a form streak toward the far side of the Haul, catch it with its face, then carom, flipping. The entire bark kicked and swayed upon the chain. Oinaral fell to one knee. Sorweel clasped at the swine carcasses, caught one of the legs above the cloven feet; it was stiff as wood for rigour. The Boatman merely swayed counter to his vessel the way an ancient mariner might, and continued singing.

And he heard her say unto her brother,
"Lay with me, tend to my fallow plot,
make my barrens bloom, sweet Cet'moiol!
Let our Line suffer no iniquity, no alien earth or seed.
Let us aim our children as spears!"

Sorweel and Oinaral each stood on the rear portion of the deck gazing upward, hands against the peering light. The youth saw the last ring of engravings climb into the murk, a band consisting entirely of heads massed upon hairless heads, all of them watching. Raw stone ruled beneath, scarps jumbled and hanging. He glimpsed an iron catwalk rising from the obscurity below, a brace of scaffold across the wall, a pillared recess—

A nude figure flickered past the prow.

Clack ... Clack ... Clack ...

Oinaral cried out. Sorweel looked up, saw at least seven forms plummet from shadow into stark light, limbs flailing, bodies somersaulting, eyes glittering for the peering light, incredulous. The nearest slammed into the stern directly behind the Siqu. The Haul kicked up, tossed Sorweel against the stacked carcasses. He glimpsed a flashing miss, then another ghoul sheared across one of the iron braces, torso exploding into violet haze behind the Boatman. Another hurtled into the stacked pigs almost immediately before Sorweel. The impact slapped him backward. The Haul rocked and danced, swung on a ragged arc. Others slipped past without sound. Sorweel teetered on the gunwale as the bark wagged about, felt his stomach pitch. Any instant, it seemed, the lacquered bark would snap the chain and they would drop into the black.

But Oinaral was up, seizing his shoulder, even as the Haul's motion rounded into a pendulous swing, one heaved slower and slower by the torsion of the Fathoming chain. He stared in horror at the pulverized pit where the wretch had landed upon the pigs. A hand lay miraculously intact on the floor at his feet, laying palm up as though holding a stylus.

All this time the Boatman had simply grasped the length of chain hanging beside him, swinging so as to seem motionless while the deck rolled and bucked beneath his shod feet. And for all the dangling violence of his bark, he did not once falter in his song ...

Thence to the cruel House they fled,
the bastion that turns aside seasons—

"What happens?" Sorweel cried out. "Are they leaping?"

"No," Oinaral replied, keen on the void above them once again. "They were not suicides."

"How do you know?"

"Because they were Nonmen."

"What? Nonmen can surrender dignity, but not life?"

"All dignity and more!" the ghoul cried, his face twisted into something nearly frantic with grief. "*We would all be dead*—Ishterebinth would be naught but a mouldering tomb!—were suicide something our nature permitted!"

Clack ... Clack ... Clack ...

Sorweel stood glaring, his limbs stuffed with straw, his heart still hammering. To think he had bemoaned the madness of his quest with Serwa and Moënghus!

"So if they didn't leap—then what?" He paused, realizing the dread alternative. "Were they *thrown*?"

Oinaral glanced at him sharply, then resumed staring upward, the swales of his face shining for the radiance of the peering.

"Were they *thrown*?" Sorweel pressed. "Could Nin'ciljiras somehow *know* what we attempt?"

Oinaral remained silent, avoiding his gaze as ever.

"We have reached the Qûlnimil," he finally said in semblance of resolution. "The great Mine of Ishoriöl ..." A grimace marred his chiselled mien. "We shall reach the Mere soon."

The false Believer-King turned from him in dismay. *Grace*, the Siqu had said. He would save himself by stalking his blessed shadow, by following the path that Yatwer had marked for the Son of Harweel, the boy doomed to murder the Aspect-Emperor. But what grace could be found in a pit so deep, amid horrors so sordid and appalling? If anything, he owed *his* life to Oinaral—not otherwise!

The Haul-hammer resounded through the black, its crack ragged for echoing across the fractured surfaces now soaring about them, counting out the unrelenting beat of the Boatman's ancient song.

And far from the Starving,
in the deepest of the Deep,
they brought forth their accursed spear.
Cu'jara Cinmoi, a soul ever aimed
at this, our desolation,
for they had lain together, brother and sister,
in mockery of Tsonos and Olissis.

The Incest Song of Linqiru, Sorweel realized. A version he—or the soul he had become—had never heard, one bearing the warp of the future ... of doom come true.

The Nonman Apocalypse. A *whole race* locked in the lightless depths, wailing for losses, raging against bargains sealed in bygone ages, souls drifting from defeat to folly to tragedy, ever more at sea, ever more removed from the shores of the now. Soon the last of the Intact would Succumb to the Dolour, the Emwama would abandon them, the last of the peerings would wink out, and silence and blackness would rule the vacant heart of Ishterebinth.

The Mountain would cease weeping.

And Sorweel *understood*, seized the fact that outran most all Men until ruin at last ran them down. *The End will have out.* The Nonmen, for all their staggering age, were no more immortal than their engravings. Despite all their pious might and ingenuity, the ages had laid waste to their dominion, had made smoke of their breathtaking splendour. They were the stronger race, the wiser, and yet doom and degradation had claimed them. The wolves had fallen. What hope was there for mongrel dogs such as Men?

And upon a single forgotten breath, the ancient grudges of the Amiolas and the perplexing facts of the Great Ordeal came together. He had a sense of being taken up, of *being aimed anew*, turned toward a reality as gritty and as grim as truth. There was no deception here. Oinaral did not dissemble. Ishterebinth was not some absurd pantomime. The End was not some daring fancy, a way to pass impiety off as courage.

It was simply inevitable.

And so it came to pass that the Son of Harweel apprehended the horizon of a new and terrifying world from the very bowel of the Mansion, one where the Unholy Consult was real, the extinction of Men was nigh, and

Anasûrimbor Kellhus was the only *hope*—the one true Saviour of Men! A world where the fraction that the Dread Mother could see had blinded Her to the fraction She could not ...

A world where he could love Anasûrimbor Serwa.

He need only survive and escape this mad and vicious place ... Flee!

For all hope had fled the Weeping Mountain.

Other than Lord Harapior, she did not know any of the nimil-armoured Nonmen who came for her. But she knew from their looks that they had heard of her, who she was, and what she had done. There was lust in their darkling gazes, but curiosity and apprehension too.

They placed a sack over her head, one woven of Injori silk as soft as rose petals across her cheeks and forehead. Her body they left uncovered, save for shackles of iron about her ankles and wrists—and the Quyan variant of the Agonic Collar welded about her neck.

They did not speak, and she did not resist.

But the hatred she had incited in the Lord Torturer was too profound to be ruled.

"Sing for us!" Harapior growled. "Sing for us, witch! Score our hearts with your foul impersonations!"

She did not oblige him—but not out of spite, for she cared nothing for the ghoul. She did not sing simply because the watch *she had sung for* had come and gone.

Her next song would command fire and ruin.

The Nonmen threaded a pole between the crotch of her elbows and her spine and bore her thus from the Thresholds.

"Noooooooo!" she heard her eldest brother, long broken, snuffle and cry. "*Leave her!*" he roared with sudden, bestial ferocity. "Let her be! *Let! Her! Beeeeeeee!*"

And it cut her far more than any indignity she had so far suffered that he might yet cry out his devotion thus, despite all the degradations, all the mutilations. Finding her body useless, the Lord Torturer had sought to make Moënghus an implement of her torture. And she had sang songs of blessing in Ihrimsû as they cut him ... as they brutalized the dark boy who had worshipped her for as long as she could remember.

She had sung in celebration while watching him sob and shriek for torture ...

And still he loved—the same as Sorweel.

Anasûrimbor Serwa pondered this as the company of ghouls bore her blind into the heights of the Weeping Mountain ... the love of troubled brothers and orphaned kings.

And the cruelty demanded by the future.

Sorweel watched as the Boatman, still singing, began gripping the carcasses about the ankles, then whirled about on quick steps to pitch them out over the gunwale.

The clacking drew them like larva from holes in the rotted walls. They groused and gesticulated, perched upon precarious ledges or iron gang-stages, rooting the air like blind pups. As wretched as those above had been, these were far worse: emaciated, ulcerated, adorned with scabs, clad in nothing but raiments of filth, their knees and palms as black as Zsoronga's shoulders, their scalps as jaundiced as human bone. The pallor of each had been scuffed from blackened skin in a manner peculiar to each, lending ornamental distinction to what misery had ground to meal otherwise. For eccentricities in motion aside, they all leaned out to the Haul with the same compulsive sway, and they all ate with identical frenzy.

These Mines had been the glory of Ishterebinth, what brought embassies from all other Mansions to reside within their mountain. For nimil—the famed silver of the Nonmen, more doughty than steel, as soft and warm as cotton against the skin—had ever been the great obsession of their Race. Once the Vast Ingressus had thronged with Hauls laden with ore bound for the furnaces and smithies of the Chthonic above. Peerings had burned. Emwama had teemed about iron walks and platforms, cringing beneath the harsh cries and cracking whips of their immortal overseers.

And now this ... this ...

Perversity.

"These are the Reduced," Oinaral said. "In a thousand years hence, this is what will become of those who yet survive in the Chthonic above."

The youth bit back on abhorrence, said only, "They do not weep."

"What we call the Gloom has fallen upon them. Centuries of reliving memories wear them to dust. The clarity of the horror endured is leached, until nothing but a dark fog remains—an obscurity that *is* their souls ..." He paused as though struck by some novel implication.

"Yet another living Hell!" Sorweel cried in incredulous retort. "Your Boatman performs no mercy, casting swine to them. It-it's *obscene* allowing such misery to persist! A *Man* would just let them die!"

The Siqu stiffened at the rail. He turned from the congregation wagging across the pitched stone to regard the apparition where Sorweel's face should lie.

"And what of the Hells?" he asked.

The question surprised the youth. "What of them?"

Oinaral shrugged. "We have spurned your infernal Gods ... and we have sinned."

"Pfah!" the youth spat. "What do we care for Gods?"

"But the Hells—we *do* care for them. The paths to Oblivion are few—as tight as the arrow's notch, Emilidis would say. Tell me, Son of Harweel, who is to decide when these wretches should hazard *damnation*?"

Sorweel stood dumbstruck.

Oinaral looked away, glanced about the limits of the peering's light, from the ghastly forms level to them to those rending and gorging above. "The most wasted souls are the eldest," he continued, "the most tragic—the friends and rivals of the one who feeds them. The Boatman *knows*, mortal: Even the Gloom is a blessed interval compared to what awaits."

Understanding cracked the youth's heart, knowing this World could countenance such misery at all, let alone as a *lesser evil*. It deadened him, hammered blunt yet another inner edge.

Clack ... Clack ... Clack ...

Their descent did not slow, nor did the Boatman relent in his grisly toil. To preserve the balance of the vessel, he drew from the forward and rear spates equally, forcing the Siqu and his ward to retreat to the blood-greased stern. In unending succession, the Most Ancient Warrior hurled the wooden bodies out on what seemed impossible arcs given their bulk. His accuracy was likewise miraculous: time and again Sorweel thought a carcass would spin short, only to watch it skid into sudden, bloodless immobility upon the very lip.

Both watched mesmerized, the throwing and the feeding, listening to the Boatman's effort lunge and release through his voice as he sang:

Let this song as unguent flow,
fly as sunlight upon virginal snow,
Sing breath sing! Declare our dissolution,
at the horned hands of Men,
how we raised one thousand sticks of light
against them,
how our heroes waded into their clamour,
until our dying buzzed as flies in our ears.

Sing! Declare golden Siöl's smashing
the Breaking of the Mountain Most-Holy
and our long exile beneath the Starving,
and how our brothers embraced us
upon the iron shoulder of Injor.
Flow! Make such perfume as might be made,
from ruin and an hour …

And Sorweel found himself gazing at Oinaral—the last of the Siqu—and pondering the will that might make peace with a Race so artless and so rapacious as Man. The Boatman sang the Lay of Little Teeth, the recounting of Siöl's fall in the first of the great migrations of Men from Eänna. The Amiolas knew well the bitter toll of those years, how darkness had crawled across the great, vacant empire of the Mansions, how the Men multiplied and multiplied, forever encroaching and invading, sacking Mansion after Mansion, hunting the False Men to extinction … through all the World save *here*, the last refuge remaining.

Ishterebinth.

And there was no end to them,
for endless were the Eännites, endless and accursed
Strong was their hatred, reckless were their heroes—
mad to prove a trifle of life!
And cunning was their claim,
for as their teeth,
so too were their thoughts both little,
and sharp.

The Haul continued clacking relentlessly downward. The Reduced dwindled in number, until no more forms puled from the tunnel-pocked walls. The Boatman resumed his station beneath the peering, his eyes lost to the shadow of his brows, his forehead and cheeks white and scrotal, his mouth working about the intonations of another ancient old song. The Haul seemed transformed for the dispensation of so many swine carcasses. The spates now piled no higher than the knee, so that the whole of the bark could be assayed from stern to prow in a single glance, at once battered and bright, lacquer peeling, wood bruised with violet, crimson, and watery pink, the whole endlessly sinking into the Stygian blackness below.

Of the three captive waterfalls that had rifled the walls of the Great Entresol above, two had vanished, redirected to different underworld regions, leaving only a third, immured in a chimney that serviced communal water grottos, recesses set along the entirety of the Mines, possessing walls as pocked with graven imagery as any of the galleries above. Some kind of cataclysm had shattered the chimney mere fathoms below the last of the Reduced, exposing the white cataract, which became ever more hairy and diffuse as it plummeted. Everyone was quickly sodden. Moisture clung as a mucous. Oinaral gleamed as a fish in his nimil hauberk and gown. Soon a scintillant haze was all that remained, a mist that the peering transformed into a prismatic infinity, pinprick colours conjured from gaping space. Sorweel seized upon the spectacle as an excuse to avoid the roiling that was his heart, extended his fingers to comb the infinitesimal lights. It seemed at once proper and criminal that beauty could only be found in things so small, so deep. The haze thinned and thinned until it was no more than a luminous fog, and then nothing at all ...

Sorweel clutched the gunwale for vertigo, cast his gaze from side to side.

But the wraparound cliffs of the Ingressus were nowhere to be found.

"We have come to the Holy Deep," Oinaral Lastborn said.

Like spiders riding silk from the mouth of a mountainous spout, they dropped into a perfect void. Looking up, Sorweel saw the rim of the Ingressus recede into a ceiling that made him hunch for scarped enormity. The clacking expanded into an echoic gas.

"Our pilgrimage is almost done?"

The Siqu nodded, his eyes likewise searching the dark.

"Aye. Pray to your Goddess, mortal, for peril is nearly upon us."

"I am done praying," he said, more vacant than alarmed. "The blind yield no favour."

Oinaral regarded him, concerned rather than relieved. The Nonman had known he would capitulate all along, Sorweel realized, that the Weal would blot Harweel's murder. Was it the degree that worried him?

"It is the Amiolas," Oinaral said in explanation. "The soul you have become is resolving contradictions between your commingled beliefs."

That word ... *contradiction* ... caught as ice in Sorweel's breast.

"But if I no longer believe," he exclaimed, "then what of Her *Grace*?

Oinaral made no reply.

"You said your only hope was to walk in my shadow," Sorweel pressed, "to find shelter in Yatwer's Grace! But if I no longer ... *believe* ..."

Oinaral hesitated, stared, the youth knew, upon the face of an *imprisoned soul*, a ghastly shred of the criminal his beloved King had so cruelly judged in days of yore.

"Fear not," the Nonman said. "You need only remember why it is we are here."

The youth scowled.

"So the Dolour renders one glib as well?"

Clack ... Clack ... Clack ...

Where the stone had snapped as raw and immediate as a clamp about his nape in the Ingressus, it now *sounded* the void, each strike falling into the great cavern of the former. Their descent suddenly seemed a preposterous invasion, a deliverance that was at once anathema. They were naught but a speck in the aphotic black, a spark thrown by the sky, and yet they came promising conflagration.

Oinaral Lastborn had seized his throat and by the time the youth realized his fury, had already slammed him across the swine.

"*Say* it!" the Ishroi barked above his vicious grip. "Tell me why we are here!"

"Wha-what?"

"What outrage have we come to redress?"

"N-Nin'ciljiras," the youth stammered on swelling ire. "He-he has allied the Mountain with Golgott—"

"With the *Vile*," the Lastborn snapped. "He has surrendered Ishterebinth *to the Vile*. You must remember this!"

Clack ... Clack ... Clack ...

Sorweel glared speechless.

Clack ... Clack ... Clack ...

Oinaral released him, staggered back a step, horrified. Suddenly—almost madly—the Boatman ceased singing. The hammer cracked once more, and the Haul abruptly jerked short. Sorweel looked up, saw Morimhira clamber astride the peering's blaze, his arms reaching to the wheels above ...

"There is no speaking on the Mere," Oinaral said, still reckoning what he had done. "If you speak on the Mere, Morimhira will kill you."

A final crack of metal. The deck dropped from beneath Sorweel's feet, then punched both his heels. They landed upon an airy whoosh. Sorweel tripped back onto the swine carcasses. The Haul rocked from side to side, buoyant.

The meat was cold, flabby about an unyielding core. He scrambled back to bare deck, found himself staring out appalled ...

For all its intensity, the peering could reveal no more than a slick of water some few hundred cubits wide. A corpse lay no more than a length from the starboard gunwale, floating just beneath the water, its pallor testifying to the rust-foulness of the water—water that had once been lucid as mountain air! Debris clotted the surface elsewhere, ropes and braids of putrefaction still undulating for the Haul's intrusion. He glimpsed another corpse farther to the stern, bloated as a dead steer, its face a murky scribble.

The part of him that had once been Immiriccas lay numb ... or dead.

The Mere become a cesspit! The Deep was holy no more.

When he looked to Oinaral, the Siqu raised three fingers to his lips beneath a stern glare: the Nonman gesture for silence.

The Boatman had moved to the prow, where he drew a beaten oar from beyond the carcasses forward. Bracing himself with a foot on the rail and one knee to his chest, he swung the oar out and down, then heaved back and about on the oar. Almost immediately the chain clattered free of the mechanism above. The Haul barged forward. Sorweel was forced to duck the kicking tip as the vessel slipped beneath. He glanced up, watched the chain needle the upper void as they drew away.

Then he looked to the ruined water, as black as pitch save where gagged with scum. He stepped to the rail.

He leaned over to stare into the brackish water.

They moved slowly enough that the reflection was bowed without real distortion. The brilliance of the peering rendered him in silhouette: he saw the Amiolas rise as a tapered square from his shoulders, its interior blessedly black. But a glimmer wavered in the void, one that kindled as he leaned closer. He watched stupefied as it waxed moon-bright, then terrified as it wobbled into the charnel visage he had only glimpsed before ...

A white face indistinguishable for Oinaral's—or a Sranc's—staring back up at *what looked down*.

And it horrified, for nowhere could the King of Sakarpus perceive himself —who he was!—in that unholy circuit of reflected and reflecting. What was human in him whimpered, begged for this mad nightmare to end. What was Immiriccas, however, recoiled in disgust and monolithic contempt—

The peering flickered out.

No one spoke.

The silence was that of breathing beneath blankets, punctuated by the brittle string of droplets falling from the Boatman's oar. The blackness was absolute, as indifferent to eyes as to water or rock. At first he *tried* to see, to force some concession from what was impervious, but that stoked the intimation of blindness—terror. So he looked without straining to look, stared without the bigotry of focus. The beads upon the oar ceased dripping. The silence was of a stone deeper than mountains. And in that darkness he saw the Darkness that is the fundament of all things, the shadow within the light, the Darkness that doffs and dons Men as masks, that always claws *outward* and never in.

Oblivion.

An urge to kick or to scream seized him ... to prove the existence of echoes. But he remembered his Siqu's warning, leaned riven against the gunwale.

The peering fluttered back to fierce life, and the sewer that was the Mere lay revealed about them once again, the glitter of greasy, swollen things. His hood heaped about his shoulders, Morimhira stood gazing and scowling at the brilliance, aglow like an angel against the black mire beyond, his eyes sparking as a sorcerer's might.

He too had been surprised.

The ancient Nonman resumed paddling the Haul forward, his back pulling into a broad V with every alternating stroke. Sorweel found himself returning to the mirroring waters, drawn by some strange will to gratify horror—not simply to regard the horrid aspect, *but to see through its eyes ...*

But the armoured Siqu clapped a long hand upon his shoulder, drew him around. Whatever rebuke his gaze held faltered the instant he looked into the Cauldron.

The Boatman toiled just over his shoulder, and, glancing at him, Sorweel saw a band of grey resolve from the far-forward limit of the peering's light—a strand. Stagnant beach climbed from the blackness, the sand white and grey, the waterline black with viscous coagulum. He followed the light's expanding margin, watched the tracts of sand unfurl, shadows shrinking into countless dimples. He spied a heap of some kind coming into murky materiality just as he realized the Haul was about to strike. He reached out to the Siqu's sleeve, seized a fistful of nimil links ...

Held him as the Haul lurched to a halt on the underworld beach.

Rather than thank him, Oinaral averted his eyes and turned to the prow, gesturing for him to follow. The Boatman barged past them on his way aft, and Sorweel found himself shocked by his *density* as much if not more than by his creased face. It was as if an engine of war lay primed within him, torsions as mighty as he was old. The youth glanced backward one last time before leaping from the Haul in pursuit of the Siqu.

Sorweel landed on the prow's furthest shadow, just beyond the fouled waters. The sand was neither warm nor cold, as fine as silk. He watched his shadow stand as he stood, only elongated across the trampled strand. The brightness of the peering was enough to render the filth of the surrounding waters translucent, and to reveal the mire of *floating bodies* clotted about the shore. Here and there some had been rolled out of the water, beached—most likely by the Haul itself, given the septic stillness of the Mere. Though intact within the water, their bodies had been rotted to sodden bone and leather once exposed to air.

He turned to Oinaral, who stood several paces inland, gazing out into the black.

The Boatman shocked him scraping about on the prow above and behind. He watched the Most Ancient Warrior launch a carcass to land with a dusty thump mere paces from Sorweel on the sand. The youth hastened to join his Siqu where he stood.

Oinaral turned to his approach, murmured, "Listen."

Sorweel paused, his ears pricked. "I hear nothing."

"Indeed," the Nonman replied. "That is what makes the Deep our only Temple. *Silence* is what we count as most holy."

He knew this, but it stood among the many things that bewildered for knowing.

"Silence ... Why?"

Oinaral's face tightened.

"Oblivion," he said. "It is where we would hide, if we could."

Serwa hung limp from the pole wedged between her arms and back, her covered head slung low, her breath hot on the fabric. The peerings passed as a succession of luminous bruises through the silk hood as her captors bore her through the mazed ways of Ishterebinth.

She pondered, not without care, the brief tragedy of her life, how circumstances could blunt, fracture, and obliterate even the most painstaking designs. She contemplated how the number-sticks ruled all ...

Everything save the Shortest Path.

The Niom had been a ruse for her father as much as for what remained of the Nonmen—she realized that now. It was merely a vessel, a thing possessing no significance aside from the terrible cargo it bore. Sorweel and Moëngus had been sent to vouchsafe her father's artifice, nothing more. They were little more than dupes in the end, witless tokens of a far more daring ambit ...

She. She was the masterstroke ... the monstrous cargo.

Anasûrimbor Serwa, Grandmistress of the Swayali, the greatest Witch to ever walk the Three Seas.

Lord Harapior called the Nonman company to heel from someplace near. The sack was whisked from her head; she found herself blinking against raw brilliance. They were still in a corridor, she noted, with no little alarm—a grand one to be sure, but a corridor nonetheless. The Upper Luminal, she reckoned.

The Lord Torturer crouched before her, his waxen features close enough to nip. Wrath splashed as agony across his face. In a single motion, he raised his right fist and struck the left side of her face.

"From the King-under-the-Summit," he growled. "He asked that I drive down your price."

She glared at him, left eye fluttering for tears.

He raised a hand to her throat, scratched the ensorcelled metal about her neck instead. Her Agonic Collar.

"Emilidis himself wrought this," he said. "No one who has tested it has survived." His glittering black look faded for a heartbeat, straying into thoughts both awful and inscrutable. "You would die were you to shed the least light of Meaning ... Certainly! To suppose otherwise would be to blaspheme the Artisan."

He swallowed, his gaze roaming down to the points of her breasts and beyond.

The great pupils once again locked upon her own.

"But then I know that you are *Dûnyain* ... I know that every blunted edge you bare conceals a poison pin."

He sighed in mockery.

"I was a fool for thinking that knowledge would make me your master ... So now I'm suspicious beyond all reason. I obsess, wondering where I might find the poisoned pin. And I ask, *What will my King do* when he at last lays eyes on you? What would any soul do when presented a famed songbird as a gift?"

He sneered.

"Of course, he would *bid it sing*."

He seized the back of her head, jammed the silken sack deep into her mouth and throat. She gagged and convulsed as someone human might. His eyes gleamed for satisfaction.

"No voice," he said. "No poison pin."

The Gods were wolves baying beyond the ageless gates of death, gluttonous and all-powerful. The Nonmen, the progeny of Imimorûl, would deny them the leathery meat of their souls, such was their pride. So where Men asked how they might live so as to become prized pets in Heaven, they asked how they might live so as to *die invisible*, to plummet beyond the Outside and vanish into the Deepest Deep.

"That is why your father came down here," the youth asked, "to find Oblivion?"

They followed the black path of their shadows into regions of dwindling light, toward the heap Sorweel had spied earlier.

"All seek it," Oinaral replied softly. "He came here because he is Tall, and all the Tall come to the Mere when they Succumb."

"Why?"

"The Dolour affects them differently: their confusion is less profound, but their violent humours rule them more completely. They come here because only the Tall can hope to survive the mad humours of the Tall."

They crossed into a debris field on the verge of the Haul's failing light, an accumulation of thousands upon thousands of bones strewn and piled across the sands. Sorweel initially assumed they all belonged to pigs, but the sight of two black *sockets* staring up from the sand informed him otherwise. A skull the size of his torso ...

"Then how do you know your father yet lives?" he murmured to his Siqu.

For the first time the youth noticed the pale luminance upon the ground before him and him alone. The Amiolas, he realized.

"Because only Ciogli the Mountain could throw him from his feet."

The Nonman strode ahead to scrutinize the heap. The great skull Sorweel had noticed earlier sparked a second bolt of terror as the Lastborn stepped around it: the pate climbed as high as his nimil-gowned knee!

Sorweel shrugged against rising hackles, threw glances across what little he could see.

The Nonman stepped around the heap the way one might a corpse found in a field. Obscurities resolved into crisp features as Sorweel hastened to follow. The Cauldron's funereal light waxed more horrific with every step. A great hauberk comprised the body of the heap, laying folded across the curve of a shield immense enough to deck half the Haul. A helm large as a Saglander barrel crowned the bulk, intricacies dimpling a hide of dust. A sword as long as he was tall—a full Siölan cubit—jutted from the sand immediately behind it, as though it were a cairn or grave. The youth gave the whole a wide berth, thinking this was how a hero's discarded armour might seem to a toddler or a cat.

He glanced back to the Haul beneath the radiant peering, saw the Boatman casting swine, his existence a tireless sliver in the angle he occupied relative to the light. He watched a carcass slap onto the heap, glimpsed the snout jiggle in the bright. He noted the parallel bird tracks he and Oinaral had inked walking from the shore ... Suddenly the monstrous *gait* that had trampled the strand surrounding became plain. Everywhere, pits had been stamped like fuzzy memories in the sand, elephantine impressions.

The blackness about them throbbed with hazard.

"What now?" he asked Oinaral on a tremulous voice.

He knew what awaited them. With his own eyes he had witnessed Oirûnas at Pir Minginnial, bellowing shouts that swatted the ear, casting ruined Sranc above the mobs with each colossal blow—crushing the throat of a Bashrag with a single hand!

The *Lord of the Watch*—he had seen him thus! With his own feet he had followed his rampage beneath the golden enormity of the Horns!

"He is here," the Siqu said, still scanning the black. "Those are his arms."

Many were out there, the youth realized. Monstrous souls in the dark, watching, waiting. This was where the Boatman came—where he delivered his ministry of swine and sustenance.

So this was where Oirûnas had carved his empire.

"So what now?" the youth repeated.

Oinaral stood rigid in the manner of those who cling to standing.

"Tell me, Manling ..." he said, his voice curious. "Tell me ... if you were you to find your father's shade rotting in this desolate place, what passion would own you? If you found *Harweel* lingering here, would terror squeeze away your breath? Numb your limbs to lead?"

Sorweel gazed upon the Nonman's profile.

"The very same."

"And what," the darkling figure asked, "would be your reason?"

It seemed he could taste something sour and despairing.

"For shame," the youth replied. "For failing to be what his glory demanded."

Oinaral pondered these words for what seemed a very long time.

Deep, my sons, delve deep,
Fortify the very bones,

Wed hope to what is solid,
Trust to space made,
Not emptiness stolen ...

The Nonman drew Holol at last, waved it as a glowing revelation across the bleak regions before them. Pins of light carved the strand sterile white, uncovered bones and more bones, cracked and splintered, tossed through the pale sand.

Holding the arcane blade before him, the Nonman set off into the black. Silver shimmered along his chain-mail rim as he dwindled.

Sorweel hastened to follow on legs that seemed braided from straw. What *would* he do, were it his father hidden in the black before them? Would he rush forward, cast himself sobbing at his feet, beg for an undeserved forgiveness? Or would he flee as fast as his legs could carry, flee the truth of the Holy Deep?

Would he even still love Harweel, the wise and strong King of the Lonely City? Or would he hate him for having suffered so long the curse of his example? For abandoning his little boy to days so hard, a Fate so perverse and cruel.

Could Harweel still love him?

These questions precluded breathing.

Man and Nonman wandered across the wrack of bone and sand, into zones where the sand shallowed, pooled in great scallops of arid rock. Holol's light whisked without sound over increasingly mangled terrain: gravel skirts heaped and bowled, stone shelves terraced the deepening darkness, climbing as a stair might. The visible limit brushed what seemed some kind of vast pier hanging above, detached from any other visible stone.

Oinaral Lastborn halted him with a restraining hand. After a moment of peering hesitation, the Siqu continued forward alone, his pace ginger, stalking the ascending clutter with the reverence of desperate souls at Temple. Just what he stalked eluded the youth for thirty heartbeats or more. A joint of stone reared from the foot of the shelves, angled so as to conceal the line dividing what breathed from what did not. Thus did the famed Lord of the Second Watch seem to be an extension of these, the deepest roots of the Weeping Mountain.

The ancient Hero lay naked with his head bowed to his chest. He seemed to slumber, but his posture—reclined with his wain-wide shoulders bent upright against unseen rock—warned otherwise.

Oinaral came about a mound of gravel, then followed a low rock defilade toward the hulking form. Ten thousand shadows swung on the whim of Holol's pinpoint light, some as small as palms, others as long as night. The sum of existence swung upon his every step.

The stony string of the Boatman's voice fell silent.

Oinaral paused just beyond the defilade, a scintillant beacon amid the dreck and gnawed desolation. Silence smothered all inkling of distance. His father lay some thirty paces before him on the second of the scalloped shelves, wreathed in shadow, his enormous frame motionless against his horn of rock, his face inscrutable.

Fear scorched Sorweel's breast.

The Siqu dared call out: "Mighty Oirûnas, Lord of the Watch ..."

The massive outline did not move. For the first time Sorweel noticed stacked skulls—*walls* of them, arrayed like macabre fortifications along each of the ascending shelves of stone. Pig skulls in their thousands, snouts drawn out ragged, as if belonging to a creature far more fearsome.

When had fathers become Dragons?

"It is me, Oinaral Lastborn ... Your son by fair Ûliqara."

He swayed Holol back and forth, causing the surrounding horde of shadows to kneel and stand and then kneel once again. Sorweel fairly lost his balance, feared he might swoon.

"*I know ...*" the hulking form rumbled. "*I know* ***who*** *you are.*"

Oinaral stood rigid.

"You are lucid?"

Silence, so utter as to make wet skin of souls and razors of the least sound.

"My disorder," the profile growled in a tone so deep as to knock heartbeats, "springs from but a single question ..." The silhouette shifted. Stone cracked in unseen sockets. A face as broad as shoulders bobbed into Holol's light, its lines twisted like ship's rigging for wrath.

"***Why do you soil my gaze now***!"

Sorweel retreated a step, then another as the Hero leapt onto the stone stage below. His countenance was wroth, broad in the manner of the Holca. Gore made a pit of his mouth, so that he looked a creature whose jaws lay outside its flesh. His musculature was clawed in veins, striate for hunger. His stature was so great as to make a statuette of his son.

"*Nil'giccas*!" Oinaral Lastborn cried beneath the looming presence. "Nil'giccas ha–!"

The blow was swift, the force absurd. Oinaral was swatted more than ten cubits, his body bouncing like a withered tuber from the rock face back across the slope of the gravel mound. Somehow, impossible as it seemed, he had managed to hold onto Holol, the famed Breathtaker. Sorweel could see its radiant point bobbing just over the Siqu's right thigh, blackening his twitching profile.

The light etched the nude white colossus that was his father, raving above him.

"***Weeeak***!" thundered across the Mere.

The Son of Harweel stood transfixed.

"***How could I not love something as weak and beautiful***!"

The luminous tip of Holol had slipped behind the Siqu's leg; its first warble pinned his heart nonetheless.

"***How could a father not love such a son as should be slain***!"

It flickered in a series of low pulses, each outlining the Siqu with the wrack of deeper regions, each depicting the Lord of the Watch, hairless and pendulous, across stages of murderous outrage.

"***Such a son–***!"

Sudden blackness always surprised, whether anticipated or not. Distant obscurity became near, blackness leapt, and the white-skinned furor of Oirûnas raging over his dying son died with his son.

Holol had not slipped Oinaral's grasp—he had slipped from it. Somehow the Son of Harweel knew this with granitic certainty.

The Haul's fierce peering yet burned behind, but he stood upon its extinction, in a twilight underworld heaped with the skulls of pig. A greater portion of him, everything human, gibbered for terror, clamoured to flee, but some other fraction had resolved he would stand his ground.

He would not leave Oinaral Lastborn to moulder with swine. This he knew with an assurance as deep as life.

He would not abandon his Siqu.

The groan of a monstrous elk huffed from the black before him, followed by a voice like cracking timbers.

"My-*my* ... My ***son*** ..."

Silence.

Sorweel strained for some glimpse, anything, but all he could see was the luminance that fell from his false face, a spectral pool of surfaces braised with faint detail.

A sob burst upon the dark, raw, plucked with mucous, so near as to make the youth retreat a step.

"***My sonnnn***!" the great lungs screamed.

The peering flickered as before, and in a moment of madness it seemed the entirety of existence hung upon the black as lights upon smoke. Then he found himself nowhere ... stranded in a vast nothing.

The World had shrunk to that swatch illuminated by his accursed face.

The silence rumbled as a tempest, one that could blow *through* ground.

The youth found himself whirling about, searching for the direction of the Haul. A heartbeat merely, and he was completely disoriented. The prospect of being marooned down here, lost in the Holy Deep, came as a chattering panic. He fell to his knees scanning for footprints by the light of his arcane communion, but the sand was too trampled, the porcine debris too copious.

A titanic howl sent him skittering backward across the sand on all fours.

"***Aiaaaaaaaaaaaa***!"

He was lost down here, he realized. He had come to the one place the Mother of Birth could not follow. For that was why Imimorûl had hidden his children in rock and mountains: to conceal them from the Gods!

The ground whumped in the black—concussions so powerful that the grains shivered about him. He scrambled back from the sound, turned to stand and run. He was lost ...

He was lost!

The obstruction loomed like a great black tortoise, knocked his shins and thighs—Oirûnas's arms and armour. His momentum pitched him to the bones and grit.

Another titanic yowl.

"***I ... have ... mur-murdered him, Brother ... Murdered mine own son***!"

The blackness roared in its wake, thrummed with intimations of hovering, hanging doom. The *light of the Amiolas*, he realized, scrambling across dimpled sand to find refuge behind the Nonman Hero's great, empty helm. The Amiolas was what would kill him! Across the Mere's every shore, the ghastly visage of Immiriccas was the only thing visible! He was the lone silver lure in the deep—jigged and dandled by his own frantic efforts no less!

Sorweel cringed behind the helm, found his eye drawn to the sullen hint of polish beneath the dust. In spite of himself he drew a sleeve across the obese curve ... and saw the luminous apparition that was his own aspect staring from the shining frame of the Amiolas. He gawked at the reflection, dumbfounded.

Mother. *He saw his mother*, the wane beauty she possessed in his most sunlit memories.

He recoiled, scrambled back until blackness had obliterated it, and found himself marooned nowhere once again, his heart hammering, his thoughts grasping thoughts grasping thoughts, like a children's finger game.

"***What happens, Brother***?" boomed hoarse from the dark.

From across the desolate, underworld strand, the Boatman's voice scrawled the guttural intonations of a new song:

They did hoist Anarlû's head high,
and poured down its blood as fire.
And the ground gave forth many sons,
Ninety-nine who were as Gods,
and so bid their fathers
be as sons ...

Sorweel dared stand. He whirled about, aching to hear, to locate the direction, but the Amiolas baffled the sound the way it baffled his other senses ...

Great Oirûnas, Lord of the Watch, leaned from blackness into materiality immediately before him. Sorweel tripped backward to the sand and bones—and the gargantuan form *followed*. Massive fists pummelled the strand to either side of his head, elephantine arms pumping, pounding. "***Nooo!***" cracked the smothered deep. The colossal face blotted the blackness, a pallid aspect as broad as a Columnary shield, wrought with anguish, nostrils flaring, alien teeth clenched as a shipwright's vice, eyes thick with what seemed dreamlike exhaustion, the pulping dismay of knowing it could not be undone. The horror he had just authored, the crime, the unthinkable …

"Nooo!"

It could not be undone.

Sorweel cringed, arms crossed before his face. Anvil fists struck smoke from the ground. The Cauldron's harrowing visage gleamed as foil in the ink of each appalling eye. "**Why**?" the hole of its mouth boomed.

"**Why**!"

The sand whumped.

"**Why**!"

The voice beat as wings across his tripping heart.

"**Why**!"

And then the mammoth fury was gone … swallowed by the blackness.

The void hummed for absence of echoes.

Somewhere in the black the Boatman sang, his voice sawing yet more ancient wood, another song of Imimorûl and the oldest of the old.

"Nil'giccas has abandoned th-the Mountain!" Sorweel coughed into the dark.

Oinaral lay sprawled as clothing over bones, the only kind of suicide a Nonman could be.

"Nin'ciljiras! Nin'janjin's accursed seed, *he* rules …"

He was never a charm for Oinaral! He was surety *that truth would be heard*, so that terrible consequences might follow.

"He has surrendered Ishterebinth to Min-Uroikas—*to the Vile*!"

The Vile—only now could he taste the *violation* that name tokened.

He looked down to the spectral illumination his face cast upon his hands. Dust and grit bearded both palms. The left one bled black in the light.

"All hope and honour have fled the Mountain!"

The giant swooped into the small light, clapped him in monstrous digits. The Lord of the Watch, who had ceded all sanity to the Dolour so long ago, hoisted the Son of Harweel slack, and then wrenched him in two.

The Sky-Beneath-the-Mountain.

As Seswatha, she had supped with Nil'giccas upon this, the pinnacle stage. She had clutched his breast for terror at hearing the Nonman King's dark tale.

But Nil'giccas no longer ruled. At Harapior's command they strapped her head to the iron-grille floor with a leather belt.

She would not bow otherwise.

The air nipped with the chill of malice. The gilded and graven facades of the Hanging Citadels sloped overhead and down across her right periphery, while to her left the tumbling void of the Ilculcû Rift pulled her against the pinching floor. Nin'ciljiras she recognized by his armour of golden scales—which glistered for being wetted. She could see him conversing with Harapior, casting avid glances in her direction. They had pinned her for display on an annex to the higher stage, so that she could see both the Nonman King's chair and the broader, petitioning floor below, all of it miraculously hooked over the Rift's dizzy plummet. Some hundred or more Ishroi and Quya stood congregated on the lower platform, each gowned in splendour, each an effete image of manly perfection.

She felt rather than saw them bringing Moënghus out to join her. She had heard him bull-shouting what Ihrimsû curses he knew in the corridors earlier, so she wasn't surprised to see him also gagged when they thrust him to his knees mere paces away, naked and bound as she was.

What surprised—even appalled—was his condition ... that he *could still draw breath*, let alone wrench and war against his restraints. The ravaged face turned to her, rising and falling on heaving breaths, black locks pasted to wounds. The glacial eyes seemed mad, overbright.

Was this what had she had wagered on her mad throw? A *brother*?

What Father had wagered.

And it descended as lightning, the realization the *she had failed*.

Harapior had guessed her gambit. Very soon, they would become the plaything of some decrepit and inhuman will, something to *sin against* and so purchase some brief term of sanity.

His gored arms wrenched back, Moënghus swayed upon his great and macabre frame, staring as if she were something he should remember.

It rose from the darkness, then, clawed her face from the inside. It kicked each of her lungs ... *shame* for what was ... *terror* of what would be ...

Her mother's inheritance.

For the first time in her brief life, Anasûrimbor Serwa grimaced for darkness, not artifice.

A sob kicked through her. And it was as if she had spilled grain in times of famine. On a heartbeat, the sonorous thrum of Nonman voices fell silent, leaving her gagged cry stranded in the void of Ilculcû, a hitching note more profound than any she had yet to sing, if not more beautiful. The sound of feminine despair ...

And it seized their black hearts, compelled their senescent fascination.

"The black-haired brother!" a crimson-armoured Siölan Ishroi cried, hooking her from her grief. Sûjara-nin, a detached fraction of her realized. "I would hear him weep as w—!"

The hanging iron frame shuddered.

To a soul the assembled ghouls whirled about. Nin'ciljiras bolted golden from his kingly seat ...

Serwa peered across the congregation, blinked for the hairs of light obscuring her gaze ...

And saw *one the Tall* stride from a crouch to his full, gargantuan height as the slope of image-pitted stone above permitted. His steps resounded through the iron platform, sent dust raining from the iron anchors above. The assembly shrank from his titanic approach. The giant should have gleamed with the same lustre as his fellows. He was decked in full battle armour, wearing a great slit-faced helm and a monstrous hauberk of stamped plates set in mail—accoutrements that had not seen the field ere Far Antiquity. But all of it was skinned in rotted pelts of dust ...

Not that it mattered, given the four points of perfect oblivion that had been affixed to it ... Chorae, set upon either thigh and either shoulder.

"Lord Oirûnas!" Nin'ciljiras cried with surprising alacrity. He spared Harapior an intent look before stepping to the edge of his penultimate platform. "You honour us!"

Oirûnas ...

The twin of Oirinas. The Lord of the Watch. The legendary Hero of the first wars against the Inchoroi.

"**Honour**," the giant boomed from his helm, "**is the sum of my purpose here**." The platform grille bit her cheek at the impact of his following step.

Nin'ciljiras retreated an involuntary step. "The Dolo—" he began, only to slip on the oil that doused him.

"What of it?" the Hero asked, pausing to tower over the Nonman King.

"Are—?" the usurper asked, attempting to raise himself, only to slip into Harapior's arms. "Are your thoughts ... ordered?" he asked, regaining his feet.

The giant loomed fearsome across the silence. The assembled Ishroi and Quya watched stunned; even the most Wayward among them blinked in awe, for Memory itself had risen from the grave that was the Mountain.

"I suffer but one disorder ..."

For some reason, this seemed to occasion some kind of relief for Nin'ciljiras. For the first time, Serwa glimpsed the *body* laying slack in the Hero's mighty left hand.

"And what might that be?"

"The armour you wear ..."

The Nonman King stared up, blank about a heartbeat of hesitation. "It ... it is a gift."

"The gold ... that sheen ..." the ancient Hero crooned. **"It is familiar to me ..."**

Nin'ciljiras said nothing.

"I revisit it in my thoughts ... often."

A *flaxen-haired Man* lay slumped in his hand ... Could it be?

"It *tyrannizes* me," the Lord of the Watch thundered.

"The Age has been unkind since you retired from the Mountain," Nin'ciljiras said, his voice brittle for breathlessness. "I am the last of the line of Tsonos, the la—"

"Tell me, my brothers!" the voice clapped. The Hero whirled to those assembled. **"What misfortune could excuse a disgrace so ... so *treacherous*!"**

The Nonman of Ishterebinth could make no answer.

"Tell one who has devoured ten thousand swine ..."

His shout churned with dark passion, intonations of revulsion, injury and betrayal. Many among those assembled dared raise hands to their pommels. Nin'ciljiras actually stepped *behind* a rigid Harapior. Serwa glimpsed Guardsmen jostling through the fragmenting crowd.

"Tell one who has squandered centuries reliving the golden horror—the *golden obscenity*!"

Without warning, the giant Hero stepped directly *toward* her, and with a deftness of someone far smaller, deposited the unconscious form he held between her and her brother. Then, even as the guardsmen converged, the

Lord of the Watch raised an oak-branch arm to point at the grandson of Nin'janjin. Serwa did not need to see the helmed face to know the violence of its sneer.

"***Tell me***," Lord Oirûnas bellowed, "***how the Vile have come to rule the Mountain***!"

The accusation boomed across the gaping Ilculcû, an interval the Hero used to draw his monstrous sword, Imirsiol. A gleaming array of weapons appeared across the platform. Harapior's eyes flared with radiant meaning. But the giant swung his immense blade up across the ceiling, shattering a legion of graven figures, sending debris raining—and *sparks* tapping—across the oil-drenched Nonman King ...

The first flames were ghostly. Nin'ciljiras hooted and began slapping in panic regardless. The sheen across the golden scales, caught ...

The Nonman King burst as a torch, began screaming like a live-braised lamb. Harapior rushed to assist him, but flame caught upon the scalps adorning his neck. He paused to beat at his neck and chest ... and was cloven in twain by the legendary Hammer of Siöl.

"***So it ends***!" the Lord of the Watch roared over the shouting clamour, and he laughed and wept both.

Nin'ciljiras thrashed and screamed. The soggomantic gold blackened.

And from regions unknown, a single point of nothingness swung on an arc—a Chorae *cast at her*, she realized. But she could not move! She could only track its nearing course against a field of heaving, scissoring motion. It bounced across the grill immediately before her, clattered through a wagging groove directly toward her face, oblivion promising oblivion. A concussion wracked the platform, and, somewhere, an anchor snapped, and the whole *dropped*, tilted to her left. The Chorae chipped to a halt a mere cubit from her face. She followed the fingers clasped about the emptiness of the thing, and saw *Sorweel*, his face blooded for flayed skin, his blue eyes fluttering as he strained to focus upon her ...

"***This!***" the Lord of the Watch boomed laughing. "***This is our cannibal fate***!"

Suddenly the Horse-King *smiled*. Chaos ruled the Sky-Beneath-the-Mountain—death and screams, but her eyes were consumed by *him* ... for he was *real* ...

As was the stained and blooded hand that he floated to her face.

A warrior's hand.

"*Sing*," he croaked through the uproar, yanking the black-silk gag clear her mouth and throat.

She gasped, drew deep the taste of smoke and war. The air reeked of burned mutton.

And she sang.

Made demonstration of her father's dread portion.

CHAPTER THIRTEEN

Dagliash

Even the God must eat.

—CONRIYAN PROVERB

Late Summer, 20 New Imperial Year (4132, Year-of-the-Tusk), the Urokkas

Not in the Near Antique days of Imperial Cenei, nor in the Far Antique days of Holy Trysë, never had the World beheld such a congregation, such a concentration of arcane might. The Sranc had at last been backed into the final corner of Yinwaul, and the Schoolmen of the Three Seas advanced upon them. The very ground smoked before the Magi, seethed. They had wrapped their faces with cloth soaked in sage and horse urine, so they might blunt the septic fumes. Otherwise, their billows flared in material contradiction of their phantom Wards, bolts of hanging cursive, a calligraphy that wooed the dawning sun with poetic threads of light. The chorus of their singing maddened the ears, drew eyes to unseen quarters. As *one* they walked upon a neck-breaking fall, *one thousand sorcerers-of-rank*, each a floating wildflower dissolving into stages of obscurity, each setting sorcerous spade to obscene earth.

The enormous fronds of the Shroud consumed everything save the pastel flash and flicker of their lights.

The Schoolmen vanished, and the Sranc burned.

Rather than fanning out as they did when Culling, the sorcerers *climbed* in fearsome procession, followed the fractured spine of the Urokkas into masses of the Horde. The Exalt-Magus, Saccarees, took the lead with his Mandate, blasting the heights, gutting the ravines with Gnostic geometries. Temus Enhorû and the Saik followed close behind, with Obwë Gûswuran and the Mysunsai arrayed behind him. The Blind Necromancer Heramari Iyokus followed in the van with the Scarlet Spires. Nothing save the lay of the mountains opposed them. The crowns themselves had been battered into domes, but their torsos were a welter of broken stone and gravel enormities. Even though sorcerers could smooth their passage by picking between echoes of the ground beneath, precipitous terrain was often lethal. For this reason, the Schoolmen abandoned the sky as soon as the Sranc were cleared beneath and found that *real* ground was treacherous footing enough.

And so the sorcerers of the great Southron Schools began seizing the high places—four mountains that were in reality a dozen in their decrepitude. Yawreg was the first and lowest, a ramp for the others, gathering the edges that clench land into fists. The second, Mantigol, was the highest. Here, Saccarees witnessed the dread majesty of the Horde *entire*, the Shroud rearing, bulging summits of ochre, the blighted tracts beneath, the insect stain, innumerable clans herded by rage and terror across the very curvature of the World. The weak shoulders and splintered head of the third, Oloreg, provided a veritable maze of passes linking the northern to the southern slopes. And lastly, Ingol, whose bulk crowded the Sea, possessing a humped summit that gazed down upon slovenly Antareg—and Dagliash.

Across unkempt leagues they pressed, each School taking a summit as a violent station, each summit perpetually besieged. Lightning bleached the slopes, blinding threads that took seizing bodies for beads. Crested heads reared, apparitions spewing fire that lit skinnies as candles. At times it was absurd, the sight of old men tottering up the slopes, cursing skinned shins and palms. At times it was legendary, the vision of entire mountains surmounted in fire and light. Gullies, gorges, and slopes burned as though dowsed in pitch. Sranc were heaped for their own pyre, forming berms in places, twitching dunes too bloody to burn. The creatures themselves were emaciated—many raced naked, limbs bulbous for joints, torsos fluted for ribs, phalluses arched into scalloped abdomens—and crazed for it, gifted with a bird-like quickness, as though their bodies had consumed the contents of their bones. Many Schoolmen endured the terror of whole bands bounding *through* the catastrophes they wrought, falling directly upon their Wards, hacking like crazed monkeys. But the pallid creatures always relented, fleeing whatever direction safety afforded. And the Horde, possessing only the brute intelligence of mobs and herds, milled upon the foundations of the Urokkas, drawn in ever greater concentrations by the promise of rutting murder, but cowed by the displays of arcane destruction above. The Schoolmen garrisoned the passes and established eyries upon each of the summits, impromptu camps where the sorcerers could tend to their injured and recoup their strength. None could hear a mundane word, even when shouted into hands and ear. A cacophony of sorcerous cries never ceased to knot the freakish din, but otherwise nothing *human* could be heard.

The mountains were wrested from the Horde one-by-one. The Scarlet Schoolmen defended the bull-skull summit of Yawreg, watched in horror as the putrid masses overran their only path of retreat. The Mysunsai occupied the greater heights of Mantigol adjacent, their numbers thinned for assisting their Anagogic confreres. The Imperial Saik held the ruined archipelago of scarps that was Oloreg; they more than any others found themselves continuously embattled. Meanwhile the Mandate cleared the crawling heights of Ingol with razors of light, Abstractions, then draped their triunes as a sparking shawl about the mountain's shoulders. Both the day and his men exhausted, the Exalt-Magus of the Great Ordeal finally halted his advance and took the measure of what he had achieved.

Wherever the World held dirt, it plumed skyward for the scribble of violent millions, but nowhere else. Saccarees peered out across a great hollow in the Shroud, a cavern as deep as the sky was tall, born of sea, stone, and stony earth. The clarity was unnatural, *pure* for the septic obscurity that caged it. The long, knifing curve of the River Sursa was scarcely visible. Dagliash seemed a monolithic bark upon Antareg below, a barge stripped to the hull, floating upon a Sranc tide. The intervening tracts *sizzled* for condensing so much fury—a thousand screeching faces in every tessera, a thousand shaking cleavers and a thousand bared teeth, on and on, forming a mosaic that vanished into the Shroud, into numbers that broke the back of reason.

Fearing the dismay the spectacle sparked within his own breast, Saccarees himself climbed Ingol's highest echo to rally the other Schools. "*I hope you're hungry*," he signalled to his brother Grandmasters.

So much Meat.

Then he sent word to his Holy Aspect-Emperor ...

What their Lord-and-God coveted, the Schools had seized. The heights above Dagliash had been taken. With the exception of Antareg, the Urokkas belonged to the Great Ordeal.

Assuring they remained such until the following dawn would prove a nightmarish toil, one that crowned each of the four mountains in glimpses of putrid masses rushing beneath weirs of slaying light. After sunset, the Ordealman knelt en masse upon the ravaged earth, and gazing upon the flaring summits, they beseeched the God to fortify their arcane brothers, lest the morrow end in ruin.

They would sleep in their armour that night.

Even if he is false, this ... *this is real* ...

Proyas and Kayûtas swayed side-by-side in their saddles, each trailing their respective entourages. Masses and columns of infantrymen trotted about them. The Sea reached into violet obscurity to the south beyond, a dark and endless procession of rollers, each bearing brilliant filaments of morning across its back. To the north on their right, the summits of the Urokkas piled westward, little more than sepulchre shadows through the Shroud. Scowling lights crowned them, the flicker of distant sorcery. A great river of Men, arms and banners flooded across everything between, the booted glory of the Three Seas, hastening with a vitality borne of the Meat into the jaws of more Meat.

This has to be real!

"What ails you, Uncle?"

Proyas gazed long and hard at his Lord-and-Prophet's remarkable son, then looked away wordlessly.

Trust, he now knew, was but a form of blessed blindness. How many times had he ridden thus? How many times had he led simple souls to some complicated doom? He had always trusted then, in the greater cunning, the greater glory, and, most of all, the greater righteousness of his cause. He had simply *known*—known for not knowing otherwise!—and he had executed with an unfailing hand.

Now balling his hands into fists could scarcely quiet the tremors.

"I cannot see as far or as deep as Father," the young man pressed. "But I can see enough, Uncle."

His anger came upon Proyas suddenly. "The fact that you accompany me says enough," he snapped in reply.

Kayûtas did not so much look at him as observe.

"You think Father has lost faith in you?"

The Exalt-General averted his gaze.

He could feel Kayûtas watch him, his eyes lucid and amused.

"You fear *you* have lost faith in Father ..."

Proyas had known Kayûtas since infancy. He had spent more time with the boy than with his own wife, let alone either of his own children. The Prince-Imperial had even apprenticed under his command, learning things far too hard, he had thought, for such a tender age. It was not possible to relieve a child of so much innocence and not come to love him—at least for a soul such as his.

"Your father ..." Proyas began, only to trail, horrified by the quaver in his voice.

This much is real! Real!

It had to be.

The Horde warbled on the wind, a chorus spackled with nearer screams. He cast his eyes across his command, convinced himself he had no need to fear prying ears. Besides, Kayûtas would not have broached the matter otherwise.

"We endlessly pondered him when we were children," Kayûtas continued, speaking as if to while away long watches. "Me. Dodi. Thelli. Even Serwa when she was old enough. How we debated! And how could we not? when he loomed so large, and we saw him so very little." The man fluttered his eyes in response to Proyas's manic glare. "Father this," he said, wagging his head in boyish sing-song. "Father that. Father-father-father ..."

Proyas felt a smirk crack the numb planks of his face. There had always been an ease to Kayûtas, a kind of impervious assurance. Nothing troubled him—ever. And this, the very thing that made loving him so effortless, was also the thing that made it seem—on occasion, at least—that he would vanish like a coin if you turned him on his side.

"And what were your scholarly conclusions?" Proyas asked.

Kayûtas groaned, shrugged. "We could never agree ... For *years* we argued. We considered everything, even *heretical* possibilities ..." The long face seemed to purse about the thought.

Dûnyain.

"Did you ever think to *ask* him?" Proyas said. Here he was, leading the flower of a faith he no longer believed into the jaws of a battle that poets would recount for the ages ... and he found himself pinned breathless to a childhood anecdote ...

What was happening to him?

"*Ask* Father?" Kayûtas laughed. "Sweet Sejenus, no. In a sense, though, we had no need to: *he could see* the debate in us. Whenever we dined with him, he would make some declaration that managed to contradict whatever theory we happened to fancy at the time. How it would drive Moënghus wild!"

In some ways, the young man's resemblance to his father made their differences that much more stark. But in other ways ... Proyas shuddered for sudden memories of his last encounter with Kellhus. He found his gaze shying from the nimil-draped image of the Prince-Imperial ...

Lest he see.

"Of course it was Thelli who figured it all out," Kayûtas continued. "She realized that we could not solve Father because *he did not exist*, that Father was, in point of fact, *no one at all* ..."

A cold tongue licked the Exalt-General's spine.

"What do you mean?"

Kayûtas appeared to scrutinize the climbing Shroud. "It *sounds* like blasphemous nonsense, I know ... But I assure you it is anything but." The blue eyes turned to appraise him, wet and iridescent. "Look ... the thing to always remember about Father, Uncle, is that he is always—and only—*what he needs to be*. And that need is as ephemeral as Men are ephemeral, and as capricious as the World is capricious. He is what circumstances make of him. Only his *end* binds his myriad incarnations together. Only his *mission* prevents his soul from dissolving into the mad foam of what happens ..."

Speech is impossible without breath, so Proyas clung to his pommel without reply. With the Ordeal in his periphery, it seemed they floated in the wreckage of a great flood. The rumble of sorcerous dispensations poked through the growing wail. Both of them peered at the grim shadow of the

Urokkas, saw the flutter of rose luminance through the bowel of the black-and-ochre Shroud.

"Did you devils ever ponder the truth of me?"

The Prince-Imperial graced him with a wicked grin. "I fear you've only *just* become interesting."

Of course. One never need ponder what one trusted.

"You dwell on your grievances," Kayûtas added after a moment—a pale approximation of his father. "You're dismayed because you've learned that Father isn't what he claimed to be. But you've simply made the discovery that Thelli made—only without the benefit of her unerring sense of fashion. *There is no such man* as Anasûrimbor Kellhus ... No such *Prophet.* Only an intricate web of deceptions and stratagems ... bound by one inexorable—and as you know, quite ruthless—principle."

"And that would be?"

Kayûtas's look was mild.

"Salvation."

The land that the Sons of Men came to call Yinwaul had leapt with life in those days, rugged and astringent. Boreal forests had darkened every horizon north of the Sea, cloaking the Erengaw Plain, sooting the shoulders of the Yimaleti. Lions had stalked deer in the meadows, ambushed muskox in the fens. Bears had swatted pickerel and salmon from the streams. Wolves had sung eternal songs beneath the Void.

And Nin'janjin had ruled in Viri.

Though populous, Viri lacked the monumental grandeur and ostentation that so characterized Mansions like Siöl, Ishoriöl, or Cil-Aujas. "*Ji'milri,*" Cu'jara Cinmoi would famously call her, "That Anthill." Her Sons were peculiar also, at once ridiculed for their rustic ways and archaic legalism and revered for the spare profundity of their poets and philosophers. They cultivated a modesty that was indistinguishable from arrogance, that reflex to judge all things in excess as excessive. They eschewed ornamentation, despised gratuitous display. They scorned slavery, seeing a more shameful enslavement in the dependence of the master. They bent their backs and dirtied their hands, blackened their nails in ways that made their southern cousins chortle and sneer. They alone embraced the Starving and the Scalding, the sky and the sun that their race had taken as their bane. No matter where they travelled, the Sons of Viri were instantly known by the broad, wicker bowl of their hats.

Wisi, the shipwright Sons of Illiserû called them—"Nails".

Only on the hunt and in the subsequent feast did the Viroi yield to *elhusioli*, the Nonman daimos of excess. Their expeditions were things of song and legend, so much so that Hûsyelt, the Dark Hunter, was said to hunt *them* from time to time. The Hoar-Pelt, the great white bear-skin the Nonmen Kings of Viri wore in a crown's stead, was held to be a gift of the jealous and mercurial God.

Nin'janjin's astrologers had spied Imburil, the star that Men call the Nail of Heaven, long before it waxed. But they had no forewarning of the calamity to come three years following. How could they, when the very Gods had been confounded?

Arkfall changed everything.

Those who witnessed and survived the event claimed that the cataclysmic impact of the Ark somehow *preceded* the Ark, that the great golden vessel dropped no quicker than an apple *into* the flash and upheaval of an earlier, far more tumultuous strike. The sound blew around the World. Chroniclers from as far as Cil-Aujas record a tremendous crack, a noise that scrambled still waters, struck dust from mortices.

The flash blinded, the concussion deafened. Ground-quakes killed tens of thousands in the Mansion Deep. Those on the surface sought refuge in the Mansion, even as those in the Mansion battled to reach the surface. A conflagration expanded as a bubble of soap, an inferno flying on a perfect arc, consuming all land and sky in charring fire. Only those caught within the wrecked underworld Manse were saved.

Mountains were thrown up. Forests were levelled where not vaporized altogether. All that had thrived was either struck dead, or left stricken. A dozen tribes of Men vanished. The World burned for a thousand leagues in all directions, engulfing Ishoriöl, and reddening the skies as far away as Siöl.

As the *Isûphiryas* relates, Nin'janjin appealed to Cu'jara Cinmoi, whom he hated, such were the straits of the Sons of Viri:

The Sky has cracked into potter's shards,
Fire sweeps the compass of Heaven,
The beasts flee, their hearts maddened,
The trees fall, their backs broken.

Ash has shrouded all sun, choked all seed,
The Halaroi howl piteously at the Gates,
Dread Famine stalks my Mansion.
Brother Siöl, Viri begs your pardon.

But Cu'jara Cinmoi, who prized vengeance before honour, shut his heart and his Mansion against his cousin. And so cruelty begot wickedness, and betrayal, betrayal. Nin'janjin and the surviving Viroi turned to the Ark. Wars raged. The Inchoroi forged weapons out of perverted life. A darker epoch passed, and Viri became but another name for folly and sorrow, the first and some say the deepest grave in the long shadow that the Incû-Holoinas has cast over this World.

When so much is so mad, what can become of proportion?

The Raft swept out over the Misty Sea, its deck crammed with Swayali witches wrapped in their golden billows, and Saubon's householders, freighted for armour, bristling with arms. They seemed a motley band, the Knights of the Desert Lion, but no Believer-King could boast a more deadly collection of souls.

The World swayed and levelled about the platform's beam. Saubon caught himself peering at his Lord-and-Prophet the same hunted way Proyas had the day previous, a look that did not so much seek to see as to *solve*, as though the image were a cipher revealing less invisible and more terrifying things. He tore his gaze away, glimpsed a naked white carcass, Man or Sranc, lurching in the black swells.

What was this adolescent mooning?

One does not clutch at ribbons tripping down a stair. Men reach for what is *stronger*—and that is simply the way. They flail for what is slow and great to better brace themselves against madness of the small and quick. Proyas had been overthrown for the same reason the sight of the

Horde so offended the heart: for want of something greater *that was not insane*.

A meaning so vast as to be empty, so slow as to be dead.

A Frame.

But everything was quick and everything was small and only distance or delusion made it seem otherwise. What was the Horde if not the manifestation of this, the way obscenities could be piled upon obscenities and still be desired, *even craved*?

Proof that one can eat and shit one's frame.

Unlike Proyas, Saubon had always expected as much of the World. In a perverse sense, his Lord-and-Prophet's confessions had not so much overthrown as *confirmed* his faith. That Kellhus was small and that Kellhus was quick in no way altered the fact that he was *so much the stronger*. The haloed man soaring backward into the gnawed monstrosity of Antareg *had conquered the Three Seas*. No matter what he was, he was greater than any martial soul to have trod good green earth. No matter what he was, he was *Anasûrimbor Kellhus*. The more Saubon had pondered it, the more it seemed that he had not so much believed the words *as the power*—the thing that could not be denied. The *conquests* of Anasûrimbor Kellhus were the only revelations that mattered, the only truths posterity could examine. As he had said to Proyas, who *else* should hew their future?

The hand of Triamis. The heart of Sejenus. The intellect of Ajencis. Kellhus *dwarfed all other souls*. It was that simple.

So why did he harbour this horror within him ... the sense of hands too frail to fist?

The World abruptly dipped and rolled, taking his purloined stomach with it.

And *there it was*, floating up around the poised form of Anasûrimbor Kellhus, before sinking below the line of the Raft.

Dagliash .... another dead corner of a dead civilization.

The cliffs of Antareg loomed black over the booming surf, only to whisk beneath the timber deck. The Swayali about the perimeter began singing, and it was peculiar to be *surrounded* by feminine voices possessing no place. Like tiles in tipping succession, the Nuns stepped from the Raft onto the echo of the ground, where they wricked their billows open, and uncoiled into something greater for the beaming sun.

Saubon gawked with the others for the way the demented vista transformed their beauty into something rare and lapidary. The Urokkas had cut a region of vast clarity from the Shroud. Reeking sheets pinned every limit, strata of dust that craned and twined like film in water, decohered. And the distances beneath *shook* for agitation, like sand in the box of a racing wain. Sranc ... everywhere they raged in scabrous mats that disintegrated and reformed about cloven ramps, clenched heights, and sprawling meadows alike. The mountain slopes burned as if slagged in bitumen, yet still the creatures could be glimpsed, in clots if not individually, scraping their way upward. Fishhook brilliance winked about the crown of mount Ingol adjacent, the razor-white so characteristic of Gnostic slaughter.

This ... This *was their Frame*, a World of poisonous pins, as small and vicious in substance as in extent.

Kellhus stood with his back to the enormities, still facing the direction they had come, his hands yet extended to either side, as if welded to the golden discs that darkened them. He steered and slowed the Raft to better trail the expanding chevron of witches. The rotted bastions of Dagliash loomed ever more near. Saubon could clearly see the defenders brimming upon the walls, Sranc of a different breed clotted about battlements reduced to gumlines. Ensconced within serpentine coils of gold, the Nuns advanced on the decrepit fortifications, more than eighty gilded wildflowers thrown wide. Their keening, high and feminine, perforated the suffocating thunder. Sorcery glittered across the interval, lines like incandescent hairs. Blinking against the glare, Saubon saw walls and turrets ignite as torches, shedding sparks that flailed and screamed.

Even Sranc perished clawing for something ...

Reaching.

Viri lay dead an age ere the Mangaecca—the most grasping of the ancient Gnostic Schools—came to its derelict halls. Using debris as their quarry, they raised a citadel about the legendary Well of Viri, the enormous shaft that plumbed the Mansion to its dregs. Nogaral, they dubbed their new stronghold, the "High Round".

Their fellow Schoolmen had scoffed and sneered, called them "grave-robbers", an affront without compare among the Cond, let alone the Ûmeri they strove to emulate. Despite their demonstrations of outrage, the Mangaecca secretly celebrated the appellation, for it concealed their far darker ambition. In sooth, Viri was nothing more than a brilliant misdirection, a *false* grave to obscure the true, a cover for the Mangaecca's evacuation of Sauglish, not to mention the endless northward trickle of chattel and supplies. For all its immensity, Nogaral was nothing but artifice, a way to *plunder the Incû-Holoinas*, the Ark itself, under the guise of ransacking Viri.

With the destruction of Nogaral, the ruse came to an end, and the cancer that had replaced the Mangaecca, the Unholy Consult of Shaeönanra, Cet'ingira, and Aurang, declared itself to those they would exterminate. And so Viri faded into shadow and scholarship once again, a grave marking the loss of a second innocence—the innocence of Men—and the rebirth of an original terror, Min-Uroikas, or as the High Norsirai would come to call it, *Golgotterath*.

Where greed for the Ark had moved Men to reclaim Viri as a sham the first time, then fear and hatred of the Ark would move them to reclaim the dead Mansion as a *bulwark* the second. After centuries of intermittent war between Golgotterath and the High Norsirai, Anasûrimbor Nanor-Mikhus, High-King of Aörsi, laid the foundations of Dagliash, or "Shieldhold", the fortress whose fame would all but blot Viri from the fickle histories of Men.

As the nameless poet of the *Kelmariad* writes,

Set upon woe, hewn from deceit, garrisoned by hope,
Our Shield against the Legions of the Dying Sun,
Pray to her, our fortress, our House of Thousands,
Implore her as you would any other sacred idol!
For her miracles are numbered by our children.

But no God was ever so generous or so reliable as Dagliash. For centuries she would be the very bastion of Men, a lone beacon raised against the nightmarish gloom of Golgotterath. The ancient Norsirai called her by many names: the Obstinate, the Unconquerable—even "the Lilac" for the violet that perpetually stained her walls. The shores below mount Antareg were beached in splintered bones instead of sand, such were the numbers cast down the cliffs. Time and time again the Consult threw their inhuman legions at the fortress. Time and time again they were thrown back reeling. As Viri dwindled in human memory, Dagliash became the very emblem of Mannish ferocity and resolve, a name traded in rice paddies and mountain vales, in temple processions and booming harbours throughout Eärwa.

And so word of her overthrow reverberated as far as the courts of Mehtsonc, Iothiah, and Shir. Swart Kings cried for silence and bent their ear. And somehow they *knew*, those hard and archaic Men, knew what they should not know given the way conceit trivializes faraway foes. Somehow they understood that the long-besieged Gate, not of Aörsi, but of *humanity itself*, had finally fallen. And though they as yet knew nothing of the No-God, their skin pimpled for brushing its absolute shadow.

The Exalt-General salivated for the smell of burning lamb.

Kellhus beached the Raft on lichen-pitted stone, and with a lurch, Saubon's householders leapt from the timber platform incredulous, disbelieving ... much as Saubon did himself. The Witches had assaulted the fortifications in a manner too methodical to be described as furious, and yet all the more furious for it. After spreading wide, they had rushed the eroded stoneworks, closed the interval with fifty cubit strides, laving the ramparts with blistering arcs and amputating lines. Nothing had survived to slow them, so they had simply stepped over the smoking walls and bastions to prosecute their scintillant extermination within.

Now Saubon stood gawking up with his fellows at the scorched walls soaring about them. A bare hand seized his plated shoulder and he saw his Lord-and-Prophet grinning as he pressed by, walking out among the smoking carcasses that matted the courtyard. Dagliash had fallen in mere heartbeats, thanks to the Swayali, but the clamour of the Horde grew more swollen with each heartbeat following.

Saubon waved his war-party to take positions flanking the Holy Aspect-Emperor. They were here, Saubon knew, but for a single purpose: to protect their Lord-and-Prophet and the Nuns from Chorae. The Knights of the Desert Lion numbered some forty-eight in all, some hulking, others reed thin, and a few (like his unlikely Scylvendi scout, Skunxa) comically rotund. Saubon had spent more than fifteen years assembling them, plucking only the most ferocious souls from those serving him through the Unification

Wars. Soldiers of the rank need only see his entourage to know that *merit*, as opposed to bloodline, could raise them. Give a life to the right sort of man, Saubon had learned, and that man would wager that life no matter what the throw.

They had set ground in the Ribbaral, an area that had once housed the fortress's famed workshops, but had been reduced to mounds of debris and gravel. The ruins of the Ciworal, the great redoubt of Dagliash, soared dark above the glowing form of the Aspect-Emperor. As with the outermost ramparts, the cyclopean works lay hunched as though beneath sheets, summits and heights sucked round by the ages. Saubon kicked over one of the inhuman defenders—the Ursranc so oft mentioned in the *Holy Sagas*. The thing seemed identical to any other Sranc, save its stature and the uniform nature of its weapon and armour. He peered at the Twin Horns branded into the thing's cheek—the mark of its wicked masters. He wondered what the scarred tissue would taste like, braised over a low fire ...

He shook the thought away, kicked his Amoti Swordbearer, Mepiro, for crouching to scoop grease he might lick from his fingers. He waved the rest of his Household forward, and despite his earlier misapprehensions, found himself grinning an almost forgotten grin, savouring the anxious tingle of old. It had been too long since he had commanded from the thick of peril rather than the hazy limit. Death was a beast he had known well in his youth, a wolfish possibility that had taken innumerable forms, exploiting every moment of weakness, every hasty oversight, striking down soul after unfortunate soul, but somehow always coming to heel for *him* ...

Yes ... This was where he belonged. This was his Temple.

His groin thick for the promise of mayhem, he trotted to where his Lord-and-Prophet stood among the smoking dead. The most senior of the Swayali cohort, a sturdy Cepaloran woman named Gwanwë, stepped down from the heights to join them, hastily gathering her billows into an aureate bundle before her. Soot greased her temple and cheek.

"*No Chorae!*" Gwanwë cried over the rising clamour of the Horde. She gazed at her Holy Aspect-Emperor's profile with an odd mixture of adoration and worry.

Saubon grasped the significance immediately: If you lacked the resources to hold a strong place, you crippled or destroyed it, lest it serve your enemy ...

The fact that Dagliash still stood meant that it still *served*.

"The Chorae are *below* us," Kellhus said, drawing his gaze up across the enormous walls of the citadel.

Saubon noticed the Decapitants askew against his white-felt thigh, black mouths working.

Gwanwë looked to the ground between the gnarled infantry boots shodding her feet. She could not feel the trinkets, the Exalt-General realized. "So they've reopened Viri?" she called.

"A trap!" Saubon snapped in dawning worry. "You need to *flee* this place, God-of-Men!"

The Aspect-Emperor turned in what seemed an aimless scrutiny. He reached out to either side, fingers held wide, as if flattened across the discs of phantom gold. Beyond the walls, across the slopes, the Sranc were coalescing about their intrusion. The roar piled ever louder, stunning the ear, and prodding the heart with the assurance of something titanic and impending. Sorcerous singing fluted through the air, unintelligible yet filled with dread import, like a secret whispered in unwilling ears. The Nuns had begun shoring the decrepit fortifications ...

The Horde was coming.

Unconcerned, Kellhus lowered his gaze to the ground. Saubon had long since learned to follow his Lord-and-Prophet's lead when it came to guessing threats. Gwanwë, however, could not stow her alarm. She called out to her Swayali sisters on the parapets immediately above—repeated the cry in more screeching tones when it failed to breach the waxing roar.

"A *legion* ..." Kellhus interrupted, his tone miraculously peeling aside the obstructing din. "*Thousands* lie concealed in the wrecked Viritic halls beneath our feet. Bashrag, Sranc. Sequestered here for days—weeks. Their stench rises through Dagliash as a soiled cloth."

Gwanwë, Saubon, everyone in the war-party, cast dumb looks at the ground.

"Perhaps they anticipated our gambit," the Holy Aspect-Emperor surmised. "Perhaps they hoped to catch us unawares after overcoming the Horde ..."

"Either way," Saubon cried, "we are outwitted!"

Lightning cracked from elsewhere in the fortress. It seemed all the witches were singing now.

"We need only bar their exit," Kellhus said.

Gwanwë hollered something, but her reply did not so much as dimple the hellish chorus. But Saubon knew her question for his own: *How does one barricade the ground?*

The Holy Aspect-Emperor of the Three Seas smiled in grim reassurance. "We set plow to the field," he said in reply to her unheard question. The din had swallowed all mundane voices save his own.

"We make the ground anew."

They wheezed and croaked in the dark, stamped and shuffled.

They had been fashioned from the muck of life, the filth and the offal. In an age when Men were nothing more than savages or slaves, they had been coaxed from machines that were too intricate to be called dead. Their architects began with a wicked craving, a soulless pit. About this they spun grotesqueries of flesh and bone, elephantine limbs and cauldron-skulls. They exulted in their revulsion, for they alone could see the beauty in *all* things. And they understood the power that was flesh, how it need only be loosed like a fish in a foreign stream to bring all prior life crashing to its knees.

Wheezing. Mucous snapping like lute strings. The stench of countless defecations.

They hid where such monstrosities always hid, in the deeper cracks of the World, waiting for the inevitable moment of horror, the one that swallows us all, ere the end.

The Bashrag waited with the impatience of the soulless. Little more than dim cunning glittered from their eyes ...

Bottomless hunger.

Vaka, the Ordealmen began calling the Lord-Chieftain of the Cepalorae. Sibawûl Vaka.

The cavalrymen of the Kidruhil dubbed him thus, after a form of archaic Ceneian shield that took its name in turn from scraped oyster shells. Other skirmishers quickly followed suit, until all those who dared the septic hem of the Shroud referred to him as such. One need only witness Sibawûl and his horse-thanes ride against the skinnies to understand the aptness of the moniker. The infantrymen had heard the name and the attendant tales, of course, and to a man they believed the stories, but they could not understand, not truly …

Not yet.

Even as the Schools secured their eyries across the Urokkas, the Great Ordeal had assembled into a massive column along the north shore of the Misty Sea. They began marching before dawn the day following, a procession city-broad and nation-deep hugging the northern shore, tilting ever more as the land ramped between the Urokkas and the Neleöst. The sun boiled from the misty rim of the Sea, dazzled the massed formations, transformed them into a river of silvered flotsam, great rafts of armour and arms flashing so bright as to pale the arcane diadems the Schools had slung about the mountains. Horns clawed what sky they could beneath the ascending roar of the Horde. To a man, they broke into a brisk trot, more than 150,000 righteous and violent souls.

They laughed for the vigour of their pace, raised their hearts in the fist of their voices, and thundered. Fields twinkled for shaking weapons.

Their inhuman foe shrank from their approach, yielded the boards of mount Yawreg, the first of the Urokkas. The Shroud thinned above, and the great cleft of clarity wrought by the mountains became visible. The Host of Hosts cried out in triumph once again, knowing the Horde had been *halved*, that the greater portion lay to the north of the Urokkas, trapped by lethal weirs of the Schoolmen, and that the lesser lay before them, backed against Dagliash and the Sea. And they laughed, playing monsters who had cornered children. The foremost among them could clearly spy their inhuman foe: seething, scabrous sheets of white from the shoulders of Mantigol, reeling from threads of arterial light, to the mountain's hip, spitting and stamping in bestial indecision, to the drowning strand.

The Ordealmen continued their surge, encompassing the flanged hinter of Yawreg. The Scarlet Magi who had held the orbitals above the cliffs joined their brothers defending the mountain's northern faces. More horns scratched the sky, scarcely audible. The Horde's collective shriek now tapped a nail in every ear. Not one of the trotting Zaudunyani heeded the cry—indeed their pace quickened if anything. Men panted, but more for exhilaration than for want of wind. They coughed and cackled. They followed the mailed backs bouncing before them, tramped across the polluted swamps that had once been brooks, skidded into gullies, then hauled themselves out. The soil had been shallow enough to be torn away as flesh from deeper stone. Here, more than anywhere else, the Ordealmen could see the ground as a carcass, as the remains of something eaten.

Again and again the horns raked trowels across the high din, but the Men of the Circumfix would suffer no impediment to their rush. Instead, the Cepalorae, the solitary horsemen in their midst, galloped out in advance of their glittering, land-spanning flood, following none other than Sibawûl Vaka.

It seemed ceremonial at first, more a suicidal demonstration of conviction than a stratagem. Less than a thousand of the blond horsemen had survived Wreoleth. They floated as loose strands across the intervening wastes, threads too fine to be bound into anything formidable. Beyond them, the cancerous enormity of the Horde infested the whole of the land from the mountains to the Sea, every glimpse churning, fizzing with homicidal fury. An unseemly glee animated the souls of the watching Ordealmen. The mad horsemen would be hacked into oblivion, and the masses cheered, bawled in tens of thousands, celebrating not the destruction, but the *sacrifice* of their haunted brothers.

None could imagine a more fitting way to begin a scripture—or *feast*.

The lines galloped across the ragged contours. High to the right, Sibawûl and his doomed riders could see the great gorge where Yawreg's shattered mandible rose from Mantigol's chalk waist, the points of dipping light upon the rim, and the incendiary blossoms they vomited into the slots surging below. But they had eyes only for the obscenities raving before them ...

There is a point in all battle where gazes *meet*, where "them" becomes *you*, and lives are honed to an edge. Some say it is the most decisive, that it is here, before a single blow has landed, that adversaries deem who lives and who dies. Some even think it a *temple*, the last interval before the terrible clamour of Gilgaöl, the mad racket of War. From the high-sprawling slopes to the long blade of the strand, the Men of the Circumfix fell silent for recognizing that point from afar, and they peered after the Cepalorae and their glorious charge, knowing that in a heartbeat they would vanish as dust drifting from light to darkness ...

Except that they did not.

Those who had spied Sibawûl Vaka watched as the inhuman masses first dimpled, then *opened about him*, dozens, if not hundreds of the creatures clawing in frenzied terror from his aspect, leaping, climbing, crawling over their putrid fellows in the delirium to escape. The same happened for his horse-thanes, lancer after lancer, riding unscathed, untouched, striking down stragglers, but otherwise encircled by scrambling terror, each pitting the mob with panic-rimmed cavities.

And for several remarkable instants, the Horde—or its southern portions at least—fell *silent*.

The Cepalorae plowed forward, a long necklace of gaps in the roiling mass, each clearing possessing a spearing, hacking rider in its pith, killing many forsooth, but not so many that the mobs did not reform *behind* them, and make it seem they waded into a screaming, threshing sea. The Ordealmen raced after them, continued closing the interval, their breath ragged as much for wonder as for taxed limbs. Grutha Pirag, an Ingraul swordsman from the High Wernma, crested a broken ridge, and saw the swirl and simmer of discord that had engulfed the forward ranks of their foe. Mimicking his beloved mother's call, he bellowed, in a high and plaintive voice, "*Dinnertime!*" to his kin. Scarcely a dozen souls understood, let alone heard, his call, and yet gales of laughter romped through the ranks, a mirth that trampled all scruple, all restraint—that left nations roaring with crazed fury.

It began the way it always begins, with an unruly few breaking ranks, running wild and raging ahead of the others. One Galeoth even cut loose his armour and clothing as he ran, until he leapt, phallus curved against his belly, across the desolation wearing naught but his boots.

Others joined them, like moths drawn to the light of glory. More followed, and more after them, some running to rescue their reckless brothers, others answering to the sudden hunger that gaped within them, an ancient hole uncovered ...

Kill. Few souls thought the word, but every soul pursued its dread and simple course. Kill. *Kill!* The forward ranks thinned, then dissolved altogether. Bawling officers scrambled to retrieve their companies.

Shrugging aside any vestigial discipline, the Men of the Great Ordeal surged as one glittering sheet toward their foe, their mouths watering.

Saubon followed his Holy Aspect-Emperor into the mammoth shadow of Ciworal, his ears ringing.

"Long have they prepared for my coming," Kellhus explained, his voice slipping between the din. The sorcerous paean of the Nuns echoed from over the horizon. Otherwise only His voice could be heard, tunnelling through a sound so great as to become ground, an impact without conclusion, bludgeoning, rattling tooth and bone, *always*.

"Absent the No-God," Kellhus continued, "they have no hope of overcoming me directly ..."

The entrance leered vacant, smashed into a breach long, long ago. Lichens scabbed the northward faces, while grasses ringed and limned the whole, clinging to every joist. No mortar had been used, simply great, fitted blocks. Walls rose concentrically, three shells, each hunching higher on thinner foundations, each battered into a more profound anonymity, bastions enclosing a husk enclosing a heap.

Kellhus placed a hand on his shoulder. It was strange, as always, to be reminded of his greater height. Strange and gratifying.

"Fear not for my safety, old friend."

Saubon craned his neck to spy the citadel's rugged peak, black against the bright plate of the sky. The brunt of morning was already upon them.

"Here ..." Kellhus said, casting his look about the structure. "The greater Mansion riddles the whole of the mountain, but its axle, the Great Well of Viri, lies *here*, beneath this pla–"

The Aspect-Emperor snapped his gaze toward Ciworal's smashed gate. Sranc erupted from the maw, bolted toward them, blades convulsing, silken faces crushed by frenzy.

Saubon's bones fairly jumped from his limbs, such was his shock. But Kellhus strode without the least hesitation to meet the inhuman rush, muttering in voices that chewed nerves and illumined the ground at his feet. The creatures leapt toward him, their skin fish-white and their rag-armour curiously dark in the gloom. Even as their cleavers swung high, geysers exploded from their chests, puffs of violet mist. Dozens toppled in near unison, hearts spit gasping across the ground.

Saubon stood dumbstruck, as did Gwanwë at his side.

"Gird yourself!" Kellhus called to the entire company. "I have yet to kick the hornet's nest ..."

He spake light and miraculously stepped into the glare gaping high above the ancient stronghold.

Saubon stood blinking and wondering. Though he loathed worship, despised kneeling as violently as he demanded it of others, he fairly shook for the *gratitude* welling through his veins, for the miracle of being *here*, at this moment. *Here* he stood, the Believer-King of Caraskand, within a fortress laurelled in ancient legends, raised upon an underworld city more ancient still, watching a *living God* set foot upon the sky ...

Anasûrimbor Kellhus, the Holy Aspect-Emperor.

It struck him then, the beauty of his life—the sheer *significance*. And a low and vicious pocket of his soul cackled, hunched over the moment with a miser's unbecoming glee. What did falsehood matter, when *this* was true? In the light of such power ...

In the light of such power!

He turned, saw that Mepiro, Bogyar, Scraul and the others were laughing—laughing because *he* was laughing, Saubon realized. The wail of the Horde blotted all, of course, but no sound was required to hear the joy and the savagery of their amusement. They could see it, the mania of *recognition*, not only of fortunes shared, but of *hungers*, atrocities committed in fact and desire. Never, it seemed, had the World been so ferocious with communal portent. Bogyar's face even flushed crimson, a sign that would have alarmed Saubon mere moments before, but simply piled another hilarity onto the heap now.

The Exalt-General howled into the miracle of his own silence. The Shroud hung like plague above the stumped walls. Charred Sranc sweetened the air. His ardour strained against his breeches, and his eyes strayed to Gwanwë, who also laughed, her manner as leering as any man's.

The Meat ...

A sorcerous crack—producing echoes like boulders tumbling down iron chutes. It should have knocked the mirth from the Company of the Raft, but instead they squinted up in grinning wonder, hooted and cheered soundlessly, watched dark monoliths thrown tumbling *upward*, into the sky ...

There was so much more than proof in miracles; there was *might*.

Numbers. Mad numbers.

Mad lights.

Gazing out from above the summit of mount Ingol, the Exalt-Magus, Saccarees, could almost see it whole: an oceanic mass twining and involuting like a living thing, a leviathan as vast and terrible as anything out of his Dreams of the First Apocalypse, lashing entire *mountains* with tentacular fury.

The Horde.

When the Great Ordeal had marched divided across the vacant heart of the Istyuli, the inclination of the Sranc had been to envelop, to spill about the prow of the Holy Host of Hosts and harry its flanks. Ever since marching from Swaranûl, however, the creatures had not so much parted about the prow as *turned aside*. Their advance, as the mathematician Tusullian had put it, was causing the Horde to *roll* along the Neleöst coast, a vast gyre of screaming millions, armatures ponderously cycling north and then west before catching on the coast and drawing southward once again. One could even *see* the mechanism in the Shroud when one knew how to look. Some thought this dramatic change simply expressed the dramatic change in the land. Where those on the coast could only back into their raving kin, those inland simply had more latitude to flee. Others attributed the change to the *knowledge they were now being eaten*. If room for elbows determined where the Sranc fled, then the Host's flank offered the most room of all. Depraved as they were, the beasts could still speak. Perhaps *rumour* drove them back—terror of larding the gullets of Men!

Though this transformation had rendered the Great Ordeal's advance far less perilous, it served to remind all that the simplicity of the Sranc in no way made them *predictable*—any more than intellect made Men unpredictable. "The Horde must lay its belly upon *your* fire," the Holy Aspect-Emperor had told him two nights previous. "If it chases any other danger, if it begins *moving east*, the day will go hard for the Ordeal."

So the Exalt-Magus had studied more than battled, standing upon the highest echo Ingol offered. Age had yet to dull his eyes, so he peered for the most part, conjuring distance-bloating Lenses only to resolve ambiguities. He watched the Horde swarm and coalesce as far as the sepulchral curtains of the Shroud allowed. And given the time he had spent Culling, he could even reckon the migratory immensities that lay beyond. With guesses and glimpses, he tracked the far northern horn curling back upon the River Sursa like a slow-twisting nail. More importantly, he saw the masses to the east fall inward, then fold into the great black bolus that blotted the Erengaw Plain immediately below the mountains.

And he rejoiced in the knowledge that the Sranc, at least, had followed his Saviour's bidding.

Unlike the Men.

They were as reapers in the field, the blond-braided Sons of Cepalor. The masses shrank from them, exposing those skinnies too weak or too unlucky, those the horsemen speared like fish as they waded forward. Mobs heaved between, before, and now even behind them, Sranc screaming, shrinking in the simulacrum of terror, clawing kin to flee the vacant gaze of the Cepalorae.

Vaka himself was the first to lose his pony to the treacherous ground. He went down with his mount, slapped as a palm from a slack wrist, and for an instant the pocket about him lost its rind of inhuman panic. Slicked in violet, the Lord-Chieftain pulled himself from the ground, his head down and helmless, his flaxen hair swaying in tangled sheets. Wrack lay about his feet. His lamed pony kicked and bucked across the ground behind. His nimil corselet shimmered pristine in the sunlight. His eyes, when he revealed them, did not so much pinpoint the near as absorb the distance. Tails of hair formed a cage about his brow, scribbled nonsense against his beard. Without expression, he drew his father's broadsword and sprinted into the pale-skinned surge to escape his terrible aspect.

The Shadow of Wreoleth.

To the Mysunsai ensconced above, the horsemen seemed unnerving violations, effects that floated without causes—magic—only without expense or consequence. Their impossible charge seemed as much a warning as a triumph. But to the Ordealmen bounding breathless in their wake, the Cepalorae were nothing less than *instruments of the God*, and the ruin they worked the *wages* so long awaited. Their miraculous charge could be nothing but the booming shout of Heaven!

The God Himself delivered the skinnies to their wrath.

The cloven ramps grew more steep about mount Mantigol, which, in addition to looming taller, crowded closer to the Misty Sea. Whether one stood on high or below, everything could be seen: the Horde shivering across the diminishing coasts to the west, the summits smoking above, sparking with hundreds of sorcerous dispensations, and the Great Ordeal spilling like a dragon's hoard from the east. The delirium of the rush was such that some Men of the Circumfix far outpaced their brothers and barrelled swinging into the Sranc entirely alone. Most of these souls were cut down in moments—for Sranc do not tarry between terror and fury as Men. To a man they died astonished, panting about some cut or puncture, before being hacked and bludgeoned into darkness.

Death came swirling down.

The Sons of Men fell upon the pale obscenities, first in bellowing flurries, then en masse, faces red with exertion and fury, loins swollen. The Sranc answered fury with fury, but the Shining Men bayed and raged and hammered like souls possessed, spittle flying from ranting mouths. Melee engulfed the beam of the coast, a great twining ribbon that was more butchery than battle. A grunting, roaring, clatter. Shields cracked. Blades shattered. Warding hands rolled like spiders. The Ordealmen speared slots in crude armour, stamped heads, shouldered Sranc screaming to the ground. They bellowed in exultation, cast looping violet into clean morning blue.

The Southron Men fell into threshing lines. What resolve the Sranc possessed evaporated before them. Oiled eyes rolled. Fused teeth gnashed. Vicious to kill became vicious to flee. Clan heaved against clan, and witless panic embroiled those regions caught between the Cepalorae and the invincible thousands that followed. Men hollered for triumph, hacked their way into the frenzied mobs, lopping, stabbing, pulping what was wicked and soulless. Tempests of sorcerous light consumed the skinnies that bolted for the heights of Mantigol. Surf bowled those fleeing into the Sea, drowned the creatures in mats, threw them broken upon the rocks, rolled them onto the strand.

Vaka and his Cepalorae continued striding into the screaming tracts, sowing the disarray that would be reaped as millet and wheat behind them.

Here and there, in pockets scattered across the fray, the most base plundered their twitching foe, gorged on raw meat, lapped violet blood as dogs in the gutters of some massacre.

The Judges would execute only those they found coupling with the carcasses.

The Schoolmen defended the very sky, or so it seemed. Never had the World witnessed such a battle: a string of a thousand Men—the Once-Accursed Few—defending mountain ramparts against the lunatic assault of a *thousand* thousand Sranc. As the creatures buckled beneath the Ordealmen on the coasts, the multitudes that blackened the Erengaw Plain assailed the ramparts of the Urokkas with fury and numbers that dwarfed anything the Schoolmen had hitherto seen. It was as if the creatures somehow *knew* the straits of their inhuman brothers to the south, understood the destruction they could wreak falling upon the unsuspecting Ordealmen from *above*.

Triunes hung singing above the passes, on ledges overlooking skewed slopes and high mountain trails. The most daring took positions endlessly pelted with black arrows; with their billows unfurled they seemed flowers set upon high-heaved stone. Others orchestrated their butchery from more remote vantages, their billows bound. And on and on, the leprous mobs surged beneath, shrieking outrage as they leapt and clambered, clawed and slavered.

Up to this point, the Southron Magi had left the steepest cliffs and precipices undefended. Now they discovered the obscenities scaling them, clinging to the plummets like swarms of frigid bees. One neck and two backs were broken in the rush to plug these precarious breaches; other stations were left undermanned. Two more arcane souls were lost for brute vertigo, missteps made for the illusion of grounds moving.

Sranc stormed the gorges and the crevasses, crept through the fractures, scrabbled over bulbous slopes. Conflagration enveloped it all, skeins of lightning, cords of decapitating light. Clan after clan surged up, through, and between the stacked heights only to vanish, consumed in squalls of radiance.

The Exalt-Magus suffered no illusions. The Ordealman's rank disorder on the coasts below meant the consequences of failure were absolute. Saccarees had *been* at Irsûlor—survived the heartbreak. He knew what would happen should the Sranc win through.

He had garrisoned each of the mountains according to estimations of a peril that refused to remain fixed. He initially held fast on Ingol, dispatching what Mandate Schoolmen he could spare according to necessity. Oloreg, which was more the ruins of a mountain than a mountain, proved the greatest trial. He even removed his eyrie to Mantigol, so he might attend to the perpetually threatened mountain from a better vantage. With his own eyes he saw the *blind cunning* of the Horde, how it shrank westward across the Erengaw, funnelling vigorous thousands into the smashed mouth of Oloreg—their greatest point of vulnerability. Soon, fully half of the Mandate found itself positioned across the broken summit with Enhorû and his Imperial Saik. Crimson billows hung next to black. The glitter of Gnostic Abstractions threaded the baleful incandescence of the Anagogis. Dragonheads vomited fire between the sweep of Cirroi Looms. Clouds of arrows—ineffectual against Wards—chipped and clattered across bare stone or quilled gravel inclines. Entire scarps teetered out into the void, crumbled into blood-slicked avalanches. Light greeted the ascending tide, sliced and consumed, pierced and exploded. Whole fields of gibbering obscenities perished, each figure a shining combustion.

The Schoolmen of the Three Seas cried out between their exertions, laughing, cackling. Weariness had addled them. They were at once children burning insects with lenses, stomping them in chortling fury, and old men coughing sorcerous words, hunched like lechers about illicit visions of destruction. Something crazed and ragged climbed into their cacophonous singing, a licentious barbarity that contradicted their exhaustion.

Those most taxed would be relieved, allowed to recline for a time upon one of the eyries, where they found water for their throats and salve for their burns. They found themselves gazing across the hanging voids at their brothers, fire-spitting motes suspended about neighbouring summits. They breathed deep the tainted air, closed their eyes, saw the sparking of mad afterimages. They listened to Cants they knew through the shrieking din, the whoosh and crack of sorceries both ancient and deadly. They gawked, despite the profundity of their erudition, that mountains could be skirted in living sheets of light, that the carcasses of their enemy could be heaped so high as to be visible across the convex curve of the Urokkas, like the blackened gums of scorched teeth ...

They marvelled that they had come so far.

A Mandate Schoolman called Nume would be the first to see it, gazing out from the eyrie Saccarees had abandoned upon Ingol. Even as a boy Nume had taken pride in the sharpness of his eyes: he had dreamed of becoming an archer, ere the Mandate had spirited him away. He waved to his fellows for confirmation, pointed out over the festering distance, but they could only see that *something* rode the skies high above the roiling plate of the Horde.

A sorcerous Lens would claw all of them to their feet.

The slaughter beggared his heart as much as the intellect, but for *proportion*, not pity. Even lives that are meaningless can stab the conscience when heaped into mountains.

These were *Sranc*. Why should he not feel the joy—nay, *rapture*—that so unmanned all the others?

Because he knew the truth?

Proyas and Kayûtas had led their troupe of officers and messengers high on the southward slopes, where they could see the glittering bulk of the Ordeal carpet the knuckled tracts below, Men marching shoulder to shoulder, bound one to the other like knots on a rope by their training. "*The Line!*" the Imperial Drillmasters hollered endlessly. "*The Square!*" These were the only sacred things in battle, the only things worth absolute sacrifice. Hold the Line, Preserve the Square, and all the sundry things they prized beyond battle would be saved: wife or king, son or prophet.

Die for the Line, and you shall be Saved, for Gilgaöl is as generous as He is ruthless.

Abandon it at damnation's peril.

In each of their contests with the Horde, the Men of the Ordeal had kept faith with that training, even at Irsûlor, where, according to Saccarees, the foe had been forced to engulf their obstinate formations, digest them like morsels of bellicose meat. In all the planning sessions in all the years prior to this expedition, *resolve* had been the paramount question, the concern that dwarfed all others save supply. They had read and reread *The Holy Sagas*, poured through what fragments of ancient chronicle that survived, even studied the Mandate accounts of Seswatha's Dreams, trying to understand how it was nation after Far Antique nation had succumbed to Mog-Pharau.

Resolve. Not cunning. Not arcane might. Apart from the whorish caprice of happenstance, luck, only resolve—*discipline*—had sorted those who had survived from those who had perished.

The very thing that had vanished before Proyas's horrified eyes.

It had been like watching a painting made of wax cast into some fire: a great canvas of formations, phalanxes perfect save for the terrain beneath, sagging, weeping, then sloughing into oily disarray. Time and again he had gestured—for no human shout could be heard—for the horns to be sounded, for the advance to be halted. He was gesticulating like a madman ere Kayûtas had clasped his left forearm. And it stung, the degree to which he saw Kellhus in the Prince-Imperial's admonishing look ... The reminder that nothing blinds a man to the future more than outrage at what is past. The realization that he had become one of those requiring such reminders.

Now they found themselves picking their way across one of Mantigol's many shoulders, their haste impeded by the mangled sheets of Sranc dead. Brine pinched the air, though the Sea remained a distant, if steep, tumble. The waist of the great column shivered and pulsed below them, advancing devoid of rank or formation, a vast bolus of peoples. The battleground extended before them, ramps hoofed with ravines, curving toward the horizon. Dead Sranc spackled all but the steepest inclines. Sorcerous lights dazzled the heights below the summits, glimpses of miniature figures hanging precarious above fields of light and thrashing shadows. Ahead of them, on the cracked stoop of Oloreg, the battle raged as if upon a tipped table, great surging masses, steaming with dust. Men, amorphous with lawless numbers, singular with bloodlust.

Greater beasts come to put an end to their lessers.

The pang that Proyas had confused for his heart climbed into his throat.

Kayûtas seized his shoulder, threw a long finger out toward the vista's hazy extremes. The Exalt-General saw it, Dagliash, squatting like a dead spider upon Antareg's headless shoulders. He saw the glitter of faraway sorcery, and a long plume of ash or dust blown like opiate smoke from the lips of the earth.

Kellhus, he realized.

He blinked away the fingers about his throat, the anguished bolt of his unmanning ...

He was no stranger to this moment, Proyas, for he had encountered it on almost every field of battle. The moment which winds every general for racing to prevent it ...

Helplessness. Events outrun every voice ere the end.

Debris showered the ancient fortress. The Company of the Raft stood agog outside the Ciworal, the great citadel of Dagliash, their necks craned to watch their Saviour. Kellhus hung upon emptiness high above, singing thoughts no mortal could fathom, his brow, cheeks and beard bleached for meaning, his arms out as if to catch a lover's leap. Together they watched the bastion, ancient and black, crumble into a vortex of meticulous lights. They watched the debris ride arcs across the sky, fall like preposterous rain wherever their omnipotent Lord-and-Prophet so willed.

After years campaigning at his side, Saubon knew well the sound of his arcane voice: at once deep and queerly fluted, as if *two throats* called through one mouth, a strange war of vocalities, as sourceless as any other arcane singing, but sounding even more distant—as well as more near. He need only glance at Gwanwë to see the religious awe it sparked in the Few, to know that Kellhus, despite all his demurrals, was *more*, a Shaman of Old, like those so violently condemned in the Tusk. At once Prophet and Sorcerer ...

Gratitude and exultation beat like wings within him. Power. Such glorious power. To uproot one of the mighty places of the earth, to *sing away* a legendary stronghold. Pride throbbed through him, a savage conceit, held him turgid and immobile, *aching* ...

For this more than anything was the sum of belonging, a submission that empowered, a grovelling that put flight to kings.

Kellhus did not sing alone. The Nuns had taken up stations all about the toothless parapets, hanging like gold-foil anemones in the sea. Saubon could see only a handful of them, so high were the walls fencing the Ribbaral. But he could *hear* their number in the piping chorus, and the carnage they wreaked in the Horde's roar. Kellhus boomed, a chant as deep as earth, in tones like distant dragons battling, and the Swayali spun weird arias about him, fluting through the thunder of corruption ...

These were the *true* hymns, the Believer-King of Caraskand realized ...

Just as Dagliash was the one temple.

He would seize Proyas when he saw him. He would make the man wince, so tight would he clamp his arms! He would hold him, and he would explain what he witnessed *this very moment*—now—and more importantly, *what he understood.* He would make the fool see the womanish cast of his heart, how yearning for the simple and the pure was its own pollution ...

Yes! The God was a spider!

But so too were Men—spiders unto themselves.

"Everything!" he would cry. "Everything *eats*!"

Ciworal, the famed Gauntleted Heart, stronghold of strongholds, *crumbled skyward* before his very eyes. It was like watching an *edge* devour the bastion, a plummet sideways to the real, blocks and fragments falling up and out before raining in a silent deluge across the baileys. He watched his Lord-and-Prophet *eat*, until even the monstrous foundation stones let go like rootless teeth, fell toppling into the Heavens—until great Ciworal was no more. Gwanwë seized his mailed forearm in her hands, but he could make no sense of her expression, let alone hear a word she said ...

Looking back he could see it, a great circle sunk into the granite, the legendary Well of Viri. Ciworal, for all its cyclopean immensity, had been no more than a scab on a deeper wound—the same as Men, perhaps. The Holy Aspect-Emperor did not cease his labour; no seam marred his embalming song. The sideways plummet simply *continued* once it reached the ground, so that the ancient mouth seemed to spew the ruin that choked it, vomit a dark and mountainous geyser of wreckage into the sky. Exhilaration scooped the breath from Saubon's chest, the sense of dangling above a torrential river flood.

Vertigo. The ground dipped beneath their feet in sensation, then shivered for clacking impacts in reality. And King Coithus Saubon found himself laughing in the teeth-baring manner of hyenas. It was the Meat, he knew, but it was the kind of careless knowing that belongs to drunks and disaster. Gwanwë still held one hand upon his forearm. A sudden longing to fuck the witch loped to the fore of his scrambled passions. He preferred slips to strong women, but the colour of her hair was so rare ...

Together they watched the great, broken bones of Nogaral tumble skyward, little more than shadows between streamers of dust and lesser debris. The Aspect-Emperor floated above in the morning sun. Conviction fairly *pulsed* through the Believer-King.

What God worth worshipping was *weak*?

Power. Power was the Mark of transcendence. What did it matter if it was diabolical or divine or even mortal?

So long as it was greater.

One tomb plundered to fashion another. Shivers through oceanic stone.

The slip of fractures as old as old. The spit of dust from the ceilings.

Some halls collapsed, be they humble or majestic, rooves clapping down, pounding wails and velvet dust through all the forking, subterranean hollows. And the beasts beat their cheeks for the stinging of slovenly eyes. The mulish barks of the dying set them baying in their thousands, strung and clotted through the veined deep. Anguish and outrage popping through sputum. The bellowing of elephantine lungs.

Where were the Old Fathers?

It sailed across the ochre glow, tracing circles over the violent pitch of the Erengaw.

A vision that crippled thought, exhaled numbness as smoke through gut and limbs ...

Saccarees stood riven before his sorcerous Lens, incredulous despite all that he had seen and horrified for everything he had Dreamed. The image dipped and dwindled, swung around to slowly bloat into clarity once again, dark and ragged, claws slack and twitching, scabrous wings hooked about unseen winds ...

A sight that made old scars itch and sting. An *Inchoroi*. The bone of the greater skull plain through intestinal skin, the lesser skull nested within its flared mandible ...

Evil Aurang, the Horde-General of old.

It could be none other.

Like any vulture, he wallowed in the sky, kiting upon gusts. He was more than abhorrent; his mere appearance panicked, somehow, did not so much set skin as *bones* crawling. There was something—a corruption in its pallor, perhaps, or an uncanniness of movement, manner—something that sickened for witnessing, unnerved for eluding clean human sensibility. The monstrosity peered down upon the gruesome multitudes when gliding northward, appraising the inscrutable, but as he swung to the south, he turned to the ramparts of the Urokkas—to the corpses belching black smoke, to the wink of murderous lights, and to Saccarees high upon Mantigol.

The Inchoroi even mouthed words in derision.

The Exalt-Magus should have signalled his Lord-and-Prophet. He and the other Lords of the Ordeal had spent watches discussing this very contingency. The Great Ordeal's gravest peril, they had decided, lay in the deployment of the Schools. Once scattered across the Urokkas, *there they must remain*, lest the Horde descend upon the Ordeal's nude flank and drive it into the Sea. This meant the Consult, who could never hope to match the sorcerous might of the Schools otherwise, could ignore them outright, throw their cunning or their might at some other weakness. And as Saccarees himself had seen at Irsûlor, a single breach was all that utter ruin required.

"They will come," Kellhus had warned. "They will not abandon such might as the Horde manifests to our design. The Unholy Consult will *intervene*. At long last, my brothers, you will vie with our foe *in the flesh*, grapple with the Cause that moves you."

Words that had balled hearts as fists!

At least it had then. Now Saccarees needed only turn on his heel to see Dagliash, to see his Lord-and-Prophet shining white from an exhaust of black ruin. He could have informed him, or any of his peers for that matter, in multiple ways ... but he did not.

For all his power and erudition, he was a Man of the Circumfix the same as any other. And like other Men he had the sense of *regions*, the passage of places and powers. Home had dwindled in his intellect, becoming little more than a muffled spark, ink spilled upon a page. For the longest time they had marched across the interval between, twilight regions that recognized no power save brutality. But now ... *Now* they had passed into the bower of their ancient and implacable enemy. And here ... *Here* the earth answered to a will more wicked, more monstrously horrific, than any the World had known. The Great Ordeal stood upon the very threshold of Golgotterath ... the outermost gate.

And like other Men of the Circumfix, a *wildness* had been kindled within Saccarees, a darkening of what was *awake*.

For he too had partaken of the Meat.

High upon Mantigol, gazing out over raving plains, Apperens Saccarees laughed heedless of his staring fellows, laughed in a voice the World had not heard for two thousand years ...

Aurang ... *Aurang*! Foul beast. Old foe.

At last.

Proyas had chosen the heights to station his command, where he could observe the Holy Host in a glance, but that had proven to be a mistake, particularly as the slopes reared ever more fractured and steep. The disaster Proyas had feared never came to pass. Even exhausted for running, pressed into blind mobs, the Ordealmen proved unstoppable, a hacking tide that swept into the roiling masses of Sranc and *over*, leaving fields of trampled violet in its wake. As individuals they roared and they cut and they hammered, but as a host they *consumed*, did not so much throw into flight as trammel. Proyas had lost three in his entourage in his attempts to pace the advance—for he could do nothing more, he had come to realize, than be where he needed to be when this headlong rush finally, inevitably sagged to its knees. And so he had struck for the beaches, driving his pony down the still-crowded slopes.

At last reaching the clotted beaches, he spurred his pony westward, trusting Kayûtas and the others would match his pace. He fairly cried out for relief, so clean was the sea breeze. But the sea itself was as soiled as could be, the breakers flapping with shining limbs, the retreating waters glinting black in silver sunlight, revealing its violet tincture in tidal pools. Sranc bobbed and bumped, knotted the waters like coagulum. The surf heaved carcasses into crashing gyres of slicked skin and fatted foam. The sight was almost narcotic, drowned faces rising from the blur, breaching the gleam, the waves rolling and dumping, dragging and engulfing, rolling and dumping ...

Narrow lozenges of beach had been cleared by the shrugging waters, allowing Proyas's sturdy little steed to chop unhindered across the sand flats, leaping the embroidery of dead along the line of the tide.

Fingers of wind combed his beard, and something began galloping within him.

Rising about him as though upon a vast bowl, the Sons of Men butchered the Sons of Ninjanjin across the cracked shoulders of the Urokkas. Anasûrimbor Kellhus was no more than a spark in the distance, immobile as a navigator's star, a knife too thin to be seen, piercing the jetting deep.

The Exalt-Magus stepped from one height to another, felt his belly swing from his throat for the way the ground dropped into churning leagues before him. He descended the stairs of the mountain, following Mantigol's many echoes. He ignored his floating brothers, threaded their ministries of light and death. Then he was striding beyond them, a dozen cubits in a step, over the heaps and mats of smoking dead, around gorges choked with flesh and char.

So did the Grandmaster of the Mandate come down from his mountain, a marble of solitary light treading over dark and ravenous tracts—pearl scalps, gesticulating limbs, masticating rage. They scratched at his image, screamed their outrage, disgorged numberless arrows and javelins, so that for those watching horrified from the mountains, he seemed a lodestone sucking up filings in black, bristling clouds.

But Saccarees felt no alarm. Nor did he enjoy the glee that comes with impunity, the wonder of passing uncut through an assembly of hated foes. A kind of solace hummed through his bones instead, the easy breathing of those who awake with no cares outstanding. Someday it would be thus, a dwindling fraction of his soul realized. Someday one Man, one Survivor, would wander out alone into a world of smoke and soulless fury.

And so he dwindled into the pestilential expanse. So he walked into the threshing depths of the Horde.

A lonely figure. A beacon of precious light.

Be they sons of cruel old Eryeat or his fellow Believer-Kings, Saubon had always stood apart from his brothers. For as long as he could remember, he had never been capable of ... *belonging* ... At least not the way other men—such as Proyas—seemed capable. His curse was not the curse of the awkward or fearful, who shied from camaraderie for the way others punished lack of grace. Nor was it the curse of the learned, who knew too much to allow ignorance to close the interval between disparate hearts. Even less was it the curse of the desperate, who reached and reached only to find backs turned against them.

No. His was the curse of the proud, the overweening.

He was no bombast. He did not, as that wretch Ikurei Conphas had done, gloat between his every breath. No. He had been born *with a calling*, a desire that unmoored all others, that anchored his very being. What he sought cast no reflection in polished silver. Greatness, for him, had always been something he would *conquer* ...

He had wept when Kellhus had told him as much on the Plains of Secharib. "*I have raised you above others,*" his Lord-and-Prophet said, "*because of what you* are ..."

A man who could never quite worship another.

All this time, bowing his head in prayers he could never speak, standing solemn for ceremonies he could scarcely *bear*, let alone celebrate—murdering hundreds, thousands in the name of a faith he found more expedient than compelling ...

Only to fall to his knees truly *now*? *Here*? Gnawed Dagliash as his Temple, the scraping Horde as his choir, worshipping, choking for brimming passions. What kind of perversity was this?

Who discovered worship only *after* their prophet declared himself False?

It was the Meat—almost certainly.

But he did not care. He *could not* care, not with Anasûrimbor Kellhus standing astride the sky, brilliant for booming meaning, drawing out the entrails of the earth—eviscerating a mountain!

The Maker of Grounds.

The Well of Viri was now as deep as Ciworal had been high—deeper. Its mouth had been smashed and cratered, but below this rim, it became a cylindrical pit, its sides ornamented in totemic reliefs that seemed too spare and shallow to belong to the Nonmen. Arms out and head thrown back, the Holy Aspect-Emperor compelled the Pit, evacuated the deep. The ruins of Nogaral dropped skyward, tumbling to the plume's summit, falling outward, riding chutes that no eye could see. Ruin crashed about the walls and towers of Dagliash, a cyclopean downpour that pelted and heaped. The debris seemed tossed like half-coppers to beggars, with only the merest concern where it landed, but such was not the case. A *legion* lay concealed in the consumptive depths, and their Holy Aspect-Emperor entombed them—shut them in! Made the ground anew!

The Consult. What cunning could they hope to devise? What trickery or deceit?

The urge to communicate his joy seized him, and he turned to his household. His Holca Spearbearer, Bogyar, was roaring soundlessly to the others, his face shining crimson—the fearsome colour of the Flush. The Company of the Raft stood scattered about the Ribbaral, exchanging looks and staring agog at their Lord-and-Prophet atop his tower of sky-tumbling ruin. His angular Shieldbearer, Ûster Scraul, was the lone defector. Ever odd, he stood with his shoulders square to the spectre of Ingol heaving over the northeastern wall, with only his face turned to the pluming ejecta. However incidental his pose, his look exposed a soul roundly stumped, not by what he witnessed—the eyes would have to be focussed—but by what he did not, by the crushing sum.

The crimson-skinned Holca stood gesticulating before the upward torrent, his great fists balled and trembling, his shoulders as broad as the Swayali were tall. He bellowed, his face a crazed rictus, twisted with ferocity ...

Alarm seized Saubon as a bolt through delirium. He lurched into action for action's sake, clapped a firm hand upon Bogyar's left shoulder, not so much to calm the giant as to gain time to think. The red-bearded Holca whirled violently, throwing spittle. He stood for a breathing instant, monstrous and looming, eyes pinned too wide to see anything but murder.

Only the Horde could be heard.

"*Master yourself!*" Saubon roared at his Spearbearer, only to find himself crashing backward. The insane Holca loomed above him, hefting his massive battleaxe. Incredulous, Saubon realized he was about to die ...

Light flashed in his periphery—low and brilliant.

Then the Bashrag were upon them.

Rather than kill him, Bogyar saved him instead, leaping over his prostrate length into the misbegotten assault. The Holca swung his axe as a javelin thrown, leveraging his leap so that the blade snapped as a lash, chipped from iron, and lopped the goliath's neck to the least tendon. The beasts stampeded into their midst. Great shags of hair. Lurching, shambling things, deformed in ways great and small. Their stench tinctured every breath with fish, rot, and feces. Saubon scrambled to his feet, saw Mepiro duck a crashing cudgel. The Exalt-General came about, broadsword drawn, saw the festering, lumbering rush, a wave of tottering, heaving obscenities, swinging crude axes and hammers, dead faces drooling from either cheek. He glimpsed Bogyar, a crimson dervish fending brackish limbs. He saw Gwanwë carved in miraculous white—realized the creatures bore *Chorae*. He saw fragments of stone, a crushing curtain, rain upon the obscenities lurching across the Ribbaral beyond. An abomination floated up out of the confusion, cudgel raised to twice his height, bull-snorting, rattling for its hauberk of iron-plates. Ulcerating moles pocking exposed skin. Furs so rotted as to grease its flesh. A senescence of motion declared the depravity of its composition. Saubon danced about the descending hammer, hacked the monstrosity high on the arm, a blow that would have amputated a human limb ...

But merely severed one of the Bashrag's trinity of bones. The foetid goliath squealed, crouched in a roar, struck out wildly.

Saubon ducked, heard the tink of pitted iron against his helm, and found himself *laughing*, shouting ...

"*Good!*"

He thrust the point of his broadsword into its mangled knee, danced spinning from a second frenzied strike. He clove one of the mucoid faces upon its cheek, leaping forward as it staggered back, bearing the shrieking beast down, cleaving adulterine flesh.

"*I'm tired of eating chicken!*"

He whirled, roaring for the impiety of his wit. The Knights of the Desert Lion chopped at what seemed a copse of nightmarish trees about him. Saubon glimpsed Scraul turn too late to a dropping cudgel, vanish beneath it, even as Bogyar's battleaxe struck the miscreant's basin skull. The thing pedalled backward, tripped into the Well, only to be caught tumbling in the upward deluge.

A glint caught Saubon's eye.

That was when he first saw it falling skyward from the gut of the Well, gleaming and intact in the helter of debris ...

A golden coffer.

The Erengaw crawled with simmering multitudes, a foul pulver that matted all that could be seen. What had appeared a morass of indeterminate horrors now pricked with the glitter of eyes and teeth, fingers that could be counted. Mauls and cleavers shaking like epileptic sons.

Above it all, *Aurang* hung black and ragged, a flake of ash hooked high on brown winds.

Apperens Saccarees pulled the knot on his Menna sash, loosed his billows, which opened into a blood-red flower, curlicues for petals, bellied and hooked like the irises so prized in Shir. The Lord Librarian was free; *Seswatha* walked the ways of the present bearing ancient totems of doom. He gave voice to his heart-cracking fury, diagrammed the distance with sun-silver brilliance. The Ninth Merotic ...

His crimson billows glowed like coloured glass set before the sun. The Inchoroi's Wards luminesced for the impact of the Abstraction, nothing more. The alien abomination laughed with the lungs of the Horde.

"**Aurang!**" the Sohonc Grandmaster thundered. "**I call upon thee! I demand a Disputation—as in days of old!**"

And at last the monstrosity dared swoop low.

"***The days are* new *Chigra ...***"

His passage sparked rapture in the swarms of Sranc below, an ejaculatory wake.

"***And far shorter than the old.***"

The Horde-General banked on a tangent to the wind, turned north and west as if on the arc of a great, invisible wheel. The standards of the clans jerked and heaved above oceans of crushed white faces.

"**Aurang!**" Saccarees cried out to the receding image, his face crimped in anguish, dreaming and not dreaming.

The wretched multitudes screamed in derision, their limbs spitting like muck beneath torrential rain.

The Holy Aspect-Emperor ceased singing. The soaring wreckage instantly slowed, then slumped crashing back into the throat of the Well, leaving only the smoky apparition of the geyser. The vibration of fracturing immensities faded. Veils of dust twisted across the Ribbaral, lending the air the taste of dust and rot.

The Company of the Raft stood astonished and hard-breathing among the giant carcasses. Though several of their brothers floundered upon the ground, they had eyes only for his Lord-and-Prophet, who floated above them at the height of flying gulls or geese ...

Holding the golden coffer suspended just beyond the reach of his haloed hands, he came to ground on the Well's western limit. Saubon held out his arms to restrain his Knights, then moved to follow his Lord-and-Prophet alone. The salt statue that had been Gwanwë clubbed his heart as he sprinted near, but the sight of Kellhus setting the golden receptacle upon the back of a dead Bashrag filled him with far more apprehension.

Never had Saubon seen him handle anything with such ghostly care.

It was not made of gold—he could see that now. It had the exhumed look of something drawn from crushing depth—it was chalked in whorls of dust and grit—and yet had not been *scuffed*, let alone bent, nicked, or dented. It was no larger than a dollhouse, but seemed larger for the piping that enclosed it—a scaffold that somehow held the interior cube *without touching it*. Eye-squinting filigree had been etched into almost every surface, geometric impressions that somehow jarred scrutiny. But nothing was so remarkable as the plate of polished obsidian forming the top of the receptacle, and the luminous characters scrolling both within and across it—a kind of script inked in light.

Kellhus paid him no regard whatsoever. The maw of the Well smoked to his left, mere paces distant. The noon sun conjured transparent gowns of shadow from high-climbing tatters. "What is it?" the Exalt-General asked, knowing he need only speak for the man to hear. His Lord-and-Prophet looked to him, his manner catastrophic for the utter absence of expression.

Three heartbeats passed.

"An Inchoroi object," Kellhus said, his voice no less miraculous for how it punctured the bottomless din. "A Tekne artifact."

Saubon had to think to breathe, breathe to think. "The writing that glowers upon it ... What does it say?"

The Horde stole each and every one of these words.

The Holy Aspect-Emperor of the Three Seas stood, retreated a single pace as if to better appraise the thing. Though his eyes remained fixed on the receptacle, Saubon knew that he stared at nothing present before him.

"That not everyone can be saved," Kellhus said.

Fear skittered as a many-legged chill across the Believer-King's skin.

"What do *you* say?" Saubon asked, too numb to be properly bewildered.

The leonine profile lowered in contemplation, his gaze wet and rigid.

The Nuns continued singing from points about the ancient perimeter, continued weaving meaning into patterns of murderous radiance. The ink of fat-fuelled fires now scribbled above the crest of every wall. Dagliash was their mountain—the most perilous eyrie of them all.

His Saviour turned to him, smiled what might have counted as an apology had they played number-sticks.

"That this is a good thing."

Kellhus glanced at the coffer and the intricate threads racing across it one final time. Light speared from his mouth. The hood was yanked from the lanterns in his eyes.

His shout, when it came, concussed. Saubon fell back, threw up arms against the blazing aspect that spake it. The walls spat dust from every slot and seam.

"Fleeee!"

Saubon gawked in horror. Bogyar was already hauling him to his feet, screaming without sound. The Holy Aspect-Emperor stepped in the empty air above the Ribbaral, his mouth a pit of white brilliance in his beard, his voice *booming from nowhere*, or at least no place in Creation:

"Sons of Men, hark!"

Cracking the Horde's wail ...

"Set aside your fury!"

Silencing it.

"*Fleeeee!*"

There was no echo, for it had shouted into each soul as a sock. And it seemed that Saubon could only exhale, that the power to draw air had been wrested from his lungs.

No, a thought called through him.

Threads of light uncoiled about Anasûrimbor Kellhus as he ascended, hooked into a spider-leg cage, then cinched him into nothingness.

No ...

"Then what does it matter, whether I sanction you or not? Truth is truth, regardless of who speaks it ..."

"I ask only for your counsel, for what you see ... Nothing more."

"But I see many things ..."

"Then tell me!"

"Only rarely do I glimpse the future. The hearts of men ... that *is what they ... That is what I'm moved to see."*

"Then tell me ... What do you see in my *heart?"*

Proyas had raced with Kayûtas and the others along the autumn-bright beaches. He would catch the foremost Ordealmen, he told himself, rally and reorganize them. But his soul only had eyes for the murderous fray. His manhood ached for the kneading grip of the gallop. To his right, the Zaudunyani clogging the beaches climbed in ascending thousands, skirting Oloreg's tangled thighs in quicksilver. Flickering sorceries rimmed the blunt summits against the fume of the Shroud above. The first tracts of trampled gore lay exposed in the Host's wake, smeared as a paste across the flanks of an entire mountain, black and purple, like overripe beets pulverized. Pitched melee braided the Column's fore, lines of remorseless threshing, Men spearing and hacking their way into reeling mobs of Sranc. Of the voids Sibawûl and his Cepalorae had wrought in the crazed expanse, few remained that he could see.

For a time Proyas could almost believe he looked *down*, so favourable was the bias of the land. Dagliash remained the armature, a canker of stone upon Antareg, whose pate extended beyond the shoulders of Ingol, equally overrun. He could see Kellhus pinned brilliant astride the black spew, and the Swayali triunes arrayed across the faraway ramparts, casting Abstractions like miniature sigils onto the ground. His heart leapt for the sight, and his imagination sparked as vivid as prophecy: how he would hew a path through the skinnies, how he would climb carcasses to gain the parapets, so he might call down to Saubon, crying, "See!"

See!

But for every cubit he gained, it seemed another obstacle plagued his advance. The black cliffs loomed nearer. The beaches grew more stony and steep, more prone to roll the carcasses directly back into the surf that deposited them. The waves battered him and his pony for attempting to circumvent the semi-submerged tangles. But as the coast narrowed, greater numbers of Ordealmen found themselves shouldered into the violet waters as well. He tried to *force* his way through the polyglot masses, a gambit that nearly cost him his life. His horse stumbled, broke his leg. Proyas was thrown—the lolling spear of a nearby Shigeki terrorized his eye as he toppled, but slit his cheek instead. Black water swallowed him. Brine pinched his lips, ignited the cut on his cheek. A profound weight slammed into his back, pestled him against the gravel bottom. Threads of air fluttered over his face. Maybe he screamed.

Then arms hauled him gasping and sputtering to the surface. Sunlight stung his tears, cracked the World into filaments of brilliance and shadow. He saw *Kellhus* resolve from slurry, started for panic only to realize it was *Kayûtas*—Kayûtas looking away to the west—to Antareg. The waters churned with wading Ordealmen. In a glance, he saw countless bearded faces turning with the Prince-Imperial's.

He looked back to Kayûtas, realized he had never seen anything resembling fear or surprise in the Prince-Imperial's expression—even in his childhood.

Until now.

Then he heard it, impossibly clear through the crazed din.

The once-beloved voice.

Antareg. The land strangely broken, slopes ravined against the ageless laws of erosion, heights heaped southwestward, as if an overthrown mountain had huddled against the shoreline to die. The Neleöst Sea. The aquamarine of placid tracts become white-backed shoals, become matted carcasses and the swirl of violet scum. Dagliash. The towers and turrets, hanging crisp against the slow-surging distances. The Horde. The moulting distances, vast and terrible, a leprous smear hardening into figures and faces pale as spider-bellies.

Sibawûl Vaka picked a solitary path through the inhuman tumult, staring forward with ghoulish vacancy. Rank after putrid rank peeled away before him, communally leapt and scratched and scurried from his approach. Paralysis seized those the crush delivered to his vicinity; they could do no more than twitch, blubber, and wheeze in his shadow. He speared them as he passed, piercing the joints in their crude armour, their necks and their faces ... and continued onward.

A mile behind, the heedless run of the Great Ordeal had bogged into melee along the cleft demarcating the torsos of Ingol and Oloreg. Archery formed spectral tangles over the fighting. Sensing vulnerability, Mandate Schoolmen began burning their way down the slopes of Ingol, each a floating point disgorging light and fire. The Sranc melted before them. Their flank relieved, the Men of the Circumfix surged forward anew, beat the caterwauling skinnies to the shadows beneath their feet. Some hollering, some sobbing, they cut and hammered their way onto the greased pitch of Ingol. Men clutched wounds in grimacing silence. Sranc twitched and kicked where they fell.

A shout cracked Creation. Men and Sranc hesitated alike ...

Ears whined for abrupt silence. Eyes rolled skyward. And then, over it all, *a light appeared*, like something dropped from an indescribable direction. White brilliance glaring from blue ...

Becoming a man ... the *Holy Aspect-Emperor*, hanging high and windblown beneath the blue vacancy of autumn, his edges smoking with otherworldly brilliance.

"***Flee Dagliash!***" his voice boomed. Across the Erengaw and the root of the Urokkas, the combatants looked up and wondered.

"***Flee! Hide yourself from its sight!***"

The Schoolmen turned immediately, striding the heights, abandoning all terrestrial plight. The Men of the Ordeal hesitated, wavered as more and more of their kinsmen abandoned the mobs behind them. The hardhearted stood their ground, knowing that retreat meant doom. They fell into battling circles and squares as the formations about them dissolved in racing slaughter.

The Sranc hacked the earth, reconquered the sky with screeching ululation—and surged forward.

Kurwachal, the ancient Aörsi had called the squat tower, the "Altar". With Ciworal destroyed, it was the mightiest bastion remaining—at least to the panicked eye. Saubon's household had wasted the Horde's silence bellowing at the Witches striding above the fortress, at first begging and then cursing their gold-ribboned passage. A handful looked askance as they fled, extending the gift of their pity perhaps, but no more. In an inkling, they were gone.

Saubon, meanwhile, concentrated on scaling the parapets to assess their straits. He hauled himself up wreckage heaped by Kellhus himself, stood upright upon a gantry wall enclosing the Ribbaral, surveyed the absurd proportions of their doom.

The Urokkas piled before him, bereft their diadems of ephemeral sorcerous light. The last of the Swayali blew as golden flakes across the raving multitudes. Even as he reeled for its preposterous extent, for the gnashing *miles* it encompassed, the Horde resumed its titanic wail, trammelled any hope of human sound. North. South. East. West. The land itself had been stippled in howling white faces.

He will come back, a fraction of him insisted.

You need only survive long enough.

He required no voice to direct his householders. The Knights of the Desert Lion had sought him out as soon as the last Nun had vanished over the walls. Even now they looked to him, grasped the doom reflected in his blue eyes. He pointed at Kurwachal. And so, from points scattered across the gutted heart of Dagliash, they mustered upon her last, truly mighty tower.

Hold on.

Saubon, who had to teeter picking his way along the interior wall, would be the last to gain the blunted summit. They set about securing the toothless parapets. Ingol heaved skyward to the east, as if the World were naught but a hide drawn over a mammoth tree stump. Oloreg was all but obscured, but Mantigol loomed in oceanic silhouette beyond, its flanks swagged with fire. The plate of the Neleöst extended southward, wind-scuffed and gleaming. To the north the Erengaw Plain flared out into the obscurity of the Shroud. Sranc smothered all the World between, from those screaming and raving directly below, to those clotting the distances, mutilated sheaves cast over bare stone and breathing earth. Maggot-teeming, worm-twisting ...

He is coming.

They found themselves standing upon a different raft in far more perilous seas—one that was sinking. Riven with the others along the parapet, Saubon watched the leaping, scrabbling flood. His breath had become a rope of frayed hemp drawn to and fro, something that sawed at his heart. Swinging and bounding, the creatures swamped the outermost defences, bloomed in the baileys, gushed through the ruined inner gates. Saubon suffered the peculiar, dislocated sense of horror that comes with watching doom unfold at a distance—a cavernous knowledge ... A recognition like a hole.

He will return!

They could see the Witches recede over the screeching tracts, like golden wildflowers for their billows. They could see *Him* sparking into existence upon the peaks, or at points above the sun-scaled coast. They could hear His dread exhortations ...

Dagliash was engulfed in scribbling activity. Everywhere he looked he spied Sranc scaling the rotted mortices as quick and limber as adolescent boys. He watched the inhuman masses fan loping across the Ribbaral, saw Gwanwë's salt effigy vanish into a fist of rutting fingers. He even glimpsed Bashrag lurching from the gutted pit where Ciworal had stood—the Well of Viri. The surge all but swallowed the unearthly golden glint of the receptacle.

The very *ground* was rotted, infested ...

Please … How could I not believe you?

Saubon turned to see Bogyar leaning perilously out on the ledge, screaming inaudible outrage, hammering his chest—his face nearly as crimson as his beard. Spittle winked in the sunlight.

You knew my heart better than I.

Like an apple core tossed upon an ant nest, Dagliash *crawled.* Sranc filing, mobbing, thronging, closing upon Kurwachal from all squares of the compass. Black arrows already pelted them. Several of his men wrested blocks from the battlements to send clacking down upon those climbing the tower's thighs ...

The Holca made a show of rubbing a large stone against his mail-clad rump, then hurling it viciously at the skinnies flying atop the very wall Saubon had used to reach Kurwachal. *Three* were felled—and instantly, the whole company cheered as if at number-sticks. And the Exalt-General *saw,* with a profundity that fairly throttled him. Death. He understood. Death! He fathomed the enormity of the *gift* he had been given.

"*Praise Him!*" he cried laughing to Men who could not hear him—only believe. "Hail our *Holy Aspect-Emperor*!"

Death comes. Death always comes. But it is meted in so many ways ...

Few as glorious as this.

And his Company, the Company of the Raft, *saw with him.* The impossible light of their Lord-and-Prophet leapt from look to look, heart to heart. They laughed and cheered, even though all the World bristled and screamed—even as the first of their number slumped to his knees, an arrow in his eye ...

"Praise! Praise to Him!"

The Sranc came scratching up, throwing themselves over the parapets.

"Hail Anasûrimbor Kellhus!"

Death came swirling down.

Saubon hacked against the onslaught, shattered wagging cleavers, cracked black helms. For a brief time, it seemed easy, hewing and chopping the snarling faces as they crested the battlements. They seemed invulnerable upon their bastion, casting Sranc like screaming cats from the heights. The rain of black arrows killed as many if not more the obscenities. Thirty-eight souls remained to the Company. They arrayed themselves about the Altar's circuit according to necessity, a line that was drawn thinner as increasing numbers of Sranc shinnied various quarters of the tower. Kurwachal was soon engulfed in crawling skirts of Sranc, and it became little more than an octagonal shaft jutting from the seething assemblage. The creatures surmounted the parapets from all directions. The defenders were forced to close their line into a besieged circle, each man separated by paces from his gasping brother. Saubon continued crying out the name of his Lord-and-Prophet, but whether to rally or beseech he did not know. None could hear him, not in the rotted throat of the Horde. The name had become something empty, a reflex borne of outrage and horror and all the other darknesses that came before. There was his Company, little more than shadows that stood battling shadows that crawled or leapt. The World had *imploded* otherwise, become a bladder sucked tight about the points of life and murder. The tip of his nimil broadsword plunged and plummeted, slicing fish-belly skin, puncturing cheeks, shattering teeth. Arrows tinked from his helm, clattered from his ancient Cunûroi hauberk. He kicked the decayed masonry before him, sent a section tipping out, locked gazes with one of the clinging obscenities. Eyes like black marbles in sockets of oil, an expression like silk crushed in a fist, a sneering, spitting frenzy, leaning out and out, into the scabrous distances, then dropping on a sheer, slipping, vanishing ... Fate begrudged him any respite or momentary exultation. More obscenities clambered over the lip—like human-faced lice they *teemed.* His blade swooped and struck, notching pitted iron, loosing strings and sheets of violet from maiden-pale skin. *Kellhus!* he bellowed. *Kellhus! Kellhus! Kellhus!* But his breath became more and more difficult, something he had to yank burning from the bottom of his lungs. Clutching agony seized his left arm. He faltered. Mepiro grovelled on his belly nearby, a javelin staking his back. Something resounded through his bones—a blow to the head. The ground swung vertical, slapped his cheek for his presumption ...

Kellhus!

He pushed himself to his knees, despite the mountain across his shoulders.

He saw Bogyar, a red-skinned fury upon the parapet, one foot upon the battlements, his mouth watering blood, a javelin jutting from his mail-armoured shoulder. The Holca held his left arm extended to the heavens, a nude Sranc impaled through the jaw upon a broken sword, shaking over the abyss, erect even in its instant of death. His right arm carried his great battleaxe down, delivering gore and ruin to the pale beasts thronging about him. From nowhere, it seemed, a Sranc leapt onto his back, and hacking and shrieking carried the red-haired warrior over the plummet.

In the vacant place remaining, he saw a Sranc cresting the battlements, its face passive and porcelain, as beautiful as anything graven—until hatred crushed it into something inhuman.

A concussion sent him rolling. A crawling, encrusted World, thrown in sheets.

A sense of inner things *leaking*.

Kellhus ...

Across a landscape of stamping legs and unshod, horned feet, he saw Mepiro's face, blank beneath wild shadows, jerking to rhythmic thrusts.

No.

Something happened. Something ...

Too loud to be sound. Too bright to be light ...

So quick, so absolute as to circumvent perception.

Dagliash was gone—along with his breath, his heartbeat.

He suffered an absence of sensation that could only be called falling. Void was a spinning place, or so he learned, for he did not move, and it spun about him.

Then a mad, *existential* jarring, as if he had slipped from a precipice to be swatted motionless caught upon a ledge ...

He opened eyes within *already opened* eyes ... Cheek against the turf, shadows thrashing about and above, a scissoring forest of horse-legs ... Men battling Men? Yes. Galeoth knights vying with golden-armoured Coyauri.

Mengedda?

By the God, his fury felt so empty, *so frail against the earth ...*

He was already gazing across trampled turf. Motionless, he saw a young man fallen the same as he, heavily armoured in the old style, sandy-blond hair jutting from his mail hood. He watched him reach out in horror and confusion and grasp his own hand, squeeze the leathery fingers, the glass nails. He felt nothing ...

A nightmarish moment of recognition, too surreal to be terrifying.

It was *his* face! His *own hand* had clasped him!

He tried to scream.

Nothing.

He tried to move, to twitch ...

Absolute immobility encapsulated him. He felt only void across his exterior skin, but within ... It seemed a door had swung or swollen open.

And he knew the way all the Dead knew, with the certainty of timeless recollection.

Hell ... rising on a bubbling rush. Agony and wickedness chattering with famished glee ...

Demons, come to pull his outside through his inside, to invert and expose, to bare his every tenderness to fire and gnashing teeth ...

Damnation ... *in spite of everything.*

There was no describing the horror.

He tried to clutch with dead fingers ... to hold on ...

Don't! he tried to call across the space of a dead man's reach. But his ribs were a breathless cage, his lips cold soil. *Don't let go ...*

Please! he screamed at his younger self, trying to communicate the whole of his life with sightless eyes ... *Fool! Ingrate!*

Don't trust Hi—

Flash of light.

So bright, so blinding, that it seemed nothing more than a peripheral flicker.

The image of Dagliash hung, a shadow wrapped about radiance, curtain walls blown to gaseous oblivion.

Air sucked to dizzying altitudes.

Ears shut to all sound.

Radiating concussions, blowing souls in their thousands from the crests and summits, puncturing the very clouds, blasting them outward, dilating the iris of the sky.

A moment of paradoxical sunlight.

Vast and luminous and golden. Lancing across emptiness, painting the back of the erupting earth, a pillar of particulate and ejecta—a mountain flying upward and out. Plumes like octopus arms, black about brilliance, surging into Heaven's vacant arch. The cooling tendrils bowed outward, fanning, descending, while an inferno scaled the obscured heights within.

Circles and rings of obliteration. The swirling ash. The charcoal slopes, all the smoking forms thrown outward. The croaking regions, fingerless hands pawing. Burning Schoolmen, stumbling from the sky.

Then the fields of screaming, Men and Sranc, raising blistered faces, melted eyes, shaking skin from their arms, so that it seemed they warred with rags.

The smell of smoke and burnt lamb and cooking pig.

Mouths round with lamentation.

CHAPTER FOURTEEN

The Demua Mountains

To be a Man is to take the frame of Man as firmament, to be immovable unto oneself. And to know Man as a Man is to be blind to this common frame, to be without knowing. Thus is knowing the corruption of being. And so to learn what it is to be a Man is to cease to be a Man.

—*Treatise on Diremption*, ANONYMOUS

Early Autumn, 20 New Imperial Year (4132, Year-of-the-Tusk), the Demua Mountains

Ishuäl destroyed. His father rediscovered. The Doctrine utterly overthrown.

This was a Study like no other.

The mountain wind fluted through as much as across the Survivor's skin. Slices. Incisions. Sickle-shaped and puckered. Intersecting. Even his scarring bore scars. Had his memory not been perfect he could have used his body as a map, a cipher. Every desperate stand. Every vicious encounter. His trial had been carved into the very meat of him, the residue of a thousand thousand shortest paths. Decisions without number.

He had become a hieroglyph, a living *indication* of things both invisible and profound. No matter how bright the sun burned, darkness surrounded him. No matter how deep the distance, slavering beasts encircled him. No matter how peaceful the birdsong, how quiet the jackpine and high stone, cutting edges whistled in the black, points gutted the near-emptiness.

Cuts and cuts and cuts and cuts and cuts ...

He had become a *walking word.* The only one that mattered now that Ishuäl was gone ...

Survival.

He and the boy followed the old man and the woman, their ears pricked to the brief exchanges between them. Lexicons were expanded. Grammars were considered and revised. They correlated tones and expressions, and began milking ever more meaning from the raw sounds.

They ascended slopes, followed switchback paths, labouring through high-altitude shadows.

By some fluke of their approach, the sun breached the mountain along the line of the glacier, so that all the world seem dazzled. They climbed toward the fields of hanging shimmer.

Shriekers bubbled up through the black. The Survivor blinked—flinched.

The boy observed.

Cuts and cuts and cuts ...

Despite their apparent infirmity, the worldborn couple scarcely paused for respite. They climbed with alacrity, trotted with relentless wind—so much so that the boy was taxed on occasion. It was the substance, the Survivor realized, the drug they administered with an exchange of fingertips: it deepened their lungs as much as it quickened their wits and their limbs.

Another mystery ...

More promising than the others.

The ink of knowledge blots the page. The couple understood what they were, but only in rough approximation. Their concepts could only touch, never grasp, the principles of the Dûnyain. They lacked the required precision.

But as partial and incomplete as their understanding was, they nevertheless assumed that they knew everything they *needed* to know—and so were safe, or at least shielded from the refugees. They could no more fathom their straits than a crow could read.

They would succumb. The Survivor need only aim his soul and they would succumb—eventually. The woman's madness was naught but a complication. The old man's hatred and knowledge were even less so.

They would succumb, he quickly realized, the way the World had succumbed to his father. They dwelt in worlds pocked and limned and partitioned with darknesses they could not see. The unity of things, they thought, was something hidden *beneath*, a vast analogue to the false unity of their souls. And so they assumed *they*, at least, stood apart, believing that it belonged to souls to hang themselves by their own hair. They did not understand how Cause nested within Cause, how all that was real—and mundane—transpired across a singular plane, the *after* forever following upon the before.

So they thought *words* were the sole avenue of conquering souls, that they could, through vigilance and a wilful refusal to believe, guard this gate and so keep their souls safe. They could not see what they could not see, and so were blind to the way they became mere moments in a greater mechanism in the presence of the Dûnyain. Like chips of ice in warm water, their secrets would melt, their principles would dissolve, and they would become continuous with the whole, all but indistinguishable.

They would succumb.

"How can you know this?" the boy asked the first night of their exodus. They had camped on the shoulder of a giant, high enough to dare the teeth of the cold. The old man and his woman lay curled one about the other on a higher tier, finding solace of sorts, the Survivor knew, in their greater elevation.

"Because they are less," something within him replied, "and we are more."

"But what of *sorcery*?" the boy asked. "You said the Singers had changed everything."

"True," the Cause-within said. As cause, it was also effect, selected from a chattering cacophony of causes. As it passed, another was selected to be voiced, a lone survivor of inner savagery. The soul was nothing more than congeries of brutalized survivors ...

"The Doctrine is incomplete."

"So how can you know?" the Cause-nearby pressed.

"Because the Doctrine yet rules the *meat* of the World," yet another survivor said. "And because," the one following added, "they succumbed to my father ..."

Yet another Cause monitored this process of selection, the sorting of the living and spoken from the dead and unvoiced, ever alert for evidence of madness ...

Nothing.

"So what will you do?"

When they succumb ... a survivor added.

"That depends on the manner of their capitulation," the Cause-within replied.

"How do you mean?" the Cause-nearby asked.

And the monitor happened upon a wane flare of solace, a mad survivor, rooted in murk. They had always been a single engine, this place and the boy, from the day they had fled into the Thousand Thousand Halls.

"Whether they love."

Cuts and cuts and cuts ...

The woman, Mimara, stalked ahead of the old man, Achamian, leading the small party with a haste borne of fury. The Survivor paced him for a while, thinking the Wizard would eventually say something, offer some ingress ...

Silence, the Survivor had noted, weighed heavy against the old man.

But he said nothing, though his motion and demeanour shouted with an awareness of the Survivor's proximity, one that dwindled as the labourious watches wore on. The shadow of the mountains rose up around them, drawing veils across orange faces of stone.

"She still wants you to destroy us ..." the Survivor finally ventured. "Destroy us with your light."

"Yes ... She does."

They were stunted—only a fraction of themselves. The legionary engines of speech lay in the darkness *preceding* their souls, he realized. They began the very instant they spoke and not before. And so their speaking seemed all that was required to *be*.

"Will you execute her wishes?" he asked as a provocation, since he already knew the answer.

The Wizard squinted at him. He *knew* he betrayed himself, that he stood before a being he could not quite conceive. He even understood the contingency of his soul, and yet he could not convince himself of his peril. And how could he, when blindness to that contingency comprised the very foundation of what it meant "to be." What could it mean to begin *before* you begin?

"Perhaps ..."

A faltering gaze. A face struggling to maintain a semblance of resolution. *Knowing* was what made the old man weak, his inkling of the vast disproportion between them.

"My father stole something from you."

This was not so difficult to see.

A quivering slackness about the eyes, fleeting. Welling tear ducts. And deeper, a knotting of thought and passion, a flexing that slipped into release.

"Yes ..." the Wizard said, looking to the scarped distance.

The first true admission. The more of these he could prise from the man's nebulous confusion, the Survivor realized, the more thoroughly he could possess him.

Little truths. He must gather them ... like one hundred stones.

The old man coughed, more to provide time to think than to clear his throat.

"Yes, he did."

The mother of the pregnant woman, Mimara. Kellhus had taken her.

The Survivor's ruminations had generated a variety of explanatory schema, each weighted according to the evidence at hand. With each Cause selected, the competitors were pitched into the dark, and new cycles of speculation were triggered, wheels within wheels within wheels ...

Why had Kellhus taken her? To coerce this man? To breed? To condition some other ground?

There was only one possibility. Always only one. For this was the very structure of apprehension: appraisal, selection ...

Slaughter.

That second night they camped upon a knoll that swelled from the long-wandering ridge-line they had followed for a better part of the afternoon. Balance seemed especially precarious. Dusk had thinned the already emaciated air, lending fingernails to the encircling soar and plummet. Void leered, tugged with the lurch of vertigo. Across the emptiness, the sun flared with geometric precision, slighting the chill wind, tanning the surrounding peaks with gold and spangled vermillion. The scuff of boots across stone and gravel pricked the ear.

Since more than a watch remained before nightfall, the pregnant woman demanded—through Achamian—that the Survivor run down one of the mountain goats they had spied on the broken slopes below. This had already become a custom of hers, making demands of the two Dûnyain.

He killed the animal with a single stone.

When he returned he found the boy plying the old man with questions while Mimara watched uncomprehending. She was troubled, the Survivor could see, by the ease with which the boy had donned and doffed the terror he had feigned the previous day. When privacy afforded, he would remind him not to exchange his tools so quickly.

They sat on the hunched spine of the World, watching the flames slick the carcass with grease and sizzle. The discomfort of the woman and the old man was palpable, such was the madness of sharing fire and dinner with those they would murder. Their quest had been long, fraught with death and deprivation, and they had yet to realize what their losses demanded of them, let alone the significance of their present situation. Possibilities besieged them. The Survivor could see them flinching from errant thoughts—misgivings, horrors. They lacked the insight to clearly distinguish between various courses of action, let alone the foresight to map them into the future. They lacked the discipline to resist seizing upon whatever fragments the darkness of their greater souls offered up to them. The Survivor realized that he could, given time, *make these decisions for them.*

They were that frail.

But his study was far from complete. He remained ignorant of all save the grossest details regarding their lives, let alone the world from which they hailed. What was more, the Logos that bound and articulated their thoughts yet eluded him. *Associations*, he had come to realize, determined the movements of their souls. Relations of resemblance in place of reasons. Until he learned the inner language that drove the outer—the grammar and the lexicon of their souls—he could do little more than shove their thoughts in brute directions.

Perhaps that was all that he needed—at this juncture at least.

He turned to the old man. "Have you discov—?"

"*Thiviso kou'pheri*," the pregnant woman interrupted. She often watched him with predatory distrust, so perhaps this was why he had overlooked the transformation that had crawled into her face.

The old man turned to her, his frown of disapproval vanishing into anxious recognition—an expression he had come to know well. Achamian did not so much fear the woman, the Survivor realized, as he feared *her knowledge* ...

Or was it the *source*?

The old Wizard turned back, his heart racing against the blankness of his face. "She says that she sees the Truth of you," he said, licking his lips.

He could hear sparrow-thrum of his old-man heart, smell the pinch of his sudden, old-man apprehension.

"And what is that?"

Numb, the Survivor realized. His lips were numb.

"Evil."

"She is misled by my skin," the Survivor replied, assuming that for souls so primitive, visual abomination would imply spiritual. But he saw his error even before the old man shook his head.

The sorcerer turned to her, translated.

The hilarity in her eyes was genuine but momentary. She did not even trust his ignorance, her suspicion of him and the boy ran so deep. But there was something else as well, crabbing her expression, throttling her thought ... a visceral reaction to what she *saw*, what had fooled him into thinking she found his aspect revolting.

"*Spira*," she said. "*Spira phagri'na*."

He required no interpretation.

Look. Look into my face.

"She wants you to gaze into her face," the old Wizard said, a sudden fascination hooking his voice. The Survivor regarded him for one heartbeat, two ... and understood that for Drusas Achamian a *great contest* was about to waged, a pitting of principle against principle, horror against horror, trust against hope.

The pregnant woman did not so much stare at as *regard* him, her expression now raw with inexplicability. Absence gutted the pitch and summit of the distance gloaming beyond her. Against such vacancy, she could only seem too near—so perilously close.

"*Spira phagri'na.*"

And the Survivor could see it all, the legionary welter that was the Cause-within. The fraction that spoke, uncomprehending. The fraction that heard this speaking and made it her own. The fractions that bring forth. The fractions that consume ...

Look into my face.

And he could see it *nowhere* ... the origin of her assurance ... the Cause.

Madness, just as he had presumed.

"*Pilubra ka*—"

Can you see it? Reflected in my eyes—can you see it?

The question bobbed through him. He caught it in the nets of his face.

Her smile could have been Dûnyain so devoid was it of anything outside the ruthless fact of observation.

"*Tau ikruset.*"

Your damnation.

She was defective—but in some profound and obscure way. Something buried deep, a fraction that feared, had seized the fractions that saw, producing hallucinations that seized the fractions that spoke and reasoned—undeniable visions. She would be far more difficult to solve than he had initially anticipated, the Survivor realized. So much so, he would have relegated the task ... had she not possessed such a hold on Drusas Achamian.

Wind braided the fire, combed sparks from its extremities. Her face pulsed orange. "*Dihunu,*" she said smiling, "*varo sirmu'tamna al'abatu so kaman.*"

The old Wizard scowled.

"She says that you gathered one hundred stones ..."

An involuntary blink. A catastrophic lapse.

Impossibility ... Only this time without the curious intimation of deformity that seemed to mar all things sorcerous. An *absolute* impossibility ...

"*Yis'arapitri far*—"

Cuts and cuts and cuts ...

"She says you only *think* you survived the Thousand Thousand Halls," the old Wizard said.

The Survivor blinked ... fell back and away, dissolving into the fractional multitudes he had always been, pieces glimpsing pieces, splinters of what would happen ... each a living claim, yearning to be raised up from the multitudes—and to exult in the flesh of the real.

He gazed at the pregnant woman, a new assemblage, clustered like winter bees about a new resolution. All the world fell to shadow and rags about the fixed point of her gaze.

His grin was both easy and sad, the smile of one who understands the errors of the heart too well not to forgive the hatred of another.

"*Resirit manu cousa*—"

"She says," the old Wizard said scowling, "that you just decided to murder her."

Cuts and cuts and cuts.

He watched the couple through the dancing, windswept pulse of their fire. They sat one about the other facing the night. Mimara huddled armour and all in the old Wizard's arms, though she was the stronger, clutching one of his hands to her golden belly. Achamian stared out, his bearded profile daubed in orange, his gaze baffled by the wonder beneath his palm. The awe that was the future.

Wolves barked and bickered and crooned, yelping cacophonies that were pared into long solitary wails. Only predators dared call out to the void of night, beasts that were never eaten. Until this evening, he had not imagined the void could answer ...

That it harboured entities every bit as predatory ... more.

"How did she know?" the boy whispered in the dark.

Only Cause could effect knowledge.

"This World," a fraction replied, "possesses directions the Dûnyain could not fathom."

He was known—he who had confounded his Elders with his gifts. She had looked upon him, and had sounded him to his dregs.

"But how?"

Shadows roiled in the darkness.

The Survivor turned away from the wavering image of Mimara and Achamian, immured the boy within the vast apparatus of his scrutiny. He reached out, curved his palm about the arc of the boy's cheek. A fraction peered at the scarred, puckered skin against smooth.

"The Soul is Many," another fraction said.

"And the World is One," the boy replied, perplexed, for this catechism had been among the first he had learned.

The Survivor let slip his hand, turned to resume his scrutiny of the couple.

"But I don't understand," the small voice pressed from his periphery.

Always so open, the boy—so trusting.

"Cause measures the *distance* between things ..." one fraction said, while another continued scrutinizing the couple. "This is why the strength of the Dûnyain has always lain in grasping the Shortest Path ..."

"But for her to know about the stones ..." the boy said. "What possible *path* could deliver that knowledge?"

The fraction that listened nodded.

"None," whispered the fraction that spoke.

The fraction that watched presided over the labour of yet others, whisking scenarios of act and consequence, all of them involving the death of the pregnant woman. By simply announcing his intent she had disastrously complicated its execution ...

"But what does that mean?" the boy asked.

Cuts and cuts and cuts ...

"That the World ..." a voice began, "is one *in every respect.*"

Fractions mewled and screamed in the dark.

"What are you saying?"

Something, the desperation hidden in the fluting striations of the boy's voice perhaps, suspended the numberless labours dividing his soul. Why? a fraction asked. Why begin plotting her death before comprehending the *ground* of what had transpired?

The Survivor pinned the boy with his regard.

"That all of this has somehow already happened."

The old man moaned in his sleep—cried out.

The pregnant woman stirred from his side, yanked herself upright in bleary alarm. She made no move to rouse him, electing to hang at his side instead, her face drawn with exhaustion. She had grown accustomed to these momentary, nocturnal vigils, thoughts freighted with the sloth of unconsciousness.

She laid a hand upon the old Wizard's breast, a reflex borne of thoughtless intimacy. A palm like an ear held against his heart.

The old man grew still.

The fire had wheezed into oblivion. The encircling night howled with wind, altitude, and gaping emptiness. The Heavens illumined all ...

Nothing sensible cued the sudden look she shot in the Dûnyain's direction. She was blind again—a fact made clear by the swarming indications of fear and indecision. Fully human.

She locked eyes with the fraction watching.

The World is One, a fraction recalled a fraction saying ...

The boy?

She turned away from its scrutiny, resumed her position at the Wizard's side. The fraction watched her eyes sort through the infinity yawing above. Seventeen heartbeats passed, then, with a kind of grim fury, she clutched her blanket to her chin and rolled to her side.

This too, one fraction whispered to the others, *has already happened.*

The wind thrummed and roiled, rushed in invisible cataracts about the hanging heights.

The Survivor rolled onto his back. *She says*, a fraction whispered in the old man's voice, *that you gathered one hundred stones*. How could such a thing be known? Sorcery, another fraction realized. Sorcery was the least among the Dûnyain's many oversights. Long had he pondered the Singers and their cataclysmic song: none of the Brethren had risked so much as he in the futile attempt to capture one for interrogation. An errant fraction glimpsed lightning and thunder in the labyrinthine black. Why? Why would the worldborn founders of the Dûnyain deny their children knowledge of something so significant as sorcery? What could motivate dooming their progeny to millennial ignorance?

Perhaps some paths were *too* short. Perhaps they had feared their descendants would forswear the more arduous harvest of Cause, when the fruits of sorcery hung so low.

As profound as it was, sorcery did naught but complicate the metaphysics of Cause. But this ... The *knowledge* that had apprehended him through the eyes of the pregnant woman.

This changed everything.

Even now, as he gazed without sight into the oceanic cavity of night, a fraction retrieved her image, and he relived the impossibility of her gaze, of a scrutiny utterly unconstrained by the incestuous caprice of the here and now. A look unbound by time and place. A look *from everywhere* ...

And nowhere.

And he knew: there existed a *place* without paths of any kind, without differences ...

An *absolute* place.

Cuts and cuts and cuts ...

The four of them ascended ways slung across the face of the heavens. Falls, some sloped and tumbling, others abyssal, framed every glance they shared. Summits dizzied the sky about them, great cleavages of rocks thrust towering into the high blue. Thin air taxed their lungs and limbs.

"It hunts us," a fraction said to the old Wizard.

An apprehensive squint.

"The darkness that comes before thought and soul," another fraction explained.

The man's face seemed of a piece with the mountains, a dark miniature.

"I did plot her murder," a fraction resumed.

These words took the old man aback—according to their design. By beginning with a cryptic utterance, he had engaged the Wizard's curiosity and attention, as well as provided a foil of obscurity for the clarity of his subsequent confession.

"And now? Do you still wish her dead?"

He needed Drusas Achamian to *listen.*

"No matter what I answer, you will not believe me."

Trust was a habit for these people. If he spoke enough truth, his voice would *become* true.

"Sounds like a dilemma," the old Singer said.

A luminous look. Smiles only called attention to the Survivor's grotesquerie.

"It need not be."

Achamian cast a worried glance at the pregnant woman several paces above. They toiled up the shoulder of a mountain, following a ravine of larger stones and boulders set into what were otherwise gravel slopes. Dislodged stones clacked down in their wake, gaining speed and kicking out onto the surrounding ramps, where they triggered small cascades of gravel, skirts woven of incalculable threads.

The old man had just resolved to ignore him, the Survivor knew.

"As much as you distrust me, you *trust* her sight more."

The shadow of some bird plummeted across the slopes.

"So?"

Truth.

"Tell her," the mutilated son of Anasûrimbor Kellhus said, "to gaze upon me while I speak."

Honesty was the way in.

"And why would I do that?"

The Shortest Path.

"Because my father stole your wife."

Cause ...

Cause was but the *skin*.

The skein.

A scab on the knuckle of the boy's left index finger, already ancient for three days healing.

The small mole to the left of the pregnant woman's chin, the one that vanished those rare times she smiled.

The swelling joints in the old Wizard's hands, and the ache that he tested without awareness, again and again, flexing and relaxing his fingers ...

Flexing and relaxing.

Each of these things had origins and destinations. Each of these things caused and had been caused. They were points that knotted the shag of the past and fanned into a hollow future. But he knew them only insofar as they were his origin, his past. He knew not the scrape that had wounded the boy's finger, the defect that marred the woman's skin, or the malady that afflicted the old Wizard's hands.

He was bound to the skin of these things—the skein.

All else was Darkness.

After generations of training and breeding for Logos, the Dûnyain could do no more than pierce this skin, cut and cut and cut. They could only lick the blood of knowledge. They could never hope to drink so deep as the woman had the evening previous. They could not so much as *raise* the cup, let alone drain it.

The Dûnyain, seeing only the skin of Cause, the pulsing webs, had assumed that Cause *was everything*, that it occupied the whole of darkness. But they had been fools, thinking that Darkness, even in this meagre respect, *could be seen*. For all their penetration they were every bit as abject before their ignorances as beasts, let alone worldborn Men.

A different blood throbbed through the infinite black, one that bled from all points equally.

He need only look at the pregnant woman to see it now, scarcely perceptible, like the stain of dawn on the longest watch of the night, or the first flutter of sickness.

They descended a broad pasture, their heads bobbing as the headlong fall pulled their steps downward. She walked below, wild for the pelts draped about her shoulders, boyish for the shortness of her hair. Unlike the old Wizard or even the boy, whose paths wandered like bumblebees, she walked with the assurance of one who followed a track both ancient and habitual ...

Her every step trod Conditioned Ground.

She did not *know* this knowing, of course, which was what made it so much more remarkable ... even *miraculous*. She bore an assurance that was *not her own*—and how could it be? How could anything bottomless be owned, let alone fathomed, by a soul so finite, so frail?

She says, a fraction whispered from the dark, *that you intend to murder her*.

Tell her, another answered, *to gaze upon me while I speak.*

The boy drew *his* crabbed hand across a throng of goldenrod ... and the Survivor felt the tickle of embroidered petals *across his own palm* ...

As did something greater. Incomprehensibly greater.

Absolute.

Pick any point in space—it does not matter which.

The only way to make that point the *measure* of the surrounding space, the Dûnyain had realized, *was to call it zero*, the absence of quantity that anchored the enumeration of all quantities. Zero ... Zero was the source and centre of every infinity.

And it was everywhere.

Because zero was everywhere, measure was everywhere—as was arithmetic. Submit to the rule of another and you will measure as he measures. Zero was not simply nothing; it was also *identity*, for nothing is nothing but the *absence of difference*, and the absence of difference is nothing but the *same*.

Thus the Survivor had begun calling this new principle *Zero*, for he distrusted the name the old Wizard had given it ...

God.

The great error of the Dûnyain, he could see now, was to conceive the Absolute as something *passive*, to think it a vacancy, dumb and insensate, awaiting their generational arrival. The great error of the worldborn, he could see, was to conceive it as something *active*, to think it *just another soul*, a flattering caricature of their own souls. Thus the utility of *Zero*, something that was not, something that pinched all existence, every origin and destination, into a *singular* point, into *One*. Something that commanded all measure, not through arbitrary dispensations of force, but by virtue of *structure* ... system ...

Logos.

The God that was Nature. The God that every soul *could be*, if only for the span of a single insight ...

The Zero-God. The absence that was the cubit of all creation. The Principle that watched through Mimara's eyes ...

And had found his own measure wanting.

Cuts and cuts and cuts ...

A mountain lay between them and the setting sun, brute ground lunging into the sky. White water blasted through a gorge below, a snaking of ravines and crevasses that made a hoof of the mountain's roots. The boy sat tending to their fire, his eyes reflecting twin miniatures of the flame, his face flushing orange as night wicked the colour from the distances beyond his shoulders. The old Wizard and the pregnant woman stood bickering above, perched on a flange of granite that curled like a great, slumbering cat about their camp.

"*Pit-pit arama s'arumnat!*" her voice fluted shrill across the stone.

"Why do they argue now?" the boy asked, raising his pupils from the reflected fires.

The Survivor had made no pretense of discretion or disinterest. He stood opposite the boy, his back to the coniferous gloom of the valley below, gazing up with cold fixity.

"I offered to submit to her gaze," a fraction replied to the boy. "And its judgment."

Another fraction tracked the serpentine interplay of outrage and incredulity flexing across her expression, warbling through her voice, twitching through her stance and gesture. Her Gaze, she was explaining to the old Wizard, had *already* passed judgment, had already found them wanting ...

"And she balks?" the boy asked.

"They have suffered too much to trust anything we offer them. Even our capitulation."

"*Mrama kapu!*" the woman cried, sweeping wide the blade of her right hand. Once again stumped by the violence of her ingenuity, the old Wizard stammered in reply.

He was losing this contest ...

"I can hear them!" the Survivor cried, his tone modulated to provoke communal alarm.

The worldborn couple stared down at him, rimmed in the violet of incipient night. The burning scrub popped, to his right, coughed points of light, constellations drawn out on the wind.

"I can hear them *in your womb*," the Survivor repeated—this time in the woman's tongue. Though he was far from mastering the language, he knew enough to say at least this much.

She gawked at him, too shocked to be dismayed—to be anything other than disarmed.

"*Taw mirqui pal—*"

What do you mean ... them?

One fraction registered the success of his stratagem. Others reaped the signs blaring from her form and face. And still others enacted the remaining articulations of this ploy ...

The Survivor smiled the old Wizard's most endearing smile.

"You bear *twins* ... Sister."

You are right to be terrified.

The Dûnyain exceed any rule that you possess ... We outrun your measure.

You are the neck of a bottle. The World but drips into your soul.

We dwell in the deluge.

You come to us as a cataract. You assume you are unitary and alone, when in sooth you are a mob of blind men, crying out words you cannot comprehend in voices you cannot hear. For the *truth* is that *you are many*—this is the secret of your innumerable contradictions.

This ... This is where the Dûnyain labour, in the darkness that comes before your souls. To converse with us is to *submit* to us—there is no other way for you to dwell in our presence. Given our respective natures, we are *your slavers*.

You were right to want to kill us ...

Especially *me*, one who was broken in the deepest Deep.

Even this confession, this speaking of plain truth, is woven from knowledge that would terrify you, such is its penetration. My very voice has been fashioned *into a key*, using manner and intonation as teeth to unlock the tumblers of your soul. You are rapt because *you have been so instructed.*

Despite the brief span of our acquaintance, despite your will to conceal, I know so very much about you. I can name the Mission you call your mission, and I can name the Mission you know not at all. I know the twists of circumstance that shape and bind you; that for much of your life abuse was the only sincere rule; that you hide the tender beneath the bitter; that you carry your *mother's children* ...

But I need not enumerate what I know, for I see also that you know.

I see that you wonder what is to be done, for in speaking the truth, I also make the case for my destruction.

And so are my own limits made plain. Though the night ranges infinite above us, a fraction of me still wanders the Thousand Thousand Halls, a dark fragment, as obscure as it is elusive, one that argues *death* ... death as the Shortest Path to the Absolute.

And I wonder, *Is this what you call sorrow?*

Thus are the limits of the Dûnyain made visible ... also. For the desire that burns so bright within you has been stamped into the merest embers within us, bred into insignificance with the passing of generations, leaving but one hunger, one flame, one mover to yoke the Legion-within ...

A single Mission.

This, Sister ... This is why I bare my throat to the blade of your judgment. This is why I would make myself your slave. For short of death, *you*, Anasûrimbor Mimara, wife-daughter of Anasûrimbor Kellhus, who is also my father ... *you*, Sister, *are the Shortest Path.*

The Absolute dwells within your Gaze. You ... a frail, worldborn slip, heavy with child, chased across the throw of kings and nations, *you are the Nail of the World*, the hook from which all things hang.

Thus do I kneel before *it*, awaiting, accepting, death or illumination—it does not matter which ...

So long as I am at last *known*.

Cuts and cuts and cuts ...

A fraction kneels before her, Anasûrimbor Mimara. And a fraction, one of a *hundred* stones, could see it ... as if it were rising up, like lead pouring into the husk and tatter of a mortal frame, an immobility as profound as oblivion.

Zero.

Sranc squealing in the black, the air rancid with sweat and exhalation, cleavers whooshing, felling brothers for lunatic fear. Feet slapping stone.

Zero ... Opening as an Eye.

The blackness, savage and greased. A point passes through it, plunging down lines and sweeping across curves. The shrieks are contagion, like fire upon the back of an arid hill.

Beauty ... not of flowers or animal form, but of *stillness*, of vast mechanisms, the threshing, pounding, scraping, dwindling into the patter of mice.

Cuts and cuts and cuts ...

Beauty ... the effortlessness of freefall, the reduction of all riddles to a single, far-falling line.

The point is sentient. It *speaks*, spinning tales of hewn ribs and deflected cleavers, punctured bowels and broken teeth, extremities sent spinning into the void of irrelevance.

The Survivor gazes into the Gaze, *sees* the lie that is sight.

Cuts and cuts and cuts …

Judge us, a fraction whispers.

Raise us up.

Strike us down.

Anasûrimbor Mimara stands above him, little more than a halo, a smear of meat and hair about the Judging Eye. An excuse. An *occasion* …

Holding, a fraction notices, a sorcerous knife.

Thronging, mewling blackness. A path picked—pursued. A calligraphy too murderous to be real. Threats isolated, plucked from the deluge, pinched like candle wicks—snuffed.

So many cuts.

Zero, trembling with feminine mortality.

Too many.

"You are *broken*," she sobs. "The same as me …"

A fraction reaches out, makes a pommel of the slender hand about the pommel of the knife. *Judge*, a fraction murmurs. *End our ingrown war* …

But she is weeping—openly now. Why does she weep?

The Gaze knows no sorrow.

"But I do," she whispers.

Cuts and cuts and cuts …

The knife clatters against stone. And somehow she is kneeling with him, embracing him, so that he can feel the sphere of her belly enter the cavity of his own. A fraction counts four heartbeats: one ponderous and masculine, another fleet and feminine, and two prenatal. She exhales into his neck, and a fraction tracks the creeping bloom of heat and humidity. She shudders.

I am lost, a fraction whispers …

Though her face is buried in his shoulder below his jaw, the Gaze *has not moved*. It watches as before, infinite scrutiny hanging from the *memory* of where her eyes had been.

"Yes …" she says. "As are we."

Zero, glaring from nowhere, showing him his measure … and how disastrously far the Dûnyain had wandered.

The rank folly of the Shortest Path.

I am damned.

Her small fists twist knots into his tunic, make rope of a portion. The boy watches, for once immaculate and inscrutable. "I forgive you," she cries into his shoulder.

I forgive.

Awareness has no skin.

No fists or fingers.

No arms.

So much must be ignored.

The boy watches him stare into the bowl of night—watches him float. "So you have succeeded?" he whispers.

A fraction hears. A fraction responds.

"Everything I have taught you is a lie."

All that you know ... another murmurs without voice. *All that you are.*

And another ...

And another ...

They deferred to the old Wizard's reckoning, following the northward wend of a great valley rather than pass out of the mountains.

"Beyond lies Kûniüri," he explained, "and Sranc without number."

The meaning was plain ...

And invisible.

Crime, a fraction postulated. Crime divides the innocent from the ignorant.

The four of them sat cross-legged, knees touching knees, upon a promontory overlooking the black velvet folds of yet another valley. Jackpine clung to the outcrop's lip, leaning out like ravaged antlers. The chill made fog of their mingling breath. The old Wizard, who had not yet grasped let alone accepted what had happened, hefted the pouch he guarded so jealously in his left palm. A fraction sorted through the varieties of alarm that muttered through his look and gesture, plucked the one belonging, almost in its entirety, to the substance in the pouch. A puling spark, a greed almost infant in extent, poised to set the horizon aflame ...

But there was veneration as well, the wince of hard memories ... unwanted lessons.

The great project of the Dûnyain was conceived by Men, worldborn souls bent on pursuing an inkling of their own finitude. Their impulse was imperial. They had seen the encroaching darkness, the oblivion from which their every thought and passion had sprung; they had reckoned the servile fact of their dependency, and they would undo it if they could.

Thus had they transformed the Absolute into a *prize*.

"*Qirri*," the pregnant woman said, her voice a bolt of silk, a banner for her mongrel fortitude. "*Pa thero*, Qirri ..."

She touched the tip of her index finger to the bulb of her tongue, then reached into the interior of the pouch.

The boy watched witless—and trusting.

Ignorance, a fraction resolved. Ignorance was the foundation. The First Principle.

Proof of this lay in the very *meat* of the Dûnyain, for they had been bred in pursuit of deception. No intellect is orphaned, despite all the foundling hearts. All sons are born stranded because all fathers are sons. Every child is *told*, even those suckled on the teats of wolves. Even Dûnyain children. To be born is to be born upon a path. To be born upon a path is to *follow* that path—for what man could step over mountains? And to follow a path is to *follow a rule* ...

To find all other paths wanting.

She pulled her fingertip from the pouch's throat, held it in the light of the Nail. A woolen smudge of powder—*ash*, so fine as to dissolve in the least wind ...

But the sky had forgotten how to breathe.

Not even an entire World of madmen could chart the infinite vagaries of belief and action. Thoughts, like legs, were joined at the hip. No matter how innumerable the tracks, no matter how crazed or inventive the soul, only what could be *conceived* could be seen. *Logos*, they had called it, the principle that bound step to step, that yoked what would be aimless to the scruple of some determinate destination. And *this* had been the greatest of the Dûnyain's follies, the slavish compliance to reason, for this was what had *shackled* them to the abject ignorance of their forefathers ...

Logos.

"What is it?" the boy asked.

"Not for *you*," the old Wizard snapped—with more vehemence than he intended, a fraction noted.

Reason was a skulking beggar, too timid to wander, to leap, and so doomed to scavenge the midden-heap of what had come before. Logos ... They had called it *light*, only to find themselves blinded. They had made it their ancient, generational toil, confusing its infirmities for their own ...

Thinking the *human* was the obscuring shroud.

She reached toward him, her palm down and her finger out so that he might take the tip of her finger between his lips. A fraction surprised her by clasping her wrist and guiding the powder to his nostril ...

The inhalation was quick, sharp enough to make the old Wizard flinch. Anasûrimbor Mimara pulled her finger back, frowned in marvelling surprise.

"Ingestion delays onset," a fraction explained. "This way ..."

A lesser fraction blinked.

The Legion-within groaned, reeled, fumbled the World they bore as burdens upon their backs.

"This ... This way ..."

This way, boy ... Follow me!

Cuts and cuts and cuts. Teeth cracking in the black, gnashing, chewing. A demonic chorus bubbles down through the corridors, filters through the descending levels, viscous with lust and fury—savage with desperation. What the darkness obscures, the darkness welds *together as one*. So they seemed a singular thing, the Shriekers, more insect than human.

Don't leave me.

The child was defective, as the Assessor had predicted. A fraction gloated for the fact of Ishuäl's undoing, knowing that the child had been saved ... for ... for ...

For what?

Bestial and inhuman, grunting as they loped through the black, lost and starving, endless thousands of them, snorting the air, shrieking for the scent of *vulnerability*. In the early days, the surviving Brethren had set out pots of their own blood and excrement as lures, and the creatures swarmed to their own destruction—though the toll proved too high: one Dûnyain for a thousand Shriekers. Scent hooked one, perhaps two, and the caterwauling seized the rest, the legions scattered through the chambered deep ...

So it was always easy at first, fending them off, raising barricades of carcasses. Easy at first, impossible after. The Brethren abandoned the strategy, elected to flee, following the parse of fork and junction, using their intellect as their eyes, dividing their pursuers again and again—until the beasts were fractured into meagre bands. The boy had been suckled on such sounds, hearing his kind hunted to extinction beneath the very roots of the earth.

They would have cracked open his skull, had Ishuäl not fallen. The boy would have been pinned as all other Defectives were pinned to the subtlety of some forbidden affect, strapped for the scrutiny of others, nailed as if a drying hide to the outer expression of some inner frailty.

It was always easy at first.

I cannot breathe ...

He danced through pitch blindness, climbed through the threshing of cleavers, climbed until he could climb no more.

Is this fear?

Sometimes he would pause and make a place, raise twitching ramparts. And sometimes he would *run* ... not so much *from* as *with* the creatures, for he had learned to mimic them, the cadence of their galloping stride, the labial quaver of their snorts, their peeling screeches—everything save their stench. And it would drive them to the very pitch of frenzy, the scent of something *almost* human in their roiling midst, set them hacking the vacant black, killing one another ...

Yes. Tell me what you feel.

Even then he had understood.

I shake. I cannot breathe.

Even then he had known that Cause had never been the Dûnyain's First Principle.

And what else?

And Logos even less.

My eyes weep ... weep for want of light!

They had settled upon these things simply because they could be *seen*. Even then he had understood this.

Yes ... This is fear.

Darkness was their ground, their foe and foundation.

What is it?

The shrieking black.

The most simple rule.

Cuts ...

And cuts ...

And cuts ...

There was a place high on the shoulder of a mountain where a boy, an old man, and a pregnant woman knelt and observed as another man, a scarred grotesquerie, convulsed and voided his bowel.

Perhaps it was real—a real place—but the fractions, who were legion, who rutted and rampaged through the black, did not care, could not.

Too many cuts. Too many divisions of skin.

Run was a rule.

Hide was a rule.

Know was a rule.

Desire was a following.

Existence was a heap.

One hundred stones, too round to lock one into the other. Rounded like thumbs. Those on top warm for sunlight, like lobes or lozenges of living meat between the fingers. Those below *chill*, like the lips of the dead. Eyes scanning the coniferous gloom, isolating the ink of avian shadows. One hundred throws, arm snapping, sleeve popping, hand flicking ... A buzzing line, comprehended more in after-image than seen, spearing through the seams between branches.

Ninety-nine birds struck dead. Numerous sparrows, doves, and more crows than anything else. Two falcons, a stork, and three vultures.

"Killing," a fraction explains to the wondering boy. "Killing connects me to what I am."

And what are you?

"The Survivor," another fraction replies, and yet another registers the network of scar tissue across his face, the tug and tension of unnatural compromises.

"The Heaper of the Dead."

There was more horror than concern in their faces when his eyes fluttered open. The boy especially.

The Survivor drew a sleeve across his hideousness, looked to him, his son. The Legion-within howled and clamoured, stamped and spit. Only now did he understand ...

Ignorance. Only *ignorance* had sealed the interval between them. Only blindness, the wilful idiocy that was worldborn love. A fraction relives the flight of the Brethren before the thunderous onslaught of the Singers. Dûnyain leaping before billowing geometries of light, fleeing into the mazed gut of the World, hunted by stone-cracking *words*, utterances, the violation of everything they held to be true. Dûnyain do not panic. Dûnyain do not reel, broken and bewildered. And he yet he had found himself in the nursery *without thought*, scooping up this very babe *without thought*, the one that smelled of him, of *Anasûrimbor*, the most promising of the Twelve Germs. He clutched this wailing burden to his breast, this impediment, *without thought*, as if it were *no less a fraction of his own soul*, a part that had wandered ...

Zero. The difference that is not a difference. Zero made One.

He had *survived*. He, the one burdened, the one tasked, the one who refused to illuminate the interval between him and his son. The fractions of the Dûnyain had been sorted, and he, the *least able*, the *most encumbered*, had been the one Selected ... the Survivor.

He who had *refused to know* ... who had embraced the darkness that comes before.

The boy clutches his tunic with both hands, hale and halved. He cannot help himself. He is defective.

And so it was with the Absolute. Surrender. Forfeiture. Loss ... At last he understood what made these things *holy*. Loss was advantage. Blindness was insight, revelation. At last he could see it—the *sideways step* that gave lie to Logos.

Zero. Zero made One.

The Eye watches. Approves.

He gestures to the boy, who obediently comes to him.

He does not speak for a time, electing instead to gaze across the crumpled condensations of earth, dark beneath the silvering arch of the sky. They have finally come to the end of the mountainous throw and steep, the terminus of tyrannical ground. The trackless forests below were just that, *trackless*, demanding judgment, decision, for being so permissive. Only one scarp remains, one last perilous descent.

The wind is warm with the dank rot that promises life, with the taste of surging green.

It will be better there.

"What is it?"

"Things ..." he murmurs to the panorama, "are *simple*."

"The madness worsens?"

He looks back to the boy. "Yes."

He draws the hundredth stone from the waist of his tunic.

"This is yours now."

The boy, the *most blessed fraction*, looks to him in alarm. He would deny the interval between them, if he could.

He cannot.

The Survivors stands, begins sprinting. He marvels at the magic that joins will to flexing limbs.

A cry, spoken in a tongue that even animals know.

The Survivor does not so much move as the ground runs out. But the *leap* ... Yes. That is his.

That is his ...

As is the yawning plummet, the drop ...

Into the most empty arms.

So quickly ...

The events that transform us slip ...

So quickly.

The face, cut into all expressions, all faces.

Eyes gazing wet from mutilation.

Fixed upon something that runs as he runs, a place he can only pursue, never reach ...

Unless he *leaps*.

The Eye understood, even if the woman did not.

Achamian could see the Dûnyain's body about thirty cubits below, a motionless swatch of skin and fabric draining crimson across fractured stone. He struggled to breathe. It seemed impossible ... that a being so formidable ... so *unnerving* ... could break so easily.

"*Sweet Seju!*" he cried, retreating from the dizzy edge. "I *told* you! I told you not to give any to him!"

Mimara knelt beside the crab-clawed boy, held his blank face against her breast, a hand splayed across his scalp. "Told *who?*" she snapped, glaring. It belonged to her infuriating genius, the ability to condemn one instant then console the next.

The old Wizard grabbed his beard in frustration and fury. What was happening? When had this damaged girl, this *waif*, become a *Prophet of the Tusk?*

She began rocking the boy, who continued gazing at nothing from nowhere—witless.

Achamian cursed under his breath, turned from her glare, understanding, in a turbulent, horrified way, that the futility of arguing with her had become the futility of arguing *with the God*. He wanted nothing more than to call her on the rank contradiction of mourning a death she had clamoured for mere days previous. But all he could do was fume instead ...

And shake.

The wisdom, as always, came after. And with it the wonder.

The Eye had always been a source of worry, ever since learning of it. But now ...

Now it had become a terror.

There was her *knowledge*, for one. He could scarcely look at her without seeing the fact of his damnation in her look, the sluggish blank of someone wracked with guilt and pity for another. Between a woman's scorn and her truth, the look of the latter was by far the most unmanning.

There was the monolithic immobility of her judgment, for another, the bottomless *certitude* that he had once attributed to impending motherhood. It was pondering this that he gained some purchase on his newfound fear. Before coming to Ishuäl, he had lacked any measure external to his exasperation, and so had the luxury of attributing her rigidity to obstinance or some other defect of character. But what he had witnessed these past few days ... The madness of making—once again—a travelling companion of a

Dûnyain, only to watch him shatter like pottery against the iron of the Judging Eye ... A Dûnyain! A *son of Anasûrimbor Kellhus*, no less!

"*The eye*," he had told her in the chill aftermath of Cil-Aujas, "*that watches from the God's own vantage*." But he had spoken without understanding.

Now he had no choice. He could no longer feign ignorance of the fact that in some mad, unfathomable manner, he walked—quite literally—with *the God* ... with the very Judgment that would see him *damned*. Henceforth, he realized, his every step would be haunted by the shadow of his sacrifice.

"Do *you* know why?" he asked Mimara when they resumed their descent, the mute boy in stumbling tow.

"Why he killed himself?" she asked, either preoccupied with her downward footing or pretending to be. She was genuinely great with child now, and even with the Qirri, she seemed to find steep descents labourious in particular.

The old Wizard grunted his affirmation.

"Because the God demanded it," she offered after several huffing moments.

"No," he said. "What were *his* reasons?"

Mimara graced him with a fleeting glance, shrugged. "Do they matter?"

"Where do we go?" the boy interrupted from above and behind them, his Sheyic inflected with Mimara's Ainoni burr.

"That way," the startled sorcerer replied, nodding to the north. What did a Dûnyain child *feel*, he wondered, in the watches following his father's death?

"The world ends that way, boy ..."

He hung upon that final word, gawking ...

Mimara followed his scowl to the horizon—the cerulean haze.

The three of them stood transfixed, gazed with numb incomprehension. The forests of Kûniüri swept out from the crumpled gum-line of the Demua mountains, green daubed across ancient and trackless black. Several heartbeats passed before Achamian, cursing his failing eyes, conjured a sorcerous Lens. And so they saw it, an impossibility painted across an impossibility, a vast plume, spewing its fell innards outward and upward, far above the reach of mountain or even cloud ...

Like the noxious shadow of a toadstool, bulging to the arch of Heaven, drawn across the curve of the very World.

CHAPTER FIFTEEN

The River Sursa

No bravery is possible in Hell, and in Heaven, none is needed. Only Heroes wholly belong to this World.

—KORACALES, *Nine Songs Heroic*

Late Summer, 20 New Imperial Year (4132, Year-of-the-Tusk), the Urokkas

The monstrous plume sailed into dissolution above the Sea.

It seemed Hell itself had taken Dagliash.

Saccarees greeted Proyas upon the summit of Mantigol, his manner blank with incredulity. The eyrie resembled a scene embroidered across some heroic tapestry: survivors milling in the aftermath of catastrophe, damaged souls who would have been illustrious, were it not for the toll exacted. This was what Men did in the wake of disaster, be it the loss of a battle, the death of a loved one, or anything that knocked their lives from the pins of workaday assumption: they communed, if not with words then with looks or simple breathing.

Turning from the mute Exalt-Magus, Proyas gazed out over what seemed perfect circles of obliteration, rings burnt into the very frame of the Urokkas, flung outward across the floodplains. The earth itself burned where Dagliash had stood. Pelts of viscous smoke streamed upward, as if an upside-down World dangled its innards in ashen skies. The ground about this boiling centre had been burnt to chalk and obsidian. The first of the visible dead began some distance away, fields of char, little more than stumped torsos that became recognizable as remains in the shelter of ravines or depressions, which were choked with dead like gutters with rotted leaves. Farther still, near the rutted foundations of Oloreg, he glimpsed survivors crawling or shambling across otherwise lifeless slopes ...

Naked souls stumbling, hands out.

Agongorea burned beyond the far shore, smoking like sodden rags thrown over a fire. The River Sursa spilled black as ink into the Sea. Great clots of Sranc clotted its course, rafts of interlocked carcasses bumping and rolling like scum across the surface of a sewer. This, at least, relaxed one of the many fists clenched within Proyas's breast. The Ordeal had suffered, certainly, but the Horde was no more.

Cataclysm.

Lights that scratch blind. Cracks that swat deaf. Concussions that slap hale bodies into pulp and mist ...

Cataclysm shows Men the truth of their pitiful proportion, how their pulse hangs upon the sufferance of more monstrous things.

If Golgotterath had such weapons or allies, what did it matter, the zeal of Men?

Proyas turned to the blanched faces about him, his dismay plain.

No one seemed capable of asking the obvious.

"Has anyone seen Him?" he called, sorting between them with his gaze.

Not a soul answered.

"*Anyone!*" he cried, his voice cracking.

"I-I saw him ..." a feminine voice stammered. "M-moments be-be"—an eye-fluttering wince—"before it ... it-it happened." One of the Swayali regarded him, teetering, her gowns burnt to a fluted husk, her once luxurious hair scorched to a shag.

Somehow he knew she would not live out the night.

"He-he ... was w-warning us! Telling us to—"

Coughs battered her, spilling blood as bright as poppies across her chin.

"And *since?*" Proyas snapped, looking from face to face. "Has anyone seen Him since ... since ..." He raised a slack hand to the mountainous plume behind him.

Not a soul among them possessed words for what they had witnessed.

Dread silence. Someone on the periphery of the small crowd began sobbing. A twist in the wind swept the summit with the reek of ash and copper filings.

No, a small voice whispered within him.

Proyas swayed, took a numb step to recover, then fairly swooned for vertigo. Far more than his balance seemed to swing off the hooks and fly. Hopes. Nations. Someone—Saccarees?—caught his elbow, and he could feel his own obstinate weight yank against the grip, as if *willing* some kind of plummet. But the hand that held him was too strong—impossibly and thoughtlessly strong, like the clasp of a father retrieving his son from peril.

"*I am here*," the glorious voice murmured.

And Proyas looked up into the beloved eyes of his Holy Aspect-Emperor.

A tattered chorus scratched the gaping spaces—gratitude and relief punched from stomach and lungs. In his periphery, Proyas saw the others fall to their faces, and, for an endless heartbeat, he longed only to join them, to fall and weep, to release the horror whose silent claws had so girdled his heart.

But Anasûrimbor Kellhus spoke world-consuming sorcery instead, not so much embracing as *engulfing* his disciple ...

Proyas found himself elsewhere, tripping across different stones, different ground, hunching over his own vomit, grey puddles of Meat. He crouched hacking and trembling. When the nausea subsided, he looked up, swatting tears from his eyes. His Holy Aspect-Emperor stood several paces away with his back turned to him, staring out across the degrees of obliteration ...

He spat at the taste of bile, realized they stood upon one of Oloreg's precarious crowns.

"A great and tragic victory has been won here this day," Kellhus declared, turning to him.

Proyas stared witlessly.

"But the land is polluted ..." his Lord-and-Prophet continued. "Accursed. Viri has at last answered for her King's ancient treachery."

Bracing his palms against his knees, the Exalt-General pressed himself upright, battled to keep both his balance and the remaining contents of his stomach.

"Let no man stray upon it," Kellhus commanded. "Let no man breathe the air that blows across it. Stay to the *north*, old friend."

Kellhus stood before him, his white robes impossibly immaculate, his mane silk ribbons in the breeze. The vista yawned deep and necrose beyond him, pillared in tar-smoke, floored with ash, cinder, and innumerable dead.

"The sick and the blind must be culled ... Those whose skin grows leprous. Those who vomit blood. Those who lose their hair ... They too are polluted."

Golden orbs enclosed his prophetic hands.

"Do you understand, Proyas?"

It seemed a miracle.

"These past months ... our discussions ... Do you understand?"

They shared a flat gaze, one rumbling with the premonition of new horrors.

"You're leaving us," Proyas croaked.

Leaving me.

His Lord-and-Prophet nodded, crushed his plaited beard against his chest.

"Saubon is dead," Kellhus said, his manner gentle. "You *alone* know the *truth* of what happens here. You. Alone."

Proyas's face crumpled, a treacherous display that was undone the instant of its commission. It was strange, to weep without grimace or tears.

"But ..."

The sick and the blind must be culled ...

"*You* are weak, I know. *You* need the surety of the divine, and will only suffer so long as you are denied it. But no matter how much *you* lament, the Greater Proyas remains strong."

He wanted to cry out, to leap over the plummet, to collapse at His feet and to weep into His knees, but he stood cold and erect instead, somehow understanding everything while comprehending nothing ...

The Exalt-General of the Great Ordeal.

"*Seize* them, Proyas. Bring the Host to heel with whip and sword. Take up its lust, fashion it as a potter fashions clay. Consuming the Sranc has transformed its zeal into a *living* fire, one that only violence and victims can cajole and appease ..."

What was happening? What was he saying?

"*Something* must be eaten ... Do you understand me?"

"I-I think ..."

"*You*, Proyas! You alone! You must make decisions *that no Believer could.*"

The King of Conriya's eyes clotted with tears, and he turned to him, his Lord-and-Prophet, only to find the place where he had stood vacant. The Holy Aspect-Emperor of the Three Seas was nowhere to be found.

Proyas picked his way down alone ... Another naked soul, stumbling.

Word spread. But the simple fact that Proyas had seized the initiative, that he genuinely seemed to know what had to be done, assured obedience. He forbade passage anywhere near Antareg. He delegated the organization of a mass lazaret on the south side of the Urokkas, dispatched word confining anyone suffering blindness, burns, or sickness of any kind to its miserable precincts. The remainder of the Ordeal marched through the night, sometimes clearing, sometime climbing the scorched carcasses that clotted Oloreg's smashed teeth. He drafted dozens of Mandati and Swayali to cast Bars of Heaven to illumine their course. For those ailing along the coast, the spectacle inspired no little dread: the sight of their brothers carpeting the shoulders of the mountain, filing beneath haphazard pillars of brilliance, mobbing the passes in their haste to rejoin the Ordeal's horsemen on the Erengaw Plain.

"*They abandon us*!" Only one man need voice this fear for it to become the fear of all. With the passing of the watches they could see the sickness consume the most afflicted among them, stealing their hair, rotting their skin, making crimson broth of their innards. They were *accursed*. They knew as much and they despaired. They had gazed upon the infernal face of Hell itself ... and they would not live for it.

The Slough, they began calling it, for it truly seemed that they decayed, inside and out. The agony was wretched, excruciating, yet a peculiar quiet prevailed over the vast lazaret. They had no food save the Sranc, which they consumed raw. They had no shelter, no blankets, no *physicians*—only their faith and small patches of miserable earth crowded against what seemed the ends of it.

The relatively healthy set about clearing the innumerable Sranc dead: many of the sickest had simply crawled across the tangled masses, making cots of corpses. Sickened caste-nobles organized teams, while sickened Schoolmen hung sorcerous lights of their own. The blind and hale were paired with the sighted. Soon Sranc fairly rained down the scarps, crumpling and cartwheeling.

So they toiled as their brothers fled.

Hoga Hogrim, Believer-King of Ce Tydonn, assumed moral and temporal command of the impromptu host. It was as much a coup as anything else, with the fealty of potential competitors demanded at sword-point. More than a dozen dissenters were murdered (and thrown from the cliffs with the Sranc). Most, however, embraced his makeshift rule, thinking that all would be sorted with the imminent return of their Lord-and-Prophet. The survivors, sickened or otherwise, were already calling what had happened "the Great Scald" by this point. Knowing the way Men rally about a common identity, Hogrim bid his ailing householders to *name* the huddled and prone masses, and so dozens of longbeards trudged the groaning slopes and silent beaches, declaring that they were the *Scalded*.

So was a second Ordeal born that night, a host of those who could scarcely hope to survive the morrow, let alone save it. Black clouds piled in echelon across the northwestern horizon, and the sickest (those coughing and vomiting blood) lay staring in glazed wonder for the way the dark giants swallowed the constellations. The front soon formed a low, roiling ceiling above the mountainous stages of the Urokkas. The rain was not long in following.

The Men shivered and steamed. Some roared and rejoiced, while others bent their heads, too weary to care. Among the sickened on the shoreline, some wept for relief, thinking they might be cleansed, while those losing their skin began howling and shrieking in agony. Raindrops had become acid. Torrential sheets chased the slopes, flooding the ravines and gorges, rolling the dead down, draining black into the heaving sea. Muck and misery ruled the shores. The mouths of the dead were filled as cups.

An eerie quiet ruled the high and low places come the following morning. The Sea scarcely gurgled. Chill morning mists broke about the heights and drained from the ravines, revealing at every stage the crazed proportion of death and destruction. Dead burred the ridges, matted the slopes, their limbs hooked for rigour, their mouths grinning for spite of the living. Crows and gulls feasted, the black feather and the white, their ancient feud forgotten for the largesse. The passes of Oloreg lay empty, inked for the dark of morning shadow. The eyries abandoned, the summits lay barren beneath the sky.

Few among the Scalded were surprised. They had lived, as all civilized

Men had lived, with pestilence their whole lives. The sick were always left behind. That was simply the way.

So they sat in solemn resignation, too aggrieved to be aggrieved by the thought of their plight. They sucked shallow breaths, perpetually braced against the sting. They passed their innards as vomit and offal. They gasped misery. Some bickered, some railed and accused, but most gazed out across the Sea, wondering at all the horizons that lay between them and their wives and children. Those blinded by the Scald smelled and listened, marvelled that air could take on the substance of water, that purity and pollution could be tasted, or that they could *hear* the scarps before them—hear the sound of falling—in the fluted pulse of the surf below. They raised their faces to the eastern warmth, wondered that they could *see* with their skin—that no man could be blind to the sun so long as he could feel.

Some wept.

And to a man they understood their toil was at an end.

Sibawûl Vaka had sat motionless for the entirety of the night and the morning, his skin weeping, his flaxen hair tugged from his scalp strand by strand, drawn like spider webs out over the Sea. When Proyas and his entourage appeared on the shoulders of Oloreg, he turned his head and stared, watched the Exalt-General descend to meet King Hogrim, the self-proclaimed Lord of the Scalded. Without a word of explanation, Sibawûl te Nurwul stood and began stalking the cliff-face, his eyes pinned upon some indeterminate point to the west. His surviving kinsmen joined him, and others joined them, souls clawing free from the torpor of doom. Soon pestilential masses were teetering to their feet, not out of curiosity or alarm or even less duty, but because their brothers so stood, so stumbled ...

Because they too were Scalded.

Sibawûl picked his way down to the carcass-littered beaches, apparently unaware of the growing thousands in his tow. Had the Sea possessed even a fraction of its native violence, his path would have been barred, but it remained miraculously calm, placid enough to see the bloom of cadaverous oils across its surface, a shimmering film of violet and yellow. He waded eastward, mapping oleaginous worlds across the water with his passage, aqueous coastlines curling into bewilderment and oblivion.

And all those able, some twenty-thousand anguished souls, laboured after him.

The tracts of floating dead rose and fell with the rhythm of deep-sleeping children. Water slurped and suckled the vertical stone. The Great Scald had shattered Antareg's seaward faces, laying out piers of ruin. Sibawûl waded between blasted enormities, dwarfed beneath incisors of rock as great as Momemn's towers. Forever staring west, he traced the seaward limit of the mountain's thighs to the mouth of the River Sursa.

All those able followed, a great wallowing column.

He stood motionless for a time at the river mouth, gazing across the slow-twisting rafts of Sranc dead, out to the line of the far shore, *Agongorea* ... the Fields Appalling. More and more of the Scalded climbed the gravel shores behind him, black for scorching, sodden with water that dripped crimson, an assembly both spectral and appalling. Never had the World witnessed a multitude more wretched: souls with hanging skin, weeping burns and ulcerations, naked backsides clotted with excrement and blood. Their hair fell into the wind, creating a haze of black and gold filaments that was drawn out over the Sea.

No less than one hundred souls perished during the ensuing vigil. Not a man among them knew what it was they were doing, only that it was proper—the thing *demanded*. The sun crawled down from its meridian, sank low enough to match the gaze of the wasted Cepaloran Chieftain-Prince. Incredulous, the Scalded watched as the dead that had rolled *out* to Sea began drifting *back*, funnelled into the river mouth even as those upstream continued bumping south. The tides were rising, the learned among them murmured. The tides that flooded the Neleöst with brine had stalled the effluence of the River Sursa, the way they had since time immemorial. The waters became cloudy and viscous with decay.

More and more dead Sranc were rolled from the deeps, clotting and tangling, forming a macabre plate that spanned the whole of the river mouth. Here and there a glimpse of hair shocked the lithe, porpoise tangle. Sibawûl Vaka stepped upon the waterlogged carcasses. He lurched and stumbled like a toddler, but nevertheless began crossing the great and ghastly expanse, kicking loose clouds of midges and flies like so much sand from a river's bottom.

Men wept for watching the dark miracle.

And followed.

CHAPTER SIXTEEN

Momemn

It is no accident, they say, that Men pray to the Gods and the dead both: far better silence than truth. —AJENCIS, *Theophysics*

VI. The Game, as the reenacting of the whole as whole, is cruel to strangers. To lose the Game is to take loss as a lover.
—The Sixth Canto of the *Abenjukala*

Mid-Autumn, 20 New Imperial Year (4132, Year-of-the-Tusk), Momemn

The honour of awakening the Blessed Empress of the Three Seas fell to ancient Ngarau, the Grand Seneschal. His mother, however, dismissed the pouch-faced eunuch, electing to laze in bed with her darling little boy instead. And so he lay in her embrace feigning sleep, his back curled into the gentle furnace of her bosom, covertly watching the pastel colours climbing from the frescoes on the walls, the sheers glowing for the morning sun. It never ceased to astound him, the way his soul would bob and float in her embrace, a thing ethereal, tethered and safe.

She did not think herself a good mother, Kelmomas knew. She did not think herself a good *anything*, for that matter, so long and so chill were the shadows thrown by her past. But the terror of failing her damaged son (for how could he not be damaged, given the horrors he had suffered?) cut her to the quick like no other fear. The boy seized upon these maternal insecurities without fail, sometimes stoking, other times soothing, always exploiting. He would often complain of being hungry or lonely or sad, anything that might provoke her guilt and indulgence.

She was too weak to be a good mother, too distracted. They both knew that.

She could only lavish him with affection afterward ... always afterward.

So regularly did he play the neglected child that it now took effort *not to*, and he had found himself caught on several occasions, needing to escape, yet playing on her guilt anyway, trusting that her duties would force her to abandon him all the same. But sometimes, her fear for her precious son was such that it blotted all other concerns. "*Let nations burn*," she had once told him, her gaze unnerving for sudden ferocity. This was such a morning.

He needed to resume his surveillance of the Narindar, not because he still believed watching the Four-Horned Brother would keep him safe, but because he *needed* to see ... just *what* he did not know.

The happening of what happened, he supposed.

In earlier days he would have simply demanded his freedom, uttered something wicked, something cutting, knowing that her shriek or her slap, when it came, would grant him license to do almost anything, be it flee, further injure, or feast upon the comic profundity of her remorse. Little boys were *supposed* to be pompous and hurtful. Something never failed to balk within her when he played the *perfect* son. This was Mimara's great lesson ere he had finally driven her away: that the children most *flawed* were the children most loved.

But since Thelli had come to him with her threat, an aura of *delicacy* had poisoned everything he now said. He had become loathe to contradict her in the old way, fearing what might happen were his accursed sister to reveal his secrets. It would break Mother no matter what, learning that her beloved son was no different than her husband, that he too possessed the Strength she thought accursed and inhuman.

So now he played along with her spasms, making of them what he could. He lay soaking in her warmth and fussing adoration, dozing in amniotic serenity, the heat of two bodies clasped between the same silken folds. And yet, more and more it seemed he could *feel* the Four-Horned Brother abiding in the nethers below, like a rat scratching at the backside of his thought.

She kissed his ear, whispered that it was morning. She lifted the hand she had clasped, drew it up for a better view. Mothers are prone to inspect their children with the same thoughtless propriety with which they inspect themselves. He at last turned his head toward her, wondered at the paleness of his skin between her brown hands.

"This is how you spend your days," she murmured with faux disapproval, "a Prince-Imperial grubbing in the gardens ..."

Suddenly he noticed the black crescents beneath his nails, the faint lines of ingrained dirt. Why her observation should trouble him he did not know. He regularly smeared himself with soil to convince her of this very thing.

"I have *fun*, Momma."

"You are *indulged* ..." her voice began, only to trail into vapour, the papyrus whisk of the shears in the still-warm Meneanor breeze. She bolted upright, calling out for her body-slaves.

So it was Kelmomas found himself pouting in a steaming bronze tub, listening to his mother expound upon what he decided were the whorish virtues of cleanliness. The water greyed almost immediately for his filth, but he settled as deep into it as he could given the freshness of the air. He groused: the fools had set the tub upon the landing immediately before the unshuttered portico. It was autumn. Mother knelt on a pillow beside him, joking and cajoling. She had dismissed the slaves, searching, he knew, for some dregs of normalcy in the ritual of mother bathing child.

Theliopa appeared just after she wetted his hair, her mazed, lace-finned gowns zipping as much as swishing. She stood on the threshold, an explosion of grey and violet fabric, her hair a kinked halo of flax, haphazardly pinned with gaudy broaches. Her skull, the boy thought, seemed particularly indiscreet today.

If she attached any significance to his presence, she betrayed no sign whatsoever.

"General Iskaul," the sallow girl said. "He-he has arrived, Mother."

Mother was already standing, drying her hands. "Good," she replied, her voice and manner transformed. "Thelli will finish bathing you while I prepare," she said in reply to his questioning eyes.

"Nooo!" he began to protest, but his mother was already barging past his sister, calling for her slaves as she hastened to her wardrobe.

He sat rigid and dripping, gazing at his approaching sister through wisps of steam.

"Iskaul has come-come with the Twenty-ninth from Galeoth," Theliopa explained kneeling on Mother's pillow. She was forced to crush her gown against the copper-gleaming tub, such was its hooped girth, but despite the obvious amount of effort she had invested in its manufacture, she seemed to care not at all.

He could only glare at her.

Not here, the secret voice warned. *Anywhere but here.*

She has to die sometime!

"You have been plotting my murder," his pale sister said while taking inventory of the soaps and scents arrayed on the floor beside her. "You-you can scarcely ponder-ponder anything else."

"Why would you assu–?" he began protesting, only to have more water dumped over his head.

"I care-care not at all," she continued, pouring a bowl of orange-scented soap powder across his scalp, "what you think or what-what you do."

She began kneading it into a lather. Her fingers were neither cruel nor soothing–simply efficient.

"I forgot ..." he replied, resenting every nod of his head. "You don't care about anything."

She worked her way from his forehead, back along his crown, her fingernails nipping his scalp.

"I have many-many cares," she said. "But they are light, like Father's. They leave no tracks in the snow."

She bundled the hair about the back of his neck, squeezed, then began working her way forward, this time along the sides of his head, moving toward his temples.

"Inrilatas could make you cry," Kelmomas recalled.

Her fingers paused. A spasm of some kind plucked at the slack muscles of her face.

"I'm surprised you remember."

She ceased ministering to his hair, turned back to Mother's accoutrements.

"I remember."

She raised and wetted a small, rose-coloured sponge, then, using the soap congealed across his scalp, she began washing his face with gentle, even tender strokes.

"Inrilatas was-was the strongest of all of us," she said upon a spastic blink. "The most-most cruel."

"Stronger than me?"

"Far stronger."

Lying bitch!

"How so?"

"He saw too deeply."

"Too deeply," the boy repeated. "What kind of answer is that?"

Theliopa shrugged. "The more you know a soul-soul, the less of a soul-soul it becomes. For Inrilatas, we-we were little more-more than beetles, scuttling around and about-about, blind-blind. So long as we remain blind to those blindnesses, our souls and our worlds remain whole-whole. As soon as we see-see them, we see that we are nothing more-more than beetles."

Kelmomas looked at her uncomprehendingly. "The more you know a thing," he said, frowning, "the more *real* it becomes."

"Only if it was real to begin with."

"Pfah," he sneered.

"And yet you do the very thing he did."

"Which is?"

"Make-make *toys* of the souls about you."

The boy caught his breath, such was the force of his insight.

"So that was what Inrilatas did? Made you his toy?"

"Even now-now," she said on her damned stammer, "this is what you-you attempt to do."

"So I'm a beetle too!"

She paused to draw the sponge across his chin. The water was becoming tepid.

"A beetle that eats beetles."

He mulled these words while she laboured to cleanse his throat and neck, particularly about the divot between his collarbones. It struck him as an epic and beautiful thing, that brother and sister could discuss the grounds that would see one murder the other ... like a tale from the Chronicle of the Tusk.

"Why did he call you *Sranc*?" he asked without warning.

Another facial seizure.

Kelmomas smirked when she said nothing. There was only one beetle here.

"No tracks in the snow, eh?"

"Because I was-was always so skinny."

She lies ... the voice said.

Yes, brother, I know ...

The young Prince-Imperial pressed aside her wrist to peer at her. It seemed a miracle to be so *close* to a face so *hated*, to see the spatter of freckles, the pink rim of her lids, the cant of her teeth. All this time he had assumed that she had been found, only to discover that she had been *made*, that his brother had bent her—*broken* her. It seemed he could remember it so much more clearly now ...

Her weeping.

"How many times?" he asked her.

A lethargic blink. "Until Father locked him up."

A deadness had crept into her voice.

"And Mother?"

"What of Mother?"

"Did she ever find out?"

The chirp of dripping water.

"She overheard him once-once. She was-was furious ..."

She raised the sponge, but he recoiled in annoyance.

"She-she was the only one-one who never-never feared Inrilatas," Theliopa said.

He could see it all so clearly now.

"She never found out," Kelmomas said.

Her head rocked as if at a silent hiccough, only three times in rapid succession.

"Inrilatas ..." he continued, watching the name bleach her expression.

"What-what?"

"Did he *seduce* you?" He grinned. He had seen what the grown do when their blood rose. "Or did he *rape*?"

Now she was truly blank.

"We are Dûnyain," she murmured.

The young Prince-Imperial chortled, shivered for the glamour of elation. He leaned forward, placed his wet cheek against her sunken one, whispered in her ear in the same grunting manner he knew his older brother had, not so many years ago ...

"*Sranky ...*"

She smelled like sour milk.

"*Sranky ...*"

Suddenly he was sputtering soap and water, rubbing eyes that burned so fiercely he could scarcely see Theliopa fleeing, just shadows and hooped shimmering. He made no attempt to call her back ...

She had left plenty of tracks in the snow.

Kelmomas dunked his head in the embalming warmth, swatted the soap from his face and hair. He had almost certainly doomed himself, he knew, but he whooped in silent triumph all the same.

Terror had always been his soul's laggard, where his will was most weak, his heart most strong.

And it was no small feat making an Anasûrimbor cry.

Issiral was not in his chamber.

His jubilation had been short-lived. Seized by a monstrous panic, he had leapt from the tub and dressed without so much as towelling down, stealing sodden and dripping into the arterial depths of the shadow palace. Never, it seemed, had he suffered such paroxysms of dread—such vicious recriminations!

Fool! You've killed us! Killed us!

You played too! You shared in the fun!

But finding the Narindar's chamber *empty* had fairly stopped his small heart. For a long while he simply lay prone at the iron grilled vent, sapped of all strength, gouged of all thought, just peering at the shadowy corner where the Narindar *should be* ... breathing. For those first moments, the thought of the Grinning God moving in the blackness, acting outside his observation, simply exceeded his grasp.

What were the chances? Was it simply *happenstance* that he would find the Narindar missing immediately *after* goading Thelli—the woman who clasped his doom in her long-fingered hands? Did the man merely roam the halls on another of his inexplicable errands? Or ... or had all this *already happened?*

And yet again it defeated him, how he could be freer than free, and yet damned to repeat the memories of the Blasted God! Solving was *doing*, pulling the threads that unravelled the whole—driving skewers into tear ducts! But his every thought, his soul's merest movement, *had already happened*, which meant he had never solved anything! Ever! Which meant ...

He gagged for the impossibility. The hopelessness of the riddle became the hopelessness of his straits.

He wept for a time. Anyone hidden in Issiral's chamber would have heard no more than a faraway keening punctuated by sniffles, delicate and near.

He lay like a sack.

How? his twin wailed. *How could you be such an idiot?*

It was her *fault!*

There has to be somethi—

There's nothing! Don't you get it?

The Prince of Hate! Ajokli *hunts us!*

A moment of roiling horror.

Then let him find us! Kelmomas resolved with rekindled savagery.

And he was racing through the shadow palace once again, his face burning, his tunic slick as flayed skin. A fury unlike any he had ever known animated him, sent his limbs slapping into the darkness. Images of wild violence exploded beneath his soul's eye.

This was his House ...

This was his *House*!

He would sooner die than cower within it.

He flew through the narrow slots, high wells, and crooked tunnels, scrambling like a monkey from the Apparatory back to the ingrown summit of the Upper Palace. He was nearly upon his bedchamber before the manic inkling that drove him faded into sober insight. He need only ask himself *where* a young Prince-Imperial *would* be found dead to begin guessing where his murder was going to take place. And in so many lays and histories, or so it seemed, the babes of Kings and Emperors were found strangled in their *beds*.

And like an axe swung, this realization struck him in two. The bull of outrage within him continued lunging forward, but the little boy had already begun snivelling and shrinking back in renewed terror. The throat of the tunnel closed as he neared, forcing him to his hands and knees. His passage forward, which had already possessed the ethereal character of dreams, became nightmarish, an ordeal of palms. He could see the luminous print of the bronze grill across the brickwork ahead of him, and it seemed both strange and appropriate that his room be both empty and bright. His throat and chest burned. Fear compelled him to crawl forward on his belly. He began mumbling voiceless prayers to no God in particular as he shimmed forward ...

Please, his twin whispered.

Please ...

Life rarely affords us the luxury of *spying* on our terrors. Typically they come upon us unawares, bat us about bewildered before leaving us wrecked or intact according to our doom. His breath a convulsive knife held fast in his breast, Anasûrimbor Kelmomas crept to the shining grill ... peered around its edge the way a less divine child might peek above their covers. So certain was he that he *would* see the Narindar in his room that he had become equally certain that *he would not*, that this entire misadventure would simply show him up for the foolish child he was. All the familiar features swivelled into soundless view, the marmoreal walls, white with shadowy veins of blue, the pinkish marble of the trim and corbelling, the sumptuous bed, the tigers prancing across the crimson carpet, the scattered furnishings, the unshuttered balcony ...

No.

The Prince-Imperial gaped breathless, utterly insensate for horror ...

His eyes rolled for impossibility. *Issiral stood near the heart of his room*, as motionless as always, atavistic for his near nakedness, peering through the broad threshold into the antechamber where the door lay obscured. His earlobes seemed drops of blood, they were so red. The very World shuddered, rumbled like distant thunder.

No-no-no-no! his twin gibbered.

The Four-Horned Brother. The Grinning God. The Prince of Hate.

Ajokli stood in his room, awaiting his return ...

Except that he now watched Him.

Confusion crimped his horror.

All he need do was ... was ... slink away ... *never* return to his room ...

Or better yet, alert the Pillarians or the Inchausti, tell them the Narindar had invaded his chambers without permission, insinuate ... insinuate ...

But how could it be so easy? What of the Unerring Grace?

How could a *child* dispose of an *invading* God?

No. This was a *trick* of some kind ...

It had to be!

But ... but ...

He heard the latch of his door clink, the whistle of the bottommost hinge as the portal swung open. The sound fairly plucked his heart from his chest whole.

The Narindar continued staring as before, his eyes happening upon the newcomer the way his hand had happened upon the rolling apple. The boy need only hear the whisk of battling lace to know who had arrived.

Theliopa.

She appeared silk-luminous beneath the threshold, a scintillant vision compared to the watching assassin. She regarded him without the least fear, and would have owned the space had not the man buzzed with such monstrous horror. Save the archipelago of sodden fabric across her waist, she betrayed no sign of her weeping flight a mere watch prior. She merely gazed in open curiosity ...

And seemed so perilously *human* for it.

The young Prince-Imperial gazed transfixed.

"Am I supposed to know-know that you await me?" she asked, her tone familiar.

"Yes," the Narindar replied.

His voice was at once mundane and preternatural ... like Father's.

"So you-you will trust your skills against an Anasûrimbor?"

The near-naked man shook his head. "There is no skill in what I do."

A pause, brief but more than interval enough. The boy saw Theliopa's point of focus dull and sharpen as she slipped in and out of the Probability Trance.

"Because there is no skill in anything," she said.

The blue light of the outdoors limned his profile, made his sandstone immobility even more impervious.

"And my death?" Thelli asked.

"Even now I see it."

The gesture he made was curious, reminiscent of ancient Shigeki engravings, almost as though he *placed* the space he indicated.

His sister hitched back her skirts, glanced to her feet—to where the assassin pointed. The boy's heart hammered. *Thelli!*

"So I am already dead?"

Move!

"What else would you be?"

Move, Thelli! Move!

"And you-you? Who are you?"

"Someone who was there when it happened."

Afterward, the boy would decide that it had started heartbeats before, while they talked, like a bubble of some kind *growing* ... a shudder riding the knife's edge of an *explosion*.

A primordial hammer struck all points *underneath* at once. The boy bucked, curled like a tossed serpent. All was roaring motion. Issiral crouched into the quake's bosom, curtains of masonry crashing about him. Theliopa stumbled, looked up in pallid alarm, then vanished in slumping shadows of stone brick debris.

Kelmomas threw his arms about his head, heard the pop of great joists cracking.

Then the ground was still.

He kept his face buried until the roar vanished into hiss and clatter.

All was dun obscurity when he finally dared peer—he could see only that the grill and a section of the wall that had concealed it had collapsed. He coughed and waved his hands, realized that he lay upon the edge of a collapse that had carried his bed to the floor below. The Narindar was nowhere to be seen, even though the portion of floor where he had stood remained intact. He could hear a man shouting, over and over, a paean of some kind. He could hear deeper, more distant calls, the throats of those attempting to restore order.

A woman's hitching cry filtered from somewhere across the Sacral Enclosure.

Anasûrimbor Kelmomas clambered down the debris to the strewn floor of his room. He turned and stared at the broken remains of his elder sister. She lay face forward where her head had recoiled, one lifeless arm cast out, propped as though in drunken gesture, her hair a scatter of wiry flaxen, chalked white and slicked black. Kelmomas approached, blinking new tears from his eyes with every step. He peered breathless, saw no sign of the

Worshipper he had glimpsed in the eyes of the others. How much more a doll she seemed dead. A sob kicked through him on his final step, and he leaned to scoop a slate brick, which he hoisted high upon a child's grip, then cast down upon her head. The blood gratified him.

He could tell by looking that she was still hot to the touch.

"She's deeead!" he wailed on the open wind. "Thelli's dead, Momma! Momma!"

He cradled his sister's ruined head on his lap, gazed at the collapsed wineskin of her face. He ducked his chin and indulged a gloating smile.

Do you believe? his twin whispered.

Oh, I believe.

The Four-Horned Brother was his *friend.*

"*Mommaaaaa!*"

The Mbimayu Schoolman thought the day ill-omened since awakening. Nightmares had taxed what seemed every watch of the night, brawling dreams, the kind that kick away blankets—dreams he should have remembered, but had shrunken instantly into fuzzy, inexplicable horror. He even retrieved his Kizzi Bones in an attempt to divine them, so cramped and irksome was the shadow they cast across his waking. But of course the Whore had already thrown them Her way: no sooner had he found the fetishes than a grim Kianene Grandee, Saranjehoi, arrived with Fanayal's invitation to break fast with him and his Concubine.

Malowebi's subsequent (and quite indecorous) haste was simply a reflection of how profoundly the mood of the Bandit Padirajah had soured over the weeks since Meppa had very nearly died. Time was the enemy, and Fanayal ab Kascamandri knew it. The endless stream of ships entering and leaving the Imperial Capital were plainly visible—the Imperials had even begun hosting feasts on the walls as a goad! The Nansur countryside, meanwhile, had become increasingly hostile—scarcely a day passed without word of another foraging band lost to ambush. Where they had rode the miles surrounding Momemn solitary and shirtless in the early days of the siege, the Fanim now moved only in numbers and according to necessity. And it was this more than anything that *galled* their legendary Padirajah (unto near-madness, thanks to the Yatwerian witch), the fact that the idolaters refused to acknowledge their defeat, that the *Zaudunyani*, for all their wickedness, consistently displayed a heroism that made his desert-warriors marvel and fear. The Fanim spoke of it about their fires, the mad resolve of their foe, the impossibility of subduing souls that *welcomed* death and degradation.

"What kind of land is this," Malowebi once overheard a chipped, old Carathay chieftain complain, "where women throw themselves as shields for men? Where ten throats are counted as a bargain for one!"

The measure of morale, Memgowa had famously written, lay in the proportion of ends to souls. The more the ends diverged and multiplied among the ranks, the less an army could remain an army. The desert horsemen had arrived here possessing a single goal—to lop the head from the Imperial Dragon. But as the passage of the days gnawed on their numbers, so their ends had gradually multiplied. The thought of *alternatives* lie on all of their faces now—as surely as it did on the Malowebi's own. The premonition of doom had taken root in *every* heart—none more than that of their Padirajah. And as abused menials were want to beat their wives and children, so Fanayal had begun to evidence his potency in acts of capricious will. *Corpses* now hung over most all the main avenues of the encampment—Fanim executed for trifles worth only the lash weeks previous.

Desperation glares in all Men, but it burns as a beacon when it takes a King for tinder.

A votive to the dread Mother of Birth.

Curse Likaro! Curse him!

The *Harem*, the desert warriors now called their Padirajah's pavilion, and to Malowebi and his alchemist's nose, it reeked of one, the air close—even sodden—with too many exhalations, too much sweat and seed. Psatma Nannaferi was in attendance, of course: Royal Concubines were confined by Fanim law and Kianene custom. She sat both too near and too distant, as always, wearing far too much and nowhere near enough—as always. Her mood, which ordinarily swung between stony and labile, was every bit as exultant as his was troubled. For the first time she wore her voluminous hair bound back, lending a severe air to her otherwise pouting fertility.

The Mbimayu Schoolman did his best not to be snared by her vast black eyes.

He appreciated the fare—fowl, cheese, bread, and *pepper*, that great gift of Nilnamesh—but as he had feared, the honour of breakfast with the Padirajah quickly degenerated into the honour of being bullied and berated yet again. Fanayal had recently abandoned any pretence of diplomacy, resorting instead to "more direct tactics," as he generously referred to his tantrums. The Zeumi Emmisary studiously examined the cracked shell of bread on his plate before him while Fanayal leaned over him, ringed index finger stabbing heavenward, demanding High Holy Zeum send him *ships* no less!

Psatma Nannaferi watched the two Men as she always watched, sitting with the lazy indiscretion of whores and maidens, those who know either too much or too little to care. A different brand of jubilation animated her look, one unencumbered by sneering.

All the World, it seemed, was a Gift this day.

"*Who*? Who does the Great Satakhan fear?" Fanayal was shouting.

Malowebi continued inspecting his bread. The brighter Fanayal's dread, the more he had begun answering his own questions—to the point of preempting his interlocutors altogether.

"The *Aspect-Emperor*!"

He spoke as a man perpetually wounded by the keen edge of his own reason.

The Zeumi Emissary had suffered several such "negotiations" now, where he need only await the Padirajah to hear his reply.

"And here we stand—*here*! Before the gates of his Capital! All we need are *ships*, man! Ships! And the Satakhan, nay, mighty Zeum itself, *never need fear again*!"

"Even if I *could* secure such a thing," Malowebi finally cried in retort, "it would take months fo—"

The ground became as planks on water.

Fanayal toppled into his lap even as he tipped backward—together they crashed into a scrambling heap.

All was rocking madness, and yet Psatma Nannaferi somehow *stood*. "*Yessss*!" she cried across the nape of the thunder. "*Your children* hear *you*, *Mother*!"

The pavilion swayed on a groaning arc. The menagerie of plundered furnishings careened and wagged like Shakers. Delicate things chirped for breaking.

The Yatwerian witch howled with libidinal laughter. "Yes! *Yessss*!"

Then it was over, replaced with ground eerie for being inert.

The Padirajah wasted no courtesy extricating himself from the Zeumi sorcerer. A racket chorus swelled outside—hundreds of Men calling out, shouting ...

Fanayal was on his feet and leaping through the flaps of the Harem before Malowebi had found so much as his hands and knees. The Emissary was several heartbeats collecting himself, such was the tangle of his Erzû gowns. He glimpsed Nannaferi pirouetting into the shambles of the pavilion interior ...

"The sights!" she called out to him from the wrecked gloom. "The sights you shall *seeeeeee!*"

He fled her chortling ecstasy, barged blinking and squinting into direct sunlight. A baffled assembly of Fanim warriors clotted the avenue.

"Silence!" Fanayal was crying, pushing men aside and turning his ear to the northern hillcrests. He threw a hand out. "*Silence!*" He turned to the Kianene nearest him, a Grandee named Omirji.

"Do you hear that?"

He glanced toward Malowebi, then raked his manic gaze across the others.

"What are they shouting? What—?"

Creation itself seemed to catch its breath for listening. Malowebi could hear the faraway chorus, but his ears still rang for the quaking—not to mention the madness of the Cultic witch.

"The walls ..." a nameless young warrior gasped, his frown of concentration blooming into innocent wonder. "They say *the walls have fallen!*"

Malowebi watched the long-suffering son of Kascamandri comprehend these words, saw his face crack, wrung by passions greater than most any soul could bear ...

Saw the soundless scream ...

"*The God!*" he croaked upon a shudder. "*The Solitary God!*"

And it was too naked, it seemed, too wet with humanity, to be anything but holy.

The whoops and cheers from the hillcrest filled the reverent hollow. Scimitars flashed in the morning glare.

"*To arms!*" the Padirajah bellowed with sudden savagery. "*To arms! We become immortal this day!*"

And all the World fell to shouts and murderous rushing.

His grin fierce, Fanayal turned to seize Malowebi's shoulder, crying,

"Keep your accursed ships, blasphemer!" before vanishing into the Harem to grab his arms and armour.

The Blessed Empress of the Three Seas had dispensed with ceremony and bid General Iskaul to follow her out behind the Mantle, where they might assay the Capital he was charged to defend. By appearance, he was one of those grand Norsirai, his frame heroic, his hair long and greying blond, his jaw as thick as his accent. But his discourse belonged more to a scholar than a Galeoth warrior-thane: apparently Iskaul was famed in the Imperial Army both for his meticulous planning and his ability to keep tallies, to always *know* what resources he had at his disposition. He began with a barrage of questions.

With the assistance of Phinersa and Saxillas, she was able to bear the brunt of his interrogation. But absent Theliopa, it took fairly every soul present to provide even partial answers. More than a few, such as the number of clotheslines in the city (for making horse snares, as it turned out), had elicited disbelieving laughter. The atmosphere was one of mirth and mutual respect when she finally cried out, "How is it my husband has never brought you here?"

"Because I follow the Field, my Glory," the man had said, "and the Field has come *here*."

The eloquence of the observation had drawn her gaze out over the hazy intricacies of Momemn. And she had felt that tickle, the way she so often did, of all the heights that lay between her and her people–

The ground itself flapped like a blanket, again and again. Existence seized and shuddered.

She alone did not fall.

The Postern Terrace pitched like a ship's deck in a tempest, only without the cushion of water.

She stood ... while the World about her fell shaking.

The ground bucked, swatted the soles of her sandals, and yet she stood as if bound to some unseen rigging. For all his poise, General Iskaul was pitched like a toddler to his rump. Phinersa fell to his knees, then to his face for throwing out the arm he no longer possessed. Her Exalt-Captain, Saxillas, made as though to steady her, but simply floated past her toppling instead ...

Beyond, she saw whole swathes of her city slump into the smoke of their implosion; distant edifices, brute faces she knew so well—like the Tower of Ziek—slouched into haze and debris, disintegrating across slopes, exploding in streets. Afterward, she would scarcely believe that so much could be *seen*, that a disaster so monumental could be laid out for the count of a single mortal. She even saw the most catastrophic collapse of all, the one that betokened the far greater calamity to come ...

The monstrous, square shoulders of the Maumurine Gate crashing into plumes ...

The roaring trailed, and there was a lull in the shouting. The accursed throb of the Fanim drums had vanished. For an instant, the tinkle and clatter of belated debris was all that could be heard. She thought it the wind at first, so diffuse was the howl when it began. But it swelled in resonance, rose into something at once raw and human and horrific ...

Her beloved city ... Momemn ...

Momemn was screaming.

"We must evacuate the palace," Saxillas urged at her side. "My Glory!"

She tossed him a vacant glance. It was a marvel that he could speak with the same ragged calm as before.

"I survived a quaking like this as a child," he pressed. "It came as *waves*, my Glory. We must get you someplace safe, lest the very Andiamine Heights fall!"

She turned blinking, not so much to him as to her home, which loomed impossibly intact against the bright day, marred by nothing more than cracks and missing marble casements. She glanced across the Terrace, at the members of her household and her entourage, collecting themselves from the tilted ground. General Iskaul watched her intently. Phinersa was on one knee, the clipped sleeve of his tunic hanging loose, blood streaming from his nose. She looked back to her Exalt-Captain.

"My Glory ... Please!"

The Gods, she realized numbly ... The *Hundred* had done this!

"Muster every man you can, Saxillas."

The Gods hunted her family.

"We must get you to the Scuari Campus fir—"

"If you care at all about my safety," she snapped, "*you will muster every man you can!*"

She raised a finger to the gouged view beyond the Postern Terrace. Dust fogged the whole of it, as if the city were a vast plate of shaken sand. The great domes of Xothei still stood in the nearer distance, as did a large number of other structures, some solitary, others clumped together, all surrounded by tracts of tossed ruin. She looked back to her peering Exalt-Captain, saw the caste-noble blanch for horror as he realized.

"The blasted *walls* ..." General Iskaul muttered from her side. Even as he peered, he scooped his hair and bound it into a warknot.

"Our foe will soon be upon us!" the Blessed Empress yelled across the canted verandah. "We have rehearsed this—we all know our stations! Do what it is you must do! Be ruthless. Be cunning. And above all, be *brave*! Burn as a lantern for your Most Holy Aspect-Emperor! Be a beacon unto those who waver!"

Her voice hung but a heartbeat upon the lamentations welling from below. Ruin, ruin, and more ruin.

Kel ...

The towering Agmundrman fell to his knees. "My Glory ..."

"The Field is now yours, General," she said. She looked to the battery of eyes upon her, some round with incredulity and horror, others already gathering the hatred they would need. "*Kill the jackals!*"

The Men broke into a cheer that was both fierce and ragged, but someone began crying, "Look! *Looook!*" in a tone too urgent to be denied. And at the behest of someone she could not see, all eyes turned to the autumn-arid southern hills, some holding out hands to block the glare of the sun climbing high above the Meneanor. The first dark clots of horsemen had begun clotting across the rim ...

Hundreds merely, soon to become thousands.

"Iskaul," she said tightly.

"*Move!*" the General bellowed in a voice trained to crack the din of any battle.

Every soldier present made for the gloomy mouth of the Imperial Audience Hall, clearing a berth for Iskaul, who trotted to the lead. The other Apparati followed suit, a migration of shining hauberks and official gowns that left only some twelve slaves kneeling a double rank on the floor before her, their foreheads to the ceramic tile. Where was Thelli?

She stood over them, waiting for the Terrace to clear. The rising sun threw her shadow across the backs of four slaves, three clothed, one bare.

Then she let the second quake loose within her. She turned to her city, her eyes horrified rims, doubled over the sob that stomped her gut. Momemn! The brisk, Meneanorean wind had cleared the dust roiling about the black-basalt heights of Xothei and had exposed the smashed carapaces of the lesser temples surrounding. Thelli? What delayed her so? Gusts rolled back the veil from the farther tracts of destruction, revealing fins and heaps of ruin inked in morning shadow, landscapes as bewildered as the racket of battle—and as mad, given the senseless welter of buildings spared. Momemn!

And now the enemy congealed on the south, a race of evil crows.

Her mouth hung open on vomit that would not come. The wailing of distant thousands hung, eerie and impossible, feminine in pitch, resonating from the autumnal ribs of Heaven. Tens of thousands calling out, wailing.

Momemn! The Imperial Home! Stronghold of the Anasûrimbor!

Now a choir of lamentation. A smashed necropolis.

A mass grave.

Inner thunder batted her ears. She hissed spit between clenched teeth. There was no doubting anymore. Pretending was no longer possible. *Earthquakes were the province of the Hundred.* Everyone knew as much!

She was being punished ... It was no conceit to think this. Not anymore.

The Gods did this. The Gods hunted her and her children. *Hunted.*

The Blessed Empress fled after her ministers, crying out for her beloved.

"*It is a Sign!*" Fanayal roared upon entering his pavilion. "A *Miracle!*"

The Padirajah's own Grandees drew up at the threshold of the Harem, for his tone told them he spoke to *her*. Malowebi nevertheless plunged after the ranting man. Again the gloom. Again the yawing musk, the reek of sheets earthen for the debris of coupling.

Psatma Nannaferi, who sat upon her settee, regarded him without interest or surprise, then turned back to her captive captor.

"*Something* has been written," she scoffed, "just not for you!"

"Emissary?" Fanayal asked, his tone as lethally blank as his expression.

"I-I," Malowebi stammered in response, "f-forgot my, ah ..." He blinked and swallowed. "My bread."

"Tell him, blasphemer!" the Yatwerian witch cried on a chortle. "Tell him, one damned soul to another!"

Malowebi knew nothing of what happened here, save that he was bound to it.

"I ... ah ..."

But Fanayal had lain his murderous glare upon the woman. "Not this! You will not take *this*!"

She leaned forward one arm upon her knee, and spat upon his plundered carpets. "A finger cannot steal from a hand. I stand *too close* to the Mother to take what she gives."

The Padirajah wiped a hand across his face, blinked twice rapidly. "I know what I know," he grated, moving to heave his chain coat and its rack from the jumble of luxurious wrack strewn throughout the gloom. "I know what needs be done!"

"You know nothing!" Psatma Nannaferi cawed. "And you *feel* it as an abscess in your heart!"

"Silence, madwoman!"

"Tell him!" she implored the immobilized Mbimayu Schoolman. "Tell him what he knows!"

"Silence! Silence!"

Psatma Nannaferi fairly shrieked for laughter, an abomination of nubile allure and ancient rot.

"Tell him *that the Mother did this*! That his miracle is the work of an idolized Demon!"

"Fane names your ki–!"

"Fane?" the woman cried, her incredulity so thoughtless, so *complete*, that feminine timbre simply blotted all other sound. "Fane is a fraud, what happens when philosophers fall to worshipping their fevers!"

Fanayal loomed over her, his face riven, his moustaches hanging about visible teeth, his warrior's hand raised. "*The Sol-Solitary God*!" he roared. "*H-h-he wrought this*!"

"The Saw-Saw-Solitary God!" she mocked, her laughter scathing. "He-he-he!"

"I will strike you!"

"Then *strike*!" she cried, her voice raking a pitch that pimpled the Emissary's skin, rumbled in his ears. "Strike *and hear me sing*! Let *all* your kinsmen know it was a *God of the Tusk* that lowed the walls of Momemn! The *God of idolaters*!" She was up and pacing now, possessed of a sparking fury, a visceral disgust of all the obscenities she had witnessed and endured. "What is it, again? What is the name you accursed wretches call Her? 'Bulbous'? You call her *Bulbous*! Outrage! You, besmirched and as *polluted* as you are, a raper of wives and children! A murderous thief! Poisoned by the ambition of hate! You? You presume to call our Mother a Demon? An *Unclean* Spirit?"

Her eyes round for outrage, she threw out her hands to all the overturned and wrecked plunder. A growl seemed to crackle through the earth beneath their feet.

"*She! Shall! Eat! You!*"

Fanayal held his palms out in warding, for her fury was plainly no longer a thing of this World.

"*Lies!*" he cried against this bitter knowing. "*This is mine! Mine!*"

Psatma Nannaferi cawed in another gale of infernal laughter. "*Your* miracle?" she howled and raved. "You think the Mother—Bulbous!—would wrack *her own earth* for the likes of you and your misbegotten race! Hunted in this life, damned in the next!"

The ancient damsel stamped her foot and spat once again.

"You are as insignificant as you are damned! Kindling for a far, far greater fire!"

"Nooo!" the Padirajah cried. "I! Am! Destined!"

"Yessss!" she crowed and stamped. "Destined to play the fool!"

"*Son of Kascamandri!*" Malowebi boomed, seeing Fanayal seize the pommel of his scimitar. The Padirajah stood frozen in an apish hunch, wheezing through a grimace, his blade half drawn from its scabbard.

"She goads you for a *reason*," Malowebi said on a measured breath.

"Bah!" Psatma Nannaferi barked with a contemptuous sneer. "We are already dead."

Words thrown like palace trash to beggars.

Both Men froze upon a bolt of premonition, so horrifying was her tone. She had uttered what she said as though it *no longer mattered* ...

Because they were already dead?

Malowebi spared one heartbeat to savage that treacherous wretch, Likaro. Then he swallowed and carefully asked, "What do you mean?"

The Yatwerian witch regarded him with a serene expression and glistening eyes. "You will *marvel* at your blindness, Zeum," she said. "How you will rail and regret."

The Mbimayu Schoolman felt it then, the Mother's *pity*, the love for a gentle soul that had wandered violently astray. And he saw how all this time what he had taken as *evil* (even if he had never dared think as much) had only been Her dread fury ... and the terror that was her Retribution.

And then Malowebi suddenly *sensed it* ... the true Evil.

It stepped into their presence from *nowhere* ... the stain of a soul damned by its own hand, the Mark of a sorcerer ...

One more powerful, more *damned*, than any he had sensed before.

"She's right!" the Mbimayu Schoolman cried out to his tormented host. "My Lord! Your Chorae! Qui–!"

A word was spoken from inside his ear canals ...

And the back quarter of the pavilion—where Malowebi could feel the Chorae in its chest—exploded. Plunder blew outward as trash. The whump knocked both Fanayal and Nannaferi to their knees—the woman rolled in paroxysms of joyous laughter. The pavilion wagged and clattered. The presence continued keening its impossible song, concealed from mundane eyes.

Malowebi thoughtlessly seized the iron cup fetish in his Erzû gown. Cold terror clawed his innards.

"*Fanayal!*" he cried out. "Run to me!"

Then his thoughts convolved and he was chanting and *thinking against* his chanting, the sacred-and-accursed Song of Iswa. He saw the Padirajah dash toward him, only to trip as Nannaferi scissored her legs across his line of flight. He fell hard across orchards stitched gold against crimson. Malowebi was too well-trained to hesitate: the Muzzû Chalice fell as a luminous bastion about him, a spectral Analogy of the fetish clenched in his left hand ...

For he had guessed *who* had come upon them!

Nannaferi had leapt to her feet and began kicking the prone Padirajah's head, screeching, "*Pig*! *Pig*!" even as the sorcerous voice began tearing the pavilion on an arc, slow at first, but spinning like a chariot-wheel within heartbeats, until they stood within a whirlwind swinging with debris—a shield against Chorae, Malowebi dimly realized. The sky keened. The felt-panelled ceiling whipped into the cyclone, and daylight flooded the crazed tableaux, spattered it with darting shadows ...

And Malowebi finally saw *him* ...

The Holy Aspect-Emperor of the Three Seas.

His Mark wrenched, sickened. The nimil links of his hauberk seethed white and silver in the chaotic light. Otherwise his appearance bore the signs of arduous travel, the tangled mane of gold, the untended beard, the mudded boots and soil-blackened fingers. He wore a sable cloak that lashed and flapped from his arms, his shoulders. And from his war-girdle hung the famed Decapitants, miens like floating nightmares swinging about his left thigh.

Showing no concern for Malowebi, Anasûrimbor Kellhus strode toward the Padirajah and the Mother-Supreme, a vision out of the most severe of the Sagas, his eyes reflecting wind-scoured ice. And as they said, *haloes* framed his head and hands, the ghosts of golden plates ... *markless*.

The Mbimayu Schoolman stood, thoughts and innards roiling.

Curse Likaro!

The Aspect-Emperor swatted Psatma Nannaferi to the ground, hoisted the ailing Padirajah by his throat—held him as if he were no more than a child!

The two old foes regarded each other thus, seeming to fall forward for the sheets of detritus whipping behind. The air howled, a sound like sheets tearing, or wildcats screaming. Smaller gyres of dust had nested within the greater, transforming what had been the Harem into a dun bowl, one kicked into clouds by the phantom shell of the Muzzû Chalice. Fanayal lolled semi-conscious in the fluttering sunlight.

The Aspect-Emperor peered at him, as though willing the man to recognize who had conquered him.

Such a breathtaking demonstration of power! To stand in the heart of his enemy's host and dictate life and death with impunity ...

The Padirajah became conscious on a seizure, an unmanly paroxysm of terror.

"*Who conceived this*!" the Aspect-Emperor thundered.

Malowebi saw the Padirajah move his lips—

Then drop like rope to the earth. Malowebi swayed for the absolute finality of it, caught himself on a step. Fanayal ab Kascamandri was dead ...

Dead!

The Holy Aspect-Emperor of the Three Seas had turned to the laughing

Mother-Supreme, who lay limbs lolling upon the embroidered earth. He yanked her to feet, spared her the indignity he had extended Fanayal.

She stood uncowed, cackled in the shadow of his looming, wind-whipped aspect.

"Mother!" she cried to the skies over his shoulder. The gale tore her costume like dogs growling on towels. "Prepare for me my place! For I come as one who *gives*—gives without memory! One who dies for tending what is *Yours*!"

"My sister," Anasûrimbor Kellhus said, "can no longer save you."

"And yet you have come!" she cried in exaltation. "Come to collect your doom!"

"The Hundred are blind to the No-God. None more than the Mother of Birth."

"Then *why*," she shrieked laughing, "do I remember *this*? The White-Luck will *eat you* ere this day is dead!"

The Holy Aspect-Emperor of the Three Seas betrayed nothing more than wind-lashed curiosity.

"You can be Everywhere and still be blind," he said. "You can be Eternal and remember nothing."

"So says the loosed Demon! So says *filth* and *horror* made manifest! Abyssal hunger!"

"Even the Infinite can be surprised."

The Anasûrimbor seized her and spoke in a single motion, his right hand clamped about her forehead, his voice cracking Reality to the joist. Brilliance consumed the Yatwerian witch. Malowebi raised a hand to shield his eyes, but too late, and so he stood blinking as the tall shadow that was the Aspect-Emperor turned from the whipping mayhem to confront *him*.

One of the Decapitants upon his thigh mouthed fungal warnings. Psatma Nannaferi was nowhere to be seen.

"What do you think, Mbimayu?" the Aspect-Emperor called, his voice eerie for slipping through the roar. He spoke as if about a dinner table. "Do you think Yatwer allowed her to see *this*?"

The Mbimayu Schoolman stood paralytic in a manner he had never before known.

"Wh-wh-what?" he stammered.

Then he heard it as an eerie intrusion upon the ripping of winds. "*Moth-errrrrrrr*!"

A faraway call ... Nearing?

Malowebi frowned, looked skyward in a panic, saw Psatma Nannaferi pitching and kicking for the merest instant before her image exploded into pulp across the arch of his Muzzû Chalice.

"Her plummet," the Thought-dancer said.

The Zeumi Emissary coughed, for something he knew not what, then staggered to his knees.

Esmenet had to pet the girl's hair lightly, lest she make contact with the lack of substance beneath.

"*No-no-no-no-no*," she blubbered and sobbed, rocking her daughter's ruined head.

Her body trembled of its own accord, muscles dancing like coins across porcelain. She could no longer hear her beloved Capital. Her lament *for* had become wailing *with*.

"*Mommaaaa*!" Kelmomas bawled into her side.

The Gods wrought this.

"*Mommaaaa*!" Kelmomas keened ...

Kelmomas. The one that yet *lived* ...

Out of all those who had mattered.

She felt herself *divide* then, divide as she had cradling the final convulsive breath of Samarmas, broken about the fault line that fissures all mothers, the instinct to bury what was mad for *loss* beneath what was mad for *making safe*. She stared at the creviced ceiling, tried to ignore the sheeting heat of her tears. She rallied about her numb core—there was no time for this!

"Sh-sh-shhh ..." she managed to coo to her shuddering boy. She had to get him to safety—away from all this horror. Saxillas! What was it Saxillas had said? She leaned from her rump, wiped a furious sleeve across her face. The ships! She must get him to the harbour! She must be strong!

But the image Theliopa so ... *ruined* yanked her back to the shattered bricks.

"Noooooo," she moaned as though only now happening upon her daughter. "This isn't ..."

She lowered her eye to the heel of her palm, rubbed at the grit that afflicted her.

"This-this isn't ..."

She shook her head in the groggy manner of drunks.

Kelmomas detached himself, swatted his cheeks and eyes while watching her.

"M-momma–?"

"*There's so many monsters!*" Esmenet shrieked with her bones, her hair and her skin. "Wh-hy *Th-Thelli?*" she gasped on hitching breaths. "When-when there are so many *monsters?*"

Kelmomas moved to embrace her, but she was already exploding to her feet ...

"*He doesn't even care!*" she roared into emptiness, her fists balled to either side. "He has no heart to break! No will to weaken! No fury to provoke! Don't you see? You take *nothing* from him when you take his children! *Nothing!*" She fell to her knees gagging, raised a wrist to her mouth.

"You only take ... *take* ... from me ..."

The palace swung as if upon hooks about her axis, a revolving motley of gleaming splendour and chalk destruction. She thrummed as a string breaking, from skin to pit and beyond. All spears! All spears were aimed at her. A spite that dwarfed the Ages!

The Gods! The *Gods* hunted her and her children! Leering, coiling, burning, shaming, murdering, watching and watching and *sometimes touching too*, ever since she was a terrified little girl, sobbing into her terrified mother's arms, saying, "*I saw* eyes, *Momma! Eyes!*" and her mother saying, "*Shush ... I did too ...*"

"*Tomorrow we will kill a bird.*"

Sundry glories lay crashed into ruin all about her. Her gaze roamed the wreckage, fell to the simple, idiot enumeration of what exists. Her little boy had lived in this room once—her youngest. She picked items from the dreck: the leather rocking horse that had sparked so many brawls with Sammi; the Cheribi cherry wardrobe stoved in the collapse that had killed Thelli; the five porcelain Kidruhil figurines given to him by Kayûtus, miraculously intact; and there, his silver Whelming Seal tipped against a ramp of bricked debris, reflecting the image of Kelmomas himself standing behind her to the right, his face framed in a flaxen maul. A dimple in the metal collapsed one cheek into his eyebrow—otherwise his expression one of malice and ... joy?

Her eyes simply hung upon the image, awaiting the arrival of her teetering soul.

"*Kel!*"

The reflection's eyes fastened on her gaze—jubilation slumped into grief.

Her heart cramped about the jagged stone of that transformation. She whirled to confront him, floating for the heat flushing through her limbs, once again crying, "*Kel!*" She reached out to seize him, possessed by a savagery she could not feel. But he *leapt* backward, *into the air*, and landed crouching on the far side of his dead sister's body. She stumbled hard onto her knees, skinned her right palm.

No-no-no-no-no ...

"Kel ..." she called sobbing. "No ... *please*."

I can pretend!

But the Prince-Imperial turned and fled.

Remnants of Psatma Nannaferi oiled the curve of the Muzzû Chalice in smoking blood.

"*Declare!*" the Aspect-Emperor boomed.

The Mbimayu Schoolman pressed himself to his feet, confronted the soul that had roused the Gods. Anasûrimbor Kellhus—the great and terrible Aspect-Emperor.

But what *was* he forsooth? Prophetic redeemer or demonic tyrant?

Or was he the inhuman Thought-dancer described by Drusus Achamian?

"*Declare* yourself, Zeumi!"

The Dûnyain paused tall and savage before the Mbimayu Schoolman, his edges fluttering like wildfire for the sorcerous whirlwind. Golden discs shimmered about a head and hands noxious for their Mark. He stood glaring just beyond the circuit of the Chalice, near enough that Malowebi had to lean into the virulent aura to remain upright.

"Un-under ..." the Second Negotiant croaked, coughed at the panic crowding his lungs. "Under th-the provisions of the Blue Lotus Treaty struck between y-you and the Great Satakhan of High Holy Zeum ..."

There was no thought of surviving a contest with this man. The Anagogic fetish sorcery of the Iswazi was no match for the Gnosis, let alone the Metagnosis. Even still, across the limit of his arcane sensitivity, Malowebi could feel the Fanim amassing Chorae beyond the whisking cyclone. Delaying was his only hope ...

"Fanayal was no nation," the dread figure snapped, the judgment in his voice as absolute as geometry. "You stand in contempt of the very Treaty you invoke."

Time! He just needed more ti–

The Aspect-Emperor barked laughing, stepped so as to place Malowebi between himself and two of the dozen or so Chorae now surrounding the whirlwind. Even the husked demon-heads upon his hip seemed to howl.

Malowebi stood, mouth hanging, bowel churning, *knowing he was doomed*, and it *cut* him, pierced him through, thinking how Likaro would laugh. Curse his miscre–!

Words, incomprehensible, skittered chitinous across surfaces beyond the Real. The Aspect-Emperor's skull became a furnace of alien meaning–

A deafening *crack*. A piercing turquoise brilliance that blackened, blotted all that could be seen–*one striking the Aspect-Emperor*, not his Iswazi Ward!

Malowebi pulled,the *omba* stitched into his Erzû across his face. The black gauze filtered the glare, revealing the Aspect-Emperor gazing bleached for the incandescent violence that engulfed his Wards. Burning light sheared *without Mark* through the cyclone, a lance that began parallel to the earth, but angled upward as its unseen point-of-origin climbed skyward ...

Water, Malowebi realized ... Psûkhe.

Meppa!

The last of the Indara-Kishauri surmounted the whirling chaos, a shadow for his cataclysmic light. Boiling brilliance, blinding even through the *omba*, swallowed all that remained of the Aspect-Emperor's image, a blue-white inferno that was at once a hammer, a torrential burning that stole breath for sucking air, a frenzied pounding that rent ears, sending cracks down to the bone of the earth ...

And then it was gone ... as was Anasûrimbor Kellhus.

Malowebi saw the Last Cishaurim hanging exposed in the arid sunlight, still garbed in the white silks of his convalescence, his feet bare, his face twisted for raging heartbreak. Sunlight slipped and flashed from the silver band obscuring his eyes. The black asp peered downward, swaying as a dowser's stick from side to side.

"*Fanayaaaaaal!*" the man screamed. "*Nooooo!*"

"*Such power ...*" Malowebi heard a deep voice murmur—*from behind him.*

The Iswazi sorcerer turned on a panicked spasm, glimpsed the looming horror of the Aspect-Emperor *inside his Chalice.* The man clubbed him to the ground. The reality of what happened stammered about the shadows.

"*Deceitful!*" Meppa howled in wrath from above. The gleaming curl of the asp had craned toward his Ward: the Primary had realized what happened. "*Craven!*"

It was as if the sun itself crashed upon the Muzzû Chalice. Malowebi could hear nothing, but through the black gauze of his *omba* he could see him standing, Anasûrimbor Kellhus, more curious than alarmed, craning his head about to inspect the Ward that preserved him. Malowebi could have released the fetish at that moment, he knew. He need only expose his palm, let slip the miniature iron cup, and they would *both* be washed away ...

But he did not. Could not ...

Besides ... the Aspect-Emperor was no longer there.

The Chalice cracked.

Kelmomas ran, fleeing the long wire of his mother's call. He traced a line through hooped cavities of what had been his home, puckering the billows of smoke, drawing its residue through the wailing air.

Something burns somewhere, he thought.

He found himself in his mother's chambers with no memory of doubling back. He could smell her warm, earthen smell, the residue of the jasmine she had worn in his room. He knew the quake had destroyed her bedchamber before so much as setting foot upon the threshold. A turret from above had sheared through the ceiling and plummeted through the floor, leaving a ruinous pit. A hand waved like a frond in water from the heaped debris below. A great fragment of the far wall had been torn down its own slope, taking the mythic marbles of the secret entrance with it. At first he simply gaped, gazed across the void senseless to the horror.

His shadow palace lay cracked open, the mazed hollows utterly exposed.

Inrilatas crouched naked in what shadow remained, smeared with his own feces.

"*You think you seek the love of our mother, little brother—Little Knife!*"

Comprehension was slow in coming.

"You think you murder in her name ..."

The eight-year-old swallowed. Nothing secret. Nothing fun. The Andiamine Heights had been boned as a bird. Laying broken, all the covert passages, all the chutes and tunnels and wells, stood revealed in countless places, a great lung drawing in every scream, every moan or wail, a soaking of all the rampant misery, siphoning, commingling, *transmogrifying*, creating a singular and most monstrous voice, a sound inhuman for the surfeit of humanity.

He stood transfixed.

Ruined! his twin shrieked from nowhere. *You've ruined everything*!

He was the panic-stricken one, as always, the helpless baby. Kelmomas suffered only a peculiar numbness, a curious sense of having outgrown not so much his mother or his old life as *existence altogether*.

It was a stupid game anyway.

This is the only game there is, you fool!

And he began shaking then, teetering over the pit, small in the vast croak issuing from the Andiamine Heights, the hideous roar that was humanity in sum. And when he regarded his abjection, he was puzzled, for he shook upon facts that he both knew and could not speak, an unbearable emptiness ... loss ... *theft*!

Something! Something had been taken!

He glimpsed the dust-chalked hand waving from the crotch of two great stones below. Horns creased the ragged air with alarm—battlehorns ...

And he was running once again, his feet flying upon a ground that was a drum, dashing through rings of glory and ruin. Smoke hung as thick as the cries in the air. Some halls were wrecked, the marble facings cracked, or shed altogether, the floors buckled or buried under shattered masonry. The Ministerial Gallery was impassable, receiving, as it had, a good portion of the Sea Beacon, which had imploded upon its foundations. Others ran, but they were as irrelevant to him as he was to them. Some milled in a stupor, blooded, or chalked colourless. Some shouted for help as they heaved at rubble, others rocked, wailing over inert bodies. Only the dead possessed decorum.

He paused for a train of slaves and functionaries bearing an enormous body grey for dust, black for bleeding. As they passed he recognized the bulk as Ngarau, strings of blood swinging from his slack lips. The little Prince-Imperial stood agog, ignoring the bearers and their concern. A slave boy no older than he trailed in their wake, staring at him with wide, questioning eyes. Glimpsing movement past his bloodied cheek, Kelmomas saw *Issiral* crossing the next juncture down the hall—a form shadowy not for garb or speed, but for unnatural intent ...

He stood motionless, tingling, staring at the now vacant intersection. Several heartbeats passed before he could dare think what was manifest—the Truth that pricked for being so plain ...

So laden with dread portent.

The Four-Horned Brother wasn't finished with the Anasûrimbor.

Strange, the ways of the Soul.

How it kicks when it should be still.

How it resigns when it should roar and spit and grapple.

The Chalice crumbled beneath the luminous ferocity of the Water. Malowebi spat blood, his face numb for the Aspect-Emperor's blow. The fetish kicked and burned like saltpetre in his fist, but he did not release it. The great strength of the Iswazi was the way it drew on the will that bound the fetish. Rather, he raised himself to his knees, held out his fire-spitting fist, swayed against the calamitous demonstration of the Psûkhe.

He thought he could hear Meppa screaming ... somewhere.

Or maybe it was him.

Metagnostic singing clambered up out of the being of things once again, and the brilliant cataract winked into nothingness. Psûkhic thunder trailed into roaring Metagnostic winds. Malowebi pitched forward, cradled the agony of his ruined hand. Grit lashed him as the remnants of the Muzzû Chalice melted away. He huddled wincing against the root of the sorcerous cyclone. Furnishings whooshed overhead, whipping around, as did sections of the pavilion itself, flapping as rapid as bat-wings across the sun. He could no longer sense the Chorae floating about the whirlwind's circuit: it seemed the desert warriors had fled with the arrival of Meppa ...

And word that Fanayal ab Kascamandri was truly dead.

The black gauze had made shadows of what was flesh and flesh of what was light. Hunched against the tempest, the Mbimayu Schoolman watched mouth agape. Meppa hung on high as before, releasing cascades of scalding light. The Aspect-Emperor stood painted lightning-white below, Fanayal's chalk corpse not more than two paces distant. A mosaic of angular planes sheared into the Waterbearer's deluge mere cubits above them, refracting the concussive glare across an arc that impaled the heights.

"*You shall bear me, Demon*!" the Last Cishaurim raged from on high. "*For I am drawn from your accursed wheel! Your oven*!"

Malowebi tore his *omba* away—gazed upon the Water with his naked eye.

"*An outcast Son of Shimeh*!"

The man's cheeks glowed beneath the spiralling radiance, wetted with tears beneath his silver visor. The asp coiled about his neck seemed to hang him as a noose from the sky. His power was its own ground.

"*The Cant that murdered my family, I took as my name*!"

And as his rage waxed, so too did the brilliance of his Water ...

"*And I swore I would come upon thee*! *Come upon thee as a flood*!"

And the hanging Abstractions cast his light upon an ever more profound convexity, a scythe that could surmount mountains.

"*That I would deliver such* **Water**!" Meppa screamed.

All existence hissed as if it were sand and some kind of surf heaved through it.

"***As to strike thee to ash***!"

Meppa howled, maddened unto berserker frenzy. The world was darkened for the sun brilliance of his Expression. Jetting light dazzled his silhouette.

All this while the Aspect-Emperor *continued singing*, so bleached for the glare as to appear something sketched in char. The Metagnostic planes above him had long since vanished into the roiling glare ... but they miraculously cast back the Water nonetheless. And for a heartbeat, the Mbimayu Schoolman understood that this was his moment to seize. The future came to him as a crushing encumbrance, for he saw that *he was the balance*, the very grain that could tip the balance of empires and civilizations. All he need do was *sing with Meppa* ...

Strike the Aspect-Emperor!

He hung from this momentous breath.

All he need do ...

Indara's Waterbearer wailed for outrage and incredulity.

And *it was too late*, for Anasûrimbor Kellhus had thrown out his arms upon his Cant's completion. Malowebi gasped for wonder at the unfolding of Metagnostic Abstractions, the intricate extent, the searing power, geometries begetting geometries, each twining upward on an antler's curve, a dozen, all flaring out and closing upon Meppa, wracking him with volcanic lights. The man's shadow jerked.

Malowebi blinked for the Water's abrupt absence, the arid gloom of mere sunlight. He glimpsed the Last Cishaurim slump from the low heights, trailing smoke, the black asp wagging as a tassel. And he reeled, thinking how all of it—everything!—had run aground upon the fact of this Man before him—this one impossible Man! The aspirations of a dispossessed race. The final and most brilliant flame of the Psûkhe. The machinations of High Holy Zeum—even the dread *Mother of Birth*!

Then the Holy Aspect-Emperor of the Three Seas *was upon him*, hauling him like a thief from market. Malowebi's gaze caught upon the visage of a Decapitant, then Meppa sprawled semi-conscious across the wine-dark crimson of carpet. The man hoisted him by the breast of his robes, lifted him bodily. Black veils roped hypnotic beneath the sky ...

And all he could see was the haloed mien of Anasûrimbor Kellhus, the glacial scrutiny in his gaze, a doom that no mortal could fathom ...

A doom that was his.

"*What?*" the Mbimayu Schoolman gasped. "*What ... are ... you?*"

The man reached for the pommel jutting above his shoulder. Enshoiya flashed in the embattled light ...

"Weary," the grim visage replied.

The famed sword fell.

It was different now that he could not pass between the walls unseen, but it was the same outrageous game nonetheless: a boy chasing a God through the halls of his House.

The lamentations had dwindled, and battlehorns now cawed from regions not so distant. Kelmomas felt a mouse for the way he darted from blind to blind, never closing on the Narindar, never losing him either, always lingering on some glimpse of his back or shoulders. Always murmuring, *Got you* ... then flitting forward. The man's route through the half-ruin was too circuitous to be anything but premeditated, and yet it possessed no logic the boy could fathom, and seemed mad for the contradiction of the man's grim intent and rudderless passage.

Did the Four-Horned Brother *play in turn*? he began wondering. Could all this be for *his sake*? Had Hell sent him a teacher ... a playmate ... a *champion*?

The question terrified as much as elated him.

So he crept and he sprinted from place to damaged place, through halls both wrecked and intact, mooning upon the thought of the Grinning God's favour—the chance that he was Hate's darling! He followed the breadcrumb glimpses around and about, impervious to any ruin or misery, ignoring even the sudden panic that sent so many running from the Andiamine Heights screaming, "*Fanim*! *Fanim*!" He cared not because he cared for nothing other than the play before his eyes, beneath his bare feet and naked hands. The silence of his mercurial brother meant that even he understood, even he agreed. *Nothing* mattered anymore ...

Might just as well have one last bit of *fun*.

Momemn was destroyed. The Fanim were about to stack the survivors with the dead. And Mother ...

Mother, she—

Ruined! Samarmas screamed, assailed him, biting deep into his neck before vanishing into his own shadow palace, the hollow bones of the boy's own thought. Kelmomas scrunched the collar of his tunic—the one he had donned after his altercation with Theliopa—under his jaw and chin to staunch the blood.

He liked to remind him from time to time, his twin.

Remind him what it had been like *before*.

At last Issiral climbed back into the Upper Palace, this time using the Processional, the grand stair meant to wind dignitaries from fat lands and to overawe dignitaries from lean ones—or so Inrilatas had once told him. Two great silvered mirrors, the finest ever crafted, had hung at angles above the stair so that those climbing could see themselves against the gilded splendour surrounding and understand full well the base and mean truth of their origins. One of the mirrors had shattered, but the other hung intact as before. Kelmomas saw the near-naked man halt on the landing, stand as if arrested by his image hanging above. The Prince-Imperial ducked behind an overturned stone vase some two junctures back. He raised a cheek to gaze over the bevelled rim with a single eye.

The man continued standing with the same immobility that had so taxed the boy's patience before. Kelmomas cursed, loathe to believe that the Grinning God could be caught by something so crude—so thin!—as reflection. This was part of the *game*, somehow. It had to be!

Without warning, the man resumed motion as if he had never broken stride. On Issiral's third step, Kelmomas stood from behind the bulk of the vase. On Issiral's fourth step *his mother appeared* from the intersecting halls ahead of him—behind the Narindar. She paused upon a skidding slipper, almost immediately glimpsing *Him*, the Four-Horned Brother, climbing the Processional ahead. Her grand lavender gowns swung upon her turn to the monumental stair, freighted for soaking so much of her daughter's blood. Her image burned as a chip of ice in his breast, so delicate, so soft, so ... so ... dark and beautiful. She made as to call out to the Narindar, but decided against it, and her little boy dropped to a crouch, knowing how she would cast a glance over her shoulder—she was forever glancing over her shoulder—before sprinting after what she thought was her assassin ...

Grab her! his brother suddenly erupted. *Flee this place*!

Or what?

A crazed growl. *You remember fu—*!

And I don't care!

Samarmas faded, not so much into darkness as beyond the possibility of sense. He was frightened, Kelmomas knew ... *weak*. The burden was *his* to shoulder ... if not the blame.

So the little boy darted in his Empress mother's wake, devoid of all thought save cunning, for at long last he understood the game in all its particulars. And there was no way he could reckon that understanding and still play *this* ... whatever it was he played with Ajokli, God of the Gutter.

Mother had always been his stake. The only thing that mattered.

The Blessed Empress of the Three Seas slowed as she climbed the stair beneath the surviving Grand Mirror, unable to believe she at all resembled the girl who had first marvelled at her reflection in a crude copper sheen in a Sumni slum decades since. How many indignities had she survived in the interval?

How many losses?

And yet *there it was*, that face ... the face other whores had raged for ...

The eyes just as dark, each perpetually reflecting some pinprick of distant brilliance. The cheeks more severe perhaps, the brow more scored by care, but the lips just as fulsome, the neck as slender, the whole untouched ...

Untouched?

Untouched! What kind of madness was this? What kind of World would paint such *beauty* upon a thing so accursed, so besmirched and polluted as *herself*! She watched her expression wince inward upon all angles, break upon spasms of shame and grief. She fled the hanging apparition, leapt the stair, her eyes downcast. She chased Issiral to the summit of her cracked and teetering empire, pursued without knowing why, to release him, perhaps, even though he had yet to accept her absurd charge. Or to *ask* him, perhaps, given the *wisdom* implicit in the way he spoke and moved—unlike any soul she had known, the way he seemed to ... to ... stand outside passion, beyond the animal prods of mortal nature. Perhaps he could ...

Perhaps he could.

Her city and palace wailed. She crested the Processional just as the Narindar vanished between the great bronze portals of the Imperial Audience Hall. She followed him, uncertain whether she breathed. She was aware of wondering at the man, why he would steal here at such a time, but all was snow otherwise, numb obscurity. She trailed her fingertips across the line of Kyranean Lions stamped into the portal door barricaded by masonry, then stole quietly through the door ajar.

The gloom was disorienting. She peered about the vast, polished hollow, searching for some sign of the Narindar, her eyes tracing gleaming lines about the roots of pillars great and small.

He was nowhere to be seen.

She strode into the Hall's mighty aisle, making no attempt to conceal herself. She could smell the Meneanor, the sky, even the scented dregs of her morning council ...

Her son's bathwater.

Her daughter's bowel.

The missing wall shone white before her, a great silver halo about the silhouette of her husband's Circumfix Throne. She paused in its monochromatic light, unafraid even though she suddenly understood *why* the Narindar had *lured* her here.

For that was the Fate the Whore had allotted her ... to forever *attempt* to rule.

To be the plaything of forces ... *other*.

To be the leprous wretch gowned in gold—*carrion* in the guise of beauty!

She stood, so small upon the expansive floor, dwarfed beneath the great pillars raised by her husband. She even closed her eyes and *willed* her end to happen. In her soul's eye she could see the *man*, Issiral, her Narindar, her Holy Assassin, walking without the least urgency or apprehension, a *being beyond effort*, his knife floating white and watery before him. And she stood awaiting the plunge, braced both for and against, somehow knowing the ways her body would convulse about the intrusion, the shameful way she would flop upon her own unyielding floor.

But the assault never came. The high-hanging spaces were silent save for a single sparrow battling the nets that hung from the vaults of the absent wall. Her throat burned.

She fixed her gaze upon the silver-white opening, then carried her reflection across floors counted so sacred that Men had been slain for failing to embrace them. The sound of the sparrow's travail began to scratch and buffet her breast from the inside. She paused on the lowermost step of the grand dais, winded by simple being.

The Blessed Empress of the Three Seas saw him then, a silhouette standing just inside the verge of the missing wall, as though sheltering his skin from the harsh autumn sunlight. She knew him instantly, but a more stubborn fraction of her soul elected to believe he was Issiral. His every step proved an insult to this pretense, the discs of gold about his hands and face, the Decapitants bound to his girdle, the flaxen beard and mane, the looming stature ...

"*Wha* ..." Esmenet coughed about sudden horror. "Wha-what are you doing here?"

Her husband held her in his expressionless regard.

"I have come to save you," he said, "and to salvage what I might."

"S-save me?"

"Fanayal is dead. His vultures scatter to the fou—"

The belly of her vision blackened, and she collapsed at his knees—as perhaps a dutiful wife should.

"Esmi?" Anasûrimbor Kellhus asked, kneeling to catch her. He held her cupped in the bottomless bowl of his scrutiny. She watched the scowl darken his face. He released her arms, towered over her dismay.

"What have you done?"

She winced at blows that did not come. She clawed at his wool leggings, hooked fingers into the rim of his right boot.

"I ..." she began on the urge to vomit.

Let it ... a seditious fragment whispered.

"I-I ..."

Happen.

And the Gift-of-Yatwer sees himself seeing, as he steps out from where he has always awaited, the column's marmoreal bulk drawing aside as a curtain, revealing the Demon Emperor standing as he has always stood, forever awaiting. He sees the White-Luck Warrior throw his broken sword ...

Mother claps the Rug of the World ...

He climbs a stairs in a hall so great that a galley could be dragged through it, oars drawn. He looks up, sees himself standing before the great bronze doors of the Imperial Audience Hall, the one blockaded shut by ruin, the other jarred open on cracked hinges. He watches himself gaze into the stone-girded gloom, the marmoreal heights gleaming, the floor reflecting all in darkling tones. He sees the sky hang white beyond the chamber's vaulted frame, the ground behind the Mantle where light and dark wars, where the Accursed Aspect-Emperor stands before his shrinking wife. She had hidden her will from herself, but still the Demon can see.

As he has always seen.

The Gift-of-Yatwer sees himself pressed soundless to a great column, hearing, "What have you done?" echo across the polished gloom.

Mother stamps her foot upon the earth.

All of Life stumbles. The ceilings unhitch and come shrugging down.

His sword twirls broken through curtains of debris.

The Tear wells in Mother's eye. The ground hammers all things terrestrial as a mallet.

The Demon dances clear the ceilings, miraculously stands to regard his teetering wife.

"Esmi?"

His broken sword pitches, end over end, following a miraculous chute through the curtains of debris.

Mother blinks the Tear. The vast ceiling slumps, then crashes, fragments of marmoreal splendour.

"Catch," the Empress calls.

He crushes the flesh in his hands, drinks deep his Mother's *gift.*

"Esmi?"

The Tear misses, leaving a rind of salt along his throat and left cheek.

Mother stamps her foot upon the earth. Seleukaran steel pitches through sheets of ruin, following the miraculous chute it has always followed, plunges into his throat. The wicked abomination gasps, as it has always gasped … the Whore of Momemn *cries out for some passion beyond woe or joy.*

Her husband gapes, vanishes beneath tumbling piers.

Arms out, the Gift-of-Yatwer looks up to the ragged remnants of the ceiling, embraces what has already happened.

The Empress calls, "Catch."

See! the Prince-Imperial silently screeched at his twin. *See!*

The Game. It had been the Game all along!

Play was all that remained.

All that *mattered.*

He had sprinted up the Processional in his mother's wake, staring into the surviving Grand Mirror, seeing nothing but an angelic boy smeared and daubed with blood—grinning in a manner some, perhaps, might find odd. Then he crept into the cavernous gloom of the Imperial Audience Hall, where he saw his mother standing bleached swan-white in the light of the Aperture, the missing wall. He crept soundlessly between the columns and through the shadows of the lesser aisle to the west. He spied the Grinning God quite quickly, standing beside a pillar on an angle inaccessible to where she stood. Heat flushed through him, such were the possibilities … the *vulnerabilities.*

Please … Samarmas sobbed from nowhere. *Call to her* …

Their mother stood upon the nethers of the audience floor, her arms held out, her face tilted to the chill emanation of light, as if awaiting ...

Call to her!

It seemed such a dark and *delicious* moment.

No.

And then he sensed it, the stomach-dandling Mark ... and he understood the *true prize* of this game they played.

Father!

Yes. *The Four-Horned Brother hunted Father*—the one most feared, most hated!

Kelmomas stood both horrified and astounded, then fairly whooped for the rush of savage vindication. He had been *right* all along! His impulses had possessed their own Unerring Grace—*their own White-Luck*! It seemed so clear now, both what had happened, and what was about to ...

Mother crossed the expanse of kneeling tiles in a stupor, her gowns swishing as she approached the floor below the Mantle. The Prince-Imperial tracked her progress in the parallel gloom, making cramped faces of joy, malice, and fury. His soul pranced and capered while his body crept.

Of course! Today! Today was the day!

Battlehorns continued to peal in distant, metallic cascades. She paused upon the lowermost step of the dais. The sky painted the vacancy of her look white.

That was why Momemn had been cracked asunder! Why Anasûrimbor blood so flowed!

She saw Father, but chose not to recognize him as such. She awaited his approaching apparition as she would any vassal ... then abruptly crumpled at his feet. Father caught her in his arms, knelt in a pose as intimate as the boy had ever seen between them. Her very image seemed warped for the foul proximity of his Mark.

This! This was why the Prince of Hate had come! To attend the *coronation of a new and far more generous sovereign*. One who could laugh as he shovelled souls into the furnaces of Hell! The boy crooned and cackled at the thought, and in his soul's eye *he could see it*, the glory that was his future, the *history of what had already happened*! Kelmomas I, the *Most* Holy Aspect-Emperor of the Three Seas!

Rimmed in plates of ethereal gold, Father held Mother swooning upon the dais, gazed into the broken cup of her soul ...

Suddenly he released her, stood graven in white and shadow as she wailed abject at his feet.

What have you done?

A flicker of motion in his periphery. The boy's eye caught Issiral turning from behind the fluted bulk of the pillar concealing Him ... the Four-Horned Brother *preparing* ...

He would *help*—Yes! He would *distract* Father. Yes! *That* was his role. That was how it *had already happened*. He could *feel* it, somehow, like an oracular density in his bones.

A certainty hard as flint, heavy as iron ... He need only abide, *be* the happening of what happened.

"*Mommaaaa*!" he wailed from his concealment.

Both Father and Mother jerked their faces in his direction. Father took a single step ...

The Prince-Imperial looked to his infernal co-conspirator, to the Narindar, expecting ... something other than the near-naked man gawking at him ... stupefied.

Certainly something more *godlike*.

The Narindar shook his head, stared down aghast at his hands. His ears wept blood.

And this seemed a calamity greater than any the Prince-Imperial had suffered, an overturning that cast the final contents of his World askew. He had miscalculated, the boy realized. The *wrongness* lay as a frozen knife held flat across the tender of his throat ...

He glanced back to the dais, saw his father striding out toward the Circumfix Throne, peering at the now hapless assassin—and the ground exploded ...

A second quake, as mighty as the first. The penultimate vault, the one framing the missing wall, the one bearing the prayer tower that had been raised upon it, simply dropped. It fell as a cudgel wreathed in streamers of dust, a hammer the size of a bastion, crashing upon the very spot where Father had stood. The ground spanked the boy from his feet. Creation clacked and roared, dropped as torrents about every glimpse. Columns spilled into stacked drums, ceilings plummeted as sodden rags. He saw the man he had mistook for Ajokli fall to his knees between tumbling immensities. He saw it then, the terror of *ignorance* that is the curse of mortality; he apprehended the man's sickening *humanity* the instant stone clapped it into oblivion.

And he screamed, shrieked the terror and fury of a child bereft of all he had loved and known.

A child not quite human.

As a boy, Malowebi had been strangely affected upon hearing how those deemed guilty of capital offences aboard Satakhanic warships would be sewn into sacks and summarily cast into the Ocean. "Pursing", the sailors had named the practice. It haunted him the way a premonition might, the thought of being immobilized without being bound, of possessing the ability to move without the ability to swim, of jerking and clawing and drowning in the infinite chill. Years later, on the galley that had transported him to his first Tenure as a young man, he had the misfortune of witnessing the punishment firsthand. A fight between rowers had led to one bleeding out during the night: the survivor was condemned as a murderer and sentenced to the Purse. The condemned man had begged the deck for mercies, knowing that none was to be had, while three marines manhandled him into a long burlap sack. The wretch had implored in whispers, Malowebi would remember, murmurs so low as to make loud the creaking timbers, the sloshing below the gunwales, the bone-rattle of knots in the rigging. The Captain spake a short verse to Momas Almighty, and then kicked the keening sack overboard. Malowebi had heard the muffled shriek, had watched the sack twist like a maggot into the greening depths, then had fled to vomit as inconspicuously as he could over the opposite side. He would be weeks shaking the last bubbles of anxiety from his limbs. And it would be years before he stopped hearing ghosts of that muffled cry.

The dream he suffered now was like this death sentence, something dark and drowning, something he could thrash and kick within, but never escape. A Pursing both more protracted and more profound.

Somehow, from a vantage he could not quite explain, he saw himself hanging before Anasûrimbor Kellhus, the World spinning ruin around them. The man's sword scissored across the angle of the sun, and Malowebi screamed as his head tipped from his shoulders and dropped to the woven earth ...

His head! Rolling like a cabbage.

Malowebi's corpse twitched in the man's irresistible grip, spouted blood, voided itself. Casting his blade into the carpeted earth, the Aspect-Emperor seized one of the Decapitants, wrenched the diabolical trophy from his girdle, then raised the horror to the welling stump of neck ...

The unconquerable Anasûrimbor Kellhus spoke. His eyes ignited like blown-upon coals, flared with infernal meaning.

The union of desiccate tissue with warm, ebony flesh was instantaneous. Blood sluiced into and soaked the desert-rotted papyrus, transforming the Decapitant into something horrid and sodden, a bundle of pitch-soaked rags. The Aspect-Emperor released the thing, watched with utter indifference as it stumbled forward to its knees, swayed ...

Malowebi screamed, kicked and clawed at the nightmarish fabric, choked on his own terror—drowned. *This isn't happening*! *This cannot be happening*!

The abomination raised *his* hands, held them about the sorcerous turmoil of *its* face, the knitting of *his* blood to *its* blasted meat and skin. Malowebi screamed for watching *Malowebi* reborn in demonic replica.

The whirlwind roared about them both, a ruinous blur.

"*Return to the Palace of Plumes*," the Aspect-Emperor called to the unholy slave. "*End the line of Nganka'kull.*"

Without lungs, void was his only wind. He howled until void was all that remained.

Chapter Seventeen

The Demua Mountains

To stand tallest beneath the sun is the yearning of the child and the old man alike. For verily, age raises us up and strips us down. But where the child dreams as he should, the old man is naught but a miser. The curse of growing old is to watch one's passion fall ever more out of season, to dwell ever more in the shadow of perversity.

—Asansius, *The Limping Pilgrim*

Late Summer, 20 New Imperial Year (4132, Year-of-the-Tusk), the Demua Mountains

The boy flies up a nearby tree as quick as a monkey despite his crabbed hand. She and Achamian run across the forest floor, both huffing and lurching under their respective burdens, age and womb. The sun flashes through the shadowy dapple. Throngs of scrub, fern, and weed scrape and tug at their scissoring legs.

Fear not, little one ...

A Sranc screams through the bowered gloom behind them, a skinned sound, glistening with anguish, yanked short by something unknown.

Your father is a Wizard!

"There!" Achamian cries on a hoarse exhalation. He makes a gesture, palsied by exertion, to an overgrown pit at the base of an oak that some storm or tumult had toppled at the roots. They slip through a curtain of nettle, curse the sting under their breath.

One without any sense of direction ...

Another Sranc shrieks, this one to the west. She thinks of faraway dogs barking in the morning chill, the way they made a tin pot of the World. It smells dank and sweet in their trench, like sunless soil and rotting green.

"Another mobbing?" she asks under her breath.

"I don't know," Achamian peers through the fingers of their blind, searching the cavities between gnarled trunks and bands of sunlight. "Those cries. Something is different ..."

Enough!

"The boy?" she asks.

"Has survived far worse than this, I'm sure."

Nevertheless, she peers into the canopy, sorting between branches that elbow rather than wend. Ever since returning to Kûniüri she has noticed an oddness to the trees, an arthritic angularity, as if they would sooner raise fists than leaves to the sky. She can see nothing of the boy, though she was certain she knew which tree he had climbed.

A mucoid hiss draws her eyes back to the forest floor. She follows Achamian's squint.

She cannot believe it at first. She observes without breath or thought.

A man on a horse. A *man on a horse* follows the Sranc ...

Little more than a silhouette at a glance, leaning back against a high cantle, swaying to his mount's tedious gait. Then a glimpse of wild black hair, a lancer's shield across his horse's rump. His arms are bare—this is how she knows what he is. It seems she sees the scars before the skin.

"*Seju!*" Achamian curses under his breath.

Neither of them speak. They track the Scylvendi horseman through the glare and gloom, watch him pass from obscurity into plain sight, then back into interleaving obscurity.

"*Sweet Sejenus!*" Achamian finally hisses.

"What should we do?" she asks.

The old Wizard slumps backward into the earthen recess, as if finally overrun by relentless ill-fortune.

"Should we run? Climb back into the Demua?"

He smears a palm across his forehead, thoughtless of the filth.

The angularity has seized her once again, that unerring *need* she has come to identify as motherhood.

"*What*, Akka?"

"Give me a blasted moment, girl!" he cries under his breath.

"We don't have a—" she begins, but a sudden realization tosses the thought to oblivion.

Akka calls after her in alarm, far more loudly than he should. She silences him with a backward frown, then nimbly floats across the forest floor, ducking from tree to tree. She pauses twice, thinking that she hears thunder beneath her breath. In the surrounding obscurity another Sranc screeches at some insult. The sound is wet with nearness. She clenches her teeth about a hammering heart. At last she finds the tree the boy had climbed. She walks about it, alternately peering upward and casting glances over her shoulder. She sees him, as motionless as barked wood, watching her without expression. She calls him down with a violent wave of her hand. He gazes southward rather than reply, his head queerly bent. "Come!" she dares call.

The boy flies down the great elm like nothing human, legs and arms hooked about space. He thumps to a crouch on the humus. Before she can even acknowledge him, he has her arm in his crabbed hand. He yanks her back toward the old Wizard violently, his strength unlikely, his manner ruthless. The thunder is louder now. Panic pricks her from behind, sparks her stumbling gait. She sees the fallen tree, overthrown at the socket. She glimpses Achamian's wild-bearded face watching through the blind of early-autumn weeds. The rumble climbs, a thrumming monotone, then *breaks*, as if a bladder overcome, becoming a cacophony of pounding hooves and equine complaints. She runs as if perpetually falling over her belly, always catching herself, always almost ...

We are caught, a corner of her soul notes—one too weary not to be wry.

But the boy thinks otherwise. He yanks her, bruising iron in his claw grip, racing full bore. She crashes through the screen of weeds, into stinging gloom, a confusion of limbs, muck, and loam.

"*Seju!*" Achamian cries under his breath. "What were yo—"

The cacophony towers as if above them. Instinct brings her to her feet, leaning to peer at their pursuers—at the identity of their fate. But the boy has her again, pins her down, his odour sour for lack of bathing, yet sweet for youth. Paralysis. And they are in the belly of the thunder, the three huddled side by side, riven, dark save for a dragon's claw of light across her belly. Rifling shadows. Pounding hooves. Huffing snorts and pinched indignations. Intimations are all they need.

Scylvendi. The dread People of War range the dead lands of Kûniüri.

Please.

Afterward she will wonder just when her every thought became a prayer.

Because of the toppled tree, the riders give their overgrown cavity a wide berth. What seems like a watch passes, lying curled and rigid. Only the boy is perfectly motionless.

Then the thunder climbs ahead of them, and the inability to discriminate wraps the whole once again.

They lie in its receding, rumbling wake, drawing breath in the earthen gloom.

"A patrol," Achamian murmurs, pulling himself to his rump. He cautiously raises his eyes above the forest floor, renews his vigil.

She has to roll sideways onto her hands and knees, so onerous is her belly. She climbs to his side. The boy simply sits behind them, perfectly impassive, his knees caught in the circle of his arms.

"So you think there's more?" she asks the old Wizard.

"Of course there is," he says, peering. "They resemble your idiocy that way."

Her apprehension is slapped from her. She is a heartbeat in understanding.

"What? I should have *left* him?"

"That boy has survived more than you or I can scarce dream."

"And he is *still* a child! He's—"

"*Not so helpless as the one you carry in your womb!*" the old Wizard cries, turning on her with sudden savagery. She shrinks from the display, understanding instantly and utterly that he speaks out of an outrage borne of terror ... The terror belonging to fathers.

She makes to speak—just what, she does not know—but another screech, strangely piteous, yowls among the bowers from places near and unknown. Another Sranc.

They both resume their anxious peering, and despite their straits, she cannot but think that this is the way with husbands and wives. A part of her even grins ...

It is proper, she thinks, that they should be married in a grave.

"Those Sranc are called *Exscursi*," Achamian says grimly. "Their scent fills their wild cousins with lunatic terror, clearing the land. The Consult uses them to secure safe passage for their human allies ..." He glances at her, speaking this last, and something in her expression ignites a furious scowl.

"What are you smiling about?"

"You are a dear old fool," she hears herself whisper.

"You don't understand," he cries. "Somewhere ... out *there* ..."—he points toward the south, to the throng and pillared deep of forest obscuring forest—"lies the People in War *in sum* ... An entire *host* of Scylvendi!"

"I do understand," she replies, staring into his eyes as if trying to lean into his irritable old soul ... Reassure him. Even still, he refuses to *trust* what was happening.

"You do? Then you understand this means it's *really happening*! The Second Apocalypse is really hap—"

The boy is upon them, hands whole and crabbed hard upon each of their shoulders, warning them to silence. Breathless they peer across the trampled humus and debris. The sound of a pony snorting jolts her—for some reason she had assumed the boy had heard one of the Sranc.

Peering through the chaotic thatch of their blind, the three of them watch as another Scylvendi horseman, apparently alone, rides into view, sinking into a depression then climbing the swale nearest to them ... and stopping ...

She cannot hear it yet, but all the south seems to shiver with teeming portent.

The People of War in sum ...

The man almost seems to sniff the air. There is a brutality to him, the odour of an ignorant race, of souls too simple to countenance nuance or doubt. His arms are bared like the other's, but nowhere near so many scars stripe their length. A looseness in the skin about the crotch of his armpit reveals his age, but little else. Blue paint adorns his face, as pale as his eyes. Fetishes dangle from his bridle and saddle, what look like desiccate mice strung by their tails. His pony paws at the leaves and loam. Like someone hunting something glimpsed, he rakes the surrounding forest depths with his glacial gaze. There is an alacrity to his eyes, something reminiscent of a weasel's nose ...

Unerringly, it seems, his look settles upon their little pit.

No one so much as blinks. The Princess-Imperial's heart drops the length of her spine.

He is one of the Few.

Daylight dwindles, draining at a pace that matches their anxious, arboreal flight. She leads despite the late stage of her term. Just behind her, the old Wizard tramps in his anarchic way, looking for all the world like an old hermit, nimble and mad. The boy trots effortlessly in the rear, alternately peering from side to side, probing the greenery that screens their flanks.

They do not talk. The barking of distant Sranc is all they can hear above their breathing. Suddenly it has become all too familiar, fleeing from wilderness into wilderness. The premonition of disaster about the neck and shoulders. The prick in every swallow. The way the birches close the curtains on the environs surrounding, allowing fear to populate them.

They continue huffing and trotting until dusk and darkness reduces all distances to ink and wool. The decision to break for the night comes as a knuckle in the landscape: a balding dome rising to the waist of the encircling trees.

Achamian leans gasping against his knees upon the summit. "He *saw* us," he says, peering into nocturnal confusion. She cannot imagine what he hopes to see: the forest is little more than tangled hair and smeared charcoal to her eyes.

She lies against the mossy back of a log, her eyes fluttering, her hands across her distended abdomen. Her every breath pinches her throat at the clavicle. An acidic heat creeps between her ribs.

"What would you have us do," she pants. "Run through the night?"

The old Wizard turns to her. The sky is overcast. The moon is little more than a lantern in the fog, so she can see nothing of his eyes beneath the coarse line of his brow. He is inscrutable and frightening for it.

Suddenly she has difficulty seeing past the blasted ache of his Mark.

"If we took more Qirri ..." he says.

What is it in his tone? Elation. Appeal. Dread ...

The craving fills her.

"No ..." she gasps.

Yes-yes-yes ...

"No?" Achamian repeats.

"I will not risk our child," she explains, leaning her head back once again.

"But this is *exactly* what you do!"

And so he continues cajoling. The Scylvendi were a race like no other, he insists in wary tones. Godless. Worshippers of violence. As vicious as Sranc and far more cunning. "They are not the artless savages you think!" he cries on the back of worry and obstinance. "Their traditions are ancient, but not hidebound. Their customs are ruthless, but not blind. Trickery and deception are their most prized weapons!"

She lies with one hand hooked like a swing beneath her belly and another held to her forehead. Tiresome pendant!

"Mimara! We must keep running!"

She understands their peril. The Scylvendi were no small matter of concern upon the Andiamine Heights, but less so than in the days of the Ikurei. The Battle of Kiyuth had consumed an entire generation of their manhood—and more. The People of War had always depended on the Chorae their ancestors had accumulated as spoils through the millennia. Shorn of these, they simply could not cope with the sorceries of the Three Seas.

"Back to the mountains ..." he says, gazing out toward the Demua. "They'll be loathe to risk their ponies in the dark. By morning we could use bare rock to obscure all trace of our passage!"

There is a vacancy in his manner, one that repels her. She is suddenly sure that the Qirri, and not the Scylvendi, motivate his exhortations. He does not want to taste to run so much as run to taste.

A cannibal yearning for the ash clasps her as a lover might.

Even still, she will not be swayed. A sudden wave of heat afflicts her, and to the old Wizard's disgust, she pulls her Sheära corselet over her head, dumps it and begins shedding her pelts. Her skin pimples in the chill air. She strips to her tunic, which clings like sodden leather for the accumulation of filth. Within heartbeats, it feels as cold as lizard skin about the dome of her maternity. Her eyes flutter shut, and she sees tumbling purple. The lost forests of Kûniüri wobble like a top second-guessing its spin. She concentrates on breathing around her myriad discomforts.

"Are ... Are you well?" Achamian asks from the oblivion above her, suddenly penitent.

"*Now* he asks," she mutters to the boy, whom she cannot see. She undoes her belt, throws aside her scabbard, as much to infuriate the old Wizard as to relieve her belly.

Achamian eases himself to his rump, glaring, then, relying on his pelts for comfort, he rolls away from her. By some miracle, he manages to hold his tongue.

The sight of his back comforts her for some reason.

Do you see, little one? I bear you …

She lays back into her exhaustion, cooling, drifting.

And he bears me …

She sways and topples through something like a dream, a tempest flashing on some nocturnal horizon …

"*What are you doing?*"

Achamian's voice, sharp enough to crack through the suffocating felt. She starts. Mere months ago she would have simply popped upright, but her belly forbids it, so she flails like an upturned beetle.

"*Kirila meirwat dagru–*" the boy is saying.

Night has claimed all the world as its spoil. She sees the old Wizard, but more as shape than substance. His ragged silhouette stands at a cautious distance, four paces or so from her feet. She whirls to the boy, who sits cross-legged on her immediate right. His eyes are luminous, searching. He holds "Chipmunk"–the bronze knife she plundered from the Library of Sauglish–flat across his left thigh. And in his crabbed hand he holds …

"It … makes … light," the boy says in careful Sheyic.

As she watches, the boy scrapes the *Chorae* he holds in his right hand along the length of the sorcerous blade. Lightning whitens the hunched grotto of his fascination, engraving the grotesquerie of his maimed hand as vividly as the innocence of his face.

She strikes him out of some reflex, the way one might a child frolicking too near open flame. The boy catches her wrist without the least effort or worry. His look, as always, betrays nothing more than curiosity. She yanks her arm clear, fairly barges into his lap, scooping up Chipmunk and her Chorae both. She spares the boy a furious heartbeat, both glaring and grating.

"*No*," she says, as if instructing a puppy. "No!"

"The knife," Achamian says, still keeping his distance—because of the Chorae, she realizes. "Let me see it."

She tosses it to him with a snort. She suddenly realizes the old Wizard has been right all along, that they *should* have continued fleeing into the night. Shivers crash across her, and she fumbles the exposed Chorae trying to slip it back into the pouch. She curses, squats, and begins pawing through the leaves scaling the ground.

"*Emilidis* ..." the old Wizard says on a contemplative rasp.

"What?" she asks, retrieving and stowing the Trinket with its sibling. Her teeth are chattering. She bunches the back of her golden hauberk, draws the silken weight over her head. *Qirri* ... a voice whispers.

Qirri will allow them to flee through the night. Yes.

"Your *knife* was locked in the Coffers for a reason ..." the old Wizard says, still peering.

The boy, who has not moved, peers into the surrounding blackness. Perhaps he *can* feel shame. She begins slinging her pelts about her shoulders, winces for the reek.

"The greatest of the ancient Artificers made this," Achamian explains.

"What?" she asks, tugging the knife from his grasp. "Chipmunk?"

The Dûnyain boy pops effortlessly to his feet, his attention pricked to something in the dark. Both she and Akka follow his gaze into the wooded blackness, searching in vain.

"*Travellers*!" a voice booms across the clearing, one harsh with barbaric intonation.

She fairly swoons, so profound is her shock.

Voices, *human* voices, begin baying from the encircling blackness, tones of barbaric outrage and triumph, each as sharp and porcelain as teeth. Suddenly she can *feel* them, a necklace of needling absences identical to those against her breast, closing upon them from all angles. Chorae Bowmen. *Scylvendi* Chorae Bowmen.

"Three Seas scum!"

Bars of moonlight wink through the woolen sky, baring all in bloodless illumination.

She sees Achamian, a mad hermit sorcerer standing every bit as transfixed as she, only with his face held down as if in dread contemplation. She sees the figure addressing them, the blue-faced, bearded Scylvendi from before. The hard-faced tongue-walker ...

"Attend me or die!" the barbarian shouts on a curious, lupine roll of his head.

The old Wizard raises his face. "Who–?"

"Maurax urs Cagnûralka calls on you! The Childstrangler. The Great and Holy Throatcutter. *Our mighty King-of-Tribes* would scry your fate with his own cruel eyes!"

To think they had feared the Sranc.

Blue-face had bid Achamian to light their way. Now midges and mosquitoes form a scribbling halo about his Surillic Point. They follow it across bleached confusion, wading through sheaved scrub and weeds rising stark from absolute black. The surrounding trees are scabbed in white. A welter of glimpses surface from the gloom beyond them. Brutal profiles. Forearms roped in sinew and striped with scars. Figures floating on saddles. Pinpricks of oblivion swim in the greater black–she can feel them, hanging above the bottom, little fish wandering in loose schools. Sranc periodically screech and yelp from tracts unknown.

Blue-face had punched Achamian full in the mouth when he dared voice a question. So they spend watch after watch trudging in silence, a pocket of sorcerous light creeping through the tangled black, an avalanche of wild horsemen as their escort. Mimara holds her belly, squinting away the waves of dozing nausea. The unborn infant is restless, kicks continually. Twice the boy catches her stumbling. She knows it well, the slurry of dread and exhaustion, and the movements of her soul seem all the more mad for it. Solace in the Eye–the unfaltering fire of a conviction she had never known. Terror in the thought, the knowledge that these were *Scylvendi*. And so it seemed that she was assured–both of the miracle that would save them, and of the torment that would see them doomed.

It occurs to her to pray. She hugs her abdomen instead.

Fear not, little one. Shush.

Blue-face smells rancid with urine–to ward against insects, she decides, after slapping her own cheek. The shrouded sky becomes threadbare. The first stars wink through rags of supernal gauze. The ground becomes more pitched, treacherous with humped stone and crabbed earth. The canopy thins then falls away, and they find themselves on the rounded edge of a scarp, staring out across a broad floodplain, one pillared with gigantic carbuncles of stone. The fires of the encamped host are not numerous, but then the night is old.

The Nail of Heaven pierces the northern skies.

Blue-face leads them down a ramp, between cyclopean stones shagged in growth. The air smells of smoke and latrines. They loiter while Blue-face consults one of their escorts, a chieftain, by the look of him, grey-maned and sporting an antique Kianene helm. Mimara notices Achamian, how his lips work in the manner of addled old men rehearsing defeats. The weariness melts away, forms a crust about a renewed sense of alarm.

Grey-mane heels his pony, spurs galloping into the darkness before them. Blue-face signals the resumption of their march.

They filter as much as pass through the slumbering host. Few yaksh populate the murk: the plainsmen slumber in the open with their ponies, larval beneath blankets of felt. There are no paths or alleys between them, so everywhere the war-party treads they are greeted with curses and scowling looks. She is unnerved by the white-blue of their irises, how they gleam in the blanched light of the Surillic Point. For all the world, they look like the eyes of *one man* staring from the cheek and brow of many.

They all reek of piss, like Blue-face.

One of the rock towers that peg the plain rears before them, a misshapen silhouette against the infinite arch of night. She glimpses the dancing crown of a fire upon its summit. Numerous yaksh crowd the scarped base, arranged in fungal clutches through the dark. Grey-mane awaits them on foot. Blue-face whistles, and the Chorae war-party dismounts. She can feel them in groups of two or three congregating with their bearers, accursed Trinkets ... Tears of the God.

She finds herself clasping the old Wizard's arm, squeezing against his tremors. He spares her a wild sidelong look, one belonging to horses encircled by fire. The boy merely observes with the same impervious curiosity with which he observes everything. The Surillic Point brings out the boy's resemblance to his grandfather, she thinks, as does his thickening hair ...

For the first time she realizes that he is her nephew.

Blue-face begins picking his way up a ramp of tossed stone, following Grey-mane. When they hesitate, one of the Scylvendi shoves Achamian forward, hard enough to swing his beard to his shoulders. There is something ominous about the way the old Wizard collects himself from the ground. Suddenly she fears the vacant expression on his face as much their captors. The soul that is perpetually beset often loses patience with life ...

She knows this fact too well.

More yaksh crowd the uneven heights, devoid of dyed colour or the least ornamentation. The air reeks of charred lamb.

Blue-face leads them toward the lone pillar of smoke rising into chill oblivion. Embers twirl and luminesce before fading into moth wings. A reluctance creeps into her step. The escorting Scylvendi have to bully her into the presence of the bonfire. It wheezes and spits, roars like tattered sails in the wind. Through the consuming brilliance, she discerns the earthworm tangle of torsos and limbs. They burn *Sranc*, she realizes.

Achamian allows his Surillic Point to wink into nothingness.

They stand upon ruins, she decides—something more than ancient old, something beaten into the crabbed semblance of nature. A line too long uninterrupted. A cylindrical curve. A stone bent at the elbow.

Blue-face directs them past the macabre bonfire into a depression that is a rectangular pool of ink for the brightness of the flame. Men await them. Nine sit along the depression's rim, their backs to the heap of burning grease and skin, their faces bent toward oblivion. One sits alone at the far end, narrow of shoulder, large of hand. The bonfire is his sculptor, scoring his arms with tiger stripes, etching the wend of veins. Dignity is his stone.

A series of poles rise from the mound of mossed debris behind him. A pony hangs skewered upon them, punctured and weeping, a ghastly apparition in the firelight. A Scylvendi warrior lolls dead upon its saddle, propped with sticks like a scarecrow.

Following Blue-face, they wade into the blackness, peering to assure their footing. She stands where he directs: with the boy opposite the Nine. Achamian he thrusts tripping toward the centre. The old Wizard topples, vanishes as if over a precipice. Mimara cries out, thinking a pit concealed in the shadow. But she sees the rolling glint of nimil and the shag of rotted pelt. He regains his footing with surprising decorum, like that of a holy man beset by rascals. It seems the blackness should fall from him in draining sheets, it is so complete.

The Scylvendi King-of-Tribes observes without word or expression. He is younger than she had expected, as hard as the ruin about him. His mane is jet-black, wild in the manner of autumn weeds. His face is too rustic to be handsome, yeoman simple, yet harbouring an intelligence too nimble not to be vicious. His eyes are keen, the irises almost white, but quick, she senses, to become bored—and all the more ruthless for it.

Mimara stands breathing into the onerous weight of her womb. The bonfire twists and whooshes, the Nine little more than silhouettes beneath its white-glaring contortions. In her periphery, the Chorae Bowmen assemble along the depression's unoccupied rim, their shafts knocked and drawn.

No one moves, other than two warriors tossing another carcass upon the fire. The Nail of Heaven squints and glowers above them, marking the direction of Golgotterath.

Her eyes adjust. Achamian, she can see, alternately clenches and releases the nimil hauberk he drew from the ashes of Nil'giccas ...

Fat hisses in flame.

"Be done with it!" the old Wizard finally cries.

The barbaric scrutiny continues.

"Kill us and *be done with it!*" Achamian cries, his disgust so profound it verges on hilarity.

"The *woman*," Maurax says in a deep, scarcely-accented voice. "She is yours?"

The fact that he had not so much as glanced at her makes the question all the more terrifying.

Achamian glares in horror.

"Wha-what?" he stammers, then stops on a swallow, licks his lips, breathes deep. A kind of resignation seems to calm him. "What do you want?"

The Scylvendi King-of-Tribes leans forward, elbows out, hands on knees. He has the air of a man dispensing advice to a half-wit.

"Migagurit says you wear your stain deep, Three Seas ... That you are a sorcerer-of-rank."

Achamian glances at Blue-face. The bonfire makes a wiry halo of his beard and hair as he does so. "Yes."

An appraising look, one both possessing the lettered arrogance of kings and the ignorant conceit of barbarians.

"And what brings a sorcerer-of-rank and his pregnant woman to the High Wild?"

An incredulous smirk creases the old Wizard's face. He raises a hand to the back of his neck, shakes his lowered face in disbelief. He is done with madness, Mimara can tell. He would quit his ancient contest with the Whore, even at the cost of his life. Were he alone, she knows, this would all end in salt and incineration.

But he is not alone. He glances at her, and even though the bonfire's white glare obscures his expression, she knows he begs forgiveness as much as permission.

"Searching ..." he says with exhausted boldness. "Searching for Ishuäl, the hidden refuge of the Dûnyain ..."

Maurax does not so much as blink. "You risk much," he says through gravel, his eyes clicking to and from Mimara. "What does Ishuäl possess that warrants such a throw?"

Achamian stands motionless. "The *truth* of the Holy Aspect-Empe—"

"LIES!" one of the Nine booms.

The man's shadow erupts from the depression's rim. The first of the Nine towers over the old Wizard, the details of his face and figure burned into blackness for the blistering white of the bonfire. But she does not need to see to know that he is the *true* power here, the true King-of-Tribes. But it is the menace of his frame, at once lean and thick, and the grating malice of his voice that *name* him ...

"*You* ..." the old Wizard croaks.

The shadow spits. She thinks she must smell his famished grin, because she cannot see it.

Slicked in firelight, Achamian's face has been struck of all defences, stripped to the wonder. "Th-they said you were dead," he stammers.

"Aye. *Dead* ..." the figure grates.

The fire of white burning Sranc blackens him. She feels more than sees his gaze slide across her face and belly ... and then, as if on some mad whim, glide to the stars.

"Dead, I walked across the desert." His voice sounds of cracking timbers, crashing stone. "Dead, I drank deep the blood of vultures. Dead, I *returned* to the People ..."

She can actually *feel* his invisible gaze seize the old Wizard anew.

"And dead, I *conquered* ..."

The other Scylvendi warriors have averted their gaze—even Blue-face peers at his boots. Only Maurax, it seems, dares look upon him directly.

"I have not the skin," the great shadow continues, "to bear the number I have taken. I have not the bones to carry the wickedness I have wrought. The sky gags for the bodies burned. The Hells *grow fat* on the back of my wrath—my judgment!"

Posturing. Pious declarations of prowess, ferocity and might. Were this the Andiamine Heights, she would have sneered, even tittered aloud—to needle Mother if nothing else. But not here—not with this man, whose every word stabbed as a knife.

"And you, sorcerer? Is Drusas Achamian *dead* as well?"

Achamian peers at the silhouette, glances down as if cowed by some unseen fury. "And alive," he says with a meekness that makes her cringe.

And with that, *the Eye opens* ...

And she finds herself in the captivity of the damned.

"What does this mean," the King-of-Tribes asks. "Eh, sorcerer? What does our meeting portend?"

All is illumined before the Eye. It knows no shadow—the same as It knows no past, no future. She *sees him*, Cnaiür urs Skiötha, the legend, and she cannot look away. She sees him for the soul he is.

"I am a fool in this," the old Wizard retorts. "No different than you."

The Scylvendi *demon* grins. It is like staring into a furnace, watching him. Heat pinches her cheeks. She squints against the blowing of unseen sparks. The sins of the Wizard—grievous though they may be—are but trifles compared to the atrocities wrought by this one man.

A bark of laughter. "So our ends are one! You too have come to collect from our common debtor."

And she *sees* it, a flicker bound to the back of flickers, a myriad of criminal glimpses. Babes caught on sword-point. Mothers raped and strangled.

"No," Achamian replies. "To *pass* judgment, not-not ... execute it."

She sees the hard ways of the People, the criminality of *being* Scylvendi, a nation born into damnation, and all the lunatic savagery that throngs between. She sees the hand drift between the shadow of opposing thighs ...

The demon snorts. "Still a philosopher! Still using your *mouth* to recover what your hands have given."

And *hatred*, unlike any she had ever witnessed, dwarfing even that of Lord Kosoter, who never heard the *anguish* of those he killed.

"I know only," Achamian said evenly, "that the World is about to end ..."

Cnaiür urs Skiötha was the murderer who cast himself into his victims, who choked and shrieked *with them* ...

"That *the Second Apocalypse* is upon us!"

To better suckle upon the fact of his own dread power ...

The Scylvendi King-of-Tribes laughs and sneers. "And you *fear* the Anasûrimbor truly is your Saviour! That his Ordeal might save the World!"

To make the World's throat a surrogate for his own...

"I have to know for certain ... I cannot risk ... risk ..."

"Liar! *You would be his assassin*! You lay breath upon the altar of your scrolls, but you *stink* of vengeance, sorcerer. You reek of it! You would put out his eyes—*no different than I!*"

The old Wizard stands thunderstruck, alarm grappling with incredulity. The bonfire whirls and cackles, coals popping deep, like bones breaking, bone buried in meat.

"So you have answered Golgotterath's summons?" Achamian asks. "You march for the Consult?"

The King-of-Tribes turns to the noisome flames, and Mimara at last sees his face as the mundane World would have her see it. High-cheeked, broad of jaw and heavy of brow, scars like coagulations of skin. He was as old as Achamian, but harder by far, as if too jealous of his strength, too indomitable of will to relinquish anything but the superfluities of youth—the weaknesses.

He spits toward the bonfire, where his eyes linger as if upon a virgin's thighs.

"Let it all burn."

"And you actually believe you will survive?" Achamian cries at his profile. "Fool! You imagine the Consult will *suffer* the Scylven—?"

The backhand is both abrupt and fluid. Achamian drops into the blackness like a crashing kite.

"You think this a *reunion*?" Cnaiür urs Skiötha screams down at him. "A meeting of old friends?" Mimara feels more than sees the kick to Achamian's face. Terror flushes through her. "This is not another favour from your Whore, Fortune! *You are not of the People!*"

The King-of-Tribes yanks the old Wizard from the indigo black, and she sees them ...

The *swazond.*

He suspends as much as holds the sorcerer upright, raises his opposite hand high. "Why? Why have *you* come, Drusas Achamian? Why have *you* dragged your bitch across a thousand screaming, rutting leagues? Tell me, what moves a man to cast number-sticks *across his woman's womb?*"

Scars—more than the Survivor—only ritual, cut with manic care, and in the Eye ...

"To learn the truth!" the bloodied Wizard shouts.

Smoking.

"Truth?" A sneering grin. "Truth? Which one? The one that makes toys out of Nations and Schools? The one that *fucks your wife* breathless?"

"No!"

Cnaiür cackles. "Even after so many lean years, he keeps you like a mouse in his pocket!"

"*No!*"

Smoking, the beaded tissue shining with orange-glowering coals ...

"*Hatred* ... Aye ... You cannot see this because you are *weak.* You cannot see this because you dwell"—he raised two thick fingers to his temple—"*here* ... Your own eye escapes you, and so you weave excuses, plead ignorance, tell tales! You hide from your truth in the sound of your voice, foul the very spigot you would clear! But I see it plainly—as plainly as a Dûnyain. *Hatred,* Mandati! Hatred has brought you here!"

Smoking ... anguish and shrieks, the residue of innumerable battles, coiling into the blackness of the greater night, a mantle of stolen souls.

"*I do hate!*" Achamian cries, his voice blood-raw. "I don't deny this! Hatred of Kellhus, yes! But hatred of the *Consult* more!"

The Barbarian King grimaces, releases the Wizard.

"What of your grudge against them?" Achamian presses. "What of *Sarcellus*? The skin-spy who murdered Serwë! Your concubine! Your prize!"

These words seem to unnerve the barbarian, physically, like a stab in his throat.

"Who's the mouse in whose pocket?" Achamian continues with scathing fury. Blood runs freely from his nose, clotting the tangle of his beard. "Who's the *gull?*"

The great black figure regards him, horned and smoking, living and yet already a Prince of Hell.

"How can I be the gull," it grates, "when they do *my* bidding?"

For a heartbeat she actually believes this could be the case, such is the *majesty* of the Scylvendi's evil. Achamian cannot see as she sees; nevertheless it seems he knows, that in some obscurity of his heart he understands the Man before him is no mere splinter, but a mighty shard ... possessed of what would have been a *hero's* soul, were it not for Anasûrimbor Moënghus ...

For the Dûnyain.

"But the *World!*" the old Wizard protests.

"The World—pfah! Let it burn! Let babes hang like leaves from trees! Let the screams of your cities crack the Heavens!"

"But how can you sa—?"

"*My will shall be done!*" the barbarian screams. "Anasûrimbor Kellhus will choke upon my knife! I shall cut out the bowel he calls his heart!"

"So that's it?" Achamian cries. "Cnaiür urs Skiötha, Breaker-of-horses-and-Men! *Consult slave!*"

The King-of-Tribes clubs as much as strikes the old Wizard to the shrouded ground.

"*I would have let you live, sorcerer!*" he thunders, hauling the hapless man from the dark. She glimpses Achamian's face, gasping as if tossed between ocean rollers—drowning ...

Panic, like a thousand little claws scratching a heart of plaster.

"*I would have spared your bitch!*" the Barbarian King rages. "*Your unborn chi—!*"

And she hears herself screech, "*You!*"

Wonder arrests the dark and grease-burning World.

"*You* are not of the People!"

She cannot feel her face, but she can feel *them* with excruciating clarity, the Chorae, Tears-of-God no more, hanging in the dark, like lead pellets dimpling the sodden tissue of existence. A dozen little rips.

Cnaiür urs Skiötha has turned from the fallen Wizard and now faces her, a granitic shadow before white gossamer flame. He stands before her, his flesh leather strapped about conflagration. The whole night roars and marvels.

"Your entire life!" she cries. "Always thinking … thinking *one thought too many!*"

The furnace apparition looms …

"Your! Entire! Life!"

The Eye closes, and a terror overwhelms her. Her gaze is bent from the hulking shadow toward the macabre horse and rider hooked on poles … at Maurax sitting beneath the carrion display. She is transfixed …

"Yes," the Scylvendi says on a bull murmur. "You do resemble her …"

Maurax, she realizes, *is no more*. A *woman* sits in his place. Flaxen hair, long and lustrous, molten with firelight, pallid with shadow.

"*Esmenet* … Yes. I remember …"

The name seizes her attention as surely as a slap, but Cnaiür is already peering beyond her.

"Look at me, boy."

Shock. She had forgotten the boy.

The Scylvendi King-of-Tribes towers before the two of them, his shadow encompassing her whole. She can make out his savage mien, see the dim facts of his expression, the way he blinks, staring at the boy like an addict stepping from an opium pit.

"Cnaiür!" she hears Achamian cry. "*Scylvendi!*"

The Barbarian King extends a callous-horned hand to the boy's cheek … The boy does not so much as flinch from the great thumb that dents his skin. Instead, he gazes up with a bland, slow-blinking curiosity that exposes everything.

"*Ishuäl* …" she hears Cnaiür exhale on a shudder.

The Scylvendi King-of-Tribes turns to confer with the thing that had been Maurax, but was now a beautiful Norsirai girl …

Serwë, Mimara realizes. Her stepfather's other wife.

She has suffered untold absurdities since fleeing the Andiamine Heights. She has witnessed more rank impossibilities, more offenses to nature and scruple than she could hope to enumerate. She has huddled beneath raving abominations. But none of it *bruised* her quite so strangely as this … as Serwë …

In Momemn, Serwë was more than just a staple of dynastic legend, a ghost for being so intimately embroiled in the mad circus of the Anasûrimbor. She was also a *weapon*, and a shameful one. Mimara regularly used her in arguments with her mother—and how could she not, when it was a name that exposed the Empress for a fraud? The dead were always more chaste, more pure of past and intention. As the living wife, Anasûrimbor Esmenet could not but be the fallen wife ...

"Did you exult, Mother, watching her rot upon the Circumfix? Did you celebrate for having survived?"

Such cruel things we say, when we make rods of our wounds.

Without a word of explanation, Cnaiür urs Skiötha strides into the darkness beyond the depression, abandons them to Maurax-become-Serwë.

The *World*, the Zaudunyani poets called her. For as she died, so too had the innocence of Men. It seems a mockery unto sacrilege, that a skin-spy might wear her beauteous form.

The three of them watch in a stupor as the counterfeit woman begins barking commands into the night. The Scylvendi tongue is curious, at once as harsh as chipped flint and as slippery as flayed skin. Warriors, arms grilled in *swazond*, set out across the deformities of the little plateau. The Chorae Bowmen are dismissed—a fact Mimara would have celebrated were it not for the malign presence of Serwë—and the Trinket bound against her counterfeit navel.

With the boy in tow she draws Achamian into the firelight, does what she can to staunch the blood welling from his lower lip. Her head still spins for panic and confusion.

"He's not through with us," he murmurs. "Let *me* speak."

"So you can get us killed?"

The amiable old face scowls.

"You don't know him, Mimara."

"The *legendary* Cnaiür urs Skiötha ..." she says on a gentle sneer. "I think I know him better than any ..."

"How—?" the old scold begins, only to catch a glimpse of the truth in her look. He is beginning to understand the Eye, to accept what it means. "Then your silence is all the more crucial," he says, spitting blood in the blackness.

She pauses in her ministrations, suddenly realizing Drusas Achamian will never *entirely* understand. And how can he, a Schoolman—worse, a *Wizard*—someone who works miracles of destruction with breath and intellect? He will always strive, *always fight*, and forever presume that events follow upon the acts of Men.

She glimpses the boy watching.

"I'll keep my counsel," she reassures the old Wizard. "What do *you* intend to do?"

He grimaces. "What Protathis bids all Men do in the court of a mad king: lick feet."

Achamian wards away Mimara's fussing, his eyes already fixed upon the thing-called-Serwë.

The flaxen-haired abomination observes them from a position some paces distant, her waifish beauty compelling for liquid conspiracies of light and shadow.

"So," the old Wizard calls out to the creature, "are you his keeper?"

The thing-called-Serwë smiles in the demure manner of a girl too timid to admit her lust.

"Were I not *his* slave," it coos, "I would love *you*, Chigra."

"And *how* do you serve him, Beast?"

It raises a white hand, points beyond the glittering heap of fire, toward a yaksh set alone on the plateau's eastern rim.

"As all women serve heroes," it said smiling.

"Outrage!" the old Wizard spat. "Madness!" After glancing back to Mimara and the boy, he set out on a hobble toward the White Yaksh.

"That is what they are! Do you not see? With every breath they war against circumstance, with every breath they conquer! They walk among us as we walk among dogs, and we yowl when they throw out scraps, we whine and we whimper when they raise their hands …

"They make us love! They make us love!"

She follows, hands upon her gold-scaled belly. The thing-called-Serwë concedes Achamian the lead, falls in beside her instead. Even though they are of a height, the skin-spy turns only to glance at her extended belly, nothing else. Mimara ponders the perversity of lolling caught in the jaws of events twenty-years dead.

Such wonders, little one ...

The interior is more gloomy for the barbarism of its accoutrements than the absence of light. A fire crouches shining in the centre, set in a circle of blackened stones for want of a hearth. Where the tent of a Three Seas King would have exhibited a bare minimum of luxury, all-important signs of significance, nothing that Mimara can see serves this capacity in the tent of Cnaiür, breaker-of-horses-and-men. Only the cushions set across the mats ringing the fire—little more than bolts of felt folded and stitched—signify any concession to comfort. And aside from a horse-tail standard whose intricacies defeat her, everything complicating the spare hollow is devoid of ornament. Bundles have been arrayed like pastries against the southern walls. Wood has been heaped along the northern. A nimil hauberk, Kianene helm, round-shield, and bowcase hang from hemp ropes opposite the entrance. A high-backed saddle lies askew to the left of the threshold. The ground itself is sloped and broken, lending the sense of a capsized sea vessel.

The old her, the embittered Princess-Imperial, would have seen only rubbish and banditry. But then the old her would have smelled of ambergis rather than the ripe of putrid fur and unwashed woman. Barbarism, she realizes with dark humour, had swallowed her life long ago.

The King-of-Tribes is the only true ornament here. He sits cross-legged opposite the entrance on the far side of the fire. Stripped to the waist, he is at once lean and gigantic, sinister for the way the firelight illuminates his punishing physique from below. *Swazond* craze his arms and torso, lined plots of scar-tissue that resemble beaded wax.

Such tales we will tell.

Cnaiür urs Skiötha does not acknowledge them in any way. If he stares at the smoke, then he holds his focus as a finger in a stream, immobile, for his gaze does not move. Achamian shocks her by exploiting his inattention, striding to the fire and sitting to his immediate right as he might have twenty years previous, when they had shared a fire in the First Holy War. Mimara hesitates, knowing from her years on the Andiamine Heights that the old Wizard's presumption was at once provocation. Only when the thing-called-Serwë took a seat to her consort's left did she kneel at Achamian's side. The boy followed suit, sitting opposite the wicked simulacrum.

The birch logs wheezed for burning wet, sizzled steam from sodden marrows.

"You sought Ishuäl."

The Scylvendi speaks with a harsh, chopping cadence. His voice, even when conversational, is husky, wide ... as if carried on distant roaring. He continues gazing at some indeterminate point above his fire.

"I confronted him with your accusations after the Fall of Shimeh ..." The old Wizard's eyebrows pop up, the way they always do when he is surprised by some recollection. "Just after Maithanet had crowned him Aspect-Emperor upon the heights of the Juterum, before all the Great and Lesser Names, no less." He peered at the barbarian's profile as if seeking approval for his daring. "As you might imagine, I had to flee the Three Seas. All these years I've been living in exile, pondering what had happened, the prophecies, and searching for some clue of Ishuäl in my Dreams ...

"The truth of man, I had reasoned ... lies in his origins."

She has difficulty focussing upon Cnaiür, despite his seething presence. The wane image of his consort leans hard against her periphery, like menace painted in oils. *Serwë*, her sister's namesake, even more beautiful than legend, like the girl-child of some God ...

"What I told you that final night was not truth enough?"

"No," Achamian said. "It was not."

The King-of-Tribes spits gristle into the flames.

"Did you doubt my honesty or my sanity?"

Mimara's breath catches on the question.

"Neither," the old Wizard says, shrugging. "Only your vantage ..."

The King-of-Tribes grins, still staring into nothing. "My *sanity*, then."

"No," the old Wizard protests. "I—"

"Only the World makes Men mad," Cnaiür snaps. At last the brutal visage turns, and the white-blue eyes fix Achamian. "You sought Ishuäl to settle the matter of my madness."

The old Wizard stares down to his thumbs.

"Tell me, then," Cnaiür continues on a growl. "Am I mad?"

"*No* ..." Mimara hears herself say aloud.

The white-eyes seize as much as regard her.

"Anasûrimbor Kellhus *is* wicked," she says lamely.

We are tired, little one. That is all ...

Achamian turns to her with the downward manner of those beleaguered by old furies, speaks as though reprimanding her soiled knee. "And if he turns out to be the Saviour?"

"He *won't*," she retorts, her voice revealing more pity than she would have liked.

"And how could you *know* this?"

"Because I have the Eye!"

"And it told you the *Dûnyain* were evil, not Kellhus!"

"*Enough*!" the Scylvendi King-of-Tribes barks. Men who grow old in the dungeon of their hearts, she has noticed, often grind their voices into faraway thunder. Cnaiür has whetted his into one that claps the ears.

"What is this Eye?"

The question inhales all the air remaining. The old Wizard warns her to silence with one final scowl, turns back to Cnaiür, who has not finished ransacking her with his shining gaze.

"She has what is called the Judging Eye," he begins, parsing his words too carefully to sound anything but disingenuous. "Very litt—"

"The *God of Gods*," she interrupts. "The God-of-Gods looks through my eyes."

Cnaiür urs Skiötha almost seems a thing of stone, his scrutiny is so motionless.

"Prophecy?"

"No ..." she replies on a swallow, realizing that this was the masculine question. She draws an even breath to calm her demeanour. "Judgment. I see ... *judgment*."

The thing-called-Serwë does not so much as blink.

The King-of-Tribes nods. "You see the facts of damnation, then."

"This is why we hasten to Golgotterath," Achamian says in a clumsy attempt to intercede. "So that Mimara may gaze upon Kellhus with the Eye ... So that we mi—!"

"The *Eye*," Cnaiür grates. "It has apprehended me?"

She dares match his gaze. "Yes."

The great man lowers his face as though to ponder her words and a hangnail together. A shudder passes through his shoulders. "Tell me, Daughter-of-Esmenet. *What did it see?*"

She glances at Achamian ... He is begging her to "lick feet"—to *lie*. The vacancy in his expression shouts as much.

"*Tell me*," Cnaiür repeats, raising his fluted face.

She tries to match the glacial intensity of his gaze. Turquoise set in sclera shot with murderous memory. Something *pricks*, and though the very God of the Gods steeps her, her look falters, falls to her hands where they strain finger against finger on her lap.

"I have never seen ..." she murmurs.

"*What?*" A voice like a father's swat.

"I-I have never seen one-one ... so ... so *damned* ..."

The black-maned head lowers in contemplation once again, like a stone sagging upon a stalk of clay. Mimara isn't sure what her words should have provoked. The man is too mercurial and far too canny for her to trust any assumption. But she expected *some* kind of reaction—for when all was said and done, he *remains a mortal man*—a soul. He might as well have been a Sempis crocodile.

She looks to Achamian, who spares her no more than a resigned and beseeching glance. If they survive, a petulant part of her notes, she will never hear the end of this night. He will curse her for her honesty, she knows. And who could blame him?

The thing-called-Serwë has been watching her this entire time on a tangent to the flames, a vision that lulls as much as warns for its beauty.

"*Seeeee* ..." it coos to its Scylvendi lover. "*Salvation ... This is the dowry that only my father can off—*"

"Stop your tongue, abomination!" Achamian cries.

But the King-of-Tribes looks to Mimara alone.

"And when you looked upon *Ishuäl* with the Eye, what did you see?"

Inhaling hurts.

"Crimes. Unthinkable and innumerable."

A longing creeps into the brutal visage. A desire to burn ... He even turns his gaze back to the fire, as though he casts images behind his eyes to the flame. His voice surprises her, so intent is he upon the wax and shimmer of the fire.

"And the boy, here ... You took him as your hostage?"

The old Wizard hesitates. She hears her voice leap into the silence—quite against her resolution.

"He is a refugee ..."

The Scylvendi King-of-Tribes glares like someone slapped clear of delirium. His scowl is instant, the glove most worn by his face. The boy, she realizes, sensing the child's immobile presence on her left—the boy has been the mad Scylvendi's motivating concern since the episode beneath the bonfire ... when he had glimpsed the child's resemblance to his Holy Grandfather—Anasûrimbor Kellhus.

"Refugee ..." For the first time the cruel eyes slacken. "You mean Ishuäl ... *has fallen?*"

This time they both remain silent.

"N-no," Achamian begins. "The boy merely sought asylum fro—"

"*Silence!*" Cnaiür urs Skiötha screams at the old Wizard. "Ketyai scum!" he says, spitting. The flames hiss like a cat. "Always you seek advantage! Always conniving—worse than greedy wives!"

He draws a knife from his girdle—whips it with an outward arc. Mimara can scarcely blink, let alone raise warding arms ...

But the knife zips past her cheek. She does not quite see, so quick is the shining passage, but she knows the boy has batted the blade to the side with his hale hand.

The barbarian now glares at the sorcerer, and for an instant, Mimara glimpses *him*, her terrible stepfather, *Anasûrimbor Kellhus*, sitting impervious in the interval between these disfigured souls. The spectre ... the *curse* ... that shackled them, these two most unlikely of Men.

She does not like the involuntary way Achamian's jaw works. She likes the tendons finning the Scylvendi's neck even less. "You know me!" the Barbarian King booms. "You know my cruelty knows no bounds! Tell me the *truth*, sorcerer! Tell me, lest I pluck your precious Eye!"

The thing-called-Serwë smiles at her from across the flames, glances toward the boy.

Achamian looks down to his hands, though out of cowardice or calculation she cannot tell.

"We found Ishuäl ruined."

"Ruined?" The barbarian is shocked. "What? By *him*? By *Kellhus*?"

She glances at the boy, who for some prescient reason seems to be *awaiting* her look. She wants to cry out to him, tell him to run, for she *knows*, even though the thought has yet to occur to her. She knows that she and

Achamian might pray to escape, but *not the boy*, not the orphaned seed of Anasûrimbor Kellhus.

"No..." Achamian says. "By the *Consult*."

"More lies!"

"No! We-we found tunnels beneath the fortress. A labyrinth filled with the bones of *Sranc*!"

Run! she wanted to cry. *Flee*! But her voice is stilled. The golden blur in her periphery, the thing-called-Serwë, watches with bottomless black eyes, poised in soulless fixation.

"How long ago was it destroyed?" Cnaiür urs Skiötha barks.

"I-I don't know ..."

"How *long*?" the barbarian repeats, his voice more hollow ...

"Ye-years," Achamian stammers. "*Years* ago."

She sees Serwë's impossible leap before she feels the air rushing to fill the boy's absence. The abomination pirouettes beneath the radial felt ceiling, lands rolling into another explosive leap through the threshold. Mimara can scarcely snap her head about quickly enough.

She blinks tears of astonished joy, battles the urge to smile. *Of course*! she silently cries, clutching her belly. *Of course he heard her*!

He is Dûnyain.

Alarums were raised, howls, clipped and guttural, leaping from breast to breast, igniting outward across the slumbering Scylvendi host.

And the boy sprinted—ran the way his dead father had shown him, the way he had been bred ...

Alive.

He was young. He was fleet. He was neither weightless nor cumbersome, but that occult in-between, smoke when soaring, grass when twisting, stone when striking. He flew through a necklace of nocturnal grottos, Scylvendi warriors crawling to their feet, milling in confusion, gazing at random points of sky the way Men are prone when keen to distant calls. They could scarcely see, let alone seize him. They could scarcely comprehend ...

He flitted through, over and between, beyond any hope of catching. Only their cries could outrun him. Shouts of coordination rang hoarse through the forest, different throats, different positions, pinpointing him in the racing black. He sensed mobs closing into ranks.

He need only *turn*, and the coalescing order dissolved into more confusion. Soft humus underfoot. Close arboreal air. The pinched musk of warriors long on the trail. And the freedom of the long run ...

Torches wagged and glittered through ragged black screens. The Scylvendi host had morphed into a single beast, a far-flung composite, teeming like ants through detritus and dark. He would turn, and it would momentarily dissolve, then reassemble about ligaments of voice. He found his way blunted, though his feet scissored just as quick. He began as a spear thrown, but now he became a sparrow. He zig-zagged, continually tacking at intervals decreed by threat and happenstance. Glimpses of swazond girding arms in torchlight, blades bouncing moonlight, and horn bows raised. Choruses of shouts tracked him, forcing him into what pockets of obscurity the forest encampment possessed. Grim, outraged expressions. Tentacles of plainsmen twined across the tracts, curled about the most recent spate of hollering. He began doubling back, forcing the beast, vast and aggregate, to crash into itself. The sparrow became a gnat, a scribble. He took to the trees, leaping and swinging through arthritic lattices. Horses floating beneath. He heard shafts popping through foliage, ticking from bark, thudding into wood—sometimes about him, but almost always behind him. Savage faces squinting to peer. So long as he could astonish and shock the Scylvendi, so long as the darkness baffled their stunted sight, he could pass like smoke through their midst.

Only the blond woman could hope to catch him ...

The one with fists for a face.

It seemed Achamian could feel the wind of their passing long after they had vanished outside.

"Call it *back*," Mimara said dully, fixing the King-of-Tribes in a stunned gaze.

Cnaiür leaned back, casually snatched a crab-apple from a small hide sack behind him. He halved the thing with a single bite, then studied the exposed flesh, white bruised with lime.

"Call it back!" Mimara cried, this time with menace as much as urgency.

"That-that thing!" the old Wizard sputtered on the heels of her demand. "Scylvendi fool! *That thing is deceit*! As much inside as without! Lies stacked upon lies until it mocks a soul! Cnaiür! *Cnaiür*! *You lie with Golgotterath*! Don't you see?"

The barbarian seized him by the windpipe, stood from a crouch, hoisting him on a swing. Achamian kicked, gripped the strapped forearm desperate to relieve his throat of his own weight, to gain distance from the Chorae bound to his navel.

"*Enough*!" Mimara shrieked.

And to the old Wizard's floundering amazement, the mad Scylvendi *heeded* her, dumped him in a rancid sheaf upon the mats. Achamian scrambled to his feet, stood beside Mimara, who, like him, could only stare puzzled and aghast at the sight of Cnaiür urs Skiötha, breaker-of-horses-and-men, *laughing* in a manner both grotesque and maniacal—laughing *at him*.

Nausea welled through the old Wizard. For the first time he truly believed he was going to die.

"She!" the King-of-Tribes barked. "She sees too much to see *anything*! But you, sorcerer, you are the fool—*truly*! So busy peering after what cannot be seen, you forever kick upon the ground at your own feet!"

Cnaiür towered over the two Ketyai, greased for sweat, surreal for the white grill of scars shining in firelight.

"Bah! My ends are my own, and my trust has long rotted to dust and bone. My prize *belongs to me* in ways you cannot know! But what of you? What of *your* prize, *pick*?" He even spat the slur with a Tydonni chirrup, an evil little memento of the First Holy War. "How can you seize what you cannot even see?"

"So you propose to *outwit* the Consult?" Achamian cried, appalled as much as alarmed. "Is that what yo—?"

"I outwitted a *Dûnyain*!" the mad Scylvendi roared. "I *murdered one*! No soul is so devious with hate, so mazed with furies as *me*!"

The old Wizard and the pregnant woman shrank from his slicked aspect, the titanic sum of his rage and hulking frame.

"Twenty summers!" he boomed. "Twenty summers have passed since I stole into your tent, and told you, as I dandled your life between my thumb and finger, the Truth—the Truth of *him*! Twenty winters have thawed, and now you find yourself in my tent, sorcerer, every bit as lost, as baffled and dismayed!"

The mad Scylvendi's voice cracked like flint, roared of a piece with the fire. "Every bit as blind to the darkness that comes before!"

He ran, sketched impossible figures through the air, twisting like a snake thrown between swatting swords. More and more he heard the thrum of bows, the zip of archery criss-crossing the emptiness. The whole host seemed to descend upon the regions about him, until all was erratic torchlight and roiling commotion. But he could hear the nearing *limit*, the infinite well of the wilderness, plunging off in all directions, the promise of solitary flight ...

A single turn was all it took.

He would have paused, so certain was he of this newfound invulnerability. He would have fashioned impenetrable armour out of their ignorance, returned to find his companions ...

Were it not for the woman—the thing—flying like a silk scrap on a tempest behind him, *gaining* ...

He resumed sprinting across the forest floor. The ground became cramped. Elms and walnuts thinning. Stone breaching. Still she gained, and he pressed harder, sacrificing endurance for flight. The canopy became leprous, scum across the crystalline deep. Beneath, the nocturnal terrain bobbed like chips of wood upon the flood, trees and ground rising, rushing, sweeping into the oblivion of what once was ...

And still she gained.

He had fled like this before. Eleven times.

And though the blindness of the Thousand Thousand Halls had been absolute, his memories were of silver, screeching and grunting, silver twining like fish through the deep, dividing rather than deciding, and so halved by each and every forking passage, until they became a fog of pathetic individuals. He had clung to the Survivor's back the first seven occasions, monkey-clinging, whooping to a glee he could never quite feel, buoyant, air whistling through his ears, snapping his robes, blood ... *exploding* ...

The fact of the Survivor's power had been something unquestioned—unthought. Things lifted, dropped. The Survivor conquered—always and everything. He had never supposed they could be defeated, that they could succumb to the bestial frenzy. But then he had never supposed the Shriekers would dwindle and vanish, the last of their silver screams eaten by the labyrinthine black. He had never supposed there could be such a thing as sun.

The Survivor *survived*—always ...

The Survivor protected. Made safe.

The madness worsens?

The forest whipped about his running, a weave of nocturnal complexities falling into oblivion.

She was *faster*, the blond-haired thing. Hers was the deeper wind. He need only attend to the blank behind him to know, to the chitinous cadence of her strides, the advancing tick ...

He was not sure when the weeping began. He never was. He was not sure what the *feeling* was, though he had seen it innumerable times on the faces of the old man and his pregnant woman.

Never on that of the Survivor.

"*I hear your blubbering!*" it screeched in the tongue of the Dûnyain, baiting a pride he did not possess.

The rushing of things near, ground like flying moss; the ominous creep of scarps along his flank. The thing commanded Phusis—there could be no question. Logos was his only refuge ...

The Logos was his now.

Things were simple ... or could be.

"*I smell your terror!*"

The boy struck for the cliffs. *Terror?* a fraction asked.

No. Not terror.

Fury?

The thing-called-Serwë limped back to the White Yaksh, which remained standing despite the white brilliance of dawn.

Cnaiür urs Skiötha, King-of-Tribes, most violent of all Men, awaited within.

They regarded each other for a time, the Man and his monstrous lover.

"You let them go free," the thing-called-Serwë said, dripping blood.

The aging Scylvendi warrior stood, revealed the strapped and scarred glory of his near-naked form.

It licked swollen lips. "What did the Wizard say?"

He advanced on the thing, reached out and seized it by the hair, bent its face back beneath his wrath.

"That I must fathom your loyalties ..."

His crazed visage floated above white-rolling eyes. It began trembling.

"What happened to the *Anasûrimbor*?" the King-of-Tribes asked.

It went limp against his cruel grip. "He cast a stone"—tongue testing teeth—"struck me from the cliffs."

"How ..." A sneer that was a sob twisted his expression. "How can I *trust* you?"

It hooked a lithe leg about his thigh, pressed the arch of its lust against him.

Cnaiür urs Skiötha groaned, raised a great hand to her throat.

"Drink from my cup," it cooed. "Taste ... *Fathom* ..."

The hand closed upon its windpipe. The White Yaksh creaked about the force of his rage and anguish.

"Ishuäl has fallen!" the King-of-Tribes screamed, heaving his slack-limbed lover from its feet, shaking it against the light.

"*Fallen!*"

He tossed it to earth ...

Tugged loose the cloth about his inflamed loins.

The caw, rumble, and holler of the barbarian host receded behind accumulating tracts of night and forest. Achamian and Mimara fled without pause, trotting as much as striding across the heaved and cracked forest floors. Their expression, when they weren't grimacing, was one of winded incredulity—disbelief.

"But the boy!" Mimara at last dared cry.

"Is better off ..." the old Wizard huffed without breaking stride, "without us!" He subsequently cursed, realizing she had jogged to a halt behind him—out of concern for the boy, he knew, and not for being quick.

They had snorted enough Qirri to assure that neither wind nor weariness would impede them.

"But—"

"But we go to *Golgotterath*, girl!"

His skin prickled for how well he could see in the dark, how impossibly untouched and utterly ravaged she looked, her expression finally falling abreast her lesser years. The Prophetess had vanished, and she stood blinking tears, a runaway Princess-Imperial once more.

Achamian raised a scuffed and blackened hand, squinted against the swelling that was inexorably closing his right eye. "Come ..." he said, knowing the very name of their destination blotted any need for further reasons. They spared the boy nothing, lashing him to a doom so mad as Golgotterath.

She clasped his fingers, not so much smiling as setting her jaw. Revulsion flicked through her like a lash through the whip—because of his Mark, he knew.

"But the boy—"

"Is *Dûnyain*, Mimara."

They stood thus in the dark, panting. Scylvendi horns rolled like otters at the surface of hearing—to the south.

Mimara licked her lips.

"So then what?" she asked lamely. "After everything that's happened, we-we just flee into the night!"

"Pray-tell ... what *else* does one do after everything that's happened?"

She looked at him, imploring, he realized, for what she did not know. The old Wizard stamped his feet, overcome by a sudden, wild frustration. He knew full well what such looks portended.

"Sweet Seju, girl!" he erupted. "How could you be *so consistent*! When I need the prophetess, I get the runaway, and when I need the runaway I get the prophetess—every blasted time!"

Anger hardened her teary eyes, hostility flashing through sorrow. "What? Because I-I *care*?"

He blundered on, determined to see his stupidity through.

"You cared nothing about sending his father over a cliff!"

She flinched at that, blinked tears. Her eyes fell to the empty ground between them.

"That was not my invitation," she said in a low, even voice.

"I *watched* you give him the Qirri ... and I *know* you knew what was going to happen. You made it pretty clear that you want—"

"*He* jumped the cliff!" she cried. "He accepted the invitation!"

"Invit—what invitation? You mean to snort the Qi—"

"The invitation to *leap*!"

Now it was Achamian's turn to stare speechless.

"To join the Absolute," she spat before stalking off.

He stood upon the saddle of level ground they had taken as their stage, motionless for the horror plunging through him, the one he had borne since first fleeing the White Yaksh and kept afloat by refusing to stop, refusing to think.

His skin prickled, flushed where exposed to the chill. Cnaiür urs Skiötha boiled as a vapour before him.

"*And now you find yourself in my tent, sorcerer ...*"

The Dreams fell hard upon what little opportunity he had to sleep, dreams drawn from the sheath. One moment the ground beneath him was slowly revolving, pricking like thistles and humming, so much he despaired of ever falling asleep. Then he was lurching, thinking blood-clotted thoughts, climbing the throat of a moaning horn. Golden walls leaned upon warring angles, surfaces betraying different sigils on different angles, elongated etchings, each as fine as an infant's hair.

Wretches ... human wretches. A shambling line, nude, white where not soiled or scabbed or welted. The chain was drawn and he swam forward, one in a necklace of thousands.

Toothless. The shadow of fists and hammers fell upon his face.

Their captors floated as tyrannical shadows, beasts that were terrors, that reduced him and the others to automatic cringes and whimpers, hapless reflexes. Those that faltered were pried from their shackles, dragged aside, beaten, raped. He could know of others likewise taken ahead of them by the gaps in the chain, how he was sometimes hauled forward four steps instead of two. No one spoke, though some managed to scream, to hack and grunt, noises reflected raw across the unearthly gold. He more started at sounds than heard them. To flee degradation one had to flee the World entire, to become a flame that burned no fuel. The fact that he yet lived meant his body—the merest meat of him—had learned as much.

He glimpsed ciphers webbed into planes of mirror soggomant.

He was missing his teeth.

A lolling gaze revealed a skewed vacancy above, scarps of metallic babble vanishing into blackness. He swayed for cresting the final step, so deep did the blackness *gape* about him. The sound of the great hammer cracking chains erupted through the hollow, disintegrated into surf-like echoes. With each clap, there was a pause ... then the chain yanked him forward with the rest, men jointed in milk and lard. The wretched file extended before him, bare feet greasing a polished black floor, shoulders shining orange and crimson ...

And the nameless captive peered out from the refuge of his misery, blinked for the sight of a ceiling hanging suspended above them—a *ceiling of flame*.

And though he knew it not at all, the old Wizard groaned in his sleep.

Unchained figures stood transfixed beneath it, Nonmen in various states of undress, gazing up ... Tears enamelled their cheeks with furnace reflections, silken wings of saffron and crimson, damnation signed in passerine lights. They paid no heed to the mortals chained in their midst, for they were every bit as enslaved.

The hammer resounded and the brutalized captive blinked and the chain heaved the battered souls ahead of him forward with him, the same two besotted steps. Inexorably, stroke by cracking stroke, he was drawn beneath the ceiling, witless, oppressed by its lurid silence. A single glance exhausted his daring, a peek into fires burning upon fires, a bottomless regression. Otherwise, he looked only at the tumult reflected across the floor as the chain dragged him beneath its onerous canopy. For all the light it appeared to shed approaching, it formed no more than a wreath about the black pool of his face, fire pale as blowing snow. With the every haul on the chain, the mirrored lights would seem to grow as hair behind his shoulders.

He dragged his tongue about the sockets of his gums, pressing the tip into every sour pit.

And he found he *knew* the fire ... realized that his empty reflection wore Hell as a wig.

Then the hammer cracked, he stumbled forward in lurching unison, and the ceiling was behind him, and he walked glass over void once again. He dared peer ahead, out across the broken souls preceding ...

And he saw it, a *harder* black staining the gloom, a confluence of gleaming edge and surface, the oiled phantom of something black looming in blackness ...

A mighty sarcophag—

The old Wizard blinked, coughed terror, squinted as though night were daybreak. A flood of spinning relief seized him. Teeth! He had his *teeth*! He seized the slight arms that had roused him, peered at Mimara kneeling over him, her eyes welling with tears.

Achamian gasped aloud, wrung by passions indecipherable and plain.

He pressed a palm across the woman's swollen womb.

And he hung upon his terror as a smile breaking, understanding at last that fatherhood, more than anything else, was mummery, the will to be a father *needed*, not the father you happened to be.

It was happening. The Second Apocalypse had begun.

"All-all will be well ..." he croaked, trusting she would see that he lied for the right reasons, if she could see at all. "You ne-need only believe."

Character and Faction Glossary

House Anasûrimbor

Kellhus - the Aspect-Emperor.

Maithanet - Shriah of the Thousand Temples, half-brother to Kellhus.

Esmenet - Empress of the Three Seas.

Mimara - Esmenet's estranged daughter from her days as a prostitute.

Moënghus - son of Kellhus and his first wife, Serwë, eldest of the Prince-Imperials.

Kayûtas - eldest son of Kellhus and Esmenet, General of the Kidruhil.

Theliopa - eldest daughter of Kellhus and Esmenet.

Serwa - second daughter of Kellhus and Esmenet, Grandmistress of the Swayal Sisterhood.

Inrilatas - second son of Kellhus and Esmenet, insane and imprisoned on the Andiamine Heights.

Kelmomas - third son of Kellhus and Esmenet, twin of Samarmas.

Samarmas - fourth son of Kellhus and Esmenet, the idiot twin of Kelmomas.

Drusus Achamian - former Mandate Schoolman, lover of the Empress, teacher of the Aspect-Emperor, now the only Wizard in the Three Seas.

The Cult of Yatwer

The traditional Cult of the slave and menial castes, taking as its primary scriptures *The Chronicle of the Tusk*, the *Higarata*, and the *Sinyatwa*. Yatwer is the Goddess of the earth and fertility.

Psatma Nannaferi - Mother-Supreme of the Cult, a position long outlawed by the Thousand Temples.

Hanamem Sharacinth - Matriarch of the Cult.

Momemn

Biaxi Sankas - Patridomos of House Biaxi, and an important member of the New Congregate.

Caxes Anthirul - Exalt-General of the Three Seas.
Imhailas - Exalt-Captain of the Eothic Guard.
Issiral - The Narindar contracted by Esmenet.
Naree - A Nilnameshi prostitute.
Ngarau - eunuch Grand Seneschal from the days of the Ikurei Dynasty.
Phinersa - Holy Master of Spies.
Powtha Iskaul – General of the Twenty-ninth Column.
Thopsis - eunuch Master of Imperial Protocol.
Vem-Mithriti - Grandmaster of the Imperial Saik and Vizier-in-Proxy.
Werjau - Prime-Nascenti, and Judge-Absolute of the Ministrate.

The Great Ordeal

Varalt Sorweel - Only son of Harweel.
Varalt Harweel - King of Sakarpus.
Captain Harnilias - Commanding officer of the Scions.
Zsoronga ut Nganka'kull - Successor-Prince of Zeum, and hostage of the Aspect-Emperor.
Obetegwa - Senior Obligate of Zsoronga.
Porsparian - Shigeki slave given to Sorweel.
Thanteus Eskeles - Mandate Schoolman, and tutor to Varalt Sorweel.
Nersei Proyas - King of Conriya, and Exalt-General of the Great Ordeal.
Coithus Saubon - King of Caraskand, and Exalt-General of the Great Ordeal.
Gwanwë - Swayali witch promoted Grandmistress in Serwa's absence.
Sibawûl - Leader of the Cepaloran contingent of the Great Ordeal.
Siroyon - Leader of the Famiri contingent of the Great Ordeal.

Ishterebinth

Oinaral Lastborn - Son of Oirûnas, youngest of the Nonman, last of the Siqu.
Nil'giccas (Cleric) - The Nonman King of Ishterebinth, lost to the Dolour.
Immiriccas - Son of Cinial, imprisoned in the Amiolas for sedition.
Harapior - The Lord Torturer of Ishterebinth.
Nin'ciljiras - Son of Ninar, Son of Nin-janjin, last surviving heir of Tsonos.
Oirûnas - Hero of the Cûno-Inchoroi Wars, lost to the Dolour.
Cilcûliccas - The Lord of Swans, Master of the Injori Quya.
Cu'mimiral - The Dragon-gored, prominent among the Injori Ishroi.
Sûjara-nin - Dispossessed Son of Siöl, prominent among the Siölan Ishroi.
The Boatman - The Master of the Great Ingressus.

Ancient Kûniüri

Anasûrimbor Celmomas II (2089-2146) - High-King of Kûniüri, and tragic principal of the First Apocalypse.

Anasûrimbor Nau-Cayûti (2119-2140) - youngest son of Celmomas, and tragic hero of the First Apocalypse.

Seswatha (2089-2168) - Grandmaster of the Sohonc, lifelong friend of Celmomas, founder of the Mandate, and determined foe of the No-God.

The Dûnyain

A monastic sect whose members have repudiated history and animal appetite in the hope of finding absolute enlightenment through the control of all desire and circumstance. For two thousand years they have hidden in the ancient fortress of Ishuäl, breeding their members for motor reflexes and intellectual acuity.

The Consult

The cabal of magi and generals that survived the death of the No-God in 2155 and has laboured ever since to bring about his return in the so-called Second Apocalypse.

The Thousand Temples

The institution that provides the ecclesiastical framework of Zaudunyani Inrithism.

The Ministrate

The institution that oversees the Judges, the New Imperium's religious secret police.

The Schools

The collective name given to the various academies of sorcerers. The first Schools, both in the Ancient North and the Three Seas, arose as a response to the Tusk's condemnation of sorcery. The so-called Major Schools are: the Swayal Sisterhood, the Scarlet Spires, the Mysunsai, the Imperial Saik, the Vokalati, and the Mandate (see below).

The Mandate

Gnostic School founded by Seswatha in 2156 to continue the war against the Consult and to protect the Three Seas from the return of the No-God, Mog-Pharau. Incorporated into the New Imperium in 4112. All Mandate Schoolmen relive Seswatha's experience of the First Apocalypse in their dreams.

The Tutelary Lands
At the time of the Great Ordeal
Following the disastrous loss at Ursulor, the Men of the Circumfix reunited at Swaranul, where their Holy Aspect-Emperor revealed the utter exhaustion of their supplies, and inaugurated what contemporaries would come to call "the Apophagia", the use of Sranc for sustenance.
THE OCCLUSION
Golgotterath
PLAINS OF SHIGOGLI
THE FIELD APPALLING
AGONGOREA
THE BALD
YIMALETI
THE LEASH
HÛNNÛ
FAR WUOR
Ishterebinth
GIOLAL
INJOR-NIYAS
Ishual
GLACIER
ANÛNUARCÛ
Dagmersor
WUOR

AÖRSI
YINWOL
ERENGAW PLAINS
INGOL
OLOREG
MANTIGOL
YAWREG
Shiarau
HINSURSA
HIGH ILLAWOR
Wreoleth
ILLAWOR
MISTY SEA
EORUFURU
IRSHI
SWARANÛL
SPEAR FENS
OSSIDÛ
ÛNOSIRI
Trysë
R. Scott Bakker 2016

Acknowledgments

Kellhus I am not.

I'm the kind of guy who would starve for forgetting to eat. I sometimes think I'm only half a person, given the way my projects consume me and my attention. I depend on others to lend me the semblance of being whole, more than most, I think. There's my wife and my daughter, of course. My agent, Chris Lotts, and my brother, Bryan.

My other conditions of possibility include Mike Hillcoat, Zach Rice, Andy Tressler, and everyone else at the Second Apocalypse forum. Thank you all not simply for believing in the series, but for assuring it walks Conditioned Ground. If these books are remembered, it will be due to you.

I need to thank everyone at *Three Pound Brain*: though my philosophical writing may seem miles away from my fiction, they are intimately intertwined.

I need to thank Jason Deem for making my vision so brilliantly visible.

I also need to thank my beta readers, Todd Springer, Ken Thorpe, Roger Eichorn, Michael Mah, and John Griffiths. The inimitable Mike Hillcoat deserves an encore mention here.